A Cassandra Jones Novel

OF LIFE, LOVE,
AND OTHER
Noble Pursuits

Of Life, Love, and Other Noble Pursuits

The Extraordinarily Ordinary Life of Cassandra Jones

Tamara Hart Heiner

paperback edition
copyright 2023 Tamara Hart Heiner
cover art by Tamara Hart Heine

Also by Tamara Hart Heiner:
Guardian Angel Academy
Year 1: Renegade (Tamark Books 2021)
Year 2: Redemption (Tamark Books 2021)
Year 3: Rebellion (Tamark Books 2021)
Year 4: Revolution (Tamark Books 2021)

Perilous (WiDo Publishing 2010)
Altercation (WiDo Publishing 2012)
Deliverer (Tamark Books 2014)
Priceless (WiDo Publishing 2016)
Vendetta (Tamark Books 2018)

Goddess of Fate:
Inevitable (Tamark Books 2013)
Entranced (Tamark Books 2017)
Coercion (Tamark Books 2019)
Destined (Tamark Books 2019)

Kellam High:
Lay Me Down (Tamark Books 2016)
Reaching Kylee (Tamark Books 2016)
Considering Margaret (Tamark Books 2023)

The Extraordinarily Ordinary Life of Cassandra Jones:
Walker Wildcats Year 1: Age 10 (Tamark Books 2015)
Walker Wildcats Year 2: Age 11 (Tamark Books 2016)
Southwest Cougars Seventh Grade (Tamark Books 2017)
Southwest Cougars Eighth Grade (Tamark Books 2018)
Southwest Cougars Freshman Year (Tamark Books 2019)
Springdale Bulldogs Sophomore Year (Tamark Books 2020)

Springdale Bulldogs Junior Year (Tamark Books 2022)
Springdale Bulldogs Senior Year (Tamark Books 2023)

Tornado Warning (Dancing Lemur Press 2014)

Eureka in Love Series
Shades of Raven (Tamark Books 2020)
After the Fall (Tamark Books 2018)

#

Table of Contents

A Cassandra Jones Book

OF LIFE, LOVE,
AND OTHER

Noble Pursuits

EPISODE 1:
WHO WE ARE

TAMARA HART HEINER

CHAPTER ONE

Reunification

"Can I go now?"

I stand beside my car, watching my mom put a few more boxes in the trunk. We're about to head out to Branson, a resort-town two hours away, to celebrate my high school graduation.

But that's not why I'm eager to get out of here.

"Yes," Mom says, laughing a little. "Sorry you didn't get to see Owen."

Owen. Sunshine breaks through the clouds in my mind at the mere mention of his name, and I smile as if that sunshine rests directly on my head. "That's all right."

It is all right. Because he texted me moments ago and asked me to swing by his apartment before I leave.

Which is also why I can't wait to go.

I'm humming by the time I put my car in reverse and back out of the driveway.

"You and Owen got back together?" Annette asks from the back.

I cast a glance at my younger sister in the rear view mirror. She's almost an exact miniature of me but in a lighter shade. Straight brown hair, almond-shaped eyes, oval face and high cheek bones. There's not much she can do to offend me. I adore her.

And I love the answer to this question.

"We did," I chirp. "Well, kind of."

She leans closer to me. "What happened?"

I lift a shoulder and focus on the road. My phone feeds me directions to Owen's apartment. I've never been there.

"He kissed me last night at the senior graduation party," I say. "He said he's sorry we broke up and wants to be together while we can be."

Which means, basically until I leave for college in three months. My heart gives a sudden squeeze and my throat tightens. *Don't think about that. Don't think about that.*

Annette settles back into the seat and pulls out a book. "I'm glad. I like him."

"Yeah, me too."

We stop at a red light and I send a text to Farrah. *Be there in half an hour.*

I pause to rethink my math. Getting out of rural Tontitown will take me another ten minutes. Then ten to Owen's apartment, and ten after that to Farrah's house . . .

I revise my text at the next light. *Maybe forty minutes.*

That gives me about ten minutes with Owen.

I pull into the parking lot of the flat, single-story complex. Five grungy doors with faded numbers stare back at me. Trash litters the lot, and the vehicles I see look rather suspicious. I scan the lot for Owen's truck but don't see it.

"Why are we here?" Annette asks, perking up from the back.

"To see Owen."

"Why here?"

"He moved here."

"Why?"

I've run out of answers. "I don't know."

Annette pulls out her book and starts reading.

I shoot Owen a text. *I'm here. Hope this is the right place.*

He responds almost immediately. *I'm almost there! Don't go anywhere.*

I check the time. Church let out an hour ago. I'd expected him to be here by now. *I'll wait,* I respond.

But I'm feeling more anxiety now. Farrah's also waiting. My mom doesn't know I took this detour. If she beats me to Branson, she'll go into full panic mode and start hunting down my car via GPS.

Now I'm overreacting. I take a deep breath to calm myself. It's never as bad as I fear.

Owen's truck roars into the lot and rocks into a spot beside mine, missing my car by inches. I shake my head.

"You missed your calling in life," I say, getting out of the car. "You should have been a stunt car driver."

He slams his own car door and crosses to me in ten seconds, looking sharp in his white button-up shirt and khaki pants. "There's still time," he says, and then his hand is on my hip as he pushes me against my car. He kisses me, his lips bruising mine as they take the lead, pushing my mouth open, finding entry to my soul. I wrap my arms around his neck and pull him in closer, a desperate energy pulsing through me that didn't exist before.

Emotion wells up in my throat and burns my eyes, and I'm afraid I'm going to cry. I break the kiss off and bury my face in the hollow of his neck.

His arms enclose me into his chest. He holds me.

And I do cry.

My shoulders shake as the tears turn into sobs. He holds me tighter but doesn't speak. I'm aware of my sister in the car behind me and I hope she's reading her book rather than staring out the window at us.

"Come inside for a moment?" Owen asks quietly.

I pull away and wipe my eyes, looking anywhere but at him. "I have to get Farrah."

"Just for a moment. Get a drink of water or something."

I can't resist him. I don't want to resist him. "All right." I turn around and open the door long enough to tell Annette, "I'll be right back."

She doesn't even look up from her book.

Owen shoves open the apartment door.

"You don't lock it?" I ask.

"We do. Doesn't work."

Inside the lights don't appear to be working either, but then my eyes adjust and I realize they are. Just not well. A beige couch with fraying cushions sits in the front room, and Owen's friend Derek is stretched across, his lanky body taking up the whole thing. He's focused on the television.

Owen takes my hand and guides me past the dingy kitchen, and I glance back long enough to see the overflowing dishes in the sink. Then we're down the hallway and into a bedroom.

He releases my hand and closes the door while I stand in the middle of the room and take it all in. The small window with broken blinds. The water-damaged ceiling tiles above the bed. The stained, industry-grade carpet.

But Owen's bed is the same one I remember from his room, and I move toward it with a flash of nostalgia. I settle on his quilted blanket and run my fingers over the squares.

I never knew how much I loved that blanket until this moment.

He sits down beside me, his eyes, that particular earthy shade of brown and green, never leaving my face.

"Are you all right?" he asks.

In answer I reach a hand out and dig it through his tumble of wavy hair. He's grown it out since we broke up. Then I lean forward, letting my body collapse against his chest. Just to feel the strength of his embrace as his arms go around me again.

His fingers drift through my hair and tickle their way down my back. "I'm sorry."

I straighten up and take his fingers in my hands, determined not to cry again. "I'm sorry too." I didn't think any harm would come from being friends with my ex-boyfriend. But I lied to Owen about it, and when he found out, he thought more was going on than actually was.

"I should have believed you," he says.

We were both wrong. And we were both right. I shouldn't have told another boy I loved him, even if he was only a friend. I shouldn't have lied to Owen and said Tiago and I weren't talking anymore. But he should have let me make it right.

"It sucked being away from you," I say. "It hurt me that you would choose to try being with someone else over saving our relationship."

"I am so sorry," he says, taking my chin and tilting it up so our eyes meet. "I thought I was doing what was best for you. For us."

"I know you did." I close my fingers over his and pull his hand from my face.

And now I hesitate. Because there are things I need to tell him. Things that happened while we were broken up. Things that I can't undo.

He sees it on my face. He knows me that well. He lifts an eyebrow, and I say, "Some things have changed in the past few months."

He nods and then silences me by dipping his face and kissing me. "I know. You don't owe me an explanation. We were broken up."

I grab his wrist. "I want to tell you."

Uncertainty flashes in his eyes, and I know I'm not the only one dreading the conversation.

"Let's talk about it when you get back," he say. "Figure out what it means for us."

I nod and exhale. I'm relieved. I want this with Owen. I want it now.

But it's not simple anymore. If it ever was.

His mouth meets mine again, a quick kiss, and then a longer one, and then suddenly that urgency from outside reawakens, shooting through my body like a firework, and I don't resist at all when he pushes me back on his bed. He moves over me, his hand running from my shoulder to my waist to below my hip, and he's never kissed me like this before. Sections of my skin that I didn't know have nerve endings spring to life, longing to feel his touch, and I completely forget about my sister in the car, about picking up Farrah, about reining in the wildfire blowing through my body.

But Owen doesn't. He lifts himself off me reluctantly, pausing to kiss me twice more before he takes my hand and sits me up. His pupils are dark, his eyes hooded, the desire so evident on his face that it stirs a corresponding desire in my navel. Or somewhere around there.

"You make me crazy," he whispers, and he stands up, pulling me from his bed.

For me. He's keeping things in check for me. No one has ever cared so much for what I want as Owen does.

"I love you," I blurt, before I can rethink it. I want to say it first. I want him to know I mean it.

Owen grabs me and holds me against him. Holds me so tight, so stiffly, as if he's not breathing, and I suddenly wonder if he's crying. I've seen him cry once before. The day he broke up with me.

We don't move. I swallow back another lump in my aching throat and listen to the beating of his heart beneath my ear. I want nothing more than for the world to fall away and he and I to be the only two objects that exist within it. I want to stay in his arms, listening to his heart thrumming, for the rest of my life.

But of course I can't.

He releases me. "I think you're late to pick up Farrah," he says, and he's let his voice drop into his familiar Louisiana southern drawl.

I smile, my heart lighter, my soul flying. "I'm late for everything." And I don't care.

I open his bedroom door, but before I can leave, he grabs my other hand, pulling me back. And he kisses me again, and again when I start to go, as if he can't get enough. And then he says the words I've been longing to hear.

"I love you too."

He finally lets me go. I skip out the door, skip out to my car, and let my heart do the skipping all the way to Farrah's house.

CHAPTER TWO

Senior Trip

I stop to text Monica, Owen's sister, outside of Farrah's house. Although there are four years between us, Monica has become one of my best friends. I only didn't tell her about Owen kissing me yesterday because of this crazy paranoid fear that if I told someone, it wouldn't be real anymore. It would vanish away like a beautiful dream in the morning.

I know. I'm weird.

So . . . I begin. *Did Owen tell you we got back together last night?*

And then I wait.

Farrah is ready when I knock, and a bit impatient, since I'm now twenty minutes late. Her blond hair is pulled back in a ponytail, and she looks stylish in her strappy sandals and cut-off shorts.

"I'm sorry, I'm sorry," I tell her, popping the trunk to put her bag next to mine. I shoot her a mischievous grin. "I was with Owen."

"Doing what?" she asks, arching an eyebrow.

I let my grin widen.

"Cassandra!" she shrieks, and I press a finger to my lips as we get back into the car. "What's going on?"

I open my mouth to explain just as my phone rings.

It's Monica.

I hit the green sphere and answer. "Hello?"

"What?" she cries, her voice echoing off the roof of the car. "You did? How? What happened? Why am I the last to know these things?"

I laugh. A cheerful sound, one that bubbles up from my belly in delight. "You're not the last, believe me. I didn't say anything until I knew for sure . . . but I just left his apartment."

"And you're back together?" She's laughing also.

"Mostly. We still need to talk through some of the things that happened, and the new development since we broke up." I know Monica will understand the reference.

"I'm so happy." She chokes on her words. "I was starting to believe it wouldn't happen."

"Me too," I say, softly, because I still remember the suffocating hopelessness of thinking I'd lost the boy I loved the most in all the world. "I still don't know what the future brings. But I want to spend every moment with him right now."

"The future is wide open," Monica purrs. I hear wedding bells in her head, and I smile.

"Yes, it is," I agree.

The drive to Branson, Missouri, from Springdale, Arkansas, is a long two hours on dangerous, curvy roads that have me braking more often than I'd like. I'm relieved when we reach the highway and can coast at a steady speed the rest of the way.

"But you didn't tell him about Brazil," Farrah says.

I've told her everything. Everything Owen told me last night after graduation and everything that happened in his apartment this morning—leaving out a few details, courtesy of Annette's innocent ears in the backseat, of course.

"I didn't tell him about Brazil," I confirm, and I cut a look at Farrah. An intentional look.

My family doesn't know, either.

They don't know about the plane ticket to Brazil next year to visit Tiago.

She gets my meaning and nods. "What are you going to do about it?"

"Well." I let out a breath. "I'm not keeping any secrets from Owen. That's what screwed us up last time."

"And if he says he doesn't want you to go?"

She lowers her voice, but there's not enough context, so I'm not worried about Annette figuring things out.

I shrug. "I won't go." It's an easy decision. Once, before there was Owen, I loved Tiago.

But now there is Owen. I know who I choose.

"But your money!"

I wince. I did buy the nonrefundable ticket, and it still cost me more than a grand. I'm stingy by nature and hate the thought of losing all that money.

But I hate the thought of losing Owen more.

"I'll have to be okay with that," I choke out.

"Maybe Owen could go with you. You guys could make a trip of it."

"Maybe," I agree, but not really.

That doesn't feel right, either.

We pull into the resort beside my mother's van in Branson an hour late. My mom doesn't text me when I'm driving, but she kept blowing up Annette's phone, who gave me a running summary of Mother's concerns and irritation for the last half hour of the drive. I pop the trunk and grab my mom's bag first, bracing myself with a big smile and a happy attitude.

Happy attitudes go a long way to appeasing mothers.

The condo looks like a seaside cottage, multiple stories and clapboard siding, painted in pastel blues and yellows and white. A wooden rocking chair sits on the porch. I rest the bag on my hip and knock on the red door.

My step-grandma Diane answers, and I work to keep my smile in place. The first time I met this woman and my grandfather was three days prior when they flew down for my graduation. I appreciate the giant check they wrote me to help my college fund, but I don't know them, and their presence feels like an intrusion.

"You're here," she says with a delicate sniff. Her thin, curly gray hair still smells like its most recent perm. She turns around and yells into the condo, "Karen! Cassandra's here!"

My mom bustles over, her expression harried, and I repaste the smile as I hold out the bag.

"Sorry I'm late," I say, as cheerfully as I can. I scoot over to let Farrah and Annette come in behind me.

"It's my fault," Farrah says, taking the fall for me. She knows Mom won't get angry with her. "I wasn't quite ready."

Sure enough, my mom's irritation melts away. "It's fine. Text me next time. I worried."

"I'm sorry," I repeat. I follow her into the kitchen and help her unpack the dishes, stacking them into cupboards next to identical pots and pans. "Can I help with the food?"

She waves me off. "You and Farrah have one of the upstairs rooms across from Emily and Anette. We're going to the outlet mall in half an hour. Get ready."

I return to the car and grab my bag, then hike the stairs up to the second floor of the three-story building. The seaside cottage theme continues in here, with an anchor hanging on the wall and an elaborate sailboat model on the table. Farrah already claimed her side of the queen bed. She stands in the adjacent bathroom, in front of the mirror twisting up her blond hair, and I dump my suitcase beside hers.

"Thanks for inviting me," Farrah says, meeting my eyes in the mirror. "Harper couldn't come?"

Guilt, my constant companion and nemesis, hisses up in my chest. Harper was —is—my best friend. I'm not sure what we are right now, actually. We've been fighting all year, mostly because I want more of her time and attention. She ditched me at prom and graduation, hurting my feelings badly.

I don't feel like explaining all this. So I say, "Yeah, she couldn't come."

"Ah. So that's why you invited me." Farrah says it with a teasing smile. "Second choice?"

"Guilty as charged," I say, even though it's not quite true. "Thanks for coming."

Farrah isn't even my second best friend. That is Riley. But Riley made herself scarce last year, popping up when she needed something and occasionally when I needed something. I feel a pang in my gut, because I don't know what's happening in her life, and I miss her. I don't know what to do to reach her, and I feel somehow this is my fault also.

I'm in-between friends right now. And it's another reason I am really looking forward to leaving for college in Colorado three short months. I need a new start. New faces. A do-over.

The outlet mall has a handful of clothing stores and fudge shops. My brother Scott abandons all of us for the gun shop even though he doesn't know a thing about hunting. Annette and Emily tag along a short distance behind me. I peruse the racks beside Farrah, fingering shirts and dresses without much interest. I work in a clothing store. I get a discount on high-end products. These aren't cute enough to tempt me or cheap enough to make me spend foolishly.

We find my mom in front of the fudge shop, trying every flavor within. I haven't eaten since breakfast. I study the elaborate multi-colored fudges, the green and black Oreo mint with crushed cookies on top, the white and pink swirled raspberry-white-chocolate with white chocolate shavings covering it. And I fight down the urge to buy them all.

I take a careful breath. Food and I have waged a war together since I was fourteen. We love each other, and I indulge too much, and then we hate each other, and I refuse it and viciously reject any that sneaks in.

At least, that's how it was. I spent a few months seeing a psychologist during my junior year of high school, and now we are at a tenuous stalemate. I eat cautiously, minding how it makes me feel, convincing and reminding myself with every bite that I'm nourishing my body. That I need food to live. That it's okay to enjoy it also.

My mom turns and slips an arm around my waist. "Which one do you want to try?"

One. I'll try just one. "The mint Oreo."

She requests my sample, and I take it off to the corner, happy with my choice and pleased I stopped at one.

It's a mind game, and one I might have to play for the rest of my life. But it's all right. I'm in a good spot.

Owen texts me while I nibble at my spoonful of sugary fudge, and my soul beams when I see his name.

O: Did you make it?

me: I did. We're here.

O: All right. See you when you get back.

I wish he were here. But I don't say that. I sense a need from both of us to take things a bit slower this time. Changes brew on the horizon, and we need to step carefully into this ocean.

Diane wants to see a show. Branson is famous for them.

We plan our day around it. All I want to do is lie down on my bed and catch up on all the missing sleep from my senior year of high school. But I agree to the plans because I'd hate to go head-to-head with Diane.

I suspect I'd lose.

"Here's the address to the Precious Moments Chapel," my mom says, giving me a slip of paper with an address on it. "Put that in your GPS. We'll see you and Farrah there."

I nod as I put the location into my phone. It's an hour and a half away.

"Why are we going there?" Farrah says. "Isn't it full of little dolls and stuff?"

"Diane collects Precious Moments figurines," I say. "She wants to go."

"Are she and your mom close? Is that why your mom is trying to please her?"

"No, actually." I don't tell her they just met also. My mom is very secretive about her family.

Of course, it just makes me want to know more.

I glance over at my grandfather, watching a game on the television. He married my grandma. He had to know her secrets. If I can get him alone, I might learn them also.

My phone chimes. I know that app. It's the one I use for messaging internationally, since only domestic is included on my phone plan.

The only person who uses it is Tiago.

He messaged me yesterday morning. I meant to respond but forgot. I stare at the phone now as my mom drives away in the van.

I don't want to ignore Tiago. He was there for me when Owen wasn't. He helped me get through that difficult time and comforted me when I felt abandoned by Harper.

But Tiago is also the reason why Owen and I broke up. I don't want to go anywhere near that path again.

"What are we waiting for?" Farrah asks.

I pick up my phone and hold it. "Tiago messaged me."

"Oh? What did he say?"

I read the text out loud. "*Cassandra! Can we talk tonight? I miss you.*" Oh, crap.

"What are you going to do?"

I don't answer because I don't know.

Farrah feeds me ideas. "Does he know about you and Owen? Maybe tell him you need space. Maybe you're busy. You can't deal with a relationship right now, you're getting ready to go to college."

It's all true, all of it, but I feel Tiago deserves the truth.

He was my first love. That means something, right?

I text him a brief, *Hey! I'm in Branson with Farrah. We're going to be busy for a few days, so I might not talk much.*

He writes back, *Okay. So no chat tonight?*

Me: Sorry. Not tonight.

T: No problem! Talk soon. Love you.

I do not say it back.

I never will again.

"What are you going to do?" Farrah asks again as I put the phone back on the dash and drive out to the main road. "You guys aren't together, are you?"

"Does it look like we are?" I snap out the words, but it's unfair of me. Tiago's in Brazil and I'm in Arkansas, but we'd gotten closer over the past few months. Closer to dating. Closer to being boyfriend and girlfriend.

That's why I bought tickets to Brazil. To see if we could be.

"Touchy," Farrah says, unabashed.

I exhale. "Sorry. No, we're not together. But I think he expects us to be soon." I had thought myself it might happen. Owen and I were broken up . . . And he'd told me we weren't getting back together. Ever.

I had started to believe him.

I shake my head. "I'll have to make sure Tiago knows it's not going to happen."

I get us safely to the Precious Moments Chapel, where we join the other over-fifties wandering around and try not to look absolutely bored. After a quick perusal of the museum and twenty minutes in the gardens, I ask my mom if Farrah and I can go back to Branson early.

"What for?" she asks, her eyes on the cherubic statues carved into the fountain.

"Just a quick nap," I say. "I'm so tired."

She looks me over and must decide I'm trustworthy. "Meet as at the theater for the Osmond show at six."

It's barely noon. An hour and a half to get back and four hours to sleep. I resist the fist pump. "See you there."

Farrah's phone rings as we get into the car. She glances at it, then shoots me a strange look. Like she's hoping I won't notice.

"Who is it?" I ask, immediately suspicious.

"A guy."

Farrah always has a guy. She's not usually sly about it.

"Who?"

When she hesitates, I know it's someone she doesn't want me to know about. "Spill it." I pounce at her, trying to pry the still-ringing phone from her hand.

"It's Tyler Reeves," she blurts in a rush. "Can I answer it?"

I lean back, startled into submission. Tyler from church? "Of course."

She turns away from me and answers, as if facing the seatbelt makes her less audible. "Hello?"

I steal glances at her while I turn on the car and head toward the interstate. She whisper-speaks and giggles and murmurs in her corner for the next half an hour. I keep checking on her until abruptly one of the interstate signs catches my eye. A big one.

Welcome to Kansas.

I almost hit my brakes but remember the cars zipping along the interstate behind me. Instead I grab Farrah's arm and give her a shake. "Farrah."

She turns from her phone call. "What?"

"We're in Kansas."

"No, we're in Missouri."

I gulp down a rush of panic. "No. We're in Kansas. I've lost us."

CHAPTER THREE

Questions

Farrah hangs up the phone with Tyler and pulls up her GPS. "Okay. We've just crossed the border from Missouri into Kansas. Stop driving and turn us around."

"I can't!" I snap, heart racing as I survey the cars zipping past me and the abundant lack of exits. How can I head off to college by myself if I can't even figure out how to get back to a resort one hour away?

"I didn't mean stop driving right here! Drive until we get to an exit. Then turn around."

Right. Of course. I take a deep breath, aware of the tingling in my nose and fingers that means I'm breathing too fast. Panicking.

Like I did last year when Owen broke up with me.

The thought manages to calm me down. No matter how lost we are, no matter how long it takes to get turned around, this isn't life-altering.

Another exit pops up four minutes later, and I take it. We pause at a gas station for me to get my bearings.

"Did you put the wrong address into your phone?" Farrah asks.

I shake my head, chagrined, as I program my map with the resort address. "I thought I remembered the way. So I didn't use it. Then I got out on the road and turned the wrong way."

"Ah, the folly of overconfidence," Farrah teases.

"Guilty." It's a character flaw I fall prey to over and over again.

"You say that a lot," Farrah says, casually, but as her eyes assess me, I sense them probing me. "Do you have a guilt-complex?"

I open my mouth, and then I laugh, because I almost said "guilty" again. "I think I might," I admit. "I always screw things up."

She gives me a sympathetic look. "No, you don't. Be kinder to yourself."

She doesn't know. Everything that goes wrong in my life is my fault. "This is a good example of me screwing up."

Farrah shrugs. "So we'll be a bit late. Let's turn around and get going. Your mom will never know. They're still at the museum."

"True." I exhale, grateful no one else witnessed this error.

I start the map, letting it guide me as we get back on the road. We are now over two hours away. An hour taken off my nap time. Sigh.

"You didn't screw up," she says, taking the conversation back to me and my feelings. "Everyone gets confused sometimes."

I don't want to argue about this. I search for a subject change, something to get the focus off me.

Then I remember Tyler.

"So." I grin at her before facing the road again. "You've been holding out on me. You and Tyler?"

"Oh, stop smirking." She slaps my forearm. "It's nothing yet. We talked at Senior Project and he said he wishes he could have a do-over from when we dated sophomore year."

"That was a long time ago," I say, falling into the past. "I almost forgot."

"Yeah. He ditched me for that cheerleader."

"Melanie," I supply. "We all get ditched for cheerleaders." Owen's done it to me several times.

Not exactly true. He turned to the cheerleaders every time I rejected him.

Still stings.

"Yeah." Farrah scowls. "Hoochies."

I don't tell her Melanie is one of the nice ones. She went out of her way to make me feel welcome when I started dating Owen.

"Anyway," Farrah continues, "after he said that about the do-over, I couldn't stop thinking about him. I really liked him, you know?"

I nod. I remember that drama.

"So this morning at church—"

"You went to church?" I interrupt, putting a shocked expression on my face.

"I do sometimes, you know," Farrah growls, and I laugh.

"Apparently when there's a cute guy to talk to," I say.

She presses her lips together and waits for me to finish chuckling.

"Sorry," I say. "Go on."

"Yeah. Anyway. We sat by each other in church, and after the sermon he asked if I want to try again. I said yes. So." She shrugs. "We're kind of dating again."

I shoot her a satisfied smile. "Like me and Owen."

"Similar. We all bring past dramas to the relationship."

Now I grimace. "I bring a lot."

"Yeah, you do."

We laugh at my expense this time.

"I hope it works out for you," I say, sincerely. "Tyler is one of my favorite people."

"We'll see what happens."

No one else is at the resort when we finally pull in, so no one is the wiser that I went the wrong way and took an extra hour to get here. Farrah and I snap pictures of each other, posing like models in front of the resort fountain. I smile as I look through the pictures, but they feel wrong.

Guilt, my familiar nemesis, sighs and licks my conscience. I'm having a great time with Farrah, but . . .

It should be Harper here with me.

I want to call her, but I feel stupid. She doesn't know anything about my life lately. I've intentionally kept her out of its because a) I was mad at her and b) I didn't feel close to her. How do I bridge that gap now?

I start with a text. I'm better at those anyway.

Hey Harper! I'm in Branson. I wish you were with me. I miss you. Can we do something when I get back?

She still hasn't responded when we return home from the show that evening. I brush my teeth and study my dark brown eyes in the mirror, wondering how mad she is at me. We made up at Senior Project. But we haven't fixed things.

Farrah giggles at her phone on the couch, probably sending photos to Tyler. I could send some to Owen. I know he'd make me feel better. But a boy can never replace a best friend. I am about to leave her for the next four or five years. Probably forever.

I spit the toothpaste out and sigh.

My phone dings, and I look down at it.

H: Hey! I miss you too. I hope you're having fun. We're headed out of town next week, but I'd love to spend time with you when we get back. I'll let you know when I'm home. How are things?

Oh, how I'm itching to talk to her. To tell her I bought a plane ticket to Brazil. To tell her Owen and I got back together. To tell her no one could ever be as good of a best friend as she is, even with her shortcomings.

To tell her how much I'm going to miss her when I go to college.

I swallow back a sudden urge to cry.

Me: It's all right! We'll talk soon.

I fall into bed feeling the enormity of what lies in front of me. I've looked forward for years to escaping Arkansas and having the chance to carve out a life independent of my family and my past. And now it scares me. I'll be all alone.

With Camila. For a moment I forgot my summer camp friend would be at PYU with me. The fact that we are sharing a dorm buoys me. And my cousin Jordan will be there, also.

I won't be alone.

◌⌒◌⌒◌

We spend the next day at Silver Dollar City, an amusement park my brother affectionately refers to as "Redneck Disney." Employees in wild frontier costume greet us at every shop, banjos play over the speakers, and pulled taffy beside freshly spun cotton candy tempts us from the windows. Emily and Annette take off because they mapped out an ambitious plan to hit every ride today. My brother Scott hangs out with Farrah and me. Somewhere in the past year he grew up, going from annoying to fun, and I enjoy his adolescent companionship now.

We meet up with my parents and grandparents for dinner, minus Abuela, of course.

The adults had a different experience than us at the amusement park, since they spent the day indoors watching the various shows and musicals Silver Dollar City is famous for. Now I discover my grandfather is hilarious, and he teases Annette and Scott endlessly in line at the buffet. We all crack up at his antics.

I end up sitting next to him at the end of a long table. It's the first time since we met that we've had the chance to talk. We make conversation around the fried chicken and mashed potatoes, with him asking me about my secondary education, my friends, college.

"And such a pretty girl as yourself," he says. "You look so much like your grandmother did when I met her. Young and bright-eyed and ready to take on the world."

His tone is wistful, his smile wispy, his eyes focusing somewhere else in time.

I see it then. He might have divorced her, but he loved her once. Abuela is not a nice person now, not since the stroke. And they were young when they married. I forgive him for leaving her. I can't judge something I didn't experience.

But I see an opportunity to ask questions.

"Grandpa," I say, "why don't we talk with Abuelita's family? Did something happen?"

CHAPTER FOUR

New Insight

Grandpa pauses as he deliberates over my question. I hold my breath, not moving, afraid he'll put me off the way Mom does anytime I ask. And then he lowers his voice.

"Well, the truth of the matter is, I don't know the details. But when I met your grandmother, she had run away from home. She came into the gas station where I was working in California, and she was frightened. I took one look at her and told her she could stay with me."

I stare at him, intrigued. "So you saved her."

"Maybe. She moved into my apartment. I let her have the living room to herself while I tried to figure out what was happening. She was only seventeen. Her English was broken, but when I pressed her for details, she just said, over and over again, 'I won't go back. I won't go back.' So she stayed, and I took care of her, and I suppose it was inevitable to fall in love. And we married."

I'm carried away in this yearning tale of suffering and young love. I can picture myself as the main character, having been seventeen and desperately in love twice in my life. "She never told you anything?"

"Never. We waited until she was eighteen so no one had to give permission to marry. On occasion I'd ask questions about her family, where she came from. For years I knew only that Spanish was her native tongue. Until your aunt was born. Then she made me go out and buy a Bible so we could write our children's names in it. Because that's how it's done in Colombia. And that's how I learned where she'd come from."

"Does my mom know anything?"

He shakes his head. "Not from me. I didn't tell her any of this when she was a child, and we didn't spend time together once she grew older. If she knows anything more, it came from your grandmother."

And Mom is silent on the subject. I'm certain she knows more.

"Mom acts like I should drop it when I bring it up," I say. "It seems to frighten her."

"It frightened your grandmother too," he says. "Whatever it is, it seems to have stayed in the past. Perhaps it's best if we left it there."

I'm not ready to let it drop. "What was Abuela's maiden name?"

"I don't know, sweetie. She put a different name on her marriage papers. She put Vallay."

"How do you know it wasn't her real name?"

"Because when she had her stroke, I tried to find her family to let them know. And there were no relatives with that last name. It was a dead end."

It feels like the conclusion. My food has gone completely cold, but I'm more curious than ever.

"Thanks for sharing with me, Grandpa," I say. And I can't help adding, "I'm sorry things didn't work out between you and Abuela."

He pats my hand with his spindly fingers, the blue veins large on a peppery canvas of age spots. "You're a sweet girl, Cassandra. I'm grateful for this chance I've had to meet you."

❧⁓✦⁓❧

Farrah and I leave Branson early Wednesday morning so I can get her to work on time. I sit in my car, idling in her driveway, and text Owen.

He's all I've been able to think about. I've waited as long as I could. Now that I'm home, I can't wait to see him.

Me: I'm back

I consider offering to come over to his apartment, but there's still a part of me that's cautious. Holding back from putting my whole heart into this relationship, from making myself vulnerable again.

After all, we'll be going our separate ways soon.

Turns out I don't need to offer. Owen texts back before I've backed out of the driveway.

O: Finally. I'm at my mom's house. Come over?

He's home. I'm relieved for a number of reasons. I didn't love his apartment, and spending time alone in his room is likely to get us into trouble. And I miss his mom and sister. I haven't seen Monica since graduation.

Me: Be there in twenty.

O: Still in Branson?

Me: No, at Farrah's.

O: It's a five-minute drive, Cass.

I laugh. He's teasing me about my slow driving, but from Springdale to Tontitown is twenty minutes, twenty-five if traffic is bad. I don't dare drive like he does. *Me: Only if I want to taunt death.*

O: drive slow then

I'm still chuckling when I pull into the long driveway beside the cornfield in front of his house. His brother Richard and Mr. Blaine are throwing a ball back and forth in the front yard. They watch me get out of the car, and I see the moment they recognize me.

"Hi," I say, waving.

"Cassandra." Mr. Blaine smiles. "Here to see Monica?"

So they don't know Owen and I are back together. My heart does a little tumble as I realize how new this is. Who else doesn't know?

Does Kristin know? I hope she's not his girlfriend anymore. Please, please don't let us have another incident like Suzi.

"Yes," I say, unsure of myself.

"She's here for me."

I turn as Owen steps off the porch, and I feel that familiar surge of pride and happiness that this tall, broad-shouldered, green-eyed boy likes me. He chose me.

Owen slips a hand through mine and pulls me up the steps.

"You guys back together?" Richard asks.

"Figure it out, Chard!" Owen hollers at him before we enter the house.

I don't see Mrs. Blaine in the kitchen, but Owen doesn't give me the chance to wander the house looking for anyone.

A few moving boxes are stacked in the laundry room.

"Still packing up?" I ask.

Owen doesn't answer. He leads me straight back to his room, only now it's bare of a bed or a dresser. Instead he plops down on the rug in the middle of the hardwood floor, and I sit across from him.

"I guess it's not your room anymore," I say, glancing around.

"Yeah, I guess not." He takes my hands and holds them lightly, resting our hands on his knees. "There's a lot we need to talk about."

My heart squeezes. I'm dreading this conversation. I want to keep living in the fantasy world where he and I get back together and everything falls into place for us. "Yes, I guess so."

But he doesn't speak. His eyes trace over my face. I don't move as he studies me. He sighs and squeezes my hands.

"I missed you."

"Every moment," I say, and I swallow. I will not cry. I will not cry.

"When do you leave for Preston Y?"

"August." Once upon a time, he'd planned to come to Colorado with me. "You staying here?"

He gives a slow shake of his head, his eyes still on me. "There's been a change of plans."

I want to believe he's going to say he's coming to Colorado after all. But I know from the somberness of his expression that's not it. "What change?" My heart's in my throat, battering out a nervous pattern that makes me sick to my stomach.

"I also got accepted to Louisiana State. I decided to enroll there instead of Arkansas."

"You're going back to Louisiana?" My voice falters. My throat is thick. The tears are lodged under my tongue. "But why?"

He squeezes my hands. "My dad got transferred back. The whole family is going. And I—oddly enough want to go with them."

The whole family. Gone. Not in Arkansas.

"You won't be here." Owen's been at odds with his parents for as long as I've known him. I'm happy to see him repair that relationship. But— "I thought I'd see you. At Christmas. During summer breaks." Crap, the tears escaped. They slide down my cheeks, one after the other, and I look down, but I can't hide them.

He lets go of one hand to wipe them with his thumb. "Monica's going to school at Snow College. She'll be five hours from you. She'll want to see you."

"Five hours." I try to laugh. "You say that like it's close." I can't stop the tears now.

He can't keep up with wiping them away, so he gets up and grabs a rag from the top of his desk. I use it to hide the stem of tears. He doesn't sit again. He stands by his desk instead, running his fingers over the back of the chair. "I already talked to Louisiana State about going on a mission trip. They're going to let me go as long as I keep my grades high for two semesters. So I plan to leave in a year."

In a year. Ironic. I'll be headed to Brazil, and Owen will be going on a mission. His mission will be anywhere from one to two years, and it could be anywhere in the world. When we leave for college, it's goodbye. It's over.

I put my face in my hands and cry.

Owen returns to the rug, and he tugs on my arms, prying them away from my face. "Come on, Cass. You're the one who's been encouraging me to do this. I thought you wanted it."

"I did." I nod and keep my eyes on the rug. "I do. It's just—reality is harder."

His fingers thread through mine. "We have until August."

"So." I swallow and try to keep my voice steady. "Are we dating? Officially? What about Kristin?"

"Well." His hand tightens, and I brace myself for more stings. "I broke up with Kristin. Before I kissed you this time."

We both laugh, though mine sounds wet and strained. Suzi didn't take it well last year when he broke up with her after he asked me out. I don't fail to notice he didn't answer my other questions.

"Is that a yes or no?" I ask.

"Here's the thing," he says, and his voice is quieter. "We're only eighteen and about to go separate directions with our lives. You know that, right?"

I do. I know what he's saying. I feel it too. But I hate it.

"We got pretty serious last time. The thought of you with another guy tore me up. But that's not fair. I don't think we should make promises. Let's enjoy right now. With no strings attached. Let life happen."

"I don't want to let life happen," I say, forcefully. "I want to make it happen."

"If I try to cage you, I'll lose you," he said. "I know it, even if you don't. So I won't."

"But we are dating." I need to define it. I need to know.

"Yes." He tightens his grip on my hand. "We're dating." He tilts his head, catching my gaze. "Is there anything else you want to know?"

He's offering to tell me the sordid details of his relationship with Kristin, but I can't bring myself to care. He broke up with her. That's all that matters. "No. But there is something I need to tell you."

"Okay." He sets his jaw and braces himself.

I take a deep breath and pull my fingers from his, feeling the heat of shame creep up my face. "You know Tiago and I stayed friends these past few months. Sometimes he was the only person I could count on," I say, reminding Owen that he abandoned me, reminding him of his part in this. I risk a glance at his face, but it's a solid stone, any emotional reaction hidden behind his mask. "I bought a plane ticket. To Brazil. For next May."

"Do you love him?" he asks me quietly.

I shake my head, clenching my teeth and meeting his eyes so he knows I'm serious. "No. But I thought you and I were over. And he offered me unconditional friendship."

He sighs, letting the breath fall away from his lips in a slow exhale. "You know what, I hate it. But it's fine. Maybe it's what's supposed to happen."

"It's only friendship, Owen."

He's quiet. Considering. Thinking. Then he pulls on me, tugging me off the carpet and into his lap, where he cradles me like a baby. "It's a year from now. Go to Brazil. And we'll just see."

I bob my head up and down in his shirt, but the tears begin again, running silently down my nose and into the fabric.

I know what happens when two people go different directions.

I've already lived that story.

CHAPTER FIVE

Job Hunt

eat lunch with Owen's family. Some of the heaviness in my heart lifts as I munch on a cheese sandwich and watch Owen and Richard toss chips at each other. Mrs. Blaine yells for them to stop throwing food. Monica gives me a hug and tells me she wants all the details about getting back together, but then her boyfriend calls and she leaves the room to talk to him.

I take my plate to the sink. Owen slides up behind me and wraps his arms around me, ducking as Richard chucks another handful of chips.

"Hey!" I exclaim as one stabs me in the forehead.

"Chard!" Owen hollers. "You hit Cassandra!"

"You think I don't see you there?" Richard throws more, and I spin out of the way. "So cowardly to hide behind your girlfriend!"

I giggle as Mrs. Blaine finally ends the mess by taking away the bag of chips.

"Crazy boys," she grumbles, throwing it in the trash. "Chips are gone now." She hands a broom to Richard. "Sweep before your dad sees it."

Richard obliges, and Owen turns me around and kisses me, right there in front of his family. He's not one for Public Displays of Affection, and I'm shocked.

"Owen." I glance around. "They might see us!"

"Who cares?" He kisses me again. "I get to kiss you. And I'm going to do it every chance I get until I can't."

"Get a room!" Richard yells, and he would have thrown the broom if his mom hadn't stopped him.

"Right here is better than a room," she says. "At least I know what you're doing."

Owen raises an eyebrow. "So we can do whatever we want as long as you're watching?"

"Owen!" I smack his forearm. I should have seen that coming. He loves making jokes laced with innuendo, especially when it embarrasses me.

But Mrs. Blaine just rolls her eyes and leaves the room.

"Think that's a yes?" Owen asks, and he walks me backward to the couch, where he pushes me onto it before falling beside me.

"Gross!" Richard says, and he drops the broom and leaves.

I giggle as Owen kisses me, slowly, bending his head to move his lips over mine and then lifting his face to look at me, brushing a hair off my face and trailing a finger over my cheekbone before lowering his head to kiss me again.

"I'm still watching!" Monica yells from the sunroom. But she doesn't sound the least bit appalled, and Owen yells back, "I don't care!"

My phone rings, and he sits up to let me dig it out of my pocket. I recognize the number from Kids First, the day care I volunteered at last year.

"Hang on," I say, hitting the answer button. "Hello?"

"Is this Cassandra Jones?"

"Yes." I stand up.

"This is Linda, the hiring manager at Kids First. I got your application, and one of my employees put in a good word for you. Do you still want to work here?"

"Yes." Spending time with the special-needs children lifted my spirits last year. "Can I?"

"Well, we'd love to have you. I need you to go to the health department and get a TB test first. Once you test negative for that, bring me the results and we'll get your paperwork filled out. Can you do that?"

"Yes!" I look around for a sheet of paper but don't see one, so I catch Owen's eye and repeat, "Get a TB test at the health department."

"The sooner, the better."

"All right. Got it."

"We'll see you soon, Cassandra."

I pull up a map to the health department on my phone.

"What was that?" Owen asks.

"I have to get a TB test so I can work at Kids First. What's a TB test, anyway?"

"No idea." Owen pushes off the couch. "I have to head back into town and get a few things from my apartment. Want me to take you?"

"I'd love to, but I can't go right now." The map shows the health department is in Fayetteville. "My mom told me to be home in an hour. I have to help her unpack from Branson."

"All right." He stands by me, sliding his hands around to my back pockets, sidling me up against him. "Are you good? With us?" He brushes my nose with his.

I drop my phone on the couch and wrap my arms around his neck. "Yes. At least we have now." That was more than I expected four days ago.

"And we'll make the most of it." He kisses me again, no spaces between us.

And I think, no one's ever going to fit with me as well as he does.

❦

A big pile of mail waits for me at home. Most of it is junk, colleges still begging for my application, and I throw them away with a smirk. I'm set. Going to the school of my dreams on scholarship.

My high school sent me a big envelope. I open it, expecting transcripts or something official, but instead my prom pictures fall out.

Prom. I pick up the images of Franklin and me and feel a churn of mixed emotions.

Franklin was a close friend all year, but mostly because he was an exchange student from Brazil who reminded me of Tiago. After Owen and I broke up, Franklin took me to prom. It felt like he was doing me a favor, and the night didn't end well. He'd apparently expected something in return for the favor, and he was annoyed with me when he didn't get it.

Looking at the picture makes me remember this. And it makes me remember how much it hurt watching Owen dance with Kristin in her I-Dream-of-Genie dress.

I'll take a copy over to Franklin later this week. Before he goes home.

Tiago messages me as I'm about to drop into bed. *Hey! Are you home from Branson yet?*

He hasn't messaged me in days. It's been a difficult few months with him, but he's respected my need for space when I've asked for it.

I'm not sure he'll like my next request.

My sister Emily shares a room with me, but she's working tonight. I settle against the covers and answer. *Yes. Got home this morning.*

T: Did you have fun?

Me: I did. I wish I'd been with Harper, but Farrah and I had a great time.

T: You have good friends.

Me: I miss Harper.

T: Have you talked to her?

Me: Not yet, but I will.

I can't avoid this. I need to do it.

Me: Tiago, I need to make something clear

T: OK

Me: I'm coming to Brazil in the spring. But you know I'm not your girlfriend, right?

There is a long pause. The three dots that indicate he's responding appear, then disappear, then appear again. Finally he says, *Right.*

I exhale. *Okay. As long as you know.*

T: So why are you saying this?

Because I'm going to date other people. Because I'm dating one now.

I'm too chicken to say that.

Me: I don't want there to be this expectation that I'm yours

I realize how harsh it sounds after I send it. But he's seen it. There's no undoing it.

T: Can I call you?

I sigh. This will get harder on the phone. But I answer, *Yes.*

The phone rings in the app moments later. "Hello?" I say.

"Cassandra. Hi."

I close my eyes at the sound of his voice. I can't help it. Tiago and I shared something once, and a part of him lives in my heart. His accented, tenor voice reaches places no one else can. "Hi."

"What's going on?" he asks.

"What do you mean?" I play dumb.

"Something's different. You sound different than a few days ago."

Crap, he's right. A few days ago—the same day Owen and I got back together, actually—I told Tiago I was coming to Brazil.

Everything's changed since then.

I'm not telling him about Owen. I'm tired of pitting these two boys against each other. "I had time to think while I was in Branson. It was good to get away." An excuse springs to mind, and I grab it, spinning a realistic reason as I speak. "It made me realize I'll be leaving for college soon. Having new experiences. Meeting new people. And I want—I want to be able to experience all of that without feeling—" Now words fail me. I almost said "trapped." But that sounds harsh.

He finds the word for me. "Trapped."

"Attached," I say instead.

"You want to date other people." His tone is flat.

I feel a rush of indignation. "I want to date people, period. You and I aren't dating."

There's a pause, and I can practically hear the gears clicking in his brain, searching for something more concrete.

"Did you meet someone you like?" he asks.

It's a safe question, and I pray with all my soul he doesn't ask about Owen. I don't want to lie to him.

"No," I say. "But I saw some cute boys at the park. And there are going to be lots of them at school. Hundreds." *There.* I like my reasoning. It makes sense.

"All right," he says. Not happily. "But can I at least be one of those people you're dating?"

I want to laugh. He's in Brazil, for crying out loud. Am I going to tick him off on my fingers when I list the guys I went on a date with in the past month? "You're not even here," I say instead.

"Just . . . keep me in your mind."

It's not my mind he wants into. It's my heart. And I completely lack the courage to tell him he can't be there. "It goes both ways, you know. You can date people also."

He makes a noise on the other end. "I've done that. It makes me miss you more."

I hate it when he says things like that. It makes me feel guilty. Like I'm a bad person for not missing him like he misses me.

And then I remember that I did. When I left Brazil last summer, I died a little each day for nine months, desperate for a simple word of acknowledgment from him while he couldn't be bothered to send even an email.

Until Owen lifted me from the grave and saved me.

"Keep your heart open," I say. "Maybe it will change."

"And how will you feel if it does?"

There's a challenge in his words. Like he's calling my bluff. I don't like it. And I know I'll get jealous. Of course I will. I'm human. I like having someone's attention on me. "I'll have to deal with it, Tiago. Life is going to happen."

"All right. But you're still coming in May?"

"Yes. My tickets are bought."

"Then it'll be okay."

I know what he's thinking. That the moment I see him, no matter what guys may have stolen my heart, he'll win me back.

He better not be right.

CHAPTER SIX

Night Terrors

ebra scheduled me for a twelve-hour shift at the clothing store the next day with Nicole. The only good thing about these all-day shifts is the one-hour lunch break I get in between. I put my feet up in the break room and open a book, glad for the chance to rest.

A text dings on my phone. I risk a glance, paranoid it might be Tiago, but it didn't come from the messaging app.

It's Monica. *Want to go to the movies?*

Me: I'm at work.

M: what time are you off?

Me: closing

M: which is???

Me: ten

Silence follows. I return to my book, but the phone dings again moments later.

M: got us tickets to a thriller movie at 11:30

I have to laugh.

Me: You're crazy. Ok.

I want to invite Owen. But I also know I need some girl-time with Monica. She's not just my boyfriend's sister; she's one of my best friends, even though there are four years between us. She came home from college because she got sick, and Owen told her she should hang out with me.

I miss him already.

M: I have to house sit for this lady. I don't want to be there alone. Stay the night after?

Me: Sure. But you have to go by my house and get my stuff.

M: Send me a list.

The work day goes well. Debra's happy I'm back because somehow I always move the most inventory. I help close up the store at ten and drive to the coffee shop in Fayetteville where Monica waits.

It must be Open Mic night, because people keep going up to the microphone set up on the dark stage and reading poetry or short stories. I have my own collection of poetry in the notebook I keep in my purse. It's full of angst and heartbreak and sadness.

It's been a few days since I've written any. And I hope it will be several months more.

"Cassandra!" Monica greets me with a hug. She towers over me as she rocks me, almost the same height as her brother. Then there's me, barely taller than five feet. I wasn't gifted in height.

We settle back at the table in the dimly lit room filled with the scent of coffee and spices, and she pushes a mug toward me. The tables are more crowded than I expect them to be for this time of night, but it is a college town.

"I ordered you a hazelnut steamer," she says. "I love them, so I thought you would too."

"Thanks." I pick it up and inhale, closing my eyes as the luscious scent wafts up my nose.

"So."

I open my eyes when she speaks. She has the same brownish green eye color as Owen, but her face is all feminine angles: delicate eyebrows and a small nose. Light brown curls fall to her shoulders. She leans closer.

"What's going on with you and Owen?"

I wrap my hands around the mug and smile. "Monica. He still loves me."

She sighs and rolls her eyes. "Of course he does! But what are you guys going to do about it?"

"Spend the summer together." I shrug like it doesn't matter, though the thought of what comes after tears at my heart. "And then go off to school."

"And wait for each other?"

"Not particularly." I lower my eyes. "I mean, we want each other to feel free to have a real college experience. Not be tied to someone far away. Loneliness, right?"

Monica takes a sip of her mug and sets it down. "You suck at lying."

I have to laugh. And I shrug. "I would wait for him if he asked."

We sit in silence, sipping, contemplating. Then she says, "What about Tiago?"

Tiago. Again. Always. The wild card. I feel a flash of irritation, and I don't know who to blame. Tiago? Owen? Myself?

At least I don't have to explain anything. Monica knows every sordid detail of my complicated relationship with Tiago.

"I'll go to Brazil. Because I have to close that chapter. No more back and forth."

Monica nods. "Yes, girl. You need to get him out of your system."

"I do." Now it's my turn. I meet her eyes and ask, "How's the cancer?" The doctors removed a malignant tumor last winter. But she looks good. Still has all her hair. I can tell she's lost some weight, but her skin has a nice golden color, her cheeks pink.

"The treatment is going really well!" She beams. "I still go for radiation every day. But the traces of the tumor are almost gone. We're still on track to be done by August. And no chemo!"

"Really?" I push out of my chair and hug her. Tears sting my eyes. I hate that I cry over almost everything, so I fight them back. "This is such wonderful news!"

She squeezes me tight, then twirls her hair around her finger as I sit. "I know it's vain and petty, but I didn't want to lose my hair."

"It's not vain or petty. It's normal. I wouldn't want to lose mine either."

"But the wig options they showed me were pretty. So it wouldn't be terrible."

"And Noah? Things are going well?"

"Yes, but we are kind of like you and Owen. Having a great time. Knowing it's going to end in August when I head to Utah for school."

"Everyone faces this, don't they?" I think of all the high school couples I know. Most will separate at the end of the summer.

"Come on." She stands up, shouldering her purse. "Let's get to the theater."

We head to the parking lot, and I halt when I see Owen's truck.

"Is Owen here?" I spin around, half expecting him to pop out from behind a light pole.

Monica laughs. "No, sorry! I drove his truck today."

"Ah." I run my hand along the back of it, feeling nearly as much affection for the car as for the driver. They are connected in my mind. "Did he move back in?"

"No, but he spends more time at our house than his apartment. It's small and gross. And those boys make it worse. The stench. Ugh."

"I know." I wrinkle my nose.

"You've been there?" Monica pauses by the door, casting me a look of surprise. "Owen took you there?"

I nod, my cheeks burning. "Yes."

She arches an eyebrow but says nothing more about it. "See you at the theater."

After an engaging thriller involving way too many bugs and lots of beautiful women with thick makeup and few articles of clothing, I follow Monica—in Owen's truck—back out into the rural backwoods of Tontitown. We wind our way down past the chicken farms that loan their particular smell to all of Springdale, out past the road leading to my house, continuing across the highway.

The house is at the end of a long rocky driveway. In the darkness I can't tell what it looks like. I park beside Monica in the wide concrete pad. Dogs yelp and bark somewhere nearby, and I huddle close to her as she unlocks the house to let us in.

It's pitch black inside. The moon doesn't even lend its light. Goosebumps prick my arms as I picture the plentiful array of beetles and scorpions from the movie we just watched lurking in the darkness. Something bumps up against my calf, and I shriek and jump, crashing into the wall before Monica finds the light switch.

"A cat, Cassandra," she says, laughing at me.

The bushy-tailed creature gives me a haughty look before marching away, tail straight in the air.

I press a hand to my chest, catching my breath, and Monica closes the door and locks it. Outside the dogs finally stop barking.

"Come on." Monica flips on lights as she goes, illuminating a gourmet kitchen with white cabinets, marble counters, and leather bar chairs.

We tiptoe across white carpet through a tall living room and reach the master bedroom. The enormous bed with a fluffy blanket gestures us forward. Monica collapses on it.

"Here's your bag." She motions to a small duffel at the foot of the bed.

I check the time and curl up in a big leather chair that could easily fit two of me. My eyes burn with exhaustion. And no wonder. It's after two in the morning.

"What do you have to do here?" I ask Monica, my words slurring with sleepiness.

"Just make sure no one breaks in. Feed and water the cat."

"How many nights?"

"One. Are you ready to sleep?"

"Yes." I force myself to my feet, grab the bag she packed me, and enter the master bathroom. Stage lights brighten the vanity. I ignore them as I remove my contact lenses and put on my glasses. My eyes tear up in relief. So nice to get those plastic eyeball huggers out. I peel off the tight pants and shirt I wore to work and slide into the shorts and tank top pajamas. I leave my bra on. It's padded, and I'm super embarrassed of my flat chest. It makes me feel like a boy. So the fake boobies are staying.

Monica already has the light out in the bedroom. I climb up on the bed, putting my glasses on the end table and falling into the cushy softness. I push down the blankets.

"I've been swallowed alive," I say.

Monica giggles somewhere to my right. "This is the kind of bed you get if you don't want to touch your husband all night long."

I laugh too, but her words send my thoughts in a different direction.

I do want to touch my husband all night long.

I close my eyes. Hazy night dreams fog my mind, and I know I'll be asleep soon.

A loud bang echoes outside. Something crashes to the ground. The dogs start up a ruckus, barking and growling, and I bolt upright, heart in my throat.

Monica flips on the light. "What was that?"

We look at each other across the blankets.

"Do they get intruders often?" I ask, pulse racing. I'm envisioning thieves with binoculars in the trees, watching the house, waiting for the owners to leave so they can break in.

"I don't know." Monica clutches the blankets to her chest. "Should I call the police?"

I don't answer but grab my glasses and slide them on. I want to see if we have to make a run for it.

We sit in silence for several minutes, the only sound the thrumming of my heart. I strain to hear anything else, but even the barking slowly dies down. Still, I'm reluctant to relax. What made that noise?

Monica lets go of the blanket and settles back on the bed. "Maybe it was a tree branch."

"It's possible," I agree.

It's quiet outside.

I hunker back in the covers, breathing deep. Telling myself it was nothing.

A sound like a gun shot rips through the silence. We both jerk upright again. Monica screams, I shriek, and the dogs bark and yelp into the night.

"Was that a gun?" I cry. Monica comes from a family of hunters. She'll know.

"I don't know!" she says. Her hand shakes as she grabs her phone.

"What are you going to do?"

"I'm calling Owen! I don't want to stay here alone!"

I'm instantly calmer. Somehow calling Owen is even better than calling the police. I jump out of bed and go to the dark living room, peeking out of the closed curtains, wanting him here right now. A streetlight illuminates the road beyond, but the corners of the yard around us are bathed in black shadows. I close the curtain, aware that eyes could be outside watching us.

Monica comes out of the bedroom, using her phone as a flashlight. She must have changed into pajamas while I was in the bathroom, because she's wearing drawstring lounge pants and a striped tank top. "Owen's coming," she says.

She sits at one end of the couch, and I fall into the other.

"What did you tell him?" I ask.

"That we keep hearing funny noises. He told me to go back to sleep and leave him alone. Then I told him you were scared too, and he said he was getting Mom's car keys."

We both laugh, and that delicious warm happiness carves its way up my chest, lighting up the dark spaces and chasing away my fear. Bring on the thieves.

Headlights bathe over the house ten minutes later, splashing over us. Monica goes to the front door and peeks out the window, then unlocks it and opens it a crack.

"Come in, come in!" she says, grabbing Owen's arm and pulling him into the entryway.

She locks up behind him, and he says, "Are you guys seriously just sitting here in the dark?"

"Well . . ." Monica says, and I begin to giggle.

"Bunch of biddies you girls are," Owen says. But he's not mocking us. He's teasing. There's a difference. He flips on a light, and I squint, shielding my offended eyes.

"So what happened?" Owen falls onto the couch next to me and looks at Monica.

She twists her fingers. "First there was a crash, and the dogs started barking. We thought maybe it was a tree branch and tried to ignore it. But then a gunshot went off—"

"There was a gunshot?" Owen repeats.

Monica nods vigorously. "Yes! At least, it sounded like one. I thought about calling the police, but—"

"Decided to call me instead."

I bite my lip, and she looks sheepish.

"Yes."

Owen stands up. I take in his apparel now. Checked flannel pants and a loose blue cotton T.

How can he be so sexy and adorable at the same time?

He puts a hand on Monica's shoulder, keeping his face serious.

"You did the right thing," he says.

She rolls her eyes and shoves his hand off. "Shut up."

He heads to the door. "I'm going to take a quick look around. You girls stay here."

"Did you bring a gun?" Monica shifts from foot to foot, looking nervous. I wrap my arms around my legs and watch.

He gives her a scornful look and lets himself out of the house.

CHAPTER SEVEN
Loud and Clear

Monica goes to the window and chews on her finger. "What if someone's out there? What if he needs a gun?"

I don't voice my own fears. Owen is confident no one is there. Or he's confident he can defend himself. His confidence takes the edge off my worry, but I've seen enough thrillers to know he could be wrong. My heart rate picks up and I breathe deeply, watching the door, waiting for Owen to return.

Five minutes pass. Six.

"Should I text him?" Monica asks, still peering out the window.

"No!" I exclaim. "Haven't you seen the zombie movie when his wife calls him and nearly kills them all?"

She makes a face, but at least she doesn't text him.

Four more minutes. Then she exhales.

"He's coming back."

I push up and meet him at the front door, Monica right behind me.

"Well?" Monica demands, letting him in and locking the door immediately. "What did you find?"

"You're okay." I resist throwing my arms around him.

He laughs at us. "There's a street behind the house. There's not a lot of traffic, given that it's almost four in the morning." He glowers at Monica. "Probably you heard a car backfire. Old cars do that a lot."

"And the crash?"

He shrugs. "Don't know."

"So it's likely nothing."

"Yep." He moves to the couch and crashes onto it. "Women are crazy."

"I wanted to call and check on you, but—" Monica chuckles. "Cassandra was worried we'd wake the undead and get you killed." She sinks into the couch beside Owen.

"It wasn't exactly like that!" I protest. But I'm laughing at myself also, feeling

44

like an idiot. I fall in on Owen's other side, and he puts an arm around my shoulders and kisses my temple.

I close my eyes and snuggle closer. There's a newness to our relationship, but it also feels familiar and comfortable.

"You girls go back to bed," Owen says quietly, and I can tell he's facing Monica. "I'll stay the night here on the couch."

"Thank you, Owen."

I open my eyes as she tugs on my arm, lifting me. My fingers find Owen's and I clutch his hand, not wanting to leave him. But then they slip free, and I stumble after her to the bedroom. She turns out the lights. I drop my glasses beside my pillow and curl to my side. I know Owen's in the other room, and I think it will keep me awake, but before I can even create a fantasy scenario in my mind, I'm asleep.

I wake when the dogs begin barking again. Adrenaline spikes my blood, and I stare at the drawn shades of the window, blinking, listening. Monica's breathing is steady and slow beside me.

I don't hear anything else. Darn dogs. My heart rate calms, but my mind is awake. Fluttering.

Is Owen asleep?

I reach over and check my phone. I've been asleep for two hours. It's almost six. I creep out of bed, quietly so I don't disturb Monica, and tiptoe to the living room.

A mellow pink glow from the rising sun filters across the room. Owen is stretched out on the couch, his back to the cushions, his knees bent slightly. I pad over the carpet and climb up on the couch, fitting myself into the bare space in front of him, facing him. His breathing changes and his head lifts.

"Cassandra," he murmurs.

"Sorry," I whisper. "I didn't mean to wake you."

He wraps his arms around me and tucks me into his chest. "I'm glad you did."

We are quiet. I'm not asleep and I don't think he is either, but we lay there as if we are. A car honks as it passes by, and the dogs start up their racket again.

"Damn animals," Owen murmurs.

"Owen." I shush him with a finger to his lips. "Don't swear."

"Drat animals," he says, a smile pulling at his mouth.

I laugh and then push upward and press a kiss to that mouth. I can't help it. His lips are soft, full, and very kissable.

He kisses me back. His mouth moves against mine, slowly at first, as if a bit drowsy, and then he seems to wake up. His hands slide from my back to my waist, and he hefts me upward, fitting my body closer to his.

I can feel everything. The thin layers of fabric between us hide nothing.

Owen rolls onto his back, taking me with him. I let my legs fall on either side of his waist, and I suck in a breath, pleasure spiking through me at the way my body hits his. He moves his hands under my tank top, his palms on my flesh, and he urges me down on top of him so his mouth meets mine again.

We never made out like this before. We were cautious. But we were in high school, we were young, and I didn't want to make a mistake.

I don't feel that way now. I want to throw caution to the wind.

He stops kissing me and tilts his head back, looking at my face. The hand on my back trails down my skin, along my waist, sending goosebumps across my shoulders. He brings it around to cup my cheek, then lets it drift to my collar bone, leaving tingling spots of heat in its wake. My necklace, the one he gave me, has fallen out of my shirt and dangles over his face. He touches the pearl before his fingers wander to the neckline of my tank top, then dip beneath it, teasing the exposed skin, making me want to expose more.

"Do you know how beautiful you are?" he whispers.

I smile. I dip my head and kiss him again, and he returns it, but I know he's holding back now.

"You are too," I say, keeping myself above him and studying his face.

He wraps his arms around me and crushes me to him, and I wiggle down until my head rests on his chest.

"I want you," I whisper.

I'm not sure he hears me. He doesn't say anything. I run my fingers up and down his arm, tangling my nails in the arm hairs.

The silence folds around me, and my eyes grow heavy. How many hours of sleep did I get? I close my eyes and let my fingers rest.

⟨⟩

"Wake up, you two."

I open my eyes at Monica's voice, and for a moment I'm disoriented. She stands in front of me, bright light pouring in from a window to her right, her hands on her hips, scowling. But also somehow smiling.

And I'm—I lift my head and discover I'm asleep on Owen's chest.

In a flash, I remember how I got here. And I smile.

"Owen," Monica snaps. "Wake up!"

"No," he says, not opening his eyes. "You can't make me."

"We have to leave. They said they'd be back at ten, and I don't want to be here."

"What time is it?" I ask. I see my phone on the floor by the couch, but it's facedown.

"Almost nine."

I push off the couch, but Owen's arms come up, grabbing me, holding me there. I look at Monica and shrug. "I guess I can't go anywhere."

"You have to go to work, Cassandra."

Crap, she's right. I'm supposed to open, which means I need to be there in half an hour. Looks like I'll be wearing the same thing I wore yesterday.

How embarrassing.

I shrug out of Owen's embrace. "Fine."

Owen rolls over and curls into the spine of the couch.

Monica follows me back to the master bedroom and shuts the door. I find my clothes from the day before and plop in my contacts.

"I should've known better than to fall asleep," Monica teases. "Can't leave you two unsupervised for a minute."

My face gets warm, and I avoid her gaze as I pull off the tank top. But I don't say anything.

She throws her hands up. "Hey, you're not little kids anymore. You don't need me to babysit. Just don't do anything you'll regret later."

I nod.

But I don't think there's anything I could do with Owen that I would regret later.

As if reading my mind, she says, softly, "If you give everything to him, how much more will it hurt when you don't get to be with him later?"

She's right again, and I hate it. I go into the bathroom to brush my teeth and don't answer.

⟨∿⟩ ❊ ⟨∿⟩

Nicole's eyes hone in on me when I clock in. She examines my clothes, my hair that I've pulled back into a ponytail because I couldn't style it.

"Isn't that what you wore yesterday?" she says.

"Very observant of you," I say. At least she's the only one from yesterday that's here again.

She follows me to the break room. Nicole's been a good friend since elementary school, and the past year working together brought us even closer.

"You didn't go home, did you."

"No." I hang up my purse and wait for it.

"So where did you sleep?"

I shrug demurely and head back out onto the floor. Brian, her boyfriend, was working yesterday, so I didn't get the chance to talk to Nicole.

She doesn't know yet that Owen and I are back together, and I can't wait to tell her.

She trails behind me. "Where, Cassandra Jones?"

I smile and hum to myself as I count out the bills from the till, making sure the numbers match up with the closing information from yesterday.

"Cassandra." She plants herself in front of my register, wavy blond hair cascading over one shoulder as she narrows her eyes at me. "You were with a boy, weren't you. You're glowing! You have to tell me everything. Now."

I put the money away and face her. Beaming. Knowing I look radiant. "Owen and I are back together."

"What!" She presses her hands to her mouth and gasps. "When? How?"

I shrug. "A few days ago."

She laughs. "I'm so happy for you! You're really together?"

I nod. "He doesn't want to be so serious this time, though. So we're taking it easy. We go different places in August, and he doesn't want me to feel pressured."

She arches an eyebrow and scans me from head to foot. "Staying the night with him is the opposite of not taking it seriously."

My smile dims somewhat. "I know." Maybe my heart knows it, too. Maybe that's part of why I feel this desperate need to tie myself to him intimately. So I can keep him.

But all it will do is rip me to pieces when we leave each other.

I'm not scheduled open to close since I worked all day yesterday. I hit my numbers and greet people with a wide smile. Brian comes by and he and Nicole argue in low and hissing tones by the dressing room next to the Men's Department, and then he leaves. I find her red-eyed in one of the changing stalls when I go to clean up the clothing.

"What's going on?" I ask. "Are you guys okay?"

She sniffs and catches a tear as it rolls down her cheek. "We're fighting a lot. He doesn't want me to go to college. He says it's better if we break up first."

I blink. "But you're not even leaving the area. Aren't you going to the U of A?" Fayetteville is a mere twenty minutes away.

She gives a watery laugh. "Yeah, but he thinks all the guys will hit on me and I'll choose someone else."

"So he wants to end things?" I narrow my eyes. "Sounds like an excuse to me."

I regret my words as soon as they leave my mouth. Nicole's eyes well up, and she puts a hand to her mouth to muffle the tears.

I creep over to the bench where she sits and hope our third coworker doesn't get inundated with customers at this very moment. I put an arm around her and hug her. "I'm sorry."

She leans into me. "I thought it was him. I thought we'd be together forever. I thought he was the one." She lowers her voice and whispers, "Everything changed when we started sleeping together. I thought it would bring us closer, but instead it made everything more serious. It changed the expectations of the relationship."

God is speaking to me loud and clear. I roll my eyes. *I hear you!* I shout back.

Sometimes I wander too close to the barricade that keeps me safe. I want to dip my toe on the other side . . . That won't hurt me, right?

***

I drive to Franklin's house when my shift ends at three o'clock. I should call and make sure he's home, but I don't. If he's there, great. If he's not, I'll just leave the prom photo.

I park in the driveway and knock on the front door. There's no response for several minutes. I'm about to tuck the photo into the seam of the door when I hear the deadbolt turning. A moment later it opens, and Franklin stands there.

He's Brazilian, but not dark-skinned like Tiago. He has blue eyes, pale skin, and light ash-colored hair. Yet something about the arrangement of his eyes and nose and cheekbones gives him the appearance of someone foreign.

"Cassandra!" he exclaims, and he hugs me. "Hey! Come on in!"

He ushers me inside.

"I can't stay," I say, standing by the kitchen cabinets as he grabs a glass.

"Orange juice? Soda? What can I get you?"

"Just water." I stay polite. But I won't forget how he treated me at prom, even if he doesn't know he offended me.

"What's happening? I'm so glad to see you." He puts my glass on the table and sits across from me, a can of soda in his hand. He grins brightly. "I haven't seen you in almost a week!"

I sit down. I know he's genuine. I relent a little because maybe I do share some of the blame from prom. We'd been getting friendly, even a bit cozy. I did flirt with him extensively at the dance. I even imagined what it would be like to kiss him.

But only because I'd been so dang lonely.

"I brought you our prom picture."

I pull it from the envelope and hand it to him while I sit.

His face lights up. "Thanks, Cassandra." He reaches over and gives me a side hug. "I'm so glad I know you. You were one of my favorite parts of this year."

"I'm glad." I glance around the quiet house. His host parents are elderly and rarely around. If I think I've been lonely, Franklin's had it worse. "I bet you're excited to go home."

"More than I want to admit," he says. "Speaking of which—would you be able to give me a ride to the airport on Monday?"

"Your host parents can't take you?" I recover from my surprise. "Yes, of course. What time's your flight?"

"Thank you. Ten in the morning. But I have to be there at eight."

They don't even want to come and see him off? Apparently they never saw him as part of the family. I stay and make small talk a bit longer, feeling bad for Franklin. He gives me another hug when I go to leave.

"Next time you come to Brazil, come visit me," he says.

"That's a good idea," I say. "Maybe I will."

⟡

Owen texts me Sunday morning.

O: Want to ride with me to church?

I haven't seen him since the night he slept over at Monica's house-sitting job Friday.

Two full days.

I hate how much I miss him.

Yes, I say, because even though I have no reason to ride with him, I have no reason not to.

O: Be there in half an hour.

I check the time. Church isn't until ten, and it's only eight.

Me: I'll be ready.

I put on a summer dress with a pink slip underneath the gauzy layer of floral print. It's fitted at my waist and flares at my hips, making me look curvy in all the right places.

"Owen's picking me up," I tell Emily, who's just waking. "In case you were planning on riding with me."

She shakes her head and drags herself from the bed. "That's all right. I'll take my own car."

I buckle my strappy sandals. "Tell Mom in case I don't see her." Mom doesn't usually get up this early on Sundays.

"Okay."

Owen's Toyota pulls up in the circle drive as I open the front door. He comes out to greet me, wearing his usual khaki pants. I recognize the blue polo as the one I gave him for Valentine's Day. It brightens the green in his eyes. He picks me up and hugs me, spinning me around on the brick porch.

"I swear you're getting taller," I say as he sets me down.

"I'm already six-one," he says, and he demonstrates the foot difference in height between us. "If I get any taller, I won't see you down there."

"That would be very sad." I grab his hand and hang on him as we walk to his car.

"Worse for me."

I keep quiet as we climb into his truck. He rockets out of the driveway, and I commandeer his radio, finding a station with uplifting sounds appropriate for the Sabbath. I catch him glancing at me a few times.

"What?" I demand.

"Nothing," he says, and he grins, his eyes crinkled as he faces the road again.

But he doesn't take the turn to the chapel. I don't ask. I'm here for the ride.

Instead he turns left, and I spot the little white church nestled next to the cow pastures. Today it has a dozen cars parked out front. Owen pulls in and adds his car to the group.

CHAPTER EIGHT

Sacred Places

"Are we going to church here?" I ask, raising an eyebrow. This isn't the church our families go to.

He shrugs. "Why not? This is our spot."

I hide my smile, pleased to hear him say that. The church parking lot has special meaning for me also. It's where he took me before we were dating, the first day I realized I might like him as more than a friend. We've met up here to talk, to cry, to fight. To make out. I remember the pang I felt when he dated Kristin, wondering if he was taking her to our church.

He takes my hand when I get out of the car, and I glance back at the truck parked along the building.

"You never brought Kristin here, did you?" I hold my breath as I ask. I know I should let everything that happened between us when we were broken up fall into the black hole of "Don't Ask," but if he did, this place will no longer feel so sacred to me.

"No," he says, and he squeezes my hand. "This place is ours."

I squeeze back. "If we're not at our church our parents will flip," I warn.

"We have time for both services," he says, unconcerned. I let him pull me inside.

The church is as small on the inside as it was on the outside. The flooring is raised at the front for the preacher. A handful of congregates mingle, dressed in a mixture of Southern finery or blue jeans and T-shirts. There are six rows of padded benches. Exposed wooden beams in the ceiling contrast with the whitewashed walls. A man plays a small organ up front, the music piping through the room.

A woman turns toward us, her floppy hat falling over her eyes. She steps over, bringing a waft of thick lavender perfume.

"Hello!" she says. "What brings you young people here today?"

I glance around and see we are indeed the only people in the building under the age of thirty.

"We live close by," Owen says. "We always admire this church. Thought it would be nice to come to a sermon."

She puffs out her chest and looks immensely pleased. "Well, you're in time for our nine o'clock service!"

"Great," Owen says.

And I add, because I don't want her to be offended when we leave, "But we have to go early. I have somewhere to be at ten."

She pats my hand. "I hope you enjoy what you hear." She spins to leave, then turns back to say, "You make a very fine couple."

"Thank you," Owen says.

Warmth creeps up my neck into my hairline.

He squeezes my hand, and I realize he never let go. Which is unusual for him.

I lean closer and whisper, "Do we make a fine couple?"

He puts an arm around me and tucks me into his side. "Yes."

I tap my chin thoughtfully. "I wouldn't know. I don't have any pictures of us."

He turns to look at me. "Yes, you do. You took one at graduation."

"Of you and me and all your friends."

"Homecoming, then."

I do have a lovely picture of us at the Homecoming assembly, and I'm surprised he remembers. But I scowl and poke his ribs. "We weren't a couple. We made a fine pair of friends."

He shakes his head and heaves a sigh. "This is easily rectified."

"Rectified," I say. "That's a big word. Are you sure you used it correctly?"

He holds his phone in front of us and pulls me in closer. "Stop talking."

I smile as he snaps a picture. Then another. Then I kiss his cheek, and he gets it on camera.

"Cassandra," he says, and his face actually turns red. But he looks at the picture and smiles, then tucks me under his arm.

I don't hear much of what the preacher says. My body hums with the energy that pulses between Owen and me, sitting with our bodies smashed together from shoulder to hip. I open the hymn book and sing along even if I don't know the song. The music thrums through my veins, matching the pulsing of my heart.

We slip out forty minutes later, and Owen holds my hand the whole way to the truck. He only releases me to drive, keeping both hands on the steering wheel. I hear his thoughts churning. I don't know what they are, but I'm content in the silence, the soft sounds of the radio the only noise.

We reach our chapel two minutes before the service starts. I slip out of the truck and skip over to the door, holding it open for Owen and waiting. He gives me a half grin before stepping into the hallway.

First thing I notice is Farrah and Tyler talking in a corner by the coat closet. I eye them curiously but leave them alone as I go inside. I'm sure I'll hear all about it later.

I slide into the pew where my family sits, a spot left open for me. Owen joins his family on the other side of the chapel.

Paster Mike stands up at the pulpit. "One announcement before we get started.

There's a youth retreat in three weeks for all youth ages fourteen to eighteen. This includes our group of recently graduated kids." His gaze dances over me before flitting to the other post-seniors. "It'll be two hours away in Tulsa, and I encourage all of you to go. Please contact me if you need more information."

He then goes on to give a sermon on evaluating where you are and where you want to be and not letting yourself become comfortable because that's when you start going backward. It's a great message. But all I can think is how lonely the left side of my body feels without Owen next to me.

I join my friends in the hallway after the sermon. We're in an awkward place now, us newly graduated. Technically we're adults and should go to the adult Sunday School. But none of us feel like it. We laugh and joke with each other, trying to goad someone into leading the way.

Instead we don't go. We end up on the couches in the foyer, me and Owen and Tyler and Farrah and Sue and Michelle. I feel Riley's absence. She used to be in this group. I wonder if I'll see her before I leave for school. She hasn't answered my text messages.

"This is my last Sunday in this congregation," Tyler says. "I'm going to start going to the congregation at the U of A. Since I'll start school there in September."

"Me too," Farrah says. "So this is it." She smiles, but it's tremulous, and tears well up in her eyes.

"We're going there too," Michelle says, gesturing between her and Sue. "But we're waiting until August. Why are you doing it now?"

Tyler shrugs. "Seems like a good time. Doesn't feel normal to be going to church here anymore, does it? No one our age is here."

He's right. There's a hole in our age group demographic because everyone graduates and leaves, either for college or mission trips. I belong to a congregation that encourages selfless service at a young age in the form of mission trips, and the church facilitates the opportunity for those to occur. The university I'll be going to has similar programs. It's exactly what I always wanted because someday I hope to join one of the mission trips myself.

I feel a prickle of nerves along my skin and clasp my hands together. I've been counting down for this exit scene for seven years, and suddenly I don't feel ready.

Michelle and Sue look at each other and nod.

"Maybe we'll start going there sooner," Michelle says. "If you guys already are."

No! I want to say. I want to beg everyone to stay. Steal a few more weeks of this transitional time.

Sue looks at me. At Owen. We're not holding hands. But we're sitting beside each other. Very closely. "What about you guys?" she asks.

I glance at Owen and then speak first, exhaling as I run my hands down the flimsy outer layer of my dress. "The semester starts in August at PYU. I'm going up a week early to be a part of Honor's Week. So early August. That's when I head out." It's only June. I have eight weeks in front of me.

It feels so short.

She rounds on Owen next. "Owen?"

"I switched schools," he says. "I'm going to Louisiana State now. I plan to head down right before school starts in September. Make sure my housing is situated."

They nod. And glance at me. Aware, as I am, that things will be ending for us.

"What about mission trips?" Sue asks. "Who's planning on one?"

"I am," Tyler says. "I'm doing a semester of school before going. So probably around Christmas. You?"

Sue shakes her head. "It's not for me. I don't think I'd last a week."

"Same," Michelle says. "What if I ended up in the rain forest or something? Yuck!"

Missions could be anything. Building new schools, teaching English, serving in start-up church congregations. That's part of what excites me.

I hope I end up in a rainforest.

"I don't care where they send me," Tyler says. "I'm willing to serve where I'm needed."

The girls laugh and roll their eyes and shove Tyler, because he always manages to sound self-righteous and condescending, but we know him well enough to see through it.

"I'm going," I say. My heart pounds as I admit something I've desired since I was a child. "Not right away. Maybe after I graduate college."

"You think you'll make it that long?" Michelle says.

I frown. "What's that supposed to mean?"

"That you won't last," Sue says. "You'll get married first. Happens to everyone."

I feel Owen's eyes on me. "Not me," I say, confidently. "There are too many things I want to do first. Marriage can wait."

Sue shrugs. "We'll see."

"What about you, Owen?" Farrah asks. "Doing a mission trip?" I wonder if she's asking out of curiosity or for my benefit.

"Planning to," he says. "In a year, maybe."

The conversation drifts to other topics, and I'm glad. These endings are already floating around in my mind. Do they have to be so in my face every moment?

After church Farrah hugs everyone goodbye, and she cries. Tyler looks excited, and I know she's going to the university congregation because he is, but she doesn't seem ready. She hugs Owen, crying, and then hugs me, still crying. It makes me teary.

"You're not actually gone," I tell her. "You still live right here. We can hang out before I leave."

"I know." She sniffs and wipes her eyes. "But everything is about to change."

Owen takes me home, and he's quiet again, but this time the silence feels charged. I don't turn on the music and I wait to see what he's going to say.

Instead of pulling into the circle drive, he pulls into my driveway and parks. We're the first ones home. The car idles. I study him as he studies my garage door.

"Want to come in?" I ask, more to break the silence than anything else.

He turns to face me. "You might get married."

I want to smack his head. "I'm not getting married."

"Every guy you meet is going to want to date you. Want to marry you. You might like one of them back."

"You're so ridiculous." I snort and roll my eyes. "Did you see the lines of guys I was fighting off this year? Oh, wait, there were none. Nobody's interested in me."

"We were in high school," Owen says, raising his voice a little. "All the guys were idiots after one type of girl, and you weren't it. But in college, they're going to grow up. And you're exactly what every guy will be looking for."

I'm startled. His words both sting and flatter. "I'm nobody. I'm nothing special."

He shakes his head. "The fact that you believe that is scary. It's going to take you by complete surprise."

I don't even know what to say. I feel like there's no right answer here.

He leans across the console and kisses me. "I'm saying dumb stuff. Thanks for coming with me today."

He puts the car in Reverse before I've even gotten out, and I know he wants time alone. Owen does that too. Needs space sometimes.

"Thanks for inviting me," I say, and I hop out.

I stand at the front of the driveway and watch him go, feeling a familiar ache in my chest.

I'm not getting married next year or the year after or the year after that. Not anytime soon.

But someday I will. And I know who I want it to be to.

CHAPTER NINE

Full Transparency

I pick Franklin up at seven in the morning to drive him out to the regional airport. He's goofy. Excited to be going home. Full of anxious energy.

"Are you sad your host parents aren't taking you?" I ask.

"I'm sad I didn't get to experience a real host family," he says. "Like Tiago did when he lived with you. He had a mom and a dad and brothers and sisters."

"Even a girlfriend," I smirk.

"Yeah." Franklin laughs. "An unexpected perk."

I laugh also, for a moment pulled into those delicious moments when Tiago lived in my basement and we were together. Shooting glances at each other during movie night, holding hands under the table at dinner, sneaking off into bedrooms and closets to kiss.

It had been fun.

"My host parents never felt like family," Franklin continues. "I think they were tired of me in the end. Glad to see me go."

Again, I feel sad for Franklin, and I forgive him for his moment of idiocy at prom.

I stand with him while he gets checked in. A wave of memories crashes over me, and for a moment I'm overwhelmed. I remember bringing Tiago here. He and I were the closest we'd ever been. I hadn't thought I could love anyone as much as I loved him. The only reason I didn't fall into a puddle of sobbing desperation when he went up the escalator to security is because I knew I was going to see him in Brazil a week later.

Franklin takes a good look at my face. "You're thinking of Tiago."

I force a smile. "Sometimes I remember."

He shrugs. "Nothing wrong with that." He reaches out for a hug, and I give him one. Then he surprises me by beginning to cry, his shoulders quaking as he holds on to me.

Someone else should be here. I shouldn't be the one he's crying to.

But there's no one else, so I pat his shoulder and let him cry.

"I'll miss you," he says, releasing me. "You were a great friend."

"I'll miss you too," I say. It's a harmless white lie.

Then he turns around and goes up the escalator, and I turn around and go back to my car in the short-term parking.

And that is how two people walk out of each other's lives.

❦

Harper calls me as I'm climbing into my car.

"Harper!" I exclaim, my heart leaping with excitement. "Are you home?"

"Got in last night." She yawns. "Been sleeping. So tired. Vacation drains you."

"Poor you," I say. "What are your plans today? Can we get together?" I have so much to say to her. She's not someone who I want to let go of when I leave Arkansas. But I know that means I need to make changes now.

"Yeah, sure. What are you thinking?"

"Well, I have to go to the health department. Then I can come over. Want to go to lunch? I'll pick you up."

"Sure. Text me when you're on your way."

"Great!" I put the phone away, the melancholy from Franklin's departure fading. I need some Harper time.

But first, the TB test.

The health department is half an hour away, and I'm confused as soon as I enter. A sign in the entryway has arrows pointing in three different directions. Vaccinations, WIC, and appointments.

Is this considered a vaccination? I decide it must be.

I go to the room on the left and stand in line behind a window that says "Intake." Five people are in front of me. Sticky heat clings to my skin. A fan whirls overhead, but it only stirs the hot air. I pull my hair up and secure it with a pencil I find at the window.

Finally it's my turn.

"What do you need?" the bored woman behind the desk asks.

"A TB test," I say, crossing my fingers I'm in the right spot.

"Fill this out and hand it in with your ID."

Should I sit down? I'm afraid to lose my place, so I start filling in my name and phone number and all my personal information at the window. She doesn't tell me to leave. Two minutes later I hand her the form with my ID.

"What's this test for?" she asks.

"Employment," I say.

"All right. Take a number and have a seat. We'll call you when it's your turn."

I take a number from the dispenser at the window and then look for a place to sit.

There's not one. Every seat is filled. People lean against the wall and sit on the floor.

A woman pops out of a side room and says, "Twenty-three."

I glance at the number in my hand and groan. I'm fifty-one.

There are thirty other people in front of me.

57

I sink onto the floor beside a young mom pushing a stroller with her foot. Back and forth, back and forth. I text Harper.

Me: It's not going to be fast. Long line.

She sends me back a thumbs up.

I always bring a book, but I didn't today. I look for something to do on my phone. Something to read.

There's an unread message from Tiago. I'm not sure when he sent it. I turned off notifications from that app. I feel all kinds of guilt over it. Maybe I should name my guilt. It's like a faithful pet, always on my heels. Down, boy. Not now. Go away. Why are you still here?

I open the message.

T: Hi, Cassandra! Are you around?

His icon is inactive.

I want to respond.

I like talking to Tiago.

But every time I talk to him, I feel like I'm leading him on. Just by talking. And sometimes I accidentally do with my words.

My mind and heart wrestle together, and my mind wins. I exit out of the app and text Owen instead.

Me: at the health center. Waiting on my TB test.

I play around on my phone, hoping he'll respond.

There's a new notification on the messaging app.

I click it open.

T: Hey, I saw you were online! Can you chat?

I lean my head against the wall and sigh. He saw me get on and read his message.

I can't ignore him now. I won't.

Me: for a bit. I'm at the health department waiting on a test.

T: You responded! I wasn't sure you would.

Guilt. Guilt. Guilt.

I opt for honesty.

Me: So I have a bit of a difficulty talking to you.

T: go on.

Me: I like talking to you. You are important to me. But I feel a lot of pressure from you.

T: what kind of pressure?

Me: well, to be more than a friend.

T: I'm not pressuring you

Me: no, but every time you tell me you love me, every time you tell me how you miss me, how much you want to be together, how you hope for our future—all that stuff makes me feel bad. It makes me want to avoid talking to you.

I sit there staring at the phone, my heart in my throat, wondering if I've just thrown away what remained of our friendship. The little green dot is the only indication that he's still online. Then he begins to respond.

A long response.

T: I have to admit that hurts. Something has changed with you in the past week. I thought we were getting closer. I thought you might feel something for me again. But you have completely shut me out. You are not a cruel person so I know you're not doing it to hurt me. In fact I think you are doing it for the opposite reason. Like there is something you are not telling me because you don't want to hurt me.

Crap! I suck at this.

I exit the app and leave the stuffy room, stepping outside and taking deep breaths. I don't know how to get out of this. I don't know what to do. I want advice from someone.

Harper doesn't even know.

Owen won't be unbiased.

I call Monica.

"What's up, Cassandra?" she says.

"I need help," I say without preamble. "I want to make sure I don't do the wrong thing here."

"What is it? What's going on?"

"It's Tiago. I told him we can only be friends. That I don't want him telling me he loves me or talking about the possibility of a future together. That it makes me uncomfortable to talk to him when he does all that."

"You're being honest. That's good. How'd he take it?"

I stomp my foot in frustration. "I'm not being completely honest, and he knows it. He knows something has happened. And he wants to know what."

"You didn't tell him you're back with Owen?"

I smack my head back and wince when I bang it on the brick wall behind me. "No. Is that what I should do?"

"Cassandra, I think it's time for you to be transparent with these boys. In everything you do."

"But I feel like such a jerk! Tiago was there when I needed him, and now that Owen's back in the picture, I drop him like a hot potato?"

"Isn't that what you're doing?"

I groan and tug at my hair. "Am I a terrible person?"

"The one time in your life when you deserve to be selfish is when you're choosing who you love."

I exhale. "This sucks."

"Yep."

I don't even bother saying goodbye when I hang up. I'm irate. Annoyed. Not with Monica, but with everything. The situation. There are no niceties left in me.

I go back inside just as they call, "Fifty-one."

That's me! They must have skipped around!

"Here, here," I say, scrambling over legs and playing children to get to the side door.

The moment we are through the doors and into the hallway, silence descends on the sterile corridor, and air conditioning pipes through the vents. I breathe a little sigh of relief.

"What are you here for?" the woman asks. Her black hair is tied in a messy bun and secured with a scarf, and the white uniform she wears looks a few sizes too large.

"A TB test," I say.

She checks the chart and nods, then leads me into another room. "Have you had one of these before?"

"No."

"All right." She pulls out a syringe and pokes it into a small vial. "You have to come back within two to three days to have it read."

"Okay." I nod, trying not to stare at the needle but failing. I passed out last year when I had a blood test. Not my thing. Today's Monday. I make a mental note to come back Wednesday or Thursday.

She takes my arm and flips it over, then wipes a section of skin in front of my elbow with a cotton ball. She pokes the needle into my skin, just under the surface, pushes the syringe, and pulls it out again.

I blink. That didn't even hurt. "Is that it?"

"That's it." She nods, writes on a card, and hands it to me. "Come back in three days and bring that with you."

I head out of the health department with the card in my hand. That was surprisingly easy.

I call Linda, the hiring manager of Kids First, when I get to the car, to let her know I took the TB test.

"That's great," she said. "Let's plan on having you start on Monday. Assuming your test is negative."

"Wonderful!" I say.

"We'll use you like a substitute. We'll call you in the morning, and if you're available, you come in. If you can't, you just tell us."

I'd rather have fixed hours, but this will allow Debra to set the hours she wants at Stage. "All right."

"Great. Come in after you get your test results and fill out paperwork."

"Will do."

Then I text Harper as I leave. *Finally on my way!!!*

Twenty minutes later I park at her house, in my usual spot behind her car in the middle of the front yard. She greets me at the door, her long blond hair flowing down her back, the skin around her clear eyes crinkling as she smiles. She's gorgeous, this best friend of mine, and I embrace her so hard we crash against the wall.

"Cassandra," she says, giggling.

"How was your trip?" I ask. I don't even know where she went. And I feel too lame to admit that.

"Oh, fine. I like hanging out with my cousins. But we didn't do anything special. How was your trip to Branson?"

I lower my eyes and play with the ring on my right hand. "I wished the whole time it was you with me."

"Well." Harper scrunches her brow. "You didn't invite me."

I sigh. "I'm sorry for that."

"Were you mad at me?"

I nod.

"You've been mad at me a lot," she says.

"I don't want to be mad at you anymore," I say. "We don't have a lot of time left. I want to hang out with you and laugh and be silly and share secrets. But I need you." I take her hands and squeeze them. "Sometimes I need some Harper-time. Just you and me."

She hugs me. "I know what you're saying, babe. I can do that." She pulls back. "What else is going on?"

I pull her out of the house. "So much. I'll tell you everything at lunch."

CHAPTER TEN

Who We Are

Harper pesters me in the car, knowing something big is going on, but I put off her questions. I want to see her face when I tell her.

We go to Loafin' Joe's and order sandwiches, and then she slaps the table with both hands and glowers at me.

"I am waiting. This is about Tiago, isn't it?"

I nod, very slowly. That's where it starts, anyway. I can't remember what I've told her. I've held back information because I was hurt, but in the end it meant I had one less person to count on. "You know how he and I were talking a lot."

"Yes, I know."

"I was lonely. It felt nice to know someone cared."

"I know."

I lick my lips. "Well, I bought a plane ticket to go back to Brazil."

She gasps and clutches the edge of the table. "So are you—did you guys get back together? For real?"

I shake my head. "I wanted to visit my friend. The person who has been there for me for the last few months. And I wanted to see if we could build something again."

"You don't sound so sure anymore."

"I'm not sure anymore. I know I want to see him, but I just want to be his friend. I don't know if I can be around him if he's always looking at me with hurt in his eyes, wanting something else."

Harper pats my hand and smiles. "Maybe you won't feel that way in a year. You might be ready to let him be more than a friend."

I pick up the paper napkin and begin shredding it to pieces. "Well, that's not everything."

She blinks, eyebrows lifting. "There's more?"

I laugh. "Lots more."

"Spill!"

Before I can, my phone rings.

It's Owen.

He doesn't usually call me. I hold a finger up to Harper and answer. "Owen? Is everything okay?"

He pauses before answering. "Yeeees," he drawls out slowly. "Am I not allowed to call?"

"No, of course you can," I say, slightly flustered, especially with Harper's x-ray vision on me. "You just usually text."

"Well, I texted and you didn't answer. So I'm calling."

"Oh. You must have texted while I was driving. I didn't see it."

"Great. Now that we know why . . . is this phone call allowed?"

I laugh. I can't help it. He's so funny, it might be my favorite quality about him. Or maybe it's his lips . . .

No, I can't decide.

"I'm at lunch with Harper," I say. "Can I call you later?"

"Yeah, that's fine. Or text me. So you don't worry me by calling unexpectedly. Whichever."

"All right. Thanks for all the options."

"No problem."

He hangs up, and I put my phone away, knowing I still have a goofy grin on my face.

"And the other thing you wanted to tell me is. . . ?" Harper supplies.

"Owen," I say. "We got back together."

Harper collapses backward in her chair as if she fainted. I lean toward her, but she sits up and nearly hits my face with hers.

"When did this happen?" she demands.

"After the graduation party," I admit.

Her eyes throw daggers at me as she growls, "I can't believe you didn't tell me!"

"I wanted to tell you in person," I say. "I wanted to see your expression." I take in the narrowed eyes, the clenched jaw, the flaring nostrils, and giggle. "And it's priceless."

She takes her napkin and throws it at me. "So are you all the way back together?"

"Yes and no. We've admitted what we feel for each other, but we're not making plans for the future. We are together until we can't be."

"Ah." Harper nods. "Does he know about Tiago?"

"Owen knows everything." I shake my head. "I'll never hold anything back from him again."

"Never?"

"Well, as long as he has the right to know."

"So are you still going to Brazil?"

I sigh again. "Yes. But not as cheerfully as before. I need to find something to get me excited about going."

"Maybe you can find a way to make it part of your education?"

I'd had a similar idea when I booked the tickets. "That's a good idea. I think I'll study Portuguese. Then going to Brazil furthers my education. There's one other thing."

The waiter brings our sandwiches, so she has to wait in suspense for me to continue. I take a big bite out of the hoagie covered in melted cheese and grilled jalapeños, closing my eyes and moaning in appreciation.

"Oh," I say, putting hand over my mouth, since I'm still chewing, "did I tell you I'm not a vegetarian anymore?"

She hasn't touched her sandwich. Just sits there and glares at me. "You don't tell me anything anymore."

Harper ditched me at the end of our senior year, and it's taken me this long to get over it. "That's fair. I'll tell you everything from now on. I'm trying to be honest with people."

"It's not like you've lied to me. You've just cut me out."

Guilt does its little stabby thing in my heart. Stab stab stab. I put my sandwich down and dab at my lips. "I didn't feel like I was important to you," I say softly. "So I stopped telling you things. Partly to get back at you, but partly to keep myself safe."

Her nose turns pink, and she sniffs. "I'm sorry."

"We're going to be fine." I take a sip of water and wave away her apology. I already forgave her. I understand her better now than I did a few weeks ago. "Here's the rest of the story. I told Tiago I don't want to date. But knows me too well. He says I've changed in the past week and flat out accused me of hiding something."

Harper finally takes a bite of her meatball sub and nods. She's with me. "What did you say?"

"I didn't answer him."

"So the reason you're different is because now you're with Owen."

"Yes. And I didn't tell him because I feel like a jerk."

"But he's smart enough to figure it out."

"So what should I do?"

Harper shakes her head. "That's hard."

I know the answer. I taste it bitterly in my mouth.

I have to tell him about Owen.

I take another bite, but my food doesn't taste good anymore.

⊙〜✳〜⊙

I take Harper home, and only then do I check the text from Owen. I want to be fully engaged with Harper when I'm with her, not constantly messaging back and forth with my boyfriend. Just like I want her to be with me.

Belatedly I realize she didn't mention Miles once at lunch. And I didn't ask.

I should have.

Owen's text asks if I want to meet for lunch. Before he knew I was out with Harper, of course. I text back, *My evening's open.*

He answers right away. *Dinner?*

I shake my head.

C: No. Eating out two meals in a row is no bueno for me.

64

The dots appear and disappear, and I wait, wondering what idea he'll come up with.

O: I'll pick you up and we'll figure something out.

That works for me.

Me: Sure.

O: Seven?

Me: all right.

I sing along to Sarah Brightman on the way home. She's my idol. I want to sing like her, let my voice carry upward on those high, lyrical notes.

There's just one dark spot on my joy, and I'm about to take care of it.

I text Tiago the moment I'm home. He's not online. He might not see it until tomorrow. But I say, *Call me.*

It's not ten minutes later that he does.

I'm in the kitchen loading the dishes, a job I loathe. But I try to do it when I'm home because I'm rarely home. Which means someone else is always doing it for me.

I abandon the task when I see his incoming call. My sister is in our room, so I go outside, sitting on the porch swing.

"Hello," I say.

"You told me to call you." Already he sounds suspicious. Tense. "What's up?"

I grind my teeth together and plow forward. "You're right. Something changed. I should have told you from the beginning, but I feel like a ping-pong ball and I didn't want to jerk you along with me."

"What is it?"

There's no give in his voice. He's bracing himself. Maybe he already knows.

I exhale. "Owen and I are dating again."

For a moment there is silence, and then he swears.

"Dammit, Cassandra. So it's not about wanting to be free when you go to college—it's about wanting to date Owen right now."

Do I have to answer that honestly? Really?

He's not done. "Why didn't you tell me that instead of acting like you had a sudden epiphany? Why do you treat me like I'm an idiot?"

"I'm sorry," I breathe, taken aback by his anger. Tiago never talks to me this way. "I should have. I didn't want to hurt you."

"No," he spits out. "You wanted to keep me in your back pocket so you could have both. You didn't want to feel bad for leading me on. You only wanted to protect yourself."

"I haven't been leading you on!" I protest. "I told you upfront—"

"Damn you, Cassandra," he says, and I cut off short.

He's crying.

"Damn you," he says again, softer this time. "You've been playing me. I can't talk to you anymore."

And he hangs up.

I sit on the porch swing with my phone in my hand, shaking.

I feel wretched.

I'm a terrible person.

I don't cry, but I feel the aching all the way from my stomach to my neck.

Tiago will never know what he means to me. I can't tell him. He'll take it a different way.

He'll never understand how much this hurts me.

I go inside and throw myself into the housework, distracting myself until I'll see Owen.

I yell bye to my family and go out to meet him as he comes around the front of his truck. I'm wearing flip-flops and cut off shorts and a peasant blouse. My heart still feels bruised. But I'm happy to see him, looking summery in board shorts and a T-shirt that reads "TACOCAT" and shows a cat inside a taco.

It makes me giggle.

"Nice," I say, poking his belly. "You don't even like cats."

"Monica got it for me."

"That explains it."

I fall silent as we drive. I stare out the window at the plantation-style houses set on immaculate acreage, fields full of cows and cow ponds, green with summer moss. I see the slime pit my junior high friends and I slid down our ninth grade year, and it makes me smile.

None of them are my friends now. I missed them at first, but I don't now. It took years, though.

"Where are your thoughts?" Owen asks.

I stare out the window a moment longer. My thoughts are nostalgic. More of the same. I don't want every conversation from here until August to be about our upcoming separation.

"When I was in ninth grade, my friends and I walked over to that pond." I point it out. "We had the brilliant idea to slide down the overflow concrete into the swamp beneath." I laugh as I remember how gross it was. "We got covered in slime and mud and worms and bugs. It was disgusting."

He laughs with me. "Why did you do that?"

I shrug. "Fifteen and dumb."

"Was it Harper and Riley?"

I shake my head. "I didn't know Harper yet, and Riley and I had a lot of rough times." Like now. If she doesn't answer my texts soon, I'm going to start calling her mom. "I didn't stay friends with those girls in high school."

"Why not?"

"Well." I shrug. "They were into guys and parties and being cool. And I decided that wasn't my thing."

He gives me a strange look as we go around the bend toward the light on Barrington. "Were you into that kind of stuff?"

"I tried to be. I wanted to be popular, like they were. But it just wasn't me."

We reach the light, but instead of turning right to head into Springdale, he pulls into a parking spot by the city park.

"We're going to the park?" I say, not hiding the surprise in my voice.

"Too boring for you?" He gets my door open and helps me out, his hands nearly closing around my waist as he lifts me.

"Absolutely not. I love parks."

"I bet you're a fan of the swings."

I grin. "Yes."

"Race you."

He takes off running, which is totally unfair. I'm not made for sprinting. I haul after him, panting.

"You gave yourself a head start," I say, gasping for breath, hands on my knees.

He laughs and sits in one of the swings. "Right. I'll let you go first next time."

I climb into the swing beside him and glare at him. "No next times. I don't want to do that again."

"So these friends," he says, pushing off the ground with his toes. "Do I know them?"

"Maybe." Probably. "I know you know Cara—"

"Cara Barnes?"

"Yes."

"She was one of your friends?"

"Best friends." So funny to imagine now. I kick off the ground too, not going far. I want to keep the conversation going.

"Who else?"

"Andrea Wall, Amity Stafford, Maureen Hemming—"

"They were your friends?" He sounds incredulous.

"Yep." I laugh. "We all slid down that dirty water together. Cara called it the 'crap slide.'"

"And you decided you didn't want to be friends anymore?"

"Well, it's not like I suddenly didn't like them. But I went away over the summer. I got to know myself, and I liked who I was. When I came back, they were all like, 'this guy that' and 'that party this.' I didn't fit in. And I didn't want to. It's a mosh pit, trying to stay on top of the social circle. Exhausting. And if you fall off, you get trampled. So I decided I didn't want to play anymore. I quit coming over. Quit calling. Quit texting. Eventually they quit inviting."

"You chose not to be in the—" He cuts himself off, probably afraid of offending me.

"In the popular crowd," I finish for him. "Yep. I chose it."

"Why?" He says it like he can't believe it. Like I didn't just explain it.

"I could see where it was going, Owen. I didn't want in anymore."

"But you wanted in at some point."

I bob my head. "Yes, I did. Very much so. I changed my hair, my clothes, my makeup, even the way I talked so I could be in their group. Stupid of me."

"So you figured out when you were fifteen what I didn't figure out until I was eighteen."

I laugh. "Looks like it."

He looks up at the sky. "That cloud looks like an umbrella."

I tilt my head back. "Where?"

"That one." He points. "Has a cane at the bottom, and it's all open like an umbrella."

I don't see it. I'm not sure why I'm trying to. "Okay. Are umbrellas important?"

"What do you see?" he persists.

I look up again, studying the puffy cloud formations. "A castle. On a cliff overlooking the ocean. And there's a dragon circling it."

He starts laughing. He doesn't even look at the sky, just laughs. He gets off the swing and takes my hand, pulling me off also.

"It can never be one simple thing with you, can it?"

I smile, but I'm perplexed. Why are we looking at clouds? Swinging in a park? This doesn't seem like Owen.

He lets go of my hand in the grassy section. "Wait here."

"All right."

He gets what looks like a big towel out of his truck, and then as he nears I see it's his blanket. The quilted one.

He opens it on the grass, and I sink down into it. I run my hands over the tufted edges of each square.

"I love this blanket."

He sits beside me. "You do?"

I nod. "It reminds me of you. I remember so many things when I see it."

Owen lays back on the blanket, crossing his arms behind his head and staring at the sky. "All right. I'm gonna try and see it the way you see it. I see a . . . river. And trees. And a dog . . . in the river."

I lay beside him, smirking. "Where?"

"It's gone."

"Where was it?"

He swirls his hand at the sky. "There. In the clouds."

I snuggle up next to him and rest my head on his chest. "We don't have to see the same things."

His hand falls to my head, his fingers combing through my hair. "What do you see now?"

I study the clouds again. "A boat with one mast falling inward. And a little tugboat in front of it." I point out the formations. "See?"

"I see it." He doesn't say anything for a second, and then he says, "Two months isn't enough time."

I prop my chin on his chest and look at him. "To do what?"

"To learn everything about you."

I lay back on the blanket, watching the white clouds drift over the blue sky, and weave my fingers through his. "I guess you'll have to save some things for later."

He squeezes my fingers. "I guess so."

CHAPTER ELEVEN
Life and Waiting

I rearrange the purses and belts at the front of the store and wave to the people who walk through the door. It's been three days since my TB test. I don't know what they'll be looking for when I go back in, but I plan to head to Fayetteville right after work.

"Excuse me," a woman says. She approaches the counter with a plastic grocery bag stuffed to the hilt. "I'd like a refund, please."

She adds the receipt, thank goodness. I can give her everything she wants.

Another customer gets in line behind her, and I use the phone to call Nicole and see if she can help up here.

"Sure. You paid in cash, so I can give it back to you in cash, or I can put it on a gift card," I say.

"Cash, please."

I begin counting out the bills. "I need to see an ID, like your driver's license."

"What?" Her brow furrows at me.

I pause. "Since I'm giving you cash, I have to know who I'm giving it to."

"Is my name on that receipt? Am I the only person who can get cash?"

Warmth creeps up my neck. "No, it's because corporate needs a record of who we give cash to."

"So you're going to take a picture of my ID? Because I'm not okay with that."

Now I'm sweating. "I'm just going to write your name down and have you sign a form saying you got cash. But I have to see your ID first to verify you are who you say you are."

Nicole arrives at the other register and takes the small line that formed behind the woman. I don't glance at her.

"I don't think you understand," the woman says, her tone haughty and snippish.

"I do understand," I say, still trying to keep a kind tone, but I'm holding back what I want to say. "This is company policy. If you don't want to show your ID, I can put it on a gift card."

She loses it. Her face turns a shade of purple, her eyes widen and then narrow, and she slams a fist on the counter. "Don't you smart ass me."

I panic. What have I done now? "Ma'am—"

"Call your manager right now. Right now!"

My hands shake as I phone Debra in the back. "Debra, you're needed for a return at the front." I manage to keep my voice calm. Then I hang up the phone and busy myself with unfolding and refolding her items, anything to avoid looking at her. I'm in a muted world.

Debra arrives, smiling, heels clicking. "Hi!" she says. "How can I help you?"

The woman swivels, leaving an elbow on the counter and delivering her line with pomp and sass. "I have no desire to be waited on by this young lady who just smart-assed me. I need someone with more authority and less attitude who can help me."

My face burns. My eyes tingle. Keeping my face poised, I remove myself from behind the counter. I'll let them work this out.

I walk as calmly as I can to the bathroom at the back of the store. I make it inside before I burst into tears. I've had people get mad at me before while at work, I've had people yell at me, but I've never been put down like that. In front of my boss, my coworker, and a line of customers.

I use a paper towel to mop at my eyes, but a new flood comes just as I think I'm done crying.

The bathroom door opens. I turn to flee for a stall, but it's Debra, and she grabs my arm, stopping me before I go.

"It's all right," she says. "You were right. It happens sometimes. You can't please every customer."

I sag against her. "We're supposed to please the customer!"

"They don't get to have whatever they want just because they're the customer."

I don't ask how Debra handled it. She probably let the customer have what she wanted. But Debra's the manager. She can do that.

"After she left, the customers in the other line told me you were very professional and handled it very well. So dry your eyes and come back to work, okay?"

I wipe at my red, swollen eyes again. "Okay."

I put on fake cheer for the rest of the day while my coworker Brian shoots me concerned glances.

I'm still rattled as I drive home. I make a snack in the kitchen and check my phone.

There are no new notifications. There haven't been all week. Tiago hasn't messaged me in days.

That hurts.

Can't we be friends?

I'm almost done doing the dishes when I remember I was supposed to go to Fayetteville and get my TB test read. I look at the time. I could make it if I left now, but the thought of standing in that long line is demoralizing.

I'll do it in the morning.

I don't wake up until ten, when the morning sun turns lethal and bathes my bedroom in radiant heat. Blurry-eyed, I drag myself from the bed and go through my morning routine. I check my phone as I brush my teeth.

Owen texted me about an hour ago. *Plans?*

I text back. *Have to go the health department and get my TB test read. Then go to Kids First and fill out new hiring paperwork.*

O: How long will all that take?

Me: don't know. Health department took a few hours last time. Angry face.

O: come with?

It takes me a second to realize he's inviting himself along. Then I smile because I think it's cute. I text back, *Nothing else to do?*

O: Nope.

Me: could be several long and boring hours

O: I'm game.

Me: I'm driving.

O: great. Now it will be even longer.

He doesn't add an emoji. He doesn't have to. I can hear him laughing.

Me: pick you up at your house or the apartment?

O: apartment

Me: see you soon

It's been a few days since I messaged Riley. I hate to feel like I've given up on her, but I almost have.

I text her now.

Me: are you around at all this summer? I'd love to see you before I go to college. Miss you and love you.

My messages are all themes on the same. I don't know how to reach her.

Twenty minutes later I park my silver Toyota Camry in front of Owen's apartment. If possible, it looks worse than before. I sit in the car and text him.

Me: I'm here.

O: come inside. Almost ready

I don't want to. But I get out of the car and knock on the apartment door.

Aiden opens it. The brooding expression in his dark eyes lifts when he sees me, and he grins. "It's Cassandra!" He throws his arms around me in a hug.

I laugh and pat his arm. "Hi, Aiden." Of all Owen's friends, Aiden's the nicest to me. The most accepting. We were friends before Owen and I started dating, so I think that helps.

"Cassandra's here!" he yells into the apartment.

Derek stands in the frame of the galley kitchen, a bowl of cereal in his hands. "Hey," he says, a dribble of milk escaping his mouth.

The apartment smells worse than before. A trash bag leans open and overflowing against the wall. The light in the living room is out, but a lamp is lit in the corner.

Owen comes out of the bedroom, shoulders back, sauntering. Like he thinks he's walking onto the football field. I hide a smile. He's still posing for these goons.

"Hey." He rests his arm on my shoulder. "Ready?"

In answer I turn for the door. "Bye, guys."

I have the engine running and the AC on high by the time Owen gets in.

"What?" he says, climbing into the passenger seat and scooting the chair back. "You don't like my place?"

"It might not be so bad if it weren't inhabited by three teenage boys who don't pick up after themselves."

"We're adults," he says, looking offended.

I level my eyes at him and then face the road again. "You're teenagers. Eighteen. Eight-TEEN."

"Semantics."

This time he takes over my radio station, and angry alternative music rages through my car. It's not my style. But it's Owen's, and that makes it okay. Sometimes I listen to it when he's not around because it makes me think of him.

I park at the health department. Owen takes my wrist before I turn off the ignition. I turn toward him, and he leans over and kisses me.

My body relaxes as our lips meld against each other. Kissing Owen is like taking an intoxicating drink. Everything else fades away. I lose awareness of the rest of the world.

He pulls away and runs his hand along the side of my face.

Then he opens the door and gets out. I turn off the ignition and follow.

He is memorizing every moment. Just like I am.

"How does this work?" he asks as we enter the stifling entryway with the directive signs.

"I don't know," I say, turning to the room on the right. It's even more crowded than last time. Dang it. I should have woken up earlier. "Last time they poked my arm. Today they have to read it."

"Read what?"

I lift a shoulder in response. "I don't know. I can't even tell where they poked me. There's no mark on my arm or anything."

I stand in line to explain what I need. There are five people in front of me. Owen hovers behind me, squished near me because of the lack of space. He reaches a hand out and trails it along my side. His touch is feather-light. I pretend I don't notice because I don't want him to stop. But he does, as soon as we inch forward.

The person in front of me leaves the window, and it's my turn.

"Name?" It's a man this time, and he doesn't even look away from his computer screen.

"Cassandra Jones."

"What do you need?"

"To have my TB test read."

He writes on a slip of paper and hands it to me. "They'll call you in a moment."

"Do I need to take a number?"

He shakes his head, waving me off.

I don't quite trust him, so I take one just in case. Better safe than sorry.

No seats again. Owen leans against the wall, and I sit cross-legged on the carpet beside him. He reaches down and scratches my scalp.

"How long do we wait?" he asks.

"Last time took over an hour."

"All right." He drops down on the carpet next to me.

"Sorry," I say. "I should have warned you."

He looks at me. "You did. I don't care. I want to spend today with you."

"Even if it's doing this?"

"You think life is always fun and parties?" He grins at me because that's my line. "It's mostly made up of boring stuff like appointments and waiting."

I take his hand and hold it and wait.

A young man in white scrubs with a clipboard steps out and calls, "Cassandra Jones."

"Can I come?" Owen asks as I stand up.

"You can try."

The man doesn't bat an eye as Owen follows me through. Must be allowed. "What are you here for?" he asks me, consulting his clipboard.

"TB test read."

He nods and takes me to a different small room than before. "Let me see the card they gave you."

I pull it out and hand it to him.

He frowns. "I can't read your test."

CHAPTER TWELVE
Summer Before College Forever

"Y ou can't read my test?" I tilt my head. "What? Why not?" I scan the card. Did I get it wet?

"Yesterday was the last day. Today's too late."

"Wait. I don't understand. I had to come back by yesterday?"

"Yes. We have to read the test between forty-eight and seventy-two hours or it's invalid."

My mouth drops open. "No one explained that to me!"

He looks dutifully chagrined. "I'm sorry. You can come back tomorrow and do another one."

"Can't I do one now?"

"We don't do TB tests on Thursdays. By the time the health department opened after the weekend, you'd have missed the window."

I can't believe it. I don't look at Owen because I'm embarrassed. I prefer him to think I always have it together. I want to make a fuss, but there's not anything that can be done, is there? So I nod and take back the card.

"Right. Thanks. I'll come back later."

I leave without another word, Owen on my heels. I take a deep breath when we get outside, trying to rid myself of the negative energy, but my shoulders are tight, my fingers clenched.

"Sorry," I say. "Looks like we wasted that time for nothing."

"It's all right, Cassandra." He stops me in my angry march, turning me to face him. "Sometimes, life is screwing up also."

"Yes, but I don't like doing it in front of you!" I wail.

He laughs. The wind blows my hair in front of my face, and he shoves it behind my ear. "I like you more when you screw up. Then I don't feel so bad when I do it."

I relent. We both need space to make mistakes. They're going to happen. "Let me call the manager and see what she wants me to do."

"Can we do that inside your car? It's getting hot out here."

"Yeah, yeah."

We climb inside and I turn the car on. Then I call Linda's number at Kids First.

"Hello, this is Linda," she says, answering on the first ring.

"Hi, it's Cassandra Jones," I say. "I'm at the health department. They couldn't read my TB test because I was a day late, so I have to go back and take another one."

"Oh." She pauses. Does she regret hiring me? Does she think I'm a ditzy teenager who won't remember her shift or her assignments? "That's fine. Come on in and fill out paperwork. Get your test done and we'll get you started anyway."

I want to shriek my gratitude and relief into the phone, but I hold myself back. "Great! I'm on way over now." I hang up and grin at Owen. "They're still going to let me start Monday."

"You're only going to work there for two months? And you're keeping your other job?"

I nod. "I enjoy working with these kids. Maybe you'll meet some of them. They make me happy, and I always feel like I accomplished something valuable after I'm with them." I'm on the verge of rambling, so I stop. But I'm beaming. It's been a mess, trying to set up this job. I'm glad it's finally working out.

"Huh. I suppose I could get a job for a few months."

"Yeah, you could."

"Maybe I will."

I pull into the daycare in downtown Springdale. I can almost see the high school from here. The prison that held me captive for eight hours every day for three years.

Crazy that it's over.

A small woman with light blond hair pulled into a bun at the nape of her neck greets me at the check-in window. "Are you Cassandra?"

"Yes."

"Come on in. I'm Linda."

"Is it okay if he comes in with me?" I gesture to Owen.

She glances at him. "Yes, that's fine."

We scoot in, and I begin to fill out paperwork.

"Come Monday morning and we'll train you on anything you don't know. After that we'll keep you on the on-call basis like I told you over the phone."

"How does it work?" Owen asks. "It's not a set shift?"

She raises her brow at him, like she's not sure he's allowed to ask questions. But she obliges him. "It's basically a substitute teaching position. When we need her, we call her, and if she's available, she comes in."

"It'll work well with my other job," I add.

"Can I work here too?"

I stop writing and look at him. Linda is appraising him more carefully also.

"Why do you want to work here?" she asks.

His cheeks flush pink, and I see him trying to come up with an answer.

"I need a job," he says. "This would work great for my hours. And I like kids. And—" he bobs his head at me. "She's going to be here."

She suppresses a smile, and I pray she's a fan of young love. "We do always need more substitutes. We never have enough. It's a bit of a rigorous hiring process."

"Yeah, I know all about the TB test stuff," he says, a bit dryly.

She pulls out a few more papers and hands them to Owen. "Fill these out and get your TB test. Once you've done that, call me."

A phone rings in another office, and she leaves to answer it. Owen leans toward me.

"Is that okay?"

I nod, keeping my eyes on the paper as I sign my name. I'm so tickled I think I might cry.

I need to find a way to freeze time and keep us in the summer before college forever.

⚬~⚬~⚬

I sleep through my alarm in the morning. Again. I throw my clothes on and rush out the door.

I clock in, exhaling in relief when the time shows I'm right on time.

"Lucky, that one," Laura says, coming up behind me and getting something out of a drawer. She sniffs with disdain. "You were almost late."

"But I wasn't." I smile sweetly at her and fold up my receipt.

She narrow her eyes at me. "Debra wants you in Women's. There's a sale going on, and we've set a goal for everyone to bring in a thousand dollars today. Since you're only working five hours, you'll have to work extra hard."

She says it like a taunt.

"I'll see what I can do." I walk away, knowing I'll blow that goal out of the water.

I lead a woman to a dressing room with three skirts hanging off her arm. I push the door open for her, checking to make sure no one left anything behind, and then give a startled yelp.

"What is it?" she asks, crowding behind me.

"It's a bird." I tiptoe into the room and examine the hatchling lying on the dressing room floor. Its eyes are open, tiny feathers on its body, and it squawks pitifully. I look up and see a ceiling tile has moved out of its place. There must be a nest up there, and there was enough room for the bird to fall through.

"Poor thing." The woman croons behind me. "It will die soon."

Oh no, there has to be a way to save it. "Let's use the other dressing room."

I get her and her prying eyes situated in the next room, and then I find Brian.

"What do I do?" I ask after I explain the situation.

"You should kill it," Brian says. "It's going to die."

"I can't kill it!" I squeal.

"Well, you can't keep it here!"

Someone needs to come get it. I get an idea. I go to the back and find an empty shoe box. I line it with tissue paper and grab my phone from the break room.

I can only think of one person who will do whatever I ask without question. I text Owen now.

Me: can you come by my work? I need help. Urgent.

I leave my phone on the table and return to the dressing room, remembering as

I get there that I have a customer.

"How are those skirts?" I ask her.

"Great. I think I'll get all three. What's happening with the bird?"

I scoop up the tiny thing very carefully and place it in the shoe box. "I'm having someone come get it. We'll try to save it."

"Oh, good!"

"I'll be back in a moment to ring you up."

I take the box to the back and check my phone.

There are three messages from Owen.

O: what is it?

O: Is something wrong?

O: I'm on my way.

Oh crap. I can tell from the way he texted that when he didn't hear back from me, he got worried. Now I feel dumb. Rescuing a baby bird isn't an emergency. He didn't need to drop whatever he was doing for this.

I'm about to text him and tell him so but decide not to. His apartment is near the store. By the time he gets the text, he'll be here.

I return to the dressing room, all smiles as I take the skirts and lead the woman to the register. "Will that be all for you?"

She fingers several necklaces on the display counter. "I'd like a few of these, actually."

I hardly notice that she spends more than two hundred dollars. My mind is on Owen and his pending arrival. "Thanks for shopping at Stage, have a great day!"

"Good luck with the bird!"

She walks out, but I see the tan truck pull in behind her.

Owen's here.

CHAPTER THIRTEEN

Wildlife Rescue

rush to the door and greet Owen. "Sorry, I didn't mean to worry you. You didn't need to come right away. I got busy and couldn't respond."

He gives my arm a squeeze. "That's all right, I wasn't doing anything. What do you need help with?"

"We found a bird." I lead him to the back and flinch when I see Laura checking inventory.

She straightens up, a frown falling over her face. "Cassandra, this is an employees only area. And haven't we had enough talks about you bringing boys to work?"

She makes it sound like I stuff them in my pocket and drag them around all day.

"Sorry," I say, and I put a lot of contrition in my voice. "This was important. He came to help."

"With what?"

I hesitate, then say, "I'll show you."

I've piqued her curiosity. She follows me and Owen without a word.

The little bird bobs its head around when I take the lid off the shoe box. It opens its wide beak and cries.

Laura stifles a gasp. "Where did this come from?"

"It was in a dressing room. It fell from the ceiling."

The bird chirps again, neck lengthening.

"It's hungry." I look at Owen. "Can you take it? Can you help it?"

He stares at it a moment and then looks at me, sympathy in his eyes. "Cassandra, it's going to die."

"It might not." I hold it out to him. "We can help it. You know about animals. Can you look it up? Find out some food plan for baby birds or something?"

I know he wants to tell me no. He doesn't believe he can do this. He doesn't want to get my hopes up.

Instead he takes the box from my hands. "I'll try."

His eyes cut to Laura, and he gives a quick nod. "Sorry for coming back here. I'll just take this and go."

Owen leaves, and I dump my phone into my bag and try to skirt around her for the door.

"Cassandra."

Her voice stops me, and I freeze.

"He's your boyfriend?"

I look at her and nod, holding my breath, wondering what comes next.

She pauses. "It was nice of him to come get that bird."

I'm so startled that at first I don't register her words. She's not criticizing. Or threatening to fire me.

"He's nice that way," I say carefully.

"He can't be coming by here all the time," she says, but there's no more fire in her words.

"I'll make sure he doesn't," I say.

When I leave for the health department three hours later, I have more than two thousand dollars in sales.

⚬ ⁓ ⁕ ⁓ ⚬

To my relief, the line at the health department isn't as long. Maybe it quiets down in the afternoon. I take my number and sit down, then text Owen.

Me: how's the bird?

I hold my breath, afraid he's going to come back and say it already died.

I read my other texts while I wait for his response. Harper texted, asked to come over later. And Riley—

Riley!

There's a text from Riley.

It's short. All it says is, *Sorry I haven't responded. I'd love to see you before you leave. You busy tonight?*

I call her.

Part of me doesn't expect her to answer, but she does.

"Hello?" She sounds bored. Like she answered because there was nothing better to do. I don't let that discourage me.

"Hey!" I say. "I'd love for you to come over! It's been so long since we've talked. Want to spend the night?"

"No, I can't, I have to work an early shift," she says. "But I can come over for a an hour."

"I would love that," I say. "Do you want Harper to come too? She asked what I was doing tonight."

"Oh, if you're hanging with Harper, we can try another night."

I feel Riley backing out, and I hang on tighter. "I'll tell Harper I'm busy. Want me to pick you up?"

"I know the way to your house. I'll see you tonight."

"For dinner?" I try to narrow down the window of expectancy.

"Probably after."

79

What does that mean? Seven? Eight? Nine? "Okay. See you then!"

I text Harper to tell her not today, and a text from Owen comes through.

O: Still alive. You home?

Me: at the health department. Getting a TB test. Again. Skull emoji.

O: Good luck.

The same young man from yesterday pops his head out and calls my number.

"You're back," he says when I follow him in.

"Yep." I hold out my arm and wait.

"Just remember," he says as he pokes me, "you have to come back on Monday. Or it won't count."

"Thanks for making it clear," I say sardonically.

He grins. "It's happened before that people don't realize there's a window."

I mock glare at him.

He writes on a piece of paper and hands it to me. "Where's the boy who came with you yesterday?"

"At his house, I assume."

"Is he your boyfriend?"

I smile. The thought of Owen as my boyfriend will always make me smile. "He is."

He nods. "Remember to come back on Monday."

It occurs to me as I leave that he wasn't curious about Owen. He was curious if I was available to date.

I glance back at the health department, pondering Owen's words from earlier. Is he right? Is college the place where boys will suddenly notice me?

⚬〜✵〜⚬

Owen's truck is in my driveway when I get home.

I bounce out of the car and hurry up the steps, then fling the doors open and call out, "Hello!"

Emily leans her head out of the kitchen. "In here."

I walk through the living room to the table and find my siblings clustered around the shoe box. Owen stands off to the side. I go to him when I enter, and he puts an arm around my shoulders.

"It's so cute," Emily coos.

"Has it eaten anything?" I ask Owen.

Annette turns to us. "Baby birds eat the partially digested bits of worms their moms bring back to them."

"That's so gross," Scott says.

"I did not feed it regurgitated worms," Owen says. "I took it to the vet. He gave me a meal of mashed up worms to feed it, which I haven't found the stomach to do." He nods toward the box. "The worms are in there. It ate a little at the vet's."

"You took it to the vet?" I pull my wallet from my purse. "How much do I owe you?"

Owen glowers at me. "In what world do you think I'll accept payment from you?"

I put my wallet away and hug him around the waist. He wraps an arm around

80

me and rubs my back.

"Is it going to live?" Annette asks. "Can we keep it?"

"I'm going to do my best with it." I tilt my face up to look at Owen. "Thanks for taking care of it."

"It's safer here than at my apartment."

I stick out my tongue. "When are you moving out? It's so gross there."

"We already paid this month. But maybe next month."

"Just move out now and forget about the money."

"Tempting," he admits.

I take his hand and pull him into my room, leaving my siblings to admire the baby bird. "What else did the vet say?" I ask, sitting cross-legged on my bed. "How often do I feed it?"

Owen sits across from me, same style. "He said every five hours. He also said to warn you, the bird will probably die. They need their nestmates and their moms."

"I'm aware I might not be able to keep it alive. Thanks for all you did today, Owen. I knew I could count on you."

Annette pokes her head in the room. "I'm making mac and cheese for dinner. You guys want some?"

"Yes," I say, answering for both of us. "Mac and cheese is all she knows how to make," I whisper to Owen as she leaves the room.

"Can't wait to try it." He scoots back on my bed, up against the headboard, and pulls me against him. "Sorry for getting you in trouble."

"Oh!" I straighten up and turn so I can see him. "You won't believe this. Something about rescuing the baby bird made Laura like you!"

"I don't believe it."

I nod. "Yes! She said you must be a nice guy."

"Huh. We should have tried that a few months ago."

"Who knew?" I swivel around again so my back presses against him. He wraps his arms around my waist, clasping his knuckles in front of me, and I pinch the excess skin on each finger joint.

"How is Tiago?" he asks.

If there is jealousy in the question, he hides it well. I continue pinching the skin and keep my voice level.

"He's really angry at me. He said he couldn't talk to me anymore. So we aren't talking."

"Why?"

I hate the answer. It shows I haven't grown up as much as I think I have. I still try to hide things and manipulate situations to serve me. "The short answer is because you and I are dating again."

"There's a longer answer?"

I sigh. "Because I'm stupid."

He laughs. "That's a shorter answer."

I turn to face him. "Because every time I think I'm protecting someone by hiding the truth, I end up hurting them worse. And I still haven't learned that lesson."

He nods. That was what broke us apart. "So you didn't tell him about us at first."

"Right." I don't give all the details.

"And then you did."

"He practically guessed it. And was upset. So we don't talk now."

I say it casually. With a verbal shrug. Like it's nothing.

But Owen knows me better. "He means a lot to you, doesn't he."

I take his fingers and pry them apart, then press my palm up to his. His hand could swallow mine. "Who was your first love?"

"You."

CHAPTER FOURTEEN

Declarations

My breath catches. I didn't expect that. My fingers curl up in his palm. "Me?" My words falter. "There wasn't someone before me?"

"No."

I don't know what to say.

He pulls his hand away and hugs me, squeezing me tight. "Your first always has a piece of your heart."

He's talking about me.

I will treasure my piece forever.

"But that doesn't mean you're always in love with your first," I say, and I'm speaking about myself now. "Just that they're always special to you. And if there's any possible way to have them in your life—you want it."

"I get it."

I think he does. He's not mad about Tiago. He knows I don't love him that way. I snuggle back into his embrace, and he folds me into him.

"I love you," I whisper.

He kisses the side of my face. "I know you do."

I smile. It's taken me months to convince him of that fact. I'm glad he knows it.

"Mac and cheese is ready!" Annette says, and she grins when she pops into the room and sees us wrapped around each other the way we are. She's thirteen and a hopeless romantic. I'm glad Owen's the example she sees. He's everything she should expect from a boyfriend.

I've just put my plate in the sink after dinner when the doorbell rings. I glance at the clock. A little after six.

Emily gets there first. "Riley!" she exclaims.

Crapola! How did I forget?

I dry my hands on a towel and rush from the kitchen. "Riley!" I reach her in two seconds and pull her into a crushing hug. Then I step back, holding her at arm's length, studying her.

Her blond hair, tinged with a hint of red, sits right at her chin in a straight bob. Freckles dot her fair skin, and one dainty eyebrow lifts over her green eyes. She's not too thin but still small, maybe an inch taller than me.

She looks the same, which surprises me. I guess I expected her to have changed in the months we've grown apart. I hug her again.

"You look great!" I tell her.

Her eyes drift past me to the dining room. "Owen," she says, surprise coloring her voice.

"Hi, Riley," he says, edging past us in the entry way. "I was just leaving. Good to see you."

He knows what I need before I do. He catches my eye and nods, and I nod back, then haul Riley past the kitchen to my bedroom.

"I haven't seen you in weeks!" I exclaim, climbing back on my bed. Riley puts her keys on my desk and sits beside me, reminding me of slumber parties and late night talks and sobbing emotional explosions, all that have happened on this bed. "How are you?"

"Well, I'm all right." We hear the sputter of Owen's truck, and she says, "Are you guys dating again?"

"We are." I pull a pillow into my chest and hug it.

"When did that happen?"

"It's pretty new. Two weeks ago? Graduation day."

She smiles, wistfully. "I'm glad. I felt bad when you guys broke up."

"It's like you said. Four months. Most people don't make it there."

"Will you this time?"

"What do you mean?" I straighten up. "The countdown starts over?"

"Well, yeah. You can't add your previous time to this time."

"We can't?" I'm crushed.

"How would that work? You subtract the months you were apart? No, it's all new again, you have a new honeymoon phase to work through."

"Then we'll only make it two and a half months," I say, slouching forward. "We're basically ending it when I leave for school."

"If you want to be with each other, you will be."

"Owen doesn't have a great track record for waiting," I say, keeping my voice light. I tick off on my fingers. "Started dating Emma within a few months of moving here. Took Eddie to Homecoming and had a thing with her. Started dating Suzi weeks later. Asked Kristin out seconds after we broke up."

Riley puts a hand on mine and lowers my fingers. "You're forgetting the one constant in all of those. Why do you think he dated Emma when he moved in?"

I don't answer, so she does.

"Because you were dating Tiago. Why did he ask Eddie to Homecoming?"

I still don't speak. I'd rather hear her put it together. So she does.

"Because you said you didn't want to go. Why did he start dating Suzi? Because you said you weren't ready to date. Why did he date Kristin? Because he was rebounding off you."

"I'm still the constant," I say. "We leave for college. Owen starts dating someone else. Right away. Because he won't be with me."

Riley mulls this over. "Why doesn't he change his plans and go to Colorado with you?"

"His family is moving to Louisiana and he wants to go with them. And he says we're too young to be so serious."

"No, we're not."

I shrug. "Maybe. We still have growing up to do. Changing."

"I moved in with Lucas."

So that's where she's been. I give a slow nod, though I feel my heart sink within me. "Is he the one, then? You love him?"

"Cassandra, love's a fairy tale. I've been with lots of guys and haven't loved any of them. I don't think it's real."

I can't fathom this. "I love Owen."

"And you loved Tiago. So what? You aren't going to end up with either of them."

Her words are a slap in the face. Does love matter so little?

She checks her phone. "I can't stay long. I need sleep so I can be alert at work."

I force a smile, trying to return us to neutral ground. "Where are you working?"

"A store in the mall. I'm pulling a double shift tonight, working until closing and then restocking in the morning. Then I stay until lunch and run the register. It pays well, and I have to make money to pay rent." She shrugs.

She's so different. Cynical. Jaded. Unfriendly. I want to peel back the layers and find my friend, but I feel a negative energy repulsing me from getting too close.

"At least it pays well," I say, looking for something positive.

"It's not forever. I'm getting my GED next month. And then I'm going to nursing school."

"Hey, that's excellent! Isn't your dad a nurse?"

"Yeah. He gave me the idea." She stands and picks up her keys. "I should go now. Lucas will wonder where I am." She glances around my room, and a whisper of nostalgia crosses her face.

I stand also. I want to hug her. Instead I hug myself. "Let's get together again before I leave. Go out to lunch or something. Maybe I can meet Lucas."

"I don't think so. You'll judge him."

"No, I won't!" I protest. At the same time, I wonder if she's hiding something about him. Why would I judge him?

I can't help it that I'll never think he's good enough for her.

"It was good to see you," she says. "I'll call you later."

I follow her out of my room. "What store are you working at in the mall?" I have to know how to find her, in case she doesn't talk to me again.

"Kirtland's."

I know the store. I continue with her out of the house. "Thanks for coming over, Riley. I've missed you." I hug her hard. "I love you."

She sighs, and some of the stiffness goes out of her. "I love you too, Cassie. You'll always be one of my best friends." She gives me a smile as she pulls away, and I see a glimpse of her. The old Riley.

Then she's in her truck, driving away, and I wish Owen were back so I could curl up in his arms and cry.

Monday is my first day to work at Kid's First.

I have to be there at seven. My alarm wakes me at five-thirty, and I curse my life. I've forgotten what it's like to wake up early. It's like getting up for Bible study again. I hit snooze for another half hour.

When it goes off again, I drag myself from bed, knowing I don't have any more minutes to sleep. I put my hair in a ponytail and skip the makeup. None of the kids will be impressed, anyway.

I check on the little bird before I slip out the door. Still alive. It's been three days. I'm feeding it every few hours, and my mom watches over it when I can't. It chirps but doesn't do much else. I hope it's warm enough.

"I'm giving you the best chance you're going to get, little one," I whisper. I'm afraid to name it. Should it not survive, I'll feel a lot worse if I've grown attached.

So little one it is.

The problem with that is, it's what Tiago called me. So I can't help but think of him when I say it.

I'm excited when I park in front of the day care. I already know several of the kids by name. Will I work in the baby room? Or the room where the kids wait after they get dropped off? Maybe I'll take shifts in different places.

I step up to the window, and the girl behind pushes the volunteer sheet at me.

"I'm not a volunteer this time," I tell her. "I'm working here. It's my first day."

"Oh." She checks another sheet. "Are you Cassandra?"

When I nod, she buzzes me through. "Go down the hall, turn right, and follow it to the end. Then knock on the door at the right."

"Okay." I do as she says. I don't know this part of the daycare. I haven't been in this section yet.

I pass several open doors and peak into the classrooms as I pass. Nothing has started yet. I picture the kids in the big gymnasium, where they get dropped off. I itch to be in there, reading stories and playing cars and pushing them on swings.

I reach the end of the hallway and face the door on the right. It's a split door, built so the top half can open while the bottom stays shut. I knock on it.

The top half opens, revealing a large woman with one very hairy mole on her chin and a loose hairnet.

"Yes?" she says sharply.

"Sorry, I think I'm lost," I say hesitantly. "The receptionist sent me down here."

She steps away, looks at the wall, and then back at me. "Are you Cassandra Jones?"

"Yes."

"You're in the right place." She unlocks the door the rest of the way and swings it open. "Come on in."

I step in and glance around.

I'm in a kitchen.

A small sink and cabinets line one wall. A tiered cart with dozens of orange trays sits in front of a refrigerator. And then there's the two of us, squished into the remaining space.

"All right, here's the list." She sets a piece of paper on the cart. "The ingredients are in the fridge, labeled in plastic bins. The list tells you how many trays each classroom needs. You take the left side, I'll take the right."

My head is spinning, and I stop her as she moves to the fridge. "I'm sorry. I don't understand."

"What do you not understand?" she barks.

I look at the trays, the list, the fridge, and my mind is trying to put it together. But it's not jelling. "What am I doing?"

She's heaves a sigh like I must be incredibly incompetent. "We're putting together the breakfast trays for each classroom. Today is French toast sticks. See the list of ingredients? Then you take seven trays to room two. Six trays to room three. Got it?" She waits for my slow nod before continuing. "After that we'll gather them up and clean the trays. We'll have two hours to prep the food for lunch before we deliver to every room. Since there's two of us, it'll be easy. But tomorrow I won't be here, so you'll be on your own."

I need to sit down, but there's no place. "I—I came to work with the children."

"I don't know what they hired you to do. But this is where you're needed."

I'm distressed. My heart pounds in my chest, and my throat aches. She watches me closely, and I take a steadying breath.

"Okay. What do we do first?"

She bobs her head and pulls open the fridge. "Find the small plastic cups and fill them with syrup."

CHAPTER FIFTEEN

Good Intentions

They release me at one.

The children are at recess. I sneak outside to see them before I leave, and several of them recognize me. They run to me and tug on my pants, pull on me until I bend to their level.

But I'm exhausted. My feet hurt from standing so much. My fingers smell like the chicken nuggets we served for lunch no matter how many times I washed them. And I have two hours to get my TB test read before I have to go work at Stage.

Owen calls me as I'm driving to Fayetteville. I put him on speaker.

"Hi," I say, the word exhaling out of me.

"You sound beat."

I groan. "Owen. You won't believe it. They put me on kitchen duty."

"Kitchen duty? As in, washing dishes?"

"And cooking food and playing server! It was one of the longest days of my life."

"Hate to break it to you, but it's not over."

"Oh, I know! I'm on my way to get my stupid TB test read, and then I have to go my other job."

"This sounds familiar. Do you always overbook yourself?"

I sigh. "I don't know how to live life if it's not packed."

"Well, I guess if that's where they're going to put you, you can say no when they call."

"But I don't want to," I whine. "I got to go outside and see the children for a few minutes. Somehow I have to convince them to let me work with the kids."

"Want to do something tonight?"

"Yes," I say, but I hesitate. I want to see Owen, but I can already tell how tired I'll be when I get off work. "I think."

"Don't say yes on my account. I'll survive."

I laugh and stick my tongue out at the phone. "Jerk. Let me see how I feel after work, okay?"

"No worries, Cass."

I pull into the health department and heave another sigh. There are too many cars here. I know how long the line will be. "I'm here. I'll call you later, okay?"

"Hope you pass your test this time."

"Thanks." I'm within the window. I should be fine.

I hang up and get out of the car. "I don't even know what TB is," I grumble. "Why is it so important?"

I don't have to take a number to have a test read, and instead of waiting an hour, I only have to wait ten minutes. It's the same guy as before.

"You made it this time," he says, and he gives me a friendly smile.

"Yes. Trying to abide by the rules."

He pulls out a tape measure and wraps it around my arm, then writes on a chart. "You passed. Congrats. Your test is negative."

"How do you know?" I peer closely at my inner arm.

"There's no swelling. No reaction at all."

"Oh. That's good."

He writes on a card and hands it to me. "Nice seeing you again."

"You too," I say, before I can catch myself.

Great. Is that considered flirting? I hurry out before he can say anything else.

Nothing exciting happens at Stage. I work in the dresses. It's usually my favorite department, but today I'm bored. My feet hurt. My legs hurt. My eyes hurt. My shift isn't over until we close the store, and I stagger out to my car, forcing myself to stay awake.

I'm home before I remember Owen's invite to do something. I go to my room. Emily glances up, headphones in, jiving to music, and bobs her head at me. I return the nod and feed the little bird a mixture of ground worms and water.

"Stay alive, Tweety," I whisper. Great. Now he has a name.

"Cassandra?"

I turn as my mom steps into the room. "Hi, Mom."

"I signed you up for the youth retreat this weekend."

"This weekend?" I shake my head. "I can't. I work."

"You'll have to ask off. I want you to go. It's your last one before college."

"Mom, I don't have time."

"You need to make the time. You're working too hard, and believe it or not, you're still a kid. Besides, I need you to take Emily and Scott."

That's probably the real reason she signed me up. "Why can't Emily drive them?"

"She's not a legal adult, so she can't."

"What days?"

"It's Thursday through Saturday. You'll be back Sunday."

"That's three whole days, Mom!" I press a hand to my forehead. "I can't take that long off! I have to ask off two weeks in advance, anyway."

"Riley's going. Her mom's making her."

That stops me. This is three days where I might be able to connect with Riley. Three days where she's forced to attend devotionals and maybe hear what people are saying.

It clinches it.

"Fine." I put the lid back on the shoe box. "I'll go. But will you feed Tweety for me?"

She's unsuccessful at hiding her smile. "Tweety?"

"Yes," I growl. "Tweety."

She doesn't hide her laughter. I ignore her and go to the bathroom to wash my face.

⊙∿·⟐·∿⊙

I spend the next day working in the kitchen at Kids First again. And then I go to Stage and request the time off for the weekend, and Debra agrees.

I have the afternoon to myself.

I want to go swimming. I haven't been all summer. Last year Harper and I went to the lake at least once a week, but this summer I've been working almost every day. And I don't know how to find the swimming hole she always goes to.

I wouldn't go by myself, anyway.

So I drive out to Owen's house.

I'm pulling into his driveway before I remember he doesn't live here anymore. Shoot. Hopefully Monica's here. I send Owen a text, just because I'm aggravated.

Me: why do you not live at your house anymore?

Monica's at the kitchen table with her boyfriend Noah. "Hey!" she says, getting up and giving me a hug. "I didn't know you were coming over!"

"Last-minute decision," I say. "I had a few hours with nothing going on."

"Come to the movies with us tonight," she says.

"As much as I love being a third-wheel . . ." I say, and she laughs.

"Invite Owen. We can all go."

I want to hang out with Owen. But I don't love going to the movies. You sit there and stare at the screen, ignoring the people next to you. You can't even whisper about what's going on because people get angry when you talk.

I'd rather watch a movie in my basement. "Yeah, maybe Owen and I can watch a movie together." I text him. *Want to watch a movie at my place tonight?*

"Want to stay the night?" Monica asks. "Maybe Owen can stay too and we can all have a slumber party like last time."

She smirks, and my face warms.

"Hush," I say, kicking her foot under the table.

The front door opens, and Mrs. Blaine comes in with grocery bags hanging off both arms. "Groceries, guys!" she says.

Noah pops up to help.

"Richard!" Mrs. Blaine shouts, and he appears from somewhere. She smiles at me. "Hi, Cassandra."

"Hi, Mrs. Blaine," I say.

She sets the groceries on the counter, and I follow Monica's lead in putting items in the pantry.

"Monica, I need your help on Thursday," she says. "I forgot I have an appointment in Little Rock, and I can't drive Richard to the youth retreat. I need

90

you to take him."

"Mom, I'm working at the animal shelter," Monica says.

"Take the day off. I can't take him, and I don't want him to miss it."

"Isn't Owen going?" I ask.

Mrs. Blaine shakes his head. "He and his dad have a hunt planned in Missouri. They leave Friday."

"Oh." I feel like I should have known that, but if Owen mentioned it, I don't remember. "Well, I'm going. I can take Richard."

"Great idea!" Monica says.

Mrs. Blaine turns to Richard as he comes in with groceries, Noah behind him.

"Richard," she says. "Cassandra can take you to the youth retreat this weekend."

"Yay," Richard says without enthusiasm.

"What time do you want him to be ready, Cassandra?"

"What time do we need to be there?" I don't know anything about this.

"Check-in's at one. You should leave here around ten-thirty, in case you hit traffic."

"All right, then . . . Ten-thirty."

They laugh.

"I'll be in my room," Mrs. Blaine says. She heads down the hall, and Richard disappears around the corner also.

"Next week there's a lake party for the Fourth of July," Monica says. "Noah and I are going. Want to come?"

"Yes!" I exclaim. "I was just thinking how I haven't been to the lake all summer!"

"Awesome. We'll ride together."

My phone chirps with a text, and I glance at it.

O: Because I paid rent somewhere else?

O: yes.

It takes me a second to realize he's answering two questions at once. But I catch on.

Me: it's a lot less fun to drop by your house when you're not here

Me: eight.

O: Are you at my house?

O: seven.

I settle into the couch, losing myself in a texting conversation with Owen.

Me: Yes.

Me: why are we negotiating time?

O: Dang it. I don't know why I don't live there.

O: because I want to see you sooner than eight

I smile.

"Is he going to come to the movies?" Monica asks.

I glance up and see her watching me from the kitchen. Then I check the time on the stove behind her.

It's three o'clock.

I text back, *five.*

O: see you there

"No, I don't think so," I say, suppressing a smile. "It looks like he's going to my house to watch a movie. And I'm going to meet him there."

Monica gasps and Noah laughs.

"You sold me out!" she exclaims, throwing a dish towel my direction. It lands five feet from me.

"Yeah, maybe," I say, grinning. "But I really like him."

I clean up the kitchen while I wait for Owen. Anything to keep my mom from being annoyed with me. I take a basket of towels and go downstairs to fold them.

I hear when Owen arrives. Scott answers the door, and then my mom greets him. I didn't tell her he was coming over, but she just calls down the stairs and tells me he's here.

It's like graduating from high school waved a magic wand over my parents, and suddenly they see me as an adult. For the most part, they give me space and let me make my own decisions.

"Hi," I say when Owen reaches the basement. I fold another towel and add it to the pile. "I'm almost done here."

He sits across from me and takes a towel from the basket. "How was my family?"

"They seem pretty good. Looks like I'm taking Richard to the youth retreat this weekend."

"Wait." He looks at me as he grabs another towel. "You're going?"

I nod. "My mom needs me to take my siblings. So she signed me up."

He frowns, the skin around his eyes pinching.

"What's wrong?"

"Maybe I'll ask my dad to reschedule the hunt so I can go."

I shake my head. "Don't do that. It's just a youth retreat. There will always be another."

"Not with you," he says, so quietly I almost don't hear.

I don't respond to that. I think how fun it would be to go together, like church camp was last summer. Owen wasn't there, and we weren't dating yet anyway. I met this kid, Trevor, and we went to classes together and danced together every night. Nothing came of it, but we had a blast.

I picture having that same experience with Owen, and I feel a pang in my heart.

"I'm sorry you won't be there," I say.

He does not answer. I study him as he folds towels. His jaw is clenched, his brow still furrowed, his gaze unfocused. It's his battle face. He's wrestling with something.

I leave him to it.

We finish with the towels, and I take my pile to the bathroom around the corner. I return for his pile, but he stands, holding them into his chest.

"I can take them. Where do they go?"

"Those go in the hall bathroom upstairs."

I grab the empty basket and lead the way. My parents are in the living room talking, and they glance up at us as we come up the stairs.

"Owen came over to fold laundry?" my mom asks.

"Yes, ma'm," Owen says.

I grin and show him the bathroom, then take the basket to the laundry room.

"We're going to watch a movie," I tell my parents when I return. "Holler if you need something."

"All right, sweetie," Mom says.

We head back downstairs, and I glance at Owen's face before I sit on the couch and pull my knees up.

"You good now? Need a rock to throw? We have plenty outside."

He laughs, which is a good sign. "I wasn't rock mad. Just—perturbed."

"Rock mad," I repeat. That must be what he calls it when he wants to break something. "So you didn't feel the need to throw things?"

"No." He sits on the couch beside me and rests his elbow on my propped-up knee.

"What was bugging you?" I know it has to do with the retreat. And me going. And him not.

"It's nothing."

"No, really," I persist, but he shakes his head.

"What movie are we watching?" he asks.

He doesn't want to tell me, and I let it go. I figure it's more of the same. Realizing that our time is slipping away. I pull up the streaming channels. "There haven't been any new zombie movies lately."

"What is it with you and the undead?"

"Better than vampires, right?"

He tilts his head, considering. "Yes. Better than vampires."

I pick the new release tab. "Anything look good here?"

"You pick."

I scan through the newest action flicks, musicals, and slasher films. Then I hand him the remote control. "No. Surprise me."

"Oh, I'll surprise you, all right."

The next thing I know, a Disney jingle rings out, and I start laughing. I can't believe he's put on the newest animated feature.

"For real. This is what you want to watch?"

He puts down the remote and grabs my ankle, yanking my leg down. Then he grabs the other and pulls hard enough that I slide from the corner of the couch until my head hits the armrest. Then he climbs over me and looks down at my face.

"I have no intentions of watching the movie," he says.

CHAPTER SIXTEEN

Temptress

His tone is mischievous, teasing, but when Owen kisses me, it's all seriousness. I can't get enough of his mouth. I feel his body press into mine, and he sits up for a moment, but I push up on my elbows and catch his lip with my teeth, and he's back down, flattening me beneath him on the couch. His mouth moves from my mouth to my jaw to my neck, and his hands wander under my shirt, squeezing the flesh of my belly. He kisses my collarbone, and I'm lost, arching my back to meet his touches, closing my eyes, wanting him to explore every part of me.

"Shit," he whispers, and then he's off me, sitting on the floor with his back to the couch.

No, no, it can't be over. I want more. I want it all. But I lay there, breathing hard, my hormone-laced blood pumping hot through my veins. I reach forward and touch his shoulder. "Owen. Come back."

"I can't."

I tug on him. "Come on."

He shakes his head. "It's getting harder and harder to remember to stop, Cass."

I bite my lip. Should I say the thoughts tumbling around in my head? Do I dare? "Maybe we don't have to stop."

He groans and puts his face in his hands. "Don't say that."

"But what if it's true?"

He finally gets up and sits on the other side of the couch, pulling his own legs up so they don't touch me. "You say that now. But you wouldn't after. After you would feel guilty. Sick inside. And so angry that you let it happen. Angry at yourself. Angry at me."

I consider his words. They come from someone who's been there. Someone who knows. I get that sinking suspicion again, that he's slept with someone. I shove it aside. He's told me to my face that he hasn't, and I trust him.

I do know he's fooled around, and the feelings that creates are similar. I

94

remember how I felt with Tiago. How great it felt when we were together, and then the terrible guilt I felt after. It was one of the things that tore us apart.

But everything is so different with Owen. Our love is so different. "I don't just think that way when I'm turned on. I think it all the time. That maybe we could. Maybe we should." It's in my thoughts every moment. When I'm eating. Reading. Sleeping. Praying.

He stands up and moves away from the couch, then sits down in a chair at the dining room table. I sit up straighter and watch him. The movie plays behind me, a silly chorus of singing creatures, but we're both oblivious to it. He lowers his head and stares at his open palms.

"I don't know what to do," he says finally.

I wait for more. But there's nothing else.

"Can I come sit by you?" I ask.

He nods, and I come to the table also, taking a chair next to him. I'm careful not to touch him. I feel his need for space.

"What is it you don't know what to do?" I ask.

He lifts his face and looks at me, studies me. "I'm torn. Every moment with you, I'm torn. I don't know how to love you casually. I want to love you like you're going to be mine forever. But I know you're not. And so I can't." He reaches his hand out and touches his knuckle to mine. "That's why I can't, Cassie."

I don't tolerate people calling me Cassie who didn't know me in elementary school. It's a name from my childhood, and I hate it. But somehow with Owen, it touches a soft, vulnerable spot in me.

"You can't what?" I ask.

He pulls his hand back and weaves his fingers together, then props his chin on top of them, still looking at me. "I can't sleep with you. Because you might be someone else's girl one day. And I know you. No matter how much you think you want this now, you will regret it."

I stare at him, and I feel the truth in his words. It's why I've waited this long. It's just that, in my heart, I feel Owen already is that man.

"What if it is you?" I ask, bravely voicing the thoughts of my heart. "What if you are the one I'll belong to?"

He gives me such a smoldering look that my blood runs hot again.

"Then I'll show you what it is to be loved, Cassandra Jones."

We finish the movie on opposite ends of the couch. He doesn't touch me again, not even to say goodnight. But I feel the heat in his eyes when he looks at me, and I know we tiptoed near a forbidden forest today. And somehow, instead of crossing it, it feels like we jumped straight to the other side.

I keep picturing Owen's face when he uttered those words. The words that feel more like a promise than a maybe.

I'll show you what it is to be loved, Cassandra Jones.

Those words fill me with such thoughts that I hardly sleep.

⟨∞⟩

It's a struggle to get Emily and Scott out the door Thursday morning, and by the time we leave for the Blaine's house, it's 11:33a.m. It pours rain outside. I tell

Emily to text Richard and tell him we'll be late while I take the switch-back curves as fast as I dare.

I slow down on the gravel leading up to the Blaine's house. Won't do to fishtail out here and make Mrs. Blaine regret asking me to drive. I see Owen's truck. I haven't seen him since Tuesday. I wonder if he came over because he knew I was coming.

I dash up to the porch, trying to keep from getting wet. Emily follows me, pulling her golden brown hair into a braid across her shoulder.

"Aren't you going to ring the doorbell?" she asks as I reach for the handle.

"I don't usually," I say. I look at her closer, noticing the slight breathless quality to her and the flush to her cheeks. "Are you crushing on Richard?"

"No!" she says, but her face gets pinker.

I grin and push open the door. "Richard!" I call. "Let's get out of here!"

He comes down the hall with only one shoe on. "I can't find my other shoe!"

Why am I not surprised? "Where's your bag? I'll put it in the car."

"Owen!" he shouts. "Where's my bag?"

"How am I supposed to know, Chard?" Owen shouts back. He strolls out of his room, putting his hands in his pockets. "Hey."

"Hi," I return while Emily stands behind me like a mute. "I'll take his bag if we can find it."

Owen moves past me into the sitting room. "There," he says, pointing to a red duffel under the table. "Bet that's it."

I go to pick it up, but Owen gets there first.

"Found my shoe," Richard says, dashing back in, pulling the shoe on as he runs over.

"Great," Owen drawls. "This your bag?"

"Yeah."

Owen takes it out of the house.

"I have a bag of snacks here too," Richard says, and he pulls a plastic sack from the cupboard.

"Give it to Emily," I say, inclining my head. "She needs something to carry."

"Oh. Thanks." Richard hands it to her.

"Got your phone? Toothbrush? Charger?" I ask.

"Uh, let me check." He darts back down the hall.

"Let's go." I urge Emily out of the house.

We pass Owen en route to the car. The rain pelts us. "Thanks for the help," I call as we near him. "Will you make sure Richard gets out of the house?"

"Yes." But instead he follows us back to my car. Like he totally doesn't notice he's getting soaked.

I smile to myself. I know he's intentionally putting physical distance between us. But I also know he's drawn to me like a moth to the flame.

I add Richard's snacks to the bags in the back seat. "We got it from here, Owen," I say, turning around and grabbing my door handle, holding a hand above my head like it will shield me from the water. "Have a great time on your hunt. We'll see you when you get back."

"All right," he says. Still standing there, hands in his pockets, five feet between us.

I open my car door.

And Owen crosses the space between us and pulls me into a hug.

I knew he would.

He crushes me to him and whispers, "I love you."

I stand on tiptoes and press a kiss to his wet cheek. "I know."

I dart into the car, shoving water from my seat.

"Let me get you guys some towels," Owen says.

"No, Owen, it's okay—" I begin, but he's gone.

It's cold now that we're wet, and I switch from AC to heat.

Owen returns with an armload of towels, which I hand out.

"Thanks," I say.

"Drive carefully," he says.

I acknowledge his words with a head bob and turn around in the long driveway.

⟋⌣⟍ ⁂ ⟋⌣⟍

Richard is hilarious. I don't know what he ate for breakfast, but he cracks jokes and makes silly noises the whole drive. Even Scott, who usually falls into a moody silence anytime he has to go to church, is laughing and jovial. Emily doesn't say much, but she sneaks glances at Richard and smiles a lot.

A little more than two hours later, we arrive at the conference center. It's still raining. I drove slower than usual, mindful of the group in my care.

Harper texts me right as we pull in, wanting to know if I can go to the lake tomorrow. I'm totally bummed when I tell her I'm at a youth retreat.

Can we try for next week? I ask.

Sure! she says.

Perfect.

I get us checked in, and they assign us to host families in the area.

"We have two classes this afternoon, and then dinner," the girl behind the desk says. "After dinner, come back to the foyer and look for your host family. They'll take you home."

"Get your stuff out my car, guys," I say. "I won't be driving it again until we leave."

All the luggage is locked in a big room, and then we leave for the classes.

I see lots of familiar faces. People I've known for years. I smile, wave, but I'm distracted. Looking for one person in particular.

And then I see her.

Riley sits with a group of kids from Fayetteville, all slumped in their seats, arms folded across their chests, all clearly unhappy to be here.

I move that direction, my smile bright, feeling as out of place as a flashlight in a blackout. "Riley!" I exclaim.

Her eyes land on me, and to my relief, she smiles. She even sits up a bit. "Cassandra. I didn't know you were coming."

I take her hand and pull her from her seat. She doesn't resist. We leave the dismal crowd and find a seat closer to the front. "I wasn't coming. My mom told me you were coming, so I decided to come also."

"Where's Owen?" She glances around for him.

"He's not here." I already miss him. But I also feel like this is okay. I'm going to be away from him soon, and this is what it will feel like.

"You really came for me?"

I nod.

She relaxes beside me. "I didn't want to come. I was so furious with my mom for signing me up. I don't even live at home. I told her she couldn't force me. And she told me if I didn't go, she'd report me as a runaway and make me quit my job."

"And she can do it because you're not eighteen yet."

Riley nods. "So it turns out she can force me."

I put an arm around her shoulders, tugging her close so our heads bump. "I'm so glad you're here."

The first class is a pep talk about finding the positives in our situations and expressing gratitude for the little things. The second class is a follow up, about how we need to find value in ourselves. Find the things that make us unique and special.

I take notes. Certain phrases and words touch my heart. They assuage the guilt that is my constant companion.

After the classes is a mixer. Riley steps out, feeling antisocial, and I'm not here to make friends, so I sit with her on a couch.

"It's so hard to find anything positive in my situation," she says. "Life keeps throwing things at me. It's like it's against me."

"What are you up against?" I ask.

"Well—I don't know. Maybe it's me. I keep making bad decisions."

I search for words to help her. I want nothing more than for Riley to be happy. "Where do you want to be right now?"

She looks at me, and something flashes in her eyes. "I want to be where you are."

I rear back a little. "Where I am?"

"You have everything, Cassandra. Your parents are together. You live in a nice house. You graduated high school with good grades and you're going to the school of your dreams. You have a boyfriend who adores you. Loves you. Your life comes together like a Christmas tree, waiting for you to put the star on top."

She's not angry as she says these things, but I feel overwhelmed with guilt. "I'm sorry," I say, for lack of anything else. "Is this why you don't like to talk to me?" I try not to feel defensive. Does she think somehow that my big house and my parents' marriage kept me up till two most nights finishing my homework?

"Partly," she admits, looking away. "But also you worked for this. You worked hard. I wanted to be you. I tried. But I didn't want to put in that effort." She exhales. "So it's me. I'm the failure."

I utter a quick prayer. I need inspiration to say the right things. Riley is open to me right now. I want her to stay that way. "Remember what they said? You have to find the things that make you special. We all have flaws, but we have to focus on the good things instead."

"What if there aren't any?"

I scoot so my knees touch hers and take her hands. "Do you need me to make you a list? I know your good traits. You've been my best friend since fifth grade."

"Well." She lifts a shoulder. "On and off again. Because I was a total jerk to you."

I laugh. "You were eleven! We can forget that. Then it was my turn to be the jerk."

"You were mean in junior high," she agrees.

We both know what came after. She matured, I shook off my cool friends, and Riley was my best friend through high school.

Even now, I consider her one of my best friends. Even though I rarely see her. Even though it feels stiff when we talk.

"My therapist taught me something last year," I say.

"The one you went to for your eating disorders?"

I nod. One hand comes down to clasp the charm of the necklace I wear around my neck. It contains a white pearl set inside a silver spiral with a psalm engraved in Hebrew. I treasure it above everything else I own. Owen gave it to me last year.

"She told me I had to learn to love myself."

Riley rolls her eyes. "Such a cliche thing to say."

"No, but listen, Riley." I release the necklace and lean closer. "She said if I don't love myself, I run out of love for other people. First I have to take care of me. Like putting on your oxygen mask in the airplane before you put it on your child. And she was right, Riley." I can't even remember the frail, desperate girl of a few years back. The one who hated herself and treated her body so poorly. "Now that I know my own worth, it's so much easier to be generous with others."

"But how do you love yourself?" she demands. "It's not a decision you make in the morning."

I'm out of answers.

"I love you," I say.

She doesn't answer. I know it's not enough.

CHAPTER SEVENTEEN

Soul Light

Riley and I are at different host homes. My sister is somewhere else also. I don't know the girls I'm with. We eat dinner with our host family, then go downstairs where several beds have been set up. Our chaperone tells us to read our scripture verses and pray before bed, and then she gets into a bed in the same room as us.

I want to call Owen, but I won't with her down here. I pull out my Bible and flip to the verses we're supposed to memorize.

Then I text Owen. *Hi.*

I get through one verse before he responds.

O: hi.

Me: how's it going?

O: packing for the hunt. Loading up my truck. Lots of equipment.

I shudder. It's the part of Owen's life I'm not sure I'll ever understand. But it's one of the only times he and his dad get along, and they don't waste the meat. *What are you hunting?*

O: Deer. But it's bow season. No guns allowed. Makes it harder.

Me: so you like it more, huh?

O: yep.

Me: you good with a bow?

O: I'm good with everything.

I grin at his cockiness. Anyone who doesn't know Owen would just see this front of confidence and self-assuredness.

Me: wish you were here

O: miss me?

Me: yeah

O: you too. Who's there?

Me: everyone. Except you.

O: nice. Feeling included.

Me: laughing tongue emoji

Me: Riley's here. She's really sad, Owen.

O: oh yeah. I meant to ask about her. What's going on?

Me: I don't know. From what I gather, she hates where she is in life. But she's not sure how she got there or how to get out.

O: if anyone can help her, it's you.

He has so much confidence in me. In spite of all the things I've done wrong, all the ways I hurt him, he still sees me as an amazing human being.

I close my eyes and utter a prayer. *Please, God, don't take him from me. He's the one I want in my life. Let all the roads in our futures lead us back together.*

When I open my eyes, I see he's sent another message.

O: have to get up early tomorrow. Won't have service all weekend.

Me: when will you be home?

O: Sunday night at the latest. Sooner if we get our buck.

I hope he gets one.

Me: Okay. Maybe see you Sunday.

O: Maybe.

Me: night, Owen.

O: night, Cassandra.

I go back to my memory verse, and I'm happy. It's just a text. It's not as great as being next to him. But every interaction with him lights up my soul.

⟳∼⟿

"Remember you are here for a reason," the speaker, a guy named Brett, says in our first class. "You might not know what that reason is. But you are a valiant soul. I know, I know, there are some of you who didn't want to come. Maybe your mom forced you. Or your best friend. But you still came. That means you're leaning toward the spiritual. Your soul hungers for it."

I write notes as he speaks. Riley is next to me. I don't glance at her, but I hope she's listening. I hope this reaches her.

"The battle's already won!" he exclaims, spreading his hands. "Now you just have to choose which side you're going to be on. But be careful." A note of warning enters his voice, and I look up. "Know your weaknesses. Be aware of them. Don't let them rule you."

I stop writing as I think on his words.

I have one major weakness.

I want to have sex with Owen.

My heart and my soul and my mind have been wrestling over this desire for the past few weeks. My whole life, I've promised to wait until I get married. Somewhere in the recent past, my certainty wavered, and that has become more like, until I find someone I want to marry.

I've justified it. Maybe I will marry Owen one day. We could have sex now. And it will all be fine because we'll be married in the future.

Or, even if we don't get married, we are committed to each other. We love each other. I want to show him the depth of my devotion. If we never get married, it's a small thing to have, isn't it? The knowledge of each other? I want to share that intimacy with him. To feel that closeness of knowing we've touched parts of each other, shared something together that we don't share with other people.

"But where does it stop?" the speaker says, and I tune back in. It's like he's in my thoughts. "Where do you draw the line?"

I don't know what he's talking about. But I apply it to myself. If the line isn't at marriage, then where is it? At engagement? At the four-month mark? One year? At "I love you"? Or is just whenever we feel "ready"?

Ready changes from one moment to another. I might think I'm ready for my math test only to take it and discover I wasn't.

I've had two serious boyfriends in my life. Tiago pushed for sex. I held him back. And now it's me pushing for it. Not as vocally as Tiago did, but I've made it clear my position. That I'm willing.

Owen's not.

I thought he was protecting me, but it dawns on me that's not all it is. He's also protecting himself.

I can wait for sex. It's not that hard. But if I analyze deeper, I'm jealous. I'm jealous of the girls who had sexual experiences with Owen. I'm jealous that it's their faces he pictures. Their bodies he remembers.

I want it to be me.

But I don't want to be one more in his list. I want to be the final one. His last experience, and the one he remembers forever.

I pick up my phone and wish I could text him. I want to tell him I'm sorry for pushing.

"Have you ever prayed about something and gotten an answer—and then gotten a different answer later?"

I'm focused again. Resolved. I pay attention.

"Do the answers to prayers change?" He waits, and a few murmurs echo around the room. "Of course they do. Of course! Answers change depending on your choices, your agency, and where you are in your journey. What is right for you now could change later and what is wrong for you now could be the right path in the future. Be flexible and pray always! Be willing to go where the Lord wants you to go."

By the time we break for lunch, I'm electric. This was what I needed. Reminders. I'm not living life for this moment, I'm living it for my future. And I have to keep my eye on my future.

Riley flips through my notebook at lunch. I sip from a juice box and pick at my sandwich.

"You wrote so many things," she says.

I lift a shoulder. "I'm trying to figure life out. The more clues, the better my chances of success."

"Don't you ever worry you're going to mess it up?"

I laugh out loud. "All the time! I already have messed it up. But that's what this is all about." I gesture to the notebook, to the people around us. "That's the whole point! Messing up is part of the journey. Fall of the train, get back up and catch the next one. We're still moving in the right direction."

She closes my notebook and pushes it back at me. "You should teach a class."

"Can I sit here?"

We both look up at a tall boy with a sandwich and a bag of chips in his hands standing beside us.

"Yeah, it's fine." I push a chair out.

"Thanks." He sits down and runs a hand through his brownish-blond hair, which parts down the middle and falls to his ears. His nose is his most interesting feature. It turns upward, almost like a cat's. Then he holds out a hand. "Earl."

"Earl." I shake his hand, a greeting I find humorous because we only do it at church. I don't meet kids at school and shake their hands.

Who knows? Maybe I will in college.

"Cassandra," I say. "That's Riley." She lifts her soda can.

"Sweet." He grins. "Where are ya'll from?"

"Arkansas."

"Sheesh, I'm in the wrong state. Why aren't there girls as pretty as you in Oklahoma?"

I shrug. "They hide when they see you coming."

"Dang it. I should wear a hat in public."

"You should," I say, straight-faced. "Might frighten people less."

We keep up an easy conversation. He even teases Riley and gets her laughing. The three of us move to our next class together.

"So what grade are you going into?" Earl asks as we sit.

"Freshman," I say.

His brows furrow, and I can see I've confused him. So I explain. "College."

"Oh!" He nods. "Way cool. Me too!"

"Which school?"

"Oklahoma State. You?"

"Preston Yarborough."

He whistles and does a strange hand shake. "Must be smart."

"Eh." I shrug a shoulder. "Just a nerd. I study a lot."

The chair beside him moves, pulling out of the row, and then Richard joins us. He pulls the chair back and drops in beside Earl.

"Hi," Richard says.

"Hi," Earl says, looking at him oddly.

It was a bit odd, the way Richard climbed over the chairs to get to us.

"Did you want to sit with us, Richard?" I ask.

He glowers at me.

Earl looks from Richard to me. "You guys know each other? Do you want to sit with him?"

"I'm good." Richard crosses his arms over his chest and faces the front.

On my other side, Riley covers her face and laughs.

I know what Richard's doing, and it's cute. He's defending his brother's territory.

"Hi, gang!" The next guy, a tall man with broad shoulders who looks to be in his early forties, comes out with his hands out. Unlike the last speaker, who wore a suit, this guy's in jeans and a T-shirt that says "May the Fourth be with you." "If you're thinking I'm in the wrong spot, don't worry. I'm supposed to be here. I just got my suitcase mixed up with my son's. And he's on a plane to New York right now, hopefully enjoying my collection of shirts and ties."

I laugh. So do the kids around me.

"The biggest thing I want you guys to know today is, you have to be your own cheerleader! If you're not on your side, how can you win?" He cracks jokes the entire time, and I can't stop laughing. I write his words down, because what he says is insightful.

"How many times do you try to describe something amazing and can't? No matter what words you use, it's like instead of painting a clearer picture, it gets more and more muddy? That's because human words cheapen what the real feelings are! It degrades them to try to describe them. It's pointless! You have to learn to trust your heart and soul so that you know what it is you feel."

Everything he says makes sense. Why I can feel something so strongly and utterly lack the ability to describe it, to pass that feeling on to someone else. If I could put emotions to words, could I evoke those same feelings in someone else?

It's such an interesting concept.

The class finishes, and they lead us to the gym for games.

"I liked that class," Earl says, keeping up with me. "I hate it when I'm trying to explain something and I can't find the right words."

"Yeah, me too."

He glances back because Richard is on his heels. Practically breathing down his neck.

"Hula hoops!" A counselor holds one out to us. "Everyone take a hula hoop! We're having a contest!"

"Pass." I wave them off. I will not humiliate myself this way.

"Oh, come on," Earl says, taking one. "Let's see you hula hoop."

I shake my head. "I'm not built for it. My hips don't move that fast."

He looks me over. "You're perfect for it. You could be a hula dancer. Come on." He takes my hand and pulls me back to the counselor. "She didn't get a hula hoop."

"No, I really don't want to," I protest. I shake myself free.

My protests are overruled. I'm handed a hula hoop and thrust into a mosh pit of confused teens, all holding hoops around their waists.

"All right!" a counselor in a lime green shirt says. "When the music starts, start shaking your hoop! We'll stop it at ten seconds. If you drop your hoop, you're out!"

I fume. I won't last two seconds.

Earl grins at me, holding his hula hoop. "This is gonna be great."

"Ready? And—go!"

The music starts. I toss the hoop and shake my hips, and it crashes to my ankles. Just as I expected.

I hand in my hoop and move to the spectator chairs.

I'm not the only one to get out right away. Richard doesn't make it past round one, and he laughs as he joins me.

"I thought you'd last longer than that."

"Thought wrong. You should know how nonathletic I am."

"Hula hooping isn't a sport."

"Beg to differ."

Riley joins us next.

Earl wins the contest.

I glare at him when he comes over. "You hustled me."

"I didn't lie about my abilities!"

"You didn't disclose them either. I disclosed mine—or lack thereof—with all transparency. And you withheld you own advantage, misleading me into an underhanded competition."

He stares at me unblinking for a full two seconds, and then throws his head back and laughs. "I don't think using words is a difficulty for you!"

"Yeah, she's good at them," Richard says, all humor gone from his voice.

I look at him and he's literally biting his inner cheek. Trying not to say something else.

Earl frowns at him, and I see him trying to make sense of this weirdness.

"Yeah," he says.

"Richard," I say, and he looks at me. I'm not sure what else to say. What's he doing? Trying to make sure no boys talk to me? "We're just talking, okay? Just having fun."

Comprehension crosses Earl's face. "Oh! Did you think—oh no, I'm not trying to—sheesh, this is awkward. Are you her—boyfriend? Brother?"

"Boyfriend's brother," Richard says.

CHAPTER EIGHTEEN

Protective Younger Brothers

Richard has his arms crossed over his chest, glowering at Earl.

This is annoying. "One second," I say to Earl, and I take Richard by the arm and lead him away. "Did Owen tell you to be my guard dog?"

"No." He drops his arms. "But he wouldn't like it if he saw other guys talking to you."

I give him a frustrated look. "Richard, guys are going to talk to me. You have to back off."

"But he's flirting with you!"

"No, he's not." I laugh. "We are just being friendly. It's what people do."

"Cassandra, you wouldn't know if a guy was hitting on you unless he handed you a note that said so. And then you probably still wouldn't believe him."

I find his words insulting. Owen has expressed a similar view. Like they think I'm naive and oblivious.

I can't help wondering if there's any truth to it.

"Well, trust me, then," I say, putting a hand on Richard's arm. "I'm not interested in Earl. I'm enjoying being here. And I'm going to talk to guys. I'm going to dance with them tonight. I'm going to have fun. Got it?"

"Do you have to be so friendly?"

I look at him in exasperation. "Do you expect me to be rude?"

"You could tell them straight up you have a boyfriend."

I've seen girls do that before. Sit on the sideline of a dance looking bored, and when a guys asks them, they say in a haughty, condescending tone, "I have a boyfriend." Like that means they can't dance.

"I would dance with other guys even if Owen were here," I say.

"Would you talk to them like you're talking to Earl?"

"Yes," I say, but I'm not sure. Mostly because I'd be with Owen, and he'd commandeer most of my attention. I would talk to him instead of engaging with those around me.

But he's not here.

And he won't be with me in college.

Suddenly I'm very aware of how that changes the dynamic.

⸙

I feel anxious as soon as I step into the next, and last, class of the day. Written across the board are the words, "Staying Virtuous while Dating."

I know what this one's about.

"So everything okay with your friend Richard?" Earl asks as he sits next to me. "Or do you call him your brother also?"

At least Richard stopped following me.

"Richard's fine. He wanted to make sure I was okay." I roll my eyes.

"So his brother's your boyfriend."

"Yes."

"Is he here? Is he going to be mad that I'm talking to you?"

I shake my head. "Owen doesn't care if I'm friends with guys." He's never made a fuss about it.

Except Tiago, but that's very clearly different.

"Okay. Because I hope you know—" Earl holds his hands out and looks at me with all seriousness. "I'm just having fun. I'm not trying to date you. You're nice, and I always try to find someone nice to hang out with at these things."

"Thanks." I grin, appreciating his candor. "You're nice too. And you have amazing hoop skills."

He laughs and settles back, and then he reads the chalkboard. He gives a low whistle. "Here it comes."

"Yes," I agree. "You didn't think we'd make it through this retreat without a talk on it, did you?"

"Let's see how blunt they are."

I laugh, because I know exactly what he means. Sometimes the church leaders pussy-foot around topics of teen sex, as if afraid of making our ears bleed or putting evil thoughts in our heads.

Don't they know we've already thought every single one of them?

The speaker comes in. She's a tiny woman with curly blond hair and lots of necklaces. She starts talking about holding onto your virtue, how virtue is a gift, and she loses my interest.

No one ever defines virtue. What is it, virginity? Isn't it a whole lot more than that? Honesty, integrity, loyalty?

She tiptoes around the subject, like I feared she would. My reasons for not having sex come from deep within me. I touch again the necklace Owen gave me. He says I'm a virtuous woman. If I slept with him, I believe I still would be.

It's more about wanting to save that intimacy for the right person and the right time.

"That did not inspire me," Earl says when she finishes.

"Same thoughts," I say. "I think Owen could give a better explanation than she did."

"Owen's your boyfriend?"

"Yes."

"Nice. What are your plans? Are you going to date through college?"

"We're going to separate colleges."

It's my answer, but I see Earl waiting for more.

I don't want to talk about this. "Let's get dinner."

Richard spots me at dinner and calls us over to sit by him. Earl comes. I'm surprised I haven't seen Farrah and Tyler, but since they go to the university congregation now, maybe this youth stuff is beneath them.

"These are my roommates," Richard says, introducing me to three other boys.

"Hi," one says, not hiding how he ogles me.

Richard kicks him under the table.

I spot Riley at another table and stand up. "Nice to meet you. I'm going to eat with Riley."

Earl stays, and I'm glad. I hear Richard's roommate as we leave. "What was that for?"

"She's my brother's girlfriend!"

I exhale and pinch the bridge of my nose. Richard is worse than my brother.

"How's it going?" I ask, dropping down by Riley.

She leans away from the other kids at the table. "Cassandra, how does any of this even apply to me? It's like I'm already out of the herd. I live with my boyfriend, for crying out loud."

Her words resonate with my thoughts. "So do you think that's it? What we do sexually defines us spiritually?"

She blinks. "It's how everyone makes it sound, isn't it?"

"Yeah, it is." I nod in agreement. "But I think it's because they really really want us to wait until we're married, or at least more mature, more able to take on the emotional weight that comes along with sex."

Riley rolls her eyes, but I already know she won't agree with everything I say. She's been having sex since she was sixteen.

"I don't think it means if you already have, you're not good anymore," I press on, trying to put into words the feelings I've been having. "We know the scriptures say to wait, right? We know God says we should be married. But that doesn't mean if you've broken that commandment, you should give up. There are hundreds of other ways you can still follow God—and be virtuous."

"Why doesn't someone say that?" Riley demands. "Instead I feel like everything they say doesn't apply to me because I've already broken the big one." She makes air quotes.

"I don't know, Riley." I exhale, echoing her frustration. "Maybe they're afraid we'll think it's permission to go out and have sex all we want."

"It's just sex," Riley grumbles, picking up her bottle of water and taking a sip.

I don't say anything. I don't even know how many guys she's slept with now.

I never want it to be "just sex." In my mind, it's something special. Serious. Sacred. Intimate.

Like Christmas morning or my mom's cinnamon rolls or passion fruit juice. Their rarity makes them special.

After dinner we're ushered back into the big classroom, only it's been cleared of chairs and tables so we can use it as a dance floor.

"Are you going to dance with people?" Riley asks me as the music starts.

"Yes. Are you?"

"I guess so."

As if on cue, a boy comes over and asks her to dance. He looks three years younger than us, and she agrees reluctantly. But he must be funny, because soon she's laughing, and when he brings her back her whole face has changed.

"I forgot how much fun this can be," she says.

I smile. "Yep."

A boy asks me next, and we make small talk as we try to avoid stepping on each other's feet. Then Brad, a kid from the Roger's congregation, asks me. And then Earl.

"There you are!" I say. "I thought maybe Richard scared you off."

"Whew." He shakes his head. "He's more protective than a Mexican chihuahua."

I picture Richard as one of the bat-eared little dogs, yipping at anyone who comes near. "Yes, he can be," I say, giggling.

"So you and Owen are calling it off when you go to school?"

That again. I hold back a sigh. "I guess you could say that."

"Smart. We're too young to make lasting commitments."

"I know." I know, I know, I know. Enough already.

He spins me around and dips me back, then spins me near. "Are you excited about college?"

"Yes. And nervous. I think it's going to be harder than I realize."

"But you must be pretty smart because you got in, right?"

"Here's the thing." I pull him close like I'm telling him a secret. "I'm a total fraud. I'm not smart at all. I'm very good at studying. And memorizing when I have to. But I don't retain it. So I'm kind of freaking out. They're going to see through me and I'll fail."

He shakes his head. "Ah, Cassandra, you're just like the rest of us. I'm not smart either. But I'm great at tests. I can study the night before and ace the subject even if I didn't listen the rest of the semester."

I scowl and whack his shoulder. "That's not fair! I want that talent."

He shrugs. "But we don't get to choose, do we?"

The song finishes, and he lets me go with a wave. My feet are tired. I turn to return to the chairs, but Richard intercepts me.

"Dance?"

"Sure, Chard."

He takes me in his arms and leads me onto the floor. I've danced with Owen's younger brother before. But not since Owen and I started dating. It's a little odd. Richard isn't some younger teen to me anymore. He's like my own brother.

"Only family gets to call me Chard," he says.

"So I'm out?"

He considers it. Then he shrugs. "No."

"Ah, thanks." I give him a teasing hug. "You think of me as family."

"My roommate said you were fine."

"I'm fine?" I repeat. "Yes, I think I'm all right."

Richard rolls his eyes. "Like, hot. He said you're fine. In all the ways."

"Should I feel threatened?"

He shook his head. "You still don't get it."

I don't say anything. I do get it.

We finish dancing and I finally sit down. I'm a bit moody now, and I take my shoes off to massage my feet. I sit through three songs, pointing to my shoes and politely refusing when I'm asked to dance. Where's Earl? I could use a good laugh.

I put my shoes on and stand up to find him when Brad reappears.

"Dance?"

"I'm looking for Earl, actually."

"Well, come on." He takes me hand. "We'll look for him together."

I expect us to walk through the dancers and check the foyer, but instead he pulls me into a dancing position and waltzes me across the floor.

"Earl?" he says, grabbing a dancing boy and spinning him around. "Nope. Earl?" He does it to another, and I start laughing.

"Not Earl."

I'm giggling nonstop as he pauses beside another couple and turns the boy toward me.

"Is this Earl?"

"No." I shake my head.

He's succeeded in lifting my mood.

We waltz out to the foyer looking for Earl, and Brad holds my hand up, continuing the facade of dancing while calling out, "Earl? Is there an Earl out here? Perhaps the Earl of Buckingham?"

I'm laughing so hard I can't breathe.

We return to the dance floor and finish up the song without finding Earl.

"And that was the last song!" the DJ says.

Brad shakes his head, his eyes downcast. "I'm sorry we didn't find your Earl."

<hr/>

I text Owen as soon as I crawl into bed at my host home. I'm overflowing with thoughts. I don't know who else to share them with.

Me: I know you're out on your hunt and won't see these for days

Me: but I can't wait to talk to you.

Me: sorry, I'm spamming your phone. Today's been amazing. I didn't realize how much I needed this. I needed a spiritual recharge. A reconnect. I get going, doing my own thing, and I forget to check in with God and see what I'm supposed to be doing

Me: now I feel like I'm getting back on track. Which is great. I need that guidance. I'm about to head out to college, on my own, and I want to have all the support I can get

Me: Owen, I'm sorry for sometimes being weak. For sometimes not being as strong as you need me to be. I'm going to do better. I promise.

Me: and I can't stop thinking about you. I wish you were here. I wish you could sit next to me and hear what I'm hearing. Learn what I'm learning. And then we could sit and talk about it. Because I want to grow with you. Next to you.

    Me: I love you, Owen Blaine.

    I am content when I fall into bed. I read my memory verse until my eyes blur and sleep takes me.

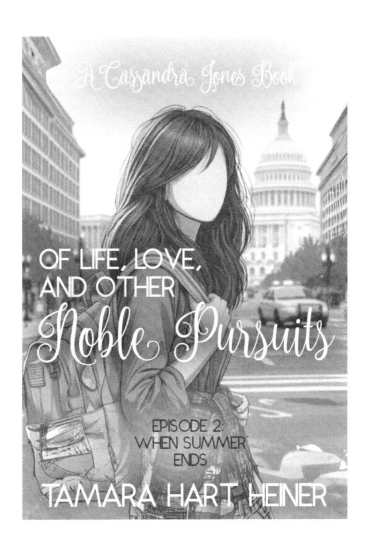

A Cassandra Jones Book

OF LIFE, LOVE,
AND OTHER
Noble Pursuits

EPISODE 2:
WHEN SUMMER
ENDS

TAMARA HART HEINER

CHAPTER NINETEEN

Walls and Fences

I t's the last day of the youth retreat where we've been held hostage for the past three days.

I've had fun, but I'm anxious to go home. I want to see Owen. I haven't heard from him since arriving, and after our tumultuous breakup and subsequent make-up, I'm not as confident in our relationship as I was before.

I need to know we're okay.

After a brief continental breakfast, the youth leaders bring us back into the gymnasium where we did the hula hooping.

"We hope you had a great youth retreat," the speaker says. "You've heard from all of us. We felt your spirits. As this is the last day, we invite any of you who would like to come to front and share your thoughts and testimonies from this weekend."

I settle back on the bleacher. I'm content to watch and listen.

"Hi, Cassandra."

It's Earl, climbing over people and legs to sit by me.

"Hi," I say. "I'm surprised you found me in this sea of people."

"I just looked for the prettiest girl here."

I snort. "Uh-huh."

A girl walks across the wood flooring and clutches the microphone. She clears her throat and begins to speak. I strain to hear her words, but the kids around me are talking, and I can't hear her.

I lean forward. "Hey, can you guys be quiet? I'm trying to hear."

They look at me like they wonder where I came from. Then they whisper for a bit before returning to normal tones.

"Idiots," Earl says. "Want to sit somewhere else?"

"No, it's fine." I suppress my irritation. I want to hear what people are saying.

Earl touches my hair, and I turn to him. "You have the shiniest hair," he says. "What color is it? It's like black but not."

"It's what we call dark brown." I tilt my head so the strands slip through his fingers. "I thought it was black when I was younger. But it's not."

He starts to say something else, but I press my finger to my lips. Am I the only person here who wants to listen?

The meeting stretches on, and eventually I give up as the kids around me get louder and louder. Earl pulls out his phone.

"Hey, give me your number. If I'm ever passing through Colorado, I'll swing by and say hi."

"Okay. Sure." I recite the number and watch him program it into his phone.

"It was nice to meet you," he says, putting it away. "You're so nice. And funny. And really pretty."

I smile. "You said that one a couple of times."

"Do you know you're pretty?"

"I—" I hesitate. "I don't think about it, actually. Some people say I am. Others don't. So I think it doesn't really matter."

He shakes his head. "You're beautiful. Like, the kind of pretty that makes people take a second look."

"You're very kind."

He laughs.

The meeting finally ends. Earl hugs me and leaves. I find Riley and give her a long squeeze.

"I'm so glad you came," I say. "It was great to have this time to connect with you."

"I'm glad for it too," she says. "The things you said to me meant more than the classes I went to."

"Maybe we should hang out more," I tease.

"Maybe."

I find Emily and Scott and get them out to the car. I hadn't seen them all weekend.

Richard is another matter.

"Has anyone seen him?" I ask them.

They shake their heads.

I search the clusters of kids before I find him in the midst of a group of girls. I march in there and grab his arm. "Richard! It's time to go!"

He scowls and shakes me free and the girls titter in amusement.

"Is that your sister?" one asks him.

I raise an eyebrow as he looks at me, wondering what he will say.

"She thinks so," he grumbles, getting his duffel bag. "She's my brother's girlfriend."

The girls smile at me. I can tell they think I have a mystical power. If I touch them with my magical wand, Richard might choose them.

"Give them your phone number," I say. "And let's go."

He glares at me, and I know I'm just as embarrassing as his own sister would be.

"Wait for me at the car," he snaps, and I head off, giggling.

Ten minutes later he's finally in the car with us, and we head back to Springdale.

"How many numbers did you get?" I ask him.

"None," he says. "But I gave mine to several girls."

"And why didn't you get any?"

"Because I'm not going to do the chasing. They are."

"Why should they have to do all the work?"

"Why should I?"

I shake my head. But I'm amused. Richard acts like Owen used to. "What about you, Emily?" I poke her thigh in the passenger seat beside me. "Meet any cute guys?"

"Lots," she says. "But I didn't ask for their numbers."

"Next time," Richard says. "You have to ask. They don't know you're interested if you don't ask."

"Okay." Her cheeks turn pink.

"And you, Scott?" I glance at my brother in the rearview mirror, but he doesn't look up from his phone.

"What about you?" Richard asks. "Did you give Earl your number?"

I meet his eyes in the mirror. "Yes. He asked for it, so I gave it."

"Why? You have a boyfriend." He doesn't hide his irritation.

"Because he wasn't asking to be my boyfriend. He just said, if he's ever going through Colorado, maybe we could get together. That's all."

Richard shakes his head and looks out the window. "You know nothing about boys."

❧

Tweety is growing.

My mom shows him to me as soon as we get home, and I'm so proud, of this little fledgling who hasn't died.

"But what will you do when it's time for him to learn to fly?" she asks.

"I haven't thought that far." I feed him his mixture of worms, which he gulps down eagerly. "I suppose I should. I'll ask Monica. She works at a vet."

Mom wants to know all about the youth retreat. I let Scott and Emily tell the details while I text Monica and ask about the bird.

M: I'll take him to work with me on Monday if you want.

I look at Tweety in his shoe box. He looks lonely. He probably needs to be with others of his kind. I text back, *Sure.* And then, *Is Owen coming home today?*

M: laughing emoji. I don't know. But I bet as soon as he has service, you'll know it.

I grin. She's probably right.

I flip over to the other messaging app. I feel that familiar twinge of sadness as I see the last of mine and Tiago's conversations. His avatar shows gray, or inactive. I think he deleted the app. Just like I did all those times last year when I kept trying to not talk to him.

There are no texts from Owen in the morning, so I assume he's not home. I try to chase away the blueness in my chest. I want to feel his arms around me. I want to close my eyes and disappear into his embrace.

Emily and Annette ride with me to church.

As soon as we park, I see Owen's truck. It's covered in mud, so I know they haven't been home long. Will he be here? Or did Monica drive it? My sisters race for the building, and I examine the truck as if I expect to find Owen hiding beneath it.

"Looking for something?"

I spin, blinking in the morning sunlight, and smile. He's here.

"No," I say. "Just feeling amazed at how anything can be so dirty." I run a finger through the mud and come away with a coating as thick as fudge icing. "If I wash it away, will there be anything underneath?"

"I'm not willing to take that chance," he says.

I want him to pull me close and hug me. But he doesn't. Still keeping physical distance between us, apparently.

The church doors open again, and Aiden comes out.

"Hello, Aiden," I say.

"Hi, Cassandra." He crosses to us and slings an arm across my shoulders. I stumble slightly.

"Are you putting on weight?" I poke his belly. He groans and sucks in. I laugh and poke him again. "It's like Jello."

Aiden releases me and backs away, holding his stomach. "I told Owen we should do some ab work."

"Might take effort," I say. Since Owen's made no move to touch me, I step around them and walk toward the church. "See you guys inside."

I find the rest of the Blaine family in the foyer. Monica's with Noah, and Mrs. Blaine turns to give me a hug. Richard ignores me as if we didn't bond over the weekend, but that's okay. I chat with Monica about the bird until Owen and Aiden join us. Aiden sits on the couch and Owen positions himself between me and Monica.

"How did your hunt go?" I ask him. "Get what you wanted?"

Monica yawns. "Oh goodness. All I've heard all morning is how the one they got isn't the one they wanted. Apparently they shot at a bigger one."

"I hit him," Owen says.

Monica rolls her eyes. "Whatever. But they couldn't find him, so they brought home a different one. Makes no sense."

"Yes, it does," Owen says. "I—"

Monica waves a hand. "Tell it to Cassandra. I've heard it enough times." She grabs Noah and pulls him into the chapel.

I clasp my fingers and smile at Owen, trying to feel out today's dynamic. "So? What happened?"

He steps past me and leans against the wall behind me. I scoot back a step and face him.

"See, we saw this buck," he says, using his hands to tell the story. "A six-point. Huge!" The hands go wide. "Dad told me to take the shot. So I did. And I shot him."

"With your bow?" I interrupt, trying to picture the scene.

Owen nods. "I saw it. The buck jumped and took off running. I was so mad because I didn't kill him, but we went after him. That happens sometimes."

I wince, picturing the injured animal running with an arrow in its flank. "What do you do?"

"You follow the blood trail until you get to the deer. They bleed out. And then you finish 'em off, put them out of their misery."

"But?"

Owen shakes his head. "We never found him. The blood trail dried up."

"How can that happen?"

"I don't know. Maybe I didn't shoot him where I thought I did. Could've been a flesh wound and he walked away to lick his wounds instead of die."

"So you shot another?"

"Dad did. I was kind of frustrated. We didn't have time to look for another six-point. Dad saw a four-point and brought him down."

"Frustrated or mad?"

"Mad," he admits.

"Rock mad?"

He laughs. "Rock mad. I may have thrown a few things." He relaxes a bit and puts his arm around my shoulders now, like Aiden did in the parking lot. "Things went well at the youth retreat?"

The organ music plays inside the chapel, and the foyer empties as congregates make their way inside.

"Yes," I say. "I told you about it."

"I saw your message."

But he didn't respond. I get that funny prickly feeling in my stomach, the one that likes to scream paranoid things at me. Like, something isn't quite right here.

But I know everything's fine. Owen just got back from a hunt. It didn't go the way he wanted. His friend is here. He didn't get the chance to respond to me. And I'm not a demanding, clingy girlfriend.

Okay, maybe I am. I try hard to pretend not to be.

"Shall we go in?" Aiden says from the couch.

"Yeah." Owen releases me.

"See you in class," I say.

"Oh." Owen touches my hand, and I turn back before entering the chapel. "I won't be in class. I have to take Aiden home."

"To your apartment?" I say. I look at Aiden, wondering why he can't stay an extra hour.

"I have to go to work," Aiden says. "Sorry."

I want Owen to invite me along. It's been three days without spending any time with him. But he doesn't, so I ask, "Can I come?"

"Um." Owen pauses, glancing toward the wall, and then gives a shake of his head. "Yeah, no, I've got to run a few other errands."

Today? On a Sunday? I push down my surprise. "Will I see you later today?" I ask.

"I'm not sure what my schedule is after that," he says, and he averts his gaze, glancing into the chapel. "I'll text you."

My chest tightens. It's like he doesn't want to spend time with me.

But I shrug. "All right. See you some time, then."

I find my family's pew and sit down, shoving down the uneasy feeling that has suddenly grown eight octopus arms and is trying to choke me.

CHAPTER TWENTY

Avoidance Issues

Sunday's silence is deafening.

I read back through the last text I sent from youth conference. My stomach churns violently in my stomach. Did I say something that might have upset him?

I can't figure out what.

Maybe I over-shared. It's a bad, bad habit of mine. But I haven't felt that fear with Owen. I've never censured what I'm thinking or feeling.

But as the sun goes down and I hear nothing from him, I know I've done something wrong.

⁂

Kids First calls me early Monday morning.

I didn't sleep well and my chest feels achy, like I fell out of a tree and got the wind knocked out of me. But I refuse to let my emotions get the best of me. I dress in jeans and a T-shirt, not sure if I'll be in the kitchen again.

"Hi," the receptionist says when I come in. Her name's Silvana, and she's friendlier now that I've been here a few times. "Cassandra, right?"

"Yes."

"You're in the baby room today."

I resist the urge to do a fist pump. "Great! Thanks for not putting me in the kitchen!"

She laughs. "Wasn't my doing. That's where the new hires go. You're not the newest anymore."

"Oh?" My interest piques. "Who is?"

"That would be me."

I turn around, and it's Owen. My heart stumbles, and every ache heals over at the sight of him.

But he doesn't smile, doesn't quite meet my eyes, and I remember something's off between us. So I just nod. "You work here now?"

"I do. Guess I saved you from kitchen duty. What room are you in?"

"The baby room." The one room he won't deliver food to. Just as well. "Thanks, Silvana."

I go through the doors, conscious of Owen in the reception behind me. Aware I'm moving away from him.

Time flies in the baby room. We start with feedings, then diaper changes, then burpings, then rocking and nap time, and then it starts over again. It's a constant motion.

One little girl cries the entire day. She's only quiet when she's eating. She doesn't sleep. I'm working with Shelley, and we take turns holding her, singing to her, cooing at her, while the other one takes care of every other baby in the room.

I'm there all day. My shift doesn't end until five-thirty after almost all the kids have been picked up.

I don't see Owen once. Something hurts quite badly inside, but I can't pinpoint it.

There's no signal inside the daycare, and my phone lights up with notifications when I step outside. But the only one I see is the message from Owen.

O: hey. Sorry I didn't get to talk to you more. My shift ended at one.

It feels like an afterthought. Like a consolation. And I'm bothered by it.

I don't respond.

And I fight tears all the way home.

⟡⟡⟡

Kids First calls me again the next morning.

"We only need you until one today," Silvana says.

"Does that mean I'm doing dishes?" I ask.

"Looks like it. It's the only spot we have open."

I sigh. I'm not scheduled for Stage, and it will be better than a day with nothing to distract me. "I'll take it."

Rain comes down so hard that I can hardly see, even with my wipers on full speed. Water overflows in the streets, little rivers hurrying across grasses to reach the culverts.

I don't want to do dishes.

Why hasn't Owen contacted me?

For once I'm glad for the lack of signal in the daycare. It means I have no reason to check my phone every twelve minutes.

It's easy to be happy when I deliver trays of food to the children. Food makes them excited. I pretend they are excited to see me. Then I clean everything up and clock out.

I try not to be anxious when I step into the parking lot, but I hold my breath as my messages load.

NOTHING from Owen.

What, did he decide to break up with me and not tell me?

And why?

I'm furious. I'm rock mad.

I'm also shaking and about to cry.

There's an email from PYU, telling me it's time to sign up for classes.

I text Camila. *Have you built your schedule yet? Can I call you tonight and you help with mine?*

There's also a text from an unknown number. I skipped it initially, but now I click on it.

Cassandra! It's Earl. Hey, I only live about an hour from you. I was wondering if you want to go to the movies with me and some friends? Just as friends.

It's such a nice invite. And it makes me feel a little better. I save his number. I'll message him later.

Camila texts me back. *Yeah! Call me. Let's do this!*

She's excited. I try to feel it.

I've just arrived home when Monica texts me.

M: You didn't bring the bird by yesterday. Do you still want me to take it?

I check on Tweety. He chirps and rustles his wings.

Me: Yes. When do you go in again?

M: tomorrow.

I don't know what tomorrow brings. I'm working at Stage in the afternoon, but I could end up at Kids First all morning.

What do I say if Owen's there?

Me: I'll bring it by now.

Owen's truck is not at the Blaine's house.

I'm relieved and disappointed.

Monica's in the sunroom watching TV. She smiles when I come in. "Hey! Ready to go to the lake tomorrow?"

I'd forgotten. "I have to work." I put the shoe box on the armrest. She leans over and takes a look at Tweety and squeals.

"Oh, he's so cute!"

"Yeah, he is." I smile briefly. "We didn't think he would live. But he did."

"I'll take him in tomorrow. They'll take care of him." She puts the lid back on the shoe box. "We can pick you up after work. What time are you off?"

I check my schedule. "Six."

"That's perfect."

I hesitate, then ask, "Is Owen going?"

"I didn't invite him. You can if you want."

I want him there. But I don't want to invite him. Because I'm afraid he'll say no, and then all my fears will be solidified. "That's all right."

I turn to leave, and Monica says, "You okay? You seem a little . . . despondent."

My eyes tear up of their own accord, and a painful lump fills my throat. "I'm fine."

"Are you and Owen fighting?"

"No."

"Want to go out and get some ice cream?"

She's trying to help me. Figure out what's wrong. But I don't want her to. "No, that's all right. I have to call Camila and plan out my schedule for school."

"All right." She nods. "Well, if you get bored later, you can come back and hang out."

I push my lips up into a smile. "Thanks."

Then I book it out to my car. Because Monica set me off, and I barely get inside before I cry.

Every car my family owns is in the driveway when I get home. I wipe my face and beeline it to the basement, avoiding everyone. Then I sit down at the computer and call Camila.

"Have you built your schedule yet?" I ask her.

"No, but I figured out how to do it. Do you have the website up?"

I click over to it. "Yes."

"You have to look at your major requirements and see what's offered for the fall semester. I built it all out on a sheet. When registration opens in two days, we have to be ready. My mom said the classes will fill up fast. So we start adding them as soon as we can."

Crap, the thought of racing against other kids to get this done sends my heart pounding. "That's how it works?"

"Yeah."

"What classes are you taking?"

She gives me her classes for the fall semester, and I write down the ones that I also need. Then I hang up. It feels like a riddle. I have a certain number of general education classes I have to take, and some I need to take for my major. But I also want to graduate in three years instead of four so I can go on a service mission when I finish.

I'm shuffling around classes and trying to figure out where things fit when Owen texts me.

O: you okay?

The text makes me angry. This is Monica's doing. She must've told him I had some kind of episode. If it weren't for her, he wasn't going to message me. He knows full well why I'd be upset, even if she doesn't. I put the phone down and try to figure out where I'm going to put Portuguese classes. I decide to focus on GEs and major classes first semester, get my feet on the ground before I add a language. That can be second semester.

The phone dings again. I check it.

O: Cassandra.

I'm busy, I think, but I don't say it. I just ignore him.

O: I know you're reading my texts.

That does it. Let's have this out.

Me: why are you texting me?

O: that's a weird question.

Me: you haven't for three days. Why now? Because Monica said something to you?

He takes too long to answer. I imagine him trying to think up a good reason. I help him out.

Me: did you break up with me without telling me?

O: no.

O: I'm coming over.

Me: don't. I stand up, grabbing my papers and going back upstairs.

O: why?

Me: I'm not staying here. I don't want to see him. I want to hold onto this anger, for reasons unbeknown to me. If he shows up here saying sorry, I'll let it all go.

And I don't trust him right now. This stunt of not talking to me, it's new territory. It makes me leery.

O: where are you going? I'll meet you.

Me: no.

O: why?

Me: because I already know what you're going to say. Just say it in a text.

I realize I do know. I scared him away with my talk of feelings and God and love. Whoa, Nellie. Now he's pulling back, and I'm left hanging out to dry, and I'm furious over it.

I get in the car. I don't know where I'm going. But I back out of the driveway and start down the road. Taking any turn.

Owen hasn't responded.

The phone rings, and I know it's him without looking. I glance at it quickly and send it to voicemail.

O: I have rocks you can throw

And just like that, he gets through to me. I start laughing. And I'm crying. I have to pull over. My hand shakes as I text back: *What's happening?*

He calls again. This time I answer.

"Yes." I keep the word clipped. I don't want him to know I've been crying. But I'm trying not to sniffle, and instead I sound congested.

"At the risk of mortal injury, can we talk in person?"

"Yes." I sniff without meaning to. Crap, now he'll know.

"Where are you?"

I glance around and feel a jolt of surprise at where I've driven myself. I pull back onto the road and into the parking lot of the little white church. "You know where I am."

"Be there in five."

He's already on his way.

I hang up and wonder what will be said. What he's thinking. How we're going to get out of this one.

If we're going to get out of this one.

CHAPTER TWENTY-ONE

Rock Mad

His truck roars in three minutes later. I keep my eyes steady out the windshield and unlock the door. The AC blows my hair from my face, and I hope it's blown the remnants of my tears away.

Owen climbs in and closes the door, then pulls out a grocery sack.

"I brought this one," he says, and I lower my gaze to see him putting a fist-sized muddy rock on my console. "And this one." He adds a bigger white one. "And I've got this one." He places a softball-sized orange and white boulder on the console. It's too big. It wobbles and then crashes into my cup holder, scattering pens. "Oops."

"Owen." I laugh in spite of myself. "Where did you get those?"

He grins. "From the bed of my truck." He's watching me. I know I haven't concealed anything. "I keep them there. Just in case."

I'm not mad anymore. Drained. Sad. "Keep them for yourself."

Silence falls between us. I don't know what to say. So I sit. Waiting.

He shifts and looks out the window.

Neither of us speaks.

I put my head on the steering wheel. This sucks.

"Say something," he says finally.

I shrug without lifting my head. "What is there to say? I'm not stupid. I know when someone doesn't want to talk to me."

He's quiet. I risk a glance, and he's staring out the window again.

"I'm sorry," he says.

I don't want to be in here with him anymore. I turn off the car, open the door, and get out. I start walking. Away. Anywhere.

It takes him a moment, but he catches up to me. Walks beside me. The tears are trekking their way down my cheeks. I don't bother wiping them.

He takes my wrist and stops me. I don't look at him as he turns me toward him. He cups my face and uses his thumbs to wipe my tears. "I'm sorry," he says again. "I didn't realize I would hurt you."

I jerk away and suck in a breath, angry again. I want to hit him, but I settle for using words instead. "You're such an idiot. Did you think I wouldn't notice? That I wouldn't care? Are you so oblivious to my feelings?"

He grabs me and hugs me, and I try to break free, even pound my hands on his chest, but he just squeezes me tighter. I fight until the fight goes out of me, and then I collapse in his arms and sob.

He pulls me down to the ground, and we sit in the gravel by the side of the road. He hands me a pebble.

"Throw it," he says. "It helps."

I give it a half-hearted toss. It tumbles along the road.

"You didn't try."

I face him. "Why?"

He blinks, and his lower lip twitches. "Why?"

"I knew we were ending." I clench my jaw as my teeth chatter. "Why did you have to do it now?"

He looks away, out over the road. "I wasn't trying to end us."

I lift an eyebrow. "That was just an unexpected consequence?"

He sighs. "It's hard to explain."

"Try."

In answer he pulls out his phone. He scrolls through text messages, then he takes a screen shot. My phone dings with an incoming text.

"Read that," he says.

I open it with my heart pounding, even though I know I haven't done anything wrong. I've been upfront and honest.

Maybe that's the problem.

But it's a text thread between him and Richard. "Chard," as it says at the top.

Chard: Every guy here wants to be w her.

O: Don't worry about it.

Chard: you should worry about it

O: why?

Chard: she doesn't know. She's just being nice and they're falling in love w her

Chard: this one guy followed her around all weekend. He didn't even back off when I told him she has a boyfriend

O: Leave her alone, Chard

Chard: that's it? You're going to let this happen?

Chard: You're dumb

O: shut up. You don't understand.

The thread stops there. I read it through again, trying to understand.

"Are you upset about Earl?" I ask. "Because I talked to him?"

"Is that his name?" Owen gives a wan smile. "No. That didn't upset me."

"What did?"

"Nothing. I didn't get upset."

"Then why did you pull away from me?"

He props his arms up on his knees and picks through the little pebbles at his feet. "I was selfish."

I shake my head, brow knitting in confusion.

He looks at the ground as he speaks. "What happened at the youth retreat is exactly what I expect to happen when you go to college. And the closer I am to you, the more it hurts. So I decided not to text you as often. Not touch you every time you're near me. After a day of that . . . it was easier to not talk at all than to talk only a little."

I hit his leg, hard. "I thought we were in this together. How dare you make a decision like that and *not tell me*. Like my feelings don't matter at all? Am I collateral damage?" I stand up. I want those rocks after all.

He comes after me. "Hey, I'm sorry."

I slip my arm free of his grip as he tries to catch me. I open my car door and grab the two small rocks. I leave the boulder there. I'm likely to drop that on my head if I try and throw it.

He steps back and stays a few feet behind me. Maybe he's afraid of my aim also.

I stand at the edge of the field and chuck the small rock. I see it land a few feet away, barely shaking the grasses it falls into. I haul my arm back to throw the next.

I nearly scream in surprise when Owen's hand closes over mine, his other hand at my elbow.

"Throw it like this. Pull your arm back," he whispers, his voice near my ear. He lets go of my elbow and drops his hand to my hip. "Swivel your body this way." He turns me with his palm.

He releases my hand. Suddenly both hands are on my hips, turning my body, pulling me closer, and then he's kissing me. I'm still clutching the rock, but I'm also kissing him back. His hands don't leave my hips, holding me in place like I'm a cement block and he's trying to keep from being swept away in a flood.

He breaks away with a gasp and pulls me into a hug.

"What does it mean, Owen?" I ask, my words tight because he's squeezing the oxygen from my lungs. "Are we together or not?"

He doesn't answer me. He takes my hand, letting the rock fall, and leads me to the parking lot. He pops the tailgate of his truck and picks me up, setting me on the edge before hopping up and joining me. Our legs dangle. I kick mine.

"I don't know," he says finally.

"That's a stupid answer."

"Help me figure it out, then."

"Well, what do you want?"

"To be with you."

I spread my hands wide. "Then let's be together while we're here."

He is quiet again.

"Owen," I prod.

"I can't touch you," he says. "But I don't know if we can be together and not touch. It might be easier not to see each other."

His words shred me like I'm string cheese he's ripping apart layer by layer.

"Why can't you touch me?" I ask.

He shakes his head.

I want an answer. "Owen."

"I can't," he says.

"Why not?"

He leans back against the truck bed. He looks weary as he peers up at the sky. "Because I'm fire and you're dynamite and we're going to explode."

I picture fireworks lighting up the sky.

I think he's picturing bloody limbs scattered across the street.

I won't press him. I promised I wouldn't push. He's drawn a line, and I'll respect it. "Okay. We don't have to touch. Can't we still date?"

He looks at me again. "Isn't that what you call being just friends?"

"We can hang out as friends but know we're more than that. I won't touch you. I promise."

"But how will you keep me from touching you?"

"Well." I had no intentions of doing so. "I guess I can scream if you touch me."

He chuckles. "That'll go over well. Have the police show up every time we get together."

I try to wrap my mind around this. Being together but not touching. Not hugging. Not kissing.

I don't like it, but I can do it. "We can still hang out. Talk."

He chews on his lower lip as he studies me. "I'm not sure I can be around you and not touch you."

I fight back my irritation. "So instead we start acting like we're already apart even though we're not yet?"

He shrugs. "Maybe. Kind of a breaking-in time."

More like a breaking-up time. "Are we going to date other people during this 'breaking-in' time?"

Another shrug. "Maybe."

I want to cry again. I swallow it back. "Will you be touching other girls?"

I see the hurt that slashes across his face before he can hide it. He shakes his head. "No."

"Then why?" I demand. "Why are you doing this?"

He doesn't answer. He lays back on the bed of his truck and stares at the sky. I don't move. I sit there and stare at him, trying to understand.

"I already explained it to you," he says, and there's snark in his tone.

"I don't get it."

"No. You don't."

Then that's that. I jump from the tailgate and move to my car.

"Cassandra."

"I'm done talking." I open my car door.

"No. Stop. Don't go." His truck rattles as he leaves it, hurdling over the side to reach me before I get in my car. "Stop. Stop." He puts a hand on my door, closing it. He inhales noisily, looks at the clouds, and looks at me. "I do not know how to explain what I'm feeling."

I cross my arms over my chest. "You've done a crap job so far. Keep going."

"I'm fighting the inevitable. And I want to give up."

"I got that part."

"I don't want to date other people. I don't want you to date other people."

I throw my hands up. "Then let's not!"

"But I don't want to hurt, either."

"I'm not going to hurt you."

He shakes his head. "It hurts, Cassandra. It already does."

"Okay." I place a hand on his arm. "I understand you. You don't want to get any closer than we are."

"And maybe less close than we are," he adds.

"All right. So we take a step back."

"No touching," he says.

"No kissing," I say.

"No touching."

I sigh. "No touching." The words come out in a whine. I love his hugs even more than his kisses. "But I'm still your girlfriend?"

"Why would you want to be?"

"Can I hit you now?" I growl.

He laughs. "No touching."

I look at my hand on his arm and let it fall. "You're not just my boyfriend, Owen. You're my best friend. And you ditched me."

He leans against my car beside me. "I'm sorry. I don't know why I thought you wouldn't notice."

"'Cause you're an idiot," I say.

"Yep."

We stand there in more silence. It's weird, not touching. I think of Tiago. When we got back together, we set rules about touching and kissing also. But ours was because we lost track of our friendship when we got physical. Our relationship got hot, hot really fast, and it blew both of us away.

Talk about carnage.

I try to think of something to say. Something to make me feel like we're still boyfriend and girlfriend. It just feels strained now.

"We're going swimming tomorrow at the lake," I say. "For the Fourth of July. After I get off work. Want to come?"

"Who's we?"

"Me, Monica, and Noah."

"A double-date with my sister?" He makes a face. "Yeah, okay."

I grin. "Great. We're meeting at Stage at six-fifteen. We're carpooling."

He nods. "I'll see you there."

"Awesome." This is so weird. I open my car door and get in. "Bye."

"Bye."

I put my car in reverse and back up. He stands there with his hands in his pockets, watching.

I've barely pulled into my driveway when he texts me.

O: you've got my rock

Me: do you need it?

O: no
Me: then why are you texting?
O: just needed an excuse to talk to you
I shake my head.
Me: you don't need an excuse for that
O: I didn't mean to make things weird between us
Me: yeah, well . . . Shrug emoji
O: sorry
At least we're talking.
Me: I'll see you tomorrow. Night.
O: night.

CHAPTER TWENTY-TWO

Lake Party

I replay yesterday's events as I drive to work at Stage the next morning. My gut always seems to know when something is wrong. Having your boyfriend not text for three days isn't a huge deal. But I knew the moment I saw him on Sunday that something wasn't right.

I'm still not quite sure what to make of it. Owen explained, and he explained again, and I know he was trying to make it clear. I don't get it, and it hurts.

I park and pull out my phone to text him. But what if it's too soon?

I hate that I'm questioning myself. Second-guessing.

I put my phone away without contacting him.

The store is packed from the moment we unlock the doors. It's the Fourth of July. We have a massive sale going on. Stephanie and Brian are both here, and I remember Nicole left for her summer trip to Europe. Stephanie spends every shift trying to one-up me and fuming when she fails. But at least Laura has been nicer to me.

I take my lunch break in the afternoon and walk over to the restaurant next door. I order a drink and hole up in a booth. I'm not hungry. I just need out of the clothing store.

I pull out my phone. Owen texted me.

O: You didn't say good morning.

I message him back.

Me: neither did you.

O: I am now.

Me: same.

O: but it's not morning.

Me: I guess I missed my chance.

O: you can try again tomorrow. Especially since I had to work the kitchens this morning because you couldn't come in.

I smile. This banter is familiar. *Me: oops! Maybe if you had another job also.*

O: one is enough. This working thing is for the dogs. Dog face emoji

Me: ....

O: crap. Was not calling you a dog.

Me: uh huh

O: facepalm emoji. Not sure how to dig myself out of that one.

Me: you're not getting a good morning tomorrow

O: I'm going to quietly exit the conversation now.

I'm happy-happy when I go back to the clothing store. It doesn't matter that I'm swamped with customers in every dressing stall and a line at my register, or that Stephanie keeps checking my stats every hour and comparing them with hers.

Owen and I are talking.

Monica and Noah come into the store as I'm clocking out.

"Do you mind driving to the lake?" she asks me. "I'm almost out of gas and have no moolah."

"No problem." I put my time sheet away. "Let me get my purse from the back and change my clothes." I give them a quick once-over. "Owen's not with you?"

"Is he coming?" Monica checks her phone. "Did you tell him what time? He wasn't at the house."

Did I tell him what time? I head to the breakroom to get my purse. As soon as I have my phone, I check it.

There are no texts. He must have decided not to come. I shove down the disappointment. I'll be with Monica. She's my friend, and she's enough.

It sounds like I'm trying to convince myself.

I come back out in a sundress, my swimsuit underneath. Even though the sun is on its way down, outside is a steamy eighty-seven degrees. The lake will feel amazing. My sandals slap across the linoleum. Monica gives me a side hug when I reach her.

"I love your dress!"

I do too. It's a white eye-let with a leather belt. It contrasts perfectly with my olive skin tone. "Thanks."

She and Noah follow me out to my car. Noah is telling her to take the passenger seat when a tan Toyota Tacoma roars into the lot and screeches to a halt beside us.

"Looks like I'll be in the back," Monica says with a smirk, and she and Noah climb in.

"I didn't think you were going to make it," I say calmly as Owen rolls down his window. As if my heart didn't leap with joy when I saw him.

"Fell asleep," he says. "Worn out from washing dishes."

"That's a job for the dogs," I say, straight-faced.

"Fits me, then." He turns his truck off and comes around the car. "You driving, killer?"

"Yep." I open my door and get in so I don't give in to my impulse to hug him. It's his nickname for me. And he hasn't called me it since we got back together.

"Better be sure I get my seatbelt on," he says, sitting up front beside me.

"She's a much better driver than you," Monica says.

"Slower driver," Owen drawls, looking over his shoulder at her. "Not better.

Slower."

"Where are we going?" I ask, pulling up my GPS.

"Here's the address." Monica hands me a slip of paper. "My friend's grandparents have a house on the lake. It's a small get-together."

I didn't realize others would be there. "Wait. It's not just us?"

"No. We were invited."

"How many people are going to be there?"

"I don't know. A few."

I program the address, but I feel an undercurrent of unease. Sounds like a party. With college kids.

"Ignore everyone else," Owen says quietly. "You're there with us."

I send him a grateful look. He must have heard the distress in my voice. Or he knows how I don't like crowds. Especially crowds of strangers.

I drive us down the highway, out past Springdale and into the smaller surrounding suburbs. Houses become more sparse and pastures and fields take over. I turn onto the county road leading to the lake house forty minutes later.

There's a cop car in the middle of the street. His lights are flashing, and he's standing in front of the car in a brown uniform and big Smoky the Bear hat. He flags me down, and my blood immediately spikes with adrenaline. I slow my car and roll my window down.

"Yes?"

"Need to see your license, please."

I put the car in Park and try to keep my cool as I sift through my purse. "Is something wrong?"

"Just a sobriety check point."

My fingers are fumbling, and I toss out hand-lotion, a piece of trash, a package of gum. Where the heck is my wallet?

Owen takes my purse from me and fishes it out. Then he opens it and pulls out my license. I take it from him, wordlessly grateful.

The officer reads it and hands it back, then leans in to peer at us through my open window.

"Any alcohol in here?"

"No, sir," I say.

He looks back at Monica and Noah and then at Owen. He gives Owen a second look.

"Have we met before?" he says.

"Maybe," Owen says evasively. "Can't remember."

The officer looks back at me. "Where are you going?"

I try to remember the name of the street I plugged into my GPS. "Cow Patty Road."

"Cow Patty Road?" he repeats. "We don't have one of those out here."

He's looking at me suspiciously and my heart's racing. I'm starting to sweat. It wouldn't be the first time a cop thought I was drunk instead of just an idiot.

"Um," I say. So inept.

"It's Cow Face Road," Monica says from the back. "Cow Face."

"Cow Face," I repeat, my face so hot I can't make eye contact.

"Cow Face Road," he echoes. He takes a step back. "All right. Stay out of trouble."

I'm pretty sure he looks at Owen when he says that, but I'm so anxious to get out of there that I hit my gas a little too hard and have to slow down to get around his car.

Monica bursts out laughing as soon as my window is up. "Cassandra! That was hilarious."

Owen grins at me. "You're a magnet for trouble."

"I'm so embarrassed!" I exclaim. "I wasn't even doing anything wrong!"

They laugh the rest of the drive to the lake house, and soon I'm laughing also.

The house has a huge green lawn with several cars parked in front of it. I park as straight as I can on a patch of grass, aware that my passengers will tease me if I'm even a little crooked. We get out, and I find sunglasses in my purse. Monica and Noah are already approaching the large single-story blue-and-white house sitting close to the shoreline. Dozens of people mill about on the wrap-around deck.

I know I need to walk over there and smile and be friendly. But I don't know any of them. It's so awkward to talk to people I don't know. I'd much rather sit here on top of my car.

"Want to go down to the lake?"

I turn to Owen, who's still standing there. "You don't want to join the party?"

He shrugs. "I've had potato salad and watermelon before."

"Yes, I want to go to the lake." That's why I'm here. Not for a stupid "get-together."

"You know the way?"

"Can't be hard to find."

Now that I know I don't have to go make small talk with strangers over hot dogs and relish, I pick up speed. We go around the house and down the rock path to the dock. Other people sit on towels or dangle legs into the water, and a handful of kids swim in the blue-green lake.

I walk to the end of the dock. I want to swim, but the thought of taking off my dress in front of Owen suddenly makes me shy. What if he doesn't like what he sees? The padding of my swimsuit isn't the same as my bra.

I turn to him. "Are you going to swim?"

He shakes his head. "I didn't bring a suit."

Then I won't either. I take my sandals off and sit down on the dock, a few feet from another couple. The girl sits on a towel in a bikini, her curly hair shining in the sun, and the boy sits next to her, rubbing the bare skin of her back with his hand. I'm envious. I want to be touched.

Owen sits next to me. He takes his shoes off, and I stare at our feet, only a few inches beneath the surface of the murky water. My toenails are still painted a shimmery purple, left over from prom six weeks ago. It's long since worn off my fingernails, but it lasts forever on my toes.

I look at Owen's feet. They're pale, and hairy, and much wider than mine. I lean over and whisper, "You have big feet."

"Cassandra Jones." He laughs. Laughs hard.

I grin. I knew he would. It's a running joke between us.

He touches my shoulder, but just briefly, like he forgot he wasn't going to and remembered just in time.

I wait to see what else he will say. Conversations are harder between us right now. Everything feels centered on the future, and our future is apart.

Someone yells, and a boy comes streaking down the dock. He cannonballs off the end, and I gasp as the cold water splashes up and over me.

"Hey!" Bikini girl shouts.

His head bobs up. "What? It's a lake party. You're going to get wet."

She stands up, looking miffed, grabbing her towel and glaring. Her boyfriend stands with her, also glaring, placing a hand on her bare shoulder, and I think they're silly.

"I hate water," she sniffs, and they walk away. Then she squeals and nearly tumbles, but her boyfriend catches her arm. "You made the dock all slippery!" she shouts at water boy.

He's under the surface again and oblivious.

"Who comes to a lake party and hates water?" I say.

"That girl," Owen says.

It's getting loud up by the house. This feels like a college party. They're probably drinking. I regret coming. I prefer quiet activities, fresh air, the sound of the wind and frogs and birds the only serenade I need. If I threw a party, I wouldn't invite anyone. Except Owen. And maybe Harper.

"What would you be doing right now if this were your Fourth of July party at your lake house?" Owen asks.

I laugh. "Did I speak out loud?"

"Your thoughts are loud."

"I don't have a lake house."

"Pretend you do."

I shift so I'm facing him. The sun is behind him, making his light brown hair shimmer like a halo. "I'd be kayaking."

"You kayak?"

"I've never been. But it looks easier than canoing, which I've done. I love being near the water. I don't have to be in it. My skin craves the sun." I close my eyes and tilt my face toward the descending rays of sunlight. I open them again and look out at the orange colors rippling across the lake. "I'd row out into the water and watch the sunset. Then I'd stay there and watch the fireworks, because they'd be twice as good from the middle of the lake, shooting off in the sky and reflecting in the water."

"Maybe they have a kayak here."

"I'm not going to take someone else's kayak. We're talking about if I had a lake house. I'd have kayaks. Lots of them."

The dock rattles as a whole herd of boys comes barreling through, yelling and shoving as they jump from the edge of the dock. They carry with them the unmistakable scent of alcohol.

"Should they be swimming while they're drinking?" I ask, worried. "Isn't that how people drown?"

"You don't lose your head with the first sip. You just get loose. A bit goofy. They're still rational, thinking people. This is more like—the fun stage."

I turn my attention back to him. Owen's looking out at the rippling green surface. At the boys who snort water and climb on each other's heads.

We haven't talked about the drinking part of his life. Not at all. I've made assumptions based on things he's said that he's not drinking anymore. My heart skips out an uncertain rhythm in my chest. I feel less certain about us than I did when we dated during high school. Everything feels new again. Am I allowed to ask such things?

I search for the least intrusive way to find out what I want to know. "Do you— did you want to get a drink?"

He turns to me, blinking, the sunlight reflecting in his greenish-brown eyes. "What?"

My face grows hot. I made a mistake, tiptoeing. I should ask what I want to know. "Do you still drink?"

He looks at me, and then he shakes his head. "I thought you knew I don't."

I'm embarrassed. Feeling like I should have more confidence in him. "Well, I know you stopped. But then we broke up. Maybe something changed." I think of prom, of Kristin, of his friends. My heart still squeezes when I remember that night, seeing them together, the way he touched her. I don't know what happened. I'm afraid to know.

Owen is quiet, and I think he senses that I'm battling insecurities. Then he says, "I didn't stop drinking because of you. You showed me the life I want to be living. Once I started living it, there was no going back."

My chest warms. I pull my legs up onto the dock so I can rest my cheek on them and look at him. "I'm glad. That it's not because of me, I mean." I falter.

"I should say," Owen says, his tone soft, "it wasn't because of you. But I don't know if I would have changed if it weren't for you. At least, not yet."

His vulnerability touches me. My soul expands, reaching toward him. I want to tell him I love him.

"Do you miss it?" I ask.

"Oh, yes." He laughs, glancing back at the boys as they try to haul themselves onto the dock. One in the water keeps grabbing them and yanking them back in. He snorts. "They're idiots. But they're also having fun."

"Was it worth giving up?"

He catches my eye, and then he rocks sideways enough to bump my shoulder. "Without a doubt."

That touch sends little sparks of joy through me. I stand up and clasp my fingers together to keep from reaching for him. "Ready to check out the potato salad?"

He stands as well. "Let's see what they've got."

The dock rocks as two of the boys manage to get themselves onto it. The third boy heaves himself up and uses one arm to hold onto the wood while the other arm snatches forward to grab the ankle of one of the boys on the dock.

A domino effect happens. The boy on deck falls and lurches a hand out to grasp at his friend beside him. His friend makes a run for it, slips on the wet dock, and grapples for anything he can find to keep from going in.

Which happens to be me.

Except he doesn't manage to grab me.

I jerk away as he clutches at my arm and lose my balance. I shoot my hands out, and there's a split second where Owen darts forward, trying to catch me.

And then I'm overboard, falling backward into the lake.

CHAPTER TWENTY-THREE

Overboard

hit the water with a splash and close my eyes, and my first thought, interestingly enough, is of my phone. I hope I left it in the car.

The lake bottom is beneath my feet, and I push upward, clearing the surface and shaking water from my face. "I'm all right," I say as quickly as I can speak, hoping to avoid an awkward save from any would-be heroes.

Owen leans over the edge of the dock, such a flurry of emotion on his face that I don't know what he's feeling. "You got it?" he asks, holding a hand out.

"Yeah." I take his hand and let him haul me out. He stands me up, grabs me by the shoulders, and looks me over. I'm soaked. My white dress is streaked with mud and weird lake weeds and clings to my body, but I'm wearing a swimsuit, so at least there's that. My sandals are brown and muddy.

"So sorry," the guy who knocked me in says, and it seems to have sobered him up. "Can I get you a towel or something?"

He shouldn't have spoken. Owen remembers him now. He releases me and spins around, and I know he's going to start dropping swear words and swinging fists.

"Owen—" I begin, reaching for him.

Too late. "Such a fff—" He trips over the swear word I know he wants to use, and it's because at least somewhere in his mind, he's aware of me right there. He gives up and continues without it.

"—idiot! Watch what you're doing!"

The boy knows danger when he sees it. His buddies are out the of the water now, backing him, and the boy holds up both hands. "Sorry. Sorry. It was an accident."

"Accidents don't make it okay!" Owen roars, and he inhales, puffing out his chest.

Time to intervene.

I get in between them, facing Owen. "I'm okay. I'm really okay."

He backs down with me in front of him. He takes a step backward and deflates, but only slightly. Looking around me, he shakes his finger in the guy's face. "Keep your head on your shoulders, asshole."

It's a mild expletive, all things considered, but as Owen turns away, the other guy doesn't appreciate it. He calls out, "Good thing your girlfriend's got her leash on you."

It's a taunt, a challenge, and I feel Owen tighten beside me, ready for the fight.

"Don't do it." I say the words quietly, but I put steel in my voice. I place my hand on his arm and dig my fingernails into his skin, the only weapon at my disposal. "Walk away. They're just a bunch of dummies."

His mental struggle is so obvious I feel the tug-of-war in his mind. I move my hand down and lace my fingers through his, and then I walk us off the dock.

He does not pull away from me.

I lead him up the steps toward the house and only let go when I'm certain we are far enough away he won't run back to the lake.

I stop and face him. "You all right?"

He takes a moment to answer. "It makes me feel weak to walk away like that."

"You're not." I want to take him in my arms, but I have to settle for catching his gaze. "It took far more courage to walk away than to fight him." And he would have looked absolutely stupid causing a fight here at the lake party.

He exhales, and I see the bluster go out of him as his shoulders relax. He reaches an arm around me, crushing me to his chest. I don't move, I don't speak, I don't dare remind him of his vow not to touch me.

Then he releases me and steps up to the French doors at the back of the lake house. I see people inside, around an island or sitting in chairs by a hearth.

"Let's find you a towel," he says.

I'm shivering. I didn't realize it until now, when I look down and see my arms wrapped around each other, goosebumps over my exposed flesh. I follow him into the house and stand in the hallway while he tracks down a towel.

He returns with a big fluffy gray one, and I loosen my ponytail to rub the towel through it.

"Should I take my dress off?" I don't mean the question to be sensual, because I'm wearing a bathing suit. But I see immediately the effect it has on him, the way his eyes sharpen and his gaze wanders down my body.

"Absolutely," he says, and he grins.

His expression is enough to make me change my mind. "On second thought." I'm suddenly shy. I take the towel and wrap it around me.

"What?" he says, looking at me quizzically.

I am not about to tell him. I keep the towel close and step into the great room beside the kitchen. I walk over to the large built-in bookshelf and drop down to the ground, the towel draping around me like a cape. I run my fingers over the spines, looking for any familiar titles. I remove the book of poetry by Shel Silverstein.

"His poems always made me laugh when I was a kid." I smile up at Owen.

He lowers himself beside me. "Which ones did you like?"

I flip through the book and stop on "Falling Up." "This one. I love the way it plays with words." I run my fingers along the words as I read aloud, and Owen leans close to me as if reading along.

"I can see why you'd like that one," he says. "But nobody trips and falls up."

"No, they fall into lakes," I say, and he laughs.

"Yeah." He flips through the book, his features softening. "Hey, I remember these. This was one of the only books I liked as a kid. I didn't know the dude's name."

I keep my eyes on his face. "Show me your favorite."

"My favorite? Don't know if I had one." He continues sifting. Then he smiles. "I liked this one." He pushes the book across my legs.

"Gardner," I say, and then I laugh as I read through the four lines. "Yes, that seems like the perfect little boy joke."

"I still think it's funny," he says, and the tightness is gone, gone from his eyes and his face and my heart. "Your turn."

I land on "Underface," and my chest squeezes. Even as a young girl, this little poem about hiding my real self so people would like me struck a chord. "This one always spoke to me."

He reads it silently. "You took the harder path, you know. Choosing to be different."

"I didn't choose it." I take the book back and give a wistful smile. "I did everything I could to not be different. I wanted to be like everyone else. It didn't work. So." I shrug. "I gave up and accepted myself. Even if it meant I was more alone."

He looks at me. "But you don't feel alone now, do you?"

I shake my head. "No. Something happens when people accept you for who you are instead of who they think you should be."

He cups the back of my head and leans toward me so our foreheads almost touch. "You accepted me first."

Then he's kissing me, right there in front of everyone, in the front room, and I'm so astonished I don't even kiss him back. Just as I catch up to him, he pulls away, resting his head against mine, his fingers playing with the wet hairs along my neck.

He doesn't say anything. We sit like that, breathing, and he doesn't have to.

☙❦❧

Friday I'm up at by seven, sitting in front of my computer waiting for the online class registration to open for Preston Y. I've got Camila on speaker phone, even though it's an hour earlier for her.

"Did you sign the Honor Code agreement?"

I pull up the form I clicked through yesterday, where I agree to abide by the school rules: the usual no cheating, no drugs, no bullying. But Preston Y has a few more stringent rules, like no cohabitation, no sleeping over with members of the opposite sex, no alcohol on campus.

None of which bothers me. It's one of the reasons I chose the school.

"Yes," I say.

"Which class are you signing up for first?"

I check my handwritten list. "I don't know. Just starting at the top."

"You should get the one that might fill up first. Then get the next."

A thread of panic wicks through me, orange and fiery. "How will I know which class will fill up?"

"You can check the registration numbers now. See how many seats it has available."

She's done more research than I have, and I try not to worry.

But my heart rate increases, and I feel myself freaking.

I shoot a text to Owen. *I have to register for classes and I'm freaking out!*

Camila is still talking. "Click on the website and put in the class you want. It'll tell you how much space it has."

I toggle over the menu and put in my first class. An English class.

My phone rattles with a text response.

O: what's got you freaking?

"Ten more minutes until it opens," Camila says, and I hear excitement in her voice. "Let's try and get our GEs together, okay?"

"Okay," I say, even though now I'm thinking organizing my schedule is going to feel like a fast-paced game of Tetris. And I'm terrible at games. I grab my phone and respond to Owen with both fingers pounding into the keys.

Me: what if I don't get the classes I want?

O: take them later.

Me: but what if they only offer them now?

O: they won't.

Me: what if I sign up for the wrong class?

O: you aren't locked in. You can change your schedule even after school starts.

Me: but what if that screws up all my other classes???

O: laughing emoji

O: you'll have to take an extra two years of college to get it straightened out

Now he's making fun of me. But he does help me calm down. Whatever I do wrong now, and I'm certain I will, it won't ruin my college career.

Me: you're a lot of help

O: you're welcome.

"Five minutes," Camila says.

"Five minutes," I breathe. I flex my fingers. I feel like I'm about to start a marathon.

O: want me to sign in as you over here and get half your classes?

It's so kind of him to offer. I'm tempted. But the control freak in me can't handle the thought of someone else picking my class schedule.

Me: I can do this. Three minutes.

O: You can do it.

I take deep breaths, eyes on the clock.

And then the bar above the registration form turns green, and Camila shouts, "It's live!"

Oh, crap. I dive in, clicking through subjects and searching for specific classes. Some classes have only one offering, and I've selected three classes before I realize my fourth class won't fit in there. I unregister and start over, planning my schedule around the fourth class this time.

But now the English class I wanted is full. Dang it! I'm sweating as I peruse the options and choose another that will fit in the Monday/Wednesday/Friday spot I have open. I don't even know what class it is. I pick it anyway.

"What religion class are you picking?" Camila asks. "I have that open."

I check my schedule. "I have a Tuesday/Thursday opening at two o'clock. Does anything fit that?"

"I have a ten or one open. Can you rearrange anything?"

I shuffle around some more, moving my physical science class from ten in the morning to two o'clock. "All right. I can do ten."

"How about the Ancient People studies?"

I scroll through the religion department and find it. "Five slots left. Hurry, Camila."

"Got it!"

I add it also, feeling like I scored an expensive item at an auction. "I'm in!"

"What GEs did you get?"

"I got English 101 and physical science."

"I thought you got a five on the AP English test?"

"I did. But since I'm majoring in English, the counselor recommended I take it anyway. So I'm doing the Honors class."

"Ah. I've got physical science at two."

"I'm in the one at ten." We have one class together. I scan over my completed schedule, the adrenaline seeping out of my system. I exhale.

"What about math?" she asks.

"Math." I make a face. "I have to take remedial math."

"You do?"

"Yeah, because I failed that section of the ACT." Me and my stupid brain. "So I'm in Pre-Algebra. Just have to get this over with."

"Don't feel bad," she says. "You can't be the only one, or the class wouldn't exist."

I laugh. "Yeah, you're right."

"Okay!" Camila sounds energized while I feel weak with relief. "This is great!"

"Really great," I agree.

"We're going to have so much fun! How are you and Owen?"

Camila knows everything. She knows about Tiago, how he broke my heart, how Owen healed it, our break up, and our reconnection. She and I met last summer at church camp, and she gets me. We understand each other.

"We're good. It's weird right now. We're together, but we know we won't be. It makes things odd."

"Do you still love him?"

I scoff at her question. "You can't stop loving someone, Camila."

"What about Tiago?"

I shift in my seat, feeling that familiar ache where he's concerned. I still haven't heard anything from him. "Love changes. But it doesn't disappear."

"That makes sense. Okay, I need to get my run in before it gets hot. Love you, Cass! See you soon!"

Camila's a runner. I'm fascinated that someone can enjoy the sport. "See you," I echo.

I exit the call and see a missed text from Owen.

O: Did you get the classes you wanted?

My chest warms at his message. I miss him so much. He lives ten minutes from me. I saw him yesterday. But there's a physical yearning inside me to be near him. To hold him close to me.

We are about to have an entire continent between us. Give or take a few miles.

I text back, *I did. This is going to be fun.*

I hate that I'm leaving him.

CHAPTER TWENTY-FOUR
Surprise Trip

'm putting my shoes on to leave for church Sunday morning when my mom calls me from the kitchen.

"Cassandra!" she calls out, her voice airy and cheerful.

I step into the kitchen, pulling on the strap to my heels and wishing I could wear flip-flops. But my mom frowns on wearing flip-flops to church, no matter how cute they are. "Yes?" I hook my hair behind my ear while noticing both my mom and dad are sitting at the table. The scent of pancakes and syrup fills the air, though breakfast has been over for an hour.

They both look at me expectantly, so I sit. "What's up?" I resist the urge to check my phone for the time. I want to leave.

"I have a business trip in Washington DC next week," my dad says.

This isn't unusual. My dad has traveled for work since I was in ninth grade. "Cool," I say. This is leading somewhere, but I'm not sure where.

"I didn't get to go with you on your senior trip, and I feel like you didn't get much of one."

"Going to Branson with grandparents you hardly know doesn't seem to count," Mom adds.

I shrug. "It was fine." Nothing exciting, but still fine.

"Well, your mom and I talked it over, and we want to do something for you." My dad's expression is serious, his tone rough, but I see by his eyes he's excited. About whatever this is.

And I'm suddenly nervous. I wait.

"So I bought you plane tickets to come with me."

And there it is.

I look at my mom, not sure what to say. Hoping she'll understand what's in my heart.

I'm in countdown mode. I have two weeks left until I leave for college. I don't want to spend one of those weeks in Washington DC.

My mom's smile softens, and I know she's reading my mind. But instead of diffusing my dad, she touches my knuckle and says, "This is important, sweetie. We want to spend time with you before you go. It's our last chance."

"Your mom is coming also," Dad says.

They're doing this for me. I know it, but I don't want to go.

"What about the other kids?" I ask, thinking of my younger siblings. "Is this a good idea, to leave them alone?"

Mom says, "They won't be alone. I asked the neighbors to stay with them. And Emily is almost seventeen."

I struggle, my thoughts warring within me, wanting to be petulant and refuse while feeling the mature thing to do is smile and be gracious.

"Won't it be fun?" Dad says. "You've never been to our nation's capital. You and Mom will explore all the museums and see the sites while I work, and then we'll spend the evenings together."

Maturity wins. I force a smile even though I feel my eyes stinging. "Yeah, great. A full week?"

"Yes, but that includes travel time," Mom says, and I feel her trying to make me understand why we will be gone for so long. "We leave Wednesday. We'll be home the Tuesday after that."

Breathe. I remind myself to breathe. "And then we leave on Friday for Colorado?"

"So we can get you checked into your dorm on Sunday. Right?"

I stand up and grip the back of the chair. They just took my twelve days and whittled it down to five.

"Okay," I croak. "Yes. Sounds great."

I'm lying through my teeth. But I won't ask them cancel this. Because they are right, I am leaving them also.

But I need to see Owen now.

*

Somehow I don't cry.

I drive to church dry-eyed, precise with every turn. I wait until I park at the chapel and see Owen's truck before I text him. I need to tell Harper, also, but my best friend has taken a backseat to my boyfriend.

C: Can you come out to my car?

O: Sure.

The outside sun roasts my dashboard. I leave the AC running, but I still sweat along my hairline. My hands feel clammy.

The passenger door opens, and I look over as Owen climbs in, moving my purse from the chair to the floor.

"What's up?" he asks, settling in and closing the door.

I am so stoic I feel nothing. "My parents planned a surprise for me."

He's watching me, guarded, knowing something's off but not sure what. "What did they plan?" he asks.

"A trip with me," I say. "To Washington DC."

He narrows his eyes, and I see him working it out in his head. "When do you go?"

"We fly out Wednesday."

"For how long?"

I lick my lips. "A week."

He doesn't say anything. He looks out the window, through the windshield, to the other cars that are filling up the parking lot.

What is there to say? We knew this was coming. Just not this quickly.

He turns to me and pulls me into his chest, so that the console shoves into my stomach. He holds me for a moment.

"All right." He releases me and puts his hand on the car door handle. His gaze catches mine again. "Come over after church?"

I nod, a painful lump in my throat.

It's our last Sunday together.

⟲∿⬡∿⟳

I don't say anything about it in church. I don't need a goodbye session or tears or people wishing me good luck in college. I need to get through today as if it were a normal Sunday.

Owen and I go to the adult Sunday school class after the sermon. We've been going every Sunday now, though I still feel like an imposter, sitting in my cushioned chair with my feet barely touching the ground.

Owen sits next to me with his Bible open, holding it across both of our thighs. I lean in close to him, inhaling the scent of spicy deodorant and musky aftershave. I run my fingernails through the golden hairs on his arm and then stop, dropping my hand to my lap.

He reaches over and gives my hand a squeeze.

I'm swept away in memories. The same scene played out last summer, only it was a different boy. And I remember what happened after we said goodbye.

Is that my future with Owen, too?

I can't speak. My throat is swollen. When the closing hymn is sung, I don't sing.

Church ends, and Owen says to me as he stands, "Are you coming over now or later?"

I pretend to think about it for a moment. "I guess I could come over now."

He grins and pushes my chin with his knuckle, a play-punch I'm very familiar with.

"Yeah. If you've got nothing else to do."

"I'll check my schedule." I keep one hand wrapped around the strap with my purse so that I don't wrap it around his hand. First I pull out my phone and text my mom.

Me: Going to the Blaines' house.

"See you there," Owen says.

I nod and head to my car. Mom texts back as I'm getting in.

Mom: Okay.

I need to call my boss at Stage and let her know I'm taking off early. My days at Kids First are numbered also.

Everything is numbered.

My head spins as I drive to Owen's house. It passes in a blur. I don't remember driving there, but suddenly I'm pulling into the gravel driveway and parking.

Owen comes to my car and opens my door before I've even put the car in Park.

"Everyone's in the house changing," he says. "We're going to play softball. Want to join?"

I look down at my white, floral-printed Sunday dress, then I smirk up at Owen. "I don't have anything to wear."

I don't do sports. Everyone who knows me knows that.

"I'm sure Monica has something."

I laugh out loud. Monica is almost as tall as Owen at five-eleven. "Right. I think I'm out."

He smirks. "My mom, then. Wear something of hers. We can make this work."

Mrs. Blaine is the same size as me. Maybe an inch or two taller.

He's got me, and he knows it. He takes my hand and pulls me into the house while I protest, trying to find some other way out of this.

His mom is just coming into the kitchen in linen shorts and a flowing blouse, and he deposits me beside her. "Mom, find something for Cassandra to wear so she can play."

"Of course!" Mrs. Blaine says, and she takes my arm and pulls me away before I can tell her how she really, really doesn't need to bother.

I glance over my shoulder to see Owen laughing at me.

I'll get him back for this.

Mr. Blaine steps into the hallway, also in shorts and a T-shirt, and she shoos him away.

"Tell the boys to get the bats and gloves," she tells him, then ushers me inside her bedroom and closes the door.

As soon as the latch clicks, she turns and puts her hands on my forearms, peering into my face. "How are you, sweetie?"

The question catches me off guard. In what way does she mean? "I'm all right."

She tilts her head, her eyes sympathetic. "These last few weeks must be hard for you two. But have faith." She squeezes my arm. "I have a good feeling about the future."

Which could mean . . . anything. "Thanks."

She releases me to open a dresser drawer and pulls out a pair of bright orange running shorts. "These will fit you."

Yay. I accept them, along with a pink v-neck T. She folds them for me and directs me toward the master bathroom to change.

"You know," she says as I'm about to shut the door, "Owen showed me those texts you sent him."

I pause. I search my memory, but nothing comes to mind. I turn back from the bathroom, one hand still on the door. "Which texts?" I hope I didn't say anything incriminating.

"The ones you sent while you were at the youth retreat."

The memory comes with astonishing clarity. They are the texts where I poured out my testimony and my feelings about God, about us. The ones that scared him away.

"He didn't even answer me," I say softly, because the reminder still stings. "I think I offended him."

"Oh, Cassandra," she says, and there's a glossy sheen over her eyes. "There are still things you don't understand about Owen. He showed me the texts when he got home from the hunt. And then do you know what he said?"

I shake my head. I don't have a clue. I can't imagine.

"He said, 'I'll never be as good as her, Mom.'"

My heart swells in my chest, and I want to cry. It hurts me that Owen thinks this way about himself. "He's everything I ever wanted," I say without thinking. And then I realize I've spoken these words to his mother, and my face burns.

But she doesn't seem to care. She looks at me with warm affection on her face and says, "If for nothing but Owen, I'm so glad we moved here."

It's a heartfelt compliment that I feel from the tips of my toes to the roots of my hair. I don't know what to say, so I nod and disappear into the bathroom to change my clothes.

"Here's an extra pair of shoes, I hope they fit!" Mrs. Blaine calls out to me from the bedroom. "I'll be outside!"

"Thanks!" I call back.

The long light above the mirror reflects in my eyes like bright squares. I blink and lean closer, examining my face in the light. I've put on weight in the past year, though I'm still slender. My cheeks are more full. My hair is long again. I search the bathroom for a hair tie and find one, and I pull the dark silky strands into a ponytail. My summer freckles are out and darkening the skin across my nose, though they are so tiny they disappear into the surface of my skin unless I look hard. My nose is pink, my eyes slightly swollen as though I have been crying or might cry at any moment.

No wonder Owen can read me so well. I wear my emotions on my face.

I find the shoes by the bed. They're a size too big, but it won't matter, I don't intend to run during this softball game. Owen will regret making me play.

Ten minutes later I'm standing behind a red plastic plate, sweat dripping down my face as I twist my hands around a wooden bat. Monica stares me down from her pitcher's mound while Mr. and Mrs. Blaine cheer for me from the outfield. Owen stands on third, waiting for me to hit the ball and bring him home.

I hate this.

"You're gonna miss," Richard says behind me.

"Shut up," I growl.

Monica winds up and throws. I swing the bat, but I'm off by a second or a minute, I don't know. The ball lands in Richard's glove, and he crows.

"Strike one!" he yells. He tosses the ball to Monica, and she readies herself again.

My heart pounds in my chest. Can't I hit the stupid ball? I've done it before. I remember my dad's words as a kid: *Keep your eye on the ball.*

Monica throws again, and I miss again.

"Strike two!" Richards sings. He's already celebrating behind me.

This sucks.

Owen cups his hands to his mouth. "You got this, killer."

I glare at him because it's his fault I'm out here.

Does he really think I have this, or is he praying he gets past third base?

And the thought makes me grin because it's laced with innuendo. Yeah, he'd like to get past third base. Or even get to third base.

Me too, for that matter.

My thoughts are all over the place now, and I almost don't see when Monica throws the ball. I swing on instinct.

The ball hits the bat with a resounding crack.

For a second I freeze, and Richard screams behind me, "Run!"

CHAPTER TWENTY-FIVE

Almost a Home Run

I drop the bat and sprint.

The ball's in the fields. Mr. Blaine is running after it.

"Go to second!" Owen shouts.

I do, and as I get there he yells, "Third!"

Can I? I race for the next base.

Mr. Blaine darts out of the field with the ball in his hand. Monica shouts and holds up her glove.

"Come home!" Owen yells at me from the safety of the porch.

Mr. Blaine throws the ball. I don't think I can make it, but I run anyway. I don't look behind me. The red plastic plate is there. I jump for it.

I land directly on it.

The plate skids out from under my feet, and I stumble, trying to catch myself. It's a valiant but futile effort. I slide across the ground, gravel eating my thigh and arm.

Richard grabs me and hauls me up, and Owen's at my side a moment later, laughing as he brushes dirt from my clothes.

"Did I make it?" I ask.

"No," Owen says. "But it sure was a good try."

"I'm sorry," Monica says, joining us. "I feel so bad. I shouldn't have caught it."

I feel a burst of disappointment. I wanted to get a home run. Be cool and athletic for once in my life.

"Great run," Mr. Blaine says, jogging over. "Great hit."

"Would have been foul in a real game," Richard says.

"But this wasn't a real game," Owen says.

"Oh, you're a mess!" Mrs. Blaine fusses over me, picking gravel out of my skin. "Owen, take her in and find some ointment for those cuts."

I didn't notice them until now, but as I twist my body to see the damage, the stinging of a dozen scrapes along my thigh and arm sings for attention.

"Come on," Owen says.

The game continues without us as he leads me into the kitchen. He picks me up and sets me on the edge of the island, then opens a cupboard and rummages through it. "Here." He dampens a rag and tosses it to me. "Get the dirt off."

I oblige, inhaling as I pick at a few pebble pieces that decided to merge with my skin.

Owen returns with a small first-aid kit in his hands. He takes the rag from me and turns my arm. His administrations are gentler than mine were as he scrapes at the dirt. "Next time don't eat the ground."

"There will be no next time," I say. I grip the edge of the counter when he wipes the rag over the road rash along my thigh. "I'm never doing that again."

He puts the rag down and opens a tube of ointment. His fingers are feather-soft as he spreads the cream along the scrapes on my leg. His hand caresses my skin, trailing down to my knee.

I don't have any scrapes there. But I keep quiet.

"There will be a next time."

He says it without even looking at me. Fact. The way it is.

And I remember him saying that same thing to me last year. When he found me in his room making his bed and I told him he wouldn't catch me in there again.

I smile at the memory, and then I seize his face, cupping his jaw in my hands. "I love you."

He steps into the space between us. I'm almost his height from up here, and he doesn't have to bend to kiss me. His lips press against mine, and mine part of their own accord, knowing this oral dance of ours. I wrap my hands around his forearms as he holds onto my hips.

The front door squeals as it opens, and Mrs. Blaine walks into the kitchen before we can do more than jerk our faces apart.

"All right, you guys, let's get back to the game!" But she beams at us, not looking the least bit distressed to find us making out on her counter.

She disappears down the hall, and Owen laughs softly. He turns my arm and puts ointment above my elbow.

"I thought we weren't touching," I say, teasing, because clearly we are. We ended the ridiculous "no-touching" charade at the lake party last night.

"Yeah, well, you see how well I resist temptation," he says.

He's being funny, but it's self-deprecating.

"Come on," I say. "You're stronger than you think."

He puts away the ointment. "How's the arm feeling?"

"I'm fine." I shake it out for emphasis.

"Nice hit. I knew you had it in you."

I start laughing. I can't help it.

"What?" He looks at me quizzically.

I'm thinking about bases again. I'm laughing too hard to answer.

"What is it?"

I shake my head. "I was motivated."

"Yeah? In what way?"

"I was imagining getting past third base."

His brow crinkles, and I see him trying to understand what I mean. His face smooths out as he gets it. "You were not thinking that."

I don't answer. I'm still laughing as I hop off the counter, take his hand, and lead him back outside.

⊙∽⋇∾⊙

Kids First calls me Monday morning, and I head in for what is likely my last time.

"You're in Michelle's room," Silvana says to me at the check-in desk. She hands me my lanyard.

"Thank you," I say.

The door opens behind me, and Silvana lifts her eyes.

"Hi," she says, and her tone is different all of the sudden. Quieter, a hint of a smile around her lips. She holds up another lanyard. "You're in Joanna's room today."

I turn to see who could cause this change and shouldn't be surprised when I see Owen. But I am. He gives me a small smile and steps around me to take his lanyard.

"You're working today?" I ask.

"Looks like it."

I watch how Silvana watches at him. She doesn't glance at me again. I step behind him and follow him through the doors.

"She likes you," I say. Is that jealousy I hear in my voice?

"Nah, she's just nice."

Insecurity washes over me. Suddenly I know how Owen felt about Earl. I'm feeling it. Owen's oblivious to her because I'm right here. But in a few short days, I won't be. And every girl with eyes will be making them at Owen.

No wonder he pulled away from me.

I don't realize I'm not moving until he stops walking and looks at me.

"Cassandra?"

I shake my head. Yes, this is happening. But I won't let it steal the moments I have now. "Have you worked in Joanna's room before?"

"No. Is she nice?"

I nod and catch up to him. "She's the one who told me to get a job here. I worked with her as a volunteer."

"Where are you?"

"Michelle's room. Arabela's in there."

"Who's Arabela?"

I picture the little girl with short dark hair and a fringe across her forehead. "She's my favorite. Absolutely adorable and Deaf. I've picked up a few signs because of her."

"Yeah? Like what?"

"Well." I laugh and stick my thumb between my middle and index finger, then swirl it around. "The essentials."

"What's that mean?"

"Toilet."

He nods. "Very essential around here."

I touch his arm and we part ways, but I wish I could sneak into Joanna's room and watch him.

It's a busy morning, with Michelle doing her best to engage the children in a preschool lesson while I get the bed sheets and accompany the children to the bathroom inside the classroom and clean up any extra messages they make. Both Michelle and I breathe a sigh of relief when lunch comes, and not because we're hungry.

Because recess comes after.

All of the classes have recess after lunch, put on a rotating schedule. My eyes search the playground as soon as I'm outside, and there is Owen. They've attached him to Carson, a very excited five-year-old who is large for his age and hangs on Owen's arms. Most of the teachers have gathered on the patio, where they laugh and talk while the kids play. I figured it's appropriate for me to approach Owen when he's working with Jordan.

"How's it going?" I ask.

Owen gives me an exasperated look as Carson climbs up the slide again. "I think it was easier in the kitchen."

I laugh and wait for him to coax Jordan off the slide. Once on safe ground, Carson takes off running.

"I don't know what I'm supposed to do," Owen says. "How do I keep him from using the equipment inappropriately?"

"Difficult question," I agreed. "I don't know how you're going to work this one out."

"You mock me."

"I would never!"

Owen shakes his head. "It takes a special person to work here. You love it. I'm realizing I'm nowhere near ready to be a father."

"Good thing you don't have to be."

Carson lets out a shriek and throws himself belly-first toward the slide. I step in front of it, blocking his body slam, and instead he crashes into my legs.

"You have to use the ladder and go up the back. Do it the right way," I tell him.

Carson pushes away from my legs and runs off.

Owen throws his hands into the air. "What, are you using mind control? You barely said anything and he obeyed you!"

I can't help but laugh.

A little girl I don't recognize hurdles over and throws her arms around Owen's legs. She buries her face in his jeans, springy blonde curls falling forward.

Owen looks down and pats the top of her head. "Hey, sis. You good?"

Something tugs at my heart strings, watching him.

She bobs her head, then releases him and runs off.

"Friend of yours?" I ask.

"My girlfriend," he says, straight-faced.

I do laugh. I can't help it.

"You'll make a great father someday," I say, and then I turn around and walk away. I'm reminded too much of last year. These goodbyes feel too real.

Same story, different boy. Is there no originality in the universe?

I spend Monday evening with Harper. I'm too tired to do anything exciting, so we veg in front of the TV and mourn my inevitable departure.

Tuesday they surprise me by throwing a goodbye party at Stage. Since I only gave them a two day notice, I don't expect it. Nicole is already gone, and it's Stephanie, Brian, Debra, and Lauren who put their money together to buy me a beautiful gold necklace with a filigreed cross on it. I put it on, letting it hang on the outside of my shirt.

Underneath is the necklace Owen gave me.

He texts me twenty minutes before I get off work.

O: I'm picking you up and we're going somewhere.

I text back, *did you ask?*

He replies, *my mom said I could.*

I don't even have a response for that, I'm laughing too hard.

I see Owen's truck pull up, and all of my focus turns to him. How can I light up at the mere thought of him sitting in the parking lot waiting for me?

Owen Blaine loves me, and that knowledge makes my world go round.

I hurry up to his truck and climb inside. "Hi," I say, a bit breathlessly.

He doesn't look at me. He guns the engine and roars out of the parking lot. "How was your last day of work?"

"It was great. Surreal. I'm done working there."

"I bet they're going to miss you."

"Yeah. Look what they gave me." I hold the gold cross in my palm.

He glances at it before he turns right onto the interstate. "Nice. Does that mean mine's been replaced?"

I dropped my hand beneath my shirt to pull out the necklace he gave me. "Never."

He turns his eyes back to the road without saying anything, but I see the smile that pushes at his lips.

I drop both necklaces back where they belong. "Where are we going?"

"I don't know. Are you hungry?"

"Not really. But I'll eat if you are."

He shoots me a probing look. "Are you eating all right, Cassandra?"

It's a loaded question, and it makes my face heat. I battled a series of eating disorders during my junior year. Even though he knows about it, it's not something we talk about. But now I know it's there in the back of his mind, a concern he has for me.

"I'm eating fine," I say, and my tone comes out more clipped than I mean it to.

Owen is not deterred. He takes the first Rogers exit and gives me a harder look at the red light. "Promise?"

"Owen." I soften my tone as I return his direct stare. "I don't struggle with that anymore." Mostly. "Promise."

He nods, and then his lip twists into a smile and he says, "Good, because we're getting ice cream."

"Not something I'm likely to ever say no to," I say.

We pull up to Andy's Frozen Custard. The benches out front are crowded with noisy kids. I order a chocolate custard with raspberries and fudge, and then stand to the side while Owen places his order, an original with peanuts and caramel. He joins me along the wall while we wait for our food.

"Chocolate custard, huh?" he says. "I didn't even know you could do that."

"If chocolate is an option, that's what I'm getting."

"Well, I knew that," he says with an eye roll. "I do know a few things about you."

I pluck at his sleeve, smiling, but I'm thinking how I didn't know he likes caramel and peanuts. What else don't I know?

The noisy kids have not vacated the premises by the time our food arrives, so we go around to his truck and drop the tailgate so we can sit on it. It's quieter here, the sky a hazy blue with the promise of sunset in the near future.

I steal a peak over at Owen's ice cream, laced with gooey caramel and salty nuts. He doesn't complain when I dig my spoon in and get a chunk of caramel.

"You'll be hooked," he warns.

"I don't like nuts."

He watches me lick the cold cream from my spoon. "But you don't mind the caramel."

"Nope. It's pretty good." I turn back to my own cup of frozen custard. I want to talk to him about what his mom said to me, about the texts I sent and what he said after. But the thought gets my heart pounding harder in my throat, and I'm not sure I can. I swirl the raspberry in my chocolate custard. "Owen."

"Yeah?"

I put my cup down on the tailgate. My stomach churns with anxiety now, and I can't eat anymore. Even after talking to his mom, maybe especially after talking to her, I want to know why Owen didn't tell me what he was feeling after the retreat. Why he preferred to give me the silent treatment instead of opening up to me.

"Why didn't you respond to my texts?"

CHAPTER TWENTY-SIX

Capital Activities

I lean against the side of the truck and face Owen, waiting to see if he'll know which text messages I mean.

He glances at me once and turns back to his custard, digging the spoon around with intent. "Which texts?"

Does he really not know, or is he stalling? I'll play. "The ones I sent at the youth retreat."

Now I know he'll know, and I wait to see if he'll answer me or avoid the question.

He shrugs. "I was on a hunt. Then I got home and knew I'd see you in church."

Looks like he's going with avoid the question, and I'm disappointed. I pick up my custard and swirl my spoon through the melting edges, keeping my eyes down so he won't see my feelings.

We are quiet, but I don't attempt to break the silence.

"What's wrong?" he asks.

My custard is completely melted now. "Why won't you just tell me the truth?"

There is no reply, and I lift my gaze to see him finishing off his dessert.

Now I can't stop talking. "I want to know what you feel, Owen. I want to know when something bothers you. I don't want you to hide things from me."

"I'm not hiding things from you."

He's defensive, but I press on.

"I opened myself up to you in those texts. I was excited, happy, and eager to share it with the person who means the most to me in all the world." He glances at me, but I keep going, not letting him linger on those words. "I felt so close to you as I sent those messages, and I anticipated you would feel the same closeness to me when you read them. I hugely overestimated my emotional reach. You ignored them. You didn't answer me at all. And I know we've talked about what was going through your head in the days that followed, but that was a moment for us to connect—and you shut me down." He opens his mouth to speak, but I'm not done.

"I worried I'd misunderstood our relationship. That I'd scared you off, even offended you. Suddenly everything felt off-kilter for me. And I'm okay." I put my hand on his thigh and lean toward him. "I'm okay. But I still don't have answers."

He picks up my custard cup and puts it into his. "Lots of big words. Give me a second to come up with a coherent response."

"I want to know why you didn't reply."

"No." He takes a bite of my melted custard. "You want to talk about feelings."

Is that it? I give a little laugh. "Yeah, maybe. Am I right? Did my texts scare you?"

"No."

"Then. . . ?"

"I didn't know what to say."

I roll my eyes. "Dumbest answer ever. A 'hey, cool' would have sufficed. Even better would have been a 'glad it's going well. Wish I was with you also.'"

"Sorry. I really did have a lot on my mind. You didn't say anything wrong."

I heave a sigh because I see that he is not going to be forthcoming with me no matter how I pry. So I decide to throw him a bone and make it easier for him. "Your mom told me what you said to her."

His gaze darts towards me. "She did, huh?"

"Yes."

"So why are you asking me if you already know?"

My frustration is getting the best of me. "Excellent question. I suppose if I want to know how you're feeling, I'll ask your mom."

"Hey, now." He puts his hand on my knee, finally meeting my eyes. "I'm not trying to be obstinate. I don't know how to talk about what I'm feeling. You're amazing. You're perfect, Cassandra. You're so much better than me. Your texts only proved it."

I stare at him, incredulous. "What are you talking about?"

He removes his hand from my knee and swirls the spoon in the custard cup again. "You've never screwed up anything in your life, and I've screwed everything up. I think one day you're gonna realize it and not want to be with someone like me."

It fits with what his mom said, but I can't fathom him thinking that's true. "So when I sent those texts, you were thinking how I'm so much better than you? Owen, you make me a better person. You make me want to be my best self because I feel so lucky to have you. I want to keep being that person who you like."

"Who I love." He corrects me quietly.

All my frustrations melt away at his words, replaced with empathy and understanding. "You're so much greater than you realize."

"If you could see yourself..." He shakes his head. "Cassandra, I'll never be the person you deserve."

"Stop saying things like that," I say, more annoyed than I mean to be. "I'm not perfect."

He grunts and finishes off my ice cream, then drops both cups into the bed of the truck. "Basically."

"Is that what your mom said? Abandon all hope?"

He gives me a classic teenage eye roll. "I'm not abandoning hope."

"So what did your mom say?"

He scoots over to my side of the truck and stretches his legs out in front of him. "She told me to go on my mission trip and serve God and see how I feel when I get back."

I pick up his hand and lace my fingers through his. "Do you know what I told your mom?"

"That I should abandon all hope?"

I lay my head on his shoulder. "That you're everything I want."

"You told that to my mom?"

I bob my head on his shoulder.

The sun drops below the horizon in front of us, masking the street in pink light. The cicadas are out in full force, their constant thrum filling the air with vibrations.

"What time do you fly out tomorrow?"

I tighten my fingers around his. "Seven in the morning."

It's our first goodbye. One week apart.

For all I know, things will already be different when I get back.

❧

I pack my bags tonight so I won't have to in the morning before my flight. I've just added my favorite pillow to my suitcase when my phone lights up with an incoming text.

O: hey

O: just in case I didn't make it clear. You can talk to me about anything. I don't want you to be afraid to say things to me. I want to know your thoughts. I'm sorry I left you hanging, left you wondering if you said too much

O: anyway. Wanted to make sure you know that

The texts come rapid fire, so I know these thoughts must've been running through his head while he drove home. I text back, *thank you*

O: night, Cassandra. Text me tomorrow when you arrive in DC. And when you leave. And anytime you feel like it

Me: I will. Night.

I fall into bed, feeling the achiness of sleeping alone, remembering the one night when we fell asleep together and I slept in his arms.

I want a thousand more of those nights. Ten thousand more of them.

But he's right. I can't make the universe bend to my will.

❧

We are up with the sun in the morning and off to the airport at an ungodly hour. In spite of the early morning torture, my dad is goofy and cheerful, and my mom keeps looking at me with an expression between happiness and tears. She touches me more than I'm comfortable, and I have to remind myself they are saying goodbye to their first child.

The last time I was on a plane, we were flying to Disney World when I was sixteen, and we had miserable experiences both coming and going. I am therefore apprehensive about what this morning brings.

157

We have no issues getting our luggage checked and marching ourselves through security. We make it to our gate on time. My mom cozies up next to me in the terminal and pulls up a travel app loaded with museums from Washington DC.

"There are so many," she says, scrolling through them. "Pick your favorites. We won't have time to go to all of them."

I take the phone from her, feeling a stirring of excitement. Our nation's capital. The Washington monument. The Abraham Lincoln statue. All things I've spent my whole life hearing about but never seen.

I stop on the Holocaust Museum. "Oh, we have to go here." I took an intensive college-level class on the Holocaust my junior year of high school. To call it life-changing is putting it lightly.

"I knew you would want to." She opens a notebook and jots the name down. "I know how much that class affected you during your junior year."

I fall silent, because thoughts of my junior year are wrapped up in Tiago. He was my best friend, the person I studied with, cried to, confided everything to. And then he became more than that, and even though I don't feel that way for him anymore, I can't erase him from my soul.

It hurts that we are not communicating.

I shove it aside. "Yeah, it changed my life. I knew the Holocaust was awful, but . . ." I have no words. The atrocities I learned about from my class gave me nightmares. I know the museum will have a similar affect on me, but I feel I must learn about it, honor the victims by remembering what they went through.

My mom asks about another museum, but the plane starts boarding. It's seven in the morning. Owen told me to text him, so I shoot one off as I buckle my seatbelt.

Me: on the plane. Next stop: Dallas.

The phone swooshes as his text comes in.

O: doesn't get more exciting than DFW

Me: may as well stop there and call it a trip

O: Then you can come home early.

I smile. He hasn't complained about me leaving. Hasn't expressed a lot of emotion, really. One could almost imagine it didn't matter to him.

And then he says things like that, and I know it does.

CHAPTER TWENTY-SEVEN

Unexpected Acquaintences

Virginia doesn't feel any different than Arkansas. It's hot and sticky when we get off the plane. Maybe more humid than back home. Bushels of green trees crowd the green spaces between the buildings outside the airport.

And there are buildings. As our taxi takes us closer to the capital, high-rise office buildings and skyscrapers dot the skyline. That's when I know I'm not in Arkansas anymore.

We go to dinner at an Italian restaurant that I think costs more than anything we've ever eaten back home, except the restaurant Owen took me to for Valentine's Day. I remember to text and tell him we've arrived, but then my parents remind me about the no-phones-at-dinner rule, and I have to put it away.

"I need to work in the hotel room and get ready for my presentation tomorrow," Dad says as a server brings dessert (a chocolate mousse with delicate cream on top and the most luscious consistency I've ever tasted). "There's a pool on the roof of the hotel. You should go check it out."

Mom looks at me. "Want to, Cassandra?"

"Sure. I haven't had a chance to go swimming this summer." I don't think getting knocked into the lake on the Fourth of July counts.

"Great, that will give me a few hours to work," my dad says, and the evening is decided.

Our hotel room is fancier than most I've stayed in. It's a suite, so my parents take the room and I take the fold out couch. There's a small kitchenette stocked with drinks in the fridge. I lock myself in the bathroom and change into my swimsuit.

It's a small spaghetti-strap affair with no padding, and I hate it the moment it's on. I'm so flat-chested I want to stuff toilet paper down the front like I used to in eighth grade, but I will look even worse when it gets wet than I did when the paper fell out of my bra in geography class.

The memory makes me laugh. Oh, how awkward and embarrassing junior high can be.

I pull a sundress over my swimsuit and meet my mom in the living room. She slips an arm around my waist, and I don't mind the physical affection. I'm feeling it too. I'm leaving them. This is my last summer with my family. I am both exhilarated and terrified.

There's not one exciting thing about the pool, even though it's on the roof. My view is the roofs of other buildings. It doesn't have a diving board and the deepest part is only four-foot. The small rectangle has no other patrons.

There's only the lifeguard, and he won't stop looking at me.

He appears about my age, eighteen or nineteen, with curly, golden-brown hair. I'm self-conscious under his gaze and spend most of my time in the water hiding my body rather than lounging on the chair with my book beside my mom, where I want to be.

He gets down from his lifeguard chair and comes to crouch next to the side of the pool, still cradling his red banana life preserver.

"Where are you from?" he asks.

I stop swimming and come to the edge of the pool. "Arkansas."

His eyes, the shade of the ocean at sunset, widen. "Arkansas! I've never met anyone from there before."

"Yeah, well." I lift a shoulder. "There's a lot us who live there."

"You guys must not travel much."

There's that note in his voice, the one I encounter sometimes when we travel and I tell people where I'm from. Like they think there can't be anything good about Arkansas.

In annoys me.

"Why travel when we have everything we want at home?" I push off the wall and backstroke away, knowing all the while my words aren't true. I'm leaving Arkansas. But not because I don't like it. Just because I want to experience something different. Something away from everyone else.

He doesn't try to talk to me again.

My mom laughs at me when we go in. "What did you say to him? Did he ask you out and you shot him down?"

"No, it was nothing like that." I explain what I said, and she laughs harder.

"I didn't expect him to get all upset," I say. "People should think about what they're saying before they insult someone's hometown."

My mom presses the button for the elevator. "The problem with you, honey," she says, "is you look like a beautiful butterfly. Every guy is immediately enamored. But it only takes a few seconds of conversation to realize you're a wasp."

I frown as I mull over her words in the elevator. "Is that an insult? I can't be sure."

"Not an insult. You don't want to lull someone in just because of your butterfly looks."

"Yeah, but I don't want to send them into shock because I poisoned them with my stinger."

Mom winks at me. "Don't worry. One sting, and they won't come around for more."

This sounds more and more like an insult.

My mom disappears into the bedroom with my dad, who is still working. I make up the sofa bed and put on a movie, enjoying my alone time, something I never get at home.

Owen calls me while I'm watching, and I mute the television.

"Hey!" I say.

"Busy day? I didn't hear from you again."

"Yeah, sorry. We were at dinner, and then I didn't take my phone with me to the pool."

"Nice. Was the pool crowded?"

My mind skips over his question entirely and flips to my mom's comment. "My mom says I have stingers."

"What?" He laughs.

I back up and try to give some context. "She said that I look like a butterfly but I'm really a wasp."

Owen laughs so hard I fear he might choke.

"Well?" I demand. "Am I a wasp?"

"Why did she say that?"

"This guy talked to me, and I guess I was rude to him. I didn't mean to be."

"What did he say to you?"

"I don't know, something about Arkansas being backward and I didn't like it."

Owen chuckles. "Well, that's one way to get on your bad side. Insult Arkansas."

"Yeah. Yeah, it is." I settle into the couch, letting my eyelids open and close lazily as sleepiness descends upon me.

"What are your plans tomorrow?"

"I'm not sure." I can't think past the next ten minutes. "Museums, I guess."

"Look for more guys to sting?"

I smile. "Only if they insult Arkansas."

"Don't forget me, all right?"

His flippant tone doesn't mask the insecurity behind the words. The sincerity.

His words hurt me. Not because they're mean, but because—is this what it will be like when I go to Colorado in a week? Will we talk on the phone like this, except as only friends? Will all we have left of each other be memories?

"Never," I say. "I'll never forget."

As long as I live, Owen Blaine will live in my heart.

☙❦❧

Thursday a town car drives Mom and me to the Metro rail.

"I'm Linda, and I know your dad well," our driver says as she squeals to a stop at a red light. "I drive him to all his meetings when he comes out here."

"Thank you for taking us today," my mom says.

The woman keeps glancing at me in the rearview mirror. I'm wearing a striped tank top and have my hair down, free-falling around my shoulders. I shove a piece behind my ear. Do I have chocolate muffin stuck on my face?

"This is your daughter?" she asks.

"Yes." Mom smiles at me. "This is her senior trip. She just graduated and leaves for college in a week."

"Oh, how wonderful!"

We stop at another red light, and Linda beams at me.

"You know what?" she says. "I have a son home from college for the summer, and he would love to take you out. Show you some of the city sites around DC."

"That would be great!" Mom says, even as I'm turning to her, wide-eyed and desperate. "How can we arrange this? I'm sure Cassandra would love to spend time with someone her age, away from her parents."

"I'll bring him by tonight when I pick up your husband for his business dinner. Then we'll let the two of them talk and decide what they want to do."

"Sure! Let me get your number so we don't get our wires crossed."

I stand outside the car beside the Metro rail while my mom talks to Linda. I hop from foot to foot, bursting with aggravation, ready to spill my thoughts at the first opportunity.

Mom closes the door and joins me, her eyes bright. She loops her arm around my waist. "What a nice offer! A chance to see the town with a boy!"

"Mom." I pull away from her. "I never said I wanted to."

"Why wouldn't you?" She frowns at me.

"Oh, I don't know, maybe because I don't know him?"

Mom waves this aside. "Your dad knows the family. He speaks very highly of them. And this is how dates work. You go out to get to know them, not because you already know them."

"But I don't want to go on a date with a guy!" I exclaim.

"Oh, Cassandra, it's not a real date. He's playing tour guide. And then you're off to Colorado and he's staying in Virginia. It's not like you're getting engaged. Try to have fun."

She's right, but I feel wrong about it. I let out a breath as we go down the stairs to the Metro. It's not real. Don't take it seriously. Just have fun.

My mom has a map in her hands that she uses to try to navigate the Metro. I'm intrigued by this noisy and dirty underground snake that carries commuters from one place to another. The man next to me has long hair and smells like oranges, and standing in the aisle holding the metal pole is a tall and statuesque black woman with shimmery gold earrings brushing her shoulders. I bet she's a super model, and I'm envious of her height.

Mom mutters to herself in her seat as she studies the map. "I can't tell which way we're going. Where is our stop?"

I look at the diagram on the wall of the train and point to the colored line. "This one's us. Here's our stop."

She folds the map and puts it in her purse, looking relieved. "Glad you're here to help."

We step off the Metro into a train station, and I'm enthralled. There's a busy hum to the people walking around, an excited energy charging the air. I see families with small children, older couples, college students like me—like me!—and tour guides leading groups of people in foreign languages.

"This is pretty cool," I say.

"Come on," Mom says. "Let's go to the Holocaust museum."

It's almost a mile walk from the Metro station. The first marker I see is the Washington Monument.

"We'll come back to it," Mom says. "The Lincoln Memorial is right there also."

I spin around, trying to take it all in. Mom points things out as we walk.

"Behind the Washington Monument is the Korean War Memorial. The Smithsonian is over there. Here's the museum of African American history."

My craving to devour knowledge awakens in me, and I hop around from foot to foot. "A week isn't long enough!" I wail.

She chuckles. "Well, let's see how long it takes you in the Holocaust Museum. Maybe we can fit in two today."

Twenty minutes later we arrive. The building is dignified if boring in its austere exterior, mostly right angles but with an entryway that resembles the Colosseum. We have tickets for ten when the museum opens, and it's only nine-thirty. We stop at a cafe and get brunch. My thoughts tumble around as I sip my orange juice.

"There's so much world to see," I say. "So much to explore and learn."

"Yes, there is," Mom says. "And now's the time to do it. It only gets harder as you get older and have a family."

I can count on one hand how many times my parents have taken a trip together without us kids. And they only went to Texas.

I want to see it all.

I tried to avoid the small-town mentality by leaving Arkansas when I went to college, but some of it eeked into my psyche anyway. Now I feel a sense of stagnation in my soul. I must get out. I must open doors and move aside curtains and hop across oceans. The world is a closed rose bud in my palm. I'm going to peel back the petals and find what's inside.

Even with our tickets, we have to wait in line to get into the museum. A woman speaks to us when we enter, explaining the layout of the museum and giving some context to the exhibitions.

I don't need it. As we enter the first room, I flashback to my Holocaust class last year. It was a college-level class taught by a visiting professor from the University of Arkansas, and no one ever expected so much from me in one semester, not even my AP English teachers.

But I learned. The horrors of the Holocaust are imprinted in my heart.

We spend five hours in the museum, exploring every floor. I'm one of those annoying people who likes to read the plaques. I want to soak it in, absorb the information. But even I am ready to call it a day when we reach the top floor. My feet hurt, and I'm hungry again.

"I got a text from your dad," Mom says. "He's going to pick us up from the Metro in an hour. Then we can go to his business dinner together."

"Wow. I can't believe we've already used our first day." I thought every minute here would feel like an eternity.

"It will take us half an hour to get back to him. We should go."

We begin the mile walk back to the station, and I'm disappointed we don't have time to go to the Lincoln Memorial or the Washington Monument.

"Tomorrow," my mom says.

There's a moment of confusion as we figure out which Metro to take, but we reach the designated meet-up location with seven minutes to spare. We sit on a bench to wait for my dad, and I check my phone.

There's a text from Owen. I wondered when I would hear from him.

O: what adventures today?

Me: spent the day in the Holocaust museum.

O: I didn't know there was one. Sounds dismal.

I tilt my head, considering his statement. It's interesting to me there existed a time when Owen wasn't a part of my life. It feels like he's always been there, but he didn't even live in Arkansas when I took the Holocaust course. He wasn't there when I went through that transformation.

Me: it was amazing. I took a class on it junior year, and the museum was like the capstone to a thesis paper.

O: whoa. Now you're talking like a college student wide-eye emoji

I laugh, because it's what I was thinking.

Me: we are college students.

O: that's crazy talk.

"Where is your dad?" my mom says, pulling me away from my text conversation. "He said he would be here twenty minutes ago."

I hadn't noticed. My stomach rumbles, seriously hungry.

My mom picks up her phone and dials my dad. "If he doesn't get here soon, we're going to go eat somewhere else."

So she's hungry too. Just to kill time, I check the local restaurants. There are plenty within a ten-minute walk.

"Where are you?" Mom is silent as she listens to Dad's response. "It would have been nice if you'd told us that before we left." She hangs up and says, "He'll be here in half an hour."

"Half an hour!" I explain. "Has he even left yet?"

"I don't know."

I breathe out a huff and cross my arms over my chest. "Do you have any snacks?"

Mom digs through her purse and shakes her head. "Looks like we have to wait."

I stew on the bench and pull my hair into a ponytail as the sun beats down on us. Sweat drips along my hairline, and I plan the verbal lashing I'll give my father when he shows up. It's hot and humid, worse than Arkansas, I think.

But when Dad shows up in his car, he greets us with jelly donuts and a big smile, and I can't stay mad when I'm holding a powdered sugar confection in the back seat of a car with sweet, sweet air conditioning blowing on me.

His business dinner is stuffy but the food is good, my dad's presentation goes well, and I have a book to read.

Then Linda the driver arrives. And she brings a tall young man with her in tow.

"Cassandra!" she says, smiling as she stops next to our table. "This is my son, Logan. I told you I would bring him by tonight!"

CHAPTER TWENTY-EIGHT
Elephants at Bay

had completely forgotten about this prearranged meeting. I look at the boy, at least a foot taller than me with a head of wild blond curls. He smiles, and judging from the shape of his jaw, he's in his early twenties.

Instantly my heart beats faster with anxiety. What's expected of me here? "Hi, nice to meet you," I say.

He extends a hand, so I do also. He clasps mine in both of his. "So nice to meet you. My mom said you're visiting for the week. She suggested I show you some of the quieter spots around here, the ones the tourists don't usually see. I think it's a great idea. Maybe tomorrow night. You game?"

"Um," I say.

"Go, Cassandra," Mom says. "What else will you do? Watch TV in our hotel room and text Owen all night?"

My face burns with embarrassment, and I'm irate she'd call me out like that. I flash her my angry look and then smile at Logan, demure again. "Sure. We can do that."

"Nice." He pats the hand he's holding. "Call me tomorrow when you're done at the mall and I'll come get you. I'll show you the boardwalk. It's got a great spot for watching the sunset."

"The mall?" I question. Am I going shopping and don't know it?

"Oh, the National Mall." He chuckles. "It's what we call the museum walk."

Dad picks up his briefcase and jacket. "I have my own car today, Linda, so I hope you're not here for me."

"Nope." She gives a white-toothed grin. "Just wanted to bring Logan by."

"Great. We'll see you in the morning, then."

My mom talks about how nice Logan seemed in the car. How adorable that head of curls is.

"I don't know him," I say. "It's weird."

"This is how you get to know people, Cassandra. Besides, his mom told me he thought you were cute."

I hadn't noticed our mothers talking.

I lie on my pulled out sofa bed after my parents retire to their room, my phone in my hand. I haven't texted Owen since we left the station, and I'm reluctant to do so now.

Things are already changing by virtue of the fact that we are not in the same place.

I shoot of a message. *Well, I'm off to bed. Walked a lot today. Tired.*

O: I'll call.

The phone rings a second later, and I answer before it can wake my parents. "Hi," I say.

"Hi," he answers. "Busy day?"

The sound of his calm, baritone voice calms my raw nerves. "Yeah. We went to my dad's work thing. I'm beat. What about you?"

"Not doing much. Didn't go into work again today."

I make a tsking sound. "You won't get a paycheck if you don't work."

"I don't need one. I was only working because I liked this girl who worked there."

"Oh? Sounds like past tense. What happened? You don't like her anymore?" I tease.

"Let me rephrase. I like this girl who worked there."

I smile. "And now?"

"Well, she quit, so you could say I'm not so motivated to get up in the morning."

"You have to find your inner strength! There must be something else that motivates you."

"Well, there's . . . No . . . Nope, not that either. Doesn't look like it."

"You got up for Bible study every day for four years."

"My life was being threatened."

I laugh. "I don't miss waking up early."

"I kind of miss it. There was this girl again . . ."

"Another girl?"

"Same girl."

Our banter is fun. But it makes me sad.

Maybe everything will make me sad.

"You should find girls that don't require so much of you," I say.

There's a pause, and I realize I put too much reality into our game. Shoot. There's nothing he can say to keep it light now.

"Maybe I like it that way," he says. "Keeps me from getting lazy."

He still managed it.

"What's on tap for tomorrow?" he says, not giving me a chance to say anything. Maybe he's afraid I'll throw another reality check at us.

"I want to see the monuments and the ponds. So maybe one of the smaller museums that won't take five hours." I pause, my heart rate suddenly escalating. What is the best way to say this? Maybe I shouldn't say it at all. I hold a split-second mental debate and remember my vow not to hide anything from Owen. "And my dad's driver arranged for her son to show me around some of the lesser known areas of DC."

The words are casual enough, but my delivery is off. I blurt the words out rapid-fire, and I think my voice goes up a notch.

"Her son, huh?" Owen says, and his tone is calm, amused, even. "Is he a tour guide? Or did he develop a sudden interest in showing visitors around his city sometime today?"

I relax into my pillow, relieved by his reaction. "I think it might be the latter," I admit. "I don't know anything about him except that he goes to school somewhere around here."

"Can't say I blame him." Owen yawns loudly. "I'd volunteer to be your tour guide also."

He's not mad or acting strange at all, which immediately loosens the knots in my stomach. "I'd rather have you."

"But I don't know that city very well. So we'd end up hopelessly lost."

Why does getting hopelessly lost with Owen sound incredibly romantic? "You can show me around Arkansas when I get back."

"Maybe I will. I know some places around here I bet you've never been."

I want to go there now. I want to be back in Arkansas, exploring new locations and places with Owen. "I think you'd better."

"Well," he drawls, slipping into his deep, southern-Louisiana accent, "it's later for you than it is for me. So you should go to bed."

"Yes," I agree, reluctantly. "Night, Owen. Talk to you tomorrow."

"Night, Cassandra."

We hang up, but the air feels thick with unspoken words. Crowded with elephants we don't want to acknowledge.

On impulse, I pick my phone up again and text him. *Love you.*

O: I love you too.

I put my phone down and turn out the lamp, feeling more at peace. The elephants are still here. But they're at bay for the moment.

❦

Mom and I sleep a little bit later today. When we do rise, I dress in my favorite brown dress, the one Martha bought me in Brazil. I can't help but think of her and Tiago when I put it on. The silence stretches between me and him, but I will wait this one out.

I pair it with a jean jacket in case I get cold in the museums. Then we call Linda to come pick us up in the town car, and she chatters nonstop about the "date" Logan and I are going on tonight. All the way to the Metro station.

"I can take you straight to the mall if you want," she says.

My mom looks ready to accept, but I can't take this chattiness any longer.

"No, that's all right, I like the walking."

Linda nods and smiles as if I have said something to agree with. "That's good. It's so good to get out and walk."

"Yes," I say.

She drops us off at the Metro, and my mom laughs at me as we take the stairs down to the train. "You couldn't stand being in the car with her another moment, huh?"

"All she wanted to talk about was Logan. It's weird!"

"Honey, she's just proud of her son."

"It's not even a real date. Sheesh."

It's too hot to walk around outside when we arrive at the mall, so we decide to explore museums first and then get ice cream and walk around the grounds. We spend three hours at the Museum of African Culture before buying hotdogs from a food stand. I haven't eaten a hotdog in about four years, and I enjoy the greasy, savory meat slathered with mustard and relish.

A few hours into exploring the war memorials, a peal of thunder makes me look up. Dark storm clouds have rolled in, promising a wet addition to our afternoon.

"We should probably get indoors," I say.

"Want to call Logan?" Mom says. "We've seen everything you wanted. You guys could go now."

I may as well get this over with. I sit on a bench and dial the number Logan gave me the day before.

He answers on the first ring. "Hello?"

I run my fingers through the ends of my ponytail. "Hi, Logan? It's Cassandra."

"Cassandra! I'm glad you called. I forgot to get your number."

I smile. "Oversight."

"So I don't know if you've noticed, but it looks like it's about to rain. I think we'll have to skip the boardwalk and go to dinner somewhere downtown. I can still show you a few things. That all right?"

"It's fine. I don't have any expectations."

"Perfect. Then I'll pick you up by the Metro station, right?"

"Sounds good."

"Is your mom with you?"

I glance at her. "Yes."

"I'll take her back to the hotel, too, so she doesn't have to ride the Metro alone."

"That's kind of you," I say, a bit startled he thought of it.

I hadn't.

We say goodbye, and I hang up, dropping my phone into my purse.

"Well? What's the plan?" Mom asked.

"He said it's fixing to rain—" I begin.

"He said it's fixing to rain?" Mom interrupts. "No, he did not."

I stare at her, a little surprised at her denial. "Yes, he did. And we can see the storm clouds from here."

"Fixing to rain?" Mom repeats, her lips twitching in humor.

I shake my head, not getting her joke. "Yes, Mother. And we should start walking to the station before we get poured on."

She laughs. "Honey. People in Arkansas say fixing to. I promise you Logan did not."

And then I understand what's so funny. I think back on the phone conversation with Logan and I laugh also. "You're right. He said it's about to rain."

We begin the walk back to the Metro station.

"Your college roommates are going to love your accent," she says.

⊙〜※〜⊙

We are almost to the station when the sky opens and the downpour begins. Neither of us has an umbrella. I take off my jacket to cower beneath it and shriek, then begin running for the station. My mom follows behind me, holding her purse above her head.

Both prove to be inefficient rain shields, and we are soaked when we step into the station. We look at each other and laugh, then hurry to the restroom to try and dry off. I'm ducking beneath the hand dryer, using it to dry my hair, when my phone chimes with an incoming text.

It's Logan.

L: I'm outside the station, small red car.

Me: on our way

I snag my mom's sleeve and haul her out the door of the bathroom. "He's here," I say, and suddenly I'm all kinds of nervous.

"Wow. That was fast," she says.

I bob my head.

The rain still wets the sidewalk outside, but it's more of a drizzle than a downpour, and now the air is thick enough to breathe, vapor rising off the hot asphalt and mixing with the falling water to create choking waves. A small red car is parked along the curb. Logan hops out to meet us when we arrive, and his face is dimples and smiles. He opens the passenger side door for my mom and then jumps back to grab my door before I can.

"That's so nice of you to pick us up," my mom says, and I'm happy to let her carry the conversation as we drive. She doesn't seem to find it hard to make small talk, a skill I am definitely lacking.

It only takes half an hour to get us back to the hotel, as opposed to the fifteen-minute drive from the Metro station after the hour ride it would have taken us otherwise. Logan pulls up at the hotel, and my mom bounces out. Logan glances back at me before she closes the door.

"Did you want to come sit up front?" Mom asks.

She gives me a pointed look, and I know my only option is yes. I unlock my seatbelt. "Of course."

She closes the door for me after I'm in and waves cheerfully as she walks up to the hotel. I'm amazed she can be so optimistic. For all she knows, I've gotten in the car with a serial killer and this is the last time she'll see me.

"Since it's raining, I don't think going on a walk is the best idea," Logan says, gesturing out the window, wipers going. "But I can take you to see the old cathedral downtown. It's one of the most historic buildings in the area."

He wants to take me to church? So much for being a serial killer.

"Yeah. That sounds great." I like churches.

But now I'm thinking of Owen and the little white church, and this ache bubbles up in my chest. I have this terrible fear that I'll never see it with him again.

I shove the thought away and focus on taking in the sights of DC. I keep my eyes peeled on the horizon, watching for a giant cathedral.

Except Logan can't remember where it is.

We drive forty-five minutes to get to Georgetown and spend another ten circling the block where Logan is certain the cathedral should be. But it's not there.

"I thought I knew where it was," he says with an embarrassed grin. "Let me put it into my GPS real quick."

I nod. I've gotten to see a lot of the area, that's for sure.

Turns out Logan doesn't know the downtown DC area well at all. We drove past the church half an hour earlier.

"I'm so sorry," he says for the umpteenth time when we finally pull up to the cathedral. "We could have been here an hour ago."

I barely hear him. The rain has stopped, and I push open the car door to gawk at the enormous building in front of me. Tall spires, flying buttresses, arched doorways, and circular windows stare back at me. The church sprawls over an entire block.

"Want to take some pictures?" Logan asks, and I turn to see him standing behind me.

I'm absolutely stunned. I pull out my camera, but I can't fit the whole cathedral in the frame. "How can this building be here? It's like something out of Europe!"

"It's the sixth-largest cathedral in the world. It wasn't built until 1907, but they mimicked the architecture of the old Gothic cathedrals."

"It's so beautiful."

"Here, let me take a few of you."

I hand Logan my phone and smile while he snaps pictures. I sit down on the grass and hop up immediately when the wetness soaks into my skirt.

"Still wet," I say.

Logan laughs and takes a few more pictures before handing my phone back to me.

We walk around the cathedral, and I wish I had pockets. Instead my hands hang at my sides, conspicuous. I clasp them together and tell myself to relax.

"Would you like to go inside?" Logan asks. "The stained-glass windows are something to see."

I do want to, but I know it will be an emotional experience, and going in with Logan feels . . . wrong. So I shake my head. "That's all right. Maybe we can get some dinner now?"

"For sure," Logan agrees. "We did take an hour detour to find this place."

We drive ten more minutes into Georgetown.

"There's a university here," Logan says. "I tried to get into it, but my grades weren't good enough."

He parks the car at a meter and I wait while he pays.

"What school do you go to?" I ask.

"George Mason. It's about half an hour from here."

"Nice."

"What about you? What school are you off to?"

"Preston Yarborough."

"Where's that?"

"Colorado."

He whistles as he holds the door to a noisy restaurant for me. "Wow! That's far away."

I shrug. "It's what I wanted."

There's a twenty-minute wait for a table, which Logan says is a blink of an eye around here. He keeps talking while we wait.

"Wanted? You don't want it anymore?"

I take a moment to answer, considering my response. "Leaving home is harder than I thought it would be."

"I'm ready for you." The hostess grabs two menus and smiles at us, so I stop talking and follow her.

She puts us at a table five feet from a stage with live entertainment. A woman in a blue sequin dress belts out blues while the band plays behind her.

We pause to study the menu. I order a pasta dish with pancetta and asparagus. He orders lasagna, and the waitress takes our menus.

"And why is it harder to leave than you were expecting?" he says, picking up where I left off. "You suddenly realize how much you're going to miss your family?" He lifts one eyebrow over his light blue eyes, and a corner of his lip quirks upward. "Or does this have to do with Owen?"

CHAPTER TWENTY-NINE

Flight Change

"What?" I keep my jaw from dropping. My hands flutter in my lap, smoothing the white napkin. "How do you know about Owen?" Did my mom actually have a conversation with his mom?

"You dad may have mentioned if you're texting a lot, you might be texting him. I'm guessing he's a boy back home?"

Logan smiles, and I realize he's teasing me in a friendly way. I smile back.

"He is a boy back home, and it has a lot to do with him. But he's not staying in Arkansas either, so in the end it doesn't matter. This transition is going to happen."

Logan exhales and shakes his head. "There's so much sadness on your face when you speak of him."

My eyes burn unexpectedly, and I drop my gaze to my lap.

Neither of us speaks for a moment, and then Logan says, "So! What are you most looking forward to about college?"

I jump at the subject change with enthusiasm. "The chance to redefine who I am. No one knows me. There are no expectations. If I tell people I'm a dancer, they'll believe me. If I say I'm an artist, no one can say I'm not. I can be whatever I want."

"Are you a dancer?"

"Well." I laugh. "Some things they might discover pretty quickly that I'm not. Like a dancer."

He laughs also.

We flow into an easy conversation, and I'm not tense anymore. He's not trying to replace Owen. We're just two college kids exploring the suburbs of DC and eating dinner together.

It's comfortable.

It's after midnight before Logan gets me back to the hotel. My mom texted a few times to make sure he hadn't kidnapped me, but when I assured her I was fine, she left me alone.

Our conversation drifts off as we near the hotel. My head throbs with exhaustion. Logan parks at the curb and runs around the car, managing to open my door while I'm still unbuckling my seatbelt.

"I had a great time tonight," he says, and he reaches out to clasp my hand. "I know you're off to Colorado and there's a lot going on in your life. So I'll probably never see you again. But just so you know, I think you're awesome, and you're going to get exactly what you want out of college."

"Thank you," I say, strangely moved. "I had a nice time also. Thanks for showing me around."

He releases my hand and steps away. That's it. He doesn't try to hug me, just waves as I walk inside. I wave back.

I let myself into the hotel room. I barely remember to take out my contacts, stopping at the bathroom to drop them into the case in a bath of saline solution.

"I'm home," I call out toward my parents' bedroom.

"Okay, honey," my mom's voice comes back, faint and sleepy.

I lay down on my couch and I'm out before I have another thought.

In the morning there's another text from Logan.

L: thanks again for the evening. Good luck at college.

And there's a text from Owen.

O: how was yesterday?

Is he asking about my date with Logan without asking?

He didn't specify.

So I don't mention it.

Me: fun. Mom and I got rained on. Hot and humid here.

O: sounds familiar. What was fun?

Me: just the museum. Using my sweater as an umbrella and getting soaking wet.

He gives a laughing emoji. I turn the conversation around to him and his day, and then I say bye because my mom tells me to get ready to leave.

He doesn't ask about Logan.

I can't imagine he forgot. Which means he intentionally didn't ask. Was he waiting for me to bring it up?

I didn't feel like it.

The last three days of our trip pass uneventfully. On our last day, my dad wins a fancy award at work, and we plan a celebratory dinner. My mom takes me shopping, and we have a blast perusing the discount racks.

Her phone rings, and she leaves me in the dressing room with an armful of clothes. When I come out, I see her by the register. I hear my name and tiptoe nearer. She spots me and says, "We'll talk later," then she hangs up.

I approach her with the clothes draped over my arm. "What was that about?"

"Oh, nothing, just some questions about Sunday school."

For real? It seems odd she would lie to me.

"You said my name."

"I wanted to make sure you found me when you got out of the dressing room."

She takes the clothing from me. "Are these the items you want?"

"Yes."

I wait for her to object to the eight articles of clothing I chose, but she nods and places them on the register without question.

I arch an eyebrow.

It's not like my mom to be sneaky. I put it from my mind.

Mostly.

⟋⟋⊱✦⊰⟍⟍

We head to the airport in the morning, and I can hardly believe an entire week went by. I had more fun than I expected, but I hate that I'm one step closer to saying goodbye to Owen.

He texts me while we're at the gate.

O: Almost home?

Me: about to get on the plane

O: great. Dad wants me to go to some church thing with him and Richard but I said I'm meeting you when you get home. So he's mad at me.

He peppers his message with rolling eye and yawning emojis, and I smile.

Me: Don't fight with your dad. Church is important. Maybe you can do both. I'll be home at three.

The three dots appear as he texts back, and I wait for it.

O: Maybe. That gives us three hours. I have to leave at six for church, then.

Me: perfect. See you soon.

I only half mean it. Yes, church is important, but I can count how many hours I have left with Owen, and I want more. I almost text him again to tell him to skip the church thing, but I don't. Any time he and his dad spend time together without fighting, it's a good thing.

The loud speaker turns on, and I put my phone away and grab my carry-on bag, waiting for the announcement that we are boarding. Instead, the woman behind the counter says, "May I have your attention, please. All passengers at gate thirty-two for flight 5555 to Dallas, this flight has been canceled."

A flurry of exclamations and shouts rise up from the people around me, but the woman just raises her voice and keeps talking into her microphone. "Please form a line behind the customer service desk, and we will be happy to help you with your travel plans."

"What?" My mom grabs my dad's forearm. "Jim! Do something!"

"What does that mean?" I say, not quite getting it. "What does that mean, canceled?"

My dad doesn't answer either of us, but he gets up and joins the line of people forming in front of the desk. I turned to Mom, who's wringing her hands anxiously, a deer-in-the-headlight look on her face.

"Mom? What's happening?"

"They canceled our flight."

I shake my head. "But why?" I'm dumbfounded. The weather outside is perfect. What would make them cancel our flight? "How will we get home?"

She looks at me, and the fear on her face dissipates as she slips into mother-mode. "The airlines will find us another flight. They're working on it right now."

The reality of what's happening descends upon my shoulders. I look at the line my dad is standing in, and it stretches away from the gate and down the hall. My dad isn't even in the first thirty people.

"But all these people are going to try to get a flight," I say, turning back to Mom. "Will the flights have room for all of us?"

My mom shakes her head. "I need to call the babysitter and tell them we won't be home yet."

She walks away to make the call, and I realize what this means.

I won't be home at three.

My heart sinks as I whip my phone out and quickly text Owen.

Me: bad news. My flight was canceled. I don't know when I'll be home.

There's no answer, and I put my phone away as a sense of sadness settles over my shoulders like a light mist.

I have two days left until I leave for college. And I was including today in my count. Today, tomorrow, and then I'm gone.

⟡

My dad manages to get us seats on a flight that leaves in five hours. We won't get home until six tonight.

I'm disappointed, but Mom is beside herself. She's close to tears as she tells my dad that we need an earlier flight.

"It's going to be all right, Karen," Dad says. "The kids will be fine a few more hours."

She turns away from him, not appeased, and I don't say anything about my own feelings. "It's all right, Mom," I say. "Just count this as part of our trip."

She gives me a tearful smile.

Dad gets food vouchers out of the airlines for our cancellation, and he lets me choose where we should eat. There is a TGIF in the airport, and I haven't been to one since I was in ninth grade. I remember that meal, hanging out with Cara and Amity and Andrea, my best friends at the time. Or the girls I was trying to be friends with. I never quite fit in, and they never treated me the way they treated each other.

But today, the giant juicy burger on the menu out front catches my eye.

I haven't had a burger in four years since I quit being a vegetarian two months ago.

I get excited.

The waitress seats us, and I choose a burger loaded with guacamole and pepper jack cheese. My phone chimes while my parents place their order.

It's Owen.

O: that really sucks.

To anyone else, it would seem like unemotional statement, but I can read Owen. His use of an adverb means he is quite disappointed.

See, I can use adverbs also.

I mean, I should hope so, since I'm majoring in English.

I text back, *I know. Sorry.*

O: I'll tell my dad I'm not going to the thing at church.

I don't say anything. Because I want him to choose me over church, but I feel guilty for wanting it. So instead I say nothing.

Right at that moment, my burger arrives. It's huge, bigger than my face. It has so much meat I feel like I'm gonna have a heart attack just from looking at it. I snap a picture of it and send it to Owen.

Me: I'm about to eat this.

O: For real?

Me: yep

O: film it

I hand my phone to my parents, and they laugh at me as I pick up the burger and try to take a bite. I can't even open my mouth that wide. I put it back down and use my fork and knife to cut off a piece, and even then when I take a bite, sauce and guacamole squirt everywhere. I catch it with my hand, but I know it's all over my face. My parents laugh as they hand the phone back and I watch the video. I'm a total disaster. I look like a child trying to eat grown-up food.

I send it to Owen. He sent me a ROFL emoji.

Then my dad makes me put my phone away because that's the rule, no phones at dinner. I enjoy my burger but only manage to eat a few more bites.

I'm so stuffed when we leave I'm tempted to unbutton my jeans. Mom says I didn't eat much, but I feel the food sitting in my stomach like a greasy lump of fat, and I go through all of my mental exercises to remind myself that food is good and meat is a protein that nourishes the body.

But I can't shake the nervous energy that wants to rid myself of what I consumed.

I wrap my arm around my mom's waist. "Come on, let's walk. We have lots of time."

Dad stays with our bags, and Mom and I walk down the terminal, with me leading a quick pace, for the next hour. The exercise both calms and energizes me. The food settles itself while we walk, and I don't feel like such a glutton by the time we return to the gate.

Then Owen texts me. *Can't get out of the church thing. Angry face emoji.*

I get it. I text back, *it's OK. Let me know when you're home.*

O: all right

It's almost five when we finally get on the plane. There's no trouble, and the only evidence that this isn't our original flight is that none of us are sitting together. Less than an hour later, we land in Arkansas.

I admire the rolling hills covered in masses of green trees as we meander down from the airport to my house, appreciating the natural beauty with new eyes. Or old eyes, eyes that realize they won't be seeing it again for awhile. Llamas graze in the pastures between Cave Springs and Tontitown. The store fronts are historic and familiar.

This is Arkansas. This has been my home since I was ten years old.

Dad drives up the hill, past the Meacham's long driveway, then around the curve leading to our house with the four pillars and the blue shutters. A plantation-style house, my mom calls it.

Half a dozen cars are parked in the circle drive. One of them is a gray Honda Civic that looks an awful lot like Miles' car.

I've barely seen Miles all summer. For that matter, I've barely seen Harper. I can't fathom why he would be here. I undo my seatbelt while I check out the other cars.

"Why are so many people here?" I say.

"I don't know," Mom says, in a fake airy voice that makes me think she does know.

I get out of the car and climb the porch steps, then push open the front door.

"Surprise!"

CHAPTER THIRTY

Round of Goodbyes

It's the most clichéd thing ever, to yell surprise at someone when they step in. But I am surprised, and I drop my carry-on bag. Gathered around the grand piano in the living room are ten of my school and church friends. I give a delighted shriek and run over to them, happily accepting their embrace. Harper is here with Miles, which explains his car. Along with Farrah and Tyler and Beckham, Nicole, Betsy, Mia, and Monica.

Riley is absent. And Owen, of course.

Mom comes in behind me. "Surprise. This is why I was upset the flight was delayed. More people would've been here."

"Owen wanted to be here," Monica says. "But there's a father/son activity at church and he told Dad he would go. He tried to bail, but my mom said it's important for them to nurture their relationship also."

I'm not sure if I agree, and it must show on my face, because Monica pinches my arm.

"No need to hide your feelings."

I shrug. "I didn't say anything." But she knows how I feel.

"Come over after. You can be at my house when he gets home."

It's a great idea, and my spirits are instantly lighter.

Mom brings out sodas, and I sit around with my closest friends. We relive memories as old as elementary school. I had a crush on Miles in sixth grade and a crush on Tyler in eighth, and we laugh because it looks like I had a crush on everyone at some point. Then we talk about our future plans and the laughter becomes heavier, weighted with expectation because we know everything is about to change.

"How was Europe?" I ask Nicole. "Work wasn't the same without you."

"Better than college is going to be, I'm sure!" she says. She pulls out her phone and shows me pictures, and my wanderlust grows. I want to see the world.

I'm the only one of my high school friends leaving Arkansas. They will still be here, connecting, bonding, and I'll be far away out west.

I made the right decision, but I feel a twist of sadness to leave this behind.

I cry when it's over. I hug each one of them tightly, and Harper promises she'll come see me before I leave on Wednesday.

I don't know when I'll see the others again.

It's after ten before the last person leaves, and then it's just me and Monica.

"Thanks for organizing this," I tell Mom as we help clean up. "I'm going to Monica's house for a bit."

She glances over at Monica. "All right. Be home by one, though. We have a lot to do tomorrow and I can't have you sleeping all day."

That's it. My only admonition.

I love being treated like an adult.

"Come on, I'll drive us," Monica says after I put a new bag liner in the trashcan.

"I'll take my car. That way I can drive myself home."

"And deprive Owen of the chance to do so?" She gives me a stern look.

I laugh. "I guess I didn't think that one through."

"No, you didn't."

Monica wants to know everything about DC, so I tell her in the car, including my date with Logan.

She doesn't judge me. Just listens.

Then she says, "Noah and I broke up."

"You did? Why?"

"I'm going out to school in Utah, and he won't be there. This way we are open to date other people."

I can't say I'm stunned, but is still saddens me. "How are you feeling about it?"

"All right. I really like him, but I didn't feel like I was going to marry him. So this had to happen, or I won't find the person I am going to marry." She keeps her eyes on the road, but her lower lip juts out. "That's not to say I didn't cry."

I pat her thigh. "It's hard."

"It's good to date. That way you know for sure you're getting what you want."

I feel like she's giving me advice, but I'm not ready to take it, so I catalog it away to think about later.

Monica pulls into the long gravel drive leading up to the Blaine's house.

"Wait." I slam my hand down on the dash so suddenly that Monica hits the brakes, and the car skids on the gravel.

"What? What is it?" she cries.

I point out the window at the big white sign in the grass. It's too dark to see the lettering. But I know what it is.

Monica follows my gaze. "Yes. We put the house up for sale a few days ago."

I crash back in my seat and swallow hard past the lump in my throat.

They are really leaving.

Monica doesn't say anything more but begins driving again. My eyes burn as I admire the single-story rambler with the makeshift softball pitch and the field of greens around it. I will miss this place like I will miss my own home.

We go into the house and find Mrs. Blaine in pink pajamas, puttering around the kitchen and wiping down the counters. She's so cute that I giggle. Mrs. Blaine is tiny like I am, and her husband dwarfs her, like Owen does me. I think his parents are adorable.

Her face breaks into a smile. "Hey!" She puts down the washrag and wraps me in a hug. "Oh, we missed you!"

Monica tugs me away. "Come see the new clothes I got for school."

"I got new clothes also," I say, following her to her room.

"Oh, I wish we had time to shop. It would be fun."

I usually do my clothes shopping with my mom. I'm not sure what it's like to do it with girlfriends. Monica and I are four years apart in age, but we share a lot of common interests. I think it might be fun.

"I'm sure we'll get the chance," I say. And I'm positive. My relationship with the Blaines does not end here.

Monica has paraded out three shirts and one dress when we hear the heavy truck tires driving over the gravel outside. We both glance toward the window as headlights flash past.

I plan to wait here, casually sitting on Monica's bed as though his arrival is no big deal.

That plan lasts exactly point-zero-two seconds, until I hear the car door slam shut. And then I'm off the bed, hurrying out of the room and down the hall.

I get to the front door just as it opens. I take a step back, not sure if it will be Owen or Richard or Mr. Blaine.

It's Owen.

His eyes land on me as he steps through, several life jackets slung over one shoulder and a cooler in his hands.

"Hey, you," he says. He drops the cooler in the kitchen, throws the life jackets off, and grabs me in a hug.

His shirt is damp, and he smells like a mixture of sunscreen and sweat, and I breathe in every bit of him.

Richard comes in behind him, shoving fishing poles into Owen's calves and saying, "Get out of the doorway!"

Owen releases me and says, "Chard! I need your help moving the kayaks into the garage."

"You got kayaks?" I ask him.

"They're not ours," he says, turning his golden-green eyes on me. "We're storing them. It was too late to take them back to the church."

"Owen!" Mr. Blaine barks from outside, and Owen backs out the door.

Richard moves around me into the kitchen to get a drink.

"Good see you, Richard," I say.

"Yeah," he says with a grunt.

I go back to Monica's room and distract myself by looking at more clothes while I wait for Owen to return. She knows what I'm doing, so she makes a game out of it by showing me every detail on the new shirt she got.

"Look at the sequin detail right here at the bottom of the flamingo," she says. "Isn't it flashy?"

"Super flashy," I say.

The front door opens, and I hear Owen's voice talking to his dad as they move down the hallway.

I exit Monica's room without so much as a goodbye, and I know she's laughing at me.

Mr. Blaine's eyes land on me when I step into the hallway.

"Hello, Cassandra. It's a little late to be over, isn't it?"

It was almost eleven when we left my house, but otherwise I haven't a clue what time it is. My face warms at the mild rebuke, but Owen says, "She's only here because I missed her goodbye party, thanks to the church thing."

Mr. Blaine grunts. "Leave the bedroom door open and don't stay up too late."

He turns down the hallway for his room. Owen takes my hand and pulls me into his room.

It's put back the way I remember it. The bed up against the wall, the dresser next to the closet door. I sit on Owen's bed and run my fingers over the fraying edges of the cotton squares on the quilt. "How was the activity? Looks like it was fun."

Owen grabs his computer desk chair and straddles it backward, facing me. "It was. You would've liked it."

He doesn't promise to take me someday, or make a comment about how we could go together next time. There will be no more promises between us. My throat tightens, and my heart aches.

"And DC?" he asks. "Was it fun?"

"It was," I say, and I give a wistful smile. "You would've liked it."

He returns the smile, and even though we are in the same room, even though we are together, I feel the distance pulsing between us, ready to take its moment and grow.

"You knew about the surprise party?" I ask.

"Yeah, I got an invite," he drawls. "It seems some people think I'm important to you."

"At the top of the list," I say.

His eyes soften, and he says, "Why are you way over there? I can't reach you."

"The bed doesn't move," I say, laughing. "You're the one who put the chair right there."

Monica appears in the doorway and gives it a tap in case we didn't notice her. "Hate to interrupt, guys," she says, "but your mom said she needed you to home by one, right, Cass?"

I fish my phone from my back pocket, annoyed. "It's only a quarter after twelve."

"Yeah, but I'm already tired," Monica says, as though she rehearsed the line. "I don't feel like driving you home. Owen, do you think you can take her?" Monica yawns and taps her mouth with her hand.

Owen smirks. "I think I got this."

"Great, then, I'm off to bed." She hugs me and then leaves the room.

"Come on." Owen rises from his chair and beckons to me.

"We don't have to go now," I protest. "Home is only ten minutes away."

"We can take the long way."

I like the sound of that. I go to him and take his hand. He tucks it into his pocket and leads me down the hall without a word.

He releases my hand when we get to his truck, and I don't wait for him to open my door. I climb inside and inhale, locking the musty overripe scent into my memory. The engine roars as Owen powers it up and spins out of the gravel driveway.

We don't talk for the first few minutes. I reach over and settle my hand on his thigh.

He glances at it and lets go of the steering wheel long enough to give my fingers a squeeze before grabbing the wheel again. "I thought of you while we were kayaking."

"You did?"

"Yeah. Because you said you want to watch the sunset from a kayak on the lake."

I'd forgotten I told him that. "Did you watch it?"

"I did."

He turns right before we get to the stop sign and pulls into the parking lot of the little white church. He parks the truck, undoes his seatbelt, and leans across the console to kiss me.

I'm totally not expecting it, but it only takes a moment for my brain to catch up with my body, and then I'm undoing my seatbelt and throwing my arms around him and kissing him back with all the feelings I have for him in my heart.

He breaks the kiss off and presses his forehead to mine, and we just breathe. His fingers trace along my collarbone and lift the chain of the necklace he gave me. He holds the charm in his palm and whispers, "I love you."

I hug him tight. I don't answer him because I'm afraid I might cry, and that would feel premature since I'm not leaving for one more day.

I hold him and whisper into his ear, "What color kayak was it?"

He laughs. He releases the necklace and leans back in his seat. "This greenish-blue color. I'm sure your English major brain can come up with a better adjective."

"Teal," I supply. "Turquoise. Maybe even azure, or cobalt."

"Yes. It was all of those."

"Have you signed up for your classes yet?"

"Not yet. My school doesn't start till the middle of September, so class registration isn't open yet."

"Did you decide what you're going to study?"

"Sports medicine, I think. I'll work on my GEs before my mission. After that I'll have a better idea what I want to do."

I run my finger over the seam in his jeans, letting my fingernail catch on each thread. "Make sure and let me know. So we can complain about our classes together."

"I will." Owen weaves his fingers through mine. His hands are so much bigger than mine, my fingers have to stretch.

"Can I come over tomorrow and help you pack?" he asks.

Tomorrow. My last day. *Don't think of it,* I tell myself. *Just enjoy right now like there's no tomorrow.* "Yeah, that would be great."

CHAPTER THIRTY-ONE
First Impressions

I'm up at the crack of dawn. Anxious energy runs through my veins and tightens my stomach. I can't sleep.

Today I pack. Tomorrow I load up my car and drive away for college.

I'm not a kid anymore.

That reality hasn't set in yet.

I eat breakfast and get dressed and then I see a text from Camila.

Camila: Text me when you're awake.

I respond. *Me: awake*

My dad brings several boxes into my room and sets them on the floor. We're quiet because my sister Emily is still sleeping. I drag clothes out of my closet and lay them on my bed and stare at them.

How many of these clothes do I actually want to keep?

I remember my goal to reframe my identity in college. The people here have known me my whole life, which doesn't leave a lot of room for a change. I don't want to be the same girl anymore. I want to be fun, and outgoing, and something besides smart and quiet.

My phone rings, and I answer quickly when I see it's Camila. I step into the bathroom and close the door so I don't wake Emily. "Camila!" I say.

"What's up? Are you excited?"

I shove my hand through my hair. "Yes! I think. Right now I'm a bit frantic. I can't figure out what to pack."

"I know exactly what you mean. How does one pack for college?"

"I'm more than a few hours from home if I forget something."

"Mailboxes exist for that purpose."

I laugh at the idea of my mom trying to find a particular item, then boxing it up and sending it to me. "It's easier to buy new."

The bathroom door opens and Emily comes in. I slip back out, giving her privacy. I turn around and look at my shelf, where my collection of beloved books sits. "How many books are you bringing from home?"

"Books? None!"

Her answer doesn't compute. "None?"

"Cassandra." Camila doesn't try to conceal her laughter. "You're going to college. You're going to have more books than you have time to read. If there's a story you absolutely love, buy the ebook."

"That's not the same as feeling the pages between my fingers," I argue.

"I'm not bringing any."

"I guess my inner book nerd is showing," I say.

She laughs again. "You're just excited. Me too! I can't wait to see you in a few days!"

"I wish you were doing the Honors Week with me." I'm headed up to campus a week before school starts to be a part of the Freshman Honors Week. It sounded like a good way for me to get familiar with campus and the structure before the other students arrive.

Of course, that was when Owen and I were broken up and I wanted to get out of Arkansas as soon as possible. Now I regret the early course.

"There's no way I'm doing the Honors program," Camila says. "But I'll be there a few days after you. The cross country coach wants us there early."

"I'm clinging to that knowledge. I'm anxious about not having someone to talk to."

"You'll be fine. You'll make friends easily."

She doesn't realize how much I hate talking to people.

"Oh hey, I have to go to work, but I almost forgot why I called! Did you see the email with our roommates on it?"

"No! I haven't checked my email."

"Take a look at it. It looks so fun, we're from all over."

"I'll definitely check it out."

"Great! See you soon, lady!"

We hang up, and I check my email. There's one from Preston Y stating "dormitory assignments." I don't know why I'm nervous as I click it open. Camila would have told me if we weren't roommates.

She's listed first. Camila Pianalto. And her address. I inhale and release the air slowly. I've got Camila.

And then there's another, a girl named Layne from California, and the fourth girl, Iris, is from Canada.

It's getting real.

There's a tap on my open bedroom door, and I look up to see Owen.

"Hey." I can't help the fluttering of butterflies in my belly that take off when I see him, the warm elixir that spreads through my veins. I climb over the empty boxes on my floor, and he meets me halfway, wrapping me up in a hug.

We stand that way for a long moment, his heart thumping beneath my cheek. I dig my fingers into the material of his T-shirt, fighting the urge to cry. I don't want to leave him.

"I like what you've done with your clothes," he says.

I pull away and have to laugh as I see my bed covered in my closet. "I'm packing. I don't want to take most of these things with me."

"Just buy new when you get there."

He sounds like Camila. "Bruh! I have to get a job as soon as I'm out there so I can pay for my dorm! Buying a whole new wardrobe is not in the budget."

"Take a few things you really like and add to it bit by bit. That's what I'm doing."

I return to the bed and begin the work of sorting through my clothing with earnest. "Not this." I toss aside a butterfly shirt with sequins that I haven't worn since the eighth grade. "No." I add to it a choir shirt from sophomore year. "No." I throw in a turtleneck sweater that always makes my head look large. "No. No. No." So many clothes I've had since junior high. They're childish and insecure and not who I want to portray in college.

Owen stands with his hands at his hips, watching my discard pile grow. "Well, you're making it easier."

"I think the only clothes I want to bring are the ones I bought in DC."

He steps over the boxes and comes to me by the bed, placing a hand on my hip and pulling us both onto the mattress. "Then bring those. You're in charge now."

I'm in charge. The thought both delights and scares me, and I shudder.

Owen pushes a strand of my hair behind my ear. I think for a moment he's going to kiss me, but then he stands and pushes back the flaps on one of the cardboard boxes. "Think we can fit your clothes in here?"

"I'm sure of it."

We end up needing two boxes for my clothing. I winnowed them down substantially, and we line another box with all of my shoes except the pair on my feet, which I will wear again tomorrow.

When I leave.

I don't pull out my pajamas or the underclothes I keep in my drawers, not with Owen here. It's not that I'm embarrassed around him—maybe a little—but it's more I figure he doesn't need to be reminded of certain, more intimate details.

I sit down cross-legged in front of my bookshelf. "Can't decide what books to bring."

He joins me on the carpet, also sitting cross-legged, and his knee bumps mine. "I wouldn't bring any," he says.

That's what Camila said also. I ignore them both. "I have to bring this one." I pull out a well-worn copy of one of my favorite *Star Wars* novels, and Owen gives a legitimate snort.

"*Star Wars*?" he says, shaking his head. "You're such a nerd."

He wraps his arm around my shoulders as he says this, and there's nothing but affection in his tone. He tugs on me so we fall against the boxes behind us.

"I know." I'll read almost anything I get my hands on. I do have a preference for science fiction and fantasy, though.

Owen releases me and leans forward to pluck a photo album from my bookshelf.

"This is fun," he says, flipping open to a page that highlights my eighth grade year.

I rest my chin on his shoulder and grin. "I look like I'm ten."

He laughs. "Yeah, you do."

"We did this in your room once. With your photo album of your friends from Louisiana." My mind flashes back to that moment over a year ago. "Do you remember?"

He tilts his head, thinking, and then he says, slowly, "I do remember. You came over for something, and we sat on my bed and I showed you pictures from Louisiana." He looks at me, a quizzical furrow to his brows. "You're the only person I showed them to."

"Really?" I pull my knees up into my chest and wrap my fingers around them, pleased to think I was special even then. "What did you think of me, when we first met?"

He leans back, a grin sliding across his face as his eyes lose focus. "Well, the first thing a guy does when he gets somewhere is scope out the girls. And you were cute. And I knew right away I wasn't your type." He meets my eyes now, the grin spreading wider.

I'm not the least bit offended. "That's for sure." Everyone loved to point that out to me when we started dating.

"Remember that time at church when I was rude, and you yelled at me in front of everyone?"

"I didn't yell!" I protest. "I simply reprimanded you."

He shrugs. "Probably. But I was totally shocked. Nobody talked to me that way. I was Owen Blaine, football all-star, king of my high school class and admired in my youth group."

I'm remembering that scene at church, and I'm caught up in his story. "So? Did you decide to totally steer clear of me after that?"

"The opposite. After that I noticed you everywhere. But you did not seem interested in me. You didn't flirt back when I flirted with you. You were just nice. Super super nice."

"And you don't ask out nice girls?" I say, amused.

"Well." He laughs again. "On occasion I do. But you gave off this 'keep your distance' vibe. And the more I talked to you, the more I realized you were dealing with something big. Something hard."

He's referring to those days after Tiago and I broke up, when I fell into a horrible depression and hated myself. My eating disorder was at its worst, my self-confidence blown. My lips press into a line. "Yeah, that was a hard time."

"I knew you needed a friend. So that's what I decided to be. Then I found out about you and Tiago." He doesn't even flinch when he says the name, and I'm impressed. "It all made sense. I told myself to leave you alone. But even though I dated other girls, I felt like I was just waiting for the right moment. And." He shrugs. "Well, you know how the rest went."

I lean forward and place my palm to his cheek, cupping his jaw, and then I press my lips to his, opening my mouth ever so gently against his.

"I think you're perfect, Owen," I say, pulling away. "You knew what I needed.

You waited for me. You let me heal on my time and you forgave me when I didn't know my heart. I think you're the best person in the whole world."

He lets go of the book and pulls me to him, wrapping his arms around me before kissing me again. It's one of the tenderest kisses he's ever given me, not hungry and full of desire, but gentle, loving, his lips caressing mine, speaking to me in a new language, telling me what's in his heart as his arms tighten around me.

Neither of us speaks when the kiss ends. I don't think there are any words they can match the emotions we just expressed to each other. I fear in my heart I will never feel this kind of connection with anyone else again.

"My turn," he says, leaning back, that familiar smirk on his face again. "What did you think of me when you met me?"

I laugh at the memory. "Are you sure you want to know?"

"I'm ready. Hit me with it."

"I didn't like you."

CHAPTER THIRTY-TWO

Unboxing Memories

Owen rolls his eyes. "And I thought you'd tell me something I didn't know. What else?"

"I thought you were an idiot. You seemed like the absolutely stereotypical arrogant jerk football player who thought he ruled the world."

Owen shrugs. "That's exactly how I was and what I thought."

"And I was so irritated that every girl at church seemed to have a crush on you that I was absolutely determined to hate you."

"Hate? Strong word."

I shrug. "Okay, not hate. I don't hate anyone. But I definitely wanted to put you in your place."

"When did you start thinking maybe we could be friends?"

I try to remember when my opinion of him changed. "I'm not sure. You acted different around me. You always sat by me at church, and you stopped making so many jokes and being so loud. It was like you quieted down around me." I pause as a memory jerks to the forefront of my mind.

"I remember. It was the night that everything changed," I say, softly.

He bumps my knee with his. "What? What did you remember?"

I cross my arms on my knees and rest my cheek on my forearm. The memory itself is hard. It's difficult to go back there. Owen only plays a small part in it, but his actions that night changed how I saw him. "I came to church to get my little sister. I was a mess, crying, my whole world falling apart. And you took one look at me and pulled me out into the hall to try to get me to tell you what was wrong. You were so kind, so caring, and in the aftermath of that night, I knew you were my friend. I knew I'd misjudged who you are. After that, we became pretty good friends, I think."

His eyes are steady on my face. "I remember that night. When I saw you crying, every instinct in me wanted to make it better. I hated seeing you hurt."

I tilt my head, studying him. "It was a terrible night, a terrible week. But I think everything happened in the timing that it needed to be."

He nods. "I wouldn't have been ready for you last year. You changed my whole life. I wasn't ready for that."

I make a fist and bounce it on his knee.

"So when did you realize you liked me?" he says, narrowing his eyes at me.

"If I'm perfectly honest, I always had a little bit of interest in you, even when I was with Tiago." I glance at him to gauge his reaction, but he has none. I continue. "When Tiago and I broke up, I almost asked you to prom."

"You did?" He sounds incredulous. "I would have gone with you."

I nod again. "I thought you would. But Riley asked me not to. She had a huge crush on you." I ended up going with Tiago anyway, for my junior prom. It was a wonderful evening, and it's one I wouldn't take back.

"Then you got back together with Tiago," Owen says, proving his thoughts are aligned with mine. "Where did I fit in?"

I shake my head. "You didn't. I didn't think about you that way again. Not until —"

"Until what?"

"There was a Sunday at church where something happened. The way you touched me, the way you looked at me, I felt something different. And Tiago was always jealous of you, and I thought, he saw what I didn't. And from that moment on, I knew I liked you."

"Well, it sure took you a long time to go out with me," he drawls.

I think of last year, how Owen and I went back-and-forth and back-and-forth on if we were together or not before we finally decided to date. I know it was me. I was the one who was not sure because I wasn't over Tiago. "Do you think you were ready? If I had been ready?"

He shrugs. "I'd never liked a girl like you. I was curious what it would be like to date someone so good. I wasn't sure if we would be compatible, you know? Because we're so different. But I figured I wouldn't know if we didn't try it."

I take his hand in mine and weave our fingers together. "I'm so glad you tried it."

We linger in silence for another moment, and then Owen says, "I lied."

I draw back and look at him in surprise. "You lied?"

He meets my gaze. "I kind of knew that dating you would change my life. I had the feeling that once I started to like you, I wouldn't be able to keep myself from falling in love with you. And that scared me."

I remember that also. I remember Owen expressing that to me. I didn't know what it meant at the time. It's incredibly flattering to think this amazing boy knew he would love me. So I snuggle in close to him and whisper, "I love you."

He turns his face and kisses my forehead.

That's how we're sitting when my mom comes in. I don't realize she's entered the room until she clears her throat, and we pull apart. There's a smile around her eyes when she says, "I'm not sure you're getting much packing done."

And . . . she is right on that assessment. We both stand up, the photo album falling to the ground.

"Sorry," Owen says. "We got distracted."

"Yes, you did," mom says. But she's not annoyed, I can tell. If anything, from the sideways glance she gives me, she feels compassion for us.

I can't accept her compassion. Owen was going to come with me to Colorado. Until Tiago happened.

But I can't even blame Tiago. It wasn't his fault. It was all mine.

I turn away from those thoughts and gather up the few books and journals I'm taking with me. "What else do I need?"

Mom shrugs. "Check your packing list."

Good idea. I find it online and realize I need to think like I'm moving, not like I'm going on a trip. "Sheet. Blanket. Pillows. Pots and pans. Towels." Everything. I will be living somewhere else.

My mom bought old kitchen supplies from the local thrift store, and Owen and I sort through them to take out what I want. I figure my roommates will have their own thing, so I grab one big pot and a large frying pan, several cups, plates, two bowls, and utensils.

"I'll have to wash dishes every day," I say.

"Or buy paper plates and throw them away."

"That will get old fast. I'm not camping."

He laughs. "At my apartment, after we all got tired of doing dishes, we went to paper products."

I remember Owen's bachelor pad and its disgusting state. "That's exactly what I'm trying to avoid."

Owen stays for another hour, and I can tell he would stay with me all day, except his mom calls needing him to go pick Richard up from something. He keeps his voice quiet while he talks to her on the phone, but I hear enough to know he's trying to get out of it. When he hangs up, he won't look at me.

"Well, I have to go."

My heart freezes. I feel my throat tighten. Is this it? Is this our goodbye? "Will I see you again?"

"Yeah. Yeah, of course. I'll call you."

He gives me a quick kiss and then he leaves.

I'm going through my evening schedule, wondering where I'll fit in time with Owen, when Monica calls me. I brighten immediately.

"Hey! What's going on?"

"Hey!" she says, just as bright as I am. "So I know it's your last night in Arkansas. I wondered if you could spend the night?"

"Are your parents okay with that?" I ask.

"I didn't ask," Monica says like it doesn't matter. "They're in Kansas City for some conference thing."

My heart skips a beat as the implications set in.

It won't be the first time Owen and I have slept in the same house.

"Absolutely! I would love to." I literally cannot think of a better way to spend my last night.

"All right! What time do you think you'll come by?"

"I'm not sure. I'll let you know."

"All right, I'll wait to hear from you."

It's a good thing I didn't give a time, because my parents want to have a special family dinner tonight.

"You pick the restaurant," my mom says, and she has that odd smile on her face, with her lip trembling slightly, her eyes glassy. "It's your last dinner living in this house."

Everything this week has been my "last." "Chinese buffet?" I suggest.

"We always go there," she says. "Let's pick something nicer. Like a steakhouse."

A steakhouse! "Like the one we ate at for my graduation?" That was the day I quit being a vegetarian.

"Well." Mom laughs. "Maybe not that fancy."

In the end we decide on a chain steakhouse that everyone at church raves about.

Harper calls before we leave, and she invites me to spend the night also. Immediately I feel terribly guilty.

"I'm so sorry," I tell her in my bedroom, surrounded by boxes. "I'm staying at Monica's tonight."

"You mean Owen's?" she says, and she cackles.

I grin. "Yes."

"You ditched me," she says.

But she's not angry. Harper understands this. She's much more patient than I was with her and Miles.

"Guilty," I say. "But we're going out to dinner. Want to come?"

"Name the place and I'll be there."

My conscience is assuaged. And I'm glad I'll see Harper.

"I'll take my own car," I tell Mom as we grab purses and keys. "I'm spending the night with Monica."

She's not fooled by my casual delivery of the news. Her eyes narrow, and she says, "Will Owen be there?"

I shrug. "I didn't ask. I'm going for Monica." It's all truth. But I'm totally counting on Owen being there.

For a moment we stare at each other, and I wonder if we're about to have a battle of wills. I don't want to fight on my last night. Will I have to back down? I'm eighteen. I should be able to sleep where I wish to.

But it doesn't come to that. She gives a small sigh and lets her lips curve upward. "Come home by eight in the morning. We have a long drive tomorrow."

I nod and give her a bright smile. I want to hug her to show my appreciation for her concession. But it might make her cry—and maybe me—so I forebear.

We arrive at the Texas chain restaurant twenty minutes later. Harper is already there, and she gives me the hug I denied my mom, and I feel those tears behind my eyes. I blink hard and swallow them back. She releases me and smiles, and I smile back. She takes me hand and doesn't let go, and any lingering negative feelings from our senior year melt away.

A hostess dressed in black from head to foot with a microphone on her collar seats us.

"Your server will be right with you," she says.

I scan the menu while we wait. The thought of consuming a plate of meat with greasy fries and sugary soda makes my stomach hurt. Instead I decide on the salmon and green beans.

"But there's no meat in that," my dad says.

"Salmon's meat," I say.

He stands his ground. "No real meat."

"There's bacon in my green beans," I point out.

Harper laughs, even if my dad scowls.

A coaster appears under my nose, followed by a glass of water. "Hello, welcome to Longhorn, my name is—"

My head is already turning toward that voice, my heart doing a strange staccato leaping in my chest.

I can't believe I still recognize the way he talks.

"Grayson," I say at the same time he does.

It's Grayson Arend. Waiting on our table.

CHAPTER THIRTY-THREE

Old Lover

Grayson Arend.

The boy who broke my heart in tenth grade.

Grayson stops speaking. His light brown eyes widen as our gazes lock, and I don't hear anything except the thundering of my heartbeat in my ears.

I thought I loved him once. But as I look at his face, golden from the summer sun, his light brown hair sporting blond highlights, I don't feel that.

I do feel the sense of unease from a relationship that ended without closure.

"Cassandra," he says.

I see it click in my mom's head when he says my name. Because he lengthens the vowels, his New Hampshire accent is foreign to our Southerner ears. Cah-ssAHN-drah. Mom shakes her menu and clears her throat, bringing me and Grayson back to the restaurant.

"Drinks and appetizers," she says. "What are we getting, Jim?"

"Oh. I think we're all trying to figure out what's going on," he says, and I groan inwardly. Why is my dad so awkward? "Do we know you, young man?"

"I do," I say, sparing Grayson from having to come up with any kind of explanation. "We were in biology together my sophomore year."

Ha. That's not even half the story.

"It's good to see you," Grayson says. He holds a tablet in his hands to take our orders, but I think he's forgotten it. "I wanted to talk to you but—"

"Drinks," I say. "You're taking our drink order." I smile to take any sting from my words, but whatever he has to say, I'm not sure I want to hear it. And definitely not in front of my family.

Harper makes a strange noise, like a cough and a laugh, and I don't look at her. I'm a ball of anxiety, and I'll either burst into laughter or tears.

"Of course," Grayson says, and he comes to his senses. "What can I get you to drink?"

We place our order, but all I can think is that Grayson is our waiter.

Grayson.

He's back minutes later with our drinks, and he keeps looking at me as he hands them out. I take the time to study him as well. He's not any taller than the last time I saw him a few years ago, but somehow he looks older. His jaw is more square, his cheeks more hollow.

"Do you live here now?" I ask him politely as he places my water in front of me.

"Only for the summer."

I remember then a conversation I had with his stepsister last year. It sparks in my memory, that moment in the school bathroom when she told me Grayson would be here in the summer.

In all honesty, I'd almost forgotten Grayson existed.

"That's right." I lean back in my seat. "Your sister told me."

"You know my sister?"

"Briefly. She recognized me. From my picture." I wonder if he still keeps it in his wallet.

My dad opens his mouth to say something, but my mom puts a hand on his arm, silencing him. I pretend my family is not there.

"Oh. She didn't tell me," Grayson says.

I nod. "It wasn't an important conversation."

I expect that will be it. He was my tenth-grade obsession, but it's over.

"I lost your number when I moved," he says. Apparently we're going to keep this conversation going. "I got a new phone. Or I would have told you."

Yes, I bet you would have, I think, but I keep the snark to myself. "That's all right."

"I'd love the chance to catch up," he says. "I go back to New Hampshire next week, but I'm not working tomorrow night. If you have a moment—"

"Sorry," I interrupt before this gets any more painful. "I actually leave for college tomorrow."

My mom clears her throat. "What do you think if we place our orders, and then the two of you step aside to talk for a minute?"

My face burns, and Grayson straightens.

"Absolutely." His voice changes to friendly and professional. "What can I get for you?"

He takes down our food requests and leaves, and Harper leans over.

"Go stand against that railing and wait for him to come talk to you."

"What if I don't want to talk to him?" I say.

She kicks my foot under the table.

"Have pity on the poor boy," she says, her eyes sparkling. "He clearly regrets losing contact with you."

"Story of my life," I huff, but I stand, placing my napkin in my chair before walking over to the railing. I stand there with my phone in my hand, checking my email and waiting to see what will happen.

Whether because he saw me there or because my parents pointed me out, Grayson comes to a stop in front of me, carrying an empty drink tray.

"I didn't mean to make things weird in front of your family," he says. "But I was afraid you'd leave before I got the chance to talk to you."

Something about his words annoys me. They bring up old wounds and hurts and lost opportunities. "I don't know why it matters to you now. You didn't take the chance when you had it before."

"You're right," he says. "I should have told you before I moved. There were things I wanted to say—after your letter."

I wince. My love-sick letter with its sappy poem. The one his girlfriend read before she let him have it. "Oh, gosh. I'm so embarrassed."

I laugh, and he laughs, and the anger evaporates out of me.

"Don't be embarrassed." He touches my arm. "We had something."

"I was such a little girl." I shift slightly so I'm out of reach. "I'm different now. You're different. But you made me feel something, back then. For a little bit, you made me feel special. Important." Right before he ripped my heart out and left me bleeding out for six months, anyway. "So thanks."

He shrugs. "Maybe we're not so different. What's your phone number? I'll be home for Christmas also. We can catch up when you get back."

Oh, no. I'm not going down this path.

"Grayson, it was good to see you." I put my hand on his to make sure I have his attention. "But I'm about to head off to college. You're going back to New Hampshire. Even if we had the inclination to see what might develop—" I don't mention that I don't— "the timing is terrible. Let's end it here. You made my sophomore year interesting."

He nods. "Of course." His gaze drops, not meeting my eyes.

I take my hand off his and put my phone away. "And can you add some coconut shrimp to my salmon plate?"

He flashes a smile. "Absolutely."

I'm shaking when I return to our table. I sit down and run my hands over my legs, letting out a deep breath. Harper puts a hand on my arm, concern on her face.

"You all right?" she asks.

I give a quick smile and nod. "Yeah. That was . . . awkward. I felt like a little girl again. It made me remember so much."

"Me too," she says. "Like how much he hurt you." She shoots a glare toward the counter, even though Grayson is gone.

"Well." Mom takes a sip of her soda. "I think he's definitely regretting his lost opportunities."

For some reason that makes me giggle. And then I can't stop. I lean on Harper's shoulder, and I'm still laughing when Grayson returns with our food.

❧

I go to Harper's house after dinner before going to Owen's. Monica's, rather. We sit on her bed and die laughing as we rehash the incident with Grayson.

"I guess he knows you're over him." She crashes back into the pillows against her metal bed frame.

"Harper! I don't know what I was thinking when I fell for him." I shake my head, remembering my pathetic fifteen-year-old self. "I never loved him. I just thought I did."

196

"You did love him."

"No. I didn't know love until Tiago."

Harper makes a tsking sound. "You're wrong, babe. It was love. Just the palest shade of it. And Tiago was such a dark color that it made it harder to see what you felt for Grayson. But I was there. I remember how you felt for him."

I consider her words. "Varying degrees of love, huh?"

"Different shades."

My thoughts fly to Owen. If Grayson was pink, and Tiago was red, then what is Owen? He makes what I felt for Tiago pale in comparison to what I feel for him.

"Enough about my pathetic love life," I say. "What about you?"

"You want to talk about my pathetic love life?" she says, and we both laugh.

Harper is anything but pathetic. She might be dating Miles, but she's got crushes on a dozen other guys, several of whom have expressed interest in her. We spend another hour imagining the kissing abilities of these various guys, and I laugh so hard I fear I'll wet my pants. Then we talk about her plans for this year. Harper's done with school. Her plan is to work and earn money so she has a good nest egg when she decides to get married.

"It's probably time for me to go," I say, my mind on my next stop.

Owen's house.

I give her another hug, holding her extra tight. This is goodbye. She's my best friend, but she won't be a part of my every day minutiae, starting tomorrow. "I'm going to miss you so much."

Her grips tightens on me, and she sucks in a breath. I feel her shoulders hitch and keep holding on. If she's crying, I'll cry, and I don't want to do that. So I hang on until she pulls away, wiping her eyes, face composed, looking mostly normal.

"The invite to stay the night still stands," she says. "One last hurrah."

"Well." I glance at my phone and then grin at her. "I could but—I'm staying the night at Owen's."

She sits up, a mischievous glitter in her eyes. "And that's far more enticing than staying here."

"Technically I'm staying with Monica at his parents' house. So nothing untoward is going to happen."

"Untoward?" she repeats. "Do you study the dictionary every morning?"

I'm used to this ribbing. I'm a book addict, and I can't help it if my daily language is peppered with the vocabulary I encounter. I don't bother responding, just give her another hug and kiss her cheek.

"But if something untoward should happen," she giggles, "will you tell me?"

I grin. "Maybe." I can think of many untoward things I would like to happen between Owen and me.

Great. Now I'll spend the twenty-minute drive to his house trying not to think about all the activities we could but won't engage in.

"I'll call you when I get to Colorado," I say, distracted by thoughts of Owen. A flutter of heat ignites in my belly, and I try to cool it. I promised Owen I'd stop trying to seduce him.

"And text me every step along the way." She squeezes me again.

"I will for sure." I scoot out of the embrace and stand up and try to think about something besides how it feels when Owen pulls me against his body.

I'm only partly successful. I sing along to my Italian opera in the car, and since I have to concentrate to remember the words, no other thoughts tumble alongside the music.

But the stirring of desire still simmers under the surface.

It dies a sudden freezing death when I pull up at the Blaine's house and Owen's truck isn't there.

I let out an exhale. I'm here for Monica. It's fine that he's not here.

But as my stomach sinks down into my toes, I know I'm lying to myself. I came here for him.

Where is he?

"Hello!" I say as I enter the house.

"Hi!" Monica comes out of the sunroom in a tank top and loose pajama bottoms. Her hair is up, only a few tendrils falling around her face. She hugs me, dwarfing me with her height. "I can't believe you leave tomorrow!"

"I know." I take my overnight bag to her room and fall across her bed.

"Are you excited?" She flops unto her belly beside me, propping herself up with her elbows.

"Yes and no. I have so many mixed emotions." Mostly because I'm leaving Owen behind.

"Oh, college is so fun, Cassandra! And I'll be at school out west too. We can meet up sometime! How was dinner with your family?"

I picture Grayson's shocked face when he saw me at the table and begin to giggle. "You won't believe what happened." I sit up and face her. "Our waiter was this guy I had a huge crush on in tenth grade."

"Oh no!" She sits up also. "Does he know you crushed on him? What did he say?"

"Oh, he knows. The crushing was mutual. But he got a girlfriend and got over me while I pined away like a love-sick schoolgirl all year."

"And now we know where the term comes from."

"Yes."

"How was it when you saw him now?"

"Honestly?" I shake my head. "I felt nothing. I'm so glad nothing more happened between us."

"Things happen the way they're supposed to."

"Sometimes." I don't think that's always true. I think sometimes we screw up the best-case scenario and have to fall back to plan B.

Like I did with Owen. I screwed up plan A. I don't know if I'll get a second chance.

"Let's watch a movie." Monica stands and leads me back into the sunroom. "There's a new horror flick I want to see."

"I don't do horror," I protest.

"You'll like this one. It's got zombies."

I grin. That's the only horror I can abide.

We settle in to watch, and I text Owen. *Where are you?*

He responds in the middle of a bloody scene where the protag axes open the stomach of a zombie to see if it ate his partner.

O: I'm so sorry. My parents went to some conference in Kansas City and Richard's ride to this stupid football convention fell through. So I had to take him. I didn't know it was going to be three hours away. Angry face emoji.

Me: That's rough. You should get a job like Monica and then they can't ask you.

O: I had a job but my girlfriend QUIT and I don't want to go anymore

I laugh. It's a very inappropriate response to the scene bleeding out on the screen, but Monica takes one look at where my attention is and smiles and shakes her head.

Me: you shouldn't text and drive. When will you be back?

O: not for an hour. Can you still do something?

It will be almost nine when he gets back. But then I realize—he doesn't know where I am.

Me: I'm spending the night at a friend's house

O: you are?

I can hear all his thoughts in those two words. Surprised, because I didn't mention this earlier. Hurt, that I would prefer a friend's company over his. Stunned, that I would make such plans when it's my last night here and our last chance to do something.

Do I clarify? If I don't, he'll spend the next hour stewing in negative emotions, thinking I abandoned him.

If I do, I'll miss the chance to see his face when he finds out I'm spending the night at his house.

I settle for a compromise. *Text me when you're close. I can meet you somewhere.*

O: OK

I turn to Monica as I put my phone away. "I need you to get Owen to come home. He doesn't know I'm here and he wants to meet me in town somewhere. I want to surprise him."

She grins. "I'll think of something."

I remember what he said about their parents being at a conference. "When do your parents get home?"

"Tomorrow morning. Their conference is over tonight, but they're staying up north so they can pick up Richard from his football thing on the way home."

I might not even see them. The thought makes me sad.

"Here we go," Monica says. She speaks out loud as she texts. "Hey, can you swing by the house real quick? I left my wallet in the truck and I need to pick up my medicine before the pharmacy closes." She hits Send and wiggles her eyebrows at me. "He's texting back. 'The pharmacy is closed.'"

She laughs, and I scoot close to read their messages.

M: Not the pharmacy I use. It closes at ten.

There is no response for a long moment. Then Owen says, *You need it tonight???*

"Oh, he doesn't want to go." Monica smirks. "I'm cutting into his precious time with you." There's an evil glint in her eye as she types, *Yes, I need it tonight! I have to take it at the same time every day or the cancer might come back!*

I know she has him with the cancer card. But I also know he's mad when he types back, *FINE*

We fall back on the couch cackling.

"Go move your car." Monica slaps my thigh. "Put it on the other side of the house so he doesn't see."

"All right," I say, grinning.

I drive around the makeshift softball field and park around the back, the fields to my left. Then I hop out and return to the house.

Monica resumes the movie, but my ears are tuned to the driveway outside. Owen's coming here.

CHAPTER THIRTY-FOUR
Broken Resolution

Forty minutes later I hear it. The gravel spitting under his tires as he screeches to a halt outside, going too fast on the loose rocks.

"Come on, come on, come on," Monica says, stopping the movie and bolting for the kitchen.

I follow and settle myself at the kitchen table.

Owen's bellowing before he even gets in the house. "Monica! I've looked all over the truck and can't find your wallet! If it's not even—"

He comes around the wall separating the entryway from the kitchen and stops abruptly when he sees me. He tilts his head as if trying to understand how I fit into what he thought was happening. "You're here?"

"I told you I was staying the night at my friend's house," I say with as much innocence as I can muster. (I had that line planned out already.)

Owen throws his head back and exhales. Then he points at Monica. "You did this on purpose."

"Why do you think I was so desperate to get you back here?" she purrs, twirling a loose strand of hair around her finger.

"Do you even need your wallet?"

"My wallet's safe in my purse. As is my medication."

Owen's shoulders relax and he shakes his head in mock frustration. Then he steps over to me, taking my hand and pulling me up from the table. "Well, since you're here . . . come on. There's something I've been wanting to do with you for a long time."

I'm startled as he leads me from the kitchen, and it's not too surprising that my mind falls instantly back in the gutter. "What?"

"You'll see."

He takes me outside, but I hear Monica yell after us as the door closes, "Keep it clean, guys!"

Owen doesn't bother responding. His truck is still running, the headlights shining over the fields. He tightens his grip on my hand and pulls me toward it.

"Where are we going?" I ask.

"You tell me." He opens the driver's side door and lets go of my hand.

I'm confused. I look at him quizzically, but he doesn't get in. He holds onto the doorframe and gestures toward the seat.

"I don't understand," I say.

"You told me you wanted to drive my truck," he drawls. "This is your chance."

"I said—"

And then I remember. The night I saw Eddie—his girlfriend? His Homecoming date? I never did figure it out—driving his truck. And I remember the tantrum I threw the next day, where I did say something about him never letting me drive his truck.

I can't believe he remembers.

"I was just mad at you, you know."

"Oh, I know."

But he doesn't move from behind his truck door, and I say, "I don't have to drive it." My heart pounds a little faster at the thought of getting behind the wheel of this big truck.

He grins. "Come on. You can do this."

He's not backing down. And then I picture Eddie, his sort-of girlfriend, sitting in this spot and driving down the highway.

I can't let her beat me.

I climb in and close the door. I immediately begin adjusting the seat, sliding it forward and raising it higher.

Owen gets in beside me. "How does it feel?"

I look out the windshield. I'm higher off the ground, and the vehicle is wider than my car, giving me the impression of taking up the entire driveway. I put my hands on the steering wheel. "It's all right."

"Great. Take us for a drive."

I shudder, unnerved. "It's so big. What if I wreck it?"

"You won't. Just keep both hands on the wheel and your eyes on the road."

I take a deep breath, my heart pounding in my throat, and move the car into Drive, making sure my foot is solid on the brake as I do so. I take my foot off the brake and tap the gas, just slightly, and the truck moves forward. I slam down on the brake, stopping the momentum.

"Keep going."

I can't see Owen's face, but I'm certain he's laughing. I put my foot on the gas again and this time push harder.

The truck responds easily, going a little too fast for my taste. I slow down and do a u-ey to get out of the driveway. Rocks kick out from under the tires, and I notice every sound and every bump more than I do when I'm in the passenger seat.

I stop when we get to the road. I feel like I'm taking up two lanes, but I'm afraid to get any closer to the shoulder. I know it's not logical. I've seen this truck from the outside often enough to know it's not that big. Owen is quiet as I ease the truck onto the curvy road, taking each turn with slow precision.

"So if you want to get somewhere before midnight," Owen says conversationally, "you should go faster than twenty miles per hour."

I laugh a little. "Shut up, I'm doing my best."

We come to a straight stretch, and I speed up, liking how it feels to go fast even though I know we're still on a country road.

"You can take it to the highway if you want," Owen says.

I'm tempted. But I don't, because I already know where I'm going, and he probably does too.

I slow down as the headlights flash over the white church. The tires squeal a little when I turn into the parking lot, and I wince. "Oops. I guess I didn't slow down enough." I put the car in Park.

"You did great." He reaches over and turns the ignition off. "Come on."

He opens his door and gets out. I follow suit, and I only have a moment to wonder where we're going before the truck bounces as Owen jumps into the bed. He leans over the side and says to me, "Come up here."

"What do you say?" I tease. I spent most of last year training Owen to stop ordering me around and start asking.

He rolls his eyes, a smile to his lips. "Will you come up here, please?"

"Absolutely." Like I wouldn't anyway. I go around to the tailgate and drop it open. Owen reaches a hand down to help me up.

The bed is full of gear from a recent fishing trip. Owen opens a metal bin and pulls out a thin blanket, then he proceeds to push the fishing poles and boxes to the back of the bed before laying the blanket over the metal ridges. He takes my hand and sits down, pulling me down to the blanket beside him.

The August night is warm, and Owen wraps his arms around me and scoots down on the blanket until he's lying on his back, cradling me against his chest. I feel every ridge of the truck through the fabric, but I don't care. I close my eyes and listen to the steady thumping of his heartbeat, losing myself in the feel of his fingers as they trail through my hair and down my shoulder, down my arm, sometimes down my back, again and again and again.

We don't speak. I could stay here forever, pretending like tomorrow isn't coming and we won't be forced to separate.

"Do you know your constellations?"

Owen's voice startles me, and my eyes fly open. The question is unexpected, and I push up with one arm to look at his face.

"The constellations?" I repeat, in case I heard him wrong.

Half of his lip quirks upward in a smirk. "The stars. In the sky."

I roll my eyes. "I know what constellations are. I'm just surprised you're asking me."

His gaze shifts from my eyes to something over my shoulder. He lifts a hand and points. "That one is Cygnus. It makes a triangle called the Northern Cross. And that one is Draco. It's a little harder to see. That bright star there? It's Vega. Fifth brightest star in the sky."

I fall back on the blanket and look up at the sky, trying to follow the trail his fingers make. It's been a long time since I looked at the stars. Thousands of them blink back at me with varying degrees of brightness. I don't recognize any of them. "I don't know anything about stars. Just the North Star and the Big Dipper."

"Everyone knows those two."

I shrug. "I guess I'm not special, then."

His arm falls around my shoulders and wiggles its way beneath my shoulder blades. His hand cups my hip and pulls me into his side. "Those three stars in a line right there? That's Orion's belt."

"Oh, of course! Orion," I say. "I've heard of him."

"Orion the great hunter."

"Is that how you know all this stuff? Do you actually use this when you're hunting?"

His fingers move beneath the fabric of my waistband, tracing small circles on the flesh of my hip. "Hunters used to. My dad would tell me and Richard stories about them when we were younger. It used to be one of my favorite things, lying under the sky and pointing out constellations with him."

It has a romantic flare to it, the way he describes it. I snuggle in closer. "Tell me more."

He points across my body, over my right shoulder. "That one is Hercules. After the strong hero who saved the world. I'm sure you know him."

"I've heard of him. Is that one your favorite?"

"I like Cassiopeia."

"Why?"

"It's easy to spot, with five bright stars. And it's named after a beautiful Greek queen. So it must represent beauty."

My eyes follow his finger as he points to different stars, but no matter how I try, I can't tell which ones are the important ones. I reach out and weave my fingers through his, pulling his hand from the sky. "I think you're so cute. I never knew you like stars so much." Every time I think I know everything about Owen Blaine, he proves me wrong.

"You are," he says.

I turn my head sideways to look at him. He's still looking up, so I study his face and profile, the square jawline, the straight nose, his full lips. "I am?" I say, perplexed. The statement comes out of nowhere. "I am what?"

"Special."

I blink at him, trying to put his words into context.

He turns his face so we're looking at each other, and he says, "You said you're not special. But you are."

I feel like he made me special because he chose me.

I close the distance between us and kiss him. The arm that is still wrapped around my waist turns me sideways. Then he pivots his hips so he faces me, and we are making out, his arms going around me, and every part of my body that touches his lights up like there are sparklers beneath my skin.

This is our last night together. Maybe ever. I remember what happened when I left Tiago in Brazil. We didn't speak for nine months. And if I'm saying goodbye to Owen tomorrow, I want to remember tonight.

I don't formulate how I want to remember it. I don't think that far. I know I want to create a memory that will last forever.

And not just for me.

Which means I abandon my resolution not to seduce him.

CHAPTER THIRTY-FIVE
Seduction

I sit up and push Owen's shoulder so he falls back on the truck bed. And then I climb on top of him, straddling his hips and letting my legs fall on either side of him.

His features are shaded by the darkness, his eyes glittering beads reflecting the light of the stars. His hands come up to my waist then slide under my shirt, and I don't stop him as they travel farther up.

I wonder if the same thoughts going through my head are going through his.

I lean forward and kiss him, and he kisses me back, his mouth opening against mine, pulling me in, and his hands move up to my shoulders and back down to my waist, and then he pulls me against him, flattening my chest to his.

I break off the kiss to breathe, and he exhales with me. I feel his palms against the skin of my back, fingers on my bare flesh.

What would he do if I took my shirt off?

I can't believe I'm even thinking that.

I can feel how turned on he is, how hard he is beneath me. His hand slides under my bra strap, pressing the space between my shoulder blades. I sit up and make it easier by reaching behind me and under my shirt and undoing my bra.

If he had any questions about my intentions, I have dissolved them.

And in case I haven't, I whisper, "I want to feel you everywhere."

Owen's hands clamp on my shoulder blades and he hugs me close, and then he rolls us so now I am underneath. The thin blanket does little to protect from the metal ridges of the truck bed, but I barely notice before Owen takes my mouth with his again. He pushes my legs apart with his knee and fits himself in the space he made. My body is on fire with need. I arch my back, craning my head back, and his mouth moves from mine to my neck. His body pushes against me with that desperate desire to get close. We are still shielded by clothing, but it doesn't prevent me from feeling. His hand trails up over the top of my shoulder, fingers falling between my bra strap and my skin, pausing on my collarbone before sliding down, down to my bare breast, and his palm closes around it, my nipple hardening under his touch. I don't have a lot of breast tissue, but Owen doesn't seem to care as he squeezes it.

He kisses my collarbone, his breath hot, and I'm yearning to feel his mouth on other parts of me. He presses his lips to the hollow of my neck and sits up, his hand sliding out from under my shirt. He touches something nestled there in the space of my neck.

The necklace he gave me. It's pooled into a puddle of silver chain.

He cups it in his palm and rubs his thumb over the pearl and my heart soars and sinks at the same moment, exhilarated from the passion we shared, from the love I feel, and terrible disappointment because I know, I know that whatever desire he allowed to take hold of him will be over now.

That necklace may as well be a chastity belt.

He doesn't move off me, but he shifts his positioning so we are no longer pressed hip to hip, and one hand comes up, his fingers trailing from my temple down to my jaw.

I watch him, his features barely discernible in the darkness. I'm still hot and breathing hard, my heart rate calming ever so slowly. I'm not sorry, I don't even feel guilty. We didn't go as far as I wanted.

Owen kisses my cheek, then my jaw, and then my mouth, but it's different now. He's got control of himself. He moves off me and sits beside me, then he pulls me into his lap, cradling me. I wrap my arms around my waist and find myself close to tears.

"I would have given you everything," I whisper.

He kisses me, long and slow, his lips moving with mine, his tongue gentle in its probing, and somehow the kiss is full of even more love than the passion-filled kisses of a moment ago. "You already have."

I do cry, because he's right. He has my heart and my soul. What more is there?

He holds me close as I sob into his chest. Neither of us speaks.

Eventually I stop crying and just cling to him. I close my eyes and inhale his scent, the sterile lemon of clean laundry mixed with the slightly tangy masculine odor of deodorant and sweat.

A phone begins ringing in the truck bed, and my eyes snap open. Owen shifts me in his arms and reaches forward, grabbing it.

"It's Monica," he says.

I sit up straight, wiping my fingers under my swollen eyes.

"Hi," he says. "Yeah, we're fine. Just talking."

Ha. Right.

I will never forget the feel of his hand on my breast.

"I know. Well, she's my friend too." He laughs. "Okay." He ends the call and turns to me. "My sister says you came over to spend time with her, not me."

I shrug. "That's the story I told her."

He gives a soft chuckle.

I reach behind me and re-clasp my bra. I feel Owen's eyes on me as I do. I've never been so close to anyone.

He helps me down from the tailgate and releases my hand to close it. "You want to drive?"

I shake my head. It was fun, but I want to remember this truck with Owen behind the wheel.

I start around the truck, and he says, "Hey."

I stop and turn to look at him. He's a few feet from me, on the other side of the truck, but in the darkness I can't make out his face.

"You know I love you, right?"

I smile and resist the urge to run back into his arms. "I know."

He disappears around the truck, and I go to the passenger side and let myself in. Owen gets in also. I grasp my seatbelt to pull it across me, but Owen grabs my forearm and turns me and then he kisses me again, kisses me so fiercely it makes my heart stutter.

"Just because I stopped doesn't mean I don't want you," he whispers.

He releases me and has his hands on the steering wheel, backing away from the parking lot before I've even gotten my seatbelt on.

He takes my hand while we drive. He never does that. Owen's a reckless driver, and he always keeps two hands on the steering wheel so he can maneuver his car with lightning fast speed. But now he drives slower, one hand on mine.

I spend the entire drive replaying our make out session, and my body flushes with heat as I remember his touches, the caress of his hands, his mouth. I'm praying it won't be the last time.

Monica is in the kitchen when we walk into the house. She glances at us over a mug of something steamy, then moves from the counter to the table. "Hi."

"Hi," Owen says. He collapses on the couch, and I follow him.

"Nice drive?" Monica asks.

Owen glances at me, and for some reason my face burns.

"Yeah," I say, and I start laughing. I don't know why. I grab a throw pillow and bury my face in it.

"She okay?" Monica says.

"Yes," Owen says, and he's laughing also. "I let her drive the truck. It was funny." He tugs on the pillow and succeeds in pulling it below my eyes.

"Oh, I remember the first time I drove it. Definitely bigger and more powerful than my car," Monica says.

"Bigger and more powerful," I say, my mind in the gutter. "More than I expected."

I can't stop giggling, and Owen punches my arm.

"Don't pay any attention to her," he says.

Monica lifts both eyebrows. "I think maybe we're talking about different things."

Owen's face flushes a shade of pink, which tickles me. I love when I manage to embarrass him. "She's crazy," he says.

"Well." Monica stands up. "I'll be in my room. I pulled out the trundle for you, Cassandra. Make sure you sleep there. My parents could come home before we wake up."

It's a polite warning to sleep in her room. Or a considerate threat. I lower the pillow and nod, keeping my face somber.

"I will."

The moment she leaves, Owen grabs me and hugs me into his chest. "What is wrong with you?"

I shake my head. I'm not telling him.

He kisses my face, right under my eye, on my cheekbone. "What time do you head out tomorrow?"

"I think as soon as I get home from here. We load up my car and go." I rest my head on his chest.

He squeezes my forearm and runs his fingers along the skin down to my elbow and back again. We are quiet a long, long moment. Ten minutes, twenty, I'm not sure. And then he says, "We should probably talk."

"You don't like the silence?" I say flippantly. But I know what he means. We should talk about what happens next. About expectations and realities for this separation. I sit up and face him, my heart already in my throat. "All right." I try to stay calm. This conversation needs to happen. Tiago and I never had it. And it made for a very lonely, uncertain first semester.

His hand stills on my arm, and he looks toward the kitchen counter. "When you go on dates, I don't want you to tell me about them, okay?"

I'm surprised. I don't know what I expected him to say, but this isn't it. "Who says I'll date?"

He faces me again. "You can't even go on a week-long trip without getting asked out. You're going to date. And you should. But—I hated hearing about your date with that kid in DC. So I don't want to know about them."

I hate this conversation already. "The same goes for you," I whisper, an ache in my throat.

His lip curves upward. "Who says I'll date?" he parrots.

"Ha." I try to laugh, but it hurts too much. So I hold up my fingers. "You didn't think I'd say yes at Homecoming, so you asked Eddie. I turned you down when you asked me to be your girlfriend, so you asked Suzi. We broke up, so you asked Kristin out. Within days. You don't know how to be single, Owen." Every word I say rings with truth. Wounds from last year, scabbed over but not healed, pulse with a dull ache, and I wrap my arms around my torso.

He doesn't take his eyes from my face. "You're right," he says, his voice soft. "Sounds like a bad habit."

I don't answer. He is who he is. And we won't be together. I think about this, my eyes drifting from his and wandering over the kitchen. Then I look back at him. "Should we break up?"

"I don't want to break up. I don't think we have to sever things like that."

"But I won't be your girlfriend," I surmise.

He purses his lips and shakes his head. "No."

"This is ending."

I can tell from the way he narrows his eyes that he doesn't like that. But it's the truth, and after a moment he exhales and says, "This is ending. For now."

I take his hand and lean back onto his shoulder. Neither one of us knows what the future holds. Maybe it will bring us back together.

But in case it's not going to, I'm not leaving Owen's side tonight. I want to treasure every moment we have.

CHAPTER THIRTY-SIX
Final Words

Eventually Owen and I stretch out on the couch and fall asleep, entwined around each other. There's not a lot of room and it's not crazy comfortable, but every time I wake up with an ache in my muscles, I remember where I am, and I lay my head back down and curl myself around him. I don't need sleep anyway.

Owen wakes me when the sun begins bathing the room in soft orange colors. "Go to Monica's room," he says. "Before my parents get home."

I nod and stumble away. My eyes are burning from sleeping in my contacts. I dig through my overnight bag in the bathroom and take the two seconds necessary to pull them out, wincing as my eyes protest. I can't find my glasses in the dark, so I use the wall to guide me to Monica's room.

Morning sunlight filters through her blinds. She is sound asleep face-down on her bed, but she set out a mattress on the ground beside it. I collapse onto it and close my eyes, falling back to sleep as quickly as if waking were part of a dream.

A phone ringing stirs through my subconscious, rousing me like my alarm waking me for Bible study.

My phone.

Monica lifts her face from her pillow. "Your phone is ringing."

"Yes. I realize that." I pick it up and hold it in front of my face.

The first thing I see is that it's my mom calling. The next thing I see is that it's 8:17 in the morning.

"Oh crap!" I say, bolting upright. "I was supposed to be home fifteen minutes ago!"

Monica rolls to her side. "What time did you come to bed?"

"To your room?" I give her a half smile. "About two hours ago."

She laughs softly. "In time to not be caught by my parents."

"Are they home?"

"I heard their car pull in an hour ago."

"Ha." I barely made it. I smile and head to the bathroom.

Monica didn't ask if anything sexual happened between me and Owen. Maybe she knows it didn't. Or maybe she figures it's time to step down as our chaperone.

Owen and I are both adults now.

That fact is both daunting and liberating.

I come out of the bathroom fully dressed and ready to go. Owen's parents are in the kitchen talking while his mom scrambles eggs, and they look over when I step in.

"Cassandra!" Mrs. Blaine says. "When did you get here?"

"I stayed the night with Monica," I say, straight-faced. I sit down in a chair at the kitchen table and pull my shoes on, a weight anchoring itself in my chest.

When I walk out these doors, it's forever.

My mom is already texting me again, reminding me I'm supposed to be home. I stand up, an ache in my throat. "I—I have to go now."

I glance toward the couch where Owen and I slept, but he's not there.

Mrs. Blaine turns off the stove and comes over to hug me. "You're a good girl. Be careful at college but remember to enjoy every moment."

I nod.

Monica comes into the kitchen. She's still in pajamas but has pulled her hair back and looks more awake. She wraps me up in her arms.

"Thank you so much for your friendship. I wouldn't have survived this year without you."

I cling to her, feeling a well of emotions at the top of my neck, the base of my throat, and just behind my eyes. *Do not cry, do not cry*, I tell myself. I'm shaking with the effort to hold it in.

Where is Owen? I pull away from Monica. "I'm going to throw my things in the car, then come back and say goodbye to the boys."

"I don't think Richard slept much last night," Mrs. Blaine warns. "He went straight to bed when we got home."

"I'll ignore him if he's rude." It wouldn't be the first time.

I toss my stuff in the car, my heart beating faster with each step. I feel nauseas. Here we go.

I go to Richard's room first. I've not been in here before, though Richard is more than my boyfriend's brother. He's my friend. I knock on the door and creak it open.

The room is set up like Owen's but in reverse, the bed near the door on the left and the dresser on the far wall, under the windows. Richard is asleep, his back to me. I tiptoe in and sit on the edge of the bed. "Richard. I'm leaving."

He rolls over, his hair mussed, and he actually reaches an arm out to me. I bend and hug him.

"Have fun at college," he says. "Be good."

I laugh. It's almost exactly what his mom said. Then I pull out of the embrace and leave the room.

My heart is hammering so hard in my chest I think I will throw up. Now I have to say goodbye to Owen.

I don't knock on his closed bedroom door but push it open quietly.

Owen is awake. He sits on his bed, leaning against the wall, his leather journal open across his thighs.

In spite of the impending farewell, my curiosity is piqued. Is he writing about me? What is he saying?

He looks up at me. "You're leaving."

I nod, finding myself at a loss of words. Perhaps he and I have already said everything.

He puts the book down and scoots off the bed, then comes to me in the doorway. He wraps both arms around my shoulders, burying my face in his chest. My hands come up to clasp his forearms and I suck in a breath, then another, holding it in to keep from sobbing.

Once upon a time, this wasn't goodbye. Owen was going with me to Colorado. We planned a future together.

Then I ruined it by lying to him. He lost his trust in me, in us, and even though he forgave me, his confidence in a future with me never came back.

And that knowledge absolutely tears me up.

I simply do not have the words to tell him everything he means to me. And how much regret I have.

But I try. "I'm sorry, Owen," I say, and my voice chokes. The sobs break free, and I cry as violently as I did when Beckham's mother died.

"Hey." He pulls back, ducking his head to catch my eyes. "What are you sorry about?"

I shake my head, unable to speak.

He rubs my back, his eyes still on me. "What is it?"

He's worried now. He still doesn't trust me. Gulping in a deep breath, I hold it until I'm a little more under control. "It wasn't supposed to be this way," I say. "We were going to be together in Colorado, and I'm sorry."

He wraps me up in his arms again. He can't deny it. We both know he lost his faith in me, in us, after the Tiago incident. He still loves me, but his heart is not the same.

He gives my shoulders a gentle shake. "Hey. None of that." He uses his finger to lift my chin up and force me to meet his eyes. "We're past that. We're going to college. We'll see each other again. It's all gonna be okay."

I know it is. But I hate this goodbye, and I'm terrible at it.

I stand up on my tiptoes and press a quick kiss to his lips. "I love you," I say.

And there is nothing else I can say, nothing else I want to say. So I turn and I flee his bedroom.

I make a beeline for the front door. I envision myself pushing the door open and making it to my car before I have a total breakdown.

But I don't get there. Mrs. Blaine intercepts me when I fly past the kitchen, and you would think she was the football player the way she hurdles herself at me and gathers me into her arms.

"Love you, Cassandra Jones," she whispers. "You always have a place in my family."

She's never told me she loves me before. "I love you too," I gasp out. I can't stay here ugly crying in the laundry room. I've got to go.

I push away from her and tear out the front door. I get my car going in record time, and my tires spin as I leave the driveway.

Leave the Blaine's house, leave the boy who owns my heart.

I don't stop crying all the way home, though I do manage to get my breathing under control.

No one reacts when they see me. My mom and my sisters are both weepy also.

Not for the same reasons, of course.

⚬⟋⟍ ⚬ ⟋⟍⚬

We load up my car. Box after box, into the trunk, the back seat, the floorboards, and I can't believe it all fits.

"Can I ride with you?" Annette asks.

My little sister is six years younger than me and probably one of my most favorite people in the whole world. I give her a squeeze and say, "Of course."

I turn to my mom as my sister hops into the car. "I'm going to walk through the house one more time." I'll be back to this house. But it'll be different when I return. I will be different.

I start in my bedroom. Emily will have a room to herself now, a luxury I've not had since her birth and doubt I ever will. I'll have a roommate in college, a companion on my mission, and eventually a spouse.

I wander through the kitchen, then walk out onto the deck. I look out over the gently sloping hills of seven acres around our house. I'm not leaving Arkansas because I don't like it. I love it here. I need to find me for a little bit, discover who I am without my family and all the people who have always known me. I want out of their box.

I turn around and go back through the living room and down the stairs to the basement.

There's only one room here I want to say goodbye to.

I enter Tiago's old bedroom and sit at his desk. I look at the spot on the floor where I used to sit and do my homework, and I remember how we would talk and laugh and he would play silly songs on his guitar. A lovely warm feeling fills my chest, and I know he was my first love and I was his. That's something we will share always even if we don't talk now, even if we never speak to each other again.

I can treasure that memory.

I stand up from the desk as my phone chimes with an incoming text. I pick it up and read a message from my mom.

Mom: Owen's here.

That's all it says, but that's all I need. I'm racing out of the room and up the stairs before the words have fully sunk in. He's here? Why did he come here? I fly outside to find Owen standing in the driveway talking to my parents, a small cardboard box in his arms.

"Owen?" I blurt. "What are you doing here?"

He turns away from my parents, those light eyes falling on me, the green more pronounced than the brown under the sunlight. He's thrown on a pair of dark blue jeans and the light blue polo I got him for Valentine's Day, but he hasn't bothered with his hair, which is still poking up on one side from sleeping crooked on the couch.

"Hey," he says. "You left in a hurry. I didn't get to finish my goodbye."

My throat closes. My parents discreetly back away, ushering everyone else into the van, and I step closer to Owen. He still holds the box. I glance at it and back at him. I don't know what to say. I can stall this separation, but it's going to happen. In the next few minutes.

Owen doesn't wait for me to find words. He talks for me. "I couldn't let you leave like that," he says, his tone soft. "I came after you as fast as I could."

"Couldn't let me leave like what?" I ask.

"Sobbing like your heart was broken." He holds the box out to me. "This is for you."

I take it. "Should I open it now?"

He shrugs. "Up to you."

I move back to my car and climb into the driver's side, holding the box in my lap. Owen follows me and leans against the open door as I rip the packing tape off the box. Then I unfold the flaps.

Owen's quilted blanket lies inside.

I gasp. "Owen, you can't give this to me!" It's probably some family heirloom.

His lip quirks upward in a half smile. "It's mine to give to whom I wish."

I laugh, but I'm also choking back tears again. I pull the blanket out and hold it to my face. It smells like late nights in Owen's room, it smells like writing essays on his bed, it smells like stolen kisses with his family around the corner.

It smells like Owen.

It smells like us.

"So you don't forget me," he says, teasing.

"I never would." I can't even tease.

There's something else in the box. An envelope. I pull it out, and Owen says, "Read it later."

I glance up at him and then look back at the paper, realizing what I hold in my hands.

A letter. From Owen.

He's never written me something before.

My heart quickens. I want to read it now.

I will wait.

Owen looks over at the van idling beside us. "Your family is patiently waiting. But we probably shouldn't keep them any more."

I put the box in the back, next to Annette, who I had completely forgotten about until that moment. "Don't touch it," I warn her. Then I climb out of the car and hug Owen. "Thanks for coming after me."

He squeezes me tight, then pulls back to take my face in his hands and kiss me. "Always remember that I love you."

I kiss him again before he can slip away. "And you always remember, Owen Blaine, that I chose you."

Then we're kissing again, only my dad must have decided he'd had enough, because he lays on the horn.

Owen pulls away, taking a step back. "Call me. Text me. The whole way."

"I will," I say.

He steps out away from the driveway and waits for us to leave. I follow my mom's van, and I honk and wave and smile as we go down the street.

Yes, I'm leaving him. But he loves me. And that gives me joy.

Plus, there's a letter in the box behind me that I can't wait to read.

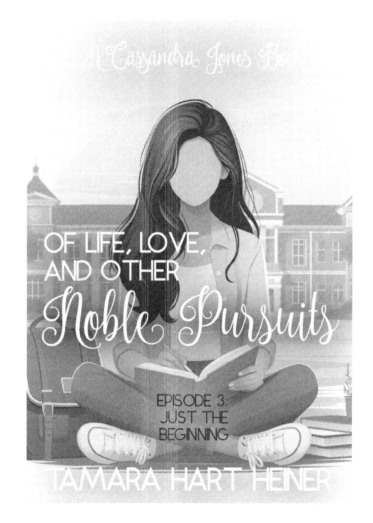

A Cassandra Jones Book

OF LIFE, LOVE,
AND OTHER
Noble Pursuits

EPISODE 3:
JUST THE
BEGINNING

TAMARA HART HEINER

CHAPTER THIRTY-SEVEN

Off to College

The letter sitting in the backseat of my car eats at me for the next four hours.

It's all I can think about as I drive behind my parents across the plains of Kansas as we head out to Colorado. I should be thinking about how I start college in one week. Or thinking about the time I'm going to spend with Camila and her family.

Instead I'm utterly focused on that letter.

Owen wrote me a letter. Something to hold in my hands as I read his words, his thoughts, his feelings. His feelings for me. It's something I can read again and again. Something I can keep and treasure forever.

It fills me with so much joy that I'm not sad anymore, even though I bawled my eyes out when I said goodbye to him and his family this morning. I've always been the one to write the letters and the notes. My soul communicates in writing. And Owen knows this. It's like he knew the one thing that would lift my spirits. He gets me.

I know, in my heart, what Owen feels for me. But sometimes my head gets uncertain. We went through a terrible break up a few months ago, and so many things changed between us after.

He is the person I thought I'd be with forever. The one I'd waited my whole life to find. Now I'm not sure. And I suppose at eighteen, I shouldn't be concerned with that anyway.

I follow my mom's van for the next three hours, me and my little sister Annette. The rest of the family is with my mom. The landscape of Kansas is flat and brown and green, with only wind generators and faded interstate billboards to break up the scenery. I almost ask Annette to open the letter and read it to me, but no. I want to read his words.

Finally, finally, we stop for gas and a bathroom break. While Annette goes to the bathroom and I fuel up my car, I drag the box Owen gave me up front and open it.

I take a moment to lift his quilted blanket to my face and inhale his scent. I think this gift must've been a last-minute decision because he didn't take the time to wash it, and I'm glad. So many warm and intimate memories are wrapped up in this blanket.

But I didn't get out the box to smell his blanket again. Instead, I want the envelope hidden underneath it.

I pull it out and open it, my heart already racing in anticipation.

Several photos and a folded paper flutter to the seat beside me. I pick up the pictures first. There's a toddler—a smiling, toothless toddler waving a fist at the camera.

My heart melts. I know from the eyes that it's Owen, and I love this little boy who grows up to be my Owen.

The next are pictures from his birthday party. Someone caught candid shots of him and me around the bonfire, and then later whispering together by the counter, a soft smile on my face.

I put them back in the envelope and unfold the paper.

Cassandra,

I changed my mind about what I said last night. Rather, I've decided to disagree with you.

This isn't the end.

I know you blame yourself that I'm not going to Colorado. Stop it. I decided to go to school in Louisiana because my family is going to be there and it felt like a good decision. I've spent the past few years breaking away from my parents, and now that I'm feeling closer to them, I want to get those years back. Coupled with the knowledge that you and I are only eighteen and with so much life in front of us, I made the decision to let the separation happen.

It's not because I don't want to be with you.

It's because I don't want to cage you. This is your year to spread your wings and discover everything about yourself without the expectation of everyone around you holding you down. That includes me.

But we are not over. You are a part of my soul, and I believe, I hope, and I expect you will be in my life forever. I hesitate to say that because I don't want that belief to tie you down, but I think it's important you know what I hope happens in my future. In your future too, hopefully.

Being with you has never taken effort. Our relationship has felt natural and easy and like the proper progression of life. That's great, it's amazing, but I don't want that familiarity to become stagnant simply because we're not reaching for anything more.

Know that I will see you again. And when I do, know that I will kiss you. Should you get married before then, warn your husband.

I love you. And I have to go now because my mom is not a fan of me chasing your family down the interstate in my truck if I don't get to your house before you leave.

My heart will always be yours. When our worlds stop spinning separate directions, I will be here to catch you.

Love,
Owen Blaine
P.S. Enjoy the photos. I hear girls get sentimental about these sorts of things.

It's all the words I needed to hear and didn't know I needed to hear. I can't stop crying, but these are not desperate tears of anguish, they are tears of gratitude. Tears of love.

I still blame myself for him not coming to Colorado. His reasoning is sound, but he only changed his mind because we broke up. If I hadn't wounded him so badly, I'm certain he would have chosen me over his family.

But I won't tell him that.

I wrap my palm around the pearl necklace under my shirt.

No matter how far apart we are, he's still here.

❦

It feels like I talk to everyone I know on the twelve-hour drive to Grand Junction, Colorado. I talk to Harper the most.

"I'm sorry I didn't spend the night with you yesterday," I tell her.

"You're sorry because you didn't have a good time with Owen?" she says coyly.

I snort. "Yeah, no. I had a great time." Even now, my chest warms with the memory. Every moment. "But I miss you already. I wish we had more time."

"We will. You had the chance to be with Owen. That's who you should have spent it with, babe."

I get her more now than I did during our senior year. She's my best friend, but Owen is—more.

"How are you guys now?" she asks.

I want to tell her everything. That I slept wrapped around him on the couch, that we made out super heavy in his truck, that he put his hand over my boob—my body grows hot and tingly at the memory. But I *can't*, not with Annette here in the car with me. "We said goodbye," I say.

"Have you talked to him?"

"I called him once. I'll wait till we arrive to call him again. I have nothing new to say and I don't want us to be those people who sit there listening to each other breathe."

That makes her laugh. "When do you get to Camila's house?"

"We are about forty minutes away."

"Video call me when you get there so I can see you both."

"I will. Thanks, Harper."

I do appreciate how supportive she has been these past few weeks. Last year she expressed insecurities about my friendship with Camila, and now that Camila and I are rooming together in college, I can only imagine her insecurity has increased. But she's given no indication of it, which helps me to feel completely at ease with her.

We got over our silly high school dramas also. Because we're not in high school anymore.

I follow the map on my phone to Camila's house. From here we are an hour and a half from Preston Yarborough University, where we both plan to go to school for the next four years. Camila bursts out of the house before I'm even put my car in park. I grin at the sight of her, as tall as me with light brown hair and an athlete's toned, slender build. Camila is a runner, and she's good enough that she got on the team at Preston Y.

She throws her arms around me and squeezes me tight. Something flutters open within me, like I was in a dark closet and someone slit open the door enough to let in a sliver of bright light.

I'm about to embark on an adventure so big it can't be contained within the confines my current mental space. I've been living in that closet my whole life, and now I get to step out and live in the world.

My parents come in with me to Camila's house, a two-story modern build made to resemble a log cabin, with rustic orange and red wood workings to decorate. We all sit as a family in the living room, Camila's family and my family, and the conversation is pleasant. It's my first time to meet her parents and brother. I met Camila at church camp last summer, and then she came out to visit me in Arkansas for a week. Camila's mom, Mrs. Pianalto, offers to feed us, but my mom begs off.

"We stopped for dinner right before we got here," she says. "And it's time to get to our hotel in Vail. We're spending the weekend there."

"But that's back the way you came!" Mrs. Pianalto says. "You have to drive back two hours!"

My mom looks at me, her cheeks flushing. "I wasn't ready to let Cassandra go."

"I hope it was worth the extra four hours of driving," I quip.

My brother, who was in the van with my parents and my other sister, guffaws loudly. "Not."

"It was," Mom says.

Maybe she means it. But this is more of what I'm looking forward to: her letting me go.

I can take a two-hour drive somewhere. By myself. A four-hour drive. Or longer. She won't be able to hover over me anymore.

We stand, and my parents hug me goodbye.

"It's not really goodbye," I say, shrugging out of their clingyness. "I'll see you in three days."

"But then we're taking you to college," Mom says, and her eyes gloss over while her nose turns pink.

I look over to see Camila snickering, and I roll my eyes. At least I know I'm not the only college-bound teen dealing with this right now.

I follow my family out onto the porch and wave goodbye, trying not to look too cheerful.

For the next three days, it's just me and Camila.

CHAPTER THIRTY-EIGHT

Touch and Go

Camila and I stay up late until the early hours of the morning catching up. Even though we connected so fiercely at church camp the summer before, life and different places have pulled us apart. We texted and talked on the phone frequently during our senior years, but there are some experiences you can't convey on the phone.

She sits riveted as I tell her the play-by-play drama of my senior year. The back-and-forth with Owen, the letting Tiago back into my life, the bullying and harassment from Owen's ex-girlfriend, our brutal break up, those terrible months in between, and finally getting back together.

Camila collapses on her bed, clasping her hands to her chest.

"Oh my goodness. Your story could have been the biggest tragedy. But instead it's got the happy ending Romeo and Juliet never got!"

"Well, it's not a perfect ending yet," I say.

Camila spreads her arms wide. "Nobody's dead! That makes it a happy ending right there."

I have to laugh at that.

"And where does Tiago fit in now? Now that Owen knows you talk to him? How are things with him?"

The smile slides from my face. "Well, they're not going so great. With Tiago, I mean. Owen was okay with us talking, but I guess—" I pause. I need to own my actions. "I kind of let Tiago think we were getting back together. I thought maybe we might. Owen and I had broken up, and it looked permanent. But when Owen and I made up and I told Tiago I just wanted to be friends, well, he got pretty upset with me. He quit talking to me completely." I try to say this stoically, but it still hurts that someone who meant so much to me is gone from my life now.

Camila reaches over and takes both of my hands. Her eyes are shiny, and I know she feels my pain. "I'm so sorry. I know what he was to you."

I lower my eyes so her compassion does not make me cry. "In the ideal world,

Tiago and I could be friends. I would have him in my life because he is so important to me, he's so special."

"But we live in the real world. And maybe it's for the best. You see him as a friend, but he still loves you. And deep down, whatever forces made you fall in love with each other in the first place, they still exist. It could happen again."

"I know. It was happening again. Until the moment Owen said he wanted to get back together."

"So we have no doubt which boy you choose."

"Yes, there is no doubt."

We share a smile, and my heart warms again by the strength of my affection for Owen.

By the time we climb into bed around two in the morning, I know all about the boy on the cross country team who Camila dated briefly and then broke up with. She had her own drama story where a few weeks after she broke up with him, she decided she wanted him back. But he'd already moved on.

"It's good, so," she says, turning out the lamp and collapsing into the sheets beside me, "I won't have to be one of those girls at every party going, 'Don't talk to me, I have a boyfriend.'"

My eyes are already closed, but I giggle. "Just once, I want to have reason to use that line."

"Here's a secret," Camila whispers next to me on the mattress. "You don't actually have to have a boyfriend to use the line!"

I'm laughing inside but only manage a soft *hmph* before sleep.

❦

Camila has our day planned out. She takes me for a drive through the national park, full of mesas and red rock buttes. It's breathtaking and beautiful and unlike anything I've ever seen before in my green Arkansas. A freak summer shower blows in, complete with pebbles of hail, and I collect the little ice rocks in my hands.

"Do you not have hail in Arkansas?" she asks me in amusement.

"It's not like this," I say, thinking of the misshapen giant hail balls that fall once a year in the spring time.

She won't let me back in the car with my ice, so we walk around exploring the park. Twenty minutes after it rained, the ice has melted, and the remaining puddles of water have soaked into the ground. I can't believe how dry it is.

"I feel like my lungs have turned into tissue paper and are wilting," I say. "How do you breathe here?"

"Remember how I felt when I got to Arkansas? I don't know how you breathe in the sauna!"

I do remember. But by the time we get home, my face is peeling, and Camila gives me a jar of Vaseline to rub on it.

"Vaseline?" I say, holding the jar and looking at her in disbelief.

"It works better than any facial cream. But I usually put it on at night so my face isn't all shiny."

"Doesn't it get all over your pillow?"

"I sleep on my back."

We're about to go to dinner, so I leave the Vaseline on the counter. I don't want to be shining like a lightbulb underneath the restaurant lights.

She drives us to Red Lobster, where her brother works as a waiter, and I'm nervous because I don't have a lot of money. I scrounged to save for college and made the impromptu decision to buy a plane ticket to Brazil, and now I have to be careful how I spend my money. First thing on my list when I get to college is get a job.

Everything on the menu looks amazing. Shrimp, lobster and salmon, crab and flounder, and all the seafood my heart could desire. And then I see the prices. Yep, no way around it, I'll have to add this one to my credit card.

"Garrett!" Camila jumps up to hug the tall boy with light brown hair the same color as hers as he stops in front of our table, grinning behind a scruff of facial hair.

"I'm so glad you guys came to eat here!" he says. "What can I get for you tonight?"

Camila releases him and returns to her seat, where she studies the menu. "What do you recommend?"

"Tonight I would recommend the flounder with asparagus and pink peppercorn cream sauce. It's divine."

"I want it." Camila closes the menu and grins at him. "Sparkling water also."

Garrett places her order, punching buttons on his tablet. "And for you, Cassandra?"

The flounder dish sounds great. But it's also thirty bucks. "I'll take the Hickory grilled salmon." It's slightly cheaper at twenty-two dollars.

"You've got it. And what to drink?"

"Oh, just water."

He nods and leaves. Camila leans across our table.

"Are you still vegetarian? I picked this place because I know you eat seafood."

"I'm not a vegetarian anymore, but I do still prefer seafood over other proteins."

"If you want to try my flounder, I'll share."

I grin. "That would be great."

"I'm so glad we'll have each other at school," she says. "We can't say we don't know anyone!"

"My cousin Jordan will be there also. He's one of my best friends."

"That's great! Now we know two people."

"I'm nervous about our roommates. I don't make friends with people very easily." At least, that's how I was at home. "Do you think you'll be different in college?"

Camila tilts her head. "Different how?"

I fold over the edges of my napkin. "I don't know. I kind of want to reinvent myself. I've always been the quiet smart girl."

"What's wrong with that?"

I lift one shoulder. "Nothing. But what would it be like to not be? To always be laughing or joking? To be someone who draws other people to them?"

Garrett returns with our drinks, and Camila thanks him.

"You're tired of hiding in the shadows. You want your life to be seen."

I like how she puts that. It's better than saying that I want attention. "Yeah."

"This is your chance to be who you want to be, Cassandra. Do you think you'll change in other ways?"

"I don't know. I suppose there's lots of ways I could change."

"People go crazy. Become sex-addicts and alcoholics." She wiggles both eyebrows at me. "Are you going to go crazy?"

I laugh. "I don't think it's within the realm of possibilities."

Garrett brings our food, and it's better than I expect. Camila cuts into her flounder and takes a bite, then closes her eyes and groans in delight. She points her empty fork at me.

"You never know who you'll be when there's no one telling you what to do."

"No one's been telling me what to do for a long time," I say.

But people have hovered over me. Made their expectations clear.

What will change without those boundaries?

I finish my salmon, which is perfectly cooked but not as good as Camila's flounder. When we pull out our cards to make payment, Garrett waves us off.

"My treat. My little sister is going to college." He beams at her. "Just a small going-away present."

"Ah, come on, Garrett!" Camila stands and hugs him again. "You're so sweet."

"Yes, thank you." I stand and offer him a hug also, even though I barely know him. "I really appreciate it." He has no way of knowing how broke I am and how much paying for my meal means to me.

Owen texts me as we're driving home. *OK to call?*

Oh, shoot. It's been a day. I never called him last night. Things got busy . . . and I'm one of the worst at remembering to contact people.

I glance at Camila. "Do you mind if I take a call from Owen?"

"No, it's fine."

I text back, *go for it.*

The phone rings a moment later with his incoming call, and I pull my knees up in the passenger seat and lean against it, curling up the best I can as I answer.

"Hey," I say.

"Hey yourself," he says back, and I don't realize how much I miss him until he speaks. Something cinched tight in my chest suddenly unravels, and my eyes grow hot. I say the first words that come to my head, not pausing to think.

"Owen. I miss you." It comes out sounding surprised.

He laughs. "I miss you too. Having some fun adventures?"

It's harder on those left behind. I remember that now, how I was still stuck on repeat inside my house when Tiago left, replaying my junior year over and over, while Tiago was already moving on to new adventures and new activities and new people.

I wonder if that's what will happen with me and Owen. I feel like I left a different person behind, not myself, but someone else. My senior year already feels distant.

And for the first time, I think maybe I was too hard on Tiago. We were only sixteen when we fell in love. Neither of us was ready for what was happening.

"Well, today we went up to the national park and got hailed on. Then Camila and I went to dinner. How about you?"

"More boring than your day. We looked at houses in the same city where I grew up."

My stomach clenches at the reminder that his family is moving. "Are you excited?"

"I don't know what I feel. I'm going to college soon. But I can't think about it yet because we have to get through this move."

I click my tongue in the back of my throat. "I hate that your family is moving."

"You're not here. So what does it matter?"

"Because that's my home base. I'll be there on breaks, and you won't be."

He's silent for a moment. Then he says, "Yeah, that part sucks."

We haven't talked about when we will see each other again. There's an understanding that we will, but no definite date.

It makes it hard to grasp.

"Are you excited to see your friends?" I say. "Will any of them be going to school with you?"

"Actually, yes. I don't know if I'll connect with them, though. I'm not the same person I was."

I'm happy he says that. I feel like I'm watching my past replay itself in front of my eyes. The moment Tiago got back to Brazil and was with his old friends, he fell into his old habits. Owen is not Tiago, but I can't shake this fear that the same thing could happen to him if he fell in with his old crowd.

We reach Camila's house. I stay on the phone as I get out of the car, chatting with Owen about going to the national park and our dinner. As we get to Camila's front door, though, I feel the need to get off the phone.

"We're at Camila's house now, so I better go." It feels rude to be chatting on the phone when I am in their presence.

"Yeah, of course. I'll call you later."

We hang up, but a sense of sadness settles around my shoulders.

This is our new relationship. Brief conversations, touch-and-go details about our days.

It's not the same.

CHAPTER THIRTY-NINE
Welcome to PYU

Camila's congregation doesn't meet for church until noon, so the two of us sleep in and have a lazy morning. I enjoy the sermon but feel like an intruder, which is odd, because church has always felt like home. I'm often more comfortable there than at my own house. Several boys surround Camila, talking to her about college, and a few ask about me, but I regard them dispassionately, as if watching a scene play out on television rather than real life. There's no point in engaging with them. They're either in high school or they live here, and I have a boyfriend.

Except I don't.

It's such a weird place to be. This odd limbo where I still feel completely committed to Owen, but . . .

I can't even explain but what.

I still manage to put on a friendly, social face, and I give no indication of my thoughts to Camila. After church we head back to her house, and her mom asks us to set the table for dinner.

I've just finished laying out the porcelain plates when my phone rings over on the counter. I pounce on it, hoping it's Owen, but it's not his special ringtone, and I suspect it's my parents.

It's Tiago.

I can't help but gasp in surprise.

"What?" Camila asks, coming over and peering over my shoulder.

I pull the phone closer to me out of instinct. "It's Tiago. I thought I'd never hear from him again."

She knows the backstory, the importance of this call. "Go in my room and take it. I'll finish with the table." She squeezes my arm above my elbow.

I don't need to be told twice.

I answer the phone as I run up the stairs to her room. "Hello?" I hear the cautious surprise in my voice. I hope it's really him.

You don't forget someone you loved just because you love someone else.

"Cassandra, hey," he says, and I close my eyes in relief, a well of emotion hot behind my eyelids.

It's him.

"Hey, you," I say softly, not wanting him to hear how happy I am to talk to him. I can't let him mistake my joy for something else. "I wasn't sure if I would hear from you again. Not after the way—" I break off. What can I say? Not after the way he told me off last time.

"Yeah, I—I wasn't too sure myself," he says, and he gives a small laugh. "But I couldn't let myself throw away my chance to be in your life. Even if you only want me as a friend."

There's so much hurt in his words, in his tone, and I feel it in my own chest. He was my first love. I was young and idealistic with stars in my eyes and fairytales in my head, and I firmly believed I would marry him.

Of course I would not. It was never even a possibility, but fantasy blurs itself with reality when you're young and in love.

"I'm glad," I say. "Thank you for letting me be your friend."

He pauses. When he speaks again, his voice is clogged with emotion. "Of course. Are you still coming to Brazil?"

"I am," I say with conviction. "I'm very excited about this trip. I've decided to study Portuguese in school." I don't know why, but I want to immerse myself in this culture. My taste of it a few years earlier awakened a desire for more.

"Great. I am excited to see you, to show you around, to help you with your Portuguese. I have something to tell you."

There's again a pause, and my heart beats faster. Is he about to tell me he has a girlfriend? I brace myself. He has a right to have one, and I have no claim over him. I tell myself I'm okay with this development.

"Go on," I say, trying my best to keep levity in my voice. But I find myself flinching.

"I spent a lot of time these past few weeks thinking. Maybe it helped not talking to you. I had time to decide what I want without you being part of it. And I started thinking more about God and his role in my life. The more I explored, the more I knew what I needed to do. So I got baptized."

Whatever I've been expecting, this isn't it. My breath freezes in my lungs, and I hear the pulsing of the blood in my veins behind my ears. "You got baptized?" Tiago got baptized.

There were a lot of things we didn't agree on, but the one that got in the way the most was our view on God. It says a lot about his willingness to change his life if he accepts God's role in it.

But I can't help the tiny worrying voice in the back of my mind whispering that Tiago did this for me.

As if hearing my thoughts, he says, "I did this to improve my life. But you are the one who set me on this path, and I hope it makes you happy."

His words put my fears to rest. "Of course I'm happy. I know this is such a big decision! I'm here for you on this journey, Tiago." I can say this with absoluteness.

"If you have any questions, let me know."

We talk a little bit longer before he says he has to go. He doesn't ask about Owen, and I don't offer anything. It's enough that we're talking. I'm so pleased when we hang up. I clutch my phone and feel the happiness bubbling in my chest.

Camila enters the room and finds me like that, still overflowing with happiness. "Good conversation?" she says.

I nod. "Camila, Tiago got baptized." I can imagine how this will change his life. He'll stop partying and maybe get further education and spend time serving the people around him.

"Wow, that's amazing." Camila sits down cross-legged across from me. "Does this change how you feel for him?"

I jump as if scalded and then scowl at her. "No. He's a dear friend. But that's all he is."

Owen owns my heart, and I'm equal parts hopeful and equal parts fearful that I will never love someone again like I love him.

⚬〜✳〜⚬

My parents show up a few hours later. I hear the car door slam and peek out the window.

"They're here," I say. I'm still reeling from Tiago's phone call.

Camila hugs me tight. "One more week, and I'll be at school with you!"

Her words bring me back to reality. My stomach erupts with butterflies. I'm about to start college. I feel like my whole life has been building for this moment. "I sure wish you were doing the Honors Program with me." I'm doubting myself now, anxious about this week alone knowing nobody.

"I'm not smart enough for that," she says cheerfully. "It's only a few days. I'll be there on Saturday for Freshman Orientation!"

I take a deep breath and gather my things. Time to be a big girl.

My parents are talking with her parents downstairs. My siblings sit on the couch, watching a show.

"Did you guys have a nice time in Denver?" I asked my mom. I'm excited to see my family, but the reunion feels surreal. In two hours they'll drop me off at Preston Y, and I won't see them again until Christmas.

I feel as if I'm at the precipice of a great cliff, my toes curling over the edge. In a moment I will throw myself from the edge and I don't know where I'm going to land. The feeling is both exciting and unnerving.

"It was great. But it didn't feel like a family trip without you," my mom says.

I know she is feeling some of what I feel.

Emily gets in the car with me, and we fill the two-hour drive with chatter. I haven't caught her up on my last conversations with Owen, or the phone call with Tiago. I do so now. She tells me all about the restaurants where they ate and the movies they saw and what else they did in Denver, but her words slide in and out of my mind as I grow more and more nervous. The mountains rise in the distance, sharp and snow-covered at the tips with lush green trees around the base.

We go around another curve and I see the university buildings, the tall bell tower, the pedestrian bridges over the roads. A smaller mountain rises behind it with the white-washed letter P emblazoned across it.

That's my school. No, that's my home. For the next four years at least, this is where I'll be.

A thrill tingles up from the base of my feet all the way to my shoulders, and I am electric with excitement.

My dad knows the campus since he went to school here also, and he leads the way to the dorm where I'll be staying during Honors Week. He parks behind a row of tall buildings. They look like an apartment complex. I park beside him and grab a box of toiletries. My whole family piles out of the cars, and I give everyone one-armed embraces, but my head is tilted toward the apartment, and I'm trying to imagine which room is mine. What will my roommate be like? If I hate her, it's all right, we're only together for one week.

Annette is crying and saying how much she loves me, but this goodbye doesn't feel real, and I want to plunge in. I'm ready to jump off the cliff.

"Love you guys. Drive home safely. I'll see you soon!" I wiggle out of their hugs, anxious to end this goodbye and start the rest of my life.

"Wait, honey." My mom stops me, grabbing my arm, her smile shaky on her face. "I made this for you."

Only then do I notice the binder in her hand. I take it, hesitant, feeling my heart in my throat where a moment ago it lodged safely in my chest.

I put down my box of toiletries to open it.

It's a photo album.

The first page shows pictures of my siblings and me, swimming, eating birthday cake, smiling on the deck of our house. The next page is my friends, graduation, my senior trip to Branson and DC. There's Harper, my house, my cat—and Owen. Lots of pictures of Owen, taken when I didn't notice. Valentine's Day, packing at my house, sitting next to him in church.

My breath catches. I run my fingers over the miniature version of him. I didn't know these pictures existed.

"Thanks, Mom," I whisper. I throw my arms around her and swallow hard because now I am close to tears. Especially when she squeezes super tight in an effort to hide the shaking of her shoulders.

I pull away, my eyes hot, averting my gaze so no one sees the wetness on my face.

My dad's face is void of all feelings, which helps me clear my emotions. I take a deep breath and concentrate on being stoic. Confident.

I follow my dad into the building, where he will check me in. And then I'll be on my own. My fingers curl into the sides of the cardboard box in my hands, and butterflies prance around in my chest.

If only Owen were here.

Missing him hits me in the chest like a rock, forcing me to take a step backward. Seeing his face has brought him to the forefront of my mind. For a moment I let him stay, let the agony of his absence dig into my soul. And then I banish him again. He's not here, and I won't go through every moment of my life aching because he's not beside me.

And yet that's exactly what I feel. I ache to feel his hand curling around my neck and pressing me forward, I ache for his hip to bump mine, I ache to see him turn slightly and give me his smirking half-smile.

For a moment I fall so strongly into the aching that I want to transfer schools and go to Louisiana.

That would be foolish.

A girl not much older than me sits behind a window marked "Registration." I follow my dad to the counter, and she looks up with a smile. Her eyes slide right past him and focus on me.

"Hi! Are you checking in?"

Me. She's talking to me. Not my dad.

Because I'm an adult now, and I'm responsible for myself.

"Yes." I swallow back any nervous filler sounds like I learned to do in my public speaking class. "I'm Cassandra Jones."

She rifles through a plastic bin on her side of the window and produces an envelope with my name written on it. "Everything you need is inside here. There's a key on a lanyard to your dorm room and your schedule for the next six days. There's a welcome ceremony tonight, you won't want to miss it, you'll find the information about it inside. Good luck, and welcome to PYU!"

She is the embodiment of excited energy, and I feed off it, bouncing slightly on the balls of my feet in anticipation.

I can't believe it! I'm in college!

CHAPTER FORTY

Make New Friends

"Want me to help you take things to your room?" my dad asks, but I shake my head. I feel like this new life begins when they leave, and I'm ready for them to be gone.

"I got it." I smile big. "See you at Christmas!"

Dad reaches over and hugs me, and I know I should feel sadness or something that I won't see them for four months, but that doesn't feel real. I can't grasp the fact they won't be in my day-to-day life anymore.

I wave until my dad disappears through the doors, then I take my box and my envelope to the elevator. I fish through the papers and find my room number. Six-thirteen. How many floors are there?

Eight.

I enter the elevator and press the button for my floor. As soon as the door opens on floor six, I'm greeted by the loud cacophony of exuberant voices. I step out as girls dart past me, chasing each other and teasing in the light-hearted, jovial way teenagers do.

None of them look at me as I make my way down the hall to room six-thirteen. The door is open, and I step inside, giving it a once-over as I do.

The room is empty. There are two twin beds, one against each wall. A tall window spanning from my chest to the ceiling faces me. A desk sits behind each bed, between the bed and the window. One of the beds has an open suitcase on it, so I set my box on the other bed. I turn around and see a closet.

"Hi!"

My eyes slide toward the door as a short, heavy-set girl with springy blond curls bounces into the room.

"You must be my roommate," she says, all dimples when she smiles. Southern twang leaks through her words. "I'm Shania. I'm from Texas."

Yep, there it is.

"Cassandra," I say. "From Arkansas. But I lived in Texas when I was younger."

"Oh, yeah?" Her blue eyes widen. "What part?"

"Watauga," I say. "Near Fort Worth."

She nods. "Nice. I live about an hour from there."

After that, the conversation dwindles. I'm disappointed. I guess I was expecting Insta-friendship. But it's only for one week. I head back to the elevator to retrieve my suitcase.

I can't help taking in everything and everyone around me as I walk through the sterile off-white hallway to the exit. A massive living room sits between the elevators and the doors, and already several teenagers lounge around the couches. I know we've all just arrived so nobody knows anyone, but several of the girls hang on the boys, legs dangling across their knees, fingers gliding through their hair.

I try not to gawk because it looks just like high school. But we are in college. Why did I think it would be different?

I go to my car and retrieve my small suitcase as well as a box of books. I feel a little silly as I do so because the box is probably overkill. I won't have time to read anything this week. With some chagrin, I remember Owen laughing at me and saying I wouldn't need books at all.

There it is, thoughts of Owen again.

I rest the box on a hip while I reach for the door to enter the dormitory, but before I can open it, one of boys unravels his legs from the couch and jumps up to get the door for me. He's tall with shaggy brown hair, and he gives me a grin as he plucks my box from my hands.

"I'll carry this for you."

"Oh, that's not—" I begin, but his lanky legs have already moved him to the elevator several strides ahead of me.

He presses the button to summon it and turns to me as we wait. "What's your name?"

I am not used to such forthright attention. I smooth back my hair with one hand, already flustered. "Cassandra. Cassandra Jones."

"Hi. I'm Mason. Where are you from, Cassandra?"

"Arkansas."

"Arkansas! You're the first person I've met from there."

The elevator arrives, saving me from having to make a response. I press the button for number six and Mason peppers me with more questions.

"Did you drive? When did you arrive? You're here for Honors Week, right? What courses are you taking?"

I answer his questions as quickly as possible before we reach my dorm room.

"This is me," I say, coming to stop.

"It was great to meet you."

Shania looks up as I take the box from Mason and place it on my bed with my suitcase.

"You too," I say, and then I stuff my hands in the back pocket of my jeans because I have a feeling Mason would like a hug and that feels awkward.

"I'll see you at the opening ceremonies tonight," Mason says. "I think a bunch of us are getting ice cream after. You should come."

I nod, not moving my hands. "Yeah, thanks."

He backs out with a wave, and I close the door, hearing the click of the lock only moments before Shania pounces.

"Oh geez, he is so cute! Look at you, here for ten minutes and already getting a guy!"

My face is blazing hot. "I didn't get a guy. He was helping me with my things."

"Oh, no, there was more to it than that. And what are you, like, not interested?"

"I literally just got here. I'm not looking for a guy." I begin unpacking my books, studiously avoiding her gaze.

"Wait a minute. I know what this is about!" She shakes her finger at me, and I look up. "Don't tell me you're going to be one of those girls who's all like, 'I have a boyfriend! Don't talk to me, don't flirt with me, I'm taken!'"

She says these words in a silly bimbo voice, and I want to disappear into my bed.

"You do, don't you! I can tell your type."

"I don't have a boyfriend," I say, and I'm not sure why I feel defensive. "But there is a boy I left behind, and I'm not ready to move on."

Her face softens with a mixture of satisfaction and sympathy. "Oh, honey, that's so understandable. I think most of the people here left someone behind! But at least you're not going to ruin your freshman year with the whole, 'I have a boyfriend' routine."

I don't know where her animosity comes from, but I can also understand the feelings behind the criticism.

Owen was wise to leave me freedom to explore this world.

Although I have no idea how to explore it without him.

I go to the window of our dorm and look outside over the parking lot, where my car sits surrounded by dozens of other unknown cars. My mom's van is gone. My family is gone. I am all alone here, and the little spike of emotion that shoots up through my chest feels very similar to fear.

⁂

A few hours later I walk with Shania and several other kids from our dorm to the building at the opposite end of campus. It's built in the Greek renaissance style, with tall columns of white marble. A slab of granite rock set out front proclaims the name of the building. I swear we walked half a mile to get here.

Inside we climb a flight of stairs to a balcony overlooking a stage. I sit down in the corner and pull out a notebook so I can write during the opening ceremony. It's a definite habit of mine.

"Excuse me. Sorry, excuse me."

I look up as a stunning girl with short red hair and big green eyes pushes her way down the row. She smiles, flashing dimples on both sides of her mouth as she asks a guy a few seats over, "Is this seat taken?"

He shakes his head.

She looks so confident and sure of herself. She drops her backpack at her feet and pops into the seat beside him and glances over briefly. Our eyes meet, and she flashes that smile my direction. I can't help but return it, though I feel inexplicably

234

shy. I want to talk to her. But I know from looking at her that I'm not in her league.

A man stands onstage and introduces himself as a professor. He give an intro about why they have the Freshman Honors Week program. All of us are very bright, most of us are on scholarship, and he believes the Honors Program is perfect for us. He's certain we will all feel the same way at the end of this week, and I'm inclined to agree with him as I take notes about the program.

"You'll attend one class for six hours every day," he says. "At the end of the week, you will have earned one college credit." On that note, he dismisses us, telling us there are cookies and punch downstairs.

"Cassandra!" Mason's voice calls out to me as I make my way down the stairs, and I turn his direction. He stands with Shania and several other kids, including the redhead who joined us late.

"Ice cream, right?" he says.

I'm feeling antisocial, and I want to find a reason not to go, but then I see the new girl is looking at me. She offers me a bright smile, and I change my mind. "Sure. Do we have to drive somewhere?"

A slightly huskier boy beside Mason shakes his head. "No, the Creamery is right here on campus."

"Oh." That's lovely.

We head out the door, the other kids chatting amiably with each other while I fall into my own world in my brain space. It's a dangerous place to be but I don't know how to avoid it, and I long to have Owen at my side because he knows how to draw me out.

The pretty redhead is talking to another girl with glasses and light brown hair pulled into a bun at the nape of her neck. They're moving slower than me, so they end up slightly behind me. When the brunette says something about the mountains, I interject with, "Yeah, that mountain pass was quite scary for me to drive through."

Stupid thing to say. Now I feel like a total idiot.

But the redhead looks at me. "You drove here? Where did you drive from?"

"Arkansas," I say.

Her green eyes go wide. "How long of a drive was that?"

"Just over twelve hours. It wasn't so bad."

"My drive was bad," the brunette says. "Nothing but switch-back roads and mountain passes for seven hours."

"Six for me," the redhead says. "I'm Abby, by the way."

"Cassandra." I fight the urge to hold out my hand in a handshake, as it's customary in formal settings at church. "Where are you from, Abby?"

"Colorado."

She flashes her dimples as she smiles at me again, and it's warm and inclusive and makes me want to be close to her. I slow my pace so I fall in on the other side of her. I look across her at the brunette, not wanting her to feel excluded, though in my mind everyone has ceased to exist except me and Abby.

"What was your name?" I ask.

"I'm Liz. I'm from Idaho."

It's amazing to me how people have come here from all over. Only a handful of people are from Colorado.

Abby carries most of the conversation as we walk. We reach the creamery almost fifteen minutes later, and Mason holds the door open to what looks like a miniature grocery store with an ice cream bar along one wall. Liz and I are the last ones in, and Mason falls in behind us, joining us in line.

I am determined not to let my previous food issues plague me in college. I study the ice cream flavors and choose two.

When the girl behind the counter with a hairnet over her black curls turns her attention to me, I say, "One scoop of blueberry swirl and one scoop of maple pecan, please." And then that feels like too much, so I change my mind. Best not to overdo it. "Scratch the blueberry. Just maple pecan."

She puts it in a cone for me without asking if I prefer a cup and rings me up, and I'm pleasantly surprised at how cheap it is. I suppose it makes sense. It's a university creamery, and we are all broke students. I'm glad it's not just me.

I fall into a table with Liz and Abby and several other kids, and Mason joins us. The conversation flows and they're funny, and I forget to be self-conscious or shy and laugh along with them.

"Curfew," someone says at another table, and suddenly everyone is checking their phones and watches.

"Crap, it's almost ten," Mason says. "We have seven minutes to get back to the dorms."

A flurry of activity begins. I wasn't even aware there is a curfew, although I didn't go through the Honors Week welcome packet they gave me earlier. I hadn't realized how late it was, but I'm fine with heading back. I need to call my parents, but I want to call Owen first.

We hustle back to the dorm, splitting into two groups when we arrive because the boys are in a separate dormitory. We're giggling, sweating, faces red and feeling exhilarated with the rush of running.

"What floor are you on?" I ask Abby as she and Liz slide into the elevator with me and Shania.

"We're on floor four," Abby says. "We're roommates. You?"

"Floor six," I say, and I gesture to Shania, sandwiched in the corner of the elevator with several other people between us. "Shania is my roommate."

"That's totally awesome!"

I want to ask her what class she's taking, but the elevator dings on the fourth floor, and she and Liz get off with several other people.

We are in our room right at ten, which is apparently our curfew this week before school officially starts. The RA, or resident assistant, strolls by to make sure everyone is where they're supposed to be. She pokes her head in our room, waves at us, and closes the door as she continues down the hall.

Shania falls into bed with a big yawn. "I'm so tired. My flight was super early this morning."

My phone is already in my hand, Owen's name pulled up. "Do you mind if I make a phone call?" I ask.

"No, go ahead, I'll listen to music." She pulls on some headphones, turns out her light, and buries herself in her blankets.

Still I hesitate to make the phone call. It feels weird to have her here, like she would be intruding on something private. I consider sneaking out to the bathroom, but the communal stalls and showerheads don't exactly encourage privacy.

So I turn the volume down low on my phone and hit call.

CHAPTER FORTY-ONE

Holy Books

Owen answers almost immediately. "Hey. I wondered when I'd hear from you."

His voice is warm, and I can picture his face in my mind.

"It's been very busy." I have to whisper.

"Where are you?" he asks.

"I'm in my dorm. My roommate's trying to sleep, and I don't want to wake her."

"Oh, the joys of a roommate. What's she like?"

I glance over at Shania's sleeping form. I can't say for fear she might overhear me. "She's nice. From Texas."

"Another southern girl. Meet any other cool people?"

I think of Mason and sense that's what he's asking without asking, because he wants to know but he doesn't. "I met this other girl. She's so pretty and so nice. She's the kind of person I wish I was like."

He makes an annoyed sound in the back of his throat. "You are like that."

I shake my head. "I'm that way with you. I want to be that way with everyone else. I want to find that confident self-assuredness so you're not the only one who knows the real me."

"I kind of like my position of honor."

I scoff. "Don't worry, you get to keep it."

"And your class?"

"It starts tomorrow. I'm doing the class on Analyzing Ancient Religious Texts as Literature."

"So it's going to be more Bible study? Haven't had enough of that?"

He's teasing, and I smile. "I don't know what it's going to be like. But I like literature, so I'm intrigued. Anything new on your end?"

"Well, actually . . ."

Owen hesitates, which makes me worry. "What is it? Is it Monica?"

He laughs. "No, but she misses you. She came in here wanting to talk about you and I told her to go away."

"At least someone misses me," I say, but I'm still wondering what he was going to say.

"I wouldn't worry about it, I'm sure my mom misses you too."

I laugh, and if he were here, I would wack him on the thigh. But my laughter makes Shania stir, so I lower my voice again. "What were you going to say?"

He's hesitant again, stalling a few seconds before saying, "We sold the house today."

My stomach clenches. I feel an uncomfortable weight in my chest. I realize a small part of me clung to the hope that they wouldn't move, and as long as the house didn't sell, I could humor that idea.

"That's great," I say, finding my voice. "Did your parents get a good deal?"

"Yeah, really good. The housing market is in their favor right now."

I'm pleased with my ability to talk about this in a level voice. As if it were run of the mill and didn't affect me on a deep emotional level. "When do you move?"

"Well, the semester starts for me in a month. So we're looking at everything in Louisiana, houses to rent, houses to buy, an apartment for me. Depending where my family is, I might live at home."

I like that idea. He's less likely to have random girls popping over if he's at home.

Stop that, Cassandra, I tell myself harshly. What Owen does with his love life now is none of my business. At least, it shouldn't be.

But I feel like it is.

"You there?" he asks.

"Yes," I say. "Taking it all in. I can't believe your family's moving."

"I know."

He falls silent, and I can't think of words to fill the space because my mind is going too fast.

Owen will be gone. I'll go home for Christmas and summer break and Owen won't be there.

When will I see him again? And should I? What if things are so different between us that it's better to remember what we had rather than suffer through a future loss?

"You good?" he says.

I've been quiet too long. A sense of sadness fills my heart.

"I miss you," I say. I didn't intend to say anything deep or emotional. I wanted to keep this conversation light and friendly. But I feel already how the dynamic of our relationship is changing, and I want him to know.

"I miss you too," he says quietly. "I'm glad we didn't waste the last three months we had together."

I close my eyes, actually close to tears, and I picture all the time we spent together in the recent past. "Me too, Owen."

We say a few more words but they are vacant, filler words to lead to the end of the conversation.

When we finally say good night, I don't say I love you. Neither does he.

But I feel the words in my heart and I know he does too and I hope he knows it for me also.

⟳⟳⟳⟳⟳

All of the Honors classes are in the building where we had the welcome ceremony on the other side of campus from the dorms. I'm ready to leave before Shania, since she takes a long shower and I skip it entirely. I take the elevator down to the lobby and begin the fifteen-minute trek toward the Honors building. I run into several other kids from the program as I walk, but I let myself fall back into my normal introverted reverie and keep my distance.

And then I remember that's not who I want to be anymore. *Look up!* I tell myself. *Smile, joke with them. Be that engaged, interesting person.*

I can't seem to find the courage to do so. I tell myself I'll do it when I get into the classroom.

But I don't. The class only has a dozen kids in it. I move myself over to the corner at least two desks from everyone else and pull out my phone, avoiding eye contact with anyone else by scrolling through notifications.

"Oh, hey, Cassandra!"

I look up in surprise that someone would know my name, and it's Abby. Her bright smile fills the room, complete with a dimple on each side of her mouth, and she pops into the desk beside me.

"How are you?" she says, reaching over to squeeze my arm.

I can't believe she's talking to me. I tingle with the knowledge that someone like her notices me. "I'm great." I put my phone away, giving her my attention. "You're in this class?"

Abby nods. "All week."

The teacher steps into the room, a tall, thin, gray-haired gentleman in light gray slacks with a button up shirt. "Hello, students!" he says, walking to the whiteboard at the front of the room. "I'm Professor Walker, and I'm so delighted to lead you in your first experience at PYU.

"The first thing we are going to do is a quick ice-breaker. Let's go around the room. Say your name, where your from, and your favorite animal."

Groans and mumbles fill the classroom, including my own. Professor Walker holds up his hand.

"You better get used to this routine," he says. "A lot of your classes, church groups, and clubs will make you do it."

The names of my classmates barely register. I'm busy rehearsing my own name for when it's my turn. Abby goes before me.

"I'm Abby Lewis, I'm from Colorado Springs, and my favorite animal is the gecko."

Crap. She's so original. And I was trying to choose between a cat and a squirrel.

All eyes are on me. Abby gives me a smile.

"I'm Cassandra Jones," I say. "I'm from Arkansas. And I like—" My mind blanks. Do any animals exist? I can't think of any, so I blurt: "turtles."

Immediately I cringe. Turtles? What's there to like about turtles? Why didn't I say cats, which are by far the animal I most want to cuddle? Even dogs, the most

240

generic favorite animal known to man, would be better than a turtle.

But my turn is over. A boy is introducing himself. My five-minutes of fame is over, and I didn't make a mark at all.

"I like turtles too," Abby says, leaning closer. "I've got a small Japanese turtle with my gecko."

My lips turn upward in a sheepish smile. "I don't know why I said that. I like cats. And squirrels. But I didn't want to say the same thing as everyone else."

Abby laughs, her shoulders bouncing. "Mission accomplished."

"Thank you for your patience while we did introductions," Professor Walker says, redirecting my attention. I shift my weight so I'm facing the front again and not Abby. "Our next task is to select which ancient religious texts we want to study. Now there's a twist to this: each of you must select a different religious text, and this week you will study it for the key points I'm going to teach you in class, and then you will give a report on the text on the last day. It's basically a week-long research assignment."

A girl in the back raises her hand, and Professor Walker nods at her.

"Yes, Devon. Question?"

"Well, I'm a little confused. I assumed we would be studying the Bible."

"And why did you assume that?" Professor Walker asks.

"Well—because the class is on religious texts, and isn't the Bible the only religious text associated with Christianity? And isn't Preston Y a Christian university?"

"I'm really glad you brought that up, Devon," Professor Walker says.

I shoot a glance back at Devon as she speaks, anxious for her. She's brave to ask such a question, and I hold my breath, wondering if she'll be chastised.

Professor Walker says, "If you selected this class thinking it was going to be a spiritual study of theology, you were confused. But that's okay. This class is a critical analysis of theological texts as if they were fiction. That means we can analyze every religious text ever written. That does mean the Bible so many of us hold dear as a sacred text will receive the same critical analysis as texts from other religions. Be prepared, students. The more you learn, the more you will question. But do not make the mistake of assuming secular learning will destroy your faith. With your knowledge comes a greater understanding and a greater ability to be firm in your belief."

He turns back to the blackboard, and I'm left trying to puzzle out his words as if he spoke in a riddle. I feel vaguely threatened by the idea of treating the Bible as if it were no more relevant than some Hindu text or Greek philosopher's writing. But I suppose that says more about my own insecurities than the validity of the religious book.

Professor Walker opens his briefcase and removes a packet of papers. He hands a stack to the boy in the front row and says, "Please take one and pass them back. You know the drill, each one of you take a packet. On the first page, you'll find a list of religious texts. They're all considered sacred by some group. Please pick one and tell me which one you choose so I can write it down."

"Do we all have to choose different ones?" the boy upfront asks.

"Excellent question, Spencer," Professor Walker says, and I am impressed with his memory. He seems to remember all our names now. "That's up to you. I don't care if you do the same text as someone else, but you may want to do a different one so that you are not presenting the same information."

The packets get to me, and I take one off the top of the stack before handing them over to Abby. My eyes scan the list.

Quran.

Vedas.

Torah.

Bhagavad Gita.

Book of Mormon.

Kama Sutra.

I've heard of most of these. The Kama Sutra rings a bell, but I can't think of why. The book is not familiar to me, and I am intrigued by the idea of learning something new. So I circle it with my pen.

CHAPTER FORTY-TWO
The Sensual Arts

"I'll give you a few more minutes. Select your first choice and a back up choice in case someone else takes your first and you want a different one," the professor says.

I study the other books on the list and pick the Apocrypha as a back up. The book, not canon in most Christian denominations, has always interested me.

"All right." Professor Walker opens a notebook. "When I say your name, tell me which book you've chosen."

He goes alphabetically, and my name is fourth down. No one else has picked my first choice, and when he says my name, I announce, "The Kama Sutra."

I expect the book to be unfamiliar to my classmates, but apparently a few have heard of it, because there are whispers around the room. I glance back but the faces are neutral, and I don't know who spoke.

Professor Walker offers no comment. He's already continued down the list names, but I am curious if the whispers regarded this book or if it was coincidental.

"Excellent," he says when we finish. "We'll spend the next hour going over critical theory and analysis, and then we will apply some of what we've learned to the religious text you are most familiar with: the Bible. After that, we break for lunch, but we will not be reconvening after. Take the time to go to the library and check out your book and began to familiarize yourself with it. You have four days to put together a presentation."

We spend the next hour dissecting the Bible. I thought this would be easy, since I've been going to Bible study religiously, no pun intended, since ninth grade.

But Professor Walker doesn't want us to search for spiritual allegories or ways to strengthen our faith. Instead, he wants us to look for literary aspects.

"A lot of it is lost on us in English," he says. "But in the original Hebrew, these verses are full of alliteration. Take, for example, psalms. The language is flowery and poetic and creates beautiful imagery in English, but we miss the repetitive sound of the consonants that the poems in Hebrew have.

"Semitic languages like Hebrew use the same root word to create an entire tree of words. The language only has eighty thousand words as opposed to the six hundred thousand we have in English. So one word in Hebrew might mean five different things, and English translators have to try to figure out which word best fits."

I'm fascinated by this. The idea that what I'm reading in English could have a different meaning in the original language because of word choice enthralls me. I never appreciated my limited knowledge of Spanish, but suddenly I'm eager to begin studying Portuguese and apply my newfound interest.

We break for lunch and head over to the Maiser Center, which is the resident cafeteria. Students on the deluxe meal plan get three meals a day served to them from here. Every meal is an all-you-can-eat buffet, and as I get in line for lunch, I'm glad I don't have this meal plan. My limited plan includes one meal a day, but I'm on the deluxe this week for the Honors class. I ate enough at breakfast that I should skip lunch, but it's here and I don't. Whatever willpower I had two years ago to resist food in front of me is completely gone now.

"What did you think of class?" Abby asks me as she loads her tray up with salad and a baked potato.

"It was interesting. I'm glad you're in there with me. I feel like a book-smart person who knows how to read the words of the Bible, but I'm not street-smart enough to understand what it actually means."

"Weird, isn't it? How we can learn new things from material we've known our whole lives?"

"I wish I had longer than a week. I could spend months studying this kind of stuff."

"Hey!" Abby's face lights up. "Professor Walker teaches this class during the semester. We could take it."

I love the idea, and I love that Abby wants to spend more time with me after this. "Let's do it!"

We walk together to the library after lunch, and we end up talking about our lives back home. She tells me about her brother in Scotland, and I tell her about Owen.

"Wow, he sounds awesome," Abby says. "I can't relate. I always lose interest in a boy after about a week." She smiles, flashing those dimples, and I wonder how many hearts she's broken.

"Not me. Every time I date a guy, I think I'm going to marry him."

"You'll marry one of them someday!"

"In the meantime, I'll break up with every one of them."

"That's how it works!"

We laugh and fall silent when we walk through the double glass doors to the giant atrium at the library. A railing cuts across the floor, and I walk up to it. I can see down four levels. I know five more stories rise above me.

"Good luck in your search," Abby says, giving me a wave as we separate.

I find one of the library computers. I type the title "Kama Sutra" in the search bar, and it directs me to the "special collections" on level three. I write down the number and head to the elevator.

It turns out that I am on level four, and level three is beneath me. The library feels like one giant maze, but I imagine by the end of my time here at the university, I will know it pretty well.

I find the section labeled "special collections" and begin searching the shelves. The room is huge, and it takes me seven minutes to find the correct row.

Except the book isn't there.

I scan from the bottom of the shelf to the top in case the book was filed incorrectly. Then I go to the beginning of the row. Finally I go back to a computer and do a quick search to check the call number.

It's right.

And it says it's not checked out. Should be here.

I'm super confused as I go back and check the shelves one more time.

It's definitely not here.

I see the reference desk with a boy and a girl working behind it, talking quietly as they flip through a Rolodex. I grind my teeth together and brace myself to ask for help. I'm nothing but a stupid freshman. I can't even find a book in the library by myself.

"Hi," I say, stopping at the desk. "I'm trying to find a book for class, and the computer says it's here, but I can't find it."

"What book is it?" the girl asks, turning to her own computer screen.

"The *Kama Sutra*," I say.

The boy looks up at me with sudden interest in his eyes, but the girl doesn't react.

"How do you spell that?" she asks.

I spell it out for her, but I took note of his reaction. There's something up with this book.

"I found it. It's in our locked collection," she says.

I focus on her. "You have a locked collection?"

"Yes. It's this way."

I follow her around the desk and down an aisle to a locked glass cabinet. She unlocks it with a key, fingers a few spines, and pulls a book out.

It doesn't look special. It's a hard cover, wrapped in some kind of red fraying cloth with no title on the spine or the front. It's not very big, maybe the size of the New Testament people sometimes gave out in high school.

"Why is it locked up?" I ask, taking it from her.

She shrugs. "I don't know. Make sure when you're done with it, you bring it back here. Don't turn it in at the front or put it in the book drop."

"Okay," I say slowly, still studying the book. I feel like I just got a book out of the "restricted section" of Hogwarts library.

She checks it out for me right there, which is unusual, I gather, since most books get checked out upfront. I slip the book into my backpack and immediately walk back to my dorm.

I'm dying of curiosity.

Shania is not in our room. I drop my backpack over the side of my bed and pull the book from within. Should I flip it open and start reading? I feel like I should prepare myself, but I have no idea for what.

I flip it open to the first page and scan the Preface. The book is broken into seven parts, beginning with "The Secrets of Love." My brow furrows and I skip to the introduction. It speaks of how the book came to be translated from Sanskrit while writing a book about love.

What kind of love? I'm familiar with brotherly love, charitable love, godly love, all the loves I've learned in church my whole life.

Is this scripture about how to be more loving? I skip ahead, past the table of contents, finally landing on Chapter One. I put together that Kama Sutra literally means Aphorisms on Love—which also means nothing to me. I continue reading, trying to make sense of it, searching for the purpose to this book. I feel like it's right in front of me, and I can't quite grasp it.

And then a sentence hits me over the head.

Sexual intercourse being a thing dependent on man and woman requires the application of proper means by them, and those means are to be learned from the Kama Shastra [or Kama Sutra].

Hold up.

What?

Does that mean what I think it does?

It can't.

I read faster now, scanning texts, piecing together, my heart pounding.

Even young maids should study this Kama Sutra along with its arts and sciences before marriage, and after it they should continue to do so with the consent of their husbands.

It sure sounds like I interpreted correctly.

This is a sex manual.

CHAPTER FORTY-THREE

Provocative Quote

We don't talk about our projects in class the next day. Instead Professor Walker has us analyze a passage of a Jewish text where a rich man invites people of means to a feast and tricks a man of poverty into remaining outside the gates and then asks what the moral is. He nods along as we share our thoughts on the point of the story, and then goes on to tell us how we are completely wrong.

"You are all approaching this story from your Christian, logical, Grecian point-of-view, which is the philosophy we've all been raised with.

"And that," he says, "is why we don't understand the Old Testament."

He then describes the lesson the Jewish writer intended with this fable—and to my mind, it feels selfish, harsh, and unfeeling.

"But you have to stop judging with your emotional brain," he tells us. "Judge with the practical, pragmatic brain. And then you'll see the helpful, caring, and supportive intent of the writer. With that in mind, I'm going to teach you two different critical theories. I want you to analyze the same passage of text and see what different ideas you extrapolate, based on what you're looking for now."

I raise my hand without thinking, and then I speak my thoughts before Professor Walker calls on me. "So you're saying we can make the text say whatever we want it to say?"

He points at me. "That's exactly what I'm saying, Cassandra. We will find whatever moral lesson we are looking for in almost any text."

I sink back in my chair, my heart rate slowing as I realize not only did I ask a question, but I just changed the way I frame the world.

Professor Walker turns his back to us and starts to say something else as he writes on the whiteboard, but another question occurs to me, and I sit up. I say, "So do we even care what the author intended when we analyze a text? Or are we just putting our own spin on it?"

He turns around and beams at me. "That is the question."

He doesn't give me an answer.

Man is divided into three classes, viz. The hare man, the bull man, and the horse man, according to the size of his lingam.

Woman also, according to the depth of her yoni, is either a female deer, a mare, or a female elephant.

I put the Kama Sutra face-down on my bed and fight the urge to laugh maniacally.

I'm in chapter one. The chapter is titled "Kinds of Sexual Union." The only way I can handle the subject matter is by giggling through it. A lingam? A yoni? I can imagine how Owen will laugh when I share these terms with him.

Except I can't do that. Thinking about him in this sexual context makes me hot with desire. Talking about it would make it unbearable.

I look at the presentation I'm building on my computer. I have to give this presentation tomorrow, and I'm not sure how to do so and keep it clean. I framed my presentation as if this book were a work of fiction. While the book has information on life and caste systems and how to decorate, that's only ten percent of it. The rest of it is on the art of pleasuring a man—and only the man, because the author and his contemporaries spend a good deal of time debating if a woman feels pleasure, and if she does, how? It's fascinating to see them trying to understand how the female body works. It's not a holy book, but it is a guide for life. It's fascinating but not spiritual.

I work on the historical context of the book. That part is easy. I talk about Vatsyayana, who created the ideas behind the Kama Sutra, though the book itself was compiled by an unknown editor after the British conquest, when the Brits found the lifestyle and methodology of the natives—shall we say, *compelling*—and wanted to know more. Thus it's not written for those already familiar with Kama Sutra and practicing that life, but foreigners who want to understand it better. As for the modern application—I'm tempted to skip that question.

At least I have the room mostly to myself. It shouldn't surprise me that Shania is something of a partier, and she's out every evening right up until curfew. I'm a bit amused and mildly worried. She and I have little in common and haven't connected. Next week I'll move into my dorm for the year and meet my permanent roommates. What if I get a wild one like Shania? Or worse?

I drag a hand through my hair and stare at my presentation. My phone chimes with an incoming text. I ignored the last one, determined to get through this paper.

But the temptation is too much. I check my phone, giving into the distraction.

There are two texts from Owen and one from Monica. My heart skips a beat, and I gladly put aside my computer. I know I should save the best for last, but I check Owen's messages first.

O: parents found a house

O: I got an apartment. We all head down next week.

And my skipping heart tumbles straight to my toes. They're leaving Arkansas. Not only that, but Owen will be living alone. Without the supervision of his parents.

I hate to think about the people he will surround himself with. The girls he will be with. He's never been good at being single. I don't expect him to be any better at it this time, and I hate it.

I know it's possible to fall in love with someone while still loving someone else.

I swallow past a painful lump in my throat and check the next text message. This one's from Monica.

M: we found a house and my parents won't stop fighting! Girl, where are you?

I tap the button to call her back.

"Hey!" Monica says, answering right away. "Long time no hear!"

I laugh, thrilled to hear her voice. "Yes. You guys have a house, huh?"

Monica makes a snoring sound. "Not that it matters to me. I can't wait to get out of here. My parents have been fighting nonstop since the house sold. And sometimes they drag me into it. Too much pressure!"

In spite of her obvious annoyance, she sounds happy. Chipper.

"How's the cancer going?" I can't pretend it's not on my mind. It always is.

"It looks like I'm in complete remission. I have an appointment with an oncologist as soon as I get out to Utah. They will keep monitoring me. But I'm doing great!"

She sounds genuine. I don't think she would say that just to make me feel better.

"And how's Owen?" I ask, because I want to know from someone other than him.

"He misses you. He's out a lot with his friends. I don't think he knows what else to do. He doesn't like to talk about you, though. I think it makes him miss you more."

I squeeze my eyes shut. We said we wouldn't talk about this. We agreed it was better not to know. So I shouldn't ask.

But I'm desperate.

"Is he seeing other girls?" I squeak out. I immediately feel guilty for asking. I'm not supposed to. And I should trust Owen a little more. I've been gone a week.

Although, past experience says it takes him about day.

"I don't think he's seeing anyone," Monica says, slowly, thoughtfully. "He wants to be with you."

And sometimes, when you want to be with someone and can't, you pick someone else to fill that space because it hurts too much to be alone.

I should know. That's how Owen and I fell in love.

"Uh-huh," I say, pretending like her words have eased my concerns.

"How has the first week been?" Monica asks. "Lots of school work?"

"I only have one class right now, so it's not so bad. I have a presentation tomorrow, though, so I'm trying to finish that up. I took a break to respond to text messages."

"Oh really? What's your presentation on?"

"The Kama Sutra," I say, wondering if she'll know what it is. So far this week, my experience has shown me that most girls don't, and a lot of boys do.

"The Kama Sutra? I've heard of it. What's it about?"

I grin. "It's a sex manual."

"What?" she screeches.

I spend the next ten minutes reading passages to her over the phone and listening to her bust up. My face flashes hot when I read the words out loud. Monica can barely breathe between laughter.

"Are you going to share that passage in your presentation?" she teases.

"I haven't even read you the worst ones."

"Read them!"

I laugh, shaking my head. "No way."

"You have to start your presentation with one of those."

"I can't!" My face burns as I imagine uttering those words to an audience.

"Cassandra, you have to! It'll be the perfect way to get their attention."

"Yeah, that it will." But I won't do it.

"Have you shared any of this with Owen?" she says mischievously.

Her words thrust Owen into the sexy narrative the book creates in my mind. Suddenly I'm all hot and bothered and have to get up and walk around the room. "I don't think that would be very productive. For either of us."

"Yeah, maybe not. Especially while you're apart. But it could be fun."

"You're supposed to be a good influence!" I exclaim.

"I'm not worried when he's in Arkansas and you're in Colorado. There's not much you guys can do besides sexting. Or do you guys do that?"

"No," I say. "I don't see what good it would do." I already want to have sex with him. Creating that kind of dialogue wouldn't ease my desires and might make me more frustrated.

"Yeah," she says. "You're right. Well, I'm going to let you get back to your little presentation. I look forward to hearing how it goes."

"I'm not going to tell you."

"I guess I'll have to get my own copy of that book."

I'm still laughing when we hang up.

And she's right. I should start with a provocative quote.

CHAPTER FORTY-FOUR

Definitely a Four

F riday morning, Professor Walker has us meet in the dorm parking lot before we begin the twenty-minute walk to his house for our presentations. I walk beside Abby, feeling frumpy in my jeans while her floral print skirt flutters around her thighs. Everything about her is feminine and delicate. I decide I want a skirt also.

Professor Walker's neighborhood is behind the football stadium. The houses look several decades old, with the seventies multi-level style of the second story jutting out above the main level. Professor Walker leads us to the front porch of a white house with tan shutters, where he serves us a brunch provided by his wife, and then we start the presentations.

I'm so intrigued by what I learn about the scriptures from various religions that I consider switching my major to theology.

Then it's my turn. I take my laptop over to the projector and connect the audiovisual cord. My heart pounds at the base of my neck, and my hand trembles as I click the first slide. It magnifies into a glowing square on the opposing wall.

"My presentation is on . . ." I draw out the title, partly to create suspense and partly because I am embarrassed by this book. I click the next slide. "The *Kama Sutra.*"

A few of the boys at the back of the room smirk at each other, but everyone else looks at me with only polite, vague interest.

I am about to change that.

I click the next slide, and my carefully chosen phrase fills the screen.

To understand the subject thoroughly, it is absolutely necessary to study it, and then a person will know that, as dough is prepared for baking, so must a woman be prepared for sexual intercourse, if she is to derive satisfaction from it.

I don't read it aloud. I wait as their eyes scan the line and gauge their reactions. I can tell when they grasp the meaning. Some eyes widen, other people gasp, a few giggle, and some do all of the above. I glance at my professor, worried I may have crossed a line, but he has his arms folded over his chest and an undeniable smirk on his lips.

"The *Kama Sutra*," I say, adopting my presentation voice, "is a scripture on the holiness of sexual intimacy." My whole face burns saying those words out loud. I feel sweat beading along my hairline but I ignore it and plow onward with confidence I don't feel. "Similar to views in the New Testament, it teaches that sexual intimacy is a holy ceremony. But the authors of the book do take a more open view of the act and its participants." I'm trying hard to act cool and collected, but I wouldn't be surprised if my embarrassment shows right through my dark skin tone.

All eyes are riveted to me like lasers burrowing into my brain. I have everyone's attention.

I clear my throat and keep going, letting the slides be my guide as I perform a literary analysis of the literature, especially pointing out where the narrator becomes a character and inserts his personal opinion.

I do not share the text where this happened. I'm not going to talk about his assessment of the tightness of a vagina on a penis. I know I would trip over the words and make my classmates think I have the sexual maturity of an eighth-grader.

I'm so very flustered when I finish that my hands shake as I unplug the cable and take my computer back to my seat on the couch. But Professor Walker claps and beams at me.

"You tackled a very challenging text, and one that is considered taboo by many in our circles. I am proud of you for stepping outside your comfort zone."

His attention turns off me as he calls the next student, and my time in the spotlight ends. I exhale quietly.

Abby pinches my arm and leans in close. "It won't be the last time. I'm getting you out of your comfort zone also."

I nod and keep my eyes on the presenter. Sometimes she scares me.

But a tiny part of me feels the slightest glimmer of excitement at what getting out of my comfort zone might look like.

⚘

The rest of the presentations go off without a hitch, though none of the others were as interesting as mine was. Professor Walker congratulates us on completing our first college credit and announces all of us earned an A. Then he dismisses us.

"That was amazing!" Abby says as we gather our books and leave his house. "I'm so glad we took that class. What are your plans for the rest of the day?"

I pull a rumpled sheet of paper from my bag. "I'm going to the bookstore to get books for my classes."

"Smart! Can't you get most of your texts in ebook?"

I nod. "Yes, but not for my major classes. I'm an English major, so most of them are still in hard form. That way I can annotate." I'm an avid reader, and I appreciate the value of ebooks. But I can't find my spot flipping back-and-forth through an ebook the way I can paperback or hardcover.

"That makes sense. Well, I'll come with you."

She hooks her arm through mine, and I hide my delight at having this instant-friend at my side. Any fears or misgivings I had about being alone in college have completely dissipated in this first week.

We talk the whole way back to campus, with Abby evaluating each boy in our class on a five-point system. She insists on knowing my opinion. It's hard to give one.

"I don't know," I say to the second boy she mentions.

She elbows me hard enough in the ribs that it hurts. "Come on. I know you're still hung up on what's-his-face that you left behind in Arkansas, but it doesn't mean you can't tell when a boy is cute."

She's absolutely right, but it makes me feel guilty to notice, or at least acknowledge I noticed.

"Just a number," Abby says. "I'm not asking you to date him. Toby."

I give in. "Three."

"Only a three!" She turns to stare at me. "What are you expecting, a Disney prince? How can you resist Toby's dark curls and his blue eyes!"

I shrug. "Not my type, I guess."

"Oh, I'm going to keep going until I find your type."

From there she insists on pointing out every boy we pass and making me rate him.

"He's a four and a half," I say, and that's the highest she gets from me.

"You rate him a four and a half? What was it that you liked about him?"

I can't picture him now that he's walked past us. "I don't know. Something about his face. The expression in his eyes."

"So it wasn't his hair color, or how tall he was?"

I shake my head. "I can't even remember."

"Do you find boys attractive?"

"Yes." I say it with enough indignation that she laughs.

We arrive on campus and cross the quad to a one-story building that houses a cafeteria on the first floor, classrooms on the second, the bookstore on the third, and a fine dining restaurant on the fourth. Like most buildings on campus, it was recently remodeled with cutting age technology and design. We take the elevator to the fourth floor and find it packed with students.

I'm immediately unnerved. So many people in one place. Abby consults my book list.

"Hey!" she says. "We have physical science together."

"Really?" I check my schedule to make sure it's on there.

"Yes. We can study together!"

"That would be great!"

We begin the tedious process of going down row after row of books, finding the required texts for each class.

"They are so expensive!" I say, dropping another two-hundred dollar book into my basket.

"Try to find them used." Abby holds up a book with a yellow sticker across the side that says "used." "They're a lot cheaper."

"A lot" is an exaggeration. I find the book I need for thirty dollars cheaper, so it's one-seventy instead of two-hundred.

Good thing I've been saving my money working two jobs all summer.

She points at a boy coming toward us in the row. He's a few inches taller than me, with golden skin and clear green eyes. He's oblivious to us, his eyes turning from the paper in his hand to the stacks of books, and Abby whispers as he passes, "Rating?"

"Definitely a four," I have to admit.

"We can work with that."

It's like she opened my eyes. I feel mercenary as we step into line and I cast my eyes over every male around me, mentally assigning a number to them. Three. Two. Four. Two. One.

Four point seven is tall with a darker skin tone, darker than mine, and a crop of short curly hair. My eyes linger on his narrow figure, the firm shoulder blades. It's my turn to pay, and I turn away only so the cashier doesn't catch me staring.

"Six-hundred and thirty-six dollars," the girl says, and my mouth drops open. I hand over my credit card, regretting my foolish decision that put a thousand-dollar plane ticket on it.

Abby joins me when I finish paying, and she starts our game again as we walk out. "What about him?"

She points at the hot guy, and I feel a predatory hunger, followed by a sinking stone of guilt in my chest. I shake my head. "I don't want to play anymore."

She catches onto something in my tone and peers at me. "Why?"

"It makes me . . . feel bad."

"Why?"

For some reason I don't want to mention Owen, and I know he's the root of my guilt.

She reads it on my face. "Because of your boy?"

I try to explain. "We're not together. We said we could date other people."

She hooks her arm through mine and squeezes my wrist. "Try telling that to your heart. Look, you're not betraying him by looking at other guys. You're not even doing anything."

"I feel like I am," I admit.

"You're not married. Give yourself permission to enjoy being in college."

She's right. I'm not doing anything wrong. I need to relax. I exhale.

It's going to take some work.

CHAPTER FORTY-FIVE

First of Many

I spend Saturday moving into my dorm for the school year. Shania's gone before I get the chance to say goodbye, but it's okay, we didn't connect. I only have one box to take down from Honors Week, but my car is loaded with things I brought from home. I drive over to the apartment-style dorms. I'll be the only one here for three days, since most students don't arrive until next week. I park my car and look up at the three-story apartment with a surreal feeling.

This is my home. I don't live with my family anymore.

It's uncanny.

I use the key I picked up at the Student Office and let myself in the front entrance. The first thing I see is a common living area. There are four apartments on each floor. I take the stairs to the second floor and open the apartment on the right. Number 208.

Mine.

Ours, I correct myself. There are two bedrooms. Four of us to an apartment. Two people to a room.

I guess I get to pick mine, since I'm the first one here.

I choose the bedroom farthest to the back and put my box on the bed next to the window. Then I explore the apartment. The other bedroom is identical to mine, with two twin beds, a closet at the foot of the bed, white-washed cinderblock walls and a large window. Shelves line the wall above the bed.

I wander out of the bedrooms and into the bathroom. There's a toilet with a shower curtain for privacy and another around the shower beside it and two sinks. Nothing special, but it will work.

I continue down the hall and into the tiny kitchen. A table for four pushes up against more cinderblock walls next to a refrigerator, a sink, and a stove with an oven. A small dishwasher is wedged between the fridge and stove. A door next to the table leads to an outside stairwell. I poke my head outside and see my car in the parking lot below.

I exit my apartment and go to the common area between the apartments. There's one on each floor. I wander the three flights, checking for people on every floor. It's quiet. No students mingle on the couches, the TVs are off. It is not like the common room on the first floor of the tower dorms where I stayed for Honors Week. I head downstairs to the basement and find a laundry room and another living room.

And that's it. I've seen the entire apartment now.

Still quiet. The dorms are only for freshman, and I'm here early.

A loneliness settles around my shoulders, making them heavy. I don't want to be alone.

I return to my car and finish unpacking, then I settle about organizing my half of the room. I get my computer out and connect it to the WiFi, wondering what my other roommates will be like. I sure hope we get along. At least I have the comfort of knowing Camila will be with me.

I step outside to the back door of the landing to see if there's anyone else outside.

There's not.

I go back inside, and the silence smacks me in the face. I lift my shoulders up and down and turn on some music for a little noise. Then I organize my room.

There's nothing more for me to do.

So I call Abby.

"Hey, you!" she says. "What are you doing?"

"Absolutely nothing. I was calling to ask you the same thing."

"Well, that's perfect," Abby says, her voice purring. "April invited me to go clubbing with her. Do you want to come?"

I remember the last time I went clubbing. It wasn't a great experience.

But what I remember most of all is seeing Owen there. It was before we dated, and my memory of him then is so different from what I know of him now.

And it makes me miss him more.

"Clubbing?" I say. "Are we even allowed to go?"

"Sure, all the college kids go. As long as we don't buy any alcohol, they don't care if we're there."

Is that true? I don't have a way to prove the veracity of her claim. "I don't want to hang with a bunch of strangers. We could do something just us, go out to dinner, go to the mall."

"I totally would! But I already promised April. Sure you won't come?"

I sigh and resign myself to the lonely, quiet evening I'm about to have with myself. "Maybe some other time."

"I'll let you off the hook this time. But next time you're going with me."

"Sure."

"And don't forget Monday night we have orientation!"

"Orientation?" My brow furrows. "I thought that wasn't until Friday."

"Honors Orientation, not Freshman Orientation."

"Oh." My head spins. "I did forget." I put it from my mind, actually. I'm not doing the Honors Program.

"I'll come to your dorm Monday at four and we can go together. I want to see your room, anyway."

And I want her to come visit me. Looks like I'm going to the orientation. "Great! See you Monday."

We hang up. I have no food, so I make a grocery list. I'll run to the store and stock up, then I'll come home and make myself soup and read from one of the books I'm so glad I brought from home. Tomorrow I'll go to church and meet new people, and by Monday my roommates will be arriving.

I'm a grown-up woman now. I can be by myself.

My phone rings as I'm about to head out. Except it's not my normal ring-tone.

It's the one that comes from my international calling app.

Only one person calls me on that.

I can't help but tense when I see Tiago's name. There's a lot of history, hurt feelings, and unexpressed regret between us. But there's also years of friendship and genuine caring for each other.

And I'm lonely.

I collapse on the couch shoved into the corner. "Tiago!"

"Hey, how are you?"

His voice is warm, friendly, and familiar, and my anxieties fade away. "Lonely," I admit. "I'm all by myself. I'm bored for someone to talk to."

"Good thing I called."

"It is. Now I don't feel so alone." I smile, but I feel that tiny stirring of worry. This isn't considered flirting, is it? I feel like I left myself open. What if he says something back that makes me uncomfortable?

"When do your roommates arrive?"

I give a quick exhale. He didn't push me, he didn't take my comment as an opening to get too familiar.

We're just two friends talking.

"Next week," I say. "Any day. We have a few days before school officially starts. I'm sure they'll move in before Freshman Orientation on Friday."

"You can endure that long."

I lose track of time as we talk until my stomach begins growling at me, reminding me that I was on my way out the door when he called me.

"I've got to get some food," I say. "But thanks for calling me."

"I can call tomorrow if you want."

I consider it. I'll be alone tomorrow also. But he's not the one I want to turn to when I'm lonely. "I think I'll try to socialize. Find people at church to hang out with."

He takes my rejection in stride. "Do it. Make friends. I'm here if you need me."

I smile. He means it. He's matured since we dated, and I feel like he's honest and open in his feelings now. "I know."

We hang up, and I use my phone to navigate me to the nearest grocery store. It's far enough away I have to get in my car and drive, which is good because I buy a lot of soup. If warm soup and crackers can be a drug, I'm going to overdose. Plus it's cheap. I make myself a bowl of clam chowder back in my apartment. When I finish, I wash my bowl and spoon and put them out to dry.

I've killed two hours. The silence wraps around me. Not even a clock to tick away the passage of time.

I turn out all the lights except the lamp by my bed. I wrap Owen's blanket around me, keeping it tucked up around my chin because it still smells like him. I read until my eyes grow too heavy for another chapter, and then I shut off the lamp and snuggle into bed.

I'm almost asleep before I realize it's the first day I've gone without talking to Owen at all.

CHAPTER FORTY-SIX

Roommate

I wake up Sunday morning with an oppressive weight in my chest. I make breakfast and get dressed for church all while feeling the heat of tears at the back my eyes, as if I might cry at any moment.

I don't want to analyze why I feel this way.

There are several congregations that meet on campus, with many of the buildings used for school converted into chapels on Sunday. I study the map and decide to go to the congregation that meets at ten. That's not too early and it meets in one of the closer buildings.

The moment I step into the makeshift chapel, nothing more than a classroom auditorium inside a brick building, a man around my father's age greets me with a handshake. A warm smile crinkles his eyes as he says, "Welcome. What's your name?"

Immediately a feeling of belonging settles over me, soothing my turbulent heart. "Cassandra Jones," I answer.

"I'm Pastor Dean. Are you a new student?"

I nod. "I'm a freshman. Just got here."

"Well, I'm delighted to have you join our congregation."

I smile and slip away as he releases me to greet the next student. My eyes slide over those gathered in the auditorium. Judging from the way their bodies lean toward each other in a familiar manner as they talk, they've probably been here all summer. Maybe even last year. They're older. I might be the only freshman here.

My introverted nature gets the best of me, and I settle into a seat near the back. I regret my decision as soon as I'm seated. Nobody will sit by me, and I didn't mean to be antisocial. But no way am I getting up and moving.

It's a long seven minutes before Pastor Dean walks down the aisle toward the podium, and the piano music starts playing. The hymns are familiar, and the loneliness seeps away from me as I sing along with the others in the congregation.

Afterward a student gets up to give the prayer, and then Pastor Dean steps to the Mic and begins to speak.

And then my phone rings.

I forgot to silence it, and the country song ringtone blasts through the auditorium. Heads turn my way.

But I don't care, because that particular ringtone is assigned to only one person, and he's someone I'm longing to talk to.

I stand and amble over knees and legs, mumbling apologies, silencing the ring before it goes off again. I barely step into the hall before I answer. "Owen," I say, and I don't try to hide the delight in my voice.

"Hey. You good?"

His voice dispels the gloom that hung over me like a dark raincloud all morning. I might not have been earlier, but I'm certainly good now. "Yes! I'm at church."

"Oh, I can call later. I didn't know what time you went to church."

"No, no," I say hurriedly. "I'd rather talk to you. I mean—church is great and all, but—"

He laughs. "Glad to know I still rank pretty high up there."

"At the top," I want to say. "You're at the top. Five stars all the way." But that doesn't feel like something I should say to him if we're not dating.

"You're still up there," I say instead, my soul smiling, feeling that warmth in my chest as if he were standing next to me and we were talking. "Thanks for thinking of me enough to call me."

"I don't really stop thinking about you," he says, so casually he might've been telling me his favorite flavor of ice cream.

And my heart melts. Owen doesn't say things to be cheesy. He says them because he feels it. Now I regret not giving into my first impulse and telling him my thoughts.

"Me too," I say, as if I can make up for not being open a minute ago. "I miss you. Everything here makes me miss you."

"Because every hot guy you see reminds you of me?" he teases.

But his words hit too close to home, and I feel a splash of terrible guilt. I swallow it back and say, quite glibly, "What cute guys?"

He laughs, an appreciative laugh, and I join him. I find a bench in the corner of the hallway and sit down. I'm clearly not going back into church.

"How did your presentation go?" he asks.

Now I can't help giggling. "I think I caught everyone by surprise."

"You always will. No one suspects what's going on in your head. By the time we realize the extent of your devious planning, we're immobilized like quicksand."

"I'm impressed. You've been studying a dictionary since I left."

"I have to. You're not around to increase my vocabulary."

I lean my head against the wall. This banter is bittersweet. It fills my heart with joy, but it also makes me ache for the real person. "I got moved into my dorm. It's pretty lonely right now. Hopefully I'll have roommates soon. What about you? What's your living situation like?"

"Well, I got moved into off-campus housing. I didn't sign up soon enough to get into the dorms. As for my roommates . . . well, they're . . . interesting."

"Interesting," I echo. "What does that mean, exactly?"

"They're all on the football team. If that doesn't say enough, let me expound to say they act like I did in tenth grade . . . except ten times worse."

"So they have the maturity of sophomore in high school and the wisdom of a toddler?"

"Yeah. That pretty much sums it up."

I laugh at Owen's assessment, but I'm hiding my concern. It's not even been a year since Owen gave up that party lifestyle. And a lot of it had to do with me. There is a chance now that he'll go back to it, if his parents aren't watching him and I'm not there to hold his hand.

That's what Tiago did.

I hate the idea, and I also don't want to bring it up.

So I say, super casual, super general, "Be careful. You never know who you can trust."

"But some people you know you can't trust. And these guys definitely fall into the latter category."

I remind myself that Owen has as much life experience as I do. He has more wisdom than I give him credit for. "How's Monica?"

"You tell me. You talk to her more than you talk to me."

He says it jokingly, but nobody makes a statement like that without some feelings behind it. He noticed, then, that I intentionally didn't respond to him the other day when they were both texting me.

"I absolutely do not. There's been one day in the past week where the topic of conversation felt more—appropriate talking to her than to you."

"Because you were talking about your sex book?"

"Owen." I'm laughing again. "Yes."

"Can't say I wouldn't mind if I was included in those conversations. You could share a little bit with me. Like your favorite line from your presentation."

Talking about sex with Owen would be oh so fun and delicious and terribly tempting.

Which is why I don't do it.

And it's why I don't respond to him now.

The doorbell rings on his side of the call, and then a male voice yells in the background, "Owen! It's for you!"

"Oh yeah?" he says, and then to me, "Guess I better go. I've got company."

Is it a girl? Who would pop over to see him on a Sunday morning? I'm dying to know. *Don't ask, don't ask!* I mentally scream at myself.

"Okay. I better get back to church anyway."

"I'll talk to you soon," he says.

I've already moved the phone away from my ear to hang up when I hear his voice through the speaker.

"Cassandra."

I bring the phone back. "Yes?"

"I still love you."

I smile. It's what I needed to hear. "Same. I love you too."

My entire mood has changed by the time I walk back into the chapel. I hum quietly in the back row, jubilant, happiness pouring through my veins like a heavy elixir.

I will come down from this high, when reality crashes upon me and I remember I'm not with the one I love.

But for now that doesn't matter. What matters is that the one I love still loves me.

I awaken Monday morning to the sound of voices in the room next to mine.

A roommate!

I tumble out of bed, catching my reflection in the mirror attached to my closet as I exit the room. I don't look too terrible, but I pause to brush my teeth before poking my head into the other bedroom.

"Hi!" I say.

A girl with jet black hair sits on the computer desk next to a man who looks like her father. A computer rests beside her, and the man presses buttons on the keyboard. A woman and a younger man in his twenties hover behind the desk, leaning over and murmuring advice. The girl lifts her face, pushing back the long curtain of hair. "Hi," she says.

I hop over to her and restrain myself from putting an arm around her shoulders and hugging her. I'm so relieved not to be alone anymore. "I'm Cassandra. I'm in the room next-door."

"I'm Iris. This is my mom, and my dad, and that's my brother."

She gestures to each person in turn. The brother waves hello, but her mom and dad only smile and nod. Her mother is a tiny woman, shorter than I am.

"Nice to meet you." I sit down on her bed. "Where are you from?"

Her dad says something to her in another language, and she nods before joining me, sitting cross-legged on the bed next to me. "Canada. You?"

My curiosity piqued when I heard her dad talk. I watch him converse with her brother, still in another language, as they assess her computer and set up a pair of speakers around it. "Arkansas. What language is your dad speaking?"

"Oh. Mandarin."

I'm impressed. My Spanish is barely passable, and my Portuguese is worse. "That's cool. I hear it's a hard language."

"My parents grew up in China, so it's easy for them. But they moved here when my brother was two, and he's the only one who speaks it fluently. He moved to Taiwan a few years ago, so he's a lot better at it than I am. I only know a few words."

I nod. "That's about how I am with Spanish."

"Where is your family from?"

"Colombia." I press my thumbs together and lower my voice, leaning toward her. "But I don't know anything about them."

"What do you mean? Like you're adopted or something?"

"No." I shake my head. "I know my immediate family, but something negative happened when my grandma left Colombia, and no one will talk about it."

"Like a secret scandal?"

"My mind has already explored a lot of options."

"It's probably something boring, like talking about Colombia makes them remember the smell of chickens and they don't like it."

I laugh, and I know I'm going to like her. "Do you need to go to the grocery store or anything? I have a car."

"Thanks, but my parents already took of me. Have you gone to campus yet?"

"Yes. I've already been here a week."

Her dark eyes grow wide. "Really? What have you been doing?"

Iris's family leaves to help her brother move into his apartment, and I spend the next half hour telling her all about Honors Week. Then we move into my room and I show her the photo album with pictures from home my mom made me. I don't plan to explain Owen, but his pictures are interspersed with my family. He appears on every page. She puts her finger on the photo of us from graduation before I can close the book.

"Who's that?" she says.

"That's Owen," I say breezily.

"He doesn't look like your brother."

"He's not." I can't help but think of his caresses, his touches that were definitely not brotherly, and I feel my face grow hot.

She's watching me, and she grins. "I see who he is. A boyfriend?"

"He was a boyfriend. Now he's just someone special."

"You broke up?"

"We agreed to be apart."

She nods. "I completely get it. I had one too. We ended things because we're going to separate schools, but it's hard to convince my mind that we're only friends now."

She does get it! I grin at her, thrilled we have this connection. "Show me pictures."

Someone knocks on the front door, and Iris jumps up to answer. I hear her talking in the hall, and then she returns.

"I'm going to dinner with my family, so I'll see you later."

"Yes!" I say, thrilled I won't be alone anymore. "See you soon!"

But after Iris leaves the room, Owen's absence falls across my shoulders like an overloaded backpack. Now is a good time to call. I can tell him about my new roommate.

His phone rings four times and goes to voicemail. I hang up feeling the weight of disappointment in my chest, and I send a text.

Me: Tried to call. First roommate is here.

There's no immediate response, and I put my phone aside, reminding myself of my resolution not to be attached to it.

CHAPTER FORTY-SEVEN

College Boys

When Abby comes over later to walk with me to the Honors Orientation, I drag Iris along.

"I already know I'm not doing the Honors program," Iris protests as we walk the twenty minutes to the Honors building.

I brush off her concerns with a wave of my hand. "That doesn't matter. This is your chance to meet people."

"Like me," Abby says, and she flashes that infectious grin, showing off both dimples.

I smile back, feeling the warmth of friendship between us. I'm so glad I've met her. "Like Abby."

I haven't seen anyone from Honors Week since the last day of class, when we all packed up and left. But as soon as I walk in the building, familiar faces call out to us, and soon a group has formed, and we are all laughing and talking and sharing our experiences about our new dorms and what our plans are for the upcoming week. It's enthralling, and the best part is I am a part of it. They include me. Abby and I stand hip to hip, the same height, me with dark hair and her with flaming red hair, and every comment, every question is directed at us. I introduce Iris and everyone is polite, but I feel a little bad because she's not in this group. I know she feels it by the way she hangs back, stepping slightly out of our circle.

We head into the auditorium and sit down as the dean of the Honors Program takes the podium, and I make sure to sit next to Iris.

I enjoyed Honors Week. It was a great way to get used to college life before the hustle and bustle started and twenty thousand other students arrived. But as the dean goes over the class requirements, and I realize I would have to take harder versions of college classes that are probably already hard enough, my enthusiasm for the program wavers. Some of the classes I would enjoy, like Honors English and reading, and some of the electives. But most of them, like Honors Math and Honors History, would challenge me uncomfortably.

In spite of that, I'm still considering the program when the dean says, "And the capstone to your Honors education will be a Master's thesis that you must complete before you can graduate with your Bachelor's degree."

A Master's Thesis? The very idea has my stomach tying in knots. There's a reason I don't intend to get a Master's degree, and it ends and begins with the thesis. Well, that and two more years of education.

Nope. Honors week was fun. I made some friends and learned a few things. But I will not be doing the Honors Program.

Mason gathers us together when it ends, throwing an arm around April's shoulder and pulling me in for a side hug. "To the creamery!" he says, releasing us to rub his hands together.

"Are you going to do it?" I ask Abby as she walks beside me. "The Honors Program?"

"I might try, but just our freshman year. I'm applying for the photography program, and if I get in, that will be time-consuming enough."

I nod vigorously. "Agreed." I turn to Iris next. "What did you think?"

"No way, it's definitely not for me! I'm here on a scholarship, I have to keep my grades up. Those classes would make it harder."

She has a very good point. "I'm also on scholarship. And I don't want to do that Master's thesis."

"So it looks like it would be a no for both of us." Iris grins. "But you got me out of the dorm on my first night in college. So thanks."

"Next," Abby says, "we are going clubbing."

Right. I forgot I promised her that. "But not tonight," I say.

Abby shoves me with her hip. "No! It's Monday. The clubs are only open on the weekend."

It looks like I have a few more days.

Owen finally responds as I'm brushing my teeth for bed.

O: sorry I missed your call. LONG day of practice. So exhausted. Finally catching a breath.

I spit before responding. *Me: yeah? Enjoying it?*

O: no. That sucked.

I chuckle. *Me: but you love the sport.*

O: I love the game. Tell me about your roommate.

I take the phone back to my room and climb into bed.

Me: she's Chinese Canadian. I think we'll be great friends.

O: you'll make friends with everyone.

He's said things like that before and I didn't believe him. That wasn't how high school went. But now I think he might be right.

Me: so far the people I've met here seem to get me

O: you're going to school with like-minded people

Truth. I am. Intentionally.

O: cass, I can't keep my eyes open. I'm glad it's going well. Talk later.

Me: okay. Have a good night.

I wait for it.

O: love you.

I smile and type out my response. *Me: love you too.*

He always says it first. That's not fair. I decide I'll say it first next time.

⟋⟋⟍※⟋⟍⟋

By Thursday, everyone has arrived.

I go outside when Camila shows up with her family, and we hug so hard we nearly topple over before we begin the process of moving boxes from their car into the bedroom we'll share.

"I took the window," I say as we put boxes on her bed. "I hope you don't mind."

She shrugs. "You got here first. I think you get first pick."

"That's what I thought too," I say, and we cackle, bumping shoulders and leaning toward each other.

The front door opens, and a fourth girl comes in, with medium-length ash blond hair and a dreamy expression on her face that makes her seem like she might be a fairy.

"Hi," she says when she sees us.

"Hi," we answer together.

"I'm Layne."

"Cassandra," I say, and then I point to Iris's room. "You're in there."

Iris pops out to meet her. Their conversation is lively and animated, and Camila and I crowd into the room with them. Layne's an only child who lives with her mom in California. I'm feeling extreme excitement and a desire to find out more about these girls who I will be living with for the next year, when I hear my phone ringing in my room. I head back to get it.

It's my cousin Jordan.

A thrill shoots up my chest. Jordan is my age, and he and I have been close since I was fifteen. For the first time ever, we live in the same state. I grab up the phone and answer the call quickly. "Jordan!" I say.

"Are you on campus?" he says. "I'm here."

"I am, yes! Where are you staying?"

"The tower dorms. I'm not even sure where I am."

"I know where you are. I stayed there when I first got here. I'm in the apartment dorms."

"Cool. I have a meal plan and no one to eat with. Want to meet up?"

"Sure."

I jaunt back over to my roommates. "My cousin just got here and wants to meet for lunch. I'll be back in a bit."

They wave at me but don't look up from their conversations. I grin as I trot out the back door.

I have a good feeling about this year.

I call Owen as I walk toward Jordan's dorm. He doesn't answer.

Jordan looks nothing like me. Somehow he's gotten even taller than last summer, and he already has a foot on me. He has broad shoulders and thick blond hair. I'm tiny, barely a hundred pounds, and my mom's Latina side shows strongly in my straight dark hair and dark skin tone.

The moment he sees me, a smile spreads from ear to ear. He rushes to the door and wraps me up in a big hug.

"Hey, little cousin," he says.

I laugh and smack his arm. "I'm almost a year older than you!"

"No one will ever believe it. Don't even try."

Even though we haven't seen each other in a year, we fall back into an easy conversation as we fill each other in on our lives. He wants all the Owen updates, and he tells me about his new girlfriend and how they plan on getting married when they turn twenty.

"That's so young!" I gape at him, astonished by his certainty.

He shrugs. "When you know . . ."

I don't finish the sentence. We're too young to know.

Or maybe I'm jealous Owen and I don't have the same commitment. "Good luck," I say.

He pulls out his phone and scrolls through it. "What's your schedule? I bet we have some generals together."

I get my schedule out so we can compare, but against all odds, we have no classes together.

"You have a gap between classes the same time as me every Tuesday and Thursday," he says, pointing it out. "Let's plan lunch."

"It's a date." I write it down so I won't forget.

He walks me back to my apartment after lunch and gives me another big comforting hug before saying goodbye.

"There's a dance on campus tonight," he says. "Want to come?"

"I would love to, actually. I love dancing." I'm just not good at it. And I'm certain the dance on campus won't be as crazy as dancing at a club.

But I call Abby and invite her anyway.

"What if it's lame, like church dances back home?" she says.

"I always loved church dances," I say, wondering if I just revealed myself to be a total geek.

"I'll go," she says definitively. "They're probably a lot more fun when you're there."

"Yes, I'm the life of the party," I say.

The very idea is hilarious.

I have two hours to kill, so I try calling Owen again. This time he picks up.

"Hey, you," he says.

"Hey, yourself!" I say back, thrilled to hear his voice. "How are you? You've been busy!"

"Yeah, sorry, it's been crazy. We're doing two-a-days."

"In this heat?"

"We take a break in the afternoons."

"Must be exhausting."

"It is. And I just got to practice, so I have to go. But I wanted to take your call."

I'm disappointed he can't talk. "That's all right. Stay hydrated out there."

"Thanks. See you later."

"Love you," I say, throwing it out there, eager to say it first.

But I'm too late. He's already hung up.

The apartment is empty. Camila is with the cross country team. I'm not sure where Layne is, and Iris says she's going to dinner with her brother and sister. And I don't want to be here anymore. I get ready for the dance and head over to Jordan's dorm by myself, where I told Abby to meet me. I wear a knee-length floral print skirt and a short-sleeved fuzzy white sweater. Jordan and I make small talk while we wait for Abby in the commons.

She walks in wearing dark jeans and a yellow top that barely touches the waistband of her pants. Every time she moves, a strip of pale skin shows above her jeans. She looks sophisticated and in college, and suddenly I feel like I'm still in high school.

But she slips her arm around my waist and says, "You look amazing! Every guy at the dance will have his eyes on you."

Not likely, not when I've got Abby next to me. She's a ball of happy electric energy, which reminds me of Harper, who was always the life of the party.

The dance is in one of the many ballrooms off of the food court. Abby enters first, leading the way into the dark room with flashing lights and bouncing people. She heads for the middle of the dance floor, leaving me no choice but to follow. She puts her hands in the air, exposing her belly button, and shakes her hips to the music. Sure enough, the guys flock over. I bob my weight from hip to hip but I don't have the confidence to dance like her, with no restraint. Jordan bounces beside me, holding a cup of punch.

"Go asks someone to dance," I tell him.

"Nah." He shakes his head. "I have a girlfriend. She's just not here."

I vacillate between envious and annoyed.

A slow song comes on, and Jordan tosses his punch in a trash can. Then he takes me in his arms and pulls me onto the dance floor. He's goofy and friendly, and if I had an older brother, I would want one like Jordan.

"I can't believe we don't have any GEs together," he says.

"I know." I nod in agreement. "What are the chances?"

His eyes drift over my shoulder, then he pulls me in close and ducks down to whisper, "There's at least five guys eyeing you."

I snort and roll my eyes. "There's never been any guys anywhere eyeing me."

"If that's true, get ready for a change. Because you're in college now, and these guys don't play by the same rules."

I swat his arm. "And how would you know? You haven't even started college."

"Oh, I know." He wiggles his eyebrows at me.

"Right."

The dance finishes, and I pop over to Abby as she steps away from a group of guys. She leans over and whispers to me, "You guys look too close out there. Two guys asked me if he's your boyfriend. You have to make yourself look available."

"But I'm not available," I want to say.

I keep it to myself. Technically, I am available.

But my heart doesn't feel like it.

CHAPTER FORTY-EIGHT

Ready or Not

School starts on Tuesday.

I'm not sure why, unless they're trying to reel us into the semester with a shorter week.

I spend Monday showing Camila around campus. Most of her classes are on the west end of campus, by the sports buildings. It seems half of her schedule is taken up by athletics.

"How will you keep up with school?" I ask her.

She shrugs. "I'll manage. I did it in high school."

"Truth."

We don't have any classes together. I consider myself lucky to have a class with Abby.

After finding all her classes, we head to the bookstore to get her books. There are ten times as many students walking around campus now as there were during Honors Week. Kids are everywhere, sitting on the walls of the quad, camping out on the grass with their laptops, laughing under the trees.

"There are a lot of people here," I say.

Camila looks up from her printed schedule and squints toward the glass building in front of us, which holds the student center and the cafeteria. "I bet there will be even more people when school starts tomorrow."

I nod in agreement. Only the new students are out touring campus right now. Everyone else knows their way around.

"Can we stop at the grocery store?" she asks. " I need a few more things."

"Of course."

We walk back to our dorm and drop off Camila's books, then we take my car off campus to the store. I'm still not used to seeing the mountains around me, and though they're impressive, the landscape is very different from back home. I miss the trees. I miss the green.

I stock up on canned soup and instant pasta. I consider buying vegetables, but I already know I'm not going to cook. My meal plan includes one meal a day in the cafeteria. I expect that will be my main meal of the day, and I'll make sure to get vegetables then.

We try to unload our groceries into the fridge in the apartment, but it's full. Full! It takes some effort to squeeze Camila's gallon of milk beside the other three.

"This is ridiculous," she says, standing back with her hands on her hips. "We should share milk."

"I'm game. It's the only thing I have in the fridge. And butter." Otherwise I have a shelf in the cupboard covered with my processed foods.

Layne comes in and says, "I think we need to assign shelves in the fridge."

Something about her tone bothers me. She sounds bossy, and my skin prickles.

Camila gives a vigorous nod and says, "I couldn't agree more. I was thinking the same thing."

"Awesome." Layne lifts her chin and presses her lips together. "I was also thinking we could take turns cooking dinner on Sundays. There's four of us, so once a month we could each cook for everyone. Iris said she'd take the first week. What do you guys think?"

I'm caught off guard, and I want to say no. It is a good idea. I'm just annoyed by her attitude.

"Yeah, that sounds great," Camila says, and I'm further annoyed that she's so agreeable.

"Looks like it's decided," I say.

Layne looks at me, and Camila lifts both eyebrows.

"Do you not want to?" Camila asks.

I backtrack before I get labeled as the difficult one of our apartment. "Of course I want to. Sounds like fun." I smile as I end my sentence and project what I want them to see of me. I'm nice, I'm friendly, we can all get along.

But dang. Keeping up the perfect persona will be hard.

⁕

I set everything out that night for my first day of college. I look over my outfit, jean shorts with a blue tank and a white button-up shirt to go over the top. I double check my backpack has my textbooks and pencils and notebooks. My heart pounds a little harder. I can't believe it. College classes start tomorrow.

"Knock knock!"

The front door opens even though we didn't answer, and I step out of the room as Debbie, our Resident Assistant, pops in. I met her when I moved in but haven't seen her since. Camila exits the kitchen, and Iris and Layne emerge from their room.

"Oh, good, you're all here!" she says. She clasps her hands together. "I want to go over a few house rules now that everyone's settled.

"First, we have monthly cleaning checks. I'll warn you a few days before they're happening, but it's a good idea to keep your area tidy.

"Second, boys are not allowed in your bedrooms. Nor are they allowed to stay the night or you to stay the night over at their places. No one's going to be watching you at all times, so a lot of this is according to the Honor Code you

270

agreed to abide by when you applied to the school."

I nod along with my roommates.

"All right, that's it! My room is on the first floor, if you need anything!"

Layne rolls her eyes when she leaves. "You'd think they'd treat us like adults now that we're in college."

I nod, but the rules don't bother me. I return to my room, climb into bed, and open my laptop. There's an email from Tiago. He didn't call me this week, which I appreciate and feel guilty for appreciating. We are friendly with each other, but I don't have room for more than that.

Even as I'm thinking this, Owen's name dances across my phone as it begins to ring. I slam my computer shut and shove it away in one motion as I answer the phone. It's been days since we talked. I curl up in his quilt and pretend he's with me.

"I was hoping you'd call," I say.

"You don't have to wait on me. You can call also."

"I know, but every time I do, you're at football practice."

"I have to be there a lot," Owen says, defensively. "I'm a walk-on. I have to put forth twice as much effort as everyone else if I hope to play."

"I know, Owen," I say, trying to defuse the sudden tension between us. "I wasn't chastising you."

"Yeah. Sorry."

And then we drift into what can only be called an awkward silence.

"Well," he says, breaking it, "you ready for the first day of school?"

Owen still has another week. He doesn't start until after Labor Day.

"Can I ever be fully ready?" I say.

"Don't take yourself too seriously, kid. You're already a pro at this."

"But college feels different."

The bedroom door opens, and Camila comes in. I clutch the phone closer to my ear, realizing having private conversations is going to be a lot harder now that I share an apartment with three other girls.

"It's not different," he says.

Camila opens her closet and sifts through her clothing, probably choosing an outfit for tomorrow, like I did. I'm distracted watching her and barely hear Owen asking about my roommates.

"They're great," I say. "I mean, I don't know them yet." I can't say what I really think, not with Camila here.

Someone starts yelling something at Owen in the background, and he hollers back, "Hang on!"

"How are your roommates?" I ask, teasing. "They sound a little louder than mine."

"Definitely messier, I'm sure. We're still waiting on two more. We rented a house, and there will be eight of us here."

"Eight!" I try to imagine a house full of eight boys. "Yeah, I remember your apartment in Arkansas. Tell me one of you boys knows how to do the dishes."

His roommate is yelling at him again, and I know he didn't hear me when yells,

"I said hang on!" To me he says, "Cass, I have to go."

Is it my imagination, or is he eager to get off the phone? "Yeah, okay," I say, and there's this funny ache at the top of my ribcage.

"Call me tomorrow and tell me about your first day," he says.

"I will," I say.

And he hangs up.

That's it. No goodbye, no I love you, no I miss you. That ache expands, swelling up in my chest.

"Was that Owen?" Camila turns around with a smile, holding a pink shirt to her torso. "How is he?"

I don't feel like expounding on my feelings. I don't feel like discussing the foreboding. "He's great. Busy getting ready for school like we are. I like that color on you."

She places it on top of her dresser. "I think I'll wear it tomorrow."

CHAPTER FORTY-NINE

Epiphany

My first class isn't until nine in the morning, but I set my alarm for six. The moment it goes off, I jump out of bed, wide awake and ready to go. My heart's already racing.

I'm so anxious I'm practically sick to my stomach. I shower and blow dry my hair and I'm about to skip breakfast when I realize I'll regret that later. I force myself to sit down and eat. I have plenty of time; it's only seven. I pull out my Bible and read a little bit to center myself, taking deep breaths as if I were meditating. Now I'm calm and I have nothing to do. It's only seven-thirty. I open my computer at the kitchen table and check my email again. I never responded to Tiago last night. I read his email now.

Hi Cassandra,

I know you start school soon. This is exciting. I hope you have a good day. I would love to know how your classes go. I'm not doing much, playing in a band and hanging out with friends. My mom sends her love. Can't wait to see you.

Love,

Tiago

It's platonic enough. I would show it to Owen without feeling guilty if he asked, but he won't ask. There's been some kind of unspoken, silent promise to give me space where Tiago is concerned.

But I don't want space. I want Owen.

I'd rather not dwell on those thoughts right now.

I type out a friendly response.

Hi, Tiago! Great to hear from you. I'm super excited/super nervous about school today. I hope my classes are not too hard. Thanks for emailing!

Cassandra

It's finally time to leave for class. I throw my computer into my backpack, double-check for my water bottle, and head out the door.

The morning is beautiful. A little bit colder then I would've expected for late

August, but the sun is shining, the birds are chirping, and I know it's going to be beautiful day.

I head to the science building for my physical science class. Students are everywhere. The sidewalk is so congested I have to slow down. It feels like there are more people on campus than in my entire hometown, although I know the student enrollment is half that. My town might feel bigger if we all got out and walked down the street at the same time.

I climb the stairs to the multi-level auditorium and find Abby waiting outside it in the hallway. She flashes her dimples in a huge smile and gives me a big hug, which instantly sooths my overactive anxiety.

"We are here! We are college students!"

We are. I squeeze her back, sharing the enthusiasm.

Together we enter the classroom, and I suck in a breath. It's huge, almost the size of the performing arts center at my high school. There's a teacher's desk with a screen for a projector set up on the wall. We take the outside steps and climb over people to find a spot with two chairs in the middle of a row. There are a few whispers here and there, but most kids remain ominously silent, staring forward with nervous, uncertain expressions on their faces. That's how I would look if I didn't have Abby. This is a freshman class, so it's the first day of school for most of us.

I feel some reassurance.

"Welcome, welcome to physical science 101!" The professor steps into the room. He wears a big, broad smile across his face and has no hair. He's a little taller than me with a tie and sweater on over his beige pants.

Abby leans over and whispers, "He is the exact picture of a stereotypical, absent-minded professor."

I can't help but giggle and nod.

"Unless you had an eight o'clock class this morning, this is your first college class," he says. "Congratulations. You picked the hardest one!"

A few titters ring out through the room, but I don't laugh. My nerves are working in overdrive. Science is not my best subject, and a difficult science class could cost me my scholarship. Although Preston Y is paying for my tuition, I have to reapply every year to renew it, and I have to keep my GPA at a 3.7.

The idea makes my teeth chatter.

"The syllabus is online, but I'm going to hand out a printed copy for anyone who prefers that." He hands two stacks of paper to the front row, and I watch as they begin to disperse among the students. I want a paper copy for sure. I don't know if I'll ever get used to everything being digital.

"Go ahead and get out your textbooks now also."

I give a small jolt of surprise. It's the first fifteen minutes of class, and he wants to get the textbook out? "I didn't think we would actually do anything today," I murmur to Abby as I bend to my backpack and pull out the book.

"Me, neither!" she says.

I guess we're not in high school anymore.

The class is interesting, at least, as he has a series of props to demonstrate the ideas behind the theories that are the foundation of physical science.

I am new to block scheduling, so I expect the two-hour class to feel like it's taking forever, but it doesn't. The time flies by, probably because I am also distracted and in my own head. When the bell rings and he dismisses us, Abby says, "Well, that was fun! I've heard horror stories about this class, but I don't think it will be that bad."

I want to share her confidence. "I have to be careful. I have to keep my grades up so I can afford school."

"Oh, are you on scholarship?"

I nod, and Abby says, "Me too. I have to maintain a three-point-five or I could lose it."

"Only a three-point-five?" I shoulder my backpack, keeping my physical science book under my arm because it's so huge. "I have to keep a three-point-seven-five."

"Ouch. What kind of scholarship are you on?"

"The kind that you have to renew every year."

Now Abby looks sympathetic. "That's ironic. I got offered for all four years, and I don't have to maintain my GPA as high as you have to."

"That's definitely ironic," I agree. And very unfair. I have to perform better than someone who showed up smarter than me in high school.

We leave the class together.

"Where are you headed?" she asks.

I have my schedule memorized, but I check it just to be sure. "Honors English. Back at the Honors building."

"I thought you decided not to do the Honors Program?"

"I did. But English is my favorite subject, so I decided to do this one class. It should be fun."

"We have different definitions of fun," she says with a laugh. "I've got biology. Talk to you later."

We hug, and then I start the long trek to the Honors building at the west side of campus.

The English classroom is right next to the room I was in during Honors Week. The teacher gives me a bright smile when I sit down. She looks two years older than me. A glance around the classroom proves we are all freshman. Most of the guys look like they can't even grow facial hair yet, except one, who sports a trimmed, short beard along his jaw. Which, for some odd reason, makes me think of Owen. If he doesn't shave, a layer of scratchy blond fuzz forms a crust on his jaw and cheeks. I love running my palms over it and feeling the contrast between his smooth skin and the tiny wiry hairs.

I shove the thought of him aside.

The teacher welcomes us to class.

"You can call me Ms. Mayhew," she says, and she explains we will be doing the same thing the other freshman English classes are doing but with more writing.

The writing is what calls to me. If it weren't for that part, I wouldn't take this class. I tested out of freshman English thanks to my AP classes. But writing is my soul-language, it's how I express myself, and I am glad to have a place where I can do so.

It's a small class of maybe twenty people, and she goes around the room and has us introduce ourselves. I recognize Mason from Honors Week, and he nods at me. The guy with the facial hair tells us he's just come home from a mission trip, so even though he's a freshman, he's in his early twenties. I tap my pencil on my desk and wonder what these mission trips are like. My dad did one. He says the only way to fully understand and love a people is to live and serve among them.

Most people in class are from Colorado, followed by California and a smattering of other states. I'm the only person from Arkansas.

"Arkansas," one boy says. "I didn't know they have public education in Arkansas."

My defenses rise, but then he winks at me, and I realize he's joking. So I smile and say, "I put my shoes on just for this class."

It's the right response. Everyone laughs, and Ms. Mayhew moves onto the next person. When we're done with introductions, she calls our attention back to her.

"The biggest thing you'll be working on this semester is a personal narrative. I want you to find a pivotal moment in your life that changed everything for you, changed your entire perspective. Maybe changed the outcome of your life. Study this word." She turns and writes on the white board, "Epiphany." "You'll also come to understand the meaning of this phrase." She writes beneath it, "paradigm shift."

She faces us again. "We're going to spend a lot of time reading examples of epiphanies and paradigm shifts, and when you write your personal narrative, I want it to encapsulate the meaning of these words, even if you don't use the actual words themselves."

I write "epiphany" on my paper and draw fancy squiggles around the word. I've heard of it, but I'm not sure I can use it in a sentence. It's slightly out of reach.

This class will be fun.

CHAPTER FIFTY

Family Relations

have lunch at noon, and then I head to the library to knock out my homework. I can't believe I already have some, but apparently in college, teachers don't know you're not supposed to get homework on the first day of school. It's another school day for them.

I get through half a chapter in my physical science text book when my stomach starts growling, and then all I can think of is food. Should I cook ramen or another can of clam chowder? These thoughts take over until I know studying is useless until I fill my belly.

I'm itching to call Owen. I have good reason to. I take my time putting my books into my backpack, deliberately drawing out the suspense until I make a leisure walk from the library to the outside.

And then I call him. My first day of school is over. I can't wait to tell Owen about it. But the exuberant smile slips from my face with each ring of the phone. And then it goes to voicemail.

I put the phone away, huffy. I shouldn't be, but I am annoyed. Owen told me to call him when I finished school. I guess I wanted him to be sitting in his room, staring at his phone, waiting for my call.

Even I know that's silly.

I walk into my apartment through the back door, taking the fire escape. I inhale the intoxicating aroma of yeast and cinnamon, closing my eyes in appreciation. When I open them, I see Iris and Layne standing in front of the dishwasher, pulling out the racks and examining the interior.

"What's going on?" I ask, dumping my backpack on the kitchen table.

Layne rises to her feet and turns to look at me. "The dishwasher flooded."

My eyes dart to the pile of rags on the floor beneath the dishwasher that I hadn't noticed until now.

"We don't see a clog or anything in the drain," Iris says. "So we don't know what's wrong with it."

I come over to squat in front of it with her, as if I have some dishwashing expertise, which I don't, in spite of being a professional dishwasher at a restaurant in high school. "Yeah, I don't know."

"I think we'll have to call maintenance," Layne says.

The back door opens again, and this time Camila walks in. "Hi, guys," she says, and I turn around to give her a big hug. She squeezes me back, then releases me to open the fridge. As she does, a tube of ground beef rolls out, and she barely catches several apples.

"Yikes!" she says. "The fridge might be a bit full."

I crane my neck and see that it's surprisingly worse than yesterday. "We definitely need to organize this," I agree.

A buzzer sounds, and Layne jumps away from the dishwasher. "Those are my muffins!" she says.

Camila and I step back, giving her the space she needs to open the oven in our tiny kitchen. She grabs an oven mitt and pulls out a tin of six muffins. She inhales, closing her eyes like I did when I entered, and the homey scent makes my stomach rumble.

"I'm happy to share," she says, setting them on the kitchen tablecloth. "Let's wait a few minutes so they can cool."

Iris stands up from the dishwasher. "How do we call maintenance? We don't want to flood the kitchen again."

Camila turns toward her. "Flood the kitchen?"

I hold back an aggravated sigh. "The dishwasher is broken." Looks like we'll be handwashing for awhile.

"I'll find out. I bet the RA knows." Camila leave the room.

Layne picks up the muffin tin and lets out a gasp. "Oh! I burned the tablecloth!"

I swivel to see six holes burned into our plastic tablecloth, in the exact location of the six muffins. I look at her, and we both start to laugh.

I think this is going to work out.

⊙〜※〜⊙

My second day is pretty much the same as my first, but with a different set of classes. My second English class is not a freshman class, and I can tell from a glance around that I'm one of the only freshman in there.

My teacher waddles in, clearly pregnant. She sits on her desk and pulls out a paper.

"I'm Ms. Cheney, and you're in English two-fifteen, critical theories and analysis. Make sure you're in the right place. I'm going to take roll real quick to see who's in here," she says.

She calls out names, and I answer, "here," when she gets to me. She pauses and looks at me.

"You're a freshman," she says.

All eyes turn to me. I force myself to hold still. "Yes."

"I assume you're in here because you tested out of freshman English. I still encourage all freshman to take English 101, especially if you're serious about English."

278

"I am," I say, though it's none of her business. "I'm taking this one also."

"Two English classes in your first semester?" Both brows shoot upward.

Does she require an answer? "Yes."

"I'm going to warn you, this is an upper level class. You'll find it challenging and might not be able to keep up. I wouldn't take it your first semester of college."

She continues to look at me over her paper like she expects me to pack my bag, stand up, and walk out. But I just nod.

"I'll keep that in mind." I refrain from telling her to mind her own business. I can do this.

"Okay. You have one week to drop the class before it's too late."

Still she stares at me. I nod again. What else can I say?

She shakes her head and turns her face back to the paper, moving onto the next name. I don't breathe until I feel the eyes of my classmates move off me, and then I relax in my seat, my heart racing.

Am I making a mistake?

But then class begins, and she has us open our text book, read a passage, and analyze it from a feminist point of view. My pulse slows. Between Miss Chapman's English class at my high school and Professor Walker's class from Honors Week, I feel prepared. It might be busy, but I'll keep up.

My math class is another matter.

I'm required to take this class because I didn't test out of it on my ACT score. It's a remedial algebra class, the same one I took in eleventh grade. But while I managed to get through it with decent marks in high school, my scores on the ACT showed I hadn't mastered it. And now here I am, sweating bullets in an air-conditioned classroom as my teacher, a lovely woman with long red hair and a Scottish accent named Jane, goes over how our assignments and testing will go.

"The midterm will be in October, and the semester concludes in December right before break," she says. "Every week we will have a test so that you are prepared for the midterm and final."

A test every week? My hands are clammy now. I'm freaking out.

"But not to worry," Jane says, her voice calm and lilting and her smile wide. "I know you're in here because math is not your strong suit. I will help you and give you opportunities to improve your grade throughout the semester. You don't have to be intimidated by this class."

Oh, I'm intimidated.

An Asian girl with long black hair and a square face turns toward me and whispers, "How are you with math?"

I bend toward her. "Terrible. This class will be my worst nightmare."

She laughs. "It won't be fun. But it could be worse. I'm Eunice."

"Cassandra." I exhale, already feeling more optimistic now that I've made a friend. "And I'm not sure how much worse it could be."

"We could be listening to an old man with a monotone grumble."

"There's that," I agree. At least it will be a pleasure to listen to Jane tutor us through every class. Even if she's reciting math precepts that may as well be a different language.

I tell myself as I leave that it won't be as awful as I think, but I have a bad feeling about this.

I'm meeting Jordan at the student center for a late lunch. I stop by the career office and fill out various applications for jobs.

Jordan already ordered food for both of us at Taco Bell, and I collapse at the table beside him. He wants to know how all of my classes are going, but I don't want to talk about school. I want to talk about his girlfriend.

"Do you still talk to each other every day?"

"Not every day," he says. "But she's still my girlfriend. I'll see her at Thanksgiving and Christmas. We know we love each other, so it's just a matter of patience."

"But aren't you worried she might find someone else?"

He shrugs. "No. She's my girl. That means she's not going to be interested in anyone else."

I won't see Owen on break.

I don't know when I'll see him again.

"I'm sure your boyfriend feels the same," Jordan says, and I know he can tell where my thoughts went. He's trying to reassure me.

It doesn't work.

"He's not my boyfriend. So things are already different."

"Maybe not so different. He'll still be the same person when you see him again."

We finish lunch and go our separate ways. I head back to the religious studies building where I have a theology class with Camila.

Camila is already seated, and I slide in beside her.

"Ready for this class?" she whispers. "I hear the religion classes are super hard."

"I'm intrigued," I whisper back. "A class that combines history in ancient cultures with religion? It's going to be fascinating. The Aztecs, Mayans, Romans . . ." The Honors class I took over the summer, with a brief overview of different holy texts from several other religions, only makes me curious to see where God fits in other cultures.

"Yeah," she says. "Should be interesting."

"Afternoon, students!" The professor jaunts forward and drops a heavy binder on his desk. He faces us with a smile, the skin crinkling around his eyes, gray hair framing his face. "You can call me Professor MacArthur! Think of this class as an in-depth Sunday School—for a grade."

"What are you doing after this?" Camila whispers.

I answer her without looking at her. I don't want to get a reputation on my first day of class. "Meeting Jordan at the library for a library tour. Want to come?"

"They do those?"

"Yeah. It's for freshman."

"No, thanks. I'll figure out where things are on my own."

She must think I'm such a nerd.

I don't care. I'm embracing my inner nerd.

My phone vibrates in my pocket as I leave my religion class, and I stop walking to haul it out, every cell in my body hoping it's Owen.

It's Abby.

My heart tumbles inside my chest. I know this pain. This is what happened when Tiago went home to Brazil. He missed me a lot, and then he quit talking to me.

I'm going to lose Owen the same way.

I swallow hard against the tightness in my throat, willing myself not to cry. It's my fault. Owen would be here with me in Colorado if I hadn't screwed things up.

I force the sadness from my voice and answer the phone with a cheerful, "Hey, girl!"

"Oh, I'm so glad you answered! Did you know there's a free theater on campus?"

No," I say, resuming my walk toward the quad.

"There is. It's an international cinema and it only shows movies from other countries. There's a Korean romance on tonight! Want to see it with me?"

Most of my homework is done, and it will keep me from sitting at home feeling sorry for myself. "All right."

"Great! It's in the cultural studies building. Starts at seven-thirty. See you there!"

"Perfect." It's only two in the afternoon. That gives me time to study for a few hours and eat dinner before going to the movie.

I meet up with Jordan in the green quad, and we head to the library together. Jordan and I signed up for tours at the same time. We stand in the atrium, leaning over the railing that peers down three levels, while we wait for our guide.

"I already know where special collections is," I tell him.

"Why? What is that?"

"It's the forbidden section of the library. Full of books on the dark arts."

He blinks, looking startled, but before I can explain, our tour guide arrives. She's too young to be a professor, so she must be an upper level student. She checks the sign-up sheet.

"Jordan Jones?"

"That's me." Jordan waves.

"And . . . Cassandra Jones?"

"Yes," I say.

She pauses and furrows her brows and looks back and forth between us with something like confusion on her face.

"You're both freshman?"

"Yep," Jordan says again.

She seems perplexed about something, and I tilt my head, trying to figure out what it is.

"Are you . . . related?" she asks.

"Yes," I say.

"You're, um, but you're . . . are you both eighteen?"

And then I realize what she's getting at, and I want to laugh.

She thinks we're married.

CHAPTER FIFTY-ONE

Heart-Melting One Liners

"We're cousins," I say.

Jordan looks at me, his blue eyes twinkling with mirth, and I suspect he would have preferred to keep her ignorant.

"Oh! Oh. Cousins. Yes. that's nice."

I smirk at Jordan. We trail along behind her as she takes us down to the subterranean levels where the glass walls of the atrium create a romantic greenhouse effect over the rows of books and study tables. Special Collections is down here, and I'm dying to tell Jordan how I know about it, but not while she's here.

We take the stairs up to the reference level, then the classical lit level, and she shows us the study rooms students can reserve. There are seven levels in total, and I'm amazed at all the information within this one building.

"And that concludes our tour!" she says, spinning to face us in front of the elevator. "Any questions?"

We both shake our heads. She pushes the button for the main level. "All right! You're welcome to ride down with me or come down when you want."

"Thank you," I say.

I turn and head for one of the tables. I've gotten comfortable here on the fifth floor.

"You're staying here?" Jordan follows me.

I nod. "Need to study. I'm already here, so I may as well get started."

"You're so . . . studious."

"So I've been told."

He stands beside the table for a moment and watches me set out my books. "Well, I'm going to go."

I'm being rude. I stand and give him a hug.

"I'm glad you're here," I say. "It's so fun to hang out."

"Have fun studying."

He leaves me, and only after he's on the elevator do I remember I didn't tell him about my adventures in Special Collections. The thought makes me smile.

I stay at the library and get my homework done, but even as I check off my last assignment, it doesn't diminish the sense of loss aching in my chest. I've been hurting for days, and I refuse to think about it, or I will cry and never stop.

"Do you come here every day?"

I lift my face from my text book, shoving an errant strand of hair from my eyes, and see a boy standing in front of me, backpack slung over one shoulder. He's tall with dark brown hair and light brown skin tone but with startling, dark blue eyes. If Abby asked me to rate him, I'd give him at least a four point five out of five, easy.

So naturally, the stupid words out of my mouth are, "It's only the second day of school."

He smiles and lifts a shoulder. "Which makes it very interesting that you've been here two days in a row."

He's noticed me. Flattery bubbles delightfully in my chest. "Your skills of observation are impressive."

"Will you be back tomorrow?"

Consider me intrigued. I stand and put my laptop and books away, then pull on my backpack. "Maybe."

"Then I'll see you maybe."

He sits down at the table I just vacated, and I steal a glance at him over my shoulder as I leave.

It's interesting how that small interaction alleviated some of the pain in my heart.

I stop by the cafeteria and grab a bowl of noodles before venturing out to the theater to meet Abby.

I expect a line, but there are only six of us. We crowd into the circular room, and I sit next to Abby near the back.

"Did you buy the sports pass?" she asks as soon as I sit.

"What sports pass?" I tuck my backpack under my seat.

"You get into all the basketball and volleyball games for a buck, and you get a discount on football tickets."

"Sounds promising. How much is it?"

"Two hundred dollars."

I balk. "That's a lot."

"One football game ticket will set you back forty bucks."

The sports pass is a good deal. But I can't afford it. "Maybe next year."

"Aren't you going to the first game? It's in two weeks."

"I'll go to that one." And maybe one other. But I can't spend that much money on sports.

My favorite quarterback won't be playing.

"What's the film about?" I ask, changing the subject.

"I'm not too sure. It's called *The Letter*, and the summary is that this woman unexpectedly falls in love with this guy, only to have him die shortly after they marry."

I draw back and wrinkle my nose. "It sounds like a tragedy. I don't do those. I have to have happy ending."

"The description said it's a romance."

The theater darkens, and I sit down in my seat, suspicious. "Maybe Koreans define romances differently."

The movie is in subtitles. At first I find it annoying, but soon I stop noticing them and fall into the plot of the movie. It's pretty cute, she's a teacher, and they meet randomly while riding their bikes home from the bus. He takes her to a park and basically says, "I'm single, you're single, I'm going to flip a coin, and if it lands heads, we should get married." She's about ready to protest when he flips the coin and it lands heads.

So they get married.

It only works because she's lucky enough to have met a stranger without anger issues who's not a narcissistic control freak. The story progresses in a sweet manner as they fall in love with each other after their wedding. It's a beautiful love story, but I have the weight of already knowing he's going to die.

My phone vibrates my pocket. A long vibration, which means it's a phone call. I haul it out, hoping against hope—

It's Owen.

I stand up. "I have to take this," I say someway apologetically. I'm glad now the theater is mostly empty so I don't have to crawl over several sets of legs to get out of the row. I bee-line for the exit and answer as I push open the door.

"Hello?"

The light in the hallway blinds me as I step out of, the theater door closing behind me with a swoosh.

"What's up, killer?"

I laugh. I want to be upset with him for not answering yesterday, for taking two days to get back to me. But it's Owen. His voice resonates in my heart, and the silly nickname warms my soul. "Not much. I'm at the movies." I sink into a bench and rest against the cinderblock wall behind me. "You?"

"At the movies, huh? Who are you with?"

It sounds like an innocent question, but I know it's not. In spite of all the words we said, we can't help digging a little, checking to see if the other is seeing anyone.

I wonder which one of us will cave first.

"My friend Abby. The one I met at Honors Week."

"Oh. Cool. Hey, I'm sorry I didn't call you yesterday. I saw your call, but I was in the middle of practice so I couldn't answer. Well, I tried, but coach yelled at me and made me mad."

It takes a moment to interpret his words. "You left practice to answer my call?"

"I tried. Your calls are important."

His words go along way to assuage the worry in my heart. But is he just saying that? Does he know it's what I want to hear, or does he really feel it?

When did I start doubting Owen? I have issues.

"You didn't call me back," I say.

He doesn't answer for a moment, and I regret saying the words. This is the way things are going to be. We won't talk to each other every day. I can't fight the distance.

"I was going to," he says. "Honest, Cass. I got home and showered, and then I lay down on the bed to do homework, and I fell asleep. I didn't even eat dinner."

"Never mind, Owen," I say, putting that false cheer in my voice that I'm becoming so good at. "You don't have to call me. And you don't need to explain why you didn't."

"I wanted to call you. I miss you."

This time I know he's genuine. Owen wouldn't fake an emotional confession for my sake. "I miss you too. So much! I wish you were here. Everywhere I go I think I see you."

He laughs, that joyful noise that rumbles up from deep in his chest. "I know exactly what you mean. For a moment, this girl in front of me at the bookstore looked just like you from behind. But then she started talking, and it was all southern twang and limited vocabulary, and the illusion ended."

I smile. "Gotta watch out for that southern accent."

"I hear girls like it," he says, turning on his southern drawl.

"Someone's been lying to you," I say breezily.

He grunts. "Dang it."

I kick my feet out from the bench and twirl a strand of hair. "How are your roommates? Are things still weird with them?"

"Weird? No, they're not weird. Just immature. Like they haven't figured out they're not in high school anymore. What about your roommates? How was school?"

"My roommates are nice enough. I have Camila, so I feel comfortable. School's not bad so far. My English teacher thinks I won't know anything because I'm only a freshman. I'm keeping up with my homework. It doesn't feel that different from high school yet."

"Must be nice to be smart."

"I'm not smart. Just—dedicated, I guess. I want to learn, and that requires time and effort."

"Yeah, she is."

His response doesn't fit my comment. And who is she? "What?"

"Oh, sorry. Just talking to myself."

"In the middle of our conversation, you start talking to yourself?"

"The thought that you're probably the most amazing girl alive just crossed my mind, so I had to respond to the thought. Yeah, she is."

"Owen." I can't stop laughing. He delivers these heart-melting one-liners as if he's commenting on the color of your jacket. I'm left without words, wanting to share my feelings with him but lacking anything clever. "I wish you were here."

"We'll see each other soon."

"When?"

"I don't know, maybe this summer. Louisiana is not that far from Arkansas. If we want to, we will."

Why did he add that caveat? Suddenly, I'm full of doubts again. If we want to? Does he think he won't? I should've ended the conversation earlier. The longer we talk, the more sadness I feel. "Well, I better go, I left Abby there in the theater by herself. Thanks for calling me. It was great to hear your voice."

"Yeah, yours too."

I hang up quickly before my sadness leaks into my voice. I'm achy because the words "I love you" are in the back of my throat.

But I didn't feel like I could say them.

How quickly things change.

CHAPTER FIFTY-TWO

Adulting

E ach school day bleeds into the next. My dreams include algebraic expressions and discourses about Newton's law.

Tiago emails me Sunday morning and asks if I would like to chat, and I almost say yes. Am I so starved for male attention? I resist the temptation to engage with him instead tell him I'm busy studying, but he's welcome to email me anytime.

He doesn't respond.

What I need is a job.

I applied for three last week with no response. Monday finds me back at the student resource center, perusing the help wanted ads, taking computer tests, and submitting more applications. Including a telemarketing one, which I would hate. I dread phone calls to my friends. How would I handle calling strangers?

But I'm getting desperate.

Nobody even calls me for an interview.

My conversations with Owen have devolved into texting. Finding time to talk on the phone discourages me. He's never available, and I don't want to be the reason he misses practice.

On Tuesday, Jordan shows up at my apartment.

"Hi," I say, opening the door wide to let him in. "Are you here for dinner? It's ramen."

He shoves his hands into his pockets and shrugs. "I have a meal plan. That includes an all-you-can-eat buffet three times a day. I don't need your ramen."

I grin back at him. "Then why are you here if you don't need me?"

"Let's go for a walk. You've seemed a bit down the past few days."

That's because I am down. But I don't say that.

Even though we've barely crossed into September, the evenings are cool here. I grab a cardigan and follow Jordan outside.

"Have you been to the life science museum yet?"

I shake my head. "No."

"Come on. I hear they have live reptiles."

He had me at "live."

The museum is a quick five-minute walk from my apartment. It's free, and stepping inside reveals a landscape of taxidermy and animals.

"I thought you said they would be alive," I say, scowling at Jordan.

"Not all of them."

"None of them," I say, spinning to look around at the spring bucks and deer, forever frozen standing at attention in their various created habitats.

But Jordan grins in the face of my displeasure. "Come on."

I follow him through the Arctic to the savannas of Africa, to the woodlands of the east, until we get to the marine ecosystem.

The wall-to-wall saltwater aquarium teams with life.

I'm transfixed. I stand in front of the glass and stare at the bright yellow and black fish, the orange ones with the fluffy fins, the neon ones that seem to glow beneath the light.

"I want a fish," I say.

"You want a fish?" Jordan repeats. "Like, to eat?"

I stomp my foot. "Not to eat, you dork!" I say, though I know Jordan understood me perfectly well. "I want an aquarium. Like this one. I want beautiful fish swimming around in my apartment."

"I should have seen that coming," he says, his expression amused. "Although I don't think this will fit in your kitchen."

I ignore him. Now that the idea has occurred to me, it's all I can think of. I follow him through the reptile exhibit, imagining a fish tank in the windowsill, or on the counter, even the kitchen table, with colorful, living objects swimming around.

We come out of the exhibit into a large auditorium, just as a woman enters from a side door. She has a massive lizard wrapped around her shoulders, which ogles Jordan and me when we step near.

I utter a gasp. "He's amazing!"

The woman pauses. She wears a tan jacket to match her tan pants, and a name badge identifies her as an employee, in case the beige uniform didn't give it away.

"This is Phil, our resident iguana," she says, holding her arm out toward me. Phil shifts on his perch around her shoulder, his eyes wobbling.

My first thought is Phil is such a boring name for a beautiful lizard.

"Would you like to touch him?" she asks.

"I'm allowed?" Suddenly I don't care what his name is. I step closer and run my fingers along his leg. The skin is firm and scaly, but somehow also soft and yielding.

Phil lowers his head and licks my hand.

I pull back and give a startled laugh, but it's because I didn't expect it.

"He likes you," the woman says.

"And I like him," I say.

"Better warn her roommates," Jordan says. "Next, she'll want a pet iguana."

I laugh, a bit sheepishly, because he's not wrong.

We leave ten minutes later, and I am significantly cheered. Somehow Jordan knew the right thing to lift my spirits.

"First few days of classes go okay?"

I shrug one shoulder. "So far so good. I won't really know until I have a test. How about you?"

"Yeah, everything is easy so far. Hey, I wanted to run this past you. At my church they announced a new class that just started. It's a Scandinavian choir. It's one credit, just once a week, and they're looking for people to join. Want to do it with me?"

"Scandinavian?" I echo. I know next to nothing about Scandinavian countries and languages. But music is in my soul, and I already miss it. "Why not? I'll do it."

"Yes, that's the spirit!" Jordan hugs me.

I notice as he drops me off at my apartment that the one thing he didn't do was ask me about my feelings or how things are with Owen. It's like he knew that wasn't what I needed right now.

⁓⁜⁓

"We think you'd be a great fit for our company," Jeff says over the phone. "Come by the office on Saturday morning for orientation and we'll fill out your paperwork."

My heart pounds too fast, my stomach knotted up.

We haven't met in person. But the job involves talking on the phone, so that's how Jeff wanted to meet. He emailed me a script and I read it to him as if he were a potential donor.

"It's not telemarketing," he continues, as if he feels my anxiety through the phone. "We're calling alumni and asking them to give back to the school that provided them with their education."

I don't want this job. But no one else has offered. And I need money.

"I'll come by Saturday," I say.

That gives me two days to get used to the idea.

As soon as Jeff hangs up, I text Owen.

Me: I got a job

It takes two hours for him to respond. I'm unloading our now fully functioning dishwasher when I hear the phone chime.

O: you can't be lazy for awhile?

I can hear his voice in his words. Picture his expression. I leave the counter and sink into the couch, curling up with the phone in my hands, losing myself in an imaginary world where he is beside me.

Me: I tried but my bank account ran dry

O: stop buying expensive wine

I laugh. It's not that funny, but to me it is. I feel my worries melting away.

Me: bad habits.

O: so what's your job involve this time?

Me: calling people

I try to picture his reaction. He'll laugh, maybe lift an eyebrow and try not to look skeptical.

O: whoa. It's like they knew that's your favorite thing

Me: almost like they did

O: are you nervous about it?

He's switched gears now, from teasing to serious.

Me: a little. Less so now that I'm talking to him. It doesn't seem important anymore.

O: it's a job. If you hate it you can quit.

Except I can't. No one else is offering, and I need the money or I can't afford everything that comes along with school. Owen doesn't know what that's like. To need money.

I don't say that. I just say, *yeah.*

He doesn't respond. My message shows delivered but unread.

He must have gone somewhere.

I put my phone down, despondent and trying not to be. I won't live this year waiting for him to respond.

I text Jordan next and tell him I got a job.

Hey, that's great! he says.

He comes over Saturday morning before I leave for my training. He sits by me on the couch while I eat a bowl of oatmeal I cooked in the microwave, one of my go-to meals.

My roommates shuffle in one by one and bid Jordan a good morning. Camila gives him a big smile, and Layne pokes his chest and elbows his ribcage.

"You'll be home in time for the game?" she asks me.

I nod. "Yes." We splurged and bought tickets together.

She shoots another flashing smile at Jordan. "Good to see you."

He watches her leave, a somewhat amused expression on his face. "Quite the flirt, isn't she?" he says after she's closed the door.

"Oh, yeah. She flirts with everyone. I told her you have a girlfriend, but that didn't phase her."

"Everyone knows people who left boyfriends and girlfriends behind are fair game."

"Do they?" I murmur. My eyes drift off, losing focus on the cinderblock wall behind Jordan.

My phone chimes, and I glance down to see a text from Owen, as if my thoughts have conjured him.

O: Good luck today. Con everyone out of their money.

I burst out laughing. "He remembered!"

"Who? Remembered what?"

I don't bother responding. I am giddy with joy. All it takes is one text from him to change my whole day. I grab my car keys. "I'll see you later."

Jordan puts his feet on the table. "No worries. I'll chill here."

I hum all the way to my new employment. The building sits in the foothills of one of the mountains, and a path winds behind it to explore the local mountain range.

I step into the building, and a woman greets me.

"Hi, I'm Becky. Keep going down the hall and you'll see a break room. That's where everyone's meeting for training."

I nod and thank her and continue down the hall. Voices greet me before I see them, and when I round the corner, I spot more than twenty people sitting at tables, already conversing.

I freeze, a moment of introverted panic seizing my nerves. They look older than me, comfortable with each other and new situations. My eyes dart to a small round table near the back with nobody at it.

Don't sit there, I tell myself. Steeling myself, I see an open chair at a table close to the front and force myself to pull out a chair and sit there instead.

A larger, dark-haired girl with broad shoulders turns to me at once. "My name is Mindy," she says, with a clear lisp and an obvious accent. "Who are you?"

"Cassandra," I say, pleating my hands in my lap.

"Cassandra, meet Jeremy, Stirling, and Jamie."

All boys. Jamie has bright red hair, Jeremy has curly dark hair, and Stirling stares off into space with a vacant expression on his face, his hair concealed by a baseball cap.

"Nice to meet you all," I say.

"Hello, new recruits!" A man steps to the front of the room, clasping his hands and smiling. "I'm your boss, Jeff! I'm the one who did the interview and tryout with you on the phone. We have twenty-four new hires! Three of you are incoming freshmen. Welcome to Preston Y! The rest of you, I don't know where you came from."

There's a spattering of polite laughter. But Jeff is funny and enthusiastic, and even though I suspect I will hate this job, I can't help liking him.

"What you're going to be doing is calling up alumni and asking them to donate to scholarships. Some of them will do so happily. Some of them will do so grudgingly. Some of them will hate your guts for calling."

This is what I'm dreading. But the way he says it makes me laugh.

"The key is not to take this too seriously. We care about the campaign, but it's not personal. Don't get your feelings hurt. If someone turns you down, hit the next number." Jeff gestures us forward. "To the training room."

We move into a room lined with cubicles. Each one has a computer screen and a headset. Becky sits down next to me.

"I'm going to be your trainer, okay?" she says.

I take a better look at her. She's only a few years older than me, with big blue eyes, blond hair in a high ponytail, and broad shoulders. A diamond ring sparkles on her finger.

"You're married?" I ask.

She smiles. "Six months tomorrow."

"How old are you?" I can't help asking.

"Twenty."

Whoa. I'm fairly certain I don't want to be married in two years.

We spend the first hour going through the screens on the computer and filling out the fields, and then we practice calling other new recruits and pretending like we are potential pledges. I call Stirling, who's sitting at the cubicle next to me. We make eye-contact, and he puts on such a thick accent when he answers the call that I have to ask him to repeat himself four or five times. He gives me a fake name and I can't stop giggling. Then he grins at me. His hat is off because he couldn't get his headset over it, and I notice the light color of his eyes, the brown waves in his hair.

"What accent were you using?" I ask.

"Icelandic," he says.

"Icelandic." I'm intrigued. "Are you Icelandic?"

He shakes his head. "No, but I did a mission in Iceland. Everyone wanted to practice their English on me, so I became familiar with the accent."

"My cousin and I joined a Scandinavian choir."

"Really? Why?"

I shrug. "I like singing and they didn't require a tryout? And it looks like an easy class."

"That's cool! Scandinavian pop music is really fun."

Becky leans between us. "Great job, Cassandra. Stirling, now it's your turn. You have to call her."

I'm not nearly as creative with my persona. It's a boring phone call where I agree to send a one-time pledge of five dollars.

Then Becky turns to me. "I think you understand the process. Now you get to listen in while I make real calls and take pledges."

I'm not nervous. At least, I'm not until I listen to the way some people react to being called. Becky remains calm as a woman screams at her for calling her number when she's on the "Do not call" list.

"Yes, ma'am, I understand." Becky hangs up and shakes her head.

"What does that mean? Are we not supposed to call them?" I ask.

"It means nothing. First, the 'Do not call' registry stopped existing in the early 2000s. Second, this isn't telemarketing, it's charity work, and the 'Do not call' list wouldn't apply."

That makes sense to me. But still . . . "So you get a lot of angry people?"

She doesn't even try to sugarcoat it for me. "Yes." She follows her words up with a smile.

I grow more anxious through every call. Next time it will be my turn.

Stirling catches up with me when our shift ends and walks with me to the parking lot. "I'm not much of a singer. But I loved Iceland. Maybe I'll come join this choir."

I laugh. "I'll be there. With my cousin."

At least I made a friend today.

CHAPTER FIFTY-THREE

Manifestation

Abby texts me as I pull out a pair of jeans for the game.

A: You better be there.

Me: I'm getting ready.

A: Next Friday we're going clubbing. I won't let you weasel out of it.

I roll my eyes.

Me: I know. Layne already told me we're doing it. She and Abby hit it off when they met. I'd be jealous except Abby still seems to prefer my company.

A: It'll be a blast.

Layne comes into my room and gives me a once-over. "You look like a country girl. Put on some make up, take down your hair."

"I am a country girl." I look down at my button-up shirt and realize I look like I'm wearing one of my dad's flannel shirts. Not wanting to be labeled the hick she thinks I am, I change into a red pleasant blouse, one of my favorites.

She laughs and shakes her head. "That's not any better."

Camila pops in, her arm hooked through Iris's. "Let's go! We need to hurry if we're going to get good seats!"

"We don't have assigned seats?" I check the tickets again and see that we don't.

"It's a mile from here. It's going to take at least twenty minutes to walk there," Iris says.

I haven't been to a football game since last fall. I will never think of them the same again.

It takes another seven minutes, but we manage to get out the door. We follow the parade of students exiting dorms and apartments along the street, all of them heading toward the football stadium.

My phone rings, and I pull it out to see it's Owen. A smile spreads across my face, and I answer while we walk.

"Owen! Every time I thought about you today, you contacted me!"

"I texted you once and I called you once. You only thought about me twice today?"

I roll my eyes. "That's not what I meant."

"Right. Now you're trying to make me feel better."

My roommates are glancing at me, very aware that I'm talking to Owen. The Owen. They know all about him. Somehow I work him into nearly every conversation, even when I'm not trying.

Is he still mine?

"Well, I don't want your head to get too big," I say, keeping with his jovial mood. "I do think about you a lot."

"Good."

And that's it. I give a little sigh. I wish he would give me affirmation and not just joke with me.

"What are you doing?" he asks.

"Walking."

"To where?"

"The football game."

"Oh." Now his tone carries a note of fondness. "Sweet. Our first game is next Saturday. Are you coming?"

My heart warms with the idea. I wish I could hop on a plane and go. "You got me a ticket?"

"Front row seat."

He's joking. Right? I want to tease back, but what if he's serious?

It makes my heart skip a beat.

It's his first college game.

I should be there.

"Hey," he says, and he sounds more serious. "I'm messing around. I know you can't be there."

I want to cry. He knows me so well that even across the country, even when I don't say a word, he knows what I'm thinking.

"I would be there if I could," I say.

"And on the off-chance that you do show up," he says, jovial again, "I'll always have front-row seats saved for you."

I don't respond. I feel wretched. I want to take out my savings and fly to Louisiana and be his devoted girlfriend.

I need that money if I'm going to stay in school.

"Cassandra?" he says.

"Sorry." I smile hard, hoping it will show in my words. "I was crossing the street. Had to pay attention."

"Don't get hit by a car," he drawls.

I can't tell if he's buying my bluff or letting me off the hook. The conversation somehow became painful. "Yeah. Wish us luck. I hear last year was a losing season."

"PYU's going to have a great one this year. Maybe you'll even play us."

"I hope so," I say. Because I will be at that game, no matter what it takes.

Layne loops an arm through mine. "Cassandra!" she shouts, leaning toward the phone. "We gotta go!"

She says it directly for Owen's benefit.

"Sounds like you better get to the game," he says.

I scowl at Layne, annoyed she brought our conversation to an end, but she's right. "Okay. I'll talk to you later."

"Have fun. See ya."

He hangs up and I put my phone away, and my friends gather around me, cackling as they guide me through the crowd to the stadium gates.

"Did he say he loves you?"

"Want to kiss him now?"

"Oh, Owen!"

They bat their eyes and make kissy noises at me, and I can't help laughing.

I also can't help noticing that he didn't say he loved me.

Again.

We show our tickets at the gate. My phone vibrates, and I pause to check it.

"Abby's in section G," I say. "Row one-hundred and fourteen. Halfway down." I glance up at the entrances to the seats.

"This way."

Layne leads us. People press in on us at all sides. The scents of roasting hot dogs, gooey nacho cheese, and buttery popcorn mingle for a not-unpleasant olfactory offering, and my stomach growls. The noise of the marching band echoes in the walkway, and the chatter of hundreds of voices vibrates through my mind. Camila takes my hand, and I grab Iris so we don't lose each other. We hurry after Layne.

I shield my eyes against the sun when we step out in section G. I'm astonished at how many sections there are, how many rows, how many people. I stand too long in the stairway, and someone knocks into my shoulder.

"Keep going!" he says.

"Sorry," I say.

"This way." Camila pulls me forward.

We spot Abby in a white baseball cap, her red hair curling around her shoulders. She's standing, and she waves and jumps up and down when she sees us. I scan the seats around her but don't see any openings.

"Where are we supposed to sit?" Iris asks.

"We make room," Layne says. She begins the uncomfortable task of pushing past people, mumbling apologies and returning dirty looks at those annoyed by our passing.

"Come on," Abby says when we arrive. She lifts several blankets from the bleachers. "I saved you spots."

A girl turns to stare at us as we climb over to Abby. "There's not room for all of you."

"We'll squish in," I say, huddling closer to Camila.

"You don't fit," she says. She turns to the boy with her. "They're taking up too much room."

"This is our spot," he says, leaning over to add his disapproval. "You can't cram yourselves in here."

"I saved this spot for them," Abby says. "You guys pushed your way in."

"We were here first!" the girl says.

"Sorry," Layne says, her tone anything but as she pushes the blankets on the bench so we take up more room than we need. "We're here now too."

The girl and her man glare at us and whisper nasty things about us under their breath. I cower against Camila and Abby and giggle into Abby's shoulder.

"They don't like us," I say.

"No, they don't," she agrees. "But they can't do anything about it."

And we both giggle, and I feel both guilty and victorious.

The energy behind the game is dynamic, electric. The whistle blows, and the players charge onto the field. I don't have a special person to cheer for, so I don't expect to get so heavily involved with game, but every time our team has the ball, I'm on my feet with my roommates and the strangers who hate us, all of us screaming and shouting, rooting for the same thing. The marching band joins the swell, blasting popular show tunes, drumming out a beat while the brass instruments pump out exciting notes that make my blood pump faster.

The other team matches us touchdown for touchdown, and we're down to the last minute of the game. Suddenly the quarterback has the ball, and he's racing down the field.

"Luke! Luke! Luke!"

The chant begins from an unknown place in the stadium, and we all take it up. I hope the kid's name is Luke, or we're cheering for the wrong person.

Thirty seconds left. Luke bolts across the line, and I scream, we throw our arms up, and we score.

The field goal follows, and my team wins.

My team.

That's why this feels so personal. I'm not cheering for an individual anymore. I'm cheering for a team.

I have a team.

It's an awesome feeling.

⟨੭ᕥᨒᩘ⟩

My throat aches from screaming.

It's after ten at night when we begin the walk back to our dorms, but we are boisterous, noisy, bumping into each other and laughing and reliving each exciting play as we join the throng of students moving toward campus.

I text Owen to tell him we won, though I'm sure he knows. He probably watched the game.

Abby joins us in our apartment, and we open several bottles of soda to celebrate.

"Let's do something," Layne says. "The night is young."

"Yes!" Abby says, sipping her soda and pumping a fist.

I glance at the clock. "It's almost eleven." I think of the assignments I didn't quite finish up. "And I have homework."

"Do it tomorrow!" Layne pulls out her phone and begins scrolling. "Black Sheep's open."

"Oh, you know Black Sheep!" Abby perks up. "Cassandra, that's the club I've been trying to get you to go to!"

"Not tonight, guys," I say, feeling a stirring of anxiety. "I've had enough of people for one day." All I want is to sit in my room and zone in on school work.

They laugh at me.

"I'll go with you," Layne says.

"I don't have a car."

Now all eyes turn to me.

Oh, crap. I'm the only one with a car.

"Next week," I say, feeling my heartbeat increase. "I promise I'll take everyone next week."

Layne heaves an aggravated sigh. "Fine."

I glance at Camila. I know what Layne thinks. I'm boring. I'm no fun. I'm a buzz-kill.

It's what everyone thinks.

Why did Owen want to date me, anyway?

I turn around and go back to my room to get started on my homework.

Camila joins me. "I think I'll go to bed," she says.

The other girls pile into Layne's room, and the sounds of a movie pump between our thin walls. They keep laughing, and I wish I was in there also. I stare at my math homework and will myself to understand the algebraic equations.

I should do more fun things.

I'm here to get an education.

I won't always have this chance.

I finish up the math and open my computer to work on one of my English essays. My plan is two English classes every semester so I can knock out these major requirements in three years instead of four. Then maybe I'll graduate early. Or maybe I'll study something else for fun.

Not that this is fun. This is work.

It's after one in the morning when their movie finishes. Camila sleeps soundly in her bed, a mask over her eyes, her deep breathing audible from my side of the room. I'm halfway through one English essay when Abby barges into my room.

"Cassandra," she says, purring. She climbs up onto my bed and pulls the computer away from me to take my hands. "Let's go to Denny's."

"Denny's?" I say, arching an eyebrow. "It's after one in the morning."

She nods. "They're open twenty-four/seven. And we're hungry. Come on!"

Layne and Iris appear in the doorway, grinning, watching me hopefully.

"It'll be fun!" Iris says.

Fun. I want to be fun. I blink at them and then back at Abby. And then I laugh. "All right." There's no one to tell us it's a bad idea. No one to say we should be sleeping. No one to forbid us going out.

I stand and get my car keys, feeling a thrilling rush of power. I'm an adult now. If I want to go out after midnight, spend my money foolishly at a chain restaurant, I can. I will.

There are worse things I could do to manifest my independence.

CHAPTER FIFTY-FOUR

Flexing her Wings

We sleep in Sunday and almost miss church. But Camila, who didn't participate in the late night extravaganza to Denny's, wakes us in the nick of time. I throw clothes on and brush my hair and head out the door.

Right away Layne finds the boys. I think I recognize one from the library, but I don't get close and he doesn't see me. Layne zooms in on them, flitting over like a bumble bee and then buzzing around, sucking energy from each one. They stare after her when she walks away as if they realize she took something from them but can't figure out what it is.

"She's such a flirt," Iris says beside me, her eyes narrowed. "It's annoying."

I don't think it's annoying until they flock over to our apartment after church. I arrive home first, and I've just sat down on the couch to read when the back door opens and five or six boys come in with Layne.

She's giggling and flushed and stops at the table to tease them, poking arms and shoving shoulders when they walk by. I try to keep reading, but two of them find me, plopping down on the couch beside me.

"Hey," one says. "We've met, right?"

I lift my eyes, and it's the boy I met at the library. Warmth creeps up my cheeks, but I pretend I don't remember. "Um."

"It's Jared."

His blue eyes reel me in, and I'm almost relieved when the other kid bumps my thigh and redirects my attention.

"What are you reading?" He plucks my book right out of my hands.

I'm incensed. "A book." I take it back from him.

He laughs. "Clearly. I'm Justin. You are?"

I glance over at Layne, who's attempting to get water for the other boys but is laughing so hard she keeps spilling it.

"Layne's roommate," I say, and I get up and leave the kitchen.

"What's wrong with her?" I hear one of them ask.

"Oh, don't mind her," Layne says. "She left a boy behind in Arkansas. She gets bitchy sometimes."

I close my bedroom door. Thanks, Layne. What am I supposed to do? I'm not interested in those boys.

⟳↝🌣↝⟲

Layne comes in to see me after the boys have left.

"Jared thinks you're cute," she says.

My mind recalls Jared's image without my permission, the way his blue eyes looked beneath his curly dark hair when he sat beside me on the couch. "Okay."

She puts her hands on her hips and huffs, blowing the hair out of her face. "He's cute too."

He is. But I'm not admitting that. "I'm not interested in dating anyone."

She comes into the room and sits at my computer desk. "It's college, Cassandra," she needles. "You need to have fun."

There's that word again. "I am having fun," I protest.

She rolls her eyes. "Go on a few dates if boys ask you out. That's all. You don't have to kiss them or promise to marry them."

"I'm not opposed to going out," I say, defensive. "But Jared didn't ask."

"Yet." She smirks. "He's a football player."

I shouldn't care. But football players make me think of Owen, and instead of driving me away from Jared, it makes me feel an affinity toward him. I turn back to my book and don't answer, but I don't fool her. I can tell from the way she laughs as she walks away.

The next night at work, Stirling, the boy who can fake an Icelandic accent and always wears a baseball cap, asks me out.

"There's a movie playing on campus," he says. "Want to see it? A bunch of us are going."

I'm so startled I forget to hit dial on my keypad. I blink at my screen, wondering why it's not calling the next person on the list before realizing I stopped mid-dial. "Um. Which movie?" I hit the button, and the number on my screen dials.

"An old Alfred Hitchcock. They're doing a classics throwback every Monday for the next few months. Tonight is *The Birds*. We can catch it right after work, then maybe get a bite to eat."

"Isn't that the one where they pluck out people's eyes?" I love Hitchcock's movies, but that's one I haven't seen, and for a reason.

He turns away to his computer and slides his microphone in front of his mouth. "Hi, I'm Stirling, and I'm calling from the Preston Yarborough student support center."

I do the same as someone on the other end of my line says, "Hello?"

"Hello! I'm Cassandra, and I'm calling from the Preston Yarborough University student support center—" I begin.

"Oh, yes, Preston Y. I loved that school."

"Yes, sir." I beam at the screen. "Well, I'm calling tonight because—"

"Cassandra? Let me stop you there. I met my darling Julia at Preston Y thirty-

299

two years ago, and she died two days ago. I'm in the middle of funeral plans, and unless you're sending flowers, this isn't a discussion I'm prepared to have today."

I gape like a fish, my mouth working with no noise. And then I sputter, "I'm so sorry. Absolutely. I'm sorry. My thoughts are with you." My throat closes up, my eyes burning, and I know I'm about to cry. "Have a good night."

I hang up and burst into tears, a perfectly typical reaction for me.

Immediately my coworkers spin toward me, concern on their faces.

"What happened?" Becky asks.

"Was someone rude to you?" Mindy says.

"No. No. It's nothing." I stand up, wiping my face. "His wife just died. That's all." I push past their chairs, into the hall and toward the bathroom.

Behind me, Becky says, "What a tender heart!" and my coworkers murmur in agreement.

I make a face, annoyed with myself.

I see them glance at me surreptitiously when I return, but everyone keeps their eyes on their computer screens and politely pretends they don't notice my red-rimmed eyes. At least I get through the rest of my calls with no further dramatic incidents.

Stirling walks with me out to my car after work. "Thoughts on the movie tonight?"

He didn't bring it up after my crying episode, and I'd hoped he'd forgotten. "Rain check?" I say. "I have a thing with eyes. Particularly loosing them." I mime poking my eye with my finger.

"Oh." He laughs. "Sure. Next week is *Room with a View*. Want to do that one?"

I've run out of excuses. Nobody loses any eyes in that one. "Yeah, if I don't have too much homework."

He unlocks his car and gets in. "Great! See you tomorrow."

Did I just agree to a date? I drive home in turmoil and feel overwhelmed as I open my apartment door. My roommates are sitting around the table talking, and I say hello before going to my room. I open my computer. I planned to do homework but find myself in my email box instead, checking out of reality by clicking on random emails.

There's one from Tiago. We haven't spoken in over a week. I open it now and read through it.

Hey Cassandra,
Hope school's going well for you!
I'd love to chat sometime. I know you're busy. Just want to see how things are.
Your friend,
Tiago

I open a response box and email back.

Tiago,
Sorry I haven't written! I'm so overwhelmed already. School gets harder every day. It takes a lot of my mental focus.
There's also so many BOYS here. They are always around my apartment, at church, at work. I want to run and hide but I can't! One asked me out today. I felt

trapped and I panicked and said yes! Now I have to go on a date and I don't want to.

This probably makes no sense to you. But I'm freaking out over it.

Cassandra

I feel better having written my feelings. I exhale and tell myself it's not a big deal, and then I open my physics book. Abby and I are working on a project together. Tomorrow we'll meet up before class to finish it up. I don't understand half of what I read, but she's brilliant, and when we talk about it, it makes sense.

A new email appears in my inbox. It's Tiago. Anything is better than physical science. I open his email.

Cassandra,

Forgive me while I laugh at you. I can't help it. Of course the guys are interested in you. You're not a kid anymore. And you're beautiful.

It's good for you to go on a few dates. We're only young once. Have fun, let them treat you special. Enjoy this time.

Don't stress about school. No one asks what grades you got ten years from now.

Your friend,

Tiago

He's so right. His words finally sink in where no one else's have. I can go out with guys. It's not much different than going out with my roommates. I'm not looking for anything.

I finish up my physical science homework, much less agitated now.

CHAPTER FIFTY-FIVE
Constant Companion

Abby meets me in the hall before our physical science lab the next morning. It's our turn to present a real-world activity that proves one of the laws of physics.

"I've got the little boats," she says, pulling out a plastic container with foil objects within it. "Do you have the other items?"

I nod and hold up the grocery sack of wind up toys and bouncy balls.

"Great. Come on." She grabs my arm and pulls me into the smaller classroom.

"So glad we're not doing this in front of everyone," I say, thinking of the large auditorium where Professor Turnbaugh teaches us.

"I hear the TAs grade hard," Abby murmurs. "We might wish we'd done this in front of everyone."

The door opens, and the TA walks in wearing a badge on a lanyard.

"I'm Aubrey," she says, flashing a smile. She checks a clipboard on the wall. "You must be Abby and Cassandra."

"Yes," Abby says. I've gone suddenly mute.

"Do you guys need anything for your presentation?"

Abby glances around the work station at the front of the room. "We need to fill this bin with water."

"There's a tap right behind you."

I take the bin from Abby and fill it up. I'd rather be the silent partner here.

Kids file in for the class, and my heart rate ratchets up a notch.

"We're ready when you are," Aubrey says, settling herself in the front row with a clipboard.

Abby looks at me, and I remember I have the first speaking part. I step forward, clearing my throat.

"We're doing an experiment involving the density, or the mass per volume, of each of our aluminum ships compared to the density of water. We'll also note what happens when we add cargo to the ships and further increase their density."

I take one of the little foil ships and place it in the water. Aubrey takes notes as I talk about what I'm doing. Then Abby steps forward.

"Not all of our boats are the same size," she says. "So we can expect different sizes to hold more and float better than others."

The experiment goes as we expect. One bouncy ball sinks the small boats, but the big ones can hold a bouncy ball and several paper clips. We didn't try it before coming to class but made our own hypothesis, which we share with the class and prove to be correct.

"Nicely done," Aubrey says when we finish. "I'll turn your score into Mr. Turnbaugh. He should have it graded later today."

"That went well," Abby breathes, dumping out the water.

I trash the aluminum foil boats. "At least I didn't freeze up."

"You're a natural in front of people. You shouldn't be shy." She holds out the bag of paper clips and bouncy balls. "Want these?"

"No. I only bought them for this."

She grabs the bouncy balls and tosses the bag with the everything else into a trashcan, then proceeds to bounce the balls down the hallway as we exit the classroom. Students turn their heads to watch and laugh when the balls pummel unsuspecting kids, and I laugh too.

"I don't think you'll get those back," I say, watching as various students pluck up the balls and stuff them into their pockets.

She shrugs. "So, how's your week going?"

"Fine." I hesitate, then blurt, "I have a date on Monday."

"Ha!" she crows. "You broke! I don't even have a date yet!"

I roll my eyes. "You could."

"I would, if anyone asked me out."

I can't fathom why no one's asked her out. Abby's beautiful and vivacious and fun. "They will."

"Are you excited?"

I shrug, and we pause in the entryway. "I only said yes because I couldn't think of an excuse fast enough."

Abby laughs. "It was meant to be. Are you going to tell Owen?"

I shake my head. "We agreed not to tell each other things like that."

"So you both knew you would date other people."

"I suppose we did." I hadn't wanted to acknowledge it then. "We are not together."

I say it with the tone of someone who has just realized, even though I've been saying it out loud for weeks.

"No, you are not," she says, and the glance she casts my direction is sympathetic. "And that's okay."

"It's okay," I repeat.

It still hurts.

We go separate directions after that, with me headed toward my English class at the Honors building.

"Hi, guys!" Ms. Mayhew says as she enters the classroom. "I'm super excited for today! We get to write!"

No one reacts, but my spirit gives a leap of joy.

She tsks. "I can see how happy this makes you. Pull out your notebook!"

"This feels like high school," Mason says.

"Good. That means your high school prepared you for college." Her smile doesn't diminish. "We're going to do a rush-write. What that means is, I give you a prompt, and you spend fifteen minutes writing about it. This is like creative writing, except you have parameters to hit. I want all five senses in here: sight, taste, touch, smell, and hearing. Bring me into the moment. Put a fake name on your paper and explore with words."

I open my notebook and get out my pen, ready.

"Here's your prompt: write a memory that makes you cringe. Maybe you're embarrassed by it. Maybe you regret it. I want something that still wounds you when you think of it. Make me feel it also."

I tap my pen on my lips, thinking. I have many regrets, many moments that shook my world.

The immediate one that comes to mind is when Owen broke up with me.

My heart skips a beat just remembering. The expression on his face when he came out of my bathroom—after he'd read the texts from Tiago—the way he crumbled when he said we were over.

It hurts too much. I'm breathing too quickly, my eyes watering, reliving everything I lost because of that indiscretion.

I shove that memory away. Besides, it's too cliche. Everyone's gone through a breakup. What's special about mine?

There was the time I broke up with him. I actually swore at him. He broke my heart that day.

I don't want to write about Owen. My heart is too tender concerning him. I don't know if there is a future with him anymore.

My mind falls back to my next worse memory. The terrible moment my parents discovered my illicit romance with Tiago.

I suck in a breath, because this memory also hurts. But the sting isn't as sharp, the pain not as poignant. I bend my head over the paper and begin to write.

In my basement, beneath the kitchen where my mom stood stirring a pot of chicken soup, the scent of onions and garlic hanging in the air, lived a boy. A teenage boy with thick black hair, curls so tight my fingers would get tangled in the coils, eyes so dark the pupils were nearly indiscernible from the irises.

My family bantered over dishes and setting the table and the amount of salt in the soup while I slunk down the stairs to the bedroom of this boy. This boy who was not my brother, but an exchange student staying in my house for a year.

This boy who I had fallen in love with.

We stole moments when no one was watching. Forced to hide our feelings, we met in dark shadows, away from prying eyes, and what started as a sweet, innocent romance quickly fermented into a drunken, lustful grab. He took me when I came into his room, the minty taste of his lips on mine, and we wasted no time falling together on the bed, hands groping our bodies' secret places, seeking satisfaction.

It was only a matter of time before we were discovered.

I write feverishly, worried I won't get to the dramatic conclusion before the fifteen minutes are up. It surprises me the strength of feelings these memories draw up. Things I haven't thought on, haven't dwelled on, in over a year. But I remember the shame when we were discovered, the agony when my parents ripped us apart, and the unbearable ache when he banished me from his heart for months.

I leave it there, in the moment of discovery, the story suspended by the weight of the consequences of our forbidden romance.

"All right, that's time!" Ms. Mayhew says. "Now I want you to split into groups of three."

The kid next to me shoves his desk toward mine. "Group?" he says, pointing to me and another girl.

I nod and we bunch up together.

"Now, pass your papers around," Ms. Mayhew says.

I freeze. What?

"Each person in your group will read your paper. You'll vote on which one uses the senses the best and which one touches you the most, and then discuss the pros and cons of each one."

My heart flutters. No. I don't want to share this. No one should know this about me. Isn't that why we put fake names?

But there is no time to write something else.

"I'm Brad," the boy says.

"Kayla," the girl says.

"Cassandra," I say.

I keep my eyes lowered as we pass our papers and pray they won't know which is mine. But my heart rattles in my throat as we read silently. I try to concentrate on the essay I hold in my hands, but my eyes keep darting to my peers. What are they thinking? We pass the papers again until we've read all of them.

"All done, right?" Brad says, looking up and taking charge. He puts the essay he holds in the middle of the table.

Mine.

Kayla and I nod and add the essays to the pile.

"So I liked this one the most," he says, holding up my essay.

"Me too," Kayla says. "I thought it was the most visual and personal."

"I could feel her pain." Brad fingers my essay. "I felt the heightened excitement. That high juxtaposed against the low of discovery made my heart heavy."

"Same," Kayla says. "It was one of the saddest things I've ever read."

They both look at me. There's no way around it. They know I wrote it. So I say, sheepishly, "Thanks."

But there's no judgment in their faces. No condescension in their eyes.

We switch groups two more times and go through the same scenario, and each time, the groups choose my essay as the best. I'm humbled. Still embarrassed—but less so.

Maybe I'm not the only one who has screwed up in their life.

I pick Jordan up after work to go grocery shopping. The store is closing, since it's a quarter to ten, and we whip through the aisles grabbing what we need. He puts crackers, chips, and dried fruit in the cart while I grab ramen, clam chowder, and instant pasta.

"That stuff will make you sick if you keep eating it," he says.

I shrug. "It's all I have time for."

"You need more meals on your meal plan."

"Then I'd get fat." I grab the skin around my belly, shoving down the noxious paranoia that it's already happening.

"Nah, you walk around too much."

I lift a shoulder. Everyone walks as much as I do. "Classes going well?"

"Pretty easy. Yours?"

I groan. "Today was so embarrassing!" I proceed to tell him about my incident with the incriminating essay in my English class, and he can't stop laughing.

"I want to read it."

"No way!" I scowl at him. "I talked about sexual stuff!"

"That's why I want to read it!"

I wack his arm, and he laughs.

"Ow," he grumbles. "That hurt. Girls hit hard."

"We don't have a lot of defenses," I point out. "How are things with your girl back home?"

"We don't talk as much. We're both busy. It gets that way in college, I guess."

"I guess." I check out my food items, and we head to my car. "I didn't think it would happen this quickly, though. It's only September, and Owen feels so far away."

"He is far away."

"You are not helping!"

Jordan laughs. We load up the car, and he says, "I know it feels like everything hinges on these moments, but it doesn't. Our lives are going to keep going no matter what we do."

"But will they keep going in the direction I want? I'm not worried about them ending."

Jordan shrugs. "In the end, you'll be happy with the direction."

"I don't buy that. Just because things turn out a certain way doesn't mean it's the ending you wanted."

I park at my apartment and we unload my groceries, but I'm not done talking. So we go back outside and settle on the stairs of the fire escape.

"Yeah, I suppose we might not end up with the ending we want," he says. "But what can you do about it?"

I think of my screw ups. "I suppose not making mistakes isn't a possibility."

"Not really."

I sigh and run my fingers along the banister. "Owen would be here. If I'd played my cards right, he'd be at a community college an hour from here right now."

Jordan studies me. "What happened? Why isn't he here?"

A knot makes my throat ache. "I hurt him, and he stopped seeing me as his future."

"All because he got hurt?"

I shake my head. "He couldn't get over it."

"That's kind of on him, then."

Jordan's too pragmatic. I can't blame Owen. Though sometimes I do.

When I say nothing more, Jordan continues. "Okay, so say that hadn't happened. He'd be out here with you. And then what? You guys would get married next year?"

"No. He would go on his mission. I'd go on one."

"And then you'd be apart for a few years like you are now. It doesn't matter how you planned it, a separation was inevitable. Unless you changed your mind and decided to get married."

"I'm only eighteen!"

"And next year you'd be only nineteen. And then only twenty. So." He shrugs. "You ended up separated faster than you anticipated. Maybe it's your fault. Or maybe it was what was meant to happen."

"I never considered it that way," I murmur. I run my hands on the rocky cement of the steps beneath me, feeling the bumps and jolts beneath my skin.

Jordan knocks my shoulder with his. "It had to happen."

I exhale. I wonder how long I will carry this guilt, this feeling that I ruined everything between us. I hear Jordan's words, but I can't grasp them. "Maybe it did."

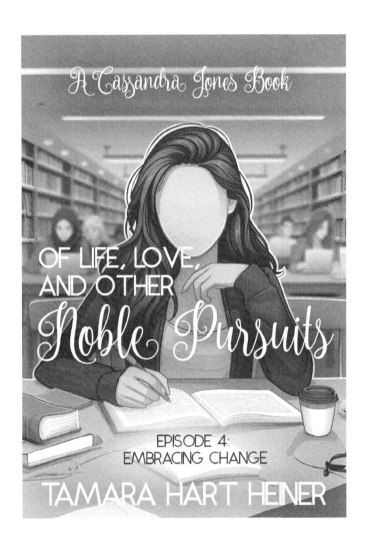

A Cassandra Jones Book

OF LIFE, LOVE, AND OTHER

Noble Pursuits

EPISODE 4:
EMBRACING CHANGE

TAMARA HART HEINER

CHAPTER FIFTY-SIX

Tender Heart

S unlight streams through the window and across my bed, waking me in the morning. I blink and stretch my arms, feeling warm and lazy after a good night's sleep. I love Saturday mornings—

It's not Saturday.

I bolt upright as I remember staying outside talking with Jordan until around two in the morning last night. Tuesday night.

It's Wednesday.

I grab my phone. My class starts in ten minutes. Ten minutes! There's no time for anything. I jump up and run to the bathroom, only to discover I've started my period.

Of course I have! Only because I'm in a hurry! I jab the tampon into place, wash my hands, brush my teeth, and throw on a change of clothes. I stuff my contacts and make up into my purse. I'll beautify myself after my first class.

I run to campus. Huffing and puffing, dragging on my water bottle, I slide into my seat beside Abby five minutes after class starts.

"You all right?" she asks, looking me over.

"I woke up fifteen minutes ago," I whisper.

"I've done that before. Did you see our presentation score? We got an A."

"Oh, that's great," I breathe. I slide my glasses off and insert my contacts while I listen to the lecture. I run a hand over my hair, hoping it looks somewhat presentable. My stomach growls, and I tell it to shush. I'll get food from the Grab'n'go after class.

"See you Friday," Abby says, shouldering her backpack and waving.

I wave back and head to the Grab'n'go, trying to decide what I want. A microwaveable burrito? A granola bar? I peruse the offerings and settle on a package of crackers and a smoothie. It can be breakfast and lunch.

There's no line at this time of day, so I step up to the register and open my backpack to take out my student ID, which doubles as a credit card on campus. It's connected to my bank account.

My flashy pink wallet isn't in the main pocket.

I open the second pocket, eyes narrowing and a frown burying into my forehead. My pulse pounds harder in my neck when I realize it's not there either.

There's one last pocket, and it's not big enough for my wallet, but I check anyway.

"Sorry," I say, faking a smile for the cashier's benefit. "Looks like I won't be getting this after all."

I shoulder my backpack and walk out of the shop, leaving the food on the counter.

All attempts as appearing casual cease there.

I run all the way back to my dorm, the second time today I've run across campus. I let myself into the apartment and tear my room apart.

My wallet IS NOT HERE.

I check the kitchen and look inside all my bags of groceries. Then I go outside and search my car, under the seats, in the trunk.

I can barely breathe. Every credit card I own is in that wallet. All my cash. There are pictures also, but at least I have the digital copies and can get reprints.

Except the ones Owen gave me when I left. His baby picture. The candid shots his friends took of us.

I sit down on the steps of the fire escape and call Jordan.

"Hey, what's up?" he says.

"Jordan," I say, gulping in breaths of fresh air, "my wallet is missing."

"Where have you looked?"

"Everywhere. My room, the kitchen, my car—Jordan, it's gone."

I'm keeping my voice even-keel. Trying to. But Jordan hears my panic.

"I'll be right there," he says.

I sit and wait for my cousin, my hero, my best friend. Tears fill my eyes and I brush them away as they creep down my cheeks.

He jogs up twenty minutes later. First thing he does is give me a hug, and then he says, "Let's look everywhere again."

I'm missing class. But I don't care. I trail behind him through my apartment, but Jordan comes up empty also.

"Did you call the school lost and found?" he asks.

"No."

"Try there."

I do, hoping against hope someone turned it in.

"Does it have your ID in it?" the girl who answered the phone asks me.

"Yes."

"Then we probably don't have it. We'd call you if it came in. But I'll check."

My heart sinks. I describe it to her, but I already know it's not there.

"I'm so sorry," she says. "Let me get your name and number, and if it shows up, I'll call you."

I shake my head at Jordan and leave her my info.

"All right," he says when I hang up. He puts his hands on my shoulders. "You must have left it at the grocery store."

I blink, and more tears trail down my face. "All my money!"

He nods. "I'll call the store and check. You call the banks and cancel all your cards."

I pull my phone out, noticing how my hand shakes. "I can put a hold on them from the apps."

"Do it."

I half listen to Jordan as he talks to the grocery store manager, asking about a pink wallet. I pause each card, one by one.

"Okay. Thanks." Jordan hangs up the phone and looks at me. "They don't have it."

I nod, sucking in a breath, my lips trembling. "There hasn't been any usual activity on my cards. I paused them for now."

Jordan pulls me into another hug. "I'm sorry, Cass."

Cass. The nickname makes me think of Owen, and I ache to talk to him. But I feel foolish for crying this much. "It's okay. I need to go to class."

He gives me a concerned look. "Will you be all right?"

"Yeah." What choice is there? "Thanks for helping."

"There's one last thing you need to do. Call the police and file a report."

"Over my wallet?" I blanch at the idea of calling the police.

"Yes. If anyone turns it in, they'll have your info."

"All right." I exhale. "After class."

I haven't finished my essay for my English class, and I stop at one of the computer labs to do it. I pull out my laptop and sit at a desk and then let my fingers do the talking. The analysis fires out of me, coherent, raw, eloquent. Somehow I do my best writing when under duress.

I feel a bit better after class. I've had my meltdown and now I'm getting myself under control. I hate that I've lost the photos, more than anything.

I head back to my apartment and call the police on the way. Just in case, I check to see if a wallet was turned in. Nothing. I leave my information and a description, but I don't have any hope left. I've reached the acceptance stage. It's time to leave for work and move on with my life.

I get into my car as my phone rings. My heart leaps with hope, but when I check, it's my mom.

Mom. She doesn't know about this, and I dread telling her about my irresponsible loss.

"Hi," I say, feigning cheer, but I know I won't keep this from her.

"Cassandra, I have a young man on the other line who says he found your wallet," she says, a perplexed note in her voice.

I shriek. I can't help it. "He did? He found my wallet? Where?"

"In a grocery cart in the parking lot. Did you lose it?"

"Yes!" I start laughing, and the tears come again, but this time they are tears of relief and incredulity. "I've been looking everywhere! I even called the police!"

"Oh, sweetie, I'm so sorry," Mom says, her tone changing to sympathy. "Where can he meet you?"

"I'm—I'm on my way to work." I'm hiccuping, I'm so ecstatic. "Can he bring it to me there?"

"Yes. I'll send him there."

My whole mood is elevated. I turn on the radio and sing as I drive, and sunshine pours down on my car. I hope he comes while I'm on break because I want to thank him in person.

"Why are you so happy?" Stirling says when I come in.

I laugh. "I lost my wallet and this guy found it and he's bringing it to me!"

My joy is contagious. My coworkers share my happiness, and I chirp with enthusiasm through each call, getting more pledges than usual.

After one of my calls, Becky comes in carrying a pink wallet in her hands. "This yours?" she asks, smiling.

"Yes!" I jump up and take it from her. "Is he gone? The guy who brought it?"

She nods. "He dropped it off and left."

I'm disappointed I don't get to thank him in person. I sit back down and start another call, my fingers trembling as I open the wallet.

The pictures are still there.

I check the credit cards, but they're less important. Still there also.

The cash is gone. All forty dollars of it. I laugh out loud. "They even stole the pennies!"

"Who did?" Stirling asks.

I wave my wallet at him. "Whoever had this. Every last cent is gone."

Thursday morning I join Camila in our religion class. We chatter about the mundaneness of our mornings so far, and then we fall silent as Professor MacArthur pulls up the timeline of ancient people in the Americas. We're discussing the indigenous groups of Mesoamerica, and this fascinates me because it pertains to my family heritage. My mother's family is from Colombia. I know from my own studies that by most definitions, Colombia isn't considered part of Mesoamerica, although some groups do include it, leaving me to deduce the prehistoric groups had to be at least somewhat similar.

I wonder if I'll have to go to Colombia to find out my family secrets.

"Pick one of the indigenous groups from the pre-Columbian era," Professor MacArthur says. "Write me a paper on their religious beliefs and practices as we understand them today. Three pages, normal formatting."

I write the assignment down and make a note to email him and ask if I can do the Muisca people. They were one of the predominant indigenous groups in Colombia and possibly my ancestors. Then I stand and leave with Camila.

"Are you heading home?" she asks.

I shake my head. "Jordan and I have our choir class tonight. I'm going to the library to study. Then I'll meet up with him for class."

"Scandinavian choir," she says, looking mystified. "Good luck."

Several hours later I have my paper outlined. Professor MacArthur approved the topic, and now I'm scouring online sites and historical journals for any information on the culture and customs of the Muisca people. The barbarity of their religion mixed with the complexity of their art and appreciation for life baffles me.

A shadow falls over my table, and I look up to see Jordan.

"At least you're always at the same spot," he says.

"For better or worse." I stand and put my computer away. "Ready to sing?"

"This will be fun."

CHAPTER FIFTY-SEVEN

Scandinavian Choir

I expect the choir class to be in the music building, but it's not. It's in a small building on the north side of campus that doesn't look like it's been upgraded since the seventies, judging from the small widows and orange coloring. The professor greets us with a smile.

"I'm so pleased so many people came!"

Jordan and I join the seven other people present. This is a lot? A few more stragglers file in, and by the time the teacher's written our names down, we have twenty-two people.

"Please divide yourselves up by what section you sing and I'll make sure we're balanced," he says.

"You don't want to hear us?" I ask.

He shakes his head. "Oh, no. I'm not worried about talent. Just numbers." His grin is huge. "So sing loud."

"Sopranos here," a tall blond woman says, raising her hand.

I join her and three other girls. They look several years older than me.

"Which language do you speak?" a brunette asks the woman.

"Swedish and Danish," she says. "But I was born in Sweden. You?"

That explains her crisp vowels.

"Norwegian, but not very well," the brunette answers. "I spent a year there as a missionary."

"It's a super hard language to learn," the woman says.

"Swedish for me also," says another woman, large with child. "But I'm sure not as well as a native."

The brunette turns to me. "What about you?"

I'm starting to sweat now. "None," I say. "I just like to sing."

Their attention swivels to me.

"And you joined a Scandinavian choir?" the tall woman says.

I nod, feeling foolish. "It sounded like fun."

314

"All right, now that you've organized yourselves into parts, let me hand out the music!" Our choir director/professor looks enthused. "We have two songs in Swedish, two in Norwegian, two in Danish, and one in Icelandic. I don't speak all of these languages, so if you do, please step up and help us with the pronunciation when we get there." He lays out sheet music on a table. "Please come take one copy of each."

We file through and grab music, then stuff it into black folders. This feels comfortable, and I fall into the familiar routine of flipping through the pages and humming, watching the notes as they go up and down, trying to sight-read the melody.

"Professor Lewis," one of the men says, and the director shakes his head.

"I'm not a professor. Not anywhere close. Just call me Mr. Lewis."

"Mr. Lewis," the man says. "What are the requirements for our grade?"

"Oh! I have a course syllabus." Mr. Lewis jumps over to a computer bag and pulls out another stack of paper. "Let's see. Come to class every week. And come to our Christmas concert. That's it."

That's it. I accept a syllabus as it comes my way and put it in the black folder.

"Now. Shall we sing?"

There is no pianist. We spend the next half an hour sounding out vowels and singing along to a recording. I wonder what Mr. Lewis had to do to get the university to offer this class. But it's fun, and Jordan and I sing the songs, correcting each other on our pronunciation, as we walk back to my apartment. He insists on dropping me off first, even though we pass his dorm on the way to mine.

My phone vibrates as we start up the stairwell. I pull it from my pocket and give a start. "It's Owen." I answer the call. "Owen, hey!"

"Hey, yourself," he says. "What are you up to, killer?"

Giddy happiness rises in my chest. We haven't spoken in a week. Maybe longer. "I'm almost home. I have a night class on Thursdays."

Jordan launches into song, except he's off-key and scratchy, and I cover my mouth to keep from laughing.

"What was that?" Owen asks.

"That was a terrible rendition of the music we're learning," I say. "It's a choir class."

"A choir class. That's great."

"It's not a serious choir class. Just for fun."

"Didn't you like my singing?" Jordan asks. "Mr. Lewis should pick me for a solo."

"Who's with you?" Owen asks.

There's an unsavory undercurrent in his voice, like he thought Jordan's singing was terribly unpleasant but he's trying to hide it.

Or he distrusts that I'm with a guy and totally doesn't want me to know.

"Jordan," I say. "My cousin." We've reached my apartment, but I stay outside.

"Oh. That's your cousin?" Owen's heard me talk about Jordan before. The unsavory undercurrent vanishes, though I hear him trying to play it cool. To act like he didn't care in the first place.

But he did, and I know it, and it makes my heart happy.

"Yeah. We're taking the choir class together."

"That's fun. I'm glad you're getting to hang out with him."

"He walks me home almost every evening. Keeps me safe."

"Good. I like him already."

"Night, Cassandra." Jordan gives me a hug and jogs down the stairwell, hitting the metal railing and making it vibrate with each step.

"Night, Jordan!" I call after him.

I unlock my apartment door and heave a sigh. Layne's having another flirt fest. She stands on a chair in the middle of the kitchen, laughing and screeching at three boys who circle around her. They yell my name when I come in, and I ignore them as I hurry to my room.

"What was that?" Owen asks.

I shut myself in and wave to Camila, who glances up at me. "My roommate and her fan club." I can still hear them. "I think I need to get earplugs."

"They sound like fun."

I'm starting to hate that word. "You would like her," I say, suddenly irritated. Is he saying I'm not fun? Because I want to hang out in my room with earplugs? "Everyone else does."

He doesn't take the bait. "I already like a girl."

I grunt and haul myself onto my bed. "Is she fun?"

"Yeah. She's fun."

"How is she fun?"

"I don't have to pretend around her. I can be myself. She makes real life interesting. She sees things differently. She's happy. It's like walking around with a rainbow."

I laugh in spite of myself. "She sounds boring."

"She's definitely not. I'm never bored with her."

"I bet she goes to bed early."

"I hear she's getting a pair of earplugs."

I laugh again, my ill-humor fading. He doesn't care that I'm not a party-girl, that I'm not the life of every activity. Owen likes who I am, and suddenly I wish Camila wasn't in the room, because I want to say what I feel to him. "She likes you too." I look over at Camila, studiously staring at her book, even turning the pages as if she's reading. But I know she hears me. "Ready for your big game on Saturday?"

"Hoping Coach lets me play. I'm not his first choice."

I can't picture that. Owen was the star of our high school team. "I'll be watching."

"You will?"

"Of course, Owen." I'll buy whatever internet sports package I need to see him play.

"What if Coach doesn't put me in?"

"Make that bench look good."

He laughs. "I will."

I hate to hang up, but I still have an essay to write, and my stomach growls, reminding me I need to brave the crowd in the kitchen and get dinner. "Thanks for calling. It was super good to hear your voice."

"Yours too, Cassandra," he says. "Have a good night."

"Good night," I echo. I hang up, and then I text him what I didn't tell him:

I love you

The three bubbles appear instantly, and then his response.

I love you too Cass

I take a screenshot, because some day this message will be deleted and I'll doubt what he feels for me. I need this text to hold as tangible proof when the silence gets too thick.

⟲⌇✦⌇⟳

I don't forget that I promised Abby we'd go to Black Sheep on Friday.

But she doesn't look so great in class, and she texts me before dinner.

A: I'm sick. You're off the hook. But we go clubbing next weekend. No excuses.

Me: No excuses

I'm resigned to going.

I head to work on Saturday morning. Jeremy greets me with a high-five, and Stirling gives me a shoulder hug.

"Are you going to the game tonight?" he asks me.

I settle into an empty chair near his and pull on my headset. "No. I'm watching the LSU game from my apartment."

"Oh. You an LSU fan?"

I consider the question. "Yes. Definitely."

"Cool. I like them too. If you want company, I could come over, bring some ice cream."

I can imagine how awkward that would be. "I'm chilling with my roommates." They don't actually know about it yet, but I'll tell them tonight.

Stirling looks disappointed. "But we're still on for Monday?"

This is my chance. He slipped it to me, the opportunity to come up with an excuse to back out. But again, it fails me. "Yeah. We're good for Monday."

I get a lot of indecisive people on the phone today, saying they want to make a pledge but don't have the funds right now. I mark them as "undecided," which means they'll get a call back later.

After the fourth one, Danielle, my supervisor, pops into the seat beside me. "Why are you marking so many undecideds?"

"A lot of people said they want to but can't right now," I say, pausing my call button.

She tilts her head at me. "Are you sure you're not marking them to keep your stats up?"

I frown at her. "How does that help my stats?"

"It doesn't count as a negative."

I gawk at her. "You mean undecideds don't count against me?"

"Not technically." She looks hesitant now as she realizes I didn't know this. "They're neutral. They don't improve your rank but they don't bring it down either."

I turn back to my screen and hit the call button. "I'm just filling out the form." I'm miffed she thought I was tricking the system.

She leaves me alone. Maybe because of her accusation, I land the next six people I talk to, managing to pull tiny five dollar pledges out of two of them so they're not a negative. By the time the shift ends, my rankings are at the top.

I fist bump my coworkers goodbye, except Stirling, who wants a hug. The physical touch makes me uneasy.

I head back to my apartment and I'm relieved to find Iris and Layne studying vocabulary in the kitchen without a posse of boys.

"Who wants to watch the LSU game with me tonight?" I say.

Iris looks up and pushes her curtain of black hair away from her face. "You don't want to go to the game? Our game?"

I shake my head and turn on the TV on our kitchen table. "The LSU game is more important tonight."

"Why?" Layne asks.

I smile as I pull up the pre-game coverage. "Because Owen might get to play."

"Who?" Layne says.

"Owen?" Iris says. "Your Owen?"

I nod. "The very one."

"Wait," Layne says, her eyes nearly bugging out. "Your boyfriend plays football for LSU?"

"He's not my boyfriend," I say. I hug myself, hating the admission. "And he's not first-string. But he's on the team. He might play tonight."

"Yes!" Iris says. "I definitely want to watch."

"I'm still trying to catch up," Layne says. She holds up a hand and she stares like she's never seen me before. "You were dating a football player?"

I roll my eyes. "Don't be so high school. Gosh, I thought I left that attitude behind."

"Why didn't you ever say he was a football player?" Layne whines.

I throw my hands up. "You've never asked me anything about him or shown much interest in our relationship."

"You lead with the football thing," Layne says. "If you say that, you get everyone's attention."

I stare at her and click my tongue. "That's exactly what I don't want. I'm so tired of people attaching those labels to us. The football player and the nerd. The football player and the choir girl. The football player and the Latina. The football player and the church mouse." My voice grows more vehement with every statement, and I force myself to calm down. "I'm sick of it. It's just me and Owen. Two people who like each other and aren't even together right now. So who we are doesn't matter anyway."

I pull up a kitchen chair and plop myself down in front of the TV, crossing my arms in front of my chest.

"Well." Layne puts away her vocab cards. "Looks like I'm watching the LSU game with you and Iris tonight."

CHAPTER FIFTY-EIGHT

Number Thirty-Two

The football team comes out and begins their warm ups half an hour before the game.

"Which one is he?" Iris asks.

I have no idea. I lean forward and squint at the players, but from this distance, one padded-shoulder helmeted football player looks like another. I should have asked Owen what his number was. I had assumed I'd know him when I saw him. I do a quick search of the roster and find him. "Number thirty-two. Owen Blaine."

I spot number thirty-two, the white numbers bright against the purple fabric. I feel a spark of nostalgia that his number isn't four anymore. "That's him." I point him out and then study him on the small screen. A lump forms in my throat as I watch him go through the familiar high knees and trots and squats I watched at a dozen football games last year. Is it my imagination, or has he gotten taller?

The players trot off the field, and I keep my eyes glued on Owen's helmet so I don't lose him on the bench.

Iris stands up and makes popcorn. The band plays. I thread my fingers together, my heart swollen in my chest. Watching him on TV makes me feel closer to him, and I ache with longing to be with him.

"Do you have pictures of you guys?" Layne asks.

"Of course I do," I say. I pull out my phone and open my pictures app. There's an "Owen" folder, and I click it. A handful of selfies of us pops up, in his truck, at the park, at his house, on the couch, in front of the old church. All are from the summer, when I realized I was lacking in photos of us. I hand the phone to Layne and swallow a lump in my throat.

"You guys are cute together," she says, handing the phone back to me. "You don't seem like the kind of girl to date a guy like that."

She has stereotyped Owen and put him in a box and added me to that box. I don't bother correcting her. I don't know her well enough to care about her opinion of me, and if she knew me better, she'd know the dynamics were different.

Iris returns with the popcorn.

Owen stays on the bench when the team goes out.

LSU gets the ball, and my roommates cheer when they score, but I'm stressing the whole time because the coach doesn't play Owen.

LSU is winning at halftime, but Owen still hasn't played.

Camila comes in and finds us crowded around the TV. "What's going on?"

Iris beckons her over. "We're watching Cassandra's boyfriend play."

"Oh!" Camila drops her backpack and pushes into the couch.

I stand up and pace the kitchen, then text Mrs. Blaine.

Me: do you think Owen will play?

Mrs. Blaine: Cassandra! Are you watching the game?

Me: yes

Mrs. Blaine: I hope so. He'll be disappointed otherwise

Yeah, he will be. He might pretend not to care, but I know how important this is to him.

Halftime finishes and the game gets going again. The veins in my temples pound with anxiety. The coach doesn't use Owen.

And then he does. Right at the start of the fourth quarter, he waves his arm and Owen shoots up from the bench. I plop into my seat and stare at the TV, chewing on the sides of my fingers, an old nervous habit. Owen trots out to the field and I exhale, the tension easing out of my shoulders. I hear my roommates yelling but I'm glued to Owen. He catches the ball and I leap to my feet, screaming.

A guy in a white jersey flies across the field and tackles Owen, taking them both to the ground.

The ball flies free and bounces back several yards.

The whistle blows. Play stops. I press my fingers together and touch them to my lips.

Owen gets to his feet. Coach beckons, and he trots off the field.

My heart sinks, and I wilt in my seat.

He played for all of four minutes.

The coach seats him and turns away. So does the camera, but not before I see Owen jerk off his helmet and toss it to the ground.

He's pissed.

It hurts my heart. I stand up and leave the kitchen.

Camila follows me to our room. "Are you okay?"

I sigh and gesture toward the kitchen. "I feel bad for Owen."

"He'll get more chances."

"I know. But today's he's upset."

Mrs. Blaine texts me. *Owen's mad.*

Me: yeah. I'm sorry for him

Mrs. Blaine: don't tell him that

She's right, Owen won't want to hear it. What can I say? He knows I was watching the game.

LSU wins, and I settle on that. I shoot him a text after the final score.

Me: congrats! Your team won!

I wait all night, but he doesn't respond.

❧⁓✦⁓❧

Monday brings on a chill and fog.

"It's too early to be cold! It's September!" I complain to Camila as I pull on a sweater.

"Only for another week. Fall comes early here."

I peek out the blinds. Outside the leaves are changing. The tips of the mountains are hidden behind a wreath of white cloud.

"Back home we'd still be swimming," I say.

"Yep. But you chose to come to school here." She grins at me.

I did choose this. But I feel the pressure of pursuing further education as I sit down beside Abby in physical science. Our first test is on Wednesday, and I want to vomit as Professor Turnbaugh goes over the terms and chapters we should know.

"Are you ready for it?" Abby asks when class ends.

I shake my head. "No. I've read all the material, answered all the questions. But when I read my answers, it's like I've never heard this before!"

"You'll do fine."

We walk together toward the exit. Visions of losing my scholarship and packing up and going home flash through my mind. "I don't think so."

"Want to study together?"

"Yes!" I grab her arm. "Please! I need that!"

She nods. "Tomorrow during lunch? After the lab?"

"Sounds like a plan."

I feel slightly more appeased with that arranged. I'll study hard and memorize everything and do fine, just like I did in high school.

Stirling greets me with a hug when I walk into work.

"You all right?" he asks, looking down at me.

His sweater is soft and I lean into it. He wears dark jeans and looks nice. He's not tall, and I fit right against his shoulder. I'm used to being swallowed up by boys when they hug me.

"It's the weather." I look over my shoulder and scowl at the lingering clouds. "What happened to the sun? I need it."

"Welcome to Colorado."

We both laugh and then I sigh. I do feel dismal today.

I know I can attribute some of that to not hearing anything from Owen all weekend. But I brush that aside. Relationships are full of ups and downs and highs and lows, and he and I are not in one anyway.

Whatever we're in is confusing.

I put on my cheerful voice for the calls and study my physical science vocab in between. I only close a few pledges, but my thoughts are on physics tonight.

Our shift ends, and Stirling stands by my station while I put away my headset.

"Want to ride with me or meet there?" he says.

"Probably best to meet there." I shoulder my purse and stand. "Otherwise you'll have to bring me back here."

"I don't mind bringing you back."

And I don't feel like driving, so I give in. "All right."

Stirling grins, revealing a dimple beneath his lips.

"What were you studying all night?" he asks as we climb into his truck.

"Physical science. I have a test on Wednesday and I'm freaking out about it."

"Wretched class." He pulls onto the street. "I hated that one."

"I feel like it's going to kill me!" I groan. "I should be studying more, not going to the movies."

"Sometimes your brain needs a break. You'll absorb more after this, trust me."

I want his words to be true. I need a break.

The theater is behind the student center. We join the line of people getting tickets, and I read the movie posters for the upcoming Alfred Hitchcock flicks. They sound intriguing.

"I want to see all of these," I say.

"We'll come back and watch them," he says.

I realize how he interpreted my words. Snap. That wasn't what I'd meant.

It's a small, old-fashioned theater with hard plastic chairs that don't lean back. I wiggle in my seat to get comfortable. At least there's a fabric cushion.

The movie, *A Room with a View,* is black and white and stars Jimmy Stewart, who I love from *It's a Wonderful Life.*

"He's in a lot of Hitchcock movies," Stirling says when I mention it. "Hitchcock was a fan."

"Fun."

It's an unexpectedly thrilling show, and I shriek and grab Stirling's arm at several tense moments, digging my nails in until he laughs and pulls away. We joke about it after the movie.

"I think you drew blood." He pulls his sleeve up. "Nope, just crescent moons."

I lean over to peer at the almost-punctured skin. "Sorry. Maybe we shouldn't see any more of these shows."

"I'll wear padding next time."

That makes me laugh, and it makes me think of Owen with all his football gear, sitting on his bedroom floor pulling out pads, or stuffing them back into his jersey. My heart constricts and I know I need to stop thinking about him in every moment, or I'll break.

Stirling checks his phone. "It's almost eleven. Want to get a bite to eat? Or go back to my place?"

Those are my options? "I shouldn't eat this late at night."

"My place it is."

Stirling turns on chipper music in a different language when we get inside his truck. The sound is upbeat and playful even if I don't understand it. I bounce my shoulders without meaning to and feel my mood lifting.

"What's this music from?" I ask. "I don't recognize the language."

"It's Icelandic. I heard it on my mission."

"Did you like it? Your mission?"

He nods as he turns into the apartments and small houses that line the south end of campus. "I loved it. It was crazy hard, you know. People love being served until you start talking about God, and then they want you to disappear off the face of the earth."

I laugh with him.

"But I learned so much about myself, about loving others, about serving God. I love Iceland, I love the language, I treasure my memories."

I hug my chest, warmed by his words. "I want to serve on a mission."

"You do? When?"

"I don't know. Maybe after college."

"Do it."

"I think I will. Was it hard to learn the language?"

"Oh, you have no idea. Icelandic is the worst. The language has four cases, ten tenses, and different moods. It's insane. Even after two years I feel like I'm still learning it."

"Wow." The idea enthralls me. "Languages are amazing."

Stirling parks in front of a series of townhouses, fancier than most of the apartments I've seen.

"These are posh," I say, climbing up the steps behind him.

"They were." He snorts. "Now a bunch of guys live in them."

We step into an entryway and I glance around. A chandelier dangles from the arched ceiling and noise from a television plays in the living room. Two boys sit on a green couch, and they give me the once-over when I step inside. Stirling doesn't introduce me but continues into an adjacent kitchen with white stone counters and red cabinets.

"The kitchen's nice," I say, sitting at a barstool.

"Ever had a purple cow?" He opens the fridge and pulls out grape juice, then the freezer for a tub of ice-cream. "I make one for myself almost every day."

I watch him toss the ingredients into a blender and mix it up, the vanilla ice cream turning a frothy purple. "Interesting."

"Try it."

It's almost like a grape milkshake, a combination I've never had before. "It's good."

He joins me with his own. "You can do orange cows, white cows, brown cows, they're all good."

"Did you learn these in Iceland also?"

"No. My brother. He made them for us when he got home from college."

He tells me all about his family, and I share a bit about mine. The conversation drifts off, and we watch the TV from the bar in the kitchen. I prop my head up with my hand. He shakes my arm when I start to nod off.

"It's almost one in the morning," he says.

"We still have to get my car." It's at the office and I want my bed.

"When do you work next?"

I rub my eyes, thinking. "Thursday."

"I'll pick you up and take you to work. You can leave it there."

My brain's too foggy to decide if this is a good plan or not. I just nod. "Yes.

That's fine."

I fall asleep on the five-minute drive to my dorm. Stirling's laughing as he wakes me again.

"Thanks," I say, and I hop out of the car. "See you later."

It occurs to me as I burrow under my blankets that I didn't give him a hug or anything. Did I want to? I can't remember.

CHAPTER FIFTY-NINE

Wall of Silence

I turn in my paper on the ancient people of Muisca on Tuesday. It's a relief to have it out of my hands, though I did find the ancient religious rituals and beliefs fascinating.

But I've no sooner opened my notebook when Professor MacArthur says, "We have our first exam on Thursday. Today will be a review session, but I'll also have essay questions where I ask you to compare and contrast the civilizations we've studied in class to the one you did your paper on."

I feel like he just ripped the carpet out from under me. I share an exasperated look with Camila. "Is there no break?" I hiss.

"College," she murmurs back.

My brain pounds by the time we leave class. I head straight to my lab with Abby, and then she and I sit in the cafeteria going over flashcards together.

"What time are you taking the test tomorrow?" she asks.

"During class time." The exam is offered at the testing center, but class is canceled so we can take it. We have until Friday, but I know putting it off will only mean I forget what I studied.

"Same. I'll see you there."

I stay in the library after class, working on an essay for English. I'm overwhelmed.

A text lights up my phone, and it buzzes across the table. I check it. It's Stirling.

S: need anyone to help you study? I'm off work at eight.

My lip curves up in half a smile. *Me: I stayed up too late last night. I'll be in bed by then.*

S: laughing face emoji

S: let me know if you change your mind. I can make you a yellow cow.

Me: yellow cow? Sound suspicious

S: made with mountain dew

I laugh and turn back to my essay. He might be onto something.

The phone buzzes again, and I glance at it.

It's Owen.

I pick up the phone and read the preview without opening the text, a dull heaviness settling in my chest. I realize I'm upset with him. We haven't spoken since the game. We didn't even talk then. I haven't let myself think about it, but I feel ignored and rejected.

O: What's up, killer?

I put the phone back down. His nickname for me doesn't light me up like it usually does. He's pretending like he didn't let a wall of silence go up between us for three days. Like he didn't ignore me.

I don't answer him. It's time he felt ignored.

⌒⍨⌒

Wednesday morning I join the line of people waiting at the testing center to take their physical science test. The line wraps around the hall like we're waiting for something exciting at Disney World. But this is much worse.

They ask for my ID when I get inside and which test I'm taking. I glance at a screen and see dozens of tests are being offered right now.

"Physical science 101," I say.

She hands me a blue booklet, a bubble sheet, and a test packet. "There's no time limit. Do you have a smart watch?"

I shake my head.

"Good. Make sure your phone is off and out of sight the entire time. If you're caught cheating, your test will be confiscated and you'll receive no score."

I nod. She gestures me forward.

I step into a room filled with rows and rows of desks. The only sound is the scratching of pencils, the occasional throat-clearing, and the shuffle of shoes against the floor. I find an empty desk and slide into it. My heart thumps so loud I think the boy beside me will hear it. I take a deep breath and open the booklet.

Multiple choice questions greet me. I read through the first one three times before it enters my brain. I need to concentrate. I think through each question and fill in the bubbles on the sheet. I have a one in four chance of getting it right even if I guess. And most of the questions are familiar. I know the answers.

The short answer questions slow me down. Suddenly I can't remember the laws or rules we studied. I close my eyes and picture the presentations and experiments we did in class. What law did they demonstrate? I answer the best I can, giving examples to try and back up my rationale.

The clock is ticking. I didn't expect to take this long. If I don't hurry, I'll be late to my English class. I can't think anymore anyway. I finish up the last two questions and jet out the door.

A boy takes my blue book and bubble sheet.

"We'll score the multiple choice section right now," he says. "You'll see your ID number and a score on the screen at the bottom of the stairs. Your TA will score your booklet."

"I'll find out right now?" My heart begins racing again, and I can't decide if this is good or bad.

"Yep."

I head down the stairs and see the large TV screen. And there's my ID number. Followed by my score.

Fifty-nine percent.

I slow at the last step and stare at the screen as if the numbers might change. Is it a mistake? I only got half of the questions right?

The fifty-nine stays there, bright green numbers, unblinking. I don't blink either, or I'll cry. I pray my essays raise my grade.

⸻ ❉ ⸻

Two days before October, the weather takes a turn.

My exam in Ancient People feels much easier than my physical science exam, but I won't hold my breath. The scores still haven't posted for the written part, and I want to cry every time I think about it.

I wear a jacket to class. I almost grab my scarf. The sun is gone, the sky a dismal gray. The clouds hang so low that I can't tell where they stop and the sky begins.

My heart is low like the clouds. Dismal. Gray.

Stirling picks me up for work but I'm not conversational. So he turns on his chipper Icelandic music. It does soothe my soul somewhat, enough that I put on a cheerful voice to talk pleasantly with potential pledgees.

Abby calls while I'm working. I wait until my break, and then I call her back.

"Hey, what's up?" I say.

"They posted our test scores online," she says. "Have you seen yours yet?"

"No." I haven't told her my multiple choice score. I told her I left in a hurry and didn't see it. I'm too embarrassed, especially since she got a seventy-two—and she wailed over it. "What was yours?"

"A seventy-eight! I can't believe it. Such a low score. I thought I'd do better."

"But the written part brought your score up, at least. That's good." I perk up slightly. It has to raise my score. Please, please, please.

"Yeah! Let me know what you get."

"I will." Maybe. Depending what it is.

I head back to work but can't concentrate on my calls. I need to know my score. I use my phone to log into the grading system and pull up my test.

A sixty-four percent.

My heart plummets. The written part did raise my score, but barely.

I bombed my first college exam.

"Are you all right?" Stirling asks after work as he walks me to my car.

"Tired." I blink wearily and unlock my car. "I need to sleep."

He gives me a hug, and I let myself lean on him. There's something so comforting about the strong, warm arms of a man.

"See you tomorrow," he says.

I nod.

We go our separate ways. I make it to the light before I burst into tears. I cry all the way to my apartment and then sit in the parking lot sobbing. It feels good. I haven't bawled in a long time.

My phone vibrates in my purse. I fish it out, betting it's Abby wanting to know

327

my score.

And then I cry harder because it's Owen.

I suck in a breath, calm my breathing, and answer. "Hello?"

There's the slightest wobble at the end of the word, and I flinch. He'll know.

"Hey." He pauses. "You okay?"

"I'm fine." I'm such a liar, and my nose is congested, so I'm not even a good liar.

"Are you crying?"

"No." Except the tears are streaming down my face again, my voice chokes, and I gasp back a sob.

"Cassandra, what's wrong?"

His voice is riddled with alarm. I don't know why he called, but I know the reason doesn't matter to him now, he wants to take care of me. Like he always has. Always there to wipe away my tears, to hold me close, to make me feel like it will be okay.

I can't tell him how much he hurt me. How distant I feel from him and how alone that makes me. How every moment I want to talk to him and know I'm only hurting myself by thinking about him.

"It's nothing. It's stupid. It's school. I'm such a failure!"

Cue the drama. I let myself sob, holding the phone away so I'm not wailing in his ear.

"No, you're not. What's going on? What happened?"

I swallow and suck in air and calm myself enough to speak. "I failed my physical science exam."

"Like, failed failed?"

"Sixty-four percent."

"That's still a D. It's a passing grade."

"Not if I want to keep my scholarship, Owen!" I lash out at him, and that feels incredibly good also. I want to scream at him. I can't do it for the right reason, so I let him feel the brunt of my emotion now. "Some of us can't waltz through life carrying a football!"

"No, no, not everyone can do that," he says. I meant it to be a low jab, but I hear the amusement in his voice and know I've failed that also. "Dancing and football are hard activities to coordinate."

I roll my eyes and groan. I'm not done lashing out, but he takes all the fire out of my blood. "School's hard. It's really hard. I don't think I can do this."

"What can't you do?"

His voice is soft, serious, and I know he's listening to me. So I share the fears in my heart.

"College," I say quietly. "High school was hard, but manageable. I studied, I got good grades. If I messed up on a test, I did better on the next one. Sometimes I got tired, but as long as I kept swimming, I knew I'd make it. I don't know that anymore. My arms are shaking. I'm gasping for breath and I'm afraid I'm going to get sucked under the surface. I thought I was prepared for this. But I was training in the kiddie pool, and now I'm in the ocean."

"Backfloat," he says.

I furrow my brow. "What?"

"Just float for a bit, Cassandra. It's all right to let the current take you while you rest. Take a breather. Then get your arms and legs going and catch up to where you need to be."

"I can't take a break."

"You can't drown, either."

I dig my fingernails into my steering wheel, feeling how he calms my heart. My soul. And I'm still angry at him for ignoring me. But I don't want to bring it up. I don't want to remind him of the game and take him back to a negative place.

I need you, I think.

But I don't speak it.

"Thank you for your words," I say. "I feel better now."

It's too formal. A silence falls between us. I wonder if he's aware of my anger toward him and realize he must be. He knows me too well. He'll know I intentionally did not answer his text.

"I wish I was there," he says. "I wish I could hold you."

The tears come unbidden to my eyes again.

"Do you?" I sniff.

He exhales, long and slow. "It's harder to talk to you than to not."

I wipe away a few more tears. "What does that mean?"

"It's hard to explain."

I know what he means, though. So I define it for him. "When you don't talk to me, I'm an ache. A dull pain. A constant soreness that you try to ignore. But then you talk to me, and it's like poking your fingers into that wound and twisting them around. Making it hurt worse than before."

"Yeah," he says, and I hear the catch in his voice.

"I feel it too," I whisper.

"This is why," he says, and he stops.

He doesn't have to finish. The same thought has been in my heart for days.

This is why people break up when they go separate ways.

We don't speak. My heartbeat thumps in my ears, pulses in my neck. We are communicating something in the silence. I feel it. I know he does.

"I'm going to take a break from calling you," he says.

He's taking a break.

We're taking a break.

I don't want him to say it. I already know. Don't make it real. "Yeah, okay," I say, swallowing hard. "That makes sense."

"And, you know, if you need someone else to be there for you—I get it."

Shut up, I want to say. *Stop talking.*

"Keep your head up," he says. "You're the smartest person I know. The best person I know. There's nothing but success in your future."

My throat clogs up. I say nothing.

"I love you," he says, his voice soft. He's saying more than that. He's apologizing. He's begging me to understand.

"I love you too," I say. I do understand. I sniff and wipe away another tear, and I hope he hears what I'm saying.

It's time to end this limboed state of confusion.

"You'll be okay. It's one test. The teachers understand. It's a hard school, but they accepted you because they know you can do it. You've got this, killer."

"Thank you, Owen." I clutch the phone to my face as if it were his hand. The tears are right behind my eyes. Will I ever hold his hand again?

I doubt this was what he intended to happen when he called, but it doesn't feel like there was any other course to take. Every path led us here, eventually. There's nothing left to say. So I'm not surprised when he says, "Bye, Cass."

"Bye, Owen," I echo.

I disconnect the call and put the phone down on my console. Then I rest my arms on my steering wheel and sob my heart out.

CHAPTER SIXTY

Non-Exclusive

U nhappily Ever After
Is that how it is?
I never should have agreed
I know how this story will end
Our love never died
But something has in my heart
Dreams are the worst intoxicant
And nothing is as it is
I love you still
I'll love you always
We didn't say it's over
But I feel it coming soon
And even the sweetest goodbye
Leaves a bitter aftertaste

I'm writing poetry again. I always do that when I'm emotionally distraught. Why can't I write happy poems?

I tell Camila what went down and no one else. I shut myself in my room for the night and Camila tells Iris and Layne I have a headache.

I dream of Owen. In my dream, we're at my house, and he's crying on my bed. I sit across from him and take his hands and ask why he's crying.

"We broke up," he says. "It's killing me."

"No, we didn't," I say. "You imagined it." Then I lean forward and kiss him. And kiss him, and he wraps his arms around me and slides my body down on the bed, then we are making out and his hands are touching me, pulling me closer, and I arch my back to meet him.

I wake up with my body on fire. I ache with desire. I'm angry at my subconscious for bringing those physical moments with Owen to the forefront of my mind. At the same time, I wouldn't mind if my subconscious took it a little further . . . and maybe a little further . . .

I splash cold water on my face in the bathroom and look into my virginal eyes and remind myself there are REASONS why we never went all the way. Good, legitimate reasons.

But a girl can dream.

I meet Abby in the hallway before class.

"Did you check your score?"

"Yeah." I sigh and shake my head as I follow her down the row. "Dismal. Not even a C."

"Ouch." Abby winces. "And I thought we were the smart ones."

I laugh. "Me too."

"Good morning, good morning!" Mr. Turnbaugh comes in and drops a huge file folder on his counter. "I know what's on your minds! Before a line of panicked students forms in front of my desk, let me reassure you! Once I average your test scores with your lab and homework scores, their bearing won't be as strong as you fear. Also, we grade on a curve in this class, and the curve can only work in your favor! In this case the highest score was an eight-six percent. So I'm raising each score by fourteen percentage points."

Fourteen points! Excited titters fill the air, and I'm not the only one exhaling in relief.

"I just got a seventy-eight percent!" I say, laughing.

"That's fantastic!" Abby doesn't mention what her new score would be, but she doesn't need to. We both know it's higher than mine.

And it doesn't matter.

Owen was right. I'm going to be fine.

I walk through the student center on my way home and notice that *Vertigo* is playing tonight. On impulse, I text Stirling.

Me: want to see Vertigo tonight?

S: You working?

Me: yes

S: what time? I'm off at seven.

That's one of the nice things about working at a call center. We're always done by eight. No one likes late night calls.

I check the time.

Me: seven-thirty. We can make it. I'll get tickets.

S: Great!

Owen—

No.

I won't think it.

I'm all smiles when I get to work, focusing on my physical science test that didn't go as bad as I thought. I'm halfway through a call that looks like it will be my fourth pledge for the day when suddenly my computer shuts down.

"Uh—" I begin.

"Jeff!" Ralph, a loud black-haired boy with glasses at the end of the row, leans back from his desk. "My computer turned off!"

"Mine too."

The voices rise from each cubicle, and I take of my headset.

"All right, all right." Jeff takes to the podium at the top of the cubicles and looks down at us. "It appears we're having a server issue," he says, holding the mic and breathing into it heavily. "Everyone sit tight."

He steps down and disappears into his office, and nothing is more exciting than being told we can't work. Someone pulls out a hacky sack, and we squeal and laugh as we toss it around the cubicles.

Jeff returns twenty minutes later. He grips the mic and looks down at us all very seriously. "I have bad news," he says. "I see dead people."

We laugh and wait for the real news.

"Server's down," he says, returning to his normal voice. "I don't know when it's coming back up, so—class dismissed."

I cheer and bolt away from my desk along with everyone present. The hacky sack comes along, bouncing from hand to hand and occasionally hitting the sidewalk as we move outside of the building.

"We have time before the movie," Stirling says, joining me. "Want to get a pizza?"

"Yes," I say. "I'm starving."

The clouds part overhead, and a tiny ray of sunlight manages to get through. I blink up at it, feeling it warm my face on its way to the sidewalk.

☙❧

"I think I'm getting into a rhythm."

I'm on the phone with my mom, walking to the religion class I share with Camila.

"I'm glad," she says. "I was worried about you."

Full disclosure: I *hate* talking on the phone. I'm terrible about keeping in touch with people. Also, I get very self-absorbed in my own life. A full week will go by before I realize I haven't talked to my mom. She says she doesn't mind; it's always a surprise when she gets a call from me.

"I was worried about me too." It's been thirteen days since Owen and I made our break up official. It still stings, but I'm coping. I pull my jacket tighter against the wind as it whispers over my neck. I suck in the cold air. It stings my throat.

"It's October. You're settling in."

"And getting cold. I'm already in a scarf."

We both laugh.

"Email me later," I say as I walk up the steps. "Tell me how everyone is."

"I will. Love you, sweetie."

"You too."

I hang up when I reach the building for my class. My throat still stings, and I start clearing it a lot because its dry and scratchy. Camila looks over at me while she takes notes.

"Are you getting sick?"

"I better not be," I whisper. "I've got choir tonight. And lots of homework."

"Never-ending," she says with a sigh.

"We should have quit while we were ahead," I say, and we both giggle.

Jordan meets me for lunch, and I order chicken soup.

"My throat hurts," I say. "I'm trying to avoid getting sick."

He makes a cross with his fingers and holds them out to me. "Stay back."

"Wrong religion," I say, shoving his hand aside. "Let's go somewhere tonight before class. I want to get out."

He makes a face. "At least you have a job. I have no reason to go anywhere."

"Sorry." I move past that. "Let's go the shopping center."

"I'm game if you're driving."

Which is funny, because I am literally the only one of my friends with a car.

Well, Stirling has one, but I'm not asking him to drive me and my cousin around.

Jordan and I meet at my apartment when our last class ends.

"What's going on with your girlfriend?" I ask him. "You haven't mentioned her in awhile."

"I guess it's like with you and Owen," he says. He, Camila, and Abby are the only ones I've confided in about that conversation two weeks ago. "We don't talk much now."

"I'm sorry." I wrinkle my nose. "I know it hurts."

"It does. But it also feels right."

Unfortunately, I know what he means by that also.

"Are you and Stirling dating now?"

I shake my head. The two of them have met a few times, even though usually I hang out at Stirling's house. He has come over to my apartment once or twice. "We go on dates. He's fun and makes me laugh. But mostly he's a good friend."

"What's holding you back?"

"Attraction," I say immediately.

Jordan laughs. "You didn't hesitate."

I grin a little sheepishly and slow my car down for the light. "I ask myself the same thing every time we go out. And it's not there. We're friends. Maybe it will change. But not so far."

"Friends are good."

We pull into the shopping center, and my eyes land on the pet store. "Oh, come on, let's go inside!"

"Why?"

But it's a rhetorical question. Jordan already knows how I am with animals.

A beautiful blue macaw sits tethered to a bare tree near the entrance. A sign says, "Stay back, I bite," and I heed it. He squawks at me, feathers opening wide, black tongue darting out.

"Your roommates wouldn't like it if you brought him home," Jordan says beside me.

"Can you imagine the mess?" I glance down at the gravel pit beneath the perch.

And suddenly I know why I'm here.

I step around Jordan to the aquariums and search for a basic one. I find one, rectangular but large enough for several fish. I grab the box, and Jordan comes over to help me.

"What fish are you putting in here?" he asks.

I grin. He already knows what I'm doing. "Let's pick a few."

An employee helps me. We pick a goldfish and a red fish and two orange ones. Loaded up with fish, an aquarium, rocks, fake plants, food, a net, and a suction vacuum, I spend too much money and skip out of the store. Jordan pushes the cart behind me, a bemused expression on his face.

"I didn't expect this," he says.

I get in the car and bounce in my seat with excitement. I hold the plastic baggies with the fish while Jordan gets in, then hand them to him. "I've wanted to do this for months."

"Mild exaggeration."

"Okay, weeks." I hum. I'm buzzing.

Layne is the only one home when I pop in. She's at the counter buttering toast.

"Wait till you see!" I crow.

"What? What is it?"

Jordan comes in behind me with the tank in his arms. I set it on the table and put the bags of fish beside it.

"A fish tank! What fun!" Layne says.

Jordan helps me set it up. We clean the rocks and put them in the tank, then add the fake plants and water. Then we put the fish in and slit the bags so they can swim out when they want. I pull up a chair and settle in to watch.

After five minutes, Jordan says, "They're boring."

"Oh, shush." I wave a hand at him, eyes glued to the tank. "They haven't left the bags yet."

He chuckles. "We have to go to class."

I whine. "We'll miss their exit!"

"They'll be swimming happily in the tank when you get home."

I sigh and rise from my chair reluctantly. "Okay."

I don't realize how sore my throat is until I have to sing. My range is lower than usual, and I lose my voice on the high notes. Instead I make frequent trips to the water fountain and gurgle lots of water and try not to breathe on anyone. I think of Stirling while I fumble through the vowel sounds of the Icelandic Christmas song. The music has a peppy feel that makes me think of boys with spiky bleached hair and dimples in their cheeks.

As much as I enjoy the music, I want to get back to my fish.

Jordan laughs at me when class ends and I hustle down the sidewalk. "You would think you got a puppy, not a fish tank!"

"Fish are better for an apartment!"

He trails behind me, and I burst into the apartment.

Iris, Camila, Layne, Jared, Brant, and a handful of other boys stand around the tank.

"Is it okay?" I push my way through. "Are the fish all right?"

They are all out of the bags, swimming through the water. Bubbles float to the top from the aerator, and the fish swivel their shiny scales in and out of the stream.

"We named them," Layne says. She points to the red one. "That one's Moby." Then she points to the goldfish. "And that one's Dick."

She busts up laughing like this is the funniest thing ever, and I lobby an eye-roll at Iris.

"We're calling him Dee for short," Camila says.

"We named these two Mic and Moe," Iris says, pointing at the orange ones.

I lift an eyebrow. "So do I get to name any of my fish?"

"They're your fish?" Jared says.

I glance at him. I stand by my initial evaluation of him: he's cute, and cuter now that his short-cropped hair is growing in. "I bought them."

"Are we going to stand here all night watching them?" Brant says.

I glower at him, and he says, "They're cool. They're just not that cool."

Layne shrugs and turns away. "I'm going to the basement to watch a movie."

Brant follows her. Iris and Camila watch the fish a moment longer and then leave the kitchen also.

Jared holds his hand out to Jordan. "Hi, I'm Jared. Are you Stirling?"

"What?" I say, and Jordan stutters out a laugh.

"No. I'm Jordan, Cassandra's cousin." He doesn't take Jared's hand.

"What do you know about Stirling?" I blink at Jared.

"Oh." Jared's face flushes pink, and he pulls his hand back to run it over his hair. "Stirling's your boyfriend, right? I just assumed."

"I don't have a boyfriend," I say, a little loudly. It shouldn't be a big deal, but this flusters me. "I'm not dating anyone."

"Gotcha," Jared says, and my face burns.

"I just go on dates," I say, trying to recover from my awkward declaration by making things more awkward. I want to hide my face.

Jordan's face is red from trying not to laugh. I avoid looking at him.

"I understand," Jared says. "Well. Nice to meet you, Jordan."

He vacates the room quite quickly.

Jordan busts up, bending over and holding his knees, he's laughing so hard.

"Shut. Up." I sit down in front of the fish tank and press my hot face against the cold glass.

"You can be so—"

"Don't say it," I growl. "Just let me watch my fish."

He gives me a hug. "Enjoy your fish! And take some Vitamin C."

I don't bother saying goodbye. I pull my phone out and snap a picture of the swimming colors. Already they brighten the room.

On impulse, I send the picture to Owen.

Me: Got a fish tank.

He hearts the message. Then he responds, *I love them.*

I smile and put my phone away.

CHAPTER SIXTY-ONE

Fish Graveyard

By Saturday morning it's clear I'm battling a cold. My throat hurts, my neck is tight, and my head feels heavy, and I pray that will be the worst of it. I work today and have tomorrow to rest and recover. I'm terrified at the thought of how behind I'll get if I miss school.

"Computers are working!" Jeff crows when I enter the building. He grins widely at each of us as we walk in.

I sit down next to Stirling and put on my headset.

"Going to the game tonight?" he asks.

I hesitate. "I spent all my money on fish," I admit. "I don't have enough for tickets."

"You bought fish?"

I nod.

"Were they like two hundred dollars each?"

"No." I laugh. "But my paychecks go to pay other bills. Not fish tanks."

He puts on his own headset, and we both begin making calls. I'm striking out.

"What bills do you have?" he asks in between dials. "Something besides tuition and rent and all that?"

"Credit cards," I say.

"You're eighteen!"

The conversation pauses as we both take calls, and then it picks up again.

"How in debt can you be?" he says.

"Well. I did an impulse buy last spring . . . and I'm almost done paying for it. This is my last month, actually."

"What was it?" he asks in a hushed voice, his eyes wide, like he expects something scandalous.

"A plane ticket to Brazil."

Now his eyebrows shoot up. We're interrupted by someone answering a call on my end, and then he's talking, but finally we are both waiting at the same time.

"Why Brazil? For how long?"

"Oh, it's complicated. I'll simplify for you. One of my best friends lives there, and we promised we'd meet up again after I graduated. But plane tickets to fly to America are too much, so as soon as I had fifteen hundred dollars, I bought a ticket." I shrug. "It wasn't the smartest thing ever, but I decided I'm going to study Portuguese and make it an educational trip."

"Wow. She must be—"

"He." I may as well clear that up right now.

I'm saved by a call. But Stirling's waiting when I get off.

"You're going to see a guy?"

"Yes."

"He's just a friend?"

I nod. "A dear friend. We don't talk much anymore, actually. But I think we'll have fun together."

"That sounds amazing. And crazy."

"It's very crazy. If I'd purchased the refundable ticket, I might back out. But I didn't."

Stirling holds up his hand for a high-five. "Here's to a grand adventure."

"Very grand." I smack his palm.

"Attention. Attention." Jeff climbs to the top of the podium. "When you get off your call, don't dial again for a moment."

We face him and wait while the calls around us finish up. Then Jeff grins and says, "I have a surprise for all of you. One of our donors visited Preston Y last week and was very impressed with the foundation. He happens to be the football coach at a school in Utah, and he's invited every one of us to come to their home game in two weeks."

"All of us?" Ralph asks.

Jeff nods. "Anyone who wants to come. We'll meet here Saturday morning and ride a bus for five hours to get there."

"What school is it?" Jamie asks.

"A little college town in Ephraim, Utah. Snow College."

My head jerks up. I know this name.

I'm pretty sure that's the school Monica goes to.

I feel a flash of guilt, because Monica, like Harper and Riley and Farrah and all my friends back home, is another person I've failed to keep in touch with. I pull out my phone and skip the pleasantries.

Me: what school are you at in Utah?

Jeff's going over logistics, but I'm staring at my phone, willing a response. And then it comes.

Monica: Hey!! Snow College.

I grin, a wide smile that stretches across my face.

Me: I'm coming to visit in two weeks.

○〜※〜○

I call Monica when I get off work and we go over the details.

"I'm so excited to see you!" she says. "It's been too long! Wait till Owen hears!"

My heart squeezes at the mention of his name, but I swallow back the reaction. I'll always feel something for him. It doesn't get to rule my life.

I step into my apartment, phone still to my ear, and find Layne and Iris standing over the fish tank, peering down at it. They look up at me, and their expressions are somber.

"I'll call you later, okay, Monica?"

"Sure! See you soon!"

I slide my phone into my purse and look at them. "What's wrong?"

They take a step back from the tank. My heart sinks when I see both the orange fish floating upside down at the top. "Oh no! What happened?"

"They're fish," Layne says. "They just die."

"Maybe they arrived sickly," Iris says.

"It's possible." I use the net to scoop them out into a plastic baggie. "There's a thirty-day return policy if they die. I'll run them back and see what they say."

"Good luck," Layne says, raising an eyebrow.

I don't waste any time but head straight back to the pet store with my dead delivery. They test my water when I arrive.

"Seems fine," the customer service rep says. "It's got the right PH for your fish. Maybe they stressed out. Does your tank have a light?"

"No." I bite my lip. Did I kill them?

"Let's get you an aquarium light."

We pick one that will fit on the side of my tank, and then I buy five tiny neon tetras, small tropical fish with shades of green, blue, and pink. They glow under the light, and I can't wait to see them in my tank.

"Good luck," she says. "Any problems, come back and see us."

"I've got it this time," I tell the school of swimming beauties. "I'm keeping all of you alive."

⚜

One of my neon tetras dies that day.

Sunday morning, another is dead.

I don't have time to worry about this. I have tests to study for, essays to write. But I come right home after physical science Monday morning and stuff corpses into plastic bags, hoping the pet store can give me an autopsy. What is killing my fish?

I stick them in the fridge and run back to English class.

"I don't do exams in this class," Ms. Cheney says. "But midterms are next week, so I'm giving you a heads up right now. I do require a five-page paper applying three different literary theories to one of the short stories we've read in here. It's a good idea to get started."

Midterms are next week.

I'm halfway through my first semester of college.

These thoughts flit through my head, followed by, when they heck am I going to have time to write this paper and study for exams?

That's more important than my fish. And yet, my fish are all I can think about. I come home, grab the bags, and hurry to the pet store.

"They could be sick," the woman says. It's a different employee, but she looks at my receipt like she's suspicious of what I'm doing to my fish. "Try this medicine."

I go home with a bottle of fish-destresser. Because fish can get stressed out also. I also bring two new tetras.

I watch them like a hawk all evening with my laptop open across my legs while I choose three literary theories for my essay. I glance up from the screen every five minutes.

They are still alive when I go to bed.

⊙〜҉〜⊙

Two of them are dead in the morning.

I want to cry.

I have a presentation on ancient people in my religion class this morning. Again, I stuff the bodies in bags and put them in the fridge.

"All right, Cassandra," Professor MacArthur says, scanning his list of names. "We're ready for you."

It should be an easy ten-minute presentation. I plug in my slideshow and turn to the board behind me.

"I'm super excited to introduce you to the Muisca people of the pre-Columbian era just south of Mesoamerica," I say, pulling up the first slide. A map lights up the screen. I zoom in on it, showing the rugged mountains and wide rivers of South America. "Like the Mayans and Aztecs—" I click another button, and the slide changes to a Mayan pyramid, "the Muisca performed human sacrifices and worshiped many gods. Unlike the aforementioned groups, however, the Muisca were a fledgling group and did not build temples, pyramids, or grand cities." A giant red x appears on top of the Mayan temple, followed by a buzzer sound. The class laughs, and I smile.

"Like the Mayans, they adored the sun and placed special emphasis on the god Chiminigagua." The name appears in bold on the screen. "Try saying that three times fast."

There's more laughter, and I click the next slide. But instead of popping up, the screen goes black.

Unexpected. I tilt my head and click the button again, but nothing happens. Professor MacArthur gets up and checks the power cord, then tries the on button.

"And that," I say, watching him try to work the projector, "is why we don't worship Chiminigagua."

My classmates bust up laughing this time. And I stand there and smile while I can't give my presentation.

Professor MacArthur straightens and shrugs. "Give us what you can without your slides."

I pull out my note cards, glad I have them as a backup. The slides were my cues. I summarize the rest, ending with why I chose the group.

"I'm fascinated by this time period and location in Colombia," I say. "My family is from there, but we don't know a lot about our ancestry." We know nothing, in my case. "A part of me feels like I'll need to get my feet on site to learn about my roots."

I sit down and the class claps politely. My face is hot. It would have gone quite well if not for the computer issues.

"Thank you, Cassandra. I enjoyed hearing about why you chose this group. Does anyone have any questions for her?"

I hope they don't, because I've already sat down. I pull out a notebook and keep myself busy. No one asks anything, and Professor MacArthur assigns pages to read.

"We'll finish up the presentations after I get the projector working again," he says.

My mind is already back on my fish. But I still have to get through my Honors English class.

"I want you to start thinking about your final project for this class," Ms. Mayhew says. "It's a personal narrative, and I need it to be deep. So this week I want you to create your outline. Then you sign up for a consultation with me. The consultation will be your midterm grade." She passes out a rubric sheet. "Challenge yourself. Make it personal."

More personal than my last assignment, when I wrote about the nuclear meltdown I had with Tiago? I study the rubric and wonder what I'll write about. I don't want it to be about Tiago. And not Owen. I want it to be about me. Something that's happened to me, something I've had to overcome.

And then I think of it.

I can write about my eating disorder.

CHAPTER SIXTY-TWO

Heartache

I forget to take the dead fish to work with me when I leave my apartment Tuesday evening. They stay sealed in body bags in the fridge, becoming less fresh by the minute.

It's not until Wednesday after school that I have the chance to get to the pet store again.

"I don't know why they keep dying," I say. "I'm trying so hard to keep them alive."

"Have you tried a protein supplement?" It's a boy this time, and he peruses the shelves and then returns with a small bottle. "Something to help them strengthen up in a new environment." He marks off two more returns on my receipt.

I return home with the protein and two more fish.

I stare at the new fish swimming with the old ones, and its as if my ability to succeed in college is tied up in their survival. If they can't make it, neither can I. But if I can build them the right environment, remove the dangerous variables and help them thrive, I can too.

I go to bed aware that I'm taking my fish way too seriously.

I clean the fish tank on Saturday, but it still looks filthy. I need something to make this easier. I google it and decide I need a sucker fish to get the algae off the sides.

The same boy as Thursday is working the customer service desk at the pet store, and he looks at me funny when I come in.

"You must like it here," he says. "You come in a lot."

"I'm trying to keep my fish alive," I say. "And keep the tank clean. Have any sucker fish?"

"A few, yeah. Some powerful suckers and some small ones."

He shows them to me, and I buy one of each, a small one and a powerhouse.

I shove the receipt in the growing pile in my purse. It's best if I don't think about all the money I'm spending on these fish.

I don't want to get my hopes up, but I count the fish on Sunday morning, and they are still there. All nine of them. I whisper them a blessing and head off to church with my roommates.

My phone chimes with a text during the sermon. All heads swing toward me, and I ignore it until the judging eyes look away. Then I slide it from my purse to my thigh to see the texter.

Owen: been awhile. How are you?

Oh, I should not text him in the middle of church, but we haven't talked in days. Weeks? I silence my phone to hide what I'm about to do, then I text back.

Me: good. In church.

O: I have good timing

Me: you do

O: heard you're going to see Monica next week

Me: I am! I'm so excited to see her

O: give her a hug for me

Me: will do

He doesn't respond to my last words. The conversation is over. I mull over his motives. Did he really want to make sure I hugged Monica? Was he trying to assert himself as my friend? Or was the knowledge that I was going to see his sister a good excuse to reach out to me?

I choose to believe it's the third option. Even though he shouldn't feel like he needs a reason to talk to me, I understand why he does. I do too.

⚬~❀~⚬

All week I'm anxious for the trip on Saturday. I finish all my assignments before I leave except for the essays, and I take my laptop with me to the bus Saturday morning with the good intentions of getting school work done. Stirling sits by me and shows me cat videos, and I tell him about my cat back home.

"How are the fish?"

I beam at him. "None of them have died in a week. I think I may have cracked the code. They're all going to live from now on."

"The fish whisperer!" He holds his fist out.

I meet his fist bump. "I worked hard for it." Then I pull out my laptop. "And now I have to work hard for my grades."

"Understood." He turns back to his cat videos.

Our friendship is comfortable but not romantic, although I know everyone at work thinks we're dating. He might think we are. We haven't talked about it.

I get sleepy forty minutes into the drive. I close my computer and try to get comfortable against the window, but the bus bumps and jolts too much. Stirling bunches up his jacket and puts it on his shoulder.

"Rest here."

I don't hesitate but let my head fall on his shoulder, and then I'm out.

He wakes me when we stop. "Time for lunch."

I look out the window. "Burger King?"

"Don't like it?"

"It's the worst of fast food places."

343

He points across the street. "There's also Taco Bell."

"That's where I'm heading."

Jeff stands up in the front. "You have a few food choices here, but eat quickly! The football coach has arranged a tour of the university before the game. It's much smaller than Preston Y, but that small school feel fosters a unique and close-knit learning environment."

Ralph snickers. "Are you reading from their brochure?"

Jeff pats down his pants and then pulls one from his pocket. "Caught me."

I'm not interested in a tour, or even food. I want to see Monica. I text her as half of us walk across the street to Taco Bell.

Me: Just pulled in. Getting food at Taco Bell

M: !!!! I can't wait. I'll come find you.

I can't wait either.

I order a chicken quesadilla and choose a table alone in the corner. I sit down to eat just as a familiar blue car zips into the parking lot.

Monica climbs out, and my heart swells. I jump out of my seat and greet her at the entrance. We throw our arms around each other and laugh.

I pull back and study her. "You look great. So great." Her ash-blond hair is in perfect waves, her face has color, and I felt the toned muscles of her arms when she hugged me. I tug her back to my table. "How is everything going?"

"I'm having a much better semester than last year," she says.

I offer her some of my quesadilla, and she accepts. "Why is that? Because you're not sick?"

She brightens. "Definitely part of it. I'm in remission, I'm feeling great, I'm even captain of the volleyball team."

"That's wonderful!" I feel dull and boring next to her.

"But mostly it's because my ex boyfriend is finally out of the picture." She sighs and rolls her eyes. "I couldn't move on with him constantly in the background."

I nod. She and I have parallel stories with our exes. "And Noah?"

She waves a hand. "We're friends, and we're fine with it. He's going to school in Missouri. I'm sure we'll meet up if we're ever in the same area."

"So are you dating anyone?"

"Lots of people," she says, and we collapse into giggles.

Then she sobers up. "And you? Dating anyone? Still talk to Owen?"

I knew this question would come up. I shrug and pick at my quesadilla, going for indifference. "Like you. I date but I'm not dating anyone in particular. Owen and I talk every once and awhile. He told me to give you a hug."

"You can check that one off." She smiles, but there's a tightness around her eyes. "Do you still like him?"

I give her an incredulous look. "Monica. I love him. There is nothing nothing nothing that will ever change that. No amount of time or distance or space. I will be seventy-five and married with grandkids and still carry love for Owen in my heart."

"Ah." Her smile is softer this time. "That's so sweet. How is school?"

"Ugh." I groan and throw back my head. "School is hard! Every class seems to think they're my only class. I hardly sleep between the reading and exams and papers. Not to mention work and church!"

"Real life, girl."

"Somehow I thought college would be easier."

"Nope. But it's more fun."

"That it is." I spot Stirling leaving the line with a tray of food. He bobs his head at me, his eyes tracking toward Monica. I gesture him over.

"Hi," he says, settling his tray beside me.

"Stirling, this is my best friend Monica. She goes to Snow College."

"No way, that's awesome! You didn't tell me you would see a friend here."

"I was afraid I might jinx it." My face warms. "Monica, this is Stirling."

"Nice to meet you," Monica says.

"That's awesome you could meet up with us." Stirling unwraps a burrito. "So you're from Arkansas too?"

"Louisiana, actually. But I lived in Arkansas last year with my family, and Cassandra and I hit it off. She's more of a sister than a best friend. She and my brother are super close also."

I nearly choke on the sip of water I just took. My eyes burn, and I grab a napkin and press it to my face. Monica looks at me, smirking slightly, and I know what she's doing. She sees Stirling as a threat, and she's trying to scare him off.

"That's great," Stirling says. "Is he here too?"

"No, but he would've come if he could've. He's home in Louisiana."

"It's hard to be away from friends. But college is a great place for making new ones." Stirling knocks his shoulder with mine. "We've gotten pretty close."

And I know that as thinly veiled as Monica's warning was, Stirling picked up on it. And he's laying down his own challenge.

"I need hot sauce," he says, rising. "Anyone else?"

We shake our heads, and as soon as he's up, Monica leans toward me.

"Are you dating him?" she hisses.

I shake my head. "I told you, I'm not dating anyone. But Stirling and I hang out a lot. And we've gone on a few dates."

She spins around to look at him and then huffs at me. "He's so short."

I press my lips together. "He's taller than me."

She pulls out her phone and takes a picture of him at the condiment stand, and I start laughing.

"Monica. What are you doing?"

"Nothing. Have you kissed him?"

"Girl, I told you. We're not dating."

"You don't have to be dating to be kissing."

I want to deny that, but then I remember how Owen and I got started. Secret kisses while he dated other girls. I give a wistful smile, full of nostalgia for those days.

"You're smiling. You are kissing someone."

"No." I meet her gaze. "I'm remembering kisses with someone else."

She leans back in her chair, but there's smug satisfaction on her face.

Stirling returns, and she must not see him as a threat anymore because no more veiled challenges are lobbied his direction. My coworkers finish their food and head back to the bus.

"We're touring the college before the game," I tell Monica as we stand. "But I'll see you there, right?"

"Yes." She hugs me again. "It's so wonderful to see you. Nice to meet you, Stirling."

"You too," he says breezily.

I brace myself.

The questions begin halfway through the tour.

"So she seems nice," Stirling says. "She's a lot older than you, to be your best friend."

"Yep. She's four years older than me." I will tell him only what he needs to know, and I don't see that as being a lot. "We were both going through a hard time when she moved out to be with her family, and we connected."

"You're close with the whole family?"

"Yeah. They're amazing."

"I'm guessing you and her brother dated?"

I'm surprised he asks so bluntly. Stirling is easy-going and friendly but never assertive or bold. "We did. We dated most of our senior year."

"Must be hard to let go."

I don't answer. This is a weird conversation with him.

"What's his name?"

"Owen." My chest tightens when I say his name. I want to say it again to see if it has the same effect.

"I still remember my high school girlfriend. She was special."

I turn to him, lowering my voice as our tour guide leads us into another building. "Where is she now?"

"Married. She got married while I was in Iceland."

I wince. "Sorry."

He shrugs. "It tore me up for a bit when I found out. But I'm fine now."

We stop talking as our guide tells us about the student activities. I'm glad Stirling's okay.

Love sure sucks.

⊙↦⋇↤⊙

I sit by Monica during the game and I don't watch any of it. Instead we go through each other's phones and share the stories behind every photo. We laugh harder than I've laughed in weeks, and I feel the heaviness and care of school lifting away from me. She makes me tell the story of my ailing fish three times.

"How much money have you spent on these fish now?" she asks.

I open my wallet and hand her the receipts. "I've been afraid to add it up. Tell me."

She thumbs through them, shaking with laughter. "No, girl. You don't want to know." She hands them back, then says, "And Tiago? How is he?"

"Fine, I assume." I put the receipts back. "We hardly ever talk, and when we do it's through email. I don't feel for him what I once did, and I'm comfortable with the friendship we have. I'm excited to go to Brazil and see the country, hear the language, and visit my friend."

"Maybe I should come with you," she says.

"Someone should," I say. "The thought of going alone makes me nervous."

"What's your mom said?"

"Funny thing, that. I keep forgetting to tell her."

"Oh, girl."

We laugh again, and then Monica snaps a few selfies.

"Hey, I've got a terrific idea," she says, her eyes lighting up. "Are you going home to Arkansas for Thanksgiving?"

I shake my head. "We only get five days off, including the weekend. Flights are expensive. I'm saving my money to see my family at Christmas."

"I'm not going home either, for the same reasons. Want to celebrate it together? You can come out here and stay in my house. All my roommates are going home."

"Yes," I say immediately. "Yes, I absolutely want to."

She squeals and claps her hands. "I am so excited! I've missed you. We have to see each other more often."

"We absolutely do."

⌒〜❀〜⌒

I'm so tired from the trip to Utah that I think I might sleep through church Sunday morning. But when my roommates shuffle through the apartment getting ready, I decide I may as well get dressed also. I open my closet and peruse my dresses.

Then Layne shouts from her bedroom. "You guys, it's snowing!"

"Snowing?" It's the middle of October. Can it really snow this early? I bounce over to my bed and peel back the blinds.

Fluffy white flakes drift lazily toward the earth. The ground is brown and dead, the trees losing their yellow leaves, but the white drizzles lend a softness to the severe landscape.

"It's beautiful," I say. I can't help but sigh a little. "But it's too early."

Camila bounces beside me. "It just gets colder from here."

She's not wrong. I'm unprepared when we step outside to walk to church. My dress is long but my legs are bare, and my exposed ears burn by the time we reach the building. I stand in the hallway shivering, trying to warm up.

"Did you see Monica yesterday?" Camila asks, waiting beside me.

"I did!" I pull out my phone and show her pictures. "It was so great to see her!"

"Aw, I'm glad you had fun."

"It made me realize how much I miss her. And Owen." I furrow my brow, annoyed. "Seeing her reminded me of him. Camila, I miss him so much. I try not to think about it, but it's there, always, like I lost my right arm and I'm functioning without it and compensating with my left arm, but I'm still aware of what I've lost!"

She gives me a sympathetic look. "When I met you, it was Tiago you felt this way for."

347

"It was a fluke that Tiago and I ever met. It was never meant to be. Owen—he is the other part of me."

She studies me, unblinking. "So you think you'll get back together someday?"

I shake my head. "I'm not saying that. I'm saying that even if we don't, even if I live my life without my right arm, I will always miss it."

She tilts her head at me like she thinks I'm being dramatic. "Maybe after awhile you won't notice it's gone."

"I'll tell you when that happens."

The sermon is energizing and inspiring. Time is measured differently in college, and this upcoming week is the season of midterms. I want to puke every time I think about it. But then the pastor reminds us to keep everything in perspective.

"Even if you fail a test," he says, "it doesn't mean your college career is over. For every opportunity missed, there is a do-over."

"But I don't want to redo physical science," I murmur to Iris.

"Same," she says. "Let's pass and get it over with."

"Game plan." I hold out my knuckles, and she bumps them.

The snow falls harder by the time we leave church. We exit together, boys and girls heading back to the dorms. I can't stop shivering, and I curse the cold.

"Jacket, Cassandra?"

Jared steps over to me and offers his long wool coat. I should say no out of niceness because he'll have nothing if I take it, but I'm so cold. I snatch it up.

"Thank you." I pull it on and sigh as I snuggle into its warmth. I pull the collar open around my face and inhale that familiar masculine scent of cologne and deodorant. Then I remember Jared and give him a sheepish look.

"Aren't you cold?" I ask.

He puts his hands in his pockets and shrugs. "You looked colder."

Jared has a pretty face, smooth features, dark hair, wide blue eyes and a firm jaw. He's huskier through the shoulders, but the body type is typical for a football player.

"Thanks," I say. "You're always kind."

He doesn't say anything else but walks with us up to the apartment. Along with Brant and Justin and two other guys.

"How's the fish tank going?" Brant asks as we enter the kitchen.

I shrug out of Jared's jacket within the warmth of our apartment and turn to my fish. Even though I cleaned the tank a week ago, it still looks dirty. The sucker fish are slow eaters. "I might have to scrape the walls."

"I made muffins!"

Layne commandeers the kitchen and the boys. I pull out a bucket and fill it with water for the fish.

"Do you need help?" Iris asks.

I glance at her. Her long black hair is pulled back, and she's put mascara on her short eyelashes. Very unlike Iris, who usually keeps her face bare. "Who are you trying to impress?" I whisper.

A small smile creases her lips. Her eyes dart toward Jared, eating a muffin in the corner with the other guys.

"Ah." I nod. Jared. Of course. "He seems like a good one." I turn back to the tank. My roommates enjoy watching the fish and they liked naming them, but all of the work has fallen to me. I guess I'm okay with that. "It's all right. I'll do it."

I make Layne take the guys out to the commons so I can do the fish tank in peace. I put the bucket on the table and empty the fish into it, then carry the tank to the sink so I can suction out the gunk with the vacuum.

"Can I help you?"

Jared appears in the kitchen, startling me.

CHAPTER SIXTY-THREE

Tepid Response

nearly drop the fish vacuum at Jared's sudden appearance but catch myself, luckily before it loses suction. "Heavens. Where did you come from?"

He shrugs. "I felt bad for you, doing all this work by yourself."

"It's not so bad." I set the half-empty aquarium on the counter. "I need to scrape the sides down, though. My algae-eaters aren't consuming fast enough."

"How do you scrape it?"

"I'm sure they sell algae scrapers at the pet store. But I don't have one."

Jared steps over to the sink and examines what we do have. "Paper towels will dissolve. What about a sponge?" He holds up the yellow rectangle.

"As long as we throw it away after." I take it from him, roll up my sleeves, and begin. "I'm buying a scraper after this." Can't wait to tell Monica. One more fish investment.

He steps over the bucket and peers in it. "How many fish do you have?"

"Nine."

He's silent a moment, and then he says, "I can only find eight."

"What?" I stop scraping and hurry over to him. "There were nine when I put them in there!" I count quickly, and my heart sinks. "Dick! Dick is missing!"

Jared smirks and then clears his face. "How?"

"He must have jumped out!" I leap backward, afraid I've crushed the fish under my feet.

We both bend down, getting on our hands and knees and searching the floor.

"Here, here, I've got him." Jared grabs the goldfish in his hand.

"Is he—" I dart over and breathe a sigh of relief when I see how the fish flops around. "Quick, put him in the water!"

Jared dumps him in, and he's laughing a little. "I'll keep an eye on them and make sure no more jump out."

"You're very helpful." I try to glare at him, but the situation is funny, and I bite my lip to keep back the giggles.

He chuckles, and then we're both laughing, and I stop cleaning and lean against the counter as we collapse in laughter. Then he helps me pour the bucket back in the aquarium and set it up on the table again.

And I feel it. That spark of interest. The simmer of chemistry.

Except I can't. Not for Jared. Because Iris likes him.

But he's the first person to make me feel anything in months, and I can't help the way it draws me toward him.

We sit in chairs in front of the fish tank when we finish and admire how it looks.

"I can see all the fish again," I say.

"They're pretty," he says.

"I can't believe Dick jumped out of the bucket."

"Dicks aren't known for their intelligence."

My eyes shoot his direction, and I bust up laughing again. "Worst joke ever!"

His eyebrows raise. "I wasn't even joking."

The kitchen door opens, and Layne walks in. She spots Jared.

"Hey, you're still here," she says. "I thought you left."

He stands and picks up his long jacket. "I was helping Cassandra with the fish tank."

Iris comes in behind her. She looks at Jared, then her eyes sweep to me, and I feel a flash of guilt.

"Nice of you," she says. "I thought Cassandra didn't need help."

"I didn't—" I begin.

"But then Dick jumped out of the bucket," Jared says. "And she had to save his life."

Layne smirks, and I try not to laugh, and Iris looks pissed.

Time to exit. "Thanks for your help," I say. "Have a good day."

I close my bedroom door quietly, then I collapse on my bed and laugh into my sheets.

⌒⟳⚜⟲⌒

Iris finds me on my way out the door for school Monday morning.

"Cassandra!" she calls, just as I'm opening the back door.

I pause with my hand on the handle. She didn't talk to me last night, and I assumed she was upset with me. "Yeah, what's up?"

"I know it's last minute, but my mom asked me to come home for her birthday. Birthdays are pretty special in Chinese culture. She booked me a flight for tonight and then I'll come home Wednesday. Can you give me a ride to the airport? My brother can pick me up."

"Um." I mentally run through my schedule. School and then work. "What time?"

"Three."

"Okay. I'm done with class at one but I have work at three-thirty, so we'll have to hurry. We'll leave here as soon as I get back from class."

She nods. "I'll be ready."

I meet with Jordan for lunch in the cafeteria and tell him all about my trip to Utah.

"And Monica and I decided to meet up for Thanksgiving!"

"That's great. Now I don't have to invite you to my house."

"Rude!" I whack his arm. "Were you going to?"

"Wasn't going to leave my cousin here alone."

"Oh." I frown. "That would be fun."

He nudges me. "Cass. Go with your friend. You see me all the time."

"Truth." I bob my head in agreement.

"Is it weird, hanging out with your ex's sister?"

I exhale and wilt in my seat. "I don't think of him that way."

"You don't think of Owen as your ex?"

"No." Suddenly I want to cry. I blink hard. "We just stopped being together. We didn't end it."

His blue eyes are large and sympathetic. "That still makes him your ex."

I pick up my napkin and shred it. "It's not weird. She's my friend."

"Excuse me."

We both look up as a teacher in a sweater vest and tie leans over our table.

"Are you married?" he asks.

Jordan and I look at each other and shake our heads. We get this question a lot.

"Boyfriend?"

"Cousin," Jordan says.

The teacher pulls up a chair. "Good, making sure I don't step on any toes. I don't mean to interrupt. Can I talk to you for a moment?" He directs the question at me.

"Sure," I say.

"I'm an art teacher." He pulls out a business card and sets it in front of me. "I specialize in live subjects, and I'm always on the lookout for a new one for my students to paint."

I blink at him. "Okay."

"You're very beautiful. I don't know if you know that."

My face warms. "I've heard it before, yes."

"But you're very exotic. Your eyes, your hair, your skin tone. What's your nationality?"

"American," I say, automatically, because it's important to me that people know. "But my heritage is Colombian."

"That explains it. The high cheekbones, the narrow nose." He gestures toward my face. "Would you consider being a subject for my class? Letting my students paint you? I'd pay you for your time, of course."

I raise both eyebrows and throw a startled look at Jordan.

"You can come to my office later," he says. "I'll show you some of my paintings. Bring your cousin with you. I promise I'm not a creep."

I'm flattered. I lower my eyes and pick up his card. "Um, sure."

"Great." He stands up again. "Give me a call and we'll set up a time."

"That," Jordan says as the teacher walks away, "was the weirdest thing I've ever seen."

"Yeah, but it could be cool."

"He should have an agency he uses to get models. People make good money from this."

"I like the idea of money."

Jordan's brow furrows. "I'm going with you. I don't trust this guy."

"It could be fun." I'll see what it's about, anyway.

I hurry home after my English class so I can take Iris to the airport.

"Ready?" I ask her. She's still in her room loading up a bag.

"Almost."

I check the time. Almost one-thirty. The airport is only half an hour away, so we should be fine.

Iris closes up the bag. "Okay, I got it."

"Awesome."

We head down to my car. I help her load her stuff, and she says, "Thanks for the ride. I appreciate it."

"It's a good thing I brought a car," I joke. "I didn't realize I'd be the only one."

"Right? Maybe I'll bring mine down from Canada."

"How's the weather out there now?"

"About the same as here, but a bit colder."

"Lots of snow?"

"Not yet."

We fall silent as I concentrate on maneuvering through traffic. I'm getting better at managing four lanes in either direction, but I still breathe a sigh of relief as we merge onto I-70.

Then the silence stretches too far. The only sound is my blinker as I switch lanes to get out of the way of cars moving faster than me. An awkward proverbial elephant sits in the backseat of the car, waiting to see if he'll get mentioned.

I exhale. "About Jared."

She looks at me.

"I'm not interested in him."

She doesn't say anything for a moment, and then she says, "It's weird how as soon as I told you I like him, you start flirting with him. That's something I would expect from Layne, not you."

I wince. My guilty conscience pokes at me. "It might look that way, but I was not flirting with him. He came into the kitchen right when Dick had jumped out of the bucket. He helped me find him and keep him alive. That was it. And it was kind of funny."

She gives a slight smile. "You didn't ask him to help you?"

I shoot her a scornful look. "No! I didn't need help."

"Of course not." She relaxes in her chair. "You promise you won't flirt with him?"

He's the first boy I've wanted to flirt with since moving out here. And the promise feels unfair. But Girl Code comes before guys, and Iris claimed him first. "I promise."

"Even if he flirts with you?"

She's making this hard. "Yep."

"Thanks."

I nod. But I'm thinking, what if Jared isn't interested in Iris? At all? Ever?

"Where are we going?" Iris says, breaking my thoughts.

"The airport." I furrow my brow at her. "Right?"

She pulls out her phone. "But we're heading east. We need to be going south."

I check my GPS. "No, the airport is off of I-70 eastbound."

Iris groans and slaps her palm to her forehead. "Oh, no! Cassandra, there are two airports! You're going to the wrong one!"

"What?" I nearly slam on my brakes but realize that's a bad idea. "Where should I be going?"

"The Aspen airport! It's south of here!"

I think words I don't say and take the next exit, parking at a gas station to reroute. "Iris! There's no way there except to go back the way we came. It's over an hour away from here!"

We both look at the time.

It's one-fifty.

Her flight's at three.

"Crap," I say.

There's nothing to add to that.

I swing back onto the interstate going back toward campus. I drive faster, keeping pace with the vehicles who would have passed me earlier. We don't talk. I don't think we'll make her flight.

"It's all right," Iris says, broaching my anxious mode. "There's another flight at six if I miss this one."

"That's good." It's all I say. I'm tense.

I take the exit near campus and then swing south onto highway 82. "Why did your mom book you out of this airport?" I want to scream. But I don't. The drive time is usually only a fifteen minute difference between airports, and if one airport has a cheaper flight than the other, I know I'd pick the cheaper one also.

Forty minutes to go. I'm racing the clock, but the GPS still says I won't get Iris to the airport until 3:02.

"Hey!" Iris says suddenly. "My flight's been delayed by fifteen minutes!"

We share a grim look.

"You're still going to have to run to catch it."

"But now I have a chance."

I laugh. "A small chance."

I manage to shave off a few more minutes. It's 2:58 when I slow down at the terminal. I'm panting like I ran a marathon, my knuckles white from taking the curves too fast.

Iris leans over and hugs me, then jumps out. "Bye!" she calls, shouldering her bag and running for the door.

"Call me if you don't make it!" I shout after her.

She waves and she's gone and I take a deep breath.

I can't drive home as fast as I drove here. I don't want to die.

I'm going to be late to work.

CHAPTER SIXTY-FOUR

Paper Weight

ris messages me twenty minutes later.

I: I'm on the plane!

I send her back a thumbs up.

I get my first warning for showing up to work late. But it's okay. My heart rate has come down, and we're allowed three warnings before we're fired.

"What happened to you?" Stirling asks after I get off my first call.

"You wouldn't believe it." I roll my eyes as I swing toward him. "My roommate needed a ride to the airport but I took her to the wrong one!"

"Rookie mistake." He nods. "Everyone learns to clarify which airport around here. One time my brother thought he booked a flight out of Eagle but he booked it out of Denver!"

"Oh no!" We both chuckle at his brother's expense. Denver is three hours away.

"He missed his flight, of course. Lesson learned."

We turn back to our calls, then Stirling says, "Want to go out this weekend?"

I log the pledge I just got. "And do what?"

"Get a bite to eat. We can go back to my place and watch *The Rope*."

"What's that?"

"An incredibly fascinating and very boring Hitchcock movie. It takes place in one room. They didn't show it at the theater. But it's a masterpiece."

In all honesty, he had me at food. I'm quite tired of the instant noodles and canned soup I've been eating every night. "I can't Saturday, I'm going to a Halloween party with my roommates."

"Friday?"

"I work. You?"

"Yeah. We can go after."

"It's a date." I grin at him.

He grins back.

Still no spark.

I get a text from an unknown number halfway through my shift.

Want to meet for lunch on Friday?

I read the text three times while I run through a call. Do they know me or is it a wrong number? I type back, *who is this?*

You mean you don't have my number in your phone? Wide eye emoji

I smile, but I'm still perplexed. I'm getting male vibes.

Me: sorry . . .

It's Jared

My eyebrows arch. Speak of the devil.

Me: Hi Jared.

Iris's face looms in my mind, shaking a finger at me, reminding me of my promise. I stick to it.

Me: I can't. I have an algebra exam in class and I have to cram for it. I hate the class.

J: I happen to be really good at math

I snort. Good thing he can't hear me. But maybe he senses my disbelief in my lack of reply, because then he says, *Yu've never met a football player good at math, huh*

He misspelled "you." It could be an accident. It could be on purpose. But it makes me think of Owen. We had a running joke of misspellings between us.

Me: I could use a study buddy. I seriously suck at it. Are you any good?

J: I actually am

Me: I'm taking a chance on you

J: I won't let you down

Me: I'll be in the library from 11-1. Fifth floor periodicals

J: I know where you sit. see you Friday

I put my phone away. Maybe I won't fail my math midterm. I've barely passed the other math tests, and only because Ms. Jane lets us rework the problems we missed for half credit.

Stirling gives me a hug goodbye at my car, and I wish I could drum up something for him.

I'm in a good mood, in spite of my harried afternoon. I pull up my playlist and sing to my music as I drive back to campus. I check on my fish and blow them kisses.

"They're still alive!" I sing to Camila as I come into the bedroom.

"You did it," she says.

"I did it," I agree. "I finally got the right balance of proteins, salts, acids, and whatever to keep them alive." I'm pleased. I pull up my computer and work on my Honors English outline. My consultation with my teacher is tomorrow.

This paper carries so much weight. Not for my grade, but for my heart. I detail the steps that led me down the path of bulimia and then the critical turning points that took me out of it.

Particularly that pivotal moment when Tiago caught me vomiting in his bathroom.

I doubt he'll ever know the impact his reaction had on me.

Why is Thanksgiving break so far away? I can't wait to see Monica. Sleep in past seven in the morning. Not think about any assignments for a few days.

I meet with Ms. Mayhew for our consultation the next day. She reads over the outline for my personal narrative and lifts her eyes to mine.

"Are you sure you're prepared to write about this?"

I nod. "You said to make it personal."

"Make sure you include all the senses like we talked about. Don't fall into the habit of telling your story. You need to show it."

Show it. Show the visual of my emaciated body. Show the act of shoving my finger down my throat. Show the undigested food falling into the toilet.

"I can do it."

"Great." She writes in her planner. "I'll give you two weeks for the rough draft. We'll meet back here right before Thanksgiving."

One more thing to look forward to before I get to see Monica.

I make an appointment after choir on Thursday to meet with the art teacher. Jordan and I walk over together from the humanities building to the visual arts building.

Several offices are open, lights flooding the halls, even if classes are over. I check my reflection in a window. My hair is long again, past my shoulder blades, straight. I should cut bangs or something to make it more interesting. I'm wearing plaid pants and a sweater that would be cropped on most girls but not me. I'm too short.

We climb up the stairs to the second story and stop beside an open office. I knock lightly on the steel frame. My heart pounds a fast rhythm. I feel anxious and on display. I want to do this, but I'm also uncertain about it.

"Come on in." The professor appears in the doorway and gestures to a couch inside. "Here's one of my portfolios. I put it out so you can look through it and see my work."

I sit down and spread the book open across my thighs. Jordan sits down next to me.

Girls in a variety of clothing in front of varying landscapes stare back at me. Some are hazy water colors, others more crisp, almost photographic. A few meet my gaze head on, while others show their profile as they gaze into the distance.

"Are these paintings done on campus?" I ask.

"No, these are done in my studio. It's a private location."

"But your class meets here," Jordan says, looking up.

"Yes. We would start with modeling for my class. But if you end up being a good model, we could do a few sessions at my studio, also."

I want to trust him because he's a professor. But that doesn't make him an automatic good guy. Still, the paintings are beautiful. Women with their hair in elaborate twists or falling around their shoulders, standing by windows, sitting at tables, lounging with a book. Anything from fancy dresses to jeans and a T-shirt. He has a few blonds, but most are brunettes like me with dark eyes and a dark skin tone.

"How much are you paying?" Jordan asks.

I steal a glance at him, glad he came along. We talked beforehand about what questions I wanted to ask, but of course I can't remember any now.

"Twenty dollars an hour."

That's not bad, since I don't have to do anything but sit there. But Jordan's brow creases, and he doesn't look pleased as he turns back to the paintings.

Then I turn the page, and one of the women is sitting on a couch with no top on, her breasts splayed out over her chest, dark nipples pointing in opposite directions. I'm so startled I just blink.

"The university uses nude models?" I say, keeping my voice neutral.

"Of course," he says. "All universities do. It's standard for figure drawing. But you wouldn't be required to be nude. No one is. Although." He adds this as an afterthought. "They do pay more. Fifty dollars an hour."

"And you would do nude sessions in your private studio, also?" Jordan asks.

"Yes, if she wanted."

I turn the page and find more nude paintings. Some with nothing on at all

"The human body is beautiful," the professor says. "It's not pornographic. It doesn't have to be sexual."

I can't picture myself posing nude for a painting, no matter how innocuous. The skin on the back of my neck prickles, little stabs of uneasiness.

Then I turn the page and find a beautiful native American in full cultural garb, standing with one hand on a table, staring outside. She's exquisite.

I could do something like that. I get to decide.

I close the portfolio and stand up. "I'm interested."

He beams. "Write your phone number here." He holds a card out to me. "I'll call you to set up the details."

"All right." I put my number on the back of the card.

"Have a great night," he says, and I follow Jordan out of the room.

"What did you think?" I ask him as we exit the building.

He shakes his head. "I don't know. Something about him made me uncomfortable."

"It's art," I say, defensive in spite of having felt the same thing. "It's not a bad thing."

"I know of no guy out there who can look at a naked woman and not get aroused. You want guys looking at you that way?"

"I wouldn't pose nude. And it's decent money."

"That's another thing. No, it's not. He's using you for cheap. A model from an agency is probably a hundred bucks an hour."

"Maybe I should charge more."

"You have time to think about it. Then you can share your thoughts when he calls you. But I wouldn't do it. I wouldn't sell yourself that cheap."

I mull over his words. The interest, the initial offer, is very flattering. I like the idea of being beautiful and special. Am I letting the praise get the best of my judgment?

"What are you wearing for the Halloween party tomorrow?" Abby asks me in physical science.

I wonder which one she refers to. It seems there's a party on each block tomorrow night. "I hate costume parties." I keep my eyes on Professor Turnbaugh, writing down answers while addressing Abby. "I have nothing."

"Put on a white sheet, paint your eyes, and say you're Egyptian."

"Not a bad idea," I admit. "But it's cold. What are you being?"

Abby and her roommate don't get along, so she spends most of her time with me and mine. "Layne, Iris, and I are dressing up as secret agents from that new alien movie. You know it?"

I nod like I do but the only movies I've watched recently are Hitchcock thrillers. "Fun. Maybe I'll get Camila to be Egyptian with me."

"It'll be so much fun! I love Halloween!"

I want the calendar to tick closer to Thanksgiving.

I head to the library after class. I wonder if Jared will show. He hasn't texted me since Monday. I prop up my book, open my folder, and sigh. Math is of the devil.

I work through three practice problems and then check the answers in the back of the book.

I got one of them right.

Great.

The table wobbles, and I glance up as Jared plops down across from me.

"I almost went to the wrong place. You could have mentioned that periodicals means magazines," he says. "I thought maybe you switched tables."

"What did you think it meant?" I ask.

"I don't know, like, seasonal stuff."

"You're not inspiring confidence."

"You asked for a mathematician, not a book nerd."

I smirk. "Guess it's hard to be both."

"I know one person who's managed it." Jared holds up a finger. "My sister. And she's fifteen and insufferable."

I chuckle and turn my notebook around for him to see. "Here are the problems I've done so far. I missed two of them. Where did I go wrong?"

"Your pencil, for starters," he says, staring at my paper. "You need much lighter lead."

I furrow my brow. "What? Why? What does that have to do with anything?"

"Because you're going to be doing lots of erasing, and these lines will show through no matter how hard you try to erase them."

I can't help laughing. "You've already figured out I'm that bad?"

"You're not doing algebra here. I don't know what it is, but it's not algebra."

"Show me the errors of my ways."

"I'm gonna try."

I end up moving over to his side of the table so we can look off the book together. He actually does know what he's doing, and he's patient with me, walking me through the steps until I understand what he did and why.

But it takes forever. Twenty minutes for one problem.

He watches me do the next problem, making noises so I know if I'm doing it correctly or going astray. With his prompts, I'm able to figure it out.

"Try the next one on your own," he says.

I take a deep breath. If I can't do this, I won't make it through my midterm. I plunge onward, stopping to analyze and erase then write again. I'm almost finished when he shifts slightly, just a bit, and I know I've done something wrong. Great. What?

I find my error clear back in step three. I erase the whole thing and start over, my heart sinking. I wouldn't have noticed the mistake except for his body language. And now I'm aware of how much time has gone by and I'm panicking.

I finally finish, and Jared says gently, "You didn't get it quite right."

I bite my lip and fight the urge to cry. "How close was I?"

"You got closer when you started over. But you still missed an important step. What time is your test?"

I glance at my phone and heave a sigh as I collapse against my chair. "In half an hour."

Jared frowns and considers, then says, "Okay. We need to focus on one or two things that will make it harder to mess up."

"Anything."

"Right here, in step three. Concentrate on completing the squares. Okay? If you remember to do that, you'll improve your chances of getting it right."

He probably thinks he's talking to me like a kindergartner, but I'm barely keeping up with him. "Let me try a few more."

I know he thinks I'm an idiot by now. I pretend he's not there as I work through three more equations, pushing myself to work fast, trying to come up with the answer and not guess at it. Because usually I get impatient and guess.

I look up at him when I finish, and he shrugs and then nods.

"Good luck."

"Did I miss all three?"

"You got two of them right."

He's worried for me, but I smile. "That's better than earlier."

I stand, shoving my book in my backpack and pulling it onto my shoulders. "Thanks for all your help."

He stands also. "You're welcome. Want to meet after your test? You can tell me how it went."

"Can't. I have work."

"After that?"

"I'm hanging out with Stirling."

"The guy you're not dating?"

"That's right. Just going on dates. Not dating anyone."

"I like going on dates."

"Good." Oh snap. What if he asks me out? Iris will kill me. I'll have to say no. That will suck.

He lifts both eyebrows. They are black, and his skin is a nice shade of brown, while his eyes are an amazing dark blue and rimmed by thick lashes. Why do guys get the perfect eyes that require no liner and no mascara?

"Well." I turn around. "See ya later."

⊙~҉~⊙

Everything Jared and I studied flees my mind when I sit down for the exam.

I feel the moment half an hour later when I give up and start guessing instead of computing. I just want to get it over with. If I can make it through this class, I never intend to do math without a calculator again.

I finish my test and hand it in without a backward glance.

Time to go to work and call people and beg for money. Something I'm good at.

The computers crash again at work.

Jeff gets on the phone with support, and they walk him through multiple steps, and we watch the computers cycle through the restart over and over again without loading any screens. Mindy pulls out a deck of cards, and we huddle on the floor playing BS and spoons, laughing and enjoying the reprieve from talking to people who don't want to give us their money.

After two hours, Jeff says, "That's a night, guys! Clock out and go home."

"Want to ride with me or drive your car?" Stirling asks as we walk out, reminding me of our date.

I want the company. "Let's drive together to get food, then grab my car before we go to your place."

"Sounds good."

I'm feeling talkative after bombing my math test. I tell Stirling about the personal narrative I'm working on. I tell him about the modeling I might start doing. I tell him about being worse than an eighth grader at algebra. He parks in front of Denny's.

"You're a very interesting person," he says.

"That's why you're buying me dinner."

He holds the door for me, laughing. "I guess so."

I order French toast and Stirling gets a sandwich, and my phone buzzes. I won't check it while I'm out with Stirling. That's rude.

Well, at least until he goes to the bathroom.

The moment he disappears, I check the message. It's from Jared. I can't help laughing as I read it.

J: did you bomb it?

Me: total fail

J: eye roll emoji sorry

Me: not your fault. Was past saving

J: you were worse than I expected

His analysis of me makes me giggle. I see Stirling coming back and put my phone away.

But I'm more smiley through the rest of our date.

CHAPTER SIXTY-FIVE

Crushing

I don't own a white sheet. The one on my bed is soft blue.

"Blue is fine," Camila says. She's dressed like a sixties GoGo girl, with a short pink paisley dress, high white boots, and a matching headband. She looks darling and her costume was effortless. Why didn't I do that?

"All right. Let's use it."

We strip my bed. Then Camila tries to wrap me in the sheet. She pins it in a dozen different places, but it continues to fall down, exposing my bra and revealing my navel.

"People will get to know me better than they're expecting," I say, glaring at my reflection.

Camila's shoulders shake with laughter as she pulls her phone out. "There has to be a way to do this." She does a quick search and shouts in triumph. "There is! Come on. We can do this now. Keep your panties on."

"They're not coming off," I say.

"But the bra has to."

I look down at my black padded bra and shake my head. "I have a white one."

"No, Cassandra, we're going to show off your shoulder."

"You don't understand." I clutch the bra to my chest and level my gaze at her. "Without this bra, I have no boobs."

She pauses as she digests that information. "But Cassandra." She shows me the image. "You don't want it showing."

I study the picture with the sexy exposed shoulder and heave a sigh. "Fine."

"I've got an idea." Camila opens her drawer and pulls out a tube top. "Put this on over your bra."

I drop the sheet and pull the tube top over my head. It fits snuggly around my torso.

"Now take your arms out of the bra straps and stuff them into the top."

I see what she's meaning. I do so, shoving the straps down so they're hidden.

362

She smiles. "Perfect. Now let's try this."

We do it again, following her tutorial, and when she finishes, my blue bedsheet is an acceptable toga.

"Want me to do your makeup?"

"I've got this." Eyeliner I am good at.

I'm extremely pleased with the final result. My skin is still dark from summer, which contrasts nicely with the light blue toga, and the eye makeup lends me the Egyptian vibe I want. We take pictures with Abby, Layne, and Iris, who wear black leather pants and body suits and have their hair slicked back.

Then we put on jackets and head out into the cold and ruin the looks entirely.

"No Egyptian ever wore boots with the toga," I say.

"I hate to break it to you," Abby says, "but Egyptians didn't wear togas. The Romans did."

"I'm mixing up my cultures. I've added boots to the mix. So?"

We laugh.

"You look hot no matter what," Layne says. "Ditch the jacket when we get inside."

We step into Brant's apartment. The party is in the basement. Lights are strung across the ceiling and smoke clogs the air. The music is loud and the voices are louder, shouting to be heard over the thumping bass.

"Layne's here!" Brant yells, and a cheer goes up.

I stop in the doorway to take off my jacket, prickles of unease creeping up my skin. Too many people crowd the small space.

"There's Jared!" Iris says, and she drags Abby after her to greet him.

Camila pauses beside me.

"Well." I glance at her. "I think I'm in the wrong place."

"We know everyone here. It could be fun." She hooks her arm through mine and leads me through the mire of bodies to Iris and Abby.

Iris is chatting it up with Jared and Justin. Both have cans of soda in their hands, which they pass around to us girls. I smile, relieved no one's tried to shove alcohol in our faces.

Jared grins at me over Iris's head. "Nice bedsheet. I mean." He fake-coughs. "Toga."

I arch an eyebrow and look him over in his shorts and striped shirt. "And you are. . . ?"

"I'm a rugby player. No, wait, look!" He dodges over to a table and returns with a football covered in colored duct tape. "See? My ball!"

"Rugby?" I repeat. "Really?"

"It's a legitimate sport in England!"

I glance down at his bare legs and look up again, arching the other eyebrow.

"What?" he says. Are his cheeks actually turning red?

"I'll stick to my bedsheets and you stick to football."

The boys hoot and slap Jared on the back, and my face warms as I hear the unintended innuendo in my words. *Think before you speak, Cassandra!* I chastise myself. But that's not how flirting works. You let fly whatever witty comment comes to mind.

Shoot. I was flirting with him.

Iris is giving me a funny look, and I turn around and walk away. Camila follows.

"Iris doesn't look happy," she says.

I sip my soda and look for someone else to talk to. Anyone besides Jared. I spot Brant and Layne and sidle over to them. Layne turns and puts her arm around my waist.

"Doesn't my roommate look awesome?"

"Not as great as you," Brant says, not tearing his eyes from Layne.

I force a smile and slide away. Camila has found a few girls from the cross country team, and they're laughing and jogging in place and kicking their butts with their boots—they're all dressed like GoGo girls.

A feeling of loneliness smacks me in the chest out of nowhere.

What am I doing here? I don't like parties. I don't like crowds. I'm not like these people.

I think I'll call Jordan and watch a movie.

I tiptoe over to Camila and touch her arm to get her attention, then lean in and say, "I'm going to watch a movie with Jordan!"

"Oh." She steps out of the huddle with her friends. "Are you sure? Already? We just got here."

I nod, smiling to keep her at ease. "Yeah, I'm good. This was fun. Thanks for helping with my costume."

"Do you want me to come?"

"No, no, of course not!" I shake my head and push her back toward her friends. "I'll see you at home."

She gives me a look like she's not sure if she should believe me, but I know she wants to stay. "All right. Where's Jordan? Is he walking you?"

I forgot I'd have to walk back by myself. I'll be fine. There are lots of lights and it's not even ten o'clock yet. "Yeah, he's meeting me outside."

"Okay." She's reassured and turns back to her friends.

I head to the exit and pull on my jacket, then slip out of the room.

As soon as I close the door, the smoke and the music and the noises fades away. I exhale and take the stairs up to the main level, breathing in the fresh air.

Is there something wrong with me that I don't like parties? If you want to connect with someone and have a conversation, shouting over a throb of a hundred people and loud music isn't the way to do it.

I step outside and pull my jacket closer, my teeth chattering. Our dorm is a seven-minute walk. I won't freeze to death before then.

"Cassandra."

I stop at the sound of a boy calling my name. A sense of deja vu washes over me, and for a moment, I close my eyes and let myself fall back into a memory.

It was my senior year. I went to a party after the game. I can see it now. Stepping into the living room and talking with Owen. Leaving because he started talking to other people and I felt out of place.

I didn't make it to my car before Owen came out after me. He told me he'd rather talk to me than them.

But this isn't Owen calling my name. I open my eyes and am not surprised to see Jared jogging toward me. In his rugby shorts and T-shirt.

My lip twists. "You will freeze out here."

He jerks a thumb toward the building behind us. "We can go back in."

I shake my head. "I'm going home."

"You're right. Boring party anyway." He shoves his hands into his pockets and trots toward my apartment.

I survey him as I walk behind. He's shorter than Owen and not as broad in the shoulders. His hair is darker and curlier. The strong jawline is similar, as are the muscles—

Why the heck am I comparing him to Owen?

He glances back and sees the distance he's put between us. "Why are you way back there?"

I gesture down at my costume. "Toga? Bedsheet? Can't run."

"Ahh!" He jogs back, rubbing his arms with his hands. "This is not algebra, you can do it! Let's hurry up!"

"I didn't tell you to come with me."

He does high-knees back to my apartment. I'm amused.

"Maybe you should tell your coach you want to do rugby now instead of football," I tell him.

"You think I'd be good at it?"

"Are you any good at football?"

"Hey." He pretends to be offended as I unlock my apartment door and go inside. "I'm on the Preston Yarborough football team. That means something, you know."

"To some people," I return. I leave him in the kitchen and go to my bedroom to change out of my toga.

"You're a bitter person, you know that?" he calls after me.

I smile as I throw the sheet back on my bed and pull on my flannel PJs.

"Bitter." I step back into the kitchen. "I haven't heard that one before."

"Maybe you're not listening."

"I hear everything that matters." I pour a bowl of cereal, pull up a chair, and sit down in front of the fish tank. Then I eat my Lucky Charms while my fish swim around.

"Are you . . . watching them?"

I give him a blank look. "I know that's a question you can answer without my help. Come on, football star."

"They're not doing anything."

I throw my arm out. "Can you not see them swimming around, flipping their fins, and opening and closing their mouths? How would you like it if someone saw you running around in your—" I cast my eyes at his legs "—little rugby shorts, kicking your feet and breathing, and said you weren't doing anything?"

He gapes at me, his mouth echoing the opening and closing motions of a fish, and then he starts laughing.

"Coming from the girl who can't complete the algebraic squares?"

"Now you're shooting low."

The banter is fun. I'm enjoying it. But suddenly it all comes together.

Why I'm enjoying it.

Why I keep comparing him to Owen.

Jared reminds me of Owen.

It's almost as if my mind is trying to fill the hole left by Owen with someone else.

Trying to fit a new arm onto my shoulder to replace the one I lost. It looks similar. It feels similar. I can pretend it's the same arm.

I want to try so badly that my breath shudders out of me. I don't want to be missing a limb anymore.

I want Jared to hold me and kiss me and take my heart and body somewhere else.

I stand up, pretending like I didn't just have a great epiphany in my head. "It's time for bed, Jared. Which means you have to go."

He gestures at the fish tank. "I can stay and watch TV a little longer."

I press my lips together, trying not to laugh. It feels so good to laugh. "I'm turning it off for the night."

"You can do that? Will they still be there tomorrow?"

"So far. Here." I go to my bedroom and return with my jacket. "So you don't have to be cold all the way home."

He shakes his head and pulls it on over his shoulders. "Cruel and bitter."

"And can't do math to save her soul."

"Luckily, that's not one of the requirements."

"Luckily."

I follow Jared to the door. He steps out, then turns around and hugs me.

I'm so startled I freeze. It doesn't feel like the shoulder hugs Stirling gives me. Or the big cousin hugs Jordan gives me.

This one lights something up inside me and makes me want to snuggle closer.

For the briefest of seconds, I give in. I close my eyes and dissolve into his arms.

It's the thought of Iris that makes me step away. As if pretending he's Owen isn't bad enough.

CHAPTER SIXTY-SIX

Boring Boys

*A*ngel of Mercy, how much farther?
I don't think I can fly anymore
You see, I've lost my Love
And Justice claimed my heart
Then threw it from its Heavenly perch
Where it tumbled to the Earth below
Breaking
Crumbling with Reality
I almost relinquished myself to Death
When Mercy came and gently lifted me up
But sweet Angel, take me no farther
I have no desire to fly
Without my Love beside me

It's a cold walk to church Sunday morning without my jacket. I don't tell anyone why I don't have it.

During the sermon they announce an upcoming school dance. This one is girl's choice. It's in two weeks, the weekend before Thanksgiving break.

Every boy in the congregation turns around and eyes every girl, as if encouraging her to ask him.

I do not look at Jared. I cannot ask him.

He, Justin, and Brant want to come over after church, but I overhear them talking to Layne about it and veto it.

"Not today, guys," I say. "I'm cooking dinner and don't want any boys over."

"She's anti-men," Brant says. "Man-hater. Feminist through and through."

"I'm a feminist," Layne says.

"I'm not a man-hater," I say. "I just like to spend Sunday with my girls."

"Nothing wrong with that," Camila says, backing me up.

"And since I'm cooking, I get to decide."

"Since when is that the rule?" Layne says.

"Can they come over after dinner?" Iris asks.

Oh, good grief. "I don't care." Then I march away.

"She hates men," Brant says.

I'm too proud to go find Jared and get my jacket back. I walk back to the apartment pretending not to shiver.

"What's for lunch, Cass?" Layne says when we walk in.

I check the time. Almost one. "Macaroni and cheese."

They laugh at me.

"Gourmet cooking for sure," Iris says.

"It is when I make it," I say.

I add chopped tomatoes and sour cream with the milk. The whole meal cooks in less than twenty minutes, but it earns the approval of my roommates.

"I didn't know you could doctor up boxed mac and cheese," Camila says.

"In more than one way," I say. "I've got several renditions of this."

"Is that what you're going to make every time it's your turn to cook?" Layne says.

"I need to expand my culinary repertoire." I'm already getting tired of my instant meals. "You guys are my guinea pigs."

Layne pokes around her food. "All right, so who is everyone asking to the dance?"

We lift our faces and make eye contact before simultaneously turning back to our food.

"I'm asking Brant," Layne says.

"I'm so shocked," I say.

We laugh.

"What about you, Camila?" Layne says.

"I don't know," Camila says. "Maybe Gary or Justin. Maybe someone from the cross country team."

"Oo, do you have cute guys on there?" Layne says. "I need to go to one of your meets!"

"They're every Saturday," Camila says. "But there's only two left."

She's never invited us. Until the Halloween party, I hadn't seen her cross country friends either. I thought she didn't want us to see her run.

Layne turns to me. "What about you, Cassandra?"

It's Jared's face that flashes through my mind. I can imagine what it would feel like to touch his hand, to have him hold me close.

"Probably Stirling," I say. "He's amenable to most things."

"Amenable," Layne snorts. "I bet he is."

They snicker but the attention turns off me as she spins to Iris.

"Iris?"

She rolls her eyes. "Is there any doubt? I'm asking Jared."

"What if he says no?" Layne asks.

Silence falls at her question. I don't look at her, but I know she's thinking of me.

Layne is keen and observant. Like Iris, she's noticed Jared's interest in me. Unlike Iris, she doesn't believe my story that there's nothing between us.

"Well, that would be rude," Iris says with a scowl. "I guess I'd ask someone else."

I stand up and clear the dishes. "I made dinner, so I don't have dish duty." I love that rule. Never more so than today.

"I have an orchestra concert on Friday," Iris says. "Will you guys come?"

"I have a study session," Layne says. "I don't think I'll make it."

I turn from the sink. I have a guilty conscience around Iris. "I'll come."

"I'll try," Camila says.

I write down the time and place, then I go to my room and curl up in Owen's blanket with my journal and scriptures.

Camila comes in and cuddles up beside me. We don't talk but read our Bibles and poke each other from time to time, giggling.

Layne sticks her head in. "Can the boys come over now?"

"Yes," I say.

She disappears, and Camila looks at me. "Why are you mad at the boys?"

"I'm not."

"You were rude to them."

"No, I wasn't." Was I? I scowl.

She pokes my ribs, and I squirm away.

"What is it?" she says.

The bedroom door is still open. I can't say. So I write in my journal, *I like Jared.*

The words stare back at me, incriminating, and I want to erase them but it's pen. I slide the book over to her.

She reads the line and looks at me with compassionate understanding in her eyes.

"It's okay to like someone, Cass," she whispers.

I pull my journal back and scratch through the words.

I have to pretend like I don't.

Twenty minutes later the back door opens, and loud boisterous male voices fill the apartment. Layne greets them with laughter and squeals. Iris bops down the hallway, and her melodic voice joins the foray. I pull out my phone and text Stirling.

Me: hey! Did you hear about the dance in two weeks?

He replies a moment later.

S: yeah, it was announced in church. I hear it's girl ask guy . . . So I just sit back and cross my fingers

Me: laughing emoji want to go with me?

S: sure!

Me: we'll plan later

Stirling is a safe place. Our friendship is platonic. I don't feel guilty for asking him.

"Cassandra!" Layne calls me.

I give Camila an aggravated look. She knows why I'm hiding in here.

Camila scoots out of the way so I can slide off the bed.

Layne turns to me as I walk in. "Jared and Justin want to sing the yodeling song from *The Sound of Music* with my karaoke machine but Iris won't sing with them. Will you?"

I look at Iris. She's a film major and already has her camera out, but I'm surprised she doesn't want in on this. "You don't want to sing?"

"I can't sing worth crap," she says. She's smiling, excited behind her lens. "But it's going to make a great video."

Layne plugs in the machine and hands me a mic. "Sorry, I only have one."

Jared puts his phone in front of the three of us and pulls up the lyrics, and the familiar intro buzz fills the kitchen. I don't recall agreeing to this, but looks like we're doing it.

Besides, I know this song. I sang it for my senior recital last year and the spring recital the year before. Tiago made fun of me for it.

I can yodel.

I launch into it as the words begin, and the boys can't even sing, they're cracking up behind me. I roll my eyes at them as they attempt to join, adding a word here or there and then howling through the yodels. Layne collapses on the couch, laughing so hard she's crying. Iris struggles to hold the camera still as her shoulders shake.

The phone wobbles in Jared's hand, and I grab his arm to steady it. I release him just as quickly. Why does touching a boy feel so good? A spike of endorphins pulses through my blood, elevating my mood and making me giddy even as I try not to feel it.

The song finishes, and we're all laughing. I try to leave the huddle, but Justin throws an arm over my shoulders and leans on me, body shaking with mirth. Then Jared wraps his arms around both of us, sheltering us in a bear hug. Iris puts her camera down and jumps in, and it's a human tent, leaning on each other and giggling. I don't know who's shoulder I'm touching or who's hand is on my waist, but it's innocent and allowable.

Layne snaps a few pictures of us with her phone, and we disengage, falling out of the huddle.

"Oh, you guys, that was too fun." She wipes her eyes. "We should do that every Sunday."

"Not until we find someone who can sing," I say. "I'm not listening to them howl along beside me again."

"We have to watch it," Iris says, grabbing the camera and loading the video.

We put the camera against the fish tank and watch our terribly hilarious music video another ten times, shrieking and pointing and rolling on the floor, uncontrollably entertained.

Brant shows up, and he and Layne leave to watch a movie downstairs.

"How much movie-watching do you think they'll actually do?" Justin asks Jared, and they both give snide laughs.

I roll my eyes. "Boys are all the same."

"Yeah, we are," Justin says.

But Jared frowns. "Not exactly the same."

"Well, that was fun." I spot my jacket on the kitchen table and grab it. I catch Jared's eye and nod at him, but I don't thank him, not with Iris there.

"Hope you weren't too cold walking to church," he says, unaware of my subterfuge.

"I was fine." I take my jacket and return to my room.

Iris' voice follows behind me. "Hey, Jared, want to go on a walk?"

"Sure."

"I'll just hang out here with the fish," Justin says. The back door opens and closes, and he calls after them, "Don't mind me. Thanks, guys!"

Camila is still on my bed. "I think I'll go sit with Justin since you guys left him there."

"Go." I snuggle back into my blankets. "He probably needs a date to the dance."

I listen to them talking and laughing and feel the ache of loneliness in my chest. I don't know how to solve this.

I message Jordan. *Bored. Want to go on a walk?*

He responds. *You know it's forty degrees outside?*

He's so right.

Me: I have to get out. Can't take it in here.

J: then let's go on a DRIVE

I can get behind that. I grab my car keys and pass Camila and Justin in the kitchen. "I'm going out with Jordan. See you guys later."

I drive to Jordan's dorm and he hops in, and we sing and bounce in the car to loud country music while I take us on a drive through the nearby canyon. He doesn't ask me what's on my mind. He knows I'll talk if I feel like it.

Jared texts me as we're driving back.

Jared: can I talk to you for a sec?

I hand the phone to Jordan. "Will you answer that for me?"

"And say what?" Jordan asks, fingers poised to respond.

"Tell him I'm out for a drive."

Jordan does so, then says, "He wants to know when you'll be back."

I'm torn with an absolute desire to be alone with Jared and the absolute knowing that I shouldn't be.

"Fifteen minutes," I say.

Jordan relays the message and hands my phone back. "Who's Jared?"

"Another guy I'm not dating," I say. Glibly.

Jordan smirks. "How many are there now?"

"Two. Unless you count the ones that I don't go on dates with, and then there's an infinite number."

"We'll leave it at two."

"You've met him. He thought you were Stirling."

"Ah. Right. Yes, he's in your fan club."

I don't respond.

I take Jordan home and park in my own complex twelve minutes later. I'm not surprised to see Jared sitting on the last step of the stairwell. He stands and comes to my car, and I unlock it so he can get in the passenger seat.

"What's up?" I warm my hands against the heater and steal a glance at him.

"At the risk of looking dumb—are you planning on going to the dance next weekend?"

"I am." My heart rate increases. He won't ask me, will he? That's not how this works.

"Iris asked me."

"Oh." I smile. "I thought she would."

He looks at me and lifts an eyebrow. "This feels very high school."

"What does?"

"I was hoping someone else would ask me."

I suspect who he means. Why else would he be in my car? "First come, first serve. Iris beat everyone to it."

"I said no."

"Jared!" My eyes widen. "You can't say no! People don't do that!"

"They should." His eyelids flutter, his lips pursing. "Why miss out on what you really want because you're being polite?"

I clasp my hands together. "Don't you know how much courage it takes just to ask?"

"Of course I do. I was gentle."

I shake my head. "Don't hold out for someone else. They might not ask."

He's quiet, watching me, and he's left me the perfect opening. If I wanted to ask him, it would be now.

And I don't.

"You should say yes to her," I say, keeping my own tone soft. Gentle, as he put it. "She likes you."

He blinks. He hears what I don't say. That I don't.

It's not true. Even now, I feel the chemistry between us. I feel the desire to reach over and cup his face, run my fingers over the dark scruff on his jaw. I know he feels it too. But now he thinks it's one-sided.

"Who are you asking?" he says.

"I already asked Stirling. And he said yes."

He nods. "Okay. Well. Sorry for the dumb questions."

He pushes open the door handle and gets out. I stay in my car and watch him in the mirror. He shoves his hands into the pockets of his long jacket and walks down the sidewalk, out of sight and away from my apartment.

My throat is tight.

I let myself inside and greet my roommates with a fake smile, but I'm sad, I'm so sad. I hurt inside.

Thirty minutes later Iris squeals from her room. "You guys! Jared just texted me! He said he wants to go with me to the dance!"

CHAPTER SIXTY-SEVEN

Knocked Up

I spend Monday evening on campus studying for my English exam. It's my literary theory class, and I feel like the five-page essay I turned in last month should count. Ms. Cheney doesn't agree.

"There will be no multiple choice on this test," she tells us, "but you're in a college English class, so I'm sure you didn't expect any. It will be short essay and one long essay. The exam shouldn't take more than two hours."

But it could take as long as two hours. I feel my GPA dropping at the very idea.

I am full of frustration, not the least being romantic.

I want to go to the stupid dance with Jared.

Instead I meet up with Stirling at his house on Tuesday when our work shift is canceled. He's in a goofy mood, and we laugh a lot as we plan this date.

"You'll have to meet us at the dorms," I say. "It's a freshman dance."

"I'll be the oldest guy there," he says.

"We'll call you grandpa," I say.

He proceeds to hobble around the house hunched over like an old man. Then he comes back to the couch and puts an arm around me while we watch a show on TV.

He never tries to kiss me.

My phone rings halfway through the show, and I'm not on a date with Stirling, so I allow myself to check it.

It's Harper.

"Oh my gosh!" I exclaim. "It's my best friend from high school!" I answer the phone as I walk into the kitchen.

"Harper!" I say. "How are you? It's been forever!"

"Long time no hear," she agrees. "You could call once in awhile."

"I *know*." I feel the encroaching guilt. "I'm so bad at it."

"It's fine. I know you're super busy with school."

I plop into a chair at the kitchen table. "I am, but it's a terrible excuse." We haven't been completely out of touch. I email her about once a week, just so we can keep tabs on each other. "What's up, lady? How are things with Miles?" I didn't think their relationship would last this long, but they are still together.

"Meh. I'm getting bored. If he doesn't pop the question soon, I'm breaking up with him."

"We're eighteen, Harper!"

"I'll be nineteen this week. I planned to be married by now."

Shoot, her birthday's this week. Is that why she's calling? I make a mental note to mail her a card.

"It will happen," I say. I think she's insane for wanting to get married now. I'm all for marriage. Someday. Not yet.

"So," she says, and I know something's up. I try to anticipate what it is. She's not getting married and she and Miles haven't broken up.

It can't be something about Owen. He's in Louisiana. And I wouldn't want to know anyway.

"Yes?" I say.

"Have you heard about Riley?"

Riley. My heart sinks at the mention of her name. She was my best friend all through elementary, junior high, and high school, give or take a few months, but I haven't talked to her since the youth retreat over the summer.

"No." I grip the edge of the table. "What's wrong? What's going on with Riley?"

"She's pregnant."

It's a blow, but it could be worse. Harper gives me the details and I hang up and sit in stunned shock. Riley is only eighteen and she's not married and the father is a total douche. Stirling comes to the kitchen table.

"You okay?" he asks.

The question breaks through my shock and then I'm crying. He sits by me and holds my hand while I tell him why I'm upset, and I'm grateful for the comfort.

But I so desperately want Owen right now.

I pull myself together and call Riley, but she doesn't answer. She probably thinks I'm a fake friend who only calls when I hear gossip and doesn't want to talk to me. I don't blame her.

"I better go," I say. I'm aching to talk to Owen. I've got to talk to him. My hands shake with the uncertain idea of calling him, just to hear his voice. "Thanks for listening, Stirling."

"Of course." He rubs my shoulders and gives me a hug.

I get in my car but I don't drive home. The awful thing about living in an apartment with three other people is they are in your business, all the time. There's no privacy. There's no seclusion. I drive out to the canyon overlook and park.

And then I call Owen.

He does not answer, and that hurts even more. It feels like a personal rejection, even though it's probably he's in class or at practice. I put my phone down and rest my head on the steering wheel and sob.

There's always Tiago.

One of the benefits of having Tiago live in my house for a year is he knows and loves my friends like I do. We have not messaged back and forth since I left for college but instead email every once in awhile. But now I want to have a conversation in real time.

So I open the messaging app and send him a text.

Me: Harper just called me. Riley's pregnant. I'm so sad for not being a better friend to her.

Tiago doesn't usually have internet in the evenings, so I don't expect a response. I sniffle and wipe my eyes and stare out at the valley below. The trees are bare, the mountains a bluish gray color from the undergrowth that will remain all winter. I see a river running through the city, and there's an austere beauty to it. But I miss the green.

The phone rings in my hand. I look down and heave a sigh.

Owen is calling me back.

"Hello?" I'm pleased my voice is steady. No sign of tears.

"Cassandra. I missed your call."

I close my eyes. How good it is to hear his voice. I pretend he is with me in the car, and I know any feelings I've entertained for anyone else shine like the dull reflection of the moon compared to the light of the sun Owen puts in my soul.

"Cassandra?"

"Hi," I say. I struggle this time keeping my voice steady. "I just wanted to talk to you." The words come out stilted and formal. It's how I'm maintaining control.

"Well, hi. How are you?"

I think of our last conversation. Of the hurt feelings, the frustrations. I don't want to talk about any of that. So I skip to the chase. "Did you hear about Riley?" I ask quietly.

"No," he says, his tone just as quiet. "What's going on?"

"She's pregnant."

He exhales. "That's tough."

"Yeah. She's our age. Younger."

"How's she handling it?"

"I don't know. She didn't answer when I called her."

"Who told you?"

"Harper."

He's silent a moment. What can he say?

"She'll be okay, Cass. She has her mom."

"I wish I was there for her." Emotion tugs at my throat, and I blink back tears. "I feel like I failed her."

"You did not." His voice is soft but insistent. "Nobody else loved her and cared for her like you did. You couldn't carry her through this life, Cassandra."

"I would have," I say. "If she would have let me. I tried."

"I know you did. She couldn't have asked for a better friend."

His words are kind. But I don't believe them. "I let her pull away from me. I didn't try to hold on when she went a different direction."

"She pushed you away. You're not remembering clearly. I was there too. She didn't want your help."

"She thought I judged her. Maybe I did. Maybe I put the wedge between us."

"Stop doing this to yourself. It's not helping you and it won't help her. She's going to need you."

"I haven't been there for her. I've been involved in my own life. I was completely unaware."

"So be there now. Cassandra, listen to me. There's nothing you could have done to prevent this. Riley's living her own life. She's lucky she had your influence for so long."

"How do you always know the right words to say to me?"

"All I'm doing is telling you what's real. Somehow you don't see it."

I want to beg him to be in my life always. To whisper the right words to me when I'm down, to give me comfort and reassurance when I'm discouraged.

"Thank you. I knew you'd help me know what to do," I say instead.

"I'm always here for you."

I believe it. But I want more.

"Okay. I'll talk to you later."

"Bye, Cass."

We hang up. I still ache for my friend, but I know this isn't my fault. I pull up her number and text her.

Me: Riley—is this still your number? Love you and miss you, girl! Text me when you can.

⁂

I'm calmer the next day. Tiago messages me, and we chat for half an hour, but my urgent need has faded, so I don't have much more to say than the basics Harper passed on to me.

Riley doesn't text back. I'll see her at Christmas time, and I'll be a better friend.

Ms. Cheney reminds us today's the last day to take our English exam, so I head to the testing center after class. In spite of the essays, it's not nearly as strenuous as my math test. I finish in an hour.

I step into my apartment and find Iris and Camila standing in front of the fish tank. That's never a good sign.

"What?" I ask, alarm shooting through me as I hurry over. "Did something happen?"

Iris points to the belly-up goldfish. "Dick died."

"Why?" I stare at him in disbelief. "Why did you die?" I shout at him. "You've got the perfect tank, no algae, protein water, and plenty of food!"

"Maybe he never recovered from jumping out of the water a few weeks ago," Iris says.

"What's going on?" Layne comes in, drawn by my voice.

"Dick died." I point at the stupid fish.

But Layne brightens right up. "I wanted to get a bigger goldfish anyway. Come on, I'll go with you to the pet store!"

I don't have work, and my homework can wait an hour, so I may as well.

As soon as we're in my car, Layne pounces. Apparently she's been waiting for this.

"So what exactly is going on between you and Jared?" she says.

I'm telling her nothing. I trust Layne as far as I can throw her, and that's maybe an inch. "I think we're pretty good friends." Until Sunday, that is. I'm not sure anymore.

"You know he turned Iris down for the dance? She was so upset, and she blamed you."

I glance at Layne. She and Iris room together, so she gets in on scoops I don't. "She blamed me? Why?"

"Everyone can see he likes you."

"Well, that's not my fault!" I say huffily.

"But then he texted her and said he changed his mind. Do you know what happened there?" She ogles me.

"No." I'm not saying a word.

We pull into the pet store parking lot. Layne knows what kind of goldfish she wants. But the moment she points out the big orange creature with the bulbous eyes, I blanch.

"No way. He's hideous."

"I'll pay for him. Please, Cassandra, I've always wanted a fish like this!"

"It's my tank," I say.

"But we all have to look at it!"

I shake my head. "It looks like his eyes are going to pop!"

"You'll get used to him. Oh, please! We can name him Dick II." She giggles and bites her lip.

"We're naming him Ahab." I glared at her.

She squeals and hugs me and prances away to get a worker.

Great. He's the ugliest fish I've ever seen.

My opinion doesn't change after we dump him in the tank. He swims around slowly, mouth gaping, like a dumb giant among my fast, colorful tropical fish. But now Layne joins me when I sit down with a bowl of cereal to watch them.

"He's my favorite," she purrs.

I try to create an analogy between my English exam and Dick dying for no reason, only to be replaced by a large, vacuous, empty-minded idiot.

CHAPTER SIXTY-EIGHT

Fishcapades

Layne invites the boys to come over and see our new fish on Thursday. I'm only home for a moment because Jordan and I have choir. I scan the boys in our kitchen and Jared is not here, so I'm not interested anyway.

Except Iris has also noticed he's not here, and she grabs me and Camila. "Justin's not here," she says, as if that's who she was looking for. "Let's go see him at the boys' dorm."

It's visiting day at the boys' dorm. Once a week girls are allowed in the bedrooms.

Justin and Jared share a room. I know what she's up to. "I have to go to choir," I say.

"In an hour," she says.

Jared's upset with me. He hasn't messaged me at all. I rejected him, even though I didn't want to. I do want to see him. I can't help it. He won't talk to me if I visit him and Justin with her, which will make me sad but will encourage Iris.

"Half an hour only," I say.

There's already a gaggle of girls at the boys' dorm. Jared and several other kids I recognize are hanging out in the commons, and about twenty girls surround Jared. Justin's not in the group, so Camila and I leave Iris with the other groupies and go upstairs to his dorm.

Justin's working on his 3D printer. He's excited to see us, and he pulls Camila over to show her the dragon he's designing.

"You built this printer?" she says.

"Yeah. I've been building them since I was thirteen. This is my favorite model so far. Back home I have a resin printer also."

He's geeking out, but she's eating it up, picking up his prints and staring at his images in wonder.

"Click through my files," he says, handing her his computer. "Pick something, I'll print it for you."

A shadow falls over the door frame, and I look up as Jared walks in.

"You got away from your fan club," I say.

"The person who counts isn't in it," he returns. It's funny but not, and he's looking at me in a perplexed way.

"Iris likes you," I say. I glance at Justin and Camila, but they are on the bed going through his files. Not paying attention to us.

Jared furrows his brow and leans against the door jamb. "She asked me to the dance. It's nothing."

"Iris likes you," I repeat.

"I'm not sure what you're saying."

I shake my head. "I think you're a great friend. I really do. I really like you." And that's it. That's all I can say.

But I see something click in his eyes. "And so does Iris."

Yes. I nod.

He steps over to me and pulls me into a hug. Oh, and it's delicious, to be held, to be folded up in a man's arms. I close my eyes and inhale him and pray Iris doesn't come looking for either of us. He rocks me gently, and it's healing and mind-numbing. *Don't let go,* I want to say.

He pulls back, his chin lowered, his eyes steady on my face.

I turn away from his probing gaze and glance over at the bed.

Camila and Justin are not looking at his computer anymore. Their eyes are steady on us. My face burns. What a show we've given them.

"I have to go to class," I say, brightly. "Great to see you guys!"

I leave the room.

Camila comes after me.

"You okay?" she asks.

I take a deep breath and prance down the stairs, skipping the elevator, anxious to put space between me and Jared. "I can't like him."

"Because of Iris?"

"Because it's wrong!"

"How is it wrong?"

"Because of Iris!"

We step out of the building, and I blink in the last vestiges of sunlight, aching inside. Wanting to cry.

"Iris would get over it," Camila says. "It's clear you like each other."

"He's not Owen," I say, and my lip trembles.

"Of course he's not. You're not doomed to never love again."

"I like him for the wrong reasons, Camila. He reminds me of Owen. When I'm with him, I see Owen. I smell Owen. I feel Owen. I don't like him for Jared. I like him for who I wish he was."

"Ah."

"See? It's wrong. I'm a terrible person."

"But you would learn to like him for him."

"I don't want to! I like the illusion of feeling like I'm with Owen!"

She nods. "That's not fair to Jared."

"No. He's better off with Iris."

"But he doesn't like her."

"He can learn to."

I walk away from her, wrapping my arms around myself and remembering how it felt to be wrapped in Jared's embrace.

Ms. Mayhew reads over the rough draft of my personal narrative at our consultation on Friday.

"I like the heart you've put into this, Cassandra." She looks up at me over the paper. "I can feel the desperation, the tunnel vision. I want to feel the actions more. Instead of telling me how you made yourself throw up, show me. Walk me through that."

I mull on my lower lip. "It might be graphic."

She leans toward me, a spark in her eyes. "We English teachers like that."

I smile, already planning the imagery I'll use.

The dance is tomorrow after work, and there's a lot I need to get done today so I'll be ready for it. I have another physical science test, and I take deep breaths in the testing center line, trying not to freak myself out.

I'll be okay, even if it's as bad as last time. I have a B in the class. I just have to keep that.

It takes me over an hour, and I scowl when the score shows up on the screen.

A seventy. How? I thought I knew the material this time.

I shrug it off. It's an improvement, after all. The written part will help.

I want to buy another fish. Layne's big dopey one annoys me.

I hurry to the music hall for Iris's orchestra performance. I'm late, so I slip in the back and stand there quietly.

She plays the cello. She looks elegant in a long black velvet dress. Her dark hair falls in her face as she leans over the large instrument, the bow flashing expertly across the strings. The sound reverberates in the hall, and I'm in awe.

My phone vibrates with a text. I check it.

Jared: want to go to the movies tonight?

I shake my head, bemused.

Me: I'm going to the pet store

Jared: again?

Me: yes

Jared: all right

I put my phone away. But I only get another thirty seconds of the concert before it vibrates again.

Jared: what time?

Me: I don't know. Maybe in half an hour

Jared: okay

Jared: movie is in two hours

Me: did I agree to go?

Jared: I invited your roommates too

He's done his due diligence. Since it's not a date . . .

Me: okay. I'll go

The concert ends, and I hurry up to hug Iris.

"It was so beautiful. I didn't know you could play like that."

"Thanks. I love all the strings, but the cello is my favorite."

"I'm way impressed."

She brings the case over and lays the cello within it, and I say, "Are you going to the movies with Jared tonight?"

She straightens. "What?"

"Oh. You probably don't know. Check your phone." He better not have lied to me.

She checks it. "Man, I want to! I can't. It's my brother's birthday. I promised I'd go."

Uh-oh. She can't go. That's not my fault.

I don't say anything. "Well, I'm off to the pet store."

"The pet store? Why?"

"Just to look at the fish."

She laughs. "Have fun. Thanks for coming! See you at home."

"Muah." I kiss her cheek and leave.

I check on my fish when I get home to make sure they're all alive. I've got nine. I can fit in one more.

I think.

There's a knock on the back door, and then it opens and Jared pokes his head in.

"Oh, hey, you're here," he says.

"Yes," I say.

"Ready?"

I tilt my head. "For?"

"Going to the pet store."

I'm slow on the intake. "Are you coming?"

"That's why I'm here."

I can't think of any good reason why he shouldn't come with me. So I gesture him out the door.

"Why are we going to the pet store?" he asks as I drive.

"I want to look at the fish."

"Why?"

"They're pretty."

"But you already have fish to look at."

"I have nine fish."

"And you want how many?" he asks.

I shrug.

We reach the pet store ten minutes later. I start at the first tank and point out the beautiful lovelies flitting around. Some are giant and would swallow my tetras in one gulp. Others are tiny, flashy little guppies.

"I want some of these," I say, pointing at the guppies with the fluffy tail fins.

"What colors?"

"The purple. And the yellow."

"Like, you want to look at them, or you want to buy them?"

I consider the question. "I want to buy them." I nod as I say it, certain.

"Wouldn't you call this an impulse buy?"

I swivel to him. "And?"

He holds up both hands. "Just saying."

"Who invited you along?"

He backs away, hands still up in surrender.

I get an employee to bag up the fish for me and find Jared examining the fish supplies.

"Here's that algae scraper you wanted," he said, holding one up.

"My sucker fish are getting the job done. It's all good now."

He tilts his head and examines the guppies. "They're kind of cute. What are you naming them?"

I grin facetiously. "Jared and Justin."

☙❧

Layne thinks it's hilarious that we named the fish after the two boys. Justin comes over to meet his namesake, and then Camila joins us and the five of us go to the movies.

My eyes are burning with the need to sleep during the movie. I'm hungry. Why didn't I eat something? I prop my chin up in my hands but my head keeps bobbing.

Jared pulls on my arm, making my head fall. Before I can complain, he puts his hand under my jaw and guides my cheek to his shoulder.

That gooey warm feeling envelopes me. I shut my eyes and sleep through the rest of the movie.

It's after eleven when the movie ends.

"Hey, my aunt said she made pizza and wants someone to come over and eat it," Justin says. "Anyone game?"

"Oh, I'm beat," Camila says. "I have one more meet tomorrow. I need rest."

My stomach is already growling. "Yes, please. I'm starving."

Layne looks up from her phone. "What are we doing?"

"Going to my aunt's for pizza," Justin says.

"Oh, fun! Brant wants to go somewhere, though. Drop me off at the bell tower."

"It's almost midnight." I fix her with a hard look.

"And you're going to Justin's aunt's house."

"Fair. Is Brant at the bell tower?"

"Yeah, he has his car."

We pile into my car. I drop Layne off first and watch as she gets in the car with Brant.

"Think she'll come home tonight?" Justin says.

"She's not in any danger," I say, continuing toward the apartment

"That's not what I meant."

"She'll come home," Camila says. "Just, really late."

"Or super early," I add.

I drop Camila off next, and then I look back at Jared in the back seat by Justin.

"Taking you to the dorms?"

"So you can eat pizza with Justin by yourself? No way."

I laugh. "Lead us, Justin."

His aunt lives literally five minutes from campus. She greets us in the living room in a long night robe, and her frizzy gray hair makes me think she's older than my mom. She sends us toward the aroma of melted cheese and pepperoni before disappearing deeper into the house. There's a living room off of the kitchen, and we take the whole pan of pizza and put it on the couch between us while we put on another movie.

"I used to be a vegetarian," I say, coming up for air after my second slice. "I can't believe it's past midnight and I'm just now eating dinner."

"Why on earth were you a vegetarian?" Justin asks.

I shrug. "Complex relationship with food."

They both laugh. The boys move the pizza to the end table beside the couch. I scoot to the edge of the sofa so I can reach the pizza. Justin monopolizes the corner of the couch, and Jared lies down, stretching out behind me.

My eyes grow heavy, and I put down my third slice of pizza. I want to lay down also, but I won't do it beside Jared. "Justin, have any blankets?" My speech is slurred. I'm exhausted.

"Yeah." He gets up and leaves.

"You can use my jacket." Jared shrugs it off and holds it out.

I shake my head.

Justin returns with big fluffy blankets. I take one and spread it out on the floor, then curl up in it like a cat. Jared swings upward.

"Cassandra, take the couch," he says.

"This is fine," I say, balling the fluff up around my neck. "I'm quite comfortable."

He lays back down, but his hand comes down off the edge of the couch and brushes along my neck. I say nothing. I pretend it's not happening.

His fingers slide down my arm and then off my body. I roll over and take his hand, sandwiching it between my arm and ribcage while still holding his fingers. I face the TV again, forcing him toward the edge of the couch because I've trapped his hand.

He clasps my fingers and says nothing.

But we can't pretend anymore.

CHAPTER SIXTY-NINE

Sleepover

A noise jars me awake. I blink and wince when I feel my contact lenses suctioned to my eyes. It happens if I sleep in them for more than an hour.

Where am I?

I sit up on a mound of soft green blankets and see sunlight pouring in from a window next to an entertainment station . . .

A rustling comes from my left, and I turn to a couch.

Jared is laid across it.

On the other side of the couch, Justin sits up, and my memory comes flying back. I gasp.

"Oh, crap," Justin says, and he starts laughing. "You guys slept over."

My eyes go wide. We can be reported for this. Freshman are not allowed to sleep over at houses of the opposite gender. "Crap," I echo, shooting to my feet. "Crap, crap, crap." I'm ready to bolt, to leave Jared there. He's not the one who will be in trouble.

He sits up, rubbing his eyes, and he squints at me. I see the moment the confusion leaves his face.

"You better go," he says. "Before anyone knows you didn't sleep at your dorm."

I check my phone. It's almost eight. I'm certain I've been missed. Where can I say I was? What won't get me in trouble?

I haven't forgotten that I held Jared's hand last night.

There's one text from Camila. Six-thirty this morning. *You okay?*

I text back. *I'm fine. Couldn't sleep.* Maybe she'll think I got up early and went for a walk or something.

"Okay. Goodbye. See you guys tonight." I slide my feet into my shoes and run out the door. My mind is tripping for an excuse. No one would believe I fell asleep in my car. It's too cold for that.

I've been through this before. The night I accidentally fell asleep in Owen's bed.

I park at my apartment and don't let myself fall into the memory. Not yet. First I need to get inside.

Layne is in the kitchen in her pajamas, getting breakfast. She turns and lifts both brows when I come in, closing the door quietly behind me.

"Don't say a word," I say, softly, imploringly. "I was here all night."

She gives a slow nod. "Of course you were."

I exhale and tiptoe to my room. She won't tell.

Camila is already gone, to her cross country meet, I assume.

I sink onto my bed and pull the blankets up to my chin. I relive the euphoria of holding Jared's hand. Feeling the heightened excitement of the touch of another person. Knowing someone liked me. Knowing I liked them.

But then it's not Jared I'm remembering. It's Owen, the night I went over after work. The way he lay me down on his bed and moved over me, the way his eyes darkened with desire as he stared at me, the way he kissed me.

I take a deep breath, reliving it again in my mind. Feeling the physical response he stirs in me. Even now.

I fell asleep at Owen's house that night and woke up in a panic, just like this morning.

My reputation was ruined that day.

But the worse part was that Owen and I broke up.

And things never went back.

The bedroom door pushes open, and Layne comes in. She carries two steaming mugs. I watch her sit down at my desk, and she offers one to me. I take it.

"Want to talk about anything?" she asks quietly.

My throat burns with unshed tears. I take a sip and make a face at the bitter beverage. "I miss Owen," I whisper. I blink, swallow, try not to cry. "For a moment, when I'm close to another guy, I don't. But when the moment's over, I miss him worse than before." I put the mug down and put my face in my hands because I can't stop the tears now. "I don't think I'll ever get over him."

The bed shifts as she sits beside me. She puts her arm around me. "You will, baby. But you never forget the first boy who owned your heart."

Funny thing is, Owen wasn't the first boy to own my heart. But he was the first boy to cradle it in his hands and treat it with care.

She squeezes me and whispers, "And you can't hide those feelings in the arms of another boy."

I know she's right.

☙ ❈ ❧

Layne does not ask where I slept or what I did. She must figure if I want to tell her, I will.

And I don't.

I get dressed for work and put on my chipper face. No one wants a sad voice calling them and asking for money.

"What are you wearing tonight?" Stirling asks beside my desk in between calls.

"My prom dress from high school," I say. "I get lots of wear out of it."

"Oh yeah? What's it look like?"

"It's light blue with beads on the bodice."

"What should I wear?"

I shrug. "Pants and a button-up shirt should be fine."

"And I meet you at your apartment?"

"Yes. We're taking pictures in the commons." I smirk. "Bring your cane."

"That's right, because I'm grandpa. Hey, how's your friend?" Concern flashes over his features as he remembers Riley.

I exhale. "I don't know. She hasn't responded to my texts." I checked with Harper to make sure her phone number hasn't changed, but Harper said she doesn't answer her either. "I hope she's all right."

"Should I bring you flowers tonight?"

I laugh at the idea. "No flowers, Stirling. It's a freshmen dance. But there is a limo that's going to take us from the dorms to the dance hall."

"That's nice. You never did say what happened with the modeling for the art classes. Are you still going to do that?"

I tilt my head. I haven't thought about it since the day at the professor's office. "He never called me, now that you mention it."

"Oh. Is that sad?"

I shrug. "It's okay, actually. My cousin got weird vibes from him and where would I fit it in? It's flattering. But not meant to be."

"Good attitude. Something to remember, though. How many girls can say that happened to them?"

"Yeah."

The shift ends with no excitement. The whole dorm is buzzing when I get home a few hours later. Layne is working the curling iron on everyone's hair, and she tells me to change so she can do mine.

"My hair won't curl," I tell her.

"Watch what magic I can do," she replies.

I slide into the prom dress I wore for junior year and remember the magical night I had with Tiago. It's a memory I treasure.

But the necklace nestled up against my collarbone is a new addition. I finger the charm, watching my reflection as I caress the pearl locked inside a silver spiral. I should take Owen's necklace off. At least for tonight. It doesn't match.

I don't. I can't. It doesn't matter what I am to Owen, he is always going to be this for me.

I step into Layne's room, where she not only curls my hair but pins it up decoratively so it falls across one shoulder in a sexy, vintage look.

"That's amazing," I say.

"Told you," she says. "You should trust me." She puts her face next to mine, and we grin at our reflections.

I like my roommates.

I help Camila and Iris with their eyeliner, and then a knock comes on the front door. We freeze and look at each other, and then all four of us pile into the hallway. Layne opens the door and throws her arms around Brant's neck. Her sparkly purple gown matches his tie, and they step into the commons to take pictures.

Jared and Justin arrive next. My stomach tightens when I see Jared. His trim body fills out the suit nicely, and his black curls are lightly tousled. He smiles at Iris and holds his hand out to her, but his eyes dart behind her to mine ever so quickly. My heart beats a little faster as she takes his hand.

Jealousy whispers through my mind.

Nobody notices a thing. Camila and Justin follow them into the commons, and Stirling comes up right behind. He looks nice with his maroon sweater over khaki pants, and I lean into him, inhaling the masculine scent of his cologne.

"Hey, you look nice," he says appreciatively.

"Why, thank you." I try to curtsy but almost lose my balance. He grabs my elbow to save me from a graceless tumble.

Dan, a photography student from the boys' dorm, takes pictures of us as couples in front of the couch. Then he has us sit with the girls in front while the boys stand.

"You're all done!" he says. "The line for the limo is downstairs."

We file down the stairs, and the four of us girls stand close together, touching hands and elbows and leaning close and giggling. We've forgotten our dates in the excitement of getting dressed up and feeling like princesses. Who needs boys, anyway?

Then they catch up to us, and each one slides their arms around our waists or around our shoulders, tucking us in against the cold night air. None of it matters, and it's fun. I hang on Stirling, resting against his chest, then snuggling up against him inside the limo as it drives the eight of us to the dance hall. I take his hand and pull him from the back of the car when we arrive. We head inside hand-in-hand. I'm light as a feather. The music jives, fun, fast-paced, music I've sung to on the radio a thousand times.

We dance fifteen minutes before taking a break. Stirling sees someone he knows and leaves to talk to him. I lean against a wall and take off my shoe, rubbing the back of my heel. Iris and Jared are dancing to a fast song, elbows moving in time to the beat, a wide grin on her face. I smile wistfully. She's happy.

I take off my other shoe and groan with relief.

Stirling returns. "Want to dance some more?"

"Almost." I gesture to my bare feet. "Just another minute."

"Sure." He spots another friend and moves off.

Layne and Brant come over, and she releases him.

"Go dance with Iris on the next song," she tells him.

"But I'm here with you."

"So? You can dance with my roommate!" She pushes him away.

Brant complies. He steps over to Iris and asks her to dance. She accepts, and Jared backs away. He glances around, spots us, and heads our direction.

"You're welcome," Layne says, and she pushes away from the wall.

Leaving me alone with him.

"Hi." He takes her place. "Where's your date?"

"Off talking to friends. I told him I needed a minute."

He lowers his voice. "Did you get in trouble for last night?"

I shake my head. "Camila hasn't asked me about it. Layne saw me come in, but she said she wouldn't tell."

"Does she know where you were?"

I weave my hand back and forth. "Not for sure. But she definitely suspects."

"Sorry." He grins. "But it was fun."

I remember the closeness I felt to him last night. How holding his hand made me feel. "Yeah."

He wanders over to a railing overlooking the student walkway below. I grab my shoes and follow him.

"You know," he says, swiveling to face me and resting his elbows behind him on the railing, "you don't actually know anything about me."

"No," I agree. "We haven't talked much. You've saved my fish and you almost saved my algebra grade. But not quite."

"What did you get?"

"Well, it was a sixty-two at first. But I redid the questions I missed and raised the score to an eighty-four."

"Lucky your teacher does that."

"She knows we're math-dumb."

He nods at Iris on the dance floor with Brant. "She's smart."

"Probably smarter than me. And she plays the cello. And she's a film student. And she's Canadian."

"I thought she was Chinese."

I lift a shoulder. "She's both."

He faces me, an errant dark curl falling over his forehead. My eyes dart to it, and my fingers twitch, wanting to push it back.

"What about you?" he asks. "No, let me guess. You seem like you're from Arizona. Maybe New Mexico. Possibly California?"

I squint at him. "You look like you're from one of those places. Or maybe Texas."

He shakes his head. "I don't fit any of the stereotypes. Smart football player, remember?"

I laugh. "Have you played in a game yet?" I think of Owen, who played for five minutes. But he's probably played more since then.

"I've had a few minutes of playing time. I'm crushed you haven't been watching."

"I've only been to three games," I admit. "They're fun. But expensive."

"I'll get you tickets to the next home game."

"You don't have to do that, Jared. Besides." I smirk. "I'll be cheering for Luke the whole time," I say, referencing the star football player whose name gets shouted across the stadium multiple times every game.

He grabs his chest, pretending to look gutted.

The song finishes. I look out at the dance floor and see Layne has intercepted Iris and Brant. Their backs are to us, but I know our time is up. On impulse, I seize his hand and tug. "Come on."

"Where are we going?" He laughs but follows me along.

I lead him down the stairs to the darkened student walkway beneath the dance hall. Tables are set up for studying, but the lights are out now. I plop down at one of them.

"We've got five minutes before Iris comes looking for you," I say. "Sit."

"Okay." He falls into the seat across from me. "What are we doing?"

"Twenty questions." I level my gaze at him. "You can't lie."

"Should I be scared?"

I shake my head. I'm being mischievous and sneaky and having way too much fun. "We'll take turns." I put my phone on the table and set a timer for five minutes. "First. Where are you from?"

"Pennsylvania," he says.

"Definitely would not have guessed that," I say. "Your turn."

"Okay. Where are you from?"

"Arkansas."

"Also would not have guessed.

"What's your ethnic background?"

"Jewish," he says, and I'm again startled. Then he laughs. "And Spanish."

His beautiful complexion makes sense now. I gesture for him to go on.

He pauses, and I glance at the clock. So far, so good. We've used thirty seconds.

"Your ethnic background," he says.

"In a question," I say.

"What's your ethnic background?" he says, lip quirking upward.

"Colombian. And British. What's your favorite color?"

"Sky blue. Like your dress. What do you like to do for fun?"

He's getting the hang of this. "Read. Sing."

"You forgot watch your fish."

I laugh. "And watch my fish." Four minutes to go. I lean toward him, getting serious now. "Who was your first kiss?"

He falls silent, and the smile wipes from his face. Oh, crap. Have I crossed a line? He glances over my shoulder and back at me, and I'm afraid he's going to bring up a heartbreaking story about his first crush who died from cancer when she was thirteen. But he says, "I haven't kissed a girl."

I'm so blown away I fall back in my chair. "What?"

"I told you I'd break all your stereotypes."

I shake my head. "You've never kissed a girl?"

"Nope."

The only thing I can think to say is, "Why?"

"Because I get nervous when a girl likes me," he says. "And I stop talking to her."

"Why are you still talking to me?" I say, and then I realize what I've admitted.

But he only smiles. "It's my turn."

I nod, still stunned.

"Why do you have an aversion to dating?"

I press my lips together. I opened myself up to any question, and I promised honesty. "I'm not over my high school boyfriend."

"Where is he now?"

I shake my head. "You only get one question at a time."

"You asked three on your turn."

"Yeah, but—" I laugh. "Okay. He's in Louisiana. Playing football for LSU."

"And how stereotypical of a football player is he?"

The question smacks hard, and it hurts. I know some of what Owen did before we dated, but not all the details.

Owen experimented a lot. Tried new experiences. Anything from girls to booze to drugs.

I haven't let it bother me. Owen changed. Owen's amazing. He's perfect.

What would it be like to be someone's first kiss?

You never forget your first kiss.

Although mine was terrible.

"He was pretty typical," I say, quietly. "But not when he and I dated. He changed his life around." I stand up, scooping up my phone even though the timer hasn't run out. "Iris would make a great first kiss."

⊙ᔕᔕ᷁ᔕ⊙

I'm determined not to talk to Jared again.

We don't speak again at the dance. But all night I think of what he told me. And how amazing it will be for the girl who gets to be his first kiss.

It won't be me.

I'm foolish enough to wish it would be.

I don't look at him at church. I go to the other side of the hall when I see him and talk to other people.

Iris sits by him in Sunday School. It's like she thinks he's her boyfriend now. She takes his pen and leans close enough to read from his Bible.

Jared does nothing to stop her. But when she rests her head on his shoulder in the hallway, he doesn't put his arm around her.

My heart is hurting. I need to be held, I need to be loved.

But I'm not ready for it.

CHAPTER SEVENTY
Tuesday in Denver

I walk home from church ahead of everyone. Before the boys can get to our apartment. I turn on my music on my phone and lock myself in my head, preparing for when I'll lock myself in my room. Everyone will say I'm rude and a man-hater, but Jared will know why.

Two days until I head to Utah for Thanksgiving. I can survive two days.

I let myself in the apartment and check on my fish. They're all doing well. Dick dying must have been a fluke. I walk to my room, shedding my jacket and unraveling my scarf as I go.

My phone rings. It's not on silent because I've been listening to music, and I freeze when I recognize the ringtone.

Owen's ringtone.

I close my bedroom door and slide onto my bed, pulling my knees up to my chest. "Hello?"

"What's up, killer?" he says, his voice warm and friendly.

We haven't talked since I called him about Riley. I'm wary. "Hey, you. Not much. Just got home from church and checked on my fish."

"They doing well?"

He doesn't know the whole drama, and I don't go into it. "Yep. Pretty little things."

"School going well?"

"Better," I say. "I made it through midterms. I feel like a real college student now."

"It's pretty real. I guess we're doing this thing."

"How about for you?"

"I'm hanging in there with grades. Wish I would've learned better study skills in high school."

"Any study skills," I say.

"Yeah." He punctuates the word with a laugh. "I had a smart girlfriend who helped me fake it."

Had. It hurts. I move on. "Not well enough. And football?"

"Have you watched any of the games?"

Not since the first one that ended in disaster for me and him. "No."

"Coach is playing me more. It's going good."

"That's great, Owen. I knew he'd see your value."

"Yeah."

Did he just call to chat? It's nice but unexpected.

"Monica said you guys had a nice time when you saw each other last month."

Honestly I'd expected him to message me about our visit weeks ago. When he hadn't, I assumed he didn't care. At all. "When did you talk to her?"

"I talk to her all the time."

"And you didn't talk about my visit until today?"

"I asked her right after. She told me if I wanted to know, I had to ask you."

"So you decided you didn't want to know." This conversation is starting to sting.

"Hang on, now, Cass, it wasn't like that." He stops. "Maybe it was a little. Of course I wanted to know. But I didn't want to call you."

"Why are you calling me now, then?" I ask, a bit testily.

"Can I see you?"

The question shocks me into silence. "What?" I finally say. "Like a video call?"

"Do you know that guys are the biggest idiots on planet earth?"

"Yes, I know," I say, still confused. "That's been well established."

"My uncle said Monica's staying in Utah and having Thanksgiving dinner with his family."

He keeps switching directions. I can't keep up. "Yes."

"Monica said you're going to be there."

"Yes." Does he have an issue with this?

"I was thinking—but I wanted to make sure it's okay with you—would it be weird if I'm there?"

I fall silent.

I picture Owen at Thanksgiving with us.

Owen in the same house as me.

"I don't understand," I say, as calmly as I can. "You didn't want to call me because you didn't want to talk to me. But now you want to come to Thanksgiving so you can see me?"

"Didn't you hear what I said earlier about guys being idiots?"

I laugh in spite of myself. "So you're trying to excuse yourself?"

"There's no excuse for me. All I know is if I start driving now, I can be in Colorado by tomorrow night. Or I can catch a flight and be there tomorrow morning. So is it all right with you if I come?"

My heart stutters. I could see Owen tomorrow.

"I have no place to put you," I say, my voice trembling.

Owen is coming.

"My break doesn't start until after school Tuesday," I continue. "And boys aren't allowed to stay in my dorm."

"Hey, look at this. I can do a round trip flight from New Orleans to Denver for less than a hundred and fifty bucks."

"It's that cheap?"

"Can you pick me up from the Denver airport Tuesday?"

THE FIRES OF HELL COULDN'T KEEP ME FROM PICKING HIM UP AT THE AIRPORT ON TUESDAY.

I don't tell him that.

"Yes." I'm so calm I sound indifferent. "It's a three-hour drive, so I might not be there right when you arrive."

"Come when you're done with classes. And then I'll ride with you to Utah. If that's all right."

I pause for a moment. He could fly straight into Utah. He'd save himself eight hours of driving.

But he's not.

Because he wants this extra time with me.

"It's all right," I say, quite placidly. "I'll tell you when I'm on my way."

"Okay, I'm booking this right now. I'll see you Tuesday."

"See you Tuesday," I echo.

I hang up and stare at the phone in my hand.

I simply cannot believe it.

I'm going to be with Owen on Tuesday.

❧

I hear when my roommates come in the door. They bring the usual flood of boys.

I'm too pent up to stay in my room.

I come into the kitchen. "Hi, guys!" I pull down the toaster and grab a loaf of bread. I'm jittery. My shoulders won't hold still and my feet are tapping.

"Hi," Brant says, giving me an odd look.

"Oh, toast me a slice too, will you?" Iris says.

I glance back at her. "Butter and jam?"

"Just jam."

Jared is behind her, his hands in his pockets, watching the fish. "Look at our namesakes play," he says, grinning. Justin joins him, and they laugh at the little guppies.

I feel nothing when I look at him.

That's not exactly true. There's something, way down in my heart. But it's more like a stirring of fondness. Nothing more.

"Those fish eat the most," I say, buttering my toast. "I'll show you. Here, Iris." I hand her bread lathered in strawberry jam and grab the fish food.

The boys step out of the way as I approach the fish tank. As soon as I open the latch, the guppies propel themselves toward the surface, little fins weaving so fast they're a blur. I drop in a smidgen of food, and they dart around like hummingbirds, gulping and spitting and gulping again. The other fish mosy on up and pick at the leftovers.

Jared and Justin laugh.

I laugh too. "See you guys."

I take my bread and head back to my room.

The mood in the kitchen is jovial. I munch my bread and hum, wiggling my feet back and forth on my bed. I'm dying to tell someone.

The boys leave half an hour later and Camila comes into the room.

"Hi," I say.

"Hi." She wakes her laptop and sits in front of it. "Dinner's in the oven. It'll be ready in twenty."

"Awesome. How was Justin?"

"Fine. We're just friends."

"That's great." I smile super big.

"You good?" She tilts her head at me. "You're kind of goofy."

"I'm great." My smile widens.

"All right. Spill it. What's going on?" She glances back toward the kitchen. "Is it something with Jared?"

"Well, if you must know." I scoot forward on my bed. "I'm spending Thanksgiving with Owen."

"What?" she shrieks.

The shriek draws our roommates.

"What is it?" Layne asks, popping in. Iris comes behind her.

I beam. Now I can tell people. "Owen's flying in Tuesday. We're spending Thanksgiving together."

"He's coming here?" Layne says.

"That's amazing!" Iris says, squealing with me.

"Where is he going to stay?" Layne asks.

"We're driving to Utah. We'll stay with his sister and his uncle."

"I'm so excited for you!" Camila hugs me. "I know how much you miss him."

"Yeah." I turn my eyes away as they tear up unexpectedly. "I miss him a lot."

"Will we get to see him?" Iris asks.

"Maybe. If you're still here when we get back from the airport."

"My mom will be here tomorrow," Layne says. "She and Dave want to take us out to dinner."

"I'm all in," I say.

My jovial mood is contagious. We flit back to the kitchen, and I pull out the photos Owen gave me when I left and show them off.

"Does he still love you?" Layne asks.

Camila elbows her. "Rude! Of course he does!"

"People fall out of love," she says.

"I honestly don't know," I say, putting the pictures away. "We haven't talked about us. I don't know what's going to happen when I pick him up. Maybe all we are is friends with a history."

A somberness descends as we consider that.

It's a possibility.

But I don't believe it.

It's not until that night when we're alone in our room that Camila broaches the subject of Jared.

"What's going on with you two?"

I steal a glance at her as I finish up my writing assignment for English. "Okay. I'll tell you." But then I fall silent. I'm not sure where to start.

"Do you like him?"

I hesitate. "If you asked me yesterday, I would have said yes. Today, the answer is no."

"But that's because of Owen."

"Yes."

"So the answer is probably still yes. If Owen wasn't in the picture, you would like Jared."

"That's probably a true assessment."

"Have you and Jared acted on your feelings?"

My face warms, and I avert my eyes. "Maybe a little."

"When? How?" Camila's tone matches mine. Quiet. In case there are spies in our closet listening.

"Friday night we held hands."

"You did?" It's a hushed exclamation.

I nod. Shame warms my body. "I shouldn't have. I was so lonely. So hungry for affection."

"Did you guys talk about it?"

I shake my head. "No. We hung out a bit at the dance. We talked. But not about that. Did you know he's never kissed a girl?"

"No way."

I nod. "Yeah." I still feel an awed reverence for that.

"What will you do now?"

"Nothing. Like I meant to do in the beginning. It's a crush. I'm not going to act on it. Besides, Iris likes him."

"Does he know about Owen coming?"

"No. Why should he?" I don't feel obligated to tell Jared anything about Owen. Owen and I aren't together. And Jared and I aren't together.

"Yeah, I suppose it wouldn't help anything." Camila sits back on her bed. "You have to tell me everything that happens with Owen."

"I will. For sure."

Monday passes at a snail's pace.

"Excited for break?" Abby asks in physical science.

"Abby." I grin so broadly my cheeks ache. "I'm going to see Owen tomorrow."

Her reaction is perfect. Wide eyes, then an excited squeal as she throws her arms around me.

"When do I get to meet him?" she asks.

"I don't know." Owen and I haven't talked since yesterday. I don't know the plan for Tuesday other than me picking him up. "When do you leave?"

"Tomorrow night."

"I'll let you know our plans."

For once my professors don't care about anything. My English teacher assigns an essay due when we get back from break, which I find annoying but doable. The rest of them know we'll forget everything between now and a week and don't bother.

My roommates and I go to an Indian restaurant for dinner with Layne's mom and her boyfriend. But I'm already too anxious to eat.

Jared messages me while we're at dinner.

J: Thanksgiving plans?

Me: going to Utah with friends. You?

J: nice. Justin's hosting at his aunt's house for those of us with no family around. If you wanted to come.

Me: thanks for the invite! Have fun!

He doesn't respond.

Finally it's Tuesday morning.

There's a text from Owen. It's a screenshot of his flight itinerary. There's nothing else, no comment, no message, no emoji. He's leaving at eleven. His flight will arrive in Denver by two p.m.

My last class is done at two.

I want to skip the whole day. I only don't because Camila drags me along to our religion class in the morning. Once I'm on campus, I go to my physical science lab.

"When are you leaving for the airport?" Abby asks me.

I'm correcting a lab I turned in and calculated incorrectly. It's extra credit to redo it, and I need all the extra I can get. "Owen will be there at two." That's in four hours. "But I'm not done with class until then."

"Cass, it's a three-hour drive."

"I know."

"So miss your last class."

"It's Honors English. It's my favorite."

"Hmm, let's see." She holds her hands out like a scale. "Go to your favorite class on the last day before break where you probably won't do anything, or leave early and pick up your boyfriend—who you haven't kissed in three months, I might add —from the airport sooner than you expected? Hard to decide."

I laugh. "You are such a bad influence!"

She grins. "Go get him, Cassandra."

That's all the permission I need. We hug goodbye after the lab and wish each other happy Thanksgivings, and then I hurry back to my apartment.

I'm skipping class.

I don't know if Owen wants to come back to my dorm or go straight to Utah, so I put my bags in the car just in case. Is there anything else I need? I don't think so. I jump in the car, take deep breaths, and program my GPS. Then I text him.

Me: I'm on my way.

CHAPTER SEVENTY-ONE
Dynamite

distract myself on the drive. I call my mom. I told her Sunday Owen was coming, and she teases me and also reminds me to keep my standards high. Right, right.

I call Monica. We've been texting to finalize plans, but I haven't talked to her since before Owen invited himself along. She doesn't answer. She might be in class.

And then I don't feel like talking to anyone else. So I put on music and breathe.

Snow begins to fall as I zoom down I-70. I didn't check the weather. What if his flight is delayed?

Heaven forbid it be canceled.

Three hours later, I slow down at the terminal entrance. I'm not familiar with this airport at all. I check my phone. Owen's flight should be here, but he hasn't texted me. I park at the arrivals and twist my fingers together. What if he changed his mind?

No. He texted me this morning. He's coming.

I pull up his flight info on the airport app and heave a sigh.

It's delayed. He'll be here in half an hour.

Now I can drive in circles around the terminal for half an hour, or I can park in short-term parking.

I opt to park.

The snow falls harder, and I'm grateful for the shelter when I get inside the covered parking garage, even though I hate these tiny spaces. I grab my entry ticket, leave my car, and head back down to the terminal. Then I sit down in the coffee shop inside the airport, pull out a book, and wait.

My eyes dart up from the book every two seconds, watching the screen of arrivals. Finally his flight shows up. My heart thumps harder in my throat.

My phone dings. I pick it up.

O: just landed.

I give his message a thumbs up.

Then I watch the escalator.

There's a pillar between me and the escalator, so I have to twist my head to see around it. My eyes scan all the men who come down. Some are old and balding, some trim in business suits. Most look haggard, tired, unexcited. All of them have their eyes down or straight ahead.

And then I see him.

I know his walk. I didn't expect to recognize him right away, but I do. He swaggers to the escalator, an LSU cap on his head. His chest looks broader, and I wonder how hard his coach works him. He shoulders a backpack and scans the floor.

He's looking for me. But I'm concealed by this pillar, and I'm content to stay out of sight for the moment.

He reaches the bottom of the escalator and pauses. He steps to the side to get out of the way of pedestrians and pulls out his phone. I watch his fingers move over the buttons. All I can see of his face is his mouth and his jaw.

Both are features I'm quite fond of.

The phone dings.

O: I'm here

Time to come out. I heft my purse and stand, then merge with a crowd of tourists, moving with them until I'm standing to his left, slightly behind him.

"Owen," I say.

He turns. His green eyes, flecked with golden brown, scan me from head to toe. He shoves his phone into his back pocket and crosses the space between us in two big steps. Then he wraps his arms around me and crushes me to him.

My breath shudders out of me, and I close my eyes, wilting against him. This is where I belong. These arms. This chest.

"Hey, you," he says, his voice deep below my ear.

I grin and take a step back. I want to keep touching him. Run my hand down his arm. Take the cap from his head and tousle his hair. Weave my fingers through his. "Hey, yourself." I clasp my fingers together so I don't grab him. "I'm parked in short-term. Do you have any luggage?"

He shakes his head. "No."

I can't believe he's here.

"Let's go, then."

He follows me to the parking garage, staying a step behind me. I unlock the car, and he throws his bag into the back.

"It's snowing," he says.

"Yeah. And it's a long drive back to my apartment. Did you want to go there or straight to Utah?"

He climbs into the passenger seat and frowns, looking thoughtful. "I want to see your place. Unless you don't want to stop."

"Either way is fine with me." I'm delighted he wants to see where I live. I program my phone and send a text to my roommates.

Me: I'm bringing Owen home! Be there in three hours.

Owen turns to watch me back out of my spot. "Good job. You didn't hit anything."

"I am a very capable driver," I say.

"A very cautious driver, you mean."

"I know how to use my vocabulary, and I meant what I said."

He laughs and turns to watch out the passenger window. "But how are you with snow?"

"That is an excellent question." I guide my car slowly down the exit ramp. "We are about to find out."

"Oh, boy. Want me to drive?"

"How are you with snow?"

He lifts a shoulder. "Never tried it. Can't be worse than mud, though."

"Maybe in a truck."

Talking with him is easy, but I feel a thread of caution between us. We're testing our connection, not sure what's changed between us in these months. We're painting a familiar landscape, but we don't have the color quite right yet.

I clear the airport traffic and merge onto the interstate. "How was your flight?"

"Uneventful. Except for being delayed. I guess I should expect that this time of year."

I bob my head.

"How was your drive?"

"Uneventful." I grin at him. "Except for being delayed."

I turn my eyes back to the road, and there's a pause. I'm not sure what to do with it. Should I turn on the radio or make mindless chatter?

"It's good to see you," he says.

I glance at him to see him studying me. "You too." My hand flutters on the steering wheel as I start to reach for him before catching myself and tightening my grip.

A gauge lights up on my dash. "Oh, I need to get gas."

I take the next exit. The snow has stopped falling but left a light dusting on the roads. My tires skid even when I take the stop sign slowly.

"Let me pay for it," Owen says, reaching into his pocket and getting his wallet. "You drove out here to get me."

"No way." I scoff at him and park at the station. "You flew all the way out here to have Thanksgiving with your sister. Your expense was bigger than mine." I grab my jacket and hop out, shivering as I shove my arms into the sleeves and start the pump.

Owen gets out also. He stuffs his hands in his jeans pockets. "By the time you get gas twice, you'll have paid the same amount as my ticket."

"Then we'll be even." I glance at his long-sleeved T-shirt. The fabric is loose around his forearms, but I see the bulge at the biceps. I bet he's ripped.

I want to take his shirt off and find out.

I banish the thought immediately. "Did you bring a jacket?"

"Forgot."

"I might have a sweater you can borrow."

He laughs. "Which arm should I wear it on?"

I grin. "They can take turns."

He comes around the car to where I stand. "Get in the car and stay warm. I'll finish this."

"You stay warm," I return. "I have a coat. You don't."

"You're shivering. I'm not."

I glance at myself. I am trembling. But it's not from the cold.

It's from him standing so close to me.

I don't want to explain that. "All right."

He comes around behind me and takes the pump, and our hands brush as I let go. I touch the sleeve of his shirt, running my fingers over the fabric for a second before turning for the car door.

"Hey."

I turn back to him, one hand on the handle.

He's got me in his gaze. Holding me with his eyes. His jaw tightens for a second, and he says, "Are you dating anyone?"

I shake my head and add a verbal, "No."

He grabs the edge of my coat and pulls me toward him. His hand comes up to cup my face and then moves around my jaw to hold the back of my neck.

And then he lowers his head and kisses me.

A hungry flutter erupts from my stomach. His tongue traces my lips, and then darts inside, tasting me, his arms wrapping around me inside my jacket, bending my body against his. I'm filled with an urgent, primal need to consume him. I slide my hands up under his shirt, pressing against his hot flesh, feeling the cords of muscle. The bill of his baseball cap knocks against my forehead, and I reach up and push it back.

The pump clicks as it finishes, and Owen glances at it. His face is flushed, his pupils large. He lets out a slow exhale and looks at me. His hands are still around me, and he tightens his embrace, pulling me against him.

I slide my arms free of his shirt and hug him back.

The chemistry hasn't lessened between us. If anything, it's crackling like dynamite, ready to explode.

"Get in the car," he says.

I don't move. "I can see you've picked up some bad habits in my absence."

He tilts his head, brow furrowing slightly. "What do you mean?"

He puts the pump away, and I lean toward him.

"You ask me to do things. You don't command."

His lip quirks upward, and my eyes fly to it. That soft, full lip, the one that was just melded to mine.

"Cassandra," he says, with all formality, "if you please, would you deign to enter the car?"

I smirk and get in.

It's warm inside, but the fire I feel is all me. I take off my coat and toss it into the back seat. Owen gets in, and I haven't even swiveled away from the console before he's grabbing my shirt around the waist and pulling me over to him.

"We can't make out at the gas station," I say, but then we are, me stretched out across the console, Owen leaning toward me, one hand on my face, the other trailing down my shoulder, squeezing my arm, trying to tug me off the console and into his seat.

If we weren't at a gas station, I would let him. I feel the same desperate need to get him close to me that he does, to fill all the aching spots in my heart with Owen. I want to touch him everywhere, feel him everywhere. I cannot get enough of Owen.

There's a warning bell going off in the far recesses of my mind. I don't know where his head is.

I'm not even sure where his heart is.

How much has changed? How has he changed?

I pull back, taking a deep breath, trying to compose myself. I didn't expect this.

"We should get back," I say.

"Yeah," he says, quietly. He takes off his baseball cap and runs a hand over his hair, which is short again, recently shaved close to the scalp. He takes my hand. "Actually, can we sit somewhere and talk for a bit?"

We have nearly a three-hour drive in front of us. There will be time for talking. But I nod and do a quick search on my phone.

"Sure. You're probably hungry, aren't you? I didn't even ask."

"I am," he admits. "I didn't eat lunch."

"Owen. Why didn't you say something?"

"I kind of forgot anything else existed when I saw you."

He's not throwing me a line. He delivers it with a quiet seriousness, and some of the worry around my heart dissipates.

He still feels something for me.

"And I didn't come here for my sister. I came here for you."

I fight hard to hide my smile.

I find a mom-and-pop sandwich shop. I'm not hungry but get a brownie to nibble on. Owen orders a foot-long with two bags of chips, a large drink, and a cookie, then joins me at the table sipping from his straw.

"You have terrible luck," he says, sitting down.

"Me?" I press a hand to my chest. "Why? What happened?"

"Because you keep ending up with douche bags who don't treat you right."

I frown at him. "No, I don't."

The guy behind the register calls his name, and Owen gets his sandwich and returns to the table.

He takes a few bites, and I wait for him to continue his earlier thought. But he eats with abandon, inhaling the first half before coming up for air. Then he looks at me, pegging me with his eyes while he takes a drink.

"Do you know," he says, "that you are a siren?"

"What?" I laugh. "Do you remember how to have a conversation? You say things that make sense, the other person responds, and you say things along the same lines."

He laughs also. Then his grin fades. "I'm not dating anyone," he says. "In case you wondered."

"I didn't let myself think about it. After the way you kissed me, I figured if you were, it was non-exclusive." I shrug. "Or I figured you didn't care. It wouldn't be the first time you kissed me while dating someone else."

"I haven't kissed anyone since you."

CHAPTER SEVENTY-TWO

Unexpected Confessions

t's an admission I didn't ask for. We agreed not to ask, and I wouldn't have anyway because I thought the answer would hurt. But I look at him in surprise. "You haven't?"

He shakes his head and turns to the rest of his sandwich.

I should let it be. But it's very unlike Owen, who always had to have a girl, even in the moments when he and I were on breaks. "Why?"

His eyes flick to me again. "A lot of reasons."

He doesn't elucidate.

"I haven't either," I say. "Kissed anyone."

"Not even Stirling?"

I smirk at the name. Monica must have told him. "Stirling's just a friend."

"Who you go on dates with."

"I go on lots of dates." That slipped out.

He's quiet, eyes down while he finishes his food. Then he stands and throws his trash away. When he comes back, he takes my hand and pulls me to my feet. His hands rest on my shoulders, and he kisses my forehead. His lips linger there, keeping the connection. Then he pulls back. His thumb traces my jaw, along my chin.

"Ready?" he asks.

I nod.

We go back to my car. The ice between us is gone. With our impromptu make out session and the unexpected confessions, we've entered a deeper realm.

"Tell me about your roommates," I say. "How are they?"

"Crazy," he says, and he laughs. "We're all on the football team. They group the sports together in student housing. Harrison's all right. He cares about his grades and he's Catholic, so he drinks a lot but doesn't always have girls over. But Steve—" He shakes his head. "He'll hump anything that moves."

"He sounds vile."

403

"No, Lewis is vile. Lewis is a rich prick who thinks everything on earth was created for him. Everything out of his mouth is a lie. Two girls accused him of assault and I'm certain he did it, but he can lie better than Satan himself."

I cast him a troubled look. "These are your roommates?"

"Just Lewis is bad. None of us can stand him. Coach told us if we find proof that he hurt any of those girls, we need to turn him in."

"Will you?"

"In less than two heartbeats."

I frown. "How often do they drink?"

"Maybe things are different at PYU, but at LSU, every night's a party. My roomies drink a few nights a week. Definitely after a game."

"Does everyone drink?"

"No. There are kids that don't."

"What do you do?"

"I'm one of those dorky religious kids that don't."

I laugh at the idea of Owen as dorky, but I'm relieved he didn't return to his old habits. "Is that hard for you?"

"Sometimes. Sometimes it's really hard. I used to love partying. Sometimes I think, one won't hurt." He exhales. "But I never stopped at one in high school. I drank hard. It took a lot to feel a buzz. I think I'd get sucked back into it. So I stay out."

I want to tell him I'm proud of him but don't want to sound like his mom. "I'm glad. It's better for you."

"What about your roommates?"

"Well, I'd call them crazy too, but in very different ways. Preston Y is a much calmer school."

"LSU is known for their party scene."

I bob my head. It's snowing again, so I have to go slower. But I wouldn't care if we got snowed in here on the interstate. I have Owen.

"I told you about Abby. She's not a roommate, but she's the first person I met during Honors week. She helped me come out of my shell. I felt so out of place all over again, and I didn't know anyone."

"Yeah, I remember."

"Then there's Camila, you met her."

"You still get along?"

"She's the best. We connect on so many levels. There's also Iris. She's Chinese-Canadian and good at everything. She can play every string instrument known to man and she's a film major. She rooms with Layne. Layne's from California and the biggest flirt you ever saw." I roll my eyes. "She's dating Brant, but rumor has it she's already kissed half the guys at church."

"Your roommates are far more interesting than mine."

"I'm blessed. We get along, even though we're all very different. And I hang out a lot with Jordan. My cousin."

"I know his voice."

I laugh. "Yeah, you do."

He reaches a hand over and scratches the nape of my neck, then lowers his hand to the console. "What else? Family good?"

"Yeah, fine."

"What about these guys you date? Where do you find them?"

I glance at him uneasily. I feel like this topic approaches a sensitive boundary. Questions I don't want to answer might be brought up. I'm not prepared to lie. I swore I'd never do that to Owen again. "Church. Class. Work."

I try to make my reticence clear with the one-word answers, and I'm relieved when his next question follows a different vein.

"And work? Are you rich now?"

"Very funny. It's not a bad job. I thought I would hate calling people, but most people are nice. They like their alma mater. Every once in awhile someone swears at me and screams and hangs up, and I say a little prayer that they don't have a heart attack and die because I called them."

Owen laughs. He touches my hand on the steering wheel, then lets his palm fall to my thigh. He gives it a squeeze, but it's not sexual. It's intimate. Connecting.

"I can't believe you're here," I exhale.

A quiet pause follows my pronouncement.

"I didn't know how much I missed you until I saw you," Owen says.

His words warm my heart, and my eyes burn. "I thought I might not see you again."

"That was never going to happen."

"We didn't make any plans."

"The future was open for us to make of it what we wanted."

"And we chose not to be together." The words are icy daggers as I speak them, but they come from regrets I carry, mistakes I can't correct. The truth is, that decision still hurts. We had a choice, and we chose this. Separation.

He doesn't answer.

His mom calls a few minutes later, and Owen puts her on speaker phone to talk to both of us. Her voice brings back memories of clandestine activities at her house, when she smuggled me over so I could hang out with Owen under the pretense of being there for Monica. She's my second mother, and I love her.

"When are you coming to visit, Cassandra?" she asks. "We have lots of room in our new house."

"I don't know," I say. "I'll have to check."

"We'll plan on it!"

We say a few more words before Owen hangs up.

"She misses you," he says.

"I miss her."

Silence descends on us again. Owen is thinking. Thinking about my words, thinking about his feelings, I'm not sure what, but I feel him sifting through thoughts. My mind is as flighty as a trapped squirrel, and I can't capture any thoughts to examine them. So I turn on the radio.

It's after six when we pull up to my apartment. I park by the stairwell, and Owen looks up, appraising its appearance. "This is it, huh?"

"Home sweet home."

"Where are you when you talk to me?"

"Either my car, my room, or the kitchen." I hop out of the car, pulling my jacket on. "Come see my fish." I take his hand and tug him forward because I can. I squeeze his fingers, feeling the warmth of his palm against mine.

"Hello?" I call as I enter the apartment. "Anyone here?" I pull Owen in behind me and scoot in front of the fish tank. "Look! Aren't they beautiful?"

He laughs. "You're a goof." He glances behind him. "Look! A couch. It's so beautiful." He falls back onto it, and he pulls me down with him. I sit beside him.

"Is there anyone else here?" he asks.

I listen but don't hear anyone. "I think we're alone," I say.

"Good." He pushes me so my back hits the armrest. His hand falls on my shoulder, and his mouth falls on mine.

How I've longed to feel this. I scoot down, bringing him with me, and our legs intertwine on the couch. He kisses me, but he's in control, his lips slow and tantalizing as they move over mine. He moves lower, kissing my jaw, the pulse point below my ear.

"I have a bed," I whisper.

"I'm sure you do," he says, and he pulls back, a hint of a smile on his lips, bright pink from the force of my mouth. "We should stay out here."

I finger the hem of his shirt and peer at him through my lashes. "I want to see you. All of you."

"You can't ask that of me," he whispers, and he kisses me again, but it's hotter this time, more demanding.

I scoot out from under him, still meeting his kisses as I sit up, and then I stand, rising from the couch. Owen sits up also, his eyes on me.

"Come on," I say, taking his hand.

"Where?"

"I'll show you my room."

He takes a hitched breath but doesn't move.

"Come on, Owen," I say, quietly, more definitively. The blood still pumps supercharged through my veins, parts of my body lit and eager to be touched. I'm desperate to do more. To feel more with Owen.

Owen stands. But he pulls his hand from mine and instead hugs me, wrapping his arms around my shoulders and squeezing me tight. Then he takes my face in his hands and kisses me again.

The front door opens down the hall, and there's an audible smack as I pull away from Owen and turn my head that direction.

"Hello?" I call.

"Hey!" Layne comes into the kitchen with bags of food. "I thought you'd be here over an hour ago!" Her eyes rake over Owen. "Hi. I'm assuming you're Owen."

"That depends on if Owen is a good guy or bad guy," he drawls.

I smile. I love his drawl.

"Apparently Owen is both," Layne says. "And much hotter than Cassandra let on, might I add. I'm Layne."

"Ha ha," I say, not impressed. Is she really flirting with my boyfriend? Is Owen my boyfriend?

"Well, thanks," Owen says. "You fit her description of you."

I purse my lips to keep from laughing.

"All good things, I hope," Layne purrs, batting her eyelashes.

"Of course."

She looks around the kitchen. "What were you guys doing in here?" She shoots me a mischievous look.

"Nothing," I say, just as Owen says, "Exactly what you think we were."

"Owen!" I sputter, and I start laughing, because this is us. This is how we've always been.

I'm filled with such happiness that I could die at this moment and feel my life was fulfilled.

Layne smirks. "You're a good influence. I wasn't sure Cassandra had it in her."

Owen looks at me, and I know what he's thinking: I'm the temptress in this relationship.

"I'm not sure you know her that well," he says, and I blush furiously.

"Really?" Layne puts away the groceries. "Are you staying for dinner? I'm the only one left. My parents are taking me out again."

Owen shakes his head.

"We're going to try to get to Utah tonight," he says.

"Better get going," she says.

I hand him the keys. "You can warm the car if you want. I need to make sure I didn't forget anything. I'll be right down."

He nods and heads out, and Layne pounces.

"Girl, he's a ten/ten! Why don't you brag about these things? You're dating a super hot football player from LSU!"

I go to my room and make sure I have my laptop charger and English book. "I don't know if we're dating."

She follows behind as I go through my things. "Okay, you're making out with a super hot football player! And I heard what he said. I think you're not the innocent goody-two-shoes you let us believe you are."

I find a phone charger and grab it in case I forgot mine. "I never said I was. You made assumptions."

"How was I supposed to know that behind the Girl Scout church veneer there is a hot-blooded vamp?"

I laugh. "I'm human, Layne. We're all hot-blooded vamps when it comes down to it."

"I don't know about that." She follows me back to the kitchen. "I see why you're not over him. You're obviously in love with him. And he's in love with you."

"He cares about me."

"If all he did was care about you, he'd screw you and be done with it. But he's still here. Because he loves you."

"He did love me. I hope he still does." This week will show.

I'm not going to put words in his mouth.

CHAPTER SEVENTY-THREE

This Moment

Owen programs the GPS while I drag my giant English lit book across my lap. He was in the driver's seat when I got to my car, and it feels so natural to have him there that I tuck into the passenger seat without question.

"What are you studying?" he asks.

"Pick the most stereotypical, well-known college English class reading material."

He considers, then says, "Hamlet."

I wiggle my finger at him. "Ding ding ding! You got it."

He laughs, then he leans over and kisses me. "Dang." He kisses me again. "I forgot how good you taste."

I grab his collar before he pulls away and kiss him hard. I'm still turned on from earlier but accepting I won't get any satisfaction. "I did not forget," I say when I release him.

He moves his hand off the transmission as if to reach for me, then shakes his head and grabs it again. "No. We need to leave."

I start reading as he drives. He goes through my radio stations and finds a country one, and I perk up and sing along when a familiar song comes on.

"Want to read to me?" he asks when the song finishes.

"Is this so I won't sing anymore?"

He smirks. "I'm trying to be helpful. Thought you might want to focus on your studies."

I read in the fading light but only manage about twenty minutes before I can't see anymore. Then I put the book away and open my laptop so I can start the essay.

"How is Tiago?"

I look over from my laptop, but Owen's eyes are on the road. "The last time I talked to him was when I found out Riley's pregnant. We chatted a bit."

"Are you still going to see him in May?"

"I'm going to Brazil in May," I say. "I'm not going to see Tiago."

"But he's the reason you're going."

"Maybe when I booked the ticket," I admit. "But not anymore. I love the city I'm flying into. Next semester I'm taking Portuguese classes. I want to study the language, the people."

"I suppose that makes sense."

"Owen." I turn to him, because this is something that excites me, and I haven't shared it with anyone. "I want to see the world. I want to try it all. I want to go places and learn languages and eat crazy exotic foods."

The street lamps flash by, casting his face in shadow and then in light, and he glances at me as he drives. But he doesn't say anything.

"I don't mean Paris or Rome or London, though of course I want to see those places too. I mean the little villages in the Swiss alps and the dirt streets of Africa and the penguins! The penguins, Owen!"

He laughs softly. "That sounds amazing."

I want him to tell me he shares that desire. That he'll travel the world with me. But he doesn't, and I settle back in my seat, a bit embarrassed by my outburst.

"What made you decide that?" he asks.

"My religion class. It's on ancient civilizations. I can't go to those places. But the remnants exist today. It made me want to see the ruins in Colombia and Guatemala and Mexico. But why stop there? There's a whole world to explore!"

There I go again. I bite my tongue to settle myself.

"I understand Tiago," he says.

I furrow my brow, confused why he's bringing him up again. "What do you mean?"

"I didn't understand him. Last year. How he could love you and then abandon you, and abandon you cruelly, not talking to you or sending you a note or anything."

I don't answer. It was a painful time in my life.

"I remember thinking to myself, if she was my girl, I would never let her slip out of my life. That guy's an idiot."

Now I know where he's going with this.

"It turns out all guys are idiots, Cassandra." He doesn't look at me but keeps his eyes on the road, and I keep my eyes on him. "I thought if talking to you brought me pain, not talking to you would make it better. If you were a drug, I needed to get you out of my system, and only time would do that. Tiago tried, and then he woke up one day and realized he'd failed completely to remove you from his heart. And I did the same exact thing. The same damn thing."

I am quiet.

He is quiet.

What does one say after such a proclamation?

I turn back to my English essay. But I'm trying to figure Owen out.

What is he saying? What does he want?

We cross the Utah border an hour later and stop at a Taco Bell drive-through for dinner.

"Sorry it's so late," Owen says.

"It's only nine," I say. "I'm in college. Some nights I don't eat dinner till midnight."

He laughs. "I hear that. What do you want?"

"A chicken quesadilla and a seven-layer burrito." My go-tos.

He orders for both of us and pulls up to the window to wait. "You look good."

"Why, thanks," I say, putting on my own drawl.

"I mean." He gives me a searching look. "How are you with the food thing?"

He knows about my history of an eating disorder.

I push the pads of my fingers together. "I'm doing all right. Sometimes I panic a bit when I step on the scale and see the weight I've gained, but mostly I'm okay with it."

"Good. I'm glad the stress of college hasn't made it worse."

"I'm writing a paper on it. For my English class."

"Can I read it when you finish?"

"Maybe. I've gained fifteen pounds. The whole freshman fifteen. Too much ramen."

He looks at me incredulously. "You look great."

"Yeah, I weigh a whole hundred and five now. But next semester I'm going to take two PE credits. Dance and swimming."

"You're already planning next semester?"

Our food arrives, and he hands it out before starting down the road again.

"Just enough to have an idea of what's available."

"I just want to survive this semester. Next semester my focus is getting ready for my mission. School feels trivial next to that."

"You're still planning on one?"

"Yes."

I touch his arm, and I can't help it. I say the motherly words. "I'm proud of you, Owen."

He rolls his eyes. "Oh, thanks, Mom," he says, and we both laugh.

"I expected that," I say.

He eats his tacos one-handed and I get halfway through my burrito before putting it away.

"There are times I've thought about not going," he says.

I'm not sure where we are in the conversation. "Where?"

"On a mission."

"Oh. You don't have to go."

"I want to go. I need to if I'm going to become the person I want to be."

"What might stop you?"

He looks at me and looks away.

He doesn't answer.

I think he did. But I'm not sure I understand.

I work on my essay and we talk about his family, my family, school, friends. He asks about Riley and I have no answers.

"I hope she's all right," I say. "Harper said she doesn't respond. I can't get an answer either. But I'll look her up at Christmas."

"I have regrets there," Owen says. "I could have been a better influence on Riley. But I was busy living it up."

"You were on your own journey. You couldn't help her on hers."

"But that's my fault for being stupid. You helped her."

"My journey was different than yours."

"You knew what was real in life."

I type a few more lines on my essay. "You're different than you were the last time I saw you."

"Good or bad?"

"Good."

"What's different?"

"You're introspective."

"Define it for me, Ms. English Major."

"You're thinking a lot. There are serious things in your head."

"Does that make me boring?"

I shake my head, my eyes on my lit screen. "It makes me like you even more."

"You like me, huh?"

He's teasing. I smile. The seriousness doesn't last long.

"Yeah, I think so," I say.

"Still deciding?"

"Hmm." I give a noncommittal grunt.

"Let me know when you figure it out."

We drift into silence as the night wears on. I pull my blanket up to the front seat and curl up in it.

"Sleepy?" he asks.

"I don't sleep much in school," I admit.

"You can rest. We have about an hour."

"Thanks." I face the window and rest my head on the seatbelt.

Owen turns on a rock station. His hand falls on my back, and he rubs my shoulder blades for a moment before the pressure disappears.

I want to ask what happens to us after this week. But I don't know what's going to happen during the next few days, so the question feels preemptive.

I wake when the car pulls to a stop. The engine turns off, and I stretch. It's dark out. We're in the driveway of a two-story house, and flood lights turn on when Owen opens the car door, but I can't see much else.

The front door opens, and a man steps out.

"You made it," he says, hugging Owen, his voice groggy. We probably woke him.

I get out and open the door to the backseat, pulling out my backpack and duffel.

"You must be Cassandra," the man says, turning to me warmly. "Call me Jake. Come on inside, I'll show you your room."

"Here." Owen takes my bags.

"I can do it, Owen," I say, voice slurring.

"I know you can." He prods me forward.

I give up and stumble after Jake. We enter a split level entryway and head down the stairs. It breaks off into a living room and several bedrooms. He leads me into a room with a bunkbed.

"Monica's asleep on the bottom," he says. "I wasn't sure if I should wake her."

I know it's sometime after one in the morning, but I didn't check the time when I got out of the car. My phone is tucked away in my purse. "That's all right. I'll see her in the morning." I turn as Owen puts my bags by the ladder.

"Owen, you're upstairs," Jake says, and my heart sinks. I want Owen here with me.

Jake leaves the room, expecting Owen to follow. Owen takes my chin and presses his lips to mine.

"Good night," he says.

"Night," I echo.

I watch him leave, then head to the bathroom to take out my contacts.

I cannot believe Owen is here with me.

CHAPTER SEVENTY-FOUR

Taking It Farther

wake up when I hear voices. The floorboards above my head creak as footsteps traipse across.

What time is it?

I don't even have my phone with me.

I peer over the edge of the bed. Monica's gone. I climb down the ladder and fish my phone out of my purse.

"Past nine!" I breathe. When was the last time I slept this late? Not during school, and not on a Saturday. Maybe on a Sunday where I've skipped church.

I rummage through my overnight bag for a toothbrush and hop over to the bathroom. Then I go through my morning routine before I head upstairs. I should change, but I want everyone to know I'm alive.

Owen's uncle Jake stands around a kitchen island with three kids next to him. By kids I mean teenagers. They have blond hair and blue eyes and bear a slight resemblance to the Blaines. Monica stands beside Jake, and she lifts her eyes when I come up the stairs. A smile widens across her face.

"You're awake!" She hurdles around the island to come to my side and hug me.

"Yes," I say, inhaling her citrusy perfume and clinging to her shoulders. She releases me, and I speak to Jake. "Thanks for letting me stay with you."

"Oh, you're welcome. We're always happy to have Jenn's kids, and their friends are welcome anytime."

Jenn. Mrs. Blaine. I never think of Owen's mom that way.

"Well, thanks." I glance around. Where is Owen, anyway?

"He went on a jog with Dane, our cousin," Monica says, answering my unspoken question. "Trying to stay in shape."

"Of course."

"You guys all right hanging out here today?" Jake asks. "We can stream some movies. Liz has most of the food being catered, so it's a relaxing day. Then tomorrow is feasting day."

I nod. "Yeah, that's fine. I have homework to do anyway."

I head downstairs and change out of yesterday's clothes, then take my backpack and laptop back to the kitchen.

"Steph, show her the den," Jake says to one of the teenagers.

"This way," she says, leading me forward.

The den is upstairs. A giant TV screen lines one wall. The windows are blacked out. I sit down in one of the oversized leather chairs.

"Here's the remote to the TV, if you want to watch something," she says. "My brothers will probably be up in a moment and put something on."

"Thanks." I set the remote on the couch. "What grade are you in?"

"Tenth. Are you enjoying college?"

"I think so. It's hard."

She laughs, flashing braces. "So you're Owen's girlfriend?"

"Sort of. We took a break to go to school."

"You're pretty."

"Thanks."

She smiles again and disappears downstairs.

I pull out my Shakespeare book and return to Hamlet.

The front door bangs downstairs, and deep voices and laughter carry to the den.

Two adolescent boys come tripping into the room, maybe twelve or thirteen years old. They glance at me and then ignore me, but not before stealing the remote. The TV clicks on, they start shouting, and it's a lot harder to concentrate.

I stand up and head back downstairs. I saw a couch in the living space outside the room where I'm staying. I'll study there.

Owen's in the kitchen talking to his uncle. He holds his wadded up shirt in his hands, sweat glistening on his abs and chest.

I stop walking and stare. He is every bit as sculpted as I imagined.

Jake notices me and smirks. I blink and shake myself out of my stupor.

"Hey, Cassandra," Jake says. "Owen's back."

Owen turns slightly and uses the wadded up shirt to wipe his face. "Hey, you," he says, a grin crossing his face.

"Hey, yourself," I answer.

"Aren't you going to give her a hug?" Jake teases.

"Not until I've showered." He snaps his sweaty shirt at me, and I draw back.

"Gross," I say.

He laughs and jogs upstairs.

"Boys too loud for you?" Jake asks.

"I'll study downstairs."

I get comfortable on the basement couch and immerse myself in Hamlet. There are two bedrooms down here and four beds, and I wonder how many kids Jake has. Steph has a friend over, and she and her sister and their friend come in and out of the living room at least seven times while I sit there. I have my laptop open, and I take notes for my essay as I read.

The couch wobbles, and Owen plops down upon it. I barely get my laptop out of the way before he drops his head in my lap. I run my hand over his buzzed head, giving into the desire I've had since yesterday.

"Did you have a good run?" I ask.

"Yeah. I hate running. But we do it a lot on the football field. So." He sits up and kisses me. Then he settles on the couch and takes my book from me. "How's Hamlet going?"

"About as well as you'd expect."

"How many different times and different ways can English majors analyze Hamlet before it's all been done and there's nothing new to discover?"

"Is this a mathematical equation? Because I suck at those."

He sets my book down and puts a hand on my shoulder, turning me so I face him. He kisses me again, opening my mouth with his, holding my face with his hand.

Steph and her friend dart in again, and they start giggling.

"Oops," Steph says.

Owen pulls back. "Move along, little cuz, nothing to see here."

"Can't we just go kiss somewhere?" I say.

"There's got to be somewhere in this big house where no one will find us." He takes my hand and pulls me up.

Steph's sister looks up at us from her bed when we poke our heads in her room. Owen waves and we move along. There's a pantry at the end of the hall filled to the brim with number ten size cans.

"We might fit in here," Owen says, pulling me in and closing the door.

We don't. He knocks over the top row when he moves his shoulders, and I can't stop laughing because when he tries to pull me close, he hits his head on a shelf.

"I knew that wasn't going to work," he says, and we exit the closet.

To find Monica and Dane standing in front of the couch peering down at my school supplies. They swivel when we come out.

"What were you—?" Dane begins, but Monica bursts into laughter.

"Cassandra left her stuff all over the couch," Owen says. "Rude."

"So rude." I go to pick it up.

"Owen," Monica says sweetly. She holds a set of house keys out. "I left my tennis shoes at my apartment. Would you go get them for me?"

"Can't one of your roommates bring them? You live ten minutes from here."

"My roommates have all gone home for Thanksgiving." She arches an eyebrow. Suggestively.

Owen takes the keys. "Cassandra," he barks.

"Yes, Owen?"

He glances at me and grins. "Come with me to retrieve my sister's shoes?"

"I will. Since you asked so nicely."

He laughs as we leave the house. "Ha!"

I can't believe Monica just provided us a place to be alone. "You still have my car keys?"

"Yep."

We get in my car, and he backs us out of the driveway.

We don't talk. The air between us is ripe with expectation.

He parks in front of Monica's apartment. It looks similar to mine, but she has a front door instead of a stairwell. Owen unlocks the door and turns on the light, flooding the small space of the entry way. He sets the keys on the counter, and I close the door.

"Want a drink?" he asks, moving around the kitchen counter. "Let's see what they have in the fridge."

I sit down at the bar. "I'll take water."

He opens a few cupboards before finding a glass. He pulls it down and fills it with water from the tap, then hands it to me.

"You been here before?" I ask.

He shakes his head. "No."

I take my water and wander into the living room. There's an armchair, a love seat, a couch, and a beanbag. Books and magazines clutter the coffee table. I set my water on the table and sit on the couch, then I pick up a magazine on photography.

Owen comes over with a brown glass bottle of root beer. He sits down beside me, and I touch the bottle.

"This reminds me of the first time I saw you drinking."

"I remember that. I think it was the first time I felt ashamed of it."

I take the bottle from him and set it on the coffee table. Then I cup my hands around his face and pull him to my level and kiss him. I run my tongue over his lips, then taste his mouth, sugary from his sip of soda.

We've both been waiting for this. He wraps his arms around my torso and lifts me up, pulling me into his lap. His mouth moves from my lips to my neck, and I reposition myself so my legs fall on either side of his thighs. He scoots to the edge of the couch, his hands on my butt, moving my hips, and I arch my neck, breathing hard, feeling him.

We are playing with fire and neither of us cares.

I have not felt this in so long.

I take the edge of his shirt and pull up, and he lifts his arms above his head so I can get it off. Finally, finally, I have access to this body I've wanted to touch.

I stand up. I know there are beds in this apartment. I take his hand and pull him up. I run my hands over his torso, across his nipples, watching how the skin puckers and tightens at my touch. He dips his head and catches my mouth, and his hands go around my back, pressing me against him.

I break the kiss and tug him down the hall. A smattering of pictures forms a collage on the first bedroom door, and I see Monica, Monica and her family, Monica and her friends. I hope this is her room. I flip on the light and step over a pile of clothes and a backpack lying on the floor. There's one bed tucked against the wall, and I beeline for it.

I'm not on birth control. We have no condoms. I've spent my whole life intending to wait until marriage.

But I want to have sex with him so very badly. I'm not doing anything to stop this.

It might happen.

I sit on the bed and pull Owen to me, and then I push him onto his back. I'm wearing a long turtleneck over black skinny jeans and a tank top under the turtleneck. I peel the turtleneck off, keeping my eyes on his. He watches my every movement. I undo my jeans and slide out of them one leg at a time, revealing my black briefs. Then I climb astride Owen again, wanting to take this slow but wanting to keep things moving also. He catches the back of my neck as I kiss him, and he groans against my mouth as I gyrate my hips over his.

"Cassandra," he breathes.

I silence his words. I sit back enough to find the buckle on his jeans and undo it, and then my fingers slide the zipper down. My heart's racing with adrenaline, and I'm nervous and excited because I've never gone this far before.

Owen stops me. His hand closes over mine. Then he rolls onto his side, taking me with him but breaking the connection between our bodies. He releases my hand and presses his palm to my temple, then runs his fingers through my hair.

"Cassandra, I need to tell you something," he says.

His tone is soft, but his voice is dead serious. And I know whatever he's about to tell me is going to change things.

The mood shifts immediately. I sit up and lean against the wall behind me, crossing my legs. I suddenly feel vulnerable and exposed in nothing but my tank top and underwear. I feel the weight of the necklace he gave me beneath the tank top.

He sits up also, the air between us entirely different.

"You are beautiful," he says.

My heart thrums too hard in my chest. I feel a bomb coming.

"And I love you."

"What is it, Owen?" I say. I snatch a pillow off the bed and pull it into my lap, concealing my legs, at least.

"I am not a virgin."

CHAPTER SEVENTY-FIVE

My Heart

His words are like a sucker punch to my gut. I've always suspected he was not. But he has defended his virginal status to my face, denying that he wasn't. So either something happened in the past three months—or he's been lying to me.

My heart stutters. I pleat my hands together and tell myself not to cry. This doesn't have to be relationship-ending.

"When?" I ask.

He stands up and paces the room, adjusts his pants.

"Go put your shirt on," I say. His toned torso is distracting me.

I pull my pants on while he's gone. It takes me a second longer, but I'm buttoning them up when he comes back.

He sits on the bed, matching my pose, sitting cross-legged in front of me.

"When?" I repeat.

"Our senior year of high school," he says, quietly. He doesn't meet my eyes.

"Were we together?"

"No." He shakes his head. "I never cheated on you."

"But you slept with someone." It's hard to describe how the irrefutable knowledge of something I've always suspected hurts. Stabs like a serrated knife. I clutch my hands together to hide their trembling.

"I did."

"While we were broken up?" A list of girls is flitting through my head.

"Before we got together."

That narrows the options. "I asked you."

"I lied."

"Lacey Gregg." Her name is asinine on my tongue.

He nods.

I exhale, and in spite of my attempt to stay stoic, when I blink, tears slide down my face.

I know this is not a big deal to the rest of the world.

But she has something of his that I will never have. I'm jealous, and I'm hurt.

"Why did you lie to me?"

"Because I wanted to pretend it didn't happen. And I didn't want you to think less of me. I was afraid I'd lose you." He adds, softer, "I know I still might."

I don't acknowledge that statement. "How did it happen?"

"It was at a party. I was drunk. Suzi and I got in a fight. I don't remember why, but I went into another room and wanted to hit something. Then the door opened, and Lacey came in." His eyes glance up to meet mine. "How much do you want to know?"

"You just decided to sleep with her?"

"I let it happen. She—" His speech slows. He shakes his head. He doesn't want to put images in my head, and I don't want them either, but I also want to know. I maintain eye contact, and he continues. "I stopped thinking. I was drunk and angry."

I know either one of those things is his kryptonite. Put them together, and you lose the rational person who is Owen.

"I realized what I'd done as soon as we finished. Like, I sobered up. Instantly. I was sick inside because, Cassandra, I never meant to do that. I've done a lot of things. I fooled around a lot. I've let girls go down on me, and I've done it to them. But that I was saving."

I know the sense of self-disappointment he felt because I've felt it before too. But my mind is conjuring images, images of Owen and Lacey, naked and sweaty and going at each other, of Suzi and the other cheerleaders giving Owen head, and the worst one, Owen between some girl's legs, eating her out.

I think I might be sick.

I stand up and push off the bed. I go to the bathroom and lock myself in it. I ball up on the toilet, put my face in my hands, and cry.

I'm not angry at Owen. He is not the same person he was a year ago when these things happened. But this knowledge tears me up.

I lean my head on the counter and sob. I cry until I'm hiccuping and there are no more tears. Owen doesn't come to the bathroom. A part of me wishes he would, but another part needs space.

I sit there in silence when I'm done crying, taking soft, gasping breaths every few minutes.

I will get over this. It doesn't affect the relationship Owen and I have now.

It only hurts this much because I love him. And I've left him out there alone, vulnerable in the face of his confession, not knowing what's in my heart.

I climb off the toilet. My necklace has come free of my tank top, and it swings over my neckline. I clasp it in my palm and catch a glimpse of my reflection.

I look terrible. My eyes are swollen and bloodshot. My nose is pink. Yesterday's mascara is streaked down my face and adhered to my cheeks with dried tears.

I take a towel off the shelf and wash my face. I press the cold, damp cloth into my eye sockets. It feels so good against my hot, throbbing eyes.

I'm freezing. There are goosebumps across my bare shoulders. I can't stop shaking. Maybe Monica's roommates turned the heat off before they left.

I open the door and step out and draw up short.

Owen is sitting in the hallway by the bathroom. His knees are drawn up to his chest, his arms resting over them. He looks up at me when I come out.

I crouch down beside him and place my hand on his arm. I lean forward and press my forehead to his.

"I love you," I whisper. "This changes nothing."

He gathers me into his arms and pulls me into his lap, cradling me to his chest. He kisses my eyes, my nose, my cheekbones, my temples, everywhere.

He's crying too.

꧁~·※·~꧂

We do not move from our spot in the hallway for a very, very long time.

He holds me, and I try not to, but I cry some more. He says nothing. Just pulls me in close, brushing the hair from my face and kissing my eyes.

I do not want to talk and he must sense that. So we don't. It's absolute silence, and as the minutes tick by, a calm descends over me. A peaceful reverence fills the space that held so much pain just moments before. I close my eyes and breathe. In and out.

A phone rings in the living room. I don't recognize the ringtone, so it must be Owen's.

He doesn't get up.

I lift my hand and run my finger over the collar of his shirt. I trace the bony ridge of his shoulders through the fabric, the line of his collar bone. The sexual hunger that nearly consumed me earlier is gone. Whatever has happened here has filled that need for intimacy.

I rest my head on his chest and listen to his heart beating above his ribcage. His heart rate still sounds elevated, but strong, steady.

The phone rings again. Owen still doesn't move, and I think he won't. He will stay here as long as he thinks I need to.

I'm not sure how long we've been in this apartment, but it's been at least an hour. Maybe two. I stir, lifting my head and twisting my legs so they fall from his lap.

He grabs me before I can stand. He crushes me to him, pressing his face into my hair.

"Do you love me?" I whisper. Just because I need to hear it. My soul needs to hear those words.

He squeezes me so tight I'm afraid he'll break a rib. "You are my heart," he breathes into my ear.

My breath shudders, and I dig my hands into his shirt.

I will not live my life without this boy.

I'm determined. He is mine. He will always be.

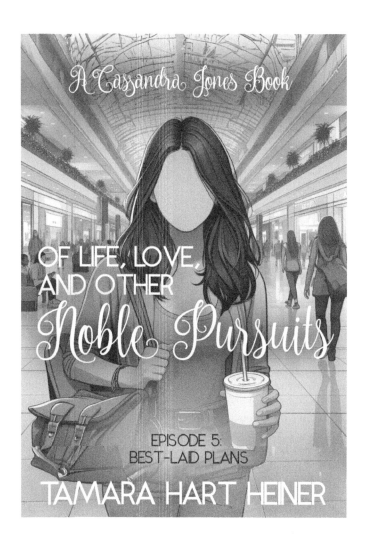

A Cassandra Jones Book

OF LIFE, LOVE,
AND OTHER
Noble Pursuits

EPISODE 5:
BEST-LAID PLANS

TAMARA HART HEINER

CHAPTER SEVENTY-SIX

After the Confession

Owen and I can't stay at the apartment any longer. We've been missed. His sister starts blowing up his phone, and then she starts on mine when he doesn't answer. It's Thanksgiving tomorrow, and whatever's going on at the main house, the family wants us there.

We still don't talk. A tenuous peace hangs between us after Owen's confession. He cradles my hand and walks me to the car, then holds the door for me while I get in.

Monica gives me a side-eye when we walk into the house. I smile to disarm any fears, but I saw my face when we got out of the car. My eyes are still swollen and probably will be for several hours. Owen stays in the kitchen and immediately joins in a conversation with his uncle and cousins.

I go downstairs. My things are on the couch, shoved to a corner because a video game console has been set up and five kids spread out on the couch and floor, yelling and jabbing arms and thumbing buttons. I gather up my computer and book and return to the bedroom I share with Monica.

My heart feels as swollen as my eyes.

I climb up on the bed and pour myself into Hamlet.

Monica comes into the room. I don't look up. She walks over to the bed and stands on the bottom bunk so she rests her arms on my bed rail.

"Are you okay?"

"Yes."

"Did you guys fight?"

I shake my head. "No. We had a long talk, and I don't feel like talking anymore." I glance at Monica. "Sorry. Not trying to be rude."

She pats my arm. "I'm here for you, okay?"

Her compassion brings tears to my eyes. "Thank you."

I'm okay. I really am. But today was hard, and I won't tell anyone why. The things Owen shared with me are private. Intimate.

They hurt. But I also feel closer to him.

And it dawns on me that was why I wanted to have sex with him. Because I wanted to feel closer to him.

Now I do.

He comes downstairs twenty minutes later. I hear his cousins yell at him, tell him to join their video game time.

"Maybe later," he says.

He enters the room. Like Monica, he stands on the lower bunk and looks over at me.

"Hey," he says.

"Hey," I answer.

He doesn't say anything, just watches me. I turn back to my book.

"Do you need any food? Lunch is out."

"I'm all right."

"Are you?"

I meet his eyes again and nod.

He touches my head, squeezes the top and runs his fingers through my hair. I grasp his wrist, turn his hand over, and kiss his palm. Then I let go.

He drops down from the bed and leaves the room.

I want to talk to Camila. I think she would understand my feelings.

I pull out my journal. I always bring it even though I don't write that often. Now I uncap my pen and scribble a few words.

This trip has not gone the way I expected. In some ways it has been much more than I hoped.

I've also learned some things that have hurt me more than I thought they could.

One thing I do know is Owen continues to be the person I want in my life.

Owen comes back half an hour later.

"My uncle's putting on a movie in the den. Everyone's going to watch. Will you come?"

"Yes." I close my book and climb down the ladder. "I should get some food, too."

"There's tons of it."

The house feels empty now that the inhabitants are congregated upstairs in the den. Sandwich fixings and lemon bars are set out on the island in the kitchen. I have no appetite, which I recognize as a sign of emotional distress. I put a sandwich together because I know I need the calories. Owen waits for me, then he leads the way to the den.

The room trembles with surround sound as a dinosaur movie plays across the screen. The couches are taken, but several blankets and bean bags dot the floor to make more viewing space. Owen sits on a blanket in the corner and gestures me to join him. I do. He settles back against the couch. I stay upright, picking at my sandwich, managing a few bites before putting the paper plate aside. Then I lean back and snuggle into his side.

He puts an arm around me and pulls me in close. His fingers trace small circles on my arm, near my elbow. I remember the first time I told him I loved him. We were at a basketball game and I wrote it on his arm with my finger. He never knew what I was doing.

I wish I would have told him. When he found out I'd been talking to Tiago, he thought it meant I didn't love him.

He shifts slightly, enough to press a kiss to my temple.

The movie finishes, and Jake suggests going to the local gym to play basketball and volleyball. I'm not into sports at all, but Monica convinces me to come along.

"Bring your school work," she says. "You can work on it while we play."

"All right," I say.

Of course the whole family is blessed with athleticism. I sit on the bleachers, wishing for a cushioned chair, and type on my essay. Monica is taller than half the boys and just as fast. I watch her and Owen in between typing. Basketball is boring, but the way they shout and cheer is amusing.

They take a water break half an hour into it, and Owen climbs the bleachers beside me.

"I'm going to have to take another shower," he says, wiping sweat from his brow.

The only witty comebacks I can think of are sexual, and anything sexual makes my swollen heart ache at the moment, so I steer clear. Instead, I say, "Remember the basketball game we went to together?"

"At Homecoming?"

"No. We didn't go together at Homecoming."

"You sat with my family and I sat by you when it was over."

"They invited me to join them. You came over after you'd safely dismissed your girlfriend."

He waves a hand. "Minor details. And she was just a date."

I roll my eyes. "Minor detail."

"So you mean the one when you and the girls met us at the game."

"Yeah, that one." I'd gone out with the girls from his group and we'd gotten our nails done. A complete waste of money, but I was making an effort to fit in.

"I remember it." He rests his elbows on his knees and looks at me, waiting for me to continue.

"Do you know that's the first time I told you I love you?"

His eyes crinkle slightly as he gives a smile. "No, you didn't."

"I did."

"I would remember."

I hold my hand out. "Give me your arm."

He does so. I turn it over and use my finger to spell letters across the flesh of his forearm.

I L O V

"Ah," he says, softly. "I remember you doing that."

I look at him beneath my lashes and finish writing. He holds still.

E Y O U O W E N

"I thought you were scribbling nonsense," he says.

"I was afraid of my feelings," I say. "I wanted you to know. But I was afraid to

424

tell you."

"Fear holds us back a lot," he says.

"It tries to keep us safe," I say.

"Owen!" Jake says. "We're ready to play again!"

He climbs down, and I return to my essay.

We will talk more. I feel it. But the talks will not be so heavy now.

⁂

The house smells like pie when we return. I haven't seen much of Jake's wife, Liz, but she's in the kitchen at the moment, and she smiles before disappearing into her bedroom in the back of the house.

"Mom doesn't like crowds," Steph says.

"Is it all right that we're here?" I ask.

"Sure, she likes family."

I'm not family. I choose not to point that out.

Jake orders pizza and starts the next Jurassic Park movie. I work on my essay while we watch it, glad that I'll be able to finish this by the time we go back to school.

After that they start another movie, but I'm bored with TV and go downstairs. It's quiet and peaceful. I lay down on the couch with a novel and lose myself in a fictional science-fantasy plot.

Monica goes into the room and changes for bed, then comes out with a deck of cards.

"Let's play," she says, sitting across from me and shuffling cards.

I've gotten better at card games because we do them at work a lot. I put my book away. I came here to spend time with Monica, and we haven't talked much at all.

"How is school?" she asks as she deals. "Getting easier?"

"I've accepted the fact that I will never have straight As again, if that's what you mean."

We laugh. Laughter is good for my heart.

"How's Stirling?" There's a mischievous twist to her mouth when she asks.

I examine my cards and choose one to play. "Who's Stirling?"

She smirks.

"He's fine," I say. "We went to a dance together last weekend." Feels like a lifetime ago. "Want to see pictures?"

"Yes."

We put the cards down and I show pictures from the dance. I point out my roommates and their dates, and I feel a twinge of guilt when I see Jared.

There was something developing there. But I don't feel it now.

"Stirling doesn't look half bad," she says. "But you're adorable."

"We called Stirling Grandpa," I say.

"Poor guy! You should show Owen."

"I'm not that mean. What about you? Managed to narrow it down to just one boy yet?"

"Why would I do that? Having options is more fun."

425

"I guess that depends on the person." I'd be happy to date only one person the rest of my life. Depending who it is.

I expect her to ask questions about Owen, but she doesn't. And for once, I appreciate that.

We play several rounds until the movie ends and people come down the stairs to go to bed. I change into my pajamas, comfortable peach lounge pants and a matching T-shirt. When I come out of the room, Owen's joined Monica on the couch. They're talking quietly but it doesn't seem like a private conversation. I fall in on the other side of Owen and tuck my feet under me, then pull out my book and read.

They're talking about their parents. I don't pay attention but catch bits here and there. I already know his parents have a troubled relationship. Owen's anger issues come from his dad, but he's aware, and he's been making a serious effort to regulate his emotions while he's still young.

"I hope you're not too bored here, Cassandra," Monica says. "Tomorrow we're just watching movies and eating."

"Sounds like a nice break," I say.

"But Friday we're going shopping!" She claps her hands and elbows Owen. "You have to come."

"Yay," he says, swirling his finger like it's a miniature flag. "Can't wait."

I echo his sentiment. I don't have money and shopping is a waste of time. But I'll go.

Monica stands up, placing a hand on Owen's shoulder. "I'm off to bed. See you guys later."

"Night," I say, not looking up.

"Night," Owen says.

The bedroom door clicks shut behind her as she leaves us alone in the sitting room.

CHAPTER SEVENTY-SEVEN

Day of Thanks

Owen's hand falls on my knee, and I put my book down. He scoots me closer to him, then pulls me in next to him. I feel his need to talk. To clarify things, to gauge where I stand. I rest my head on his shoulder and wait.

But he doesn't seem to know how to get started. We sit in a somber silence for at least ten minutes before I speak.

"When did you know you loved me?"

His hand tightens around my arm. He thinks about it a long moment. "I loved you from the first time I kissed you."

It's a cheesy answer. I sit up and dig my knuckle into his ribs. "No, you did not."

"Ow." He laughs and shoves my hand away. "I did. Maybe I loved you before then. I knew kissing you would cement the deal and I should absolutely avoid you at all cost."

"You did not love me then. You were interested in me. Getting to know me."

"There was another time you told me you loved me. Before the basketball game."

"I did?" I squint at him. "When?"

"At a church dance. Life was sucking hard at the time, and I was leaving because I felt like church and churchy people weren't my crowd. You came over and put your arms around my neck and said, 'I love you.'"

I smile as the memory comes back. "Yes. I remember."

"You startled me. Here I was feeling like no one cared, and then you out of the blue tell me you love me. And that's when I fell for you."

"What did you say back to me?"

"I don't know. I don't remember. What I remember is the sudden realization that I could love you."

I take his hand and weave our fingers together. "But when did you *know* you loved me?"

"At your Christmas recital."

"Really? Was it the crutches that did it, or the bulky pants I wore to get past my cast?"

"The crutches. I knew I needed them in my life."

I laugh. The knot in my chest unravels, coils of tension unspooling and rolling away. "Tell me."

He pulls me back into his side. "I felt something when I watched you. Something I'd never felt before."

It's fun to remember. To replay the night of my recital and realize Owen was falling in love with me.

"I didn't know I was falling in love with you," I say slowly. "Every day I felt closer to you. Happier with you. More excited by life because you were in it. I thought it was just fun. And then one day I realized it was past that point. That piece by piece, I'd given my heart to you."

"When did you realize?"

"I was practicing for the part of Maria in *West Side Story*. I could relate to her, feel what it felt like to fall in love with a boy who was so different from her and yet completed her, perfected her. And in the middle of this, I knew I could relate to her because it's what I had done."

"I should have told you about Lacey," he says, his voice going softer. "I'm sorry."

He should have told me, especially when I asked. His deception, though understandable, leaves me feeling uncertain and vulnerable. But he's not the only one who's lied before.

"What happened between you and Lacey after?" I ask.

"Nothing, absolutely nothing. I was disgusted with myself and angry with her. I told her to go away and I never, ever spoke a word to her again."

I'm less jealous of her in that moment. I imagined that being his first would make me special, someone who always had meaning to him. I see that's not necessarily the case.

"Have you slept with anyone else?" I ask this question very quietly. I'm quite afraid of the answer.

"She's the only one. It was one time. That's it."

I swivel on the couch, wrapping my arms around my knees and tucking my chin into the space between them. I face him. "I need to know I can trust you," I say. "I need to trust that whatever words come out of your mouth, they're the truth."

He blinks at me. "It guts me that you have to say that. I swear to you I've not ever lied about anything else."

"I've lied too, and I nearly lost you over it. We have to be honest with each other."

"I didn't know how to tell you, Cass, especially after you asked me and I flat out lied to you. But I felt it between us, I felt the lie hiding in every conversation, sneaking in every time we made out, and I knew any closeness between us would be fake if I didn't tell you about it."

Closeness between us . . . "You mean sex?"

His hand squeezes my arm. "I could not sleep with you with that secret between us."

The heated moments of earlier flash through my mind, and my skin grows hot at the mere memory. "Were you willing to have sex?"

He exhales and rolls his head back to look at the ceiling. "Every part of my body was screaming yes."

His secret saved my virginity today.

"What if we had?" I ask. "Would you think less of me?"

"God, no." He cups my face and kisses me, a quick, hard press of the lips. "And I wasn't swearing. That was a prayer. So God knows how I feel for you." He looks heavenward and makes the sign of the cross.

"Owen." I roll my eyes and giggle. Even in a serious discussion he can't stay serious. "We're not Catholic."

"Oh. Right. No. I would not think less of you."

"Would you love me more?"

He hesitates. "I don't know if I can love you more than I do. But I would not be able to walk away from you." He meets my eyes. "I don't know if I'd be able to leave you."

I furrow my brow, not sure I understand. "You mean, go back to Louisiana?"

"Yes. I mean go back to Louisiana. I mean go on a mission. I mean live life without you next to me."

I suck in a breath and realize how close I came to changing the course of Owen's life. And not necessarily for the better. I don't care if he changes schools. I want him to spend his life beside me.

But his mission. He's planned his whole life for it, and he's so close.

I will not ruin that.

"Well." I take his hand and tuck myself back into his side. "Sex is just going to have to wait."

He snorts, and his body shakes with laughter beside me. I smile, and I'm content. We are closer than we've ever been. I know exactly where my place is.

⟶◦⟵

Soul fire

The little fire in my heart
Fills my soul with sweet desire
And forces me to hold on
I knew I was right to believe
I never want to let go
The burning that began that day
Ran flickering through my spirit
And sent warmth across my body
The feeling has not gone away
White flames encompass me with heat
I surrender to the fire
Of his love, his beauty, his soul
Feeling my resistance retreat

I'm stronger with the fading night
As I calmly await the day
When the two souls meld into one
In a union of pure light

Thanksgiving day is less than exciting. We watch movies and eat all day.

I'm happy. I revolve around Owen whenever he's in a room, flitting near him, touching his back or his arm and then flitting away again. I like knowing he's here.

I overhear him talking about me with his uncle once. I'm not far from them, getting plates for the table with Steph while Jack and Owen carve the turkey. I'm not sure if they don't see me or if they think their voices are too quiet to overhear.

"Is it serious?" Jack says.

"It's really serious," Owen says.

"You're young, Owen. Take your time."

"We won't always be."

"So you think she's it?"

"She's it."

There's no doubt in Owen's voice. He's absolutely confident.

Liz joins us at the table for dinner, a small fair-haired woman with a pleasant smile. The food is fine but not as good as my mom's, and I'm filled with such nostalgia that I call my family and talk to all of them for more than an hour.

I try so hard to not speak about Owen the whole time that my mom asks, "How's Owen? Have things been weird?"

"No. Things are great."

"You haven't talked about him much."

I wish I could sit down with her and tell her everything. I would tell her more if I wasn't in Owen's uncle's house surrounded by his family. "I'm really happy with him. I'll tell you more at Christmas."

"Three weeks away!" she says.

Mom is far more excited for me to come home than I am. But I do miss them.

I sit on the couch and text all my friends. Harper, Riley. Abby, Iris, Camila, Layne, Jordan. For hours I sit there, carrying on multiple conversations, laughing as they share stories of what's happening around them. Owen comes over for a few minutes and tries to read the conversations, but I hide them from him.

They all want to know about him.

Things are great, I say with a devilish smiley face.

I reveal nothing more.

Stirling also texts, and we exchange pleasantries.

And then Jared texts.

Happy Thanksgiving! he says. *How are things going?*

Guilt churns like an undigested corndog in my gut. I have half the mind to ignore him. But that feels wrong. So I respond.

Me: Happy Thanksgiving! Hope it's a good one!

I ask no questions and I don't answer his and I pray he gets the hint.

He must, because he doesn't text again.

And that makes me feel bad also.

We watch more movies and eat more pie and I go to bed early because I don't think my stomach can handle any more. Owen finds me there and he says goodnight and kisses my cheek and leaves.

It's the only kissing we've done all day.

And it's very, very okay.

CHAPTER SEVENTY-EIGHT

What Next?

Monica shakes me awake when it is still dark outside.

"Cassandra," she whispered. "Time to get up. Liz wants to go Black Friday shopping."

What insanity is this? I roll over and peek out the blinds. Everything is dark. I check my phone.

"It's five-thirty in the morning!" I hiss.

"I know. But the mall opens at six, it's an hour away, and Liz says people will be lining up already."

"Have you done this before?"

"No."

"Nobody does this!" I'm cranky from waking early, but the irritation is waking me up.

"Liz goes every year. It's her tradition."

Monica says it apologetically. I relent. I can't be this sour when I'm a guest.

"This is why online shopping exists!" I grumble. I climb down the ladder, and Monica laughs at me.

It's freezing outside. I stand in the driveway shaking in my jacket over my sweater and jeans, waiting as Liz scrapes the ice from the windshield. Owen slides an arm around me, and I whisper, "This is the stupidest tradition ever."

He kisses my temple.

I fall asleep against him in the car.

I wake an hour later when we pull into the parking lot. I'm much more rested and not nearly so grumpy.

Liz turns to us in the car. "Let's meet back here at three. You have the day to yourselves!"

Liz's kids jet out.

"What store do you want to go to first?" Monica asks me, leading the way inside.

"Did you and I ever go shopping together?" I ask her.

"Only if you were working and I was shopping at your store."

"There might be a reason behind that."

She considers that statement, then says, "You only like shopping if you're working?"

"I only go shopping if I'm working."

Owen strolls along beside us, his hands in his pockets, and he laughs.

"Why? There's lots of sales. You can find new clothes, Christmas presents, things you didn't know you want," Monica says.

"Yeah, I'll look around." I can't explain to her that I don't like spending money on trivial things. I don't have enough of it to waste like that. "You don't have to wait for me."

"But it's not as much fun to shop by myself."

I wrinkle my nose. "I'm not fun to shop with."

She's not listening, though, because she spotted a friend. "Megan!" She turns to me. "Well, if you're sure. Text me if you want to meet up for lunch."

I nod, and she hurries to catch up with her friend.

Where's Owen? I spin around and spot him by the mall directory. He glances my direction.

"Come on," he says, removing a hand from his pocket to take mine. "I know a place you'll like."

I'm intrigued. I let him lead me along willingly.

And then I laugh when we stop in front of a pet store. "Of course."

"They've got fish." He points to a row of aquariums.

I start toward them and then notice the open kennels at my thighs. "Puppies!" I bend over and scoop one up. It whines and whimpers as I push my face against the fluffy, loopy ear.

"I don't think you're supposed to pick them up," Owen says. "See, there's a sign here—"

I put the puppy down and pick up another, crooning as I scratch behind its ear. "Oh, sweet thing! What a doll you are!" I give Owen a frosty look. "You were saying?"

"Nothing. Nothing at all."

I move past the puppies to the next open kennel. This one has floppy-eared bunnies. They run from me when I reach in, but there is nowhere to go except on top of each other, so I capture one easily. I nuzzle it, hug it, and put it down for another.

"Do you have to touch them all?" Owen asks. There's no concealing the laughter in his voice.

I pretend he's not there. "What are you guys?" I murmur, moving on to the next kennel. I do not recognize the animals with round bodies and ears like a giant mouse. I step back to read the sign. "Chinchillas." I touch one, and it squirms away.

I gasp. "You are freaking adorable!" It squeaks and squeals but I pick it up anyway.

"There's no escape," Owen says. "Resistance is futile. Accept your fate, little chinchilla."

I laugh. "He's so soft! Pet him!"

I hold him out, and Owen obliges.

"Yep. Soft." He lowers his voice and says, "Worker incoming. You should probably put it down."

"Fine." I put the critter down and move onto the reptiles, pretending like I hadn't just been holding animals illegally.

"Want to hold those too?" Owen asks.

"I'll pass. Did you know I was bit by a snake once?"

"I did not."

"Yep. Spent a week in the hospital."

"I got a splinter once. Cried for a week."

"Owen!" He's impossible. I can't stop laughing.

I move on to the fish. They are so big and beautiful but I know my fish tank has reached capacity. "How are your friends from high school? Do you still talk to them?"

"I talk to Aiden. That's it, mostly."

"How's he?"

"Eh." Owen lifts a shoulder and shrugs. "I guess doing all right. Acting about the same as my roommates. Drinking and carrying on like there's no tomorrow."

I turn around and hug him, just because I can, because he's here and I'm here. I wrap my arms around his torso and squeeze, and he squeezes me back.

I'm so glad he's who he is.

"What about Farrah and Tyler?" he asks when I let go. He keeps one hand at the base of my neck, his fingers rubbing the skin that stretches from shoulder to shoulder. "They still together?"

I shrug. "I don't know," I admit. "Farrah and I haven't stayed in touch."

He makes a face. "She was always a bit odd."

"She was your friend."

"Well, if we're being honest—she annoyed the crap out of me."

"She did not."

"Yeah, she did. I always felt like she was trying to get attention. I didn't tell you because she was your friend. But I thought she was weird."

"Farrah is unique," I agree. I move on to the next tank. "These are newts and salamanders! What do you think of salamanders?"

"Like, would I eat one? Or is it good hunting bait?"

"For a pet!"

He lifts both eyebrows and looks at me like he thinks I'm crazy. "Go for the gator."

⌒〜✺〜⌒

I have a super long drive on Sunday.

We leave before church. Owen's flight isn't until five, but it's an eight-hour drive back to the Denver airport. Monica packs granola bars and sandwiches for us so we don't have to stop, and then she hugs us.

"I love you," she tells me. "I hope I'll see you soon."

"Me too." I squeeze her hands.

We say goodbye to everyone, and then we leave.

Owen tries to talk me out of taking him for the first hour of our drive.

"I didn't think about how you'd have to take me to the airport and then drive home," he says. "You'll be driving all day."

"It's fine. I'll have good company for the first eight hours, at least."

"We can go to your apartment, and then I can call a taxi or something."

"For a three-hour drive?" I give him a scornful look. "It would cost more than your flight. I got this, Owen."

"All right," he says, giving up.

The last two days have been perfect. Filled with absolute nothingness. We've spent nearly every moment together, always touching, always close. We've kissed but we haven't made out, none of that tear-off-your-clothing desperation that I felt the first two days.

But now, as I drive him toward his place of departure, I feel an apprehension creeping back over my shoulders.

We're about to separate again. And we haven't talked about it.

I don't want to talk about it.

I turn on the radio and sing to old country songs that remind me of high school.

But now it's all I can think about.

The radio keeps playing but I'm in my head.

"What are you thinking?"

"Hmm?" I glance at him. He's watching me.

"You have that look." He reaches over and touches the skin between my brows. "Here." He touches the corner of my mouth. "And here. You're thinking."

"My face does not show all that."

"Yes it does."

I consider my answer. "What happens between us now, Owen?"

I glance at him to see him press his lips together and face forward.

"It was really hard to be away from you," he says.

I bob my head. "Yes. It was." I was lonely. Confused. Aching.

All. The. Time.

"I made a mistake in letting you go."

I steal a quick glance at him. "What do you mean?"

"I should have changed schools. I should have gone to Colorado with you." He exhales and scrubs his face with his hands.

"Why didn't you?"

I don't mean to ask, but the question has been eating at me all semester. "I mean, it's my fault. I know that. I screwed up, talking to another guy. But—couldn't you forgive me? Couldn't you put faith in us again?" The words come out riddled with more resentment than I intend. But this has bothered me.

"Yes. I should have. I—" He shakes his head. "I'm not saying this to make you feel bad, but you hurt me. Really bad. I tried so hard to get over you. That's why I dated Kristin so fast. Even after we got back together, a part of me was scared to get too close. I figured I would at least keep you at a distance. So you couldn't have that power over me again."

I know he's not trying to hurt me, but he is. I was wrong, and I know it, and I'm grateful that he let me back in his life as much as he did. "Okay," I say, my throat tight. "I'm sorry. It's my fault." I regret asking. I knew the answer already. "It is what it is, then. We're apart. We deal with it."

Silence falls between us, but it's tinged with pain. Owen holds onto the handle bar above his head and stares out the window. I watch the road. I turn the radio up, at least filling the space with noise.

He reaches over and turns it off. "Listen to me. We all screw up sometimes. Yeah, you did, and I got hurt, but the bigger mistake was mine. And that was never more clear to me than three days ago when I ripped your heart out because I hid something from you, and what did you do? You took about half an hour to clean up your own pain before you came out to comfort me. To make sure I was okay. Because you, Cassandra Jones, are the most amazing woman in the whole world, and I knew that, but I was so stuck in my own pain I couldn't see my way out enough to fix things for both of us. And that's my screw up. I screwed up, dammit, and that's why we're not together. It's not because of you. Do you hear me? This is not your fault."

He's angry, but it's a kind of angry I haven't heard before. He's perfectly in control. But he also wants to be understood.

"I hear you," I say, and my eyes fill with tears.

"Why are you crying?" he asks, his voice softer now.

I shake my head.

"Pull over," he says.

I find a wide shoulder on this country road and pull to the right. Owen unbuckles his seatbelt, and I've barely put the car in park before mine unclicks also. Then he pulls me into a hug.

"What?" he asks. "What did I do?"

"It's me," I say, and I pull back, wiping at my eyes.

"What's you?"

"This. Us. All of it. I can't explain it."

"Spit it out. Don't try to censor it."

So I do, letting out a rush of emotions in verbal vomit. "I've been angry. I was angry at you for not coming with me. For letting space come between us. But mostly I was so angry with myself for losing you. You are—" I'm sobbing, fighting for breath. "The piece of me I didn't know I needed. You are my other half. And you left me." I choke on my words. "Because of what I did. You made me feel not good enough—I believed I wasn't good enough—that you didn't love me as much, that you didn't believe in our love—that I ruined it. And every time I hurt, every time I ached, every time I missed you, I reminded myself that I didn't deserve you—that I did this. And that you—you would rather wait and see than take another chance on me."

Feelings I've allowed to fester deep inside boil out, overflowing in the car, running down my cheeks, and for the second time in a week I'm crying so hard I can't breathe.

He grabs me and holds me close and I sob. At least this time I'm not alone in the bathroom.

"I'm okay." I wipe my eyes and pull away. "I'm fine." I turn back to the steering wheel. "We need to go."

"Let me drive."

I shake my head. I need something to focus on. "I got it."

I pull back onto the highway. I feel a bit lighter. That heaviness had been weighing me down since March. Now it's out.

"I don't think I ever apologized to you for how things went down when we broke up," he says.

"Don't, Owen. I know what I did."

"We could have fixed us right then, Cassandra. You didn't cheat on me. You weren't in love with another boy. I thought you did and I thought you were, and I'm such a stupid idiot. If I would have stepped out of myself long enough to listen to you—"

He stops talking, but I'm already filling the silence, on a roll, airing out my own hurts and grievances.

"We missed prom," I say. "Our senior year, our chance to go together. We had it planned. Instead you took another girl. Mere days after breaking up with me. You asked another girl!" I slam my hand down on the steering wheel. "It would have hurt less if you'd slapped me in the face and called me a whore in front of the whole school. And she wasn't 'just a date.' You kissed her. You liked her. Maybe you did more than that with her." That one's a low jab, and my face flames for it, but I keep going. "We missed senior showcase and senior assembly and graduation and every opportunity in between to be together. Instead I was alone. Paying my penance. And believing I deserved it."

"You didn't deserve it," he says quietly.

I'm not done. "And then, by some miracle you decided to take me back. I'm not so terribly unworthy." I don't know where all the anger is coming from, but it turns out I'm bitter after all. Jared was right about me. "At least, worthy enough to date, but not someone to build a future with. I lost that. All because I texted 'I love you' to a boy who was nothing more than a friend. I lost you—" a sob breaks out again. "I watched my future crumble to dust because of my mistake." I say the last word hotly, letting the "k" resonate in the air.

Neither of us speaks for a long moment. I'm sobbing, trying to catch my breath. He's probably waiting to see if I'm done. I can probably think of more.

"Cassandra, I—" He breaks off, shakes his head, and tries again. "Why didn't you tell me you felt this way?"

"Well, some of it I didn't know until just now." I give a short, watery laugh. "The rest of it, I was just so grateful for what you gave me—so grateful to be a part of your life. To have whatever part you wanted to give me. I put my own feelings aside."

I exhale and stop. I've said more than enough.

"I don't know what to say. Except, I'm sorry. I'm really sorry." He touches my leg, then runs his fingers along my scalp, tucking a piece of hair behind my ear. I shake my head, pulling away from him. "You never should have carried that."

"I'm figuring that out." I sniff and nod.

"What did you mean about your future? Watching it crumble to dust?"

Now my face warms. Owen never, not ever, made promises about the future. But when he said he was coming to Colorado, when he asked if he could be with me during our college years, I made presumptions.

"I thought we'd be together through college," I admit.

"What about the mission?"

I lift one shoulder. "In my mind, we would spend freshman year together. Then you would go on your mission, I would go on mine, and we would see each other when we got back. I did not think we would break up. Ever."

"Did you want that?"

I cast him an incredulous look. "I love you. Why would I want anything else?"

"What if there is a better person out there for you?"

I growl deep in my throat. "Say something like that again and you're walking back to Colorado."

He laughs, and the sound almost makes me smile. Then he exhales.

"I want you to know—and I want you to try to understand—that the mistakes I made with you stem from fear. You make me weak. The thought of losing you turns me into a terrified toddler."

I'm listening to him. I hear the vulnerability in his voice.

"I am helpless when it comes to what I feel for you."

"I feel the same, Owen," I say.

"Do you remember our first kiss?"

I laugh, startled by the subject change and also the stupidity of the question. "Do you?"

"Yes. It was outside the church building. Before Bible study."

"Good job."

"Do you remember what I said to you?"

Like it was yesterday. "I do."

"What was it?"

"You told me you couldn't get involved with me because you would give me everything but I wouldn't give it in return."

"And do you remember when I called you a siren?"

"Yes."

"What does a siren do?"

"Lures men to their deaths by singing them into the ocean and drowning them," I say, bemused. "Are you worried I'm going to drown you?"

"I knew if I started dating you, it wasn't going to be a casual fling. Not with you. It's not possible. Because you're a siren. Any boy who loves you will never be the same. No matter how we try to break free, you have us in your clutches."

"In my fins?" I joke.

"Yeah."

"Should I be flattered or offended?"

"What I'm saying is—" he pauses. "I am saying something here."

"I'd love to know what it is."

"Don't make any more boys fall in love with you."

I sputter out a laugh. "That's your point?"

"No."

"Then what is?"

"That I'm going to marry you," he says, quietly, and it stops my laughter. "Not now. But I will. And then I won't have to worry about losing my soul to you anymore. I'll give it to you."

CHAPTER SEVENTY-NINE
The Proposal

I can't joke about what Owen said.

It is everything I ever wanted. Everything I ever hoped for.

"When?" I ask, my heart beating so hard in my chest I fear I'll have a heart attack.

"Someday. After my mission. When we have a little more school, a little more life behind us."

There's plenty of time in there to change his mind. But the words offer me the hope of a future, the hope of commitment, the hope of being together that I thought I'd lost.

More than a hope. An expectation.

I want to hold this burning light in my heart. Let it warm me. Pray nothing extinguishes it.

The conversation dwindles because I don't want to talk. The hours fly by as I replay the past few days moment by moment in my mind, starting with the car ride down to Utah.

Owen loves me enough to want to marry me. To imagine a life with me. Only me, forever.

I take his hand and squeeze his fingers.

He lets me for all of two seconds. "Two hands on the wheel. Always."

"I'm not a wannabe stunt driver like you. I'm safe with one hand."

He gives me a look of insufferable patience.

"Fine." I put both hands on the wheel. We're nearing the exit to my campus. I check the time. "Want to see if my roommates are home? I'd love for you to meet Iris."

"Sure."

I let us in the back door off the stairwell, and we walk right into the kitchen with five, six, seven people in it. It's Sunday afternoon and they are all home. Along with the parade of boys Layne brings over from church.

I should have expected that.

"Hello!" I say, hauling Owen in behind me. "I'm on my way to the airport with Owen, and we thought we'd stop by and say hi."

Layne, Brant, and Jared are on the couch. Iris, Justin, and Gary are sitting at the table, drinking sodas and watching the fish tank. Camila is at the sink, doing dishes. All seven heads turn toward us.

"Owen!" Camila drops the dishes and crosses to him, giving him a big hug. "So great to see you! Did you have a nice time?"

"Great to see you too." His smile is genuine as he hugs her back. "I think we did."

"You're giving hugs?" Layne stands up and hugs Owen also. I roll my eyes and make sure Owen sees. "Wow, nice biceps."

Brant scowls.

"This is the famous Owen, huh?" Iris says. She smiles big and holds out a hand.

"You're Iris." He bypasses her hand and wraps her up in a hug. "I've heard all about you."

Her face flushes pink. Out of the corner of my eye, I see Justin mouthing at Jared, "Who's Owen?"

I turn, heat creeping up my neck. I will owe Jared an explanation.

But he's already risen from his chair. He offers his hand to Owen. "You must be the football player from LSU."

I'm ashamed, and I hope my face isn't bright red.

"Yeah." Owen takes his hand and gives it a mighty shake. "You are?"

"Jared. I play for Preston Y."

"Hey, that's great!" Owen grins openly. He has no idea he's shaking hands with the enemy. "Maybe I'll play you sometime."

Jared smiles. It's friendly and shows no sign of malice, but I know I've hurt him. And I hate that. "Hey, that would be cool."

"And that's Justin, Gary, and Brant." I point them out, and they wave, but they don't feel inclined to greet Owen. "Well, that's all we have time for. See you guys in a few hours!"

I usher Owen back out the door, grateful for the cold winter air to cool my flaming face.

"I hoped to meet Abby," Owen says. "You talk so much about her."

"She'll be so sad she didn't meet you. But she's not my roommate."

"And no Stirling?"

I laugh as we climb in the car. "Stirling doesn't live on campus. He's twenty."

Owen raises an eyebrow and pulls his seatbelt on. "A bit old for you."

"That's why we call him Grandpa."

"How many of those guys have you gone on dates with?"

"I've hung out with all of them. I haven't actually gone on a date with any of them."

"What does hanging out entail?"

"A bunch of us went to the movies last weekend. Jared's gone with me to the pet store. A couple of us have gone over to Justin's aunt's place for pizza." And spent the night . . . but honesty doesn't require full disclosure of every detail.

Right?

"Do they come over a lot?"

"Have you met Layne?"

He laughs and bobs his head.

"Yeah. They come over all the time," I say.

He doesn't seem suspicious, and I grin, relieved.

"I'm actually not interested in dating anyone, Owen, and I tell that to any guy who acts interested. I want to hang out with people as friends. And I was saying that even before I knew I'd see you again."

"You were always going to see me again."

"I didn't know that. What I did know was I wasn't ready to move past you."

"Jared knew who I was. Is he one of the guys who acted interested?"

My face warms. I gave him a lot of information without meaning to. "Yes. He asked me why I didn't want to date anyone, and I told him I wasn't over my high school boyfriend. And apparently I told him a few things about you."

I shoot him a sidelong glance. We're not supposed to talk about this, but he's asking me questions, so I feel it's fair. "Did you date a lot?"

"No."

"Why not?"

"Didn't feel like it."

"Were there any girls that interested you?"

"Yes."

Ouch. Jealousy flares up, and I shove it down. "Why didn't you ask them out?"

"None of them were smart. They had small vocabularies."

I hide my smile. "Is that your checklist? Large vocabulary?"

"There's a few other things on it, but that's near the top."

"What else is on your list?"

"That's for me to know and you to wonder," he drawls.

Oh, and I want to know. "Tell me." I jab my knuckle into his thigh.

"You are abusive, woman." He pushes my hand away and moves his thigh so I can't reach him. "What's on your list?"

I have a list. It keeps changing. Some of the things on there are stupid, like being bilingual. Others are near the bottom but should be near the top, like able to control their temper.

"I'll tell you one thing from it."

"Ready."

"He has to make me laugh." I wonder if he'll remember.

"'I want to laugh with you every day for the rest of my life,'" he says, quoting word for word the cheesy line from my Valentine's Day card back at me.

I smile big at him. "You remember."

"That was the day I knew you loved me." He's got that serious look on his face again.

"That was my intention." I touch the necklace around my neck. The one he gave me that night. "That night was magical. Maybe the best night of my life." He, like me, had not told me he loved me. Not in so many words. But the way he talked to me, the way he looked at me, the way he touched me, I knew.

I knew Owen loved me. And I knew I loved him back.

He sits back in his seat and doesn't say anything else.

⟨ೲ⟩

"It's going to be close," I say when we're twenty minutes from the airport. "We'll be there forty minutes before your flight."

"That's plenty of time. I have no bag to check."

"If you'd been driving, I'm sure we'd be there by now."

"Like an hour ago."

I smile.

The terminal comes into view, and my heart thunders. I'm not ready for this.

"So, are you still mad at me?" he asks.

"What?" I wrinkle my nose, trying to watch the signs to the terminals. "Am I? Was I mad at you?"

"Yeah, it must have slipped your mind, but there was a major yelling-slash-crying fest where you told me off for being an insensitive jerk."

"Oh." I chuckle. "I didn't say all that."

"That's what I heard."

"I'm not mad at you. I wasn't really mad to begin with. Just sad. So sad." I furrow my brow, sad at the memory of how sad I'd been.

"But you're not sad now."

"No."

"So you're not mad either."

"No." I laugh again. "It's not fair. It's impossible to stay mad at you."

"I hate it when you're mad," he says. "But it's worse when you cry, especially if it's my fault."

"I cry a lot."

"I've noticed."

I slap his thigh. "It's usually your fault."

"I've noticed that too. I'm a jerk even when I try not to be."

I pull up to the curb, trying to smile as I park but in spite of his words, in spite of the feelings between us, I don't know what will happen when we go separate ways. I hop out of the car but forget my jacket. I wrap my arms around myself and go to his side of the car.

He pulls his backpack on and regards me as I stand there, shaking. I'm so cold. I'm so scared.

"Promise me," he says, his voice quiet, "that you won't fall in love."

"I promise," I say. It's an easy promise to give.

I won't. I can't. Not when I love Owen this much. There are no pieces left of my heart to give to someone else.

He folds me into his arms, holding me tight, momentarily stopping my shaking. "I am so sorry for everything," he whispers, his breath warm on my ear. "I love you." He pulls back, cups the back of my head, and presses his lips to mine, holding them for a solid three-second count before releasing me. "We will see each other soon. I promise."

He turns around and walks into the terminal without a backward glance. I watch until he fades from view, and then I get back into my car. I'm trembling all over. I turn up my heat and hold my hands in front of it.

My heart is aching. Already I miss him. Already I feel alone.

I am fifteen minutes from home when Owen calls me.

"Hello?" I say, putting it on speaker.

"Hey. I just landed in Louisiana."

I start laughing. "I'm not home yet."

"Dang. Takes you longer to get across a few cities than for me to get across the country."

"Totally not fair."

"Well, I wanted to tell you I'm here. Text me when you get home, okay?"

"All right."

"Listen. I know we're apart. And I know it sucks. I know sometimes it's harder to work at this than to let it go. But it's worth it, Cassandra."

"I know," I say. I don't remind him this isn't my first long-distance rodeo.

"Okay, so, goodnight. And I love you."

"Love you too, Owen."

I hang up.

I already hate this.

They are all in the kitchen when I walk in the door, every one of my roommates, doing a karaoke party. I'm relieved it's just them. No guys. The moment I walk in, they stop singing and embrace me a group hug. I pat their arms and hug them back, and they move away to let me breathe.

"So?" Layne says. "How were things with Owen?"

"Great." I can't hide my smile as I pull out a loaf of bread and the toaster. I ate Monica's sandwich three hours ago, and I'm hungry again. "Really, really great."

"I take it he still likes you?" she says.

"Um-hm." I drop my bread in the toaster. "Yes, I think so."

"Are you guys back together?" Iris asks.

"Yes. Yes, we are." Owen did say that, didn't he?

I should've asked him. Why do I need clarification?

"What about you guys?" I glance at them and then butter my toast. "Good Thanksgivings? Any new guys?"

"OMG, let me tell you about this guy back home," Layne says with a huge eye-roll.

I meet Iris and Camila's gazes over her shoulder, and they eye roll as well.

CHAPTER EIGHTY

Clearing the Air

I manage to keep everything to myself for the next hour while I hang with my roommates. Then I finally escape, citing that I need to finish my homework, and close myself in my room.

Camila comes in before I've shut the door.

"Tell me everything," she breathes, climbing onto her bed. "I kept thinking I'd get a text from you, but there was nothing until Thanksgiving Day, and then all you said was that things were good!"

I climb onto the bed beside her. "Camila, there was so much—I don't even know where to start! We talked, and talked, and talked, and we cleared the air, and everything's great between us."

"So you're doing the long-distance thing now?"

"Yes, kind of." I crinkle my nose. "I think so. I mean, he didn't say we're boyfriend and girlfriend, but he said we have to fight for what we have, and he didn't say not to date other people, but he did make me promise not to fall in love." I'm more uncertain as I speak. "We talked about everything. We had an eight-hour drive to Utah and an eight-hour drive back, and lots of time alone in the house to talk."

"Do you still love him?"

"Yes." I bite my lip as my feelings for Owen swell in my heart. "Camila, he told me some things he's done that really hurt me. That was a hard, hard day."

"What kinds of things?" Her eyes narrow like she thinks she might need to fight someone.

"Some things he did before we started dating. Sexual things."

"Was his conscience bothering him so much that he decided to tell you?"

Now my face warms. I lower my voice. "We almost had sex."

Both eyebrows go up. "How almost is almost?"

My pulse quickens at the memory. "I took my pants off. I was in the process of taking his off when he stopped me."

"Why did he stop you?"

"Because he felt guilty. He didn't feel like he could have sex with me when I didn't even know he'd slept with someone else."

"He just now told you?" Her voice is hushed.

"Even worse, I asked him specifically when we were dating, and he lied to me."

"How directly did you ask him?"

I flash back to that moment in his bedroom and give a harsh laugh. "I said, 'did you sleep with Lacey Gregg,' and he said, 'No.'"

"And now you found out he did." Camila puts her hand to her mouth. "I'm so sorry, Cassandra. What did you do?"

"Cried. A lot."

"It must have been hard to learn that about Owen, especially when Jared told you a few days ago he's never kissed a girl."

I suck in a breath. I've avoided thinking of that conversation. I don't want to compare Owen to Jared. I can't allow myself to think like that. "Jared's amazing. He'll be wonderful for some girl. But not for me. I love Owen."

"But if you didn't, you could love Jared."

"But I don't love Jared," I say, infuriated. "I don't even know him. He was just a stand-in for Owen because I couldn't have Owen."

I return to my bed, huffy. I'm frustrated now.

Owen needs to be here.

❧

Owen calls me before I go to bed. I sit down in the kitchen and curl up on the couch, but there's nowhere private to go. It's too cold to go outside, and there are groups of students congregating in the commons. But both Layne and Iris are piddling around in the kitchen. Camila's in our room. I keep my voice low as we talk, hoping no one overhears.

"You didn't text me when you got home," he says.

"Sorry. I forgot. But I'm here."

"I figured that out. You good?"

I can see every conversation turning into where I tell him how much I miss him and wish he was here.

I also think that would be incredibly dull for our relationship.

"Yeah. It's kind of weird. I was just with you, but I'm here, and it feels like last week was a dream."

"I know what you mean. But it wasn't. I can't stop thinking about you, about the things you said."

"Is this a good thing or a bad thing?"

"It's good. You should get angry at me more often. Your feelings are valid, but I'm not always aware of them until you tell me."

"I get angry at you a lot."

"But you hide it really well."

"I don't want to create a problem between us."

"There's no problem when you're telling me something I did wrong or something that hurt you. It doesn't help us when you mask your feelings and keep

446

them inside."

"Does it help to yell at you?" I murmur. Layne and Iris are talking, also in muted tones, so they don't bother me. But I still feel like this conversation is private.

"It does."

I want him to explain how it helps, but he doesn't say anything else. And then I want to beg him to come out here, but I'm half afraid he won't and I'll feel rejected and half afraid he will, uproot from LSU and transfer to Colorado in the middle of the school year, and then I'll feel guilty.

So I keep it to myself.

"What are you thinking?" he asks.

So many things. "I really enjoyed last week." A dozen more cheesy lines flit through my mind. I'm happiest when I'm with you. You're my best friend, my confidant. Nobody makes my soul rejoice like you do. Just knowing you are near makes my heart sing.

I don't say any of those things.

"When do you go home for Christmas?"

"In three weeks," I say.

"I'll come see you."

"You will?" It's more than I hoped for when we said goodbye in August.

"Check with your family, let me know what days are good. How long are you home?"

"Two weeks."

"That's a short break."

"I guess because they're trying to fit the whole semester in before break, and then winter semester finishes at the end of April."

"We'll figure it out. We'll see each other."

It's a promise, a reassurance, and it calms my heart. "Okay."

That was what upset me the most when I found out they were moving. I had counted on breaks to spend time with Owen.

Now I still would.

⊙⌒◈⌒◎

"Your midterm has been graded, we have one more exam this week, and then your final is next week before Christmas break. I recommend you study all of your exams to prepare for the final."

I hear Mr. Turnbaugh, but I'm doing my best to block him out and continue my whispered conversation with Abby.

"He says he's going to come up and see me at Christmas," I say in answer to her question.

"That's so amazing. I'm sorry I didn't get to meet him."

"He wanted to meet you also. I'm sure you'll get to chat."

I've filled all my friends in on what went down with Owen. Everyone is thrilled for me.

There is someone else I need to talk to, though. I dread any conversation between us, but I pull out my phone and text Jared.

Me: Hey, can you meet up sometime so we can talk?

He doesn't respond.

I don't stress out about the upcoming exam for physical science, and I only feel a little more apprehensive after English class when she reminds us our final paper for the personal narrative is due before the break. I am prepared.

But then I go to math class, and the next day, I go to my other English class and my religion class, and every single one of them has either a final paper, a test, or both.

I'm panicking now. I've never gone through finals before, and I understand why every college student dreads them.

It's a lot to get through before Christmas break.

These thoughts go through my head as I walk back to my dorm from the library Tuesday evening. I'm bundled up in my jacket, hood pulled low over my head, and I glance up to cross the street and see Jared moving toward me on the other side. I don't think he recognized me until the moment I looked up because he stops short when he sees me.

He never did respond to my text.

There's only one way to make this not awkward.

I put on a big smile and say, "Hi, Jared!" I have to yell to make sure my voice carries over the wind.

He smiles back, even if it looks a bit chagrined. "Hi."

"Do you have a minute?" I bob my head in the direction of the creamery two blocks away. "I wanted to talk to you. Want to get some ice cream?"

He gives a short laugh that almost sounds like a bark. "Is that how you're going to soften the blow?"

I work hard to keep my smile on my face, but my heart squeezes. I'm not sure what to say, so I say nothing.

"Yeah," he says, apparently deciding he's not going to rake me over the coals just yet. "I'll take you up on that."

He joins me on my side of the street, and we walk together toward the creamery. I search for any innocuous small talk that won't bring things back to the big painful topic between us. "Did you have a nice Thanksgiving?"

"I did. Justin's aunt is a terrific cook, and we watched movies and played games and ate enough food to induce cardiac arrest in an army for three days."

I glance over at him. "You don't look the worse for wear."

He lifts his shoulders almost to his ears. "Well, I still had football practice. Coach made sure no turkey or cranberries could slow us down."

"Of course."

But my mind has wandered to another football player. His coach is probably whipping him in shape also.

We walk in silence for a few more minutes. The wind slams into me, blowing my hair in my face and tickling my nose, creeping into the space between my head and my hood. I wish for a hat. I breathe a sigh of relief when Jared grabs the door to the creamery and opens it for us, and we are ushered into the warmth of the small store.

"What would you like?" I ask, pulling out my wallet. "My treat."

"I can buy my own."

"I know." I lift my eyes to his. I feel guilty. This is my apology. Let me do this. I hope my eyes express what I can't say.

He shrugs. "I got you next time."

That one sentence eliminates half my guilt. Whatever harm I've done to Jared, he doesn't hate me. He's even willing to go out to ice cream with me again in the future.

I want to hug him, but I refrain. He gets blueberry cheesecake in a waffle cone, and I get a pumpkin spice cup with hot fudge. Then we sit down at a table. I still dread the conversation in front of me, but I know it's going to be okay. "Excited to see your family in two weeks?" I ask.

"Yes. I've always been what you would call a mama's boy. We still talk on the phone a lot, but I can't wait to see her and tell her all about college."

There are so many great things about Jared. "I bet she's incredibly proud of you."

"Yeah, but now she's got my sister and they're spending all their time together. I don't think she misses me that much."

"I'm sure that's not true." I put a spoonful of ice cream in my mouth and relish the contrast between the smooth cold ice cream and the warm, bittersweet fudge. I lower my spoon, swallow, and say, "Jared, I'm sorry about Owen."

He shakes his head. "You don't have anything to apologize for."

I meet his eyes. "I know we didn't have anything official between us, but I definitely liked you. And I felt like something was growing between us."

"But you were fighting it the whole time. And now I understand why."

I bob my head in acknowledgment. "I knew I wasn't over Owen. I didn't know I was going to see him at Thanksgiving, though, and I really was trying to find a way to move past him."

"But now?"

"I'm not trying."

He gives a smile, and it's tinged with sadness, but it's also kind and warm. "I thought as much when I saw you two. I don't know what happened to make you want to move past him, if it was the distance or if you agreed to date other people, but I could tell whatever was going on between you and me was over."

I swallow, because somehow it still hurts to hear him say that. If I didn't have Owen, Jared is the kind of person I would want to date.

I don't say that. I don't think it will help.

"I never meant to hurt you or lead you on. I tried to be very honest in what I was feeling."

"I know, and I appreciate that. I think you're a heck of a girl, and Owen—I hope he knows how lucky he is."

I think of our conversations, of our embraces, of Owen's tender words to me. "I think he does. If it's not too weird for you, I would like it if we could stay friends." I look down at my ice cream as I speak, afraid he'll say no, knowing he has that right, and it might even be better for him, but also knowing it will hurt me if he does. Even if it's not what I want, I'll respect his answer, whatever it might be.

"I would love that."

I lift my eyes to meet his again, and this time we exchange a smile, and all the heaviness is gone from my heart. I plop back in my chair, holding my cup of ice cream in my hand.

"So you know." I take another spoonful of ice cream and then wave my spoon at him. "I have this roommate."

He laughs again.

Jared walks me back to my dorm and gives me a hug at the door. It's a friendly hug, but tinged with more, with the affection of two people who know they started to feel something for each other, but circumstances stopped it from progressing. It has a bit of an ache to it, but it's also very comforting.

I go up to my room, ready to tackle my assignments.

CHAPTER EIGHTY-ONE

Milk and Cookies

My throat starts to bother me the night before our Scandinavian Christmas concert.

I am neck-deep into studying for finals and finishing my personal narrative and I ignore it. Plus I have to work. I see Stirling at work but we don't talk, other than me telling him all the things I have to do in the next few days. Then he leaves me alone to concentrate on getting donations and homework.

But midway through the next day, I'm coughing and sneezing and I know I'm sick. The back of my neck aches and my eyelids feel made of lead. I want to curl up in a ball and sleep.

Instead, I meet Jordan on campus, me dressed in a long black skirt and him in a black button up shirt with black slacks, and we head to the concert hall.

We are not expecting a large audience, so the teacher reserved a small concert hall for us. But as soon as I step out to the raised platform, a loud cheer goes up from the crowd, and I hear my name.

"Cassandra!"

My name is punctuated by shouts and claps, and I raise my face, startled.

The entire front row is taken up by my roommates and friends. Even Stirling is there, wedged in beside Layne.

I told them about my concert, of course, but only to mention it. I didn't expect any of them to come.

Jordan elbows me, and I can't stop the grin that slides across my face.

I have people here who care about me.

By now I have accepted my fate, and my throat hurts enough that I don't try to hit the high notes. I focus on facial expressions and the pronunciation of every Scandinavian word.

Our professor/choir director looks extremely pleased when we finish. While the audience claps behind him, he says to us, "I know you're all eager to go be with your family and friends. If you'll give me a few minutes backstage, I want to go over your grade for the semester."

We nod in agreement.

He turns around, bows, and steps to the side so the audience can cheer for us again. Then we file off stage.

Behind the concert hall is a classroom. I sit with Jordan and whine about our upcoming finals until the director calls my name.

"Cassandra Jones."

I stand and go over to the desk where he has his gradebook open.

"You had perfect attendance," he says. "I was glad to have you in the choir. Did you enjoy it?"

I nod. "I always sang in school. I didn't have the time to commit to the choir here, though, so I was grateful for this opportunity."

"You get an A in the class. Go ahead and tell your husband to come up."

I stare at him, trying to figure out if I really heard those words come from his mouth. "My husband?"

I see him immediately trying to backtrack, realizing from my reaction that he said something wrong. "Yes. Jordan? Aren't you married?" He looks down at his gradebook and back at me. "Jordan Jones?"

Jordan hears his name, and I bite my lip to keep from laughing as he joins me at the desk.

"Jordan is my cousin," I say.

The poor man goes beet red. "Oh. I assumed—I'm so sorry! I thought you seemed awfully young!"

"It's all right," Jordan says, trying to ease the poor man's distress. "It happens all the time."

I pat Jordan's arm. "I'll let you talk to my cousin about his grade." I return to my desk and pull out my phone, already texting Camila to tell her what happened. I'm still laughing when Jordan comes back, and we try not to let our teacher see the merriment we get at his expense.

We leave the classroom together and find my friends. They've heard the story by now, and they tease me and Jordan about being a happily wedded couple. It's utterly embarrassing, but it's also hilarious.

"You guys all came!" I say.

"Of course we did!" Abby leans in for a hug, but I shy back.

"I'm sick," I say.

"Oh, who cares?" she says, and then she wraps her arms around me and rocks me. She releases me, and Camila hooks her arm through mine as my friends gather around to hug me also.

"I can't believe you came to see me sing." I accept Justin's hug and only hesitate slightly before also hugging Jared. My gaze settles on Stirling, who carries a bouquet of daffodils. "How was my pronunciation?"

"I could almost understand what you were saying," he says, and I laugh, then accept the vase of daffodils.

"Thanks for coming," I say.

"Flowers," Jordan says. "That's nice. No one brought me any."

"That's because you're the husband," Iris says, and we laugh.

"I've got to head," Stirling says, "but I'll see you at work." He releases me, waves, and jogs away.

Our group walks out of the building together. I'm not sure where we're going, but we move in the direction of my apartment. Jordan falls in next to Camila and Iris, and Jared ends up walking beside me.

I shoot him a grin. "It was nice of you to come."

"Of course. You are, apparently, one of my close friends."

"Apparently?" I raise my eyebrows.

"So Iris says."

"I hope it's true."

He nods at the vase in my hand. "One of your admirers?"

"Oh." I laugh. "That was Stirling."

"Ah. The guy you work with who takes you out a lot."

"Also just a friend." I steal another glance at Jared. "But not as close as you."

Jared smiles and bumps my shoulder with his.

We drift into silence, his hands in his pockets, mine wrapped around the vase. Iris glances back and notices us, and she comes to join us. Layne looks over and hollers, "Jared, steer clear of Cassandra, she's technically married!"

"To which guy?" he responds.

"To me," Jordan says, as we hoot with glee.

We arrive as a group at the dorm, and Layne pulls out a gallon of milk and a package of cookies. Abby eyes it contemptuously.

"Milk and cookies?" she says. "This is what you have to offer?"

We giggle at her dismay.

I take a cookie and sit down in front of the fish tank, watching my survivors flip around in their water. I expect Jordan to sit by me, but he won't stop messing with the string on Camila's jacket, even as she hits his hand and shoves him away.

Jared pulls out a chair and plops down beside me and offers me a glass of milk. I accept it.

"Don't drink too much," he warns. "One drink often leads to another."

"Thanks for the warning. I'll go slow on my milk intake." It's a joke, but it makes me wonder. Does Jared have a past like Owen? Owen was so stereotypical in high school. He's led me to believe even the good boys go wild during those years.

Jared doesn't seem like that though.

I drink my milk thoughtfully and bite into a cookie, letting the sugar and butter and milk-chocolate chips dissolve in my mouth as I watch my neon-colored tropical fish.

"It was a good concert," Jared says, drawing my gaze toward him. "It was fun to watch you trip over those words."

I grin and repeat one of the phrases from the song, although I'm not sure at all if I got it right.

"Did you just put a hex on me?" He presses his hands to chest. "I'm feeling a little lightheaded."

"I have that effect on people. Once I had to learn a song in Italian for a recital, but I could never remember the order of the words, so I sang whatever line came to mind."

"I bet that was fun to see."

"Maybe. Or just awkward. I hit the wrong note on the very last note the song. It was one of those performances where you wish you could delete the whole thing."

"Now I really want to see it."

"I might be able to make that happen. I think my mom recorded it."

"I bet your boyfriend thought it was funny."

I'm not sure why Jared brings him up. Is he trying to remind us both? "He actually didn't see it. We were on a break."

"Oh. Well, maybe we can sit down and have a watch party together."

The idea makes me giggle. I wonder if Jared and Owen could ever be friends. Somehow I think there would be too much rivalry between them, even without me in the picture. I take another drink of my milk. "Did you drink a lot in high school?"

"Why do you ask that?"

I shrug. I don't say anything about Owen. I don't want Jared to judge him.

But I forgot Jared's smart. "Because that's what football players do, huh?" he says.

I press my lips together and keep my eyes on the aquarium in front of me.

"No. I was one of the weird ones. I actually lived what I believed."

It hurts my heart to hear these words. I should not be comparing him to Owen, but I am. It's unfair and I despise myself for doing it. If only Owen—

I banish the rest of the thought from my head.

"I told you."

I glanced at Jared. "Told me what?"

"I told you I would make you rethink all your preconceptions of football players."

"Ha." I nod. "Yep."

I won't let him any further into my thoughts.

It turns out I don't have to. Iris comes over with a chair, placing it conveniently between me and Jared. She has a tray of cookies, and she plops her feet on the couch so she can rest the tray on her thighs.

"Cookie?" she says, offering one to me.

And that's where the conversation ends.

⟡

My throat hurts even worse in the morning. I want to sleep all day, but I have a math final and a consultation with my Honors English teacher.

The sky is dark. I look out the window as I brush my teeth. It has the shadows like an incoming summer thunderstorm, but it's the wrong season for that. I spit and put my toothbrush away and grab my things for school.

Camila is already gone, but Iris and Layne are watching TV in the kitchen while they eat breakfast.

"I don't know how you guys eat," I say, throwing a granola bar in my backpack. "I'm so nervous about finals that I'm sick to my stomach."

Layne smirks. "Nobody cares about grades anymore."

I can't make myself not care. "I have to keep my grades up or I'll lose my scholarship."

"Me too," Layne says.

I grunt in acknowledgment. Layne scored better on the ACT than I did, and her scholarship is for all four years. She doesn't have to renew it every year like I do. She just has to pass her classes.

I am envious of this.

I throw open the back door and freeze.

It's snowing.

And not a little bit of snow. It's pouring down, swirling through the air so I can't even see the parking lot.

"You guys!" I slam the door and spin back to my roommates. "It's snowing like crazy!"

"Really?" Layne is from California, and she jumps up to look also. Iris joins her.

"It's so beautiful!" Layne says.

"Oh, that's nothing," Iris says. "My mom said they got a foot last night."

I exchange glances with Layne.

"But we're not in Canada like your mom," Layne says.

"Do we still go to school?" I say, not quite hiding the alarm in my voice.

Iris laughs. "This is not enough to cancel school. Camila has already gone to cross country practice."

This is insanity. I run back to my room and grab my hat and scarf and a different jacket.

I can't help feeling a tiny bit excited. I've never seen snow like this before.

The walk to school is slow and treacherous. The wind cuts through my hat, stinging my nose and cheeks. I breathe through my scarf because the air is so cold. Burns my lungs. My gloves do not protect my fingers, which I curl into fists, trying to retain the warmth.

But there's something amazing at how beautiful campus looks covered in the thick blanket of white. The trees, dead and bare, now hold layers of the fat whiteness. Even the trash cans look pristine.

God did this. He turned everything white and pure and clean. It's amazing and fills me with wonder.

And for some reason it makes me think of Owen, and I wish he were here to share this moment with me.

By the time I reach the Honors building, my nose is running, and my sore throat has worsened into a cough. I take a drink of water and swallow it back. I still have a math final after this.

I'm meeting with Ms. Mayhew to go over my personal narrative for my Honors English final. I turned it in a few days earlier, and today is our last consultation so she can tell me how well I fulfilled the rubric.

She closes the door to the office and goes around the desk. "I want you to know," she says as she pulls her seat in closer to me, "that I admire and appreciate your bravery in sharing this experience. Only in being vulnerable can we learn from each other, but this level of vulnerability is often too difficult for people. So thank you for that."

I nod. "It was one of the most difficult things I've gone through in my life. Writing about it was actually cathartic. It made me feel like maybe something good could come of it."

"Well, the way you handle yourself, the way you speak, and the way you carry yourself tells me this experience impacted you. It made you stronger." She shuffles her papers, glancing down at them, and then flattening what I recognize as my essay on the desk in front of her. "You made significant modifications that improve the visual aspect of your narrative. My criticism last time we met was the lack of description. You went above and beyond to improve that. The moment where you describe crouching in front of the toilet, and sticking your finger down your throat —" She shudders. "I could feel it. I was horrified and fascinated that anyone could do that."

My face grows hot. "It takes someone mental."

She smiles at my own self-deprecation. "But you recognize that, and your ability to tell the story from the point of view you have now makes the reception that much more impactful."

Ms. Mayhew is full of praise and complimentary words, but she hasn't told me my grade yet.

"I also want you to know that I entered your essay into the Honors personal narrative contest. I hope you don't mind. It is by far the best I've ever read, and I'm certain it will resonate with other people."

My eyes widen. That is not something I expected. "Wow, thank you. That's quite an honor."

"Yes it is." She pulls out a grading sheet. "You get an A on the essay and an A for the semester. Your narrative wasn't perfect, but nothing ever will be. This is for you. You can look it over and see how I graded you."

I don't know what to say. She just told me how much she loves my essay and that I aced the class. Probably the easiest A I've ever gotten in my life. "Thank you so much."

"Have a merry Christmas, Cassandra. Hold on to that inner strength. I can't wait to see what you do with your life."

CHAPTER EIGHTY-TWO

Stereotypical

The snow still pours down when I leave the Honors building. My socks are wet, my shoes soaked as if I've been walking in rain puddles. I shiver the whole way to the testing center, which isn't very far, luckily. My stomach knots up when I arrive.

I dread my math final, even more than my physical science one, which I took three days ago.

I have this test and one more English paper, and my first semester of college will be behind me.

The line in the testing center winds through the hallway and down the stairs. It's a gloomy prospect, all of us queuing forward as if we march toward our execution.

I finally make it to the front of the line. The proctors send me to one of the smaller rooms branching off the large room.

There's no time limit. I can take as long as I need to hang myself on this algebra final. It's multiple-choice, but option E on every question is "none of the above."

Yep. I'm going to die.

I place my calculator next to me and begin the exam with charisma. But I hit my first snag three questions in, and everything spirals from there. If I don't come up with an answer listed in the multiple-choice options after I complete a problem, I move to the next question with the plan to go back to the ones I'm skipping and double-check my work. But an hour into the exam, I am skipping three questions for each one I answer.

I still have forty-seven problems to go, and I'm starting to panic.

Three hours into the exam, I don't freaking care anymore. I'm done. My fingers are cramping, I'm sweating, and I can't remember the difference between addition and subtraction. I give up. I start back with the first question I couldn't answer, number three, and I fill in the bubble. Anything to get me out of this room and get me off this campus.

I do that to the rest of the questions.

I hand in my score card and tell myself to leave the testing center without looking at the results. Just go home.

But I can't help myself. My eyes jump upward toward the screen as I reach the bottom of the stairs.

There is my student ID number, followed by the test score.

Thirty-six percent.

Thirty-six percent!

My heart plummets. It is by far the worst score I've ever received on any exam, maybe any assignments ever.

I hate math.

But I'm done. And I will never take another math class again.

My cough escalates as I walk back to my dorm, the cold air irritating my lungs with each breath. I step into the kitchen and breathe in the warm air. My nose reacts by running like a faucet. I open the door to the hallway and draw to a quick halt because standing directly in front of me, mouths locked in a slobbery, drooling embrace, arms wrapped tight around each other, are Layne and Brant.

They are so engrossed with each other that they don't hear me come in, and I get an eye full of their tongues chasing each other around their mouths, their hands caressing each other's shoulders and hips. It's disgusting, and I start laughing. I can't help myself.

They break away with a start, Layne crashing into the wall behind her, and I wave them off, still laughing.

"Don't mind me, I'm not even here!"

I go to my bedroom and close the door and hear them giggling over the encounter. And then it's silence, and I imagine they're making out again.

I'll stay here in my room for a bit.

But it makes me miss making out. Those passionate, stolen moments behind closed doors. I think of Owen, pulling me into the closet in his uncle's house, trying to find a private place to make out. And then I remember Tiago, in a bedroom in my uncle's house this time, the lights out as we kissed as quickly as we could before my dad walked in on us.

Being a teenager can be so hard. And now I'm an adult, but I don't feel any older.

My flight home is tomorrow, and now that my finals are out of the way, I can finally allow myself to be excited. I miss my mom, more than I thought I would, and there's been no point in dwelling on it during the semester, but now that I'm going to see her, I find myself near tears with anticipation.

Christmas break is more than two weeks long, but I still have plenty of clothes at home, so it takes me all of fifteen minutes to pack. My toiletries are there too. I can leave most things here.

I go into the kitchen to get a snack. I hear voices and assume it will be Layne and Brant, but to my surprise, it's Iris and Jared.

"Hi, guys," I say, and I hear the slight hesitation in my voice. Is that jealousy I feel? I have no right.

They sit on the couch, Iris with her knees up in the corner, and Jared with his elbows resting on his legs next to her, hands clasped together. He gives me an easy smile.

"Hi, Cassandra. We were making hot chocolate. Want to join us?"

I notice the pot of water boiling on the stove. I glance at Iris, whose face is flat, but she manages to force a smile.

"Yes. We'd love to include you," she says.

Her body language says the opposite, and I should excuse myself and return to my room, but I'm hungry, and Jared is my friend. So I settle down on the couch on his other side.

"For a minute. I came to get food."

Iris has a hold of Jared's hand and is playing with his fingers. It's so clear she likes him. He doesn't grip her hand or run his fingers along her flesh like she does to him, but neither does he pull away. He just lets her hang on him.

I don't know if I'm jealous of Iris because she gets to hang on Jared or if I'm jealous that she's got someone and I don't.

All I know is I'm jealous and it makes me cross.

"We were talking about racial diversity on campus," Jared says. "That's probably a topic you could weigh in on."

"Me? Why?"

"Well, because you're—" He seems at a loss for words and gestures the length of my body. "You," he finishes, rather lamely.

"Do you see me as different than other people?" I say, reacting defensively.

"Well, we are," Iris says. "I'm Chinese, you're Colombian."

"I'm American," I say, my tone more hostile than I need to be.

"Sure, and I'm Canadian. But I still get treated differently. People look at me and they see a minority, and they're not sure if they're supposed to act more inclusive or if they're supposed to act like they don't notice I'm different."

"I think people only treat us differently if we tell them there's something different about us," I say. I focus on Jared. "What do you think? When you see us, do you think, 'I can be myself,' or do you think, 'I have to be careful what I say so I don't offend anyone'?"

"Ah," is all Jared gets out before Iris jumps back in.

"That's not where this conversation is going. First of all, being aware of minorities isn't the same as treating them differently. No one can look at me and not know I'm Chinese."

"But do you want to capitalize on that difference or do you want people to see you as the same as them?"

"I'm not the same."

"Only because you're focusing on being different."

"I think you're awfully defensive about this."

"I think we perpetuate racism because it makes us feel special."

"That's a very one-sided opinion, and definitely not shared by the majority of people. And for you to take your opinion and say it's how most minorities feel is extremely arrogant and condescending."

I stand up. I'm not hungry anymore. And for reasons I can't explain, I'm angry. "Whatever." I grab my jacket off the hook and go outside.

Outside is frigid. The wild snow storm from earlier has calmed down to lightly drifting flakes. In my hasty exit, I didn't grab a hat or gloves, but no way am I swallowing my pride and going back into the house. Instead, I walk toward the science museum where Jordan took me at the beginning of the school year.

My anger cools as I walk, and my words come back to haunt me. I can see how they came off, bigoted and conceited and condescending. What must Jared and Iris think of me now?

It's only been seven minutes, and I haven't reached the museum, but I turn around. My face is hot with shame, and I need to apologize before I leave for break.

I reach the stairs as the second floor door opens, and Jared steps out. I halt at the bottom of the steps. He doesn't see me, and his boots clatter on the metal support of the stairwells. And then he lifts his eyes and there I am. Both eyebrows rise when we make eye contact. Then he closes the distance between us, opens his arms, and pulls me into a hug.

I let out a breath. He knows, then, without me saying anything, that I'm sorry.

I still need to say it. I pull back. "I'm sorry. I said stupid things."

"I know. I imagine there's a history behind it. It's not like you to talk that way."

How does he know? He barely knows me. We haven't had that many interactions, have we?

I suppose the ones we've had have been revealing.

"Do you wanna talk about it?" he asks.

"Yes."

I sit down on the cold cement of the first step, and he settles in beside me. The arm of his wool jacket brushes my arm, and I scoot closer so the jacket warms more of my skin. I make a fist and put my hand next to his. My olive skin tone contrasts with his lighter coloring, though he has enough pigment that I imagine in summer he gets a nice tan. "Sometimes kids say degrading things because my skin's a different shade than theirs."

He puts his hand over mine, the warm softness of his palm engulfing my fist. "You don't like seeing yourself as different, is that it?"

"No, actually, most of the time I do. But I'm just me. I want to be recognized for who I am, not because of where my grandmother was born. It's like being judged for having brown or black or blond hair. Who cares? What does it matter? It doesn't change me."

"I understand exactly what you're saying."

"I want to be seen for me. For what I do, how I act, what I accomplish. Not because I'm short or female or Latina. I think the more I call attention to it, the more people notice."

"But the truth is, people notice anyway. You're not hiding it by not talking about it." He closes his eyes. "Do you know what color my eyes are?"

"Blue," I say without hesitation.

He opens them and gives a half smile. "It's impossible not to notice."

I bob my head. "Sure. But can you understand why it might be a source of frustration for me?"

"I totally get it."

I'm cold again. My ears are numb, and the fingers on one hand burn from the freezing temperature infiltrating the bare skin.

Not the other hand.

I extract my fist from under Jared's palm and rub my hands together. "I think I better go in."

"Yeah, you probably should."

We both stand up, and Jared grabs me again. He wraps me up in a warm hug, sheltering me within his long wool jacket.

I still feel it. I still feel something for him, and I don't understand how that's possible. How I can be so in love with Owen and have feelings for Jared, as infinitesimal as they are?

I don't know what he feels, but we stay in that embrace for a long moment before I step out.

"Safe travels. Have a great Christmas break," I say.

"You too."

We separate, me going back up the stairs and him putting his hands in his pockets and heading for his apartment.

I shove him from my mind. I still have my roommate to apologize to.

CHAPTER EIGHTY-THREE

Arkansas Connections

My alarm wake me early Saturday morning. My throat aches, my eyes feel glued shut, and I do not want to get out of bed. I wrap the blankets around me and try to ignore the siren.

I am lucky Camila left last night or she would be yelling at me to get my alarm.

Or not. Camila never yells at me, even when she's frustrated with me.

I'm the only one left. Camila's parents picked her up yesterday, Layne is with Brant until her flight this afternoon, and Iris's brother left with her last night for a red-eye out of the Denver airport.

Stirling offered to give me a ride to the airport so I wouldn't have to pay to park my car, but I declined. I enjoy having my own car and being able to take myself.

My alarm is still going off, and I am more awake now, a glimmer of excitement rising in my chest at the prospect of seeing my family in a few hours.

So I get up.

My drive to the airport is uneventful. I wonder how my grades turned out. I cross my fingers I at least got a 3.7 GPA so I can keep my scholarship.

I sleep on my first flight. I'm connecting in St. Louis. The flight is only an hour, but I roll up my jacket and use it as a pillow and I'm out. I awaken as the plane lands, and anticipation fires through me.

I'm that much closer to home.

I find a food court and sit down with a sandwich just as all of the notifications I received during the flight come chiming in.

Did you catch your flight OK? Mom.

Have a merry Christmas! I love you all. Kisses. Camila to our roommate chat.

That's followed up with a heart emoji and responses from my roommates, so I add my own kissy face.

Choir grades have been updated! Jordan

Did you escape yet?

That last one's from Owen. I grin and settle into my seat, not interested in my sandwich anymore.

Me: I escaped.

O: How far did you get?

Me: So far only St. Louis.

O: St. Louis? What are you doing there?

Me: Apparently it's my connecting flight.

O: I think you're lost.

That makes me giggle.

Me: I'll be home tonight.

O: Excited to see your family?

Me: Actually, yes.

O: When do I get to see you?

A rush of bubbly delight makes my toes curl.

Me: Anytime. I'm just at home.

O: All right, let me check with my parents to make sure I have no commitments.

Me: Sure.

That one word doesn't begin to convey my giddiness at the thought of Owen coming to visit. It doesn't feel like we're together when we're apart, I guess because we're not. But at the same time, it feels like we are committed. In some way.

Or maybe I'm just not able to let go of someone who I love.

I try to sleep on the next flight, but I'm too riled up. I didn't know I could be this excited about seeing my parents and siblings. When I graduated, all I wanted was to get away, but I've missed them.

My knee bounces up and down as the plane lands on the tarmac. The small Bentonville airport is centered in front of me. I grab my bag and stand in line, taking deep breaths and pretending to be patient.

Finally we are off the plane. I want to break into a run, but that's a terrible idea because I can't run and I would look very foolish. Instead, I politely excuse myself and maneuver around the old people shuffling through the hallway.

I stop at the escalator. In a moment, I will see my family for the first time in four months. Any signs of sickness vanished on the flight, though I don't know if I'm better or just excited.

I'm ready.

They are standing at the bottom of the escalator and they spot me the same time I see them. Annette shrieks.

"There she is!" And then she bursts into tears.

I laugh and trip over myself trying to get to them, and I realize I'm crying also. Annette is twelve now and my height, and fourteen-year-old Scott's grown past my shoulders. Mom throws her arms around me. Even my dad's nose is red as he takes a turn to hug me.

My mom hooks her arm through mine, and I let her. My dad and Emily get my luggage, and Annette takes my hand. We're probably too old for that, but we're both okay with it.

Outside, the world is dead. I forgot what it looks like in Arkansas in the winter. No mountains, but the land is not flat. The rolling hills are covered with spiny arms, the bare branches of naked trees blending into the browns and gray apparent in everything in front of me. I'm filled with nostalgia for spring time, when all of these trees will be full of bright green leaves.

I love my home.

We chatter in the car. My sisters give me gossip about my peers, my parents tell me about people at church, and I share all the rigors of college classes. They already know about my roommates, but I talk about them again, going into detail on life with three strangers.

"Any boys?" Emily asks, a mischievous gleam in her eyes.

"There are lots of them," I say, which brings laughter from my family. "I've gone on a few dates. It's fun."

"But you saw Owen over Thanksgiving," my mom says.

"He's going to try to come up here," I say. "After Christmas, maybe. Is that all right?"

"Sure," Mom says.

The conversation moves off Owen and I look out the window as we drive. I'm flashing back to high school, remembering taking these roads to visit Harper or Riley, or, of course, Owen.

It feels like a different life now. But I remember it.

I don't see anyone my first night in Arkansas, and I'm glad. I'm exhausted and I've been on planes all day and I look terrible. Plus I'm still fighting my cold, though it's better than it was a few days ago. Instead, I snuggle up with my family and watch a movie while I eat popcorn, which I don't even like, but it feels perfect.

Tomorrow night I'll see everyone I know at my parents' Christmas party.

My head still feels stuffy when I wake up in the morning, and my eyes burn. I pry them open and step into my closet to lovingly finger the clothing I left behind. I decide some of these things need to go back with me.

In my bedroom, my phone rings. I dance out of the closet, wondering who it might be. It could be anyone, someone from school or someone from home.

I don't expect it to be Riley, not after all this time of silence, but it is her name I see lit up on my phone.

I grab it up and answer immediately, afraid if I don't take this call now, I'll never talk to her again.

"Riley, hey!"

"Hi, Cassie!" she says, and she sounds happy. Carefree.

"How are you?" I say. "I've been desperate to talk to you. I've got to see you!"

She laughs. "I'm free today."

I can't believe it. All these months of zero contact, a depressing goodbye, and now she's good to hang out? "I'll come pick you up! We can go shopping, get some lunch. Where are you staying?"

"Lucas and I live with his mom in east Springdale," she says. "I'll send you the address."

I hang up excited. I'm nervous also because we haven't spoken in so long and so much has happened, but I take it as a good sign that she reached out to me.

I finish getting dressed and make the forty-minute drive out to the east side of Springdale. I turn down a street in the suburbs lined with houses and park in front of a beige and white brick duplex, identical to the others on the street. I check the number to make sure I have the right one, then I walk up to the front door and knock.

Riley opens the door. She looks the same as when I met her in fifth grade, my petite friend, with girlish features and freckles across her nose. Except her hair is longer than I've ever seen it, below her shoulders, and her belly protrudes in the long-sleeved T-shirt she wears.

"Riley!" I throw my arms around her, and my eyes burn, an ache of unshed tears in my throat. Then I pull back and press both hands to the basketball of her belly. "You're pregnant," I say. "I can't believe you're going to have a baby."

"I know." Riley laughs. "It's pretty crazy."

She take my hand and pulls me into the house. A large boy, man, I suppose, sits in the La-Z-Boy beside an older woman, both of them watching TV.

"Cassie, this is Lucas, and that's his mom. This is Cassie."

Riley's one of the only people who can get away with calling me that. Their heads spin away from the television long enough to glance at me and wave, and I try not to study Lucas too carefully. He has short, wavy dark hair and a darker skin tone, similar to my own, with an olive tint to it, and he is, to put it nicely, portly.

Before I have to make any awkward small talk, Riley takes my hand again and tugs me down the hall.

"This is our room." She leads me into a bedroom with a queen bed filling up most of the space. I look at it and imagine her and Lucas, sharing that space, snuggling together at night, breathing the same air, and I'm jealous. I feel that need, that desire to be next to Owen, so fully in my soul that I ache.

"It must be nice, having him with you," I say.

Riley rolls her eyes. "Not really. We spend as little time together as possible because we're always fighting."

"Yeah, that doesn't fit with what I imagined," I agree, and we both laugh.

"But you seem happy," I say.

Riley lifts a shoulder. "I am. I'm excited to be a mom. And I don't drink anymore or anything like that because I don't want to hurt the baby."

I squeeze her hands. "You'll be a great mom."

"I'll try. We're getting married." She holds her hand out to me and shows me a solitary diamond on her ring finger. "Next month."

She says all of this without excitement. "Congratulations?" I suggest.

"Thanks."

This doesn't seem like the best scenario for her life, but it's the path she's on. So I just nod. "What's it like? Being pregnant?"

Her face brightens. "It's amazing. I feel the baby moving, and can't believe I created a life." Her hands fall protectively on her stomach. "It's another person inside of me."

I press my hands over hers, echoing that amazement. "How did you find out?"

"I was sick three mornings in a row, and the third morning as I sat in front of the toilet vomiting, suddenly I knew. I started crying. I called Lucas and told him and he sat there with me by the toilet, and we both cried."

"So is he supportive?" I ask, keeping my voice low. But I have to know that he's taking care of her.

"Yes. We are friends, at least. And he says he's going to get a job."

He doesn't have one? I fight back my criticism. That's exactly what she doesn't like about me.

"That's great," I say instead. I look over the stretchy T-shirt she's wearing. "Do you have maternity clothes?"

Her cheeks turn rosy. "It's not high on the list when we have a baby coming."

I have to tread carefully again. "That's all right. I owe you a birthday present and a Christmas present. Let's go shopping."

Her smile stretches up to her eyes. "That sounds great."

CHAPTER EIGHTY-FOUR

Homeless

I spend everything in my bank account on her.

Granted, it wasn't very much, after the plane to get home and food at the airport and Christmas presents for my family. But between buying her several expensive dresses at the maternity clothes shop and taking us both out for lunch, I've got nothing.

"What's going on with you and Owen?" she asks over our Chinese food.

"We still talk a lot. We saw each other at Thanksgiving. He said he's going to come see me for Christmas or New Year's."

"Isn't it amazing? I never would've put the two of you together when he first moved in."

"Who would've thought we would fit together so well?" I agree.

I take Riley home after lunch and squeeze her extra hard, though I'm careful of the belly.

"I hope you'll call me when she comes," I say. "I want to see pictures."

"I will! Thank you for taking me today. I enjoyed it." Riley lifts the bag of clothing we bought together. "This is really helpful."

She's more like my Riley that she has been in years. The jaded, angry, cynical side of her has faded away under her pregnancy. I know her life is far from perfect, but right now she's happy, and I hope she can stay that way.

When I get home, my mom puts me to work with the Christmas party. Harper is coming over, and a few other friends from church, and I'm excited to see them.

Harper shows up an hour early, as I'm putting out food labels and serving utensils with the food bowl. She's beautiful, my gorgeous friend, with long blond hair and bright blue eyes, wearing an oversize beige sweater with plaid leggings.

"Harper!" I greet, and then I throw my arms around her, stills clutching plastic utensils in one hand.

"Oh my goodness, I've missed you!" she says.

My throat is tight with unshed tears. There are so many distractions in college, so many new people and things and places, it's easy to think my life here in Arkansas was a dream.

"You look amazing," I tell her, pulling away.

I see Miles over her shoulder, and I feel the smile on my face start to slip. I force it to stay. I've known Miles since fifth grade, and he was my friend before hers, but I've become so jealous of her time with him over the past few years that I don't think of him as my friend anymore.

"Miles." I offer him a hug.

We move to the couch with cups of hot chocolate in our hands so we can gossip. I'm just getting caught up on Betsy's life and anything Harper knows about Mia or Nicole when the front door opens and Farrah and Tyler walk in.

More hugging ensues, and we continue talking about our peers, only now it's people from church. They want to give me the dish on Riley, but I tell them I spent the day with her, and suddenly I'm the one with information.

"She's getting married," I say. "She seems happy."

I don't mention how she and Lucas fight. How she works so hard for her family because he's a bump on a log and she deserves better.

"I got my mission call," Tyler says. "I'm leaving in February for Mexico."

"He'll miss Jason by four months," Farrah says.

"That's so hard, to not see your brother and be gone for so long," Harper says.

Tyler shrugs, and I wait for the slightly condescending spiritual comment to come out of his mouth.

He doesn't disappoint. "If that's what the Lord requires of me, it's no sacrifice at all."

I slide my eyes over to Farrah, who gives me a grin.

My parents gather everyone downstairs to put on the Christmas story like we've done every year, and I find an opportune moment to pull Farrah aside.

"How do you feel about Tyler leaving?" I ask.

She shrugs. "I'm feeling pretty comfortable in our relationship. I think he might be the one."

I squeeze her fingers. "But doesn't that make it harder to be apart?"

"Tyler has a really good attitude about it. He says if we're going to be together after his mission, then I won't find somebody else when he's gone. If I do, then I'm not meant to be with him. He's very confident in whatever God has planned."

"That sounds like Tyler. I'm not sure I'm that faithful."

"You're thinking about Owen?" she guesses.

I nod. "He's always told me I try too hard to control things. Like I think that if I desire something and work at it hard enough, I can make it happen."

"While Tyler's attitude is the opposite. Stop fighting, relinquish control, and trust in the process."

"But what if the process makes you lose each other?" I ask.

"According to Tyler, we trust that we're on the best path for our lives even if it's an unexpected outcome."

In a way, it makes sense. And it takes some pressure off, to think I don't have to force life to happen.

But it's awfully hard to relinquish the control.

⊙〜⚬〜⊙

I call Stage when I wake up Monday morning. It's been a restful weekend. I saw my friends and I went to church. Tomorrow's Christmas and today's Christmas Eve, but right now I'm restless and I have nothing to do.

Besides, it's the oddest thing, but I don't feel like I've come home. I feel like I'm visiting someone. My room is not mine. The church congregation is not mine. My parents' house is not mine.

Debra's bright, springy voice answers the phone. "Stage in Springdale, how can I help you?"

I smile. "Hi. It's Cassandra. Cassandra Jones. I'm home for Christmas and wondered if you need any holiday help."

She gives a shriek of delight. "Absolutely, I do! When can you start?"

I exhale, my heart beating a little faster as I prepare to commit. "I'm available today."

"We are swamped. Can you be here in two hours?"

I have absolutely nothing else to do. "Yup."

I'm finally over whatever cold I got during finals, but my eyes burn. Putting in my contacts hurts. I go through my closet and pick a pair of black slacks and a lacy sweater. I enjoy the feel of sliding nice, fashionable clothes on. I haven't done it in a while.

The store is crazy busy! Debra immediately puts me in charge of the women's department, and I think it's the busiest. I missed the Christmas season last year because I had surgery on my foot, so it's my first time to be thrown into this. I move in a constant rotation of helping people and cleaning dressing rooms and ringing up customers at the register.

It's the distraction I wanted, but my feet hurt after several hours, and it's not as much fun as I remember.

I finish checking out a woman who I think bought clothing for every person on her Christmas list, and I hurry to the dressing room after to retrieve the articles she decided she didn't want. I take a pile of clothing with me to the register and begin folding and hanging, all while watching for anyone else who might need help, because paying customers take priority over clean up. For a moment, everyone is taken care of, and I take my clothing and return it to the racks.

The front door swishes open again, bringing in the frigid December air, and I turn as footsteps approach my department. I already have my customer service smile in place as the words, "Welcome to Stage, can I help you find anything?" leave my lips automatically.

And it's a good thing, because everything inside me freezes when I see who it is.

Lacey Gregg and her mother just walked in.

CHAPTER EIGHTY-FIVE

Face to Face

Lacey hasn't noticed me. She's fingering the fabric of a sweater with shimmery sleeves. I don't know if she even knows me. We've never spoken to each other. But she was captain of the cheer squad. I know who she is.

I know what she did.

"We'll need a dressing room," her mom says, already retrieving items from the racks.

"Sure, sure," I say. I'm trying to maintain a semblance normalcy.

But my mind is tripping, and all I can think of is her and Owen, her and Owen . . .

My heart. It's imploding.

Lacey looks up then, and she meets my eyes. She's got chin-length dark blond hair and a smattering of freckles across her nose. She smiles, and it's friendly, but with a note of curiosity.

"You dated Owen Blaine, didn't you?"

I nod. Dating Owen brought its own semblance of notoriety. "We're still dating."

She lifts both eyebrows over her clear blue eyes. "Oh! I thought you guys broke up."

Maybe it should bother me that she doesn't know we got back together, but it doesn't. It means she and Owen don't talk at all, they're not in the same circle, she has no idea what happens in his life, and I am one hundred percent okay with that. My smile feels less frigid as I say, "We got back together after graduation."

Her mom is oblivious to us, going through the clothing, and Lacey moves closer to me.

"That's nice. Seems like the rest of us couldn't catch his eye no matter how hard we tried."

And you tried pretty hard. I literally bite my tongue so I don't say anything. I

470

don't want her to know we've talked about her. I don't want her to know that she will always have some part in our history.

But at the same time, I don't want her to think I don't know about her because Owen is embarrassed or that we don't tell each other these kinds of things.

"Yeah, well, sometimes people have to experiment a little bit before they find what they want."

I'm careful to keep my voice neutral. No Snark. No accusation. No contest.

Lacey smiles again. "Tell him I said hi."

"I will." I am not at all sure that I will. That painful conversation is too fresh on my mind, and I don't want to throw it in his face.

Lacey doesn't talk to me again until they're leaving. I let someone else take the sale and I keep busy refolding shirts at a table. She catches my eye as they walked toward the exit, and she waves.

"Bye."

Nothing bad happened during our interaction, but I'm shaken up by it just the same.

Owen will only feel bad if I tell him. So I resolve not to.

But it's still on my mind when he calls me that evening. We've been texting since I got home, but this is the first time he's called.

"My parents aren't super keen on me driving up there by myself," he drawls. "But they are too busy to come up with me."

My chest constricts at the thought of not seeing him. "What about flying?" I feel selfish for asking. I don't have the money to fly. I shouldn't ask that of him.

"It's a possibility," he says. "But I'm working on the driving. Trying to convince them I'm a super safe and cost-effective driver."

I laugh, because we both know that's not what Owen is. "What if I met you halfway? So it's a five-hour drive for both of us?"

"And where would we stay?" he says, his voice gentle but riddled with amusement. "I don't think it would go over well if we booked a hotel room for a few nights."

My abdomen tightens at the very mention. It might go very well. But I know that's precisely what we're trying to avoid for the next few months.

"Don't worry," he says. "They'll let me come. They like you."

I let out a breath. "I hope you're right."

"How was yesterday?"

I brighten, warming to the subject. "So great! I saw everyone."

I give him all the details about my shopping day with Riley. Then I transition to the Christmas party and tell him about Harper and Farrah and Tyler.

"Tyler got his mission call. He's leaving soon."

"I know," Owen says. "I actually talk to him a lot."

I'm surprised. Tyler didn't mention Owen at the Christmas party.

"Oh? Really?"

"Yeah, I pick his brain a bit about how he's preparing. Get his advice. I feel like he spent his whole life getting ready, while I've spent the last six months doing it."

"Year," I correct.

I'm referencing the fact that Owen started making changes in his life when he and I started dating, which was around Christmas time last year.

"Almost," he says.

He's right. He didn't stop drinking and turn his life around just because we were dating. It still took some time.

"And how was work?" he asks.

I hesitate, remembering my work visitor. "Fine."

"Only fine? Did the manager give you a hard time?"

"No, Debra likes me. It was just—" I search for some other reason for work to be lackluster. "It made my feet hurt and I got tired of talking to people and smiling all the time."

"Something bothering you?"

Of course, he can tell. I am the worst actress.

"A customer left me a bit rattled. That's all." There. I feel much better having said the truth but without any details.

"What did they do?"

"Oh, nothing . . ."

"Nothing, and you're still upset about it?"

I'm scrambling to come up with a reason but he's shooting holes through my excuses faster than I can make them. "Um."

"Was this a random person, or someone you know?"

Dammit, dammit, why can't he let it be? I'm trying to figure out how best to respond so we can get past this, but all I come up with is, "Um, well," and he says, "Cassandra," with that tone of voice that says he knows I'm trying to avoid something and I may as well spill it because now he's not going to stop until he gets it.

I opt for nonchalant. "It was Lacey Gregg." Like it was no big deal. like we weren't just talking about her a month ago and feeling the repercussions of the impact she has on our life.

No big deal.

But I know from Owen's silence that he's also feeling all of these effects.

"I'm sorry," he says finally, and I hate that he needled the truth out of me. "I'm sorry you ran into her, I'm sorry for—"

He doesn't finish that sentence, and I'm glad. "No, Owen, it's fine," I say, desperate to keep him from disappearing into a shell of guilt. "It surprised me to see her. But I'm okay."

Except he probably knows I'm not. He probably knows exactly what mental images I'm fighting, what's on my mind. The fact that it is still bothering me hours later says a lot.

I wait for him to ask if she and I talked. Wait for him to ask if she mentioned him. I'm prepared to answer this question.

But he doesn't ask. Instead, he says, "I better go. I'll be in touch about coming up there."

No, no, no, he better not block me out now. "Owen—" I begin, but he hangs up.

I am utterly frustrated. I hold the phone in front of me and pound out a text message.

Me: Don't hang up on me! I wasn't done talking.

He responds immediately. *Sorry. I just feel bad that you got me when you deserve better.*

Me: Stop it! That is not what I think.

O: But it's the truth, Cass.

I knew this would happen.

Are you feeling sorry for yourself or for me? I type, and it's a low jab. But his lack of confidence, this feeling of guilt, it hurts me as much as it hurts him.

He doesn't respond, and ten minutes later, I feel guilty for aiming so low. So I type out, *sorry. I hate it when you block me out. Let's deal with this together. Please?*

He still doesn't respond.

I'm forced to put Owen from my mind as my family goes out for our traditional Christmas Eve caroling and door dropping as well as looking at the lights.

But my mind is anxious, resting on Owen, wishing I had managed not to bring up Lacey, and wondering if she'll always be a hurdle in our life.

CHAPTER EIGHTY-SIX

Snowstorm

Christmas morning is a blur of tradition and memories mixing with present day. I feel like I'm trying to fit into a prescribed role as I open my stocking and unwrap the presents my family got me.

The whole time, this icky feeling descends across the top of my shoulders and over my neck, telling me this is not my home anymore. I don't belong here.

I want to go back to college, back to my own apartment.

Annette receives a set of nail wraps, and I sit with her at the kitchen table, helping her cut and shape and file the images to the tips of her nails. That's where I am when Tiago calls me.

"Tiago, hi!" I say, surprised to hear from him.

But also not. It is Christmas day, and I'm going to visit him in May.

"Hello, Cassandra," his familiar tenor voice says.

A wave of nostalgia crashes over me. I remember him. I remember laughing with him, crying over him, loving him.

It's a cozy feeling, and welcoming, but it doesn't invade my heart. I don't love him anymore.

"Merry Christmas!" I say brightly.

"Same to you!" he says. "I thought of you while we opened presents last night."

"Last night? You open presents on Christmas Eve?"

"Yes, that's always when we do it. It was strange for me to open them on Christmas morning with your family."

"Huh," I say, tucking this interesting information away. "So what will you do today?"

"We will all go to my grandfather's house. My cousins, my aunts and uncles. Then we'll eat more food and watch movies, it will be pretty casual and relaxed."

"Not so different from my day. Movies and food."

"I miss you," he says. "My mom misses you also. It will be so great to see you."

I am already uneasy about this trip to Brazil, but I try to keep it light. "Yeah, it's going to be so fun," I say, and I realize it's time I told my mom I was taking a trip.

At the same moment I'm thinking this, my phone chimes with an incoming call. My stomach tightens in a rush of anxiety when I see Owen's name.

"Tiago, I've got to go," I say. "Merry Christmas."

"Merry Christmas, Cassandra," he says, his tone warm.

He doesn't say I love you.

I thought that would hurt, but instead it fills me with a huge sense of relief. If he is finally over me, he and I can be friends, really and truly.

I answer Owen's call, keeping my tone cautious. I'm still miffed about yesterday.

"Hello?" I say.

"Hey, you," he says, all signs of tension gone from his voice.

"Hey, yourself," I say, and I get more comfortable in my seat beside Annette. "Had a good Christmas?"

"Yeah, it's been nice to be with my family. But it would be better if I were with you."

I smile into the phone and forgive him for yesterday. "That's about the only thing missing to make it a perfect Christmas. That, and maybe snow."

"You should've stayed in Colorado. They've got lots of snow."

"It was an option. But I liked my odds of seeing you better from here."

He laughed. "Good, because the odds are in your favor. How about if I come up on the twenty-seventh and stay through New Year's? Monica said she'd come with me, so my parents are cool with me driving."

I hold back my squeal of delight. "Hey, that sounds awesome. We have plenty of room for both of you here."

"Great. I'm excited to see you."

In typical manly fashion, Owen does not share his sentiments very often. When he does, I nurse them for all they're worth. "Do you miss me?"

"Ever since you dropped me off at the airport."

It's a vulnerable admission, and my smile softens. "You too, Owen. I'm so excited to see you."

"And I'm sorry about yesterday."

I shake my head. "We're good. Nothing to apologize for."

"It keeps me humble. I'll keep practicing."

I laugh at the thought of Owen being humble. "It might take a while."

"I've got time."

I hang up giddy with expectations and excitement. I stand up to tell my parents that Owen and Monica are coming for New Year's.

I think while I'm at it, I may as well tell them I'm going to Brazil.

My eyes are stinging. They've been stinging since yesterday. I stop at the bathroom to see if I have an eyelash in them. I don't see anything, though both are a little bit shiny and pink. Maybe I should take my contacts out.

⁂

I wake up and find my eyes wired shut. At least, that's how it feels. I try to pry them apart, but I can't, and I would rather not rip out my eyelashes getting my eyes open. I stumble to the bathroom and put hot water on a rag, then slowly work my eyes open.

They are swollen and red. Every time I blink, white gunk fills the corners of my eyes.

I'm either turning into a zombie, or I have pink eye.

I pray I'm turning into a zombie. Pink eye is disgusting. I sanitize my hand and wash my face and blink. There's no more gunk. I decide I'm okay and head to work.

The day after Christmas is supposed to be the busiest day of the whole year, but not for our store. It's so slow that for the first time I can remember, we close early.

And I'm so grateful for it, because my eyes are burning, and they're weepy, and the tissues I've been using to clean them are coming away sullied.

I can no longer deceive myself into thinking my eyes are okay.

I confirm what I suspected when I get in my car and flip down the mirror visor. The skin around my eyes is swollen and puffy, and there is yellowish discharge in the corners of each eye. The whites themselves are pink with inflamed blood vessels. It looks like the worst case of pink eye I've ever seen. I'm surprised I didn't send anyone screaming with terror away from the store.

I flip the visor down with alarm. Tomorrow Owen plans to drive up here.

This is not good. I have to get better fast. He can't see me like this.

I don't tell my parents when I get home. I go to my room and Google home remedies for pink eye.

What gets rid of pink eye fast? Pops up. I click it.

Go to a doctor.

Helpful.

Make a cold compress with water and a washcloth. Use eye lubricants for relief and keep this over your eyes. Stop wearing contacts and eye makeup.

Great.

I remove my contacts, make an eye bath, and then lay down on my bed with a cold compress over my face.

My phone rings. I don't want to open my eyes and see who it is, so I grab it up and answer, pressing it to my ear and hoping it's not spam. "Hello?"

"Cassandra!" Camila's warm and chipper voice fills my ear, and I almost sit up, I'm so happy to hear from her.

"Camila!" I squeal. "How are you? How was Christmas?" I miss her. I miss all of my roommates, I miss our apartment. That is home.

Not here. Here I'm just visiting.

"Oh, it was great! I got a bunch of gift cards that will come in handy at school! And did you see your grades? They posted this morning!"

"No, I was working." And now I'm fighting the desire to grab my computer and boot it up. "How did you do?" My heart races in my chest. My scholarship for next year depends on my grades last semester. So does Camila's. We have to be above average, above the 3.5 of those who got a four-year scholarship.

"3.73!" She squeals.

It's enough. She'll keep her scholarship. I scramble off the bed, removing the washrag and opening my eyes. The light stings, my vision is blurry, but I locate my computer. "Hang on. I'm getting online."

"Layne and Iris are both on probation. They only got 3.1 and a 3.2."

I make a noise of sympathy in my throat, but I'm too anxious about my own grade to worry about theirs.

My computer loads, and I log into the school system. "I'm checking now."

"What did you get?"

I tap my fingers against my thighs, chest tightening with the suspense. The circle spins and spins over my screen, and just when I think it won't load, it does. The breath washes out of me.

"Three-point-seven-eight." 3.78! I throw myself backward onto the carpet, exhaling. "I did it!"

"That's amazing! We won't have to drop out after our first semester of college!"

I join her in the cheering.

"How's the weather in Arkansas? Are you guys getting any of this winter storm?"

"Not the last time I checked." I sit back in front of my computer and read the grades for each class. "I left work a few hours ago and it was forty-five outside. Not warm but not too cold."

I got a B in math. An A minus in ancient cultures and an A minus in physical science. I can hardly believe it! I thought I would fail that class.

The rest of my grades are As.

"You might want to check the storm path. I think Arkansas was in it," Camila says. "It goes down pretty far south."

I look up from my computer, paying attention to her words for the first time. "How far south?"

"I think Alabama and Mississippi are getting hit with it also."

"Louisiana?" I ask.

"Yes, I think I heard it mentioned."

No, this can't be happening! And we never get snow storms here! Camila is still talking, but I'm distracted, and I say, "I've got to go now, but I'll talk to you later."

"Okay, stay safe and warm!"

I hang up and pull up my weather app.

Snow. Snow snow snow for the next four days.

I jump up and run to the window, half expecting to see a torrential blizzard outside, but there is nothing. I let out a short exhale.

Maybe nothing will happen. The weather frequently calls for snow, and it doesn't come. I check the weather in Louisiana and feel more reassured. It's still a balmy fifty in New Orleans, and their chance of snow in the next four days is minimal.

The snow won't happen. My eyes will be better. I can still see Owen in two days.

⁕

My eyes are not better in the morning.

I don't think my home remedy did anything. They are painful and swollen shut and I actually tell Emily to get mom to help me.

"Cassandra, your eyes look terrible," my mom says as she cleans the gunk from them like I'm four years old again. "You should see a doctor."

"Can you make me an appointment?"

"I'll call them."

My eyes burn like sand is stuck to the inside of my eyelids, and every time I blink it scratches. The grit makes its way to the corners of my eyes in great globs of yellow gunk.

"It's snowing!" Annette calls excitedly from the kitchen.

"Snowing?" Scott says in a tone of disbelief.

I echo that feeling as I go to the window and repeat, "Snowing?"

I'm praying for a little flurry. Tiny petals of dust falling from the sky.

But no. It's the wet kind. The sticking-and-dangerous kind.

My mom comes back into the room. "I got you an appointment for three o'clock this afternoon, right before the office closes for the weekend."

I move around, a little frantic. "It's snowing!"

"It sure is."

"But Owen," I whine.

"Oh, I'm sure he'll still make it. The snow is already slowing. See?" She tilts her head at me. "So are you tied up over both these boys?"

"Both?" I echo.

"Tiago and Owen."

I furrow my brow. "No. Only Owen."

"Oh? Then why are you going to Brazil?"

My face warms. My mom had a minimal reaction when I told her last night, just looked dumbfounded for a moment, and then nodded like it was par the course for college students to decide they want move to another country for a month.

Maybe it is.

"Well." I plop down cross-legged on my bed, and my mom sits across from me, as if she senses I'm about to tell a story. Even Emily goes to her bed and sits down, ready to listen. "When Owen and I were broken up, Tiago and I started talking."

She nods. "I remember you wanting to call him on graduation day."

I lift one shoulder. "He was someone I could turn to. Someone I could rely on."

"But he's never been someone you can rely on," she says, probably in one of those parenting moments where moms speak their mind without meaning to. "He's let you down and hurt you over and over again."

I consider that. "Yeah. He did. So he's just a friend. But I'm also going so I can study Portuguese and improve my understanding of Brazil."

"I see. So now it's part of your education."

I nod. "I fell in love with the Brazilian culture. I'm excited to go back."

"And Owen? What does he have to say about it?"

"He supports me."

"You know it is dangerous to go back and visit someone you used to love," she says, her voice calm and steady but full of warning. She takes my hand. "Feelings that you thought were dead might only be dormant, and they can re-awaken."

I shake my head. "Tiago and I had our chance. Whatever I felt for him is nothing compared to what I feel for Owen. I'm not worried about that happening."

She pokes her finger into the top of my hand. "And that is precisely why you should be."

I pull my hands away from her and rub at the corners of my eyes, which are already gunky. Her words annoy me. So I ignore them.

"Are the rooms ready for Owen and Monica yet?"

"Yes. We're putting Monica in the guest room and Owen in the game room. They're both set up."

"Perfect." I stand up and go to the bathroom, closing the door behind me and ending our conversation. Everything is going to work out great. It will stop snowing, I will go to the doctor, and by tomorrow, my eyes will be better and Owen will be here.

CHAPTER EIGHTY-SEVEN

Disappointments

It starts snowing harder around noon.

I sit on the couch with my family as they watch a movie, but I'm not watching. My eyes itch, and they keep gunking up. I keep them closed. I have a wet rag next to me that I use to clean them every few minutes.

"It's snowing a lot," I hear Annette say.

A lot is a relative term, especially here in Arkansas. If we get an inch, it's a lot. I'm not concerned.

The phone rings, and my mom answers it. Without my eyes, I pay a lot more attention to the noises around me. I hone in on her voice now.

"Oh? It's that bad? Yes. Yes, right now. Okay, thank you."

Even though I was half listening, I don't realize the conversation applies to me until my mom says, "Cassandra."

Now I turn toward her. "What is it?"

"That was the doctor. They're closing the office early because of the snow. They said if you want to get seen, we have to go now."

I push myself to my feet, the first thread of alarm spiraling through my chest. "How bad is the snow?" I blink one eye open and look outside. The sky is white, swirls of snowflakes falling around us.

"Not bad yet. But apparently it's going to become so."

I grab a jacket and shoes through slitted eyes, and my mom helps me slip and slide out to the car. It's treacherous, just going from the front porch to the driveway.

We already have an inch of snow.

Mom backs the van out of the driveway, but as soon as she turns for the circle drive, the tires stick. I clutch the handle above the door as she hits the gas and we slide forward, though not exactly in the direction intended. I grind my teeth and resist staring at my mother as she spins the steering wheel.

We manage to get out of the driveway.

Mom and I exchange a grim look.

"I don't know if we're going to make it there, Cassie," she says.

I don't respond.

We start up the street. The snow is coming down harder now, and she has the windshield wipers going on full blast. The car maneuvers up the steep hill where I used to catch the bus in elementary school, but as she follows the curve of the road, we lose control again. We're slipping, sliding, moving ever so precipitously closer toward the ditch.

Mom pumps the brakes, and somehow the van jerks to a halt.

I already know we are aborting the mission.

We sit in silence a few moments, letting our heart rates slow, catching our breath. She gets the van moving again, ever so slowly, and she finds the first big patch where she can begin the laborious turn back toward home.

"I'm sorry," she says. "I'll look up home remedies, I'll see what we can do for your eyes."

"I've already done that." I don't mean to snap, but I'm frustrated. And I'm in pain.

My phone rings as we drive home. I know the ringtone.

It's Owen.

The heavy weight of defeat sits in my chest as I answer. "Hey," I say, but my voice lacks the normal cheer when I talk to him.

"Hey," he says, the same tension in his voice. "What's the weather looking like up there?"

I exhale. "Pretty bad," I say honestly, and I choke back a sob. "They're shutting everything down. It looks like a blizzard over here."

"We're supposed to get it tomorrow. I can leave now. Maybe I can beat the storm."

I shake my head. Owen might escape the snow in Louisiana, but he'll find it in Arkansas. "We didn't make it a quarter of a mile from my house. It's bad. I don't want you driving in this."

"I'm a good driver."

"No." I desperately want to see him. But not at this kind of risk. "Besides, I'm sick."

"What's wrong?"

I don't want to tell him my eyes have changed into gross inflamed balls of pus. "It's a bad cold. We were on our way to the doctor, but it's snowing too much." Maybe the tears in my eyes will help heal them. "It's not a good time to see me."

"I don't care if you're sick," he says, gently.

"I do. Let's wait a few days. See what happens."

"All right," he agrees. "We'll watch the weather. I'll come up a few days later than planned. But I'll still come."

I nod in agreement, my heart in my throat. "I'll see you soon."

⚜

The snow hits us hard.

The New Year's Eve celebration on the Square is postponed because of the snow. When it finally finishes in Arkansas, it heads south and preys on Louisiana.

Owen can't come.

I spend New Year's Day in Fayetteville with my dad and grandma. Grandma is nicer to me than she ever has been, as if graduating high school suddenly deemed me respectable in her eyes, and she leaves me alone.

My eyes are in terrible shape. We get family photos done when the snow clears up, with me wincing and squinting at the bright light. My mom gets me into the doctor right after. Within hours of taking the medicated eye drops, my eyes feel better. I wake up Tuesday, and I can open my eyes again.

Iris and Layne call me from campus. They are already home, and I'm excited to talk to them. I'll be there in two days.

Home is there, not here.

But I have to figure out when I will see Owen again.

Harper takes me to lunch Wednesday, the day before my flight back to campus. I come home and sit in front of the computer and register for my second semester classes.

It is time to get serious about learning Portuguese, since I'm going to Brazil in five months.

I pull up the Portuguese class curriculum. It follows the logical sequence like most college classes: 101, 102, 201, 202, 301, 302. Once I reach the 300 level, I'll be considered an advanced student and can take literature classes and history classes in Portuguese.

The whole idea excites me.

I pull up the online portal and search for Portuguese 101.

I find Portuguese 201 and Portuguese 102, and an accelerated class that offers 101 and 102 in one semester.

I frown and read the class descriptions in the catalog. Where is 101? I need that entry level class before I can take anything else.

What I read makes my heart stop.

Language classes are offered on a rotating basis of 101 in the fall semester and 102 in the winter semester.

Now I am panicking.

I won't be able to speak Portuguese in four months if I haven't taken any classes. I can't improve a language I don't know. I turn back to the accelerated class, the combination 101 and 102.

The prerequisite is being fluent in Spanish.

I'm not fluent in Spanish. I know a lot of words and recognize a lot of phrases, but I have never had to communicate in Spanish. My abuela speaks English and doesn't like to speak in Spanish.

So that class is out.

I look at the prerequisite for 102. Take Portuguese 101 in the fall semester. Or have the equivalent foundation of beginning Portuguese.

I seize on that. Is my rudimentary knowledge of Portuguese enough to fake my way through Portuguese 102?

It might be. And if I need help, Tiago will help me.

I don't want to ask him for help, but I can.

I take a deep breath and sign up for Portuguese 102.

⟳∽⁂∽⟲

My whole family sees me off to the airport the next morning.

I'm not sad. Annette cries, clinging to me, and my mom looks weepy.

But I feel it in my bones. I am not a child and my life is not under my parents' roof anymore.

I am eager to go back.

But my first hitch happens when I try to check in for my flight. I use the automated kiosk, but instead of making a confirmation when I scan my barcode, it makes the negative noise at me.

Record locator not found. Please go to ticket counter.

I glance at the ticket counter, where already a long line forms behind it.

"Is something wrong?" Mom asks.

My newfound-confidence of five minutes ago suddenly vanishes.

"It says they can't find my ticket," I say, and I hope she hears the alarm in my voice.

"We'll get this sorted," she says. She turns to my dad. "Go ahead and take everyone home. I'll call you when I'm done here and you can come get me."

She's prepared for this to take a while.

At least she's not going to leave me.

Everyone else leaves, and we get in the long line. Now I'm anxious. I have an hour and a half until my flight, but I wasn't expecting inconveniences. I listen to the conversations around me. I'm not the only one this happened to. And some of the voices are more frantic, angrier, with flights leaving in half an hour. I want to bite my nails, but I gave up that habit a decade ago.

The line creeps forward.

Finally, it's my turn. I relinquish my need for independence as my mom steps up. I'll let her take charge on this.

"My daughter has a flight in an hour, but when we tried to check in, it said her ticket could not be found."

The girl behind the check-in counter with eyeliner like airplane wings doesn't even look up from her computer as she types. "ID?"

I dig out my driver's license and hand it over.

The girl types a few things and says, "Sorry, but I can't find her ticket number in the system."

"Yes, that's what I said," my mom says, only now her tone is irritated and impatient. "But I've got my confirmation number right here. So the problem is on your end."

The girl still doesn't look up. My eyes glance to her name tag. Alisha. Although she doesn't say anything as she types on the computer, I get the impression she already knows that. We're not the first ones to show up today with this problem.

"What is your final destination?"

"Eagle County," I say.

She continues typing, eyes on her screen. I don't think she's looked at us once.

483

"Okay." The printer whirls, and she pulls out the long paper. "I got you rebooked on an American Airlines flight going out at four p.m. You'll connect in Denver and reach Eagle County at eight." She attaches the long tags to my luggage.

"Four p.m.?" I say, my brain catching up to her words. "It's nine in the morning."

"That's the best I can do. Everything is full. Unless you want to wait until tomorrow, and then I can get you on a nine a.m. flight."

Now her tone is brusque, like somehow this is my fault and she's doing me a favor.

I open and close my mouth. I look at my mom. It's not like I have options.

"Thank you," Mom says.

Alisha finally looks up as she hands over my boarding pass. "Have a nice day." She doesn't smile, and her gaze slips away quickly as if worried she'll be caught in a lie.

I am absolutely incensed. I follow my mom out of the line. "What am I supposed to do for six hours?" I exclaim.

My mom shakes her head. "This happens all the time when flying. You'll be okay. Sit down with your book and enjoy the journey."

And now I realize she's going to leave me. I fight down the rising panic. "What if something else goes wrong? What if I'm stuck here?"

My mom looks at me with something like amusement on her face. "If you're still here tonight, I will come get you and you can sleep at home, and then I'll bring you to the airport in the morning."

She's right. I'm freaking out for no reason. I give her another hug and then make my way up the escalator to security.

It's a long day. I text all my friends, but as the hours linger, soon Owen is the only one responding. We joke and chat, but there is an aching in my chest because I didn't see him, and I feel the distance growing between us with each passing day.

We are meant to be with the ones we love.

I need to see him. Somehow I'm going to find a way. That has to be a top priority.

I arrive in Eagle County Regional Airport at eight p.m. The massive snowstorm is gone, the plane cooperated, and I land without fanfare. I haul my luggage out to my car and leave the parking lot.

I pull my car up to the open guard post and hand the attendant my ticket. She reads it, looks back at me, and says, "A hundred and twenty-four dollars."

I stifle of gasp. Say what? It costs that much money to park my car at the airport? I hand over my debit card, numb, already calculating the hours I need to work pay for this.

From now on, I'm getting rides to the airport. I'm never parking my car here again.

CHAPTER EIGHTY-EIGHT

Confidently Bilingual

I spend the two days before school starts getting ready for it. In addition to my Portuguese class, I have a modern dance class. I'm a terrible dancer, but I am excited about this class. My healthy food habits fell by the wayside in college in favor of convenience, and my meals consist of ramen and macaroni and cheese and clam chowder. I lack the motivation to incorporate cooking into my daily routine, so instead, I will add exercise. In addition to a dance class, I'm taking a swimming class. I know how to swim but not well. I'm looking forward to improving that.

I jump right back into work. Stirling is there the second day, and we have an easy conversation catching up on each other's Christmas break, but he doesn't ask me to come over.

The generous spirit of giving from Christmas is over. Every person I talk to is rude and short. I only have two donations by the end of the night, and the highest number anyone has is six. Quite pathetic.

My roommates are back, and we spend a full hour cuddling on the couch in front of the fish tank together, the four of us, sharing stories about our break. I whine about work and my terrible pink eye infections and no kissing.

"Pink eye and kissing don't go well together," Layne says.

"I wouldn't know," I say, and we laugh at my misfortune.

I hardly sleep the night before the second semester starts. I feel like I know a little bit more of what to expect from college, and it's a solid mixture of fun and difficult.

Portuguese is my first class Monday morning. I step into the room at nine a.m., nervous but excited. It's a small class, with only about twelve students. I keep to myself and sit in the back, wondering how hard it can be.

The professor comes into the room and greets us, then launches into excited chatter about the class while holding up a syllabus.

He's speaking entirely in Portuguese.

He lost me after "good morning."

I sit there through the hour class, sweat gathering beneath my arms and in my hairline. He draws a root tree on the board and goes over irregular conjugations. Even my knowledge of Spanish does not help me here.

And then finally, he switches into English. I breathe a sigh of relief as he explains our homework assignment: to write a one-paragraph essay about ourselves and why we are learning Portuguese. I lean back in my seat, feeling my heart rate slow.

I'll be able to do this.

I hang around after class ends and approach the professor as he packs up.

"I wanted to let you know, I didn't take Portuguese 101," I say.

He lifts his face to look at me. His hair is receding, but he's not old. The glasses he wears make his eyes look large and buggy.

"This is your first Portuguese class?" he says, and I hear the alarm in his voice.

"Yes, but I went to Brazil two summers ago," I say, hurrying to reassure him. "I have some familiarity with the language."

"How did class go for you today?"

I nod as I speak to lend credibility and confidence to my words. "Pretty good. I kept up pretty well."

"Well, great." He looks somewhat appeased. "I'm sure you'll do fine, then. If you change your mind, you have until the end of the week to drop the class."

"Thank you," I say.

But I'm sure of myself now. I won't need to drop the class.

My English class goes as well as I expect it to. I'm taking two every semester, trying to get through my major requirements in three years instead of four so I can leave on a mission after I graduate. At least there's no math this semester.

I head to the library after class and settle myself in my favorite spot on the fifth floor, surrounded by books and square tables. I have reading assignments, but they will be easy. The assignment occupying my mind is Portuguese. We are, of course, forbidden from using any online translation services. And the professor said he would check, and he would know if we used one, even if we tried to tweak it.

That defeats the purpose of trying to learn this language anyway. So I pull out the dictionary I bought and begin to write my essay. How hard can it be?

It's terrible. I cannot simply translate word for word.

I don't know how to conjugate the verbs. I attempt to do it the way we do it in Spanish.

I am learning Portuguese because my friend—no, no, delete that.

—*because I love Brazil and I am going there*—

I get stuck again. I find a verb, but I don't know how to conjugate it, and there are three different words for "there."

I give it my best shot.

—*this summer. I want to speak Portuguese to the people around me.*

There is no direct translation for around. I'm frustrated because the dictionary lists ten possibilities for each word. How do I know I'm using the right one? I comfort myself with the fact that most people in the class have only had one semester of Portuguese more than me. All of us will be confused.

I finish the two paragraphs and read back over it. It seems decent.

I am tempted to send it to Tiago and have him look over it. But I keep him at an arm's length, and I'm comfortable with that.

I put my laptop and my essay away. Then I turn to my reading assignments, feeling good about this semester so far.

⚬〰⚬

My classes the next day are very straightforward. I have an English class and then my history class, which is one of those giant general education classes that crams a thousand kids into one auditorium, and we watch the teacher walk back-and-forth on the stage like a little bitty stick figure with a microphone. I'm nervous about this class because it was a hard one for my roommates last semester, and everyone says the questions on the tests are tricky. My history class in high school was one of the hardest I took, and the only AP test I didn't pass.

From there I move to my next English class, British literature. This one I'll enjoy. I'm not familiar with most of these books my professor assigns as reading material, but as we analyze a passage together, something about the formal, archaic writing style appeals to me.

Then I head to my swim class, my second PE credit for the semester. As soon as I put on my swimsuit, I remember why I don't like to swim in front of people.

I have no boobs. And this swimsuit has absolutely zero padding.

I'm as flat as a boy, and my reflection embarrasses me. I'm slender with good hips, but I have no chest.

I hate it.

I try to tell myself that the boy who loves me won't care, but how can he not? Boys love boobs.

The two boys who I've been physically involved with didn't seem to care, but then, it's not like I took my shirt off and paraded my naked chest. They don't actually know.

There's nothing I can do about it.

I head to my swim class, resolving to forget about my bodily insecurities.

The class is boys and girls, but I ignore the boys and sit down by another girl on the bench. She's tiny like I am, Asian, with short, dark hair. She hunches her shoulders, as if trying to be invisible. I am immediately drawn to her.

The teacher comes out and gives us a syllabus and explains that we'll be learning every basic stroke (which means no butterfly) and survival techniques.

She hands out kickboards and tells us to jump in and kick to the other side.

I give a shudder as I jump into the water, which is only lukewarm. She demonstrates from the sideline how to hold the kickboard straight out in front of us, with our fingers clasped around the curved edge.

"Then keep your legs straight behind you and kick."

I hold my hands out in front of me with the board between my fingers and start kicking.

Around me, my classmates are moving forward a foot at a time, but I barely bob. I cheat and push off the wall behind me with my foot, and that manages to get me a few inches. I slap the water with my feet hard enough to rotate my hips, and I begin to move.

Backward.

What the heck? I cannot be this bad at swimming. I touch the bottom of the pool with one foot and again give myself a forward push. For a moment, my legs and hips and torso work together, and I give a jubilant mental shout as I rock forward.

But it doesn't last. I make it about five feet before once again, I start sliding backward.

The teacher steps over to me at the side of the pool. "Use your entire thigh to kick the water. The whole leg," she says.

I try. My legs want to bend at the knees, but I hold them firm and scissor kick in the water.

I do not go backward. But I do not go forward. I remain as stationary as if I were treading water.

She crouches beside me. "You are moving forward at the same time that you move backward," she says. "You have to learn to isolate the movement."

Yes. I will have to learn to do this. So far, I'm unable to do so.

After class, we herd ourselves to the locker rooms to change. I find myself next to the tiny Asian girl, and I glance at her as I open my locker. Somehow I find the courage to speak to her.

"Well, that was interesting."

She laughs. "Yes." Her voice is soft and heavily accented. "I know nothing with water."

We change out of our swimsuits, using our locker doors to shield ourselves out of an overabundance of modesty.

"I'm Cassandra. What's your name?"

"Call me Chris." It sounds like "crease." "You won't be able to say my name in English." She flashes a smile.

I smile back. I slide my shirt on and slip into my pants. "Where are you from?"

"Thailand."

"Wow. And you came to school all the way out here?"

She shrugs. "They provide very good opportunity for me. And I want to try all the sports."

"I hate sports," I say with gusto. "But I want to be more active. So here I am."

"And me too."

We close our lockers and shoulder our backpacks, then head out of the locker room together.

"I'll see you Thursday," I say.

"See you," she answers. "Maybe you will learn to swim forward."

I'm momentarily startled, unaware she saw my horrible swimming today. Then I laugh. "Maybe."

⁘

I turn in my Portuguese essay on Wednesday and then sit down for class. I feel confident about my work. My dictionary will get me through this class.

Or so I think.

I'm completely lost the moment the professor begins speaking. I realize he is talking slowly and annunciating his words carefully, but I don't recognize his words. No matter how slowly he speaks, I don't know this language.

He writes a reading assignment on the board, and I'm sweating with anxiety as I open my textbook.

I don't know what I'm doing.

I try to read the pages, but they mean nothing to me. It's a short story and I'm irritated, because I feel like I should be able to get the gist of it, but even the words that look like Spanish don't make sense. I haul out my dictionary and translate the best I can, but it's very slow going, and it's like having an egg and a spoonful of sugar and being told to make brownies. The key ingredients are missing.

I write down the assignment to finish at home. I need help. I will have to contact Tiago for this.

I meet with Jordan for lunch, but I don't tell him how stressed I'm feeling. He is busy watching a news clip online anyway. We make small talk over food, but his attention is elsewhere.

"And it looks like Louisiana State is headed to the championship football game," the announcer says, stealing my attention.

"What was that?" I ask.

"What?" Jordan lifts his eyes to mine.

I wave him over and lean closer, trying to watch his clip. But the announcer has moved on to something else.

I sit back in my seat and pull out my phone, then search "Louisiana State football championship game."

Owen's team made it to the championship playoffs. The game is in February, a week before his birthday.

Just like that, a plan solidifies in my mind.

I'm going there. I'm going to be at that game and I'm going to celebrate his birthday with him.

I'm so excited I push away from the table and grab my backpack.

Jordan looks up. "Where are you going?"

"Home." I shoulder my backpack. "I left my computer at home and I need it."

"Why don't you go to the library and use one there?"

I shake my head. "I need mine." All of my information is saved on it.

I speed walk back to my dorm, my legs moving ahead of my body in excitement. But first I need to talk to his mom and make sure they're okay with this.

I call Mrs. Blaine while I'm walking. She answers on the second ring.

"Cassandra!" Her voice is warm and welcoming. "What a surprise to hear from you! How are you?"

"I'm doing great." My mind is jumping, and I can't remember how to make small talk. "I heard that Owen's team made it to the playoffs."

"Yes! He's pretty excited."

"I bet he is." I let out a little exhale. "I was thinking of coming down to see the game. As a surprise. Do you think that would be all right?"

She lets out a gasp. "Cassandra, what a marvelous idea!" The excitement grows in her voice with each word. "He would be delighted! Oh, my goodness, I can just see his face!"

Me too. If I time this right, he won't know I'm there at first, he'll be busy with his game. But at some point, halftime, maybe, he'll look for his family. And he'll see me.

Best surprise ever.

"And then I thought, since I'm there, I would stay a few more days to celebrate his birthday with him."

"You'll stay with us," Mrs. Blaine says immediately. I picture her with her planner open, penciling me in. "You can take Monica's room. She's not here."

"Okay. Okay, great!" This is going smoother than I expected.

"You might even be here when he gets his mission call," she says, her tone taking on a more hushed quality. "He put in all the paperwork right after the new year."

I suck in a breath, surprised how this news both thrills me and terrifies me.

He'll be gone. A year, maybe two. We are already apart, but this is different.

I push aside those feelings. Owen going on a mission trip is amazing. "Oh, wow. He's really going."

"He really is. Let me know as soon as you have your plane ticket what time you're coming in. We'll get you from the airport and hide you at the house."

I smile, my worries fading away beneath this delicious conspiracy. "I will!"

It's the middle of the day, so I expect my dorm to be empty. But as I walk through the kitchen to the hallway I hear rapid breathing laced with whimpers coming from Layne's open room.

Alarm shoots through me. I run down the hall, wondering how I will fight off an intruder or get help if she's hurt. All I've got is my backpack, which is heavy enough that it might knock someone out for two seconds if I whack it against their head.

It turns out that won't be necessary.

Layne's back is to me, but she is naked, sitting astride a pair of legs on the bed. Also apparently naked. A groan comes from the direction of the bare legs, and she shifts slightly in an upward motion that reveals a face at the top of the bed.

It takes me all of two seconds to realize she is having sex with Brant in her room in the middle of the day.

CHAPTER EIGHTY-NINE
Lustful Embrace

dart back into the hallway and slam my hand over my mouth to muffle my gasp. I cannot believe what I just saw. I wish I could wash my eyes out with soap.

I also cannot believe she's doing that. It's against the rules to have boys in our rooms, and it is absolutely against the rules to have sex with them in our rooms. She could be kicked out of the school for this.

I don't know what to do. I'm shaking, my mind is tripping. Do I pretend like I didn't see? Am I supposed to keep this a secret? Is that what a good friend does?

I can't think. I can't stay here. I don't know if I should stop them or run away.

I grab my laptop, shove it in my backpack, and flee.

I sit myself down at a cubby in the library, but I can't get the images out of my head, and I feel nauseous. What do I do? According to the Honor Code agreement I signed when I enrolled, I'm obligated to report this. But how do I? I don't want anything to happen to Layne. And she covered for me when I slept over at Justin's aunt's house.

Even though I did nothing else there. No hanky-panky.

I need someone to talk to, someone unbiased, someone who won't judge me no matter what I decide.

I call Owen.

I hold my breath as the phone rings. Our schedules don't usually align, which is why we text more than we talk.

But Owen answers.

"Cassandra?" His voice is mellow but concerned. "Are you all right?"

"Yes, I—" I feel sheepish now for calling in the middle of the day. "Something happened, and I needed someone to help clear my mind."

"What happened?"

I hear voices around him. I keep my voice quiet because I'm in the library and don't want to be overheard. I check the time. One-fifteen. "You don't have class right now?"

"I stepped out take your call."

Of course he did. My chest warms at the consideration he has for me. "It's about my roommate."

"Is everything okay?"

I let out a short breath. "I just walked in on her having sex with her boyfriend." My face burns saying it. I am mortified.

Owen gives a low whistle. "Did she see you?"

"No. What am I supposed to do?"

"What are you thinking?"

"I don't know." I hear the desperation in my own voice. "I'm thinking how she broke the rules and now that I know, I could get in trouble if I keep it a secret. I'm thinking how she could get in trouble if I tell. I'm thinking that she probably needs me to be her friend right now."

"Those are a lot of thoughts, and they don't all match up."

"I can't think straight. All I can picture is what I saw when I walked in on them."

"I don't envy you there," he says, and I have to laugh.

"What do I do, Owen?" I say. I want him to have the answers for me. Make this easy for me.

"Do you feel like you should tell?"

I close my eyes. He knows me. I'm a rule-follower. I'm not comfortable with people breaking rules. He probably knows I'm the one who told on Beckham and his drinking party last year.

I should ask him.

But not now.

"I feel like I should," I admit. "But that makes me feel guilty. Am I more loyal to a set of rules than to a friend?"

"We all have to draw a line somewhere."

"But have I drawn the right one? In the right place?"

"What happens to Layne if you tell?"

"I don't know! I don't want her to get in trouble. I just want her to—stop having sex in our dorm!"

"Do you think you could talk to her?"

My face warms at the very idea. I would have to admit what I saw.

He talks into my silence. "What about your other roommates? Do they know?"

"I don't think so, but it's an excellent question." Has this happened before? Does Iris know? They share a room.

She's breaking the rules in our dorm room. Whether she agrees with them or not, she agreed to honor them in our house. My roommates have the right to know what's going on.

Preston Yarborough isn't like other universities where you turn your head and live and let live. We chose this school—*I* chose this school—because I didn't want to deal with things like drunken parties on campus and sorority pledges and roommates bringing boys over to exchange bodily fluids. We made a commitment not just to the school, but to respect each other's commitments.

Layne broke that respect.

"Why don't you talk to your roommates about it?"

I nod. "That's a great idea."

"It's going to be all right, Cassandra, whatever you decide. Layne made her choices. It's not your job to decide how she handles the consequences."

They are good words, and they calm me somewhat. But I know I will still bear a burden of guilt if her consequences are negative. I squeeze my phone tight, wanting to tell him I'm coming to see him. I can't ruin the surprise.

"Thank you. I appreciate you taking the time to talk to me about this."

"Of course, Cassandra. Call me anytime."

I'm less rattled when we hang up. I take a deep breath and decide I will confer with my roommates before I do anything else. I don't want to carry this burden alone.

I open my computer and take my mind back to the much more pleasant activity of purchasing a plane ticket. I'll have to fly out of the Denver airport, which is three hours away, but the flight is only two hundred dollars. It's worth it.

Of course, I'll have to take my car and leave it parked. It shouldn't cost too much since it's only four days, not two weeks.

I click the purchase button, and a hot wave of giddy anticipation rolls through my shoulders. I do not like being away from him.

⌒⁓⁂⁓⌒

I text Iris and Camila individually and ask them to meet me outside our dorm at eight o'clock tonight. This is not a conversation we can hold anywhere that Layne might hear. And I don't want to do a group text and have them realize I left Layne off.

Both of them respond individually and with curiosity, to which I reply with an ominous, *I've got something personal to talk about.*

I know they'll be there.

I'm not sure how this is going to go down.

I'm underneath the stairs outside at 7:55, wrapped in my jacket and scarf because it's freezing. Camila shows up a moment later.

"What's going on? Are you okay?"

I can feel the concern simmering beneath her skin. "Let's wait another minute."

She glances around. "Are you expecting someone else?"

I don't have to answer, because Iris pops around the corner. She sees us in a huddle there under the stairwell and comes to join us.

"What's happening?" she says.

I take a deep breath, my heart rate ratcheting. I roll my fingers and move out from under the stairwell, around the building, so we are out of view of the back door. Just in case Layne should pop out. We are in the shadows, and I hope she doesn't wander over and stumble upon us.

"It's Layne."

Camila glances at Iris, and Iris focuses on me.

"What's wrong with her?" Iris asks.

Layne is her roommate. They seem to get along very well. Maybe Iris already knows about Brant.

There's no easy way to say this, so I just go for it. "I walked in on her and Brant today—having sex."

Camila utters a gasp, and Iris's eyes go wide.

Looks like neither of them knew either. "How do you know?" Iris asks, her voice even. "Did you actually see. . . ?"

I nod. "I saw. They were both naked. She was riding him. I got a full back view."

I say the words callously, like they don't burn the back of my throat as if they were made of acid.

Silence meets my pronouncement. There can be no arguing with that.

"I didn't know they were having sex," Iris murmurs.

None of us are quite sure how to digest this information. My best friend Riley was having sex all through high school, but it wasn't in my house. She was breaking her house rules, not mine. I certainly never saw it. This is different, and it's awkward.

"Boys are not allowed in our rooms." Camila speaks calmly, but there is grit in her voice. I feel a surge of relief. The Honor Code means something to her also.

She doesn't mention that the Honor Code also says no sexual activity. We know. But what we do privately is kind of, well, private.

I certainly wouldn't report myself if I had sex with Owen over Thanksgiving.

"I don't want to have an awkward situation in our apartment," Camila says. "She can't be bringing guys over. Iris, you need to talk to her."

"I don't want to be the one to confront her," Iris says. "You're the one who saw, Cassandra."

I throw my hands up. "I don't want to confess to that."

"So let's pray on it," Camila says. "We'll meet back here tomorrow night and see if anyone has any insight."

We nod. I feel relief; the burden is not on me anymore.

We go inside the apartment one at a time. Layne is spread across the couch, eating a bowl of cereal and watching TV. She doesn't look up when I enter, and I try to banish from my mind the mental image I have of what I saw earlier.

It's impossible.

I go to my room, and I can't help wondering what Layne feels now. Is she thinking about Brant? Remembering what it felt like to touch his body, to have him touch her? Does she feel a stronger connection to him? I shiver and try not to explore the thoughts too much. I'm eighteen and a virgin and my hormones are screaming at me to share that experience with someone.

But not just anyone.

I imagine what I would feel in my heart and in my soul if it were Owen.

I want it so badly I could cry.

The bedroom door opens and Camila comes in, dragging me from my pitiful thoughts. I look at her and she looks at me and we don't speak. But I know we are both thinking about the same thing.

All thoughts of Layne vanish in the morning because I have a pop quiz in Portuguese.

"Irregular verb conjugation," my professor says. "I'll give you a verb. You conjugate it into first person, second person, third person, and then first person plural and third person plural."

I start to sweat. I don't know the verbs. I won't know how to conjugate this.

You know a decent amount of Spanish, I comfort myself. *Just transpose that knowledge.*

I exhale. I'm ready.

"*Por*," he says.

My classmates hunch over their papers, writing.

Por? Isn't that the same as the English word "for"? That's not a verb. I blink and stare at the lined sheet in front of me, aware of the scratch of pens. I guess at the spelling of the root and then add made-up conjugated endings. Poro, Pores, Porendo.

"*Fazer*."

I have no freaking idea.

"*Dar*."

I lay my pen down and wait. I'm out of my element.

He gives us three more verbs.

I don't recognize any of them. This language is not Spanish. And I'm stuck. I feel it in my heart. I'm doomed.

We pass our papers to the person behind us grade-school style. I'm so embarrassed. Now somebody besides me will know my folly in registering for this class. The professor gives us the answers, writing the spelling on the board. The paper I'm grading misses three possible conjugations.

When the paper is handed back to me, I wince at the massacre. Some of them I didn't spell the root verb correctly and thus missed the rest of it. Three of them I got the plural "we" form correct because it wasn't irregular.

That's it. I can't take this class. If I'm going to drop it, it has to be now. I suck in a breath and slouch lower, swallowing against an ache in my throat.

I go up to the teacher as soon as class is over.

"I'm going to have to drop the class," I say, trying not to let my voice tremble. I'm close to tears. "I don't know as much as I thought. I can't do it."

"I understand," he says kindly. "You have a basic knowledge. Why don't you try the accelerated class? I think you would catch up quickly."

I nod. I looked at that class, but I'm not sure I can do it. It's an eight-credit class, with Portuguese 101 in the first nine weeks and Portuguese 102 in the second nine weeks. The only requirement is that you have to be fluent in Spanish.

If I drop this class, I'll be down to ten credits. Adding that one will put me at eighteen. The maximum.

I was trying to take it easier this semester.

"Thanks for helping me," I say. "Thanks for teaching me for a week."

"Of course."

I leave the classroom in a blur. I have to put another class in place of this one and I want to study Portuguese. What am I going to do? I wander over to the bookstore in between classes and stand in front of the rows of journals and notebook. Usually looking at these pretty things make me happy, but my head isn't on right at the moment, and I stare past them. I'm discouraged and overwhelmed.

"Well, if it isn't Cassandra Jones!"

I lift my head and look over the shelf to see Jared standing across from me.

"Jared," I say, and the sight of my friend, the boy I've harbored secret feelings for during the past five months, undoes the carefully crafted emotional barrier I was attempting to hold in place. I burst into tears.

Jared's smile drops in an instant, and his face crinkles in concern. "What is it? What's wrong?"

"Oh, nothing, it's just my stupid Portuguese class!" I can't believe I'm crying over it. And I am. Right there in the bookstore, sobbing. "I signed up at the wrong time, and they only have 102 available this semester and I can't do it! I thought I could, but it turns out my limited knowledge of Portuguese is not enough, and I totally bombed the quiz today and I'm going to have to drop the class. But I don't know what to take instead, if I wait until next semester I'll be a full year behind and I'll have already gone to Brazil and I want to learn Portuguese before I go!" I'm totally rambling, the words pouring out of me.

Jared comes around the shelf to stand in front of me. I know he wants to hug me, but instead, he puts his hands on my shoulders. "You are one of the smartest people I know. Take another subject you enjoy to plug-in the spot."

I shake my head. "I only want to do Portuguese!"

"But you're dropping the class," he says, almost gently, as if I don't know. "It doesn't look like that's an option anymore."

"There is another option." I dry my eyes on my sleeves, my breathing still shaky. "I could take the accelerated class."

"What's that?"

"It's a full year of Portuguese, crammed into one semester."

Jared raises both eyebrows. "Cassandra, that's the solution! You'll get all the Portuguese you want before you go!"

"But I'll have eighteen credits. It's so much."

"If anyone can do it, you can."

I don't have as much faith in myself as he does. But I am encouraged by his enthusiasm. Maybe I can do it.

It's my only option.

"Thank you." I throw my arms around his neck and try not to notice how nice it feels when he squeezes me back.

CHAPTER NINETY
Contention at Home

I feel calmer about my Portuguese class when I leave the bookstore. I go to the administration building and drop the 102 class.

"You don't have enough credits to be considered a full-time student now," the registrar warns. "You'll lose your scholarship if you don't add more."

"I know," I say. "I'm adding another class on Monday." Now that the semester is a week old, I can't add the class online. The professor has to sign off on it.

I'm praying he lets me be in his class, even as I mourn the death of my easy credit semester and replace it with a full load.

Then I go to the library to study.

Owen texts me as I pull out my history book.

O: What went down with your roommate?

I cradle the phone in my hands and lean back in my chair, giving him my full attention. I'm tingly with anticipation. I'm going to see him in six weeks and he doesn't even know.

Me: I talked with my other roommates about it, and we're trying to figure out what to do. None of us are sure, but I feel a lot better not bearing the whole burden.

O: I'm glad. Whatever decision you make will be the right one.

He has so much faith in me it's uncanny.

Me: how are your classes going?

O: Meh

Me: Meaning?

O: I don't much care anymore. I have to finish out this semester and then I'm out of here.

Me: Are you ready?

O: I think so. Feeling good about things.

I remember the Owen I met two years ago, who only wanted to party and shake off responsibility. This boy I love is not the same one.

Me: stay focused a bit longer

I wait a moment for his response, but he's not there anymore. I turn back to my studying, but I'm glad Owen texted me. He is a stabilizing force in my life and helps keep me grounded.

I'm a bit anxious about going home and what I might find there, but my anxiety subsides when I find Layne's note on the fridge.

Spending the weekend with friends. Love y'all XOXO Layne.

I make myself a cup of soup with crackers and then go to my room to read.

Camila pops in an hour later. "How was your day?" she asks.

My drama from this morning feels like it happened a week ago, so I shrug. "Normal. I had to rearrange my schedule, but I'll make it work. How about yours?"

"I saw a sign when I went past Glendale on my run this morning," she says. "They're taking rental applications for next term."

"Is it already time to think about that?" I haven't thought past next week, let alone next term.

"We won't be able to stay in the dorms."

Who will I room with? My heart pounds a little faster, and I meet Camila's eyes. What if she doesn't want to be my roommate anymore? Will I have to make new friends?

There's a tap on our bedroom door an instant before Iris pops in. She munches on a can of chips and sits down next to Camila.

"What do you guys think about rooming together next year?" Iris says, very casually.

Very coincidentally. I wonder if they talked about it before Camila came in.

"I would love to room with you guys next year," Camila says, her face brightening. "We get along so well. You're my favorite people."

I grin at them, my spirits lifting. "I feel the same way."

"What about Layne?" Camila says. "Do we want to room with her again next year?"

I consider the question. I like Layne, I like her a lot. She's fun. She's also a total flirt and a rule-breaker.

"She isn't here," Iris says.

"I know. I saw the note," I say.

"Which friend's house do you think she went to?" Iris says, raising her eyebrows.

I look at Camila, and neither one of us responds.

"What are we going to do about this?" Camila says.

We are quiet for a moment. Then I say, "I think we should talk to her."

Camila chews on her lower lip while she mulls that over. "You don't think she'll deny everything?"

"She can't," I say. "I freaking saw them."

"She might try to say you didn't see what you thought you saw," Iris says.

I shrug. "We need to give her a chance to agree not to—do that here. And she should be the one to fess up. If she refuses, we can take it to the Honor Code office."

Again silence. Then Iris nods.

"I feel like that's right. We're bound by the Honor Code because we choose to be. We can't force her to stop doing it."

"We kind of can," Camila says. "The Honor Code office can take action."

"Like what?" I ask. "Expulsion?"

Camila lowers her gaze. "That's definitely not what I want."

"None of us do," I say. "Are we in agreement, then? We talk to Layne. And then we decide what to do based on her reaction."

Iris nods. "I'm in agreement. Who's going to be the one to talk to her?"

Both of them look at me, and my heart skips a beat.

"Me?" My voice squeaks out. "I can't talk to her about something like this." I am so non-confrontational.

"You are the one who saw," Camila says, her tone gentle. "You're the only one who can talk to her. What would I say, Cassandra told me that she walked in on you guys having sex?"

I flinch, and Iris giggles.

"Somehow I don't see that going over well," Iris says. "It's got to be you, Cassandra."

I see their point. "Fine. I'll do it."

"What should we do about next year?" Camila asks. "I mean, the rooming situation."

"I would rather not room with her," Iris says. "She keeps me awake and can be a little too crazy."

"I don't think she and I would get along, honestly," Camila says. "I like her, but we're not super close."

Again, that leaves me. "I can room with her. If she even wants to after I talk with her." Which I am so dreading.

"The other option would be leaving the fourth bed available for a new roommate," Camila says.

"I'd rather have Layne than take my chance on someone else we don't know," I say.

Camila nods. One more thing agreed-upon.

❦

Iris wants to go see the apartment Camila was talking about it, but I have to work. We plan for me to pick everyone up at two o'clock and drive over to the apartment.

Work is extremely slow. I think our entire list got spam blockers on their phone lines over Christmas, because most calls go unanswered or straight to voicemail. Stirling pulls out a deck of cards, and we play Uno, which doesn't work very well if there's only two people. He tries to tell me the reverse card means he gets to go again, but I argue that he sent the play back to me. Finally, we pull all the reverse cards out of the deck.

We haven't talked much since I got back. He said hello when he saw me after Christmas break but didn't hug me, and I didn't miss him, so there wasn't much to talk about.

We finish up the workday with only a few pledges. Stirling swings an arm around my shoulders as we walk out.

"We can get together next weekend," he says. "It's been a while since we've chilled."

I nod. "Yeah. that would be fun."

I'm at my apartment ten minutes later. Iris and Camila come tumbling out before I even turn the car off. They are full of chatter and excited to talk, and we are all anticipating the excitement of our sophomore year of college.

I pull up in front of the Glendale apartment complex. It's huge, taking up an entire block. And it's very dated. Brown siding, brown brick, brown roof.

A few vacant apartments have been left open for us to peruse. We fall into an apartment. Immediately it's better than our dorm. We don't have a living room, just a kitchen with a couch. This has a living room. I sit down on the couch behind the TV and sprawl out.

Camila goes down the hall, and Iris heads into the kitchen, which is around the corner, separated from the living room by a counter.

"At least it has a dishwasher!"

I hop up to join her. It's a tiny kitchen, with barely room for the round table shoved into the corner. The counter has been cut at an awkward angle to leave room for the refrigerator to open.

"It's so small," Iris says, and she wrinkles her nose as she surveys the kitchen space.

"The bedrooms are a decent size," Camila says, coming in.

I leave them in the kitchen so I can check out the bedrooms. There's two. I lean across the bed to look out the window over the parking lot below. Not much of a view, but it gets light. Two desks flank each bed with a closet at one side of the room.

I return to the living room. Camila is perusing the spec sheet on the counter.

"Rent is a lot," she says. "And it doesn't include utilities."

I come over and examine the spec sheet with her. Living here would take a third of my paycheck. My heart rate quickens at the logistics.

Along with that comes the realization that I don't want to work at the telefund anymore. I want a quiet, respectful job behind a desk where I don't have to convince people to part with their money.

"It says here there are twice as many female units as male," Camila says, running her finger under the data.

She and Iris exchange glances.

That means girls outnumber boys two-to-one in this complex.

It looks like they're not in love with this place. But I want to be done searching. I want to find a place and not worry about it anymore. "That's not a huge deal," I say.

"Because you're in love someone already," Iris says. "You're not looking."

"I thought you were too," I shoot back.

Her ivory skin blushes. "I like to keep my options open."

"Let's look at a few other places," Camila says. "I'll make a list."

She's got two more places to look at before we get to my car. We drive over and examine them, but one of them feels cheap and ghetto, and the other one is too far from campus.

"We'll keep looking," Camila says, optimistic and cheerful. "We'll find the perfect place. In the meantime, we need to talk to Layne."

They both look at me, and I know somehow this is still my responsibility.

"Make yourselves scarce tonight," I say. "I'll talk to her when she gets home."

But Layne does not come home until Sunday. She's there when we get back from church, making a bowl of noodles and watching TV. She looks up at us and smiles big, shoving her light hair out of her face.

"Hi, guys!" she says. "How was church?"

I feel Iris and Camila stiffen up behind me, and I glance back at them to see them looking like deer in headlights. I step on Camila's foot, which brings her back to life, even as I turn to Layne.

"It was great. How was your friend?"

"Oh, good, good." Layne waves her hand. "Everything was great."

Iris and Camila slip past me into the hallway, and I can hear them whispering. Can their behavior be any more conspicuous? But Layne doesn't seem to notice.

I sit down at the table and pleat my fingers in front of me. How do I start this conversation?

"We went and looked at apartments yesterday."

Layne looks up from her phone, her eyes brightening. "Really? That's so exciting! For all four of us?"

"Well, if you want to room with us. We weren't sure . . ."

"Of course I want to! I love you guys! We all get along so well, right?"

"Right," I say quickly, but something must show on my face, or in my voice, because fine lines form in the skin above her brows as she raises them at me.

"No?"

This is harder than I expected it to be, and I expected it to be hard. I feel sweat gathering along my hairline. "Well, the thing is, we have some concerns."

CHAPTER NINETY-ONE

Sink or Swim

Layne's eyebrows arch even higher. "Some concerns?" she echoes.

Crap, I have no idea what to say next. I feel like an idiot at my word choice. I lick my lips and hope I don't look as nervous as I feel. "Yes. Regarding Brant. Or . . . any other boy you might decide to bring home in the future."

She settles back in the couch and closes her fingers around her noodle bowl, her expression one of complete irritation. "How is it any of your business?"

"Well, it kind of is, if we live together." Her response has me digging my heels in. I'm not wrong here.

"I'm the one who's not allowed to bring guys over, but everyone else can?"

"It's not bringing them over that's the problem," I say. "It's having sex with them in your bedroom that creates an issue."

It turns out I have a flair for the dramatic.

Her blush is priceless, and she gets out, "What?"

Her shock is enough to make me doubt what I saw. "I walked in on you and Brant three days ago," I say, lowering my voice so I don't sound aggressive or attacking. "You can imagine how hard it's been to carry around that knowledge and not—"

"You don't have to carry around any knowledge!" she says, full on defensive. "It's none of your damn business what I do! Or any of the rest of you! You don't get to police me, you don't get to control me!"

She's so upset her hands are shaking, and I'm wilting. I hate fighting. This confrontation is my kryptonite.

"But you agreed to the Honor Code," I say. "Just like we did. That's not just for you, but for us. It's about respect and consideration for your roommates, so we don't have unwanted activities happening in our apartment."

"Oh, you won't have them," she says, nostrils flaring, fire-breathing. "I am not rooming with you guys!" She slams her bowl down on the floor, pushes to her feet, and exits through the fire escape.

I sit there at the table, breathing heavily, shaking, sick to my stomach over the confrontation. It did not go the way I wanted. I love Layne, and I hate for her to feel like we don't want her. What could I have done differently?

I grab my phone and I leave also. It's too cold to go walking around, so I jump in my car and crank the heater. My teeth chatter, and I want to vomit.

So I call Owen.

"Hey, girl," he says, answering on the second ring. "What's up?"

"I had a big fight with my roommate," I say without preamble, and then I burst into tears.

"Hey, hey," he says, his voice turning soft and gentle. "It's okay. What happened?"

"It's the one I told you about," I say, still weepy. "Since I'm the one who saw her with her boyfriend, everyone decided I should be the one to confront her."

"Why confront her?"

"See, I knew I did it wrong!" I cry harder. "I didn't mean to hurt her feelings or upset her!"

"Deep breaths, Cassandra. Did you go at her with your claws out and weapons drawn?"

"No. I started out talking about how the rest of us are looking at an apartment and we would like to room with her but the boy situation has to change. I wasn't trying to attack her. I did point out that we all signed the same Honor Code agreement, and that is to protect us as much as her. We shouldn't have to walk into our own apartment and be confronted with people having sex!" I can feel that I'm defensive. I want Owen to side with me.

"I agree with you. And I know you probably weren't trying to attack her. But she's not gonna hear your words as logic, she's going to hear an accusation and see it as an infringement on her rights."

"She doesn't have rights in this situation!"

He's quiet, and I regret my tone.

"I'm sorry," I say, exhaling. "I'm a bit emotionally charged right now."

"So what happens next depends on you, Cassandra," he says, very calmly. "And I think I know you well enough to know what you want. You want to make peace with her, and you want her to be your roommate, but you also want her to respect your boundaries and the rules of your school."

"Yes. How do I do that?"

"Throwing the rulebook at her won't work," he says. "The only way you're gonna win her over is by letting her know how much you care. That it's her wellbeing you're worried about."

I squeeze the phone in my hand. I screwed up. "How can I fix this?"

"She still lives with you. Go find her and talk to her. You're great at unruffling feathers. You have a gift at smoothing things over, making people feel important."

"I do?"

"Yes. You can do this."

"I will." He's given me the determination. "You're the smartest person I know."

"I've walked in her shoes."

And he came out better for it. But I refrain from waxing lyrical.

"I love you," I say. I can't hold that back.

"I love you too," he says, his voice going soft. Tender.

It's painful in its emotion. He doesn't know he'll see me in six weeks. But he knows he's leaving soon. And I feel it, on the edges of his words: he's breaking away from me.

⚬〜⚘〜⚬

Layne doesn't come back all evening.

Camila and Iris ask me how it went, but I tell them we're still talking and to ask me later. I know from the way Camila looks at me that she suspects it didn't go well, but she keeps her questions to herself.

I stay up in the kitchen with the lights off, waiting for Layne to come home. She finally comes tiptoeing in after midnight. She hits the light by the fridge and stops when she sees me.

"What?" she says, her tone frosty. "Waiting up like my mother now? Going to impose a curfew on me?"

Her tone wounds me, and I bite my lip, blinking to hold back tears.

"I wanted to apologize," I say, and I can't keep the tremble from my voice. "I said everything wrong earlier today. I love you and we want you to be our roommate next year and I'm worried. Everything else I said was me not knowing how to express my concern without sounding like an old-fashioned ninny." I'm unable to contain the hot liquid in my eyes, which spills down my cheeks.

Layne remains still, but I see the skin around her eyes softening. "I'm surprised you didn't already report me to the Honor Code office."

"We wouldn't do that." I shake my head. "We're not out to get you. We want to protect you."

She moves away from the counter and sits at the edge of the couch, adjacent from me. "Do the other girls know?"

I nod. "I felt they had the right to know also."

"I don't agree with that," Layne says, her tone fiery but contained. "It's my life. My body. My decision."

"Outside of this house, yes," I say. "But we live here. If Camila were doing drugs in the bathroom, the rest of us would have the right to know and demand she stop."

"I'm not doing drugs," Layne says softly.

"But we all signed an agreement. Boys are not allowed in our rooms—and definitely not naked ones."

She finally smiles. "But the naked ones are the best ones."

That elicits a giggle from me, and she laughs, and then I'm laughing. She reaches over and hugs me, and I squeeze her tight, so glad we're not fighting anymore.

"I'm sorry," I say. "I didn't mean to make you feel attacked."

She leans back. "So it's him being over here that's the problem?"

"He can be over here. It's just—you guys having sex here that's the problem."

504

She arches an eyebrow. "But not elsewhere."

I shrug, pushing down my motherly urges to caution her. "As you said, we don't have a say in what goes on outside of this apartment."

"All right. We can respect that boundary." She gets a dark glint in her eye. "But it's so much fun."

"What is?"

"Sex."

The desire to know makes my blood hot and my head pound. I shake my head. "I've not gone that far."

"Not even with Owen?"

"No."

"How far have you gone?"

It sounds like Layne wants to trade war stories. But I don't. I try not to let my mind wander into our carnal activities. "Far enough to want to go all the way."

"Just so you know, the first time's not so great," she says. "So you have to do it at least twice. Because it gets better."

"I'll keep that in mind." My thoughts have spiraled in a dangerous direction.

"If you need any tips—" she begins, but I raise a hand.

"I don't," I say. "We'll figure it out when the time comes."

"Are you planning on sleeping with Owen?"

All the planning we have done has been on *not* sleeping together. But I know with a certainty in my heart what I want. "He will be my first."

As soon as I say the words, I feel like I've cemented them into my future. My heart burns within me like a spiritual awakening. I've just put my deepest desire out to the universe.

She grins. "If it doesn't go great the first few times, keep trying until it does."

My phone chimes. I glance down to see a text from Owen, which means he's up super late. There's an hour difference between us.

O: did you talk to roommate?

"Speak of the devil," Layne says.

I stand. "Good night, Layne. I'm glad you'll room with us next year."

I lay down on my bed and pull the blankets up to my neck. I hear the soft sound of Camila's deep breaths on the other bed, then I turn sideways and respond to Owen.

Me: I did. It's all better. Thanks for your help

O: you're welcome. I'm glad. I knew that would bug you till you fixed it

My thoughts are full of inappropriate desires, and my fingers itch to express them. My mind is flashing back to Thanksgiving, when we gave into the pull of touching and feeling and almost, almost let it happen. My skin is alive, my body lustful. But I am in Colorado and he is in Louisiana. We are apart. We are safe.

Me: thank you for everything. You mean the world to me.

O: thanks for being you

Me: go to bed. It's late. I'll talk to you later.

O: night, cass

Me: night, Owen.

I stare at the texting conversation as my phone dims and then shuts off. Ten minutes pass. I'm too bothered to sleep.

I send one last text. *I love you.*

I'm nearly asleep when the phone chimes by my ear, jolting me to alertness. I blink and lift my head enough to see my phone go dark again. I pick it up, and it lights up as I tilt it toward me.

O: I love you too.

I smile and drift into a warm and contented rest.

⁂

Monday I show up at my new Portuguese class. Eight in the morning every day of the week. I vowed at the beginning of the school year to avoid eight a.m. classes at all costs. I'm not a morning person. Nine is early enough.

Yet here I am, eight o'clock Monday through Friday.

My heart races as I enter the room, filled with upperclassman. They joke and talk to each other and ignore me. I'm just a freshman and I missed the first week. I find a seat in the back, my add card in my hand. If the professor allows me to be in the class, he has to sign off on my card and I'll take it back to the registrar.

He comes in. He's an older man, mostly bald with a silver fringe around the sides of his head, a pleasant smile, and glasses.

"*Bom dia!*" he says, and the class echoes it back.

I know this phrase. It means good morning.

"*Sou Professor Dennis.*"

I recognize the introduction, and for a moment I'm buoyed—and then he launches into speech.

Why is he speaking Portuguese? Isn't this the intro level class? I don't have the text book yet because I wanted to make sure I got it added before I bought it, so I just listen.

I understand nothing.

"*Entenderam?*" he says.

Apparently he's expecting an answer because he looks at the class and waits. But blank faces stare back at him. So he starts again, but this time I recognize the language.

It's Spanish.

I tilt my head as I catch a few words.

Then I realize what he's doing.

He's re-explaining. Repeating everything he just said. In Spanish instead of Portuguese.

My breathing comes a little faster. This class will not be easier than the other one. My Spanish isn't good enough to help me here.

But I have no choice. If I don't take this class, I have to wait until next year. What good will that be? I leave for Brazil in four months.

It's a hopelessly daunting task. Learn this language in four months. My entire semester will be breathing, thinking, and dreaming Portuguese.

When class ends, I approach Professor Dennis's desk.

"*Sim?*" he says to me, still in Portuguese mode.

I can't fake it. I fumble along in English as though the words strain me. "I'd like to add this class."

"Do you speak Spanish?" he asks me.

I remember the class requirements. Spanish speaker. If I say no, he won't let me in the class.

"I grew up hearing Spanish," I say. "My grandmother spoke it. And I took it in school."

"But are you fluent?" he presses. "This is an accelerated Portuguese class. Most kids in here understand sixty percent of Portuguese because they know Spanish. And when there's a concept or assignment they don't understand, I explain it in Spanish. I don't speak English in here. At all."

I feel sick to my stomach.

I don't speak Spanish.

I need to take this class.

"I can do it," I say. "I understand more Spanish than I can speak."

"All right." He looks hesitant as he signs my add card. "Make sure you get the text books. You're already a week behind. I'll see you tomorrow."

I nod and slip out, queasy with what I've done.

I can still change my mind. Find some other class to fill this space.

I march into the registrar's office and turn in the add card.

It's done.

CHAPTER NINETY-TWO

Rooming with the Enemy

I see Abby at my Bible as Literature class that evening. Professor Walker greets us with enthusiasm, his only freshman in an upper level English class. I tell her all about my difficult Portuguese classes while he reviews some of the same concepts we learned in his class over the summer.

"That's so crazy," she whispers. "You're actually going to do that?"

I nod. "This weekend was crazy too. We had a fight with Layne, and we looked at apartments."

"Apartments!" Her eyes grow wide. "For next year?"

"Yes."

"Are you going to room with the same people?"

"I think so. We get along so well."

"Oh." She looks a little discouraged, which is very unlike Abby.

"What's wrong?" I ask.

"I was hoping we could room together next year," she says.

"Us?" I'm surprised. We've never talked about this. I assumed she'd want to room with her current roommate.

"Yeah. You're my best friend. It would be so fun."

"It would. I would love to room with you." My mind spins, wondering how I can appease all parties. "You get along with my roommates."

"Yeah, they're nice."

"What if we all roomed together?"

She tilts her head and considers that. "Would they want to?"

"I'll ask them."

"So either you'd have to kick someone out or get a bigger apartment."

"Right." I'd overlooked the fact there would be five of us. "I'll talk to them, see what they think. Would you be interested?"

"I totally would!"

We quiet down when Professor Walker has us open a text and begin analyzing.

It's very much like what Abby and I did in his class over the summer. But we don't mind. That was only one week. This is four months.

I'm excited for this class.

⸙

My heart races through each Portuguese class, pumping to the beat of *eu* and *tu* and *nós*. I can't focus on anything else. This class will be the death of me. Nothing else matters. I can't even daydream about my surprise visit to Owen because before that can happen, I have to get through the first nine weeks of the semester.

I may be dead by then.

By my third day, I know I am in way over my head.

I'm lost through the entire class. I wait for Professor Dennis to write the assignment on the board so I know what it is we're supposed to be doing. I spend the time calculating what will happen to my GPA if I get a C in an eight-credit class.

I can't. It will ruin me. I have to get at least a B. And even then, all my other classes have to be As if I'm going to keep my GPA at a 3.7. Any lower than that, and I won't be able to renew my scholarship.

The pressure is on.

Everything would have been so much easier if they'd offered a Portuguese 101 class this semester.

We watch a movie in American History, but I keep falling asleep. I'm exhausted. I worked last night and received the Caller of the Week award. Stirling congratulated me and asked when we're going out, and I couldn't think of any response.

I try to take notes through the movie because I know this will be important on the test later, but my eyes burn. My vision is blurred.

I look over my notes after class and see them taper into nonsense every time I fell asleep. Great. Another class to bomb.

Iris greets me when I walk in the door.

"Are you working tonight?" she asks.

"No," I say. "Why?"

"Let's go look at apartments. I found a few good ones."

She already has my keys in her hand, and she tosses them to me.

"I'm so tired," I protest. "And I have so much homework."

"I've got to get out of here," she says, dragging me down the stairs and opening my car door.

I give in. I climb in and start the car. "What's going on? Why do you need out?"

"Layne," she says, crossing her arms over her chest. "Turn left. We're heading toward Center Street."

"What's going on with her?" I glance at her and follow her directions.

"It's the whole thing over Brant. I can't get over that she did that in our room. She even admitted to using my bed!"

"Ugh." I make a face. "Yeah, that's gross."

"So we're not talking to each other. It's not cool."

"I'm sorry. If it makes it any better, she agreed not to sleep with him in our apartment." I cringe at the words.

"Yeah, that's great. But it doesn't make it better."

I can tell Iris is annoyed by the whole affair. "Are you still okay with her rooming with us?"

"Maybe."

"Because Abby wants to room with us also."

"Abby?" She turns to me. "Your friend?"

"Yeah. Would you guys be okay with that?"

"Instead of Layne?"

We can't kick Layne out. I know it would wound her terribly. "No. In addition to."

"Well." Iris glances down at a list on her phone. "None of the places we're looking at sleep more than four people."

"Hmm." I chew on my lip. "Maybe we should check out a few."

"Let's talk to Camila and see what she says."

Iris wants to kick Layne out.

But she won't. This anger will pass. None of us have fought before, not like this. It won't last.

I hope.

Layne comes into my room Sunday morning. She's dressed for church in a wrap skirt and a tank top with an off-the-shoulder sweater. I'm putting on eyeliner for the first time in months. Camila is in the kitchen with Iris.

"I'm not sure I want to room with you guys next year," she says.

She startles me. I drop the eyeliner wand and bend to pick it up. Then I turn to her.

"What? Why?"

She presses her lips together, her eyes narrowed. "Iris and I aren't getting along. She's rude and snide and treating me like I'm a sinner."

My heart sinks. "It won't last."

"She wants me to stop seeing Brant. I'm not going to."

A heaviness descends over me. "She said that?"

"She has no right, Cass. She thinks I'm evil now that we're having sex. She said I shouldn't go to church, that I'm a hypocrite. And she can't stand being in the room with me."

I step away from my mirror and sink down on my bed. I don't know what to say. "She doesn't mean it."

"Well, it looks like she does. So I'm just letting you know. I'm looking at getting my own apartment."

My throat tightens. "I thought we worked through everything."

"You and I did. And I have no issues with you. In fact, if you want to come room with me, you can."

She tilts her head and waits like she wants a response. My heart flutters in my neck. Choose between Camila and Iris, or Layne?

"Thanks for the option," I say. "I'm sorry this is happening."

She shrugs. "I'm done with it."

She turns around and walks out, but I stay sitting. I'm filled with sadness. We didn't fight the whole first semester, me and these three girls. They've become my best friends, my sisters. I wouldn't make the same choices Layne is, but I still love her.

Layne leaves for church ten minutes before us. Brant comes by in his brother's car and takes her. I gather the other girls in the kitchen for a quick powwow before we go.

"Layne doesn't want to room with us next year," I say.

"Why?" Camila says. "I thought she did."

"She said she's not getting along with all of us." I don't look at Iris as I speak, but I don't have to.

"She means me," Iris says.

I turn to her, wanting to be tactful here and remain neutral. "She doesn't feel like you're friends anymore."

"She's not interested in changing. She's going to keep doing what she does and walk over us like we're doormats."

"Her personal life doesn't have to be an offense to us," I say, gently, carefully.

"You mean her sex life? We should tell the Honor Code office what she did."

"She hasn't since then," Camila says. "And she said she wouldn't do it again."

"Here," Iris says. "But she's probably doing it elsewhere, and you know that's against the rules also."

That's true. But if it's not happening under our noses, we can pretend we don't know.

"The bottom line is, we don't have any control over Layne's personal decisions," I say. "And we shouldn't. It's her life."

"We don't have to like what she's doing, though," Iris says.

I see how their conversations get nowhere. Iris is kind and funny and smart, but on this she's unyielding. "You're willing to have her not live with us because she's sleeping with her boyfriend?"

"Yeah," Iris says.

Her acknowledgment stings. A lump forms in my throat, and I blink back the hot tears gathering in my eyes. "What if it is someone else next time?"

"What do you mean?" Iris frowns at me.

"What if it's Camila in a year? Or me in a month? Will you stop wanting to be around us because we had sex?"

"No," Iris says, but she looks troubled. "It's not like that."

Camila knows this already. So I don't look at her as I tell Iris.

"Owen and I almost had sex over Thanksgiving. I was willing. I wanted to. He stopped us. But it's interesting to know if we *had* had sex, or if it happens the next time we see each other, you won't want to be my roommate either."

Iris's brows fold inward toward her nose. Silence ticks between us, the only sound that of the bubble maker in the fish tank. "But you wouldn't still be doing it," she says. "That's the difference."

"Only because we'd be apart," I say. Baring my soul to her. Being perfectly honest.

"We have to meet people where they are in this life journey," Camila says, speaking up at last. "We don't get to decide if they've screwed up or how badly or if they're worthy of our friendship. I say we set down our boundaries—which coincide with the Honor Code anyway—and as long as we each live within those parameters, we give each other grace to figure out what's important to us individually. And we don't judge each other."

Camila's words are smart but I know each item will be a jab to Iris, whether intended or not. This conversation is because of her. I remember what Owen said. *You have a way of smoothing things over. Making people feel important.*

I step up to Iris and wrap my arms around her. "I love you and hate to think I might do something some day to make you not want to be my friend. I hope you'll still accept me no matter what I do."

She remains rigid in my embrace. "I will. I don't discard people if they make a mistake."

I don't say anything. I feel like enough has been said. She'll think on this.

Either she and Layne will work it out or they won't. But I've said my piece. Now Iris knows not just how Layne feels, but how Camila and I do.

⟲〜✦〜⟳

Layne doesn't come back to the dorm after church. The sun comes out, turning the frigid air into something more tolerable. A few boys follow us home from church, and my cousin Jordan comes over. Jared is among them, and I sit by him on the couch, enjoying the easy friendship between us. I'm grateful for it, because when two people realize they like each other and then end up not being together, you have a fifty-fifty chance of it becoming either a great friendship or something tense and awkward.

Actually, I think the friendship is less likely.

"How are the Portuguese classes going?" he asks as I settle beside him.

I fold my knees inward and bite my lip, feeling my anxiety rise from the mere mention of the class. "I'm pretty much terrified all the time."

"Terrified?" He arches one eyebrow.

"Yes. I don't understand anything in there. The text book helps, but I feel like I'm memorizing phrases rather than learning."

"Can you ask the teacher for extra help?"

"He said we can set up a meeting with the TA. I'm going to do that."

"I mean, in class. Ask for clarification?"

I pleat my fingers together. "So I kind of misled him about my foreign language abilities so he'd let me in the class."

A smile plays about Jared's lips. It draws my attention, and I remember how he hasn't kissed a girl. Or maybe he has now. Not Iris. She would have told me.

"You misled him?" he repeats. "In what way?"

"You're supposed to be fluent in Spanish to take the class. I said I was."

"Why would that help?"

I groan and run my fingers through my hair. "It would be so easy if I spoke Spanish! The languages are incredibly similar. And anytime the class doesn't understand what he's teaching, he switches languages and explains it again—in Spanish!"

"Whoa." Jared's eyes go wide. "What's your grade in there so far?"

"We've had two quizzes. The first one I only got four wrong."

"That's good!"

"Out of six."

He winces. "Ouch."

"Yeah." I give a self-deprecating laugh. "After that one I knew what to study a bit better, so I got an eighty on the next quiz."

"So what's your grade?" he says, getting back to the question at hand.

"C."

His eyes flick over my face, reading me. "C isn't a bad grade."

I let out a breath, trying to smile, but all of this feels so real and heavy. "It's an eight-credit class. Even if I get As in all my other classes—which isn't likely—I won't maintain a three-point-five with that score."

"That's all right."

"I'll lose my scholarship." The words make my throat tighten.

He nods. "That's okay too. It happens."

"I know. Layne and Iris are both on probation this semester to raise their grades, or they'll lose theirs. I don't want to be one more person who can't hack it."

"No one's going to think that about you. You're ambitious and maybe bit off more than you can chew."

I snort. "To put it mildly."

"Hey, you guys." Iris pulls up a chair and settles down across from us. "Want to go for a drive through the canyons?"

I look over at Jordan and Camila and Mike. The boys are messing with her, tugging her hair and taking her mug, making her giggle.

"Hey," I call. "We're going for a drive through the canyon." I indicate Jared and Iris beside me. "Want to come?"

The three of them look at each other in a wordless conversation, then Camila says, "We're good here!"

I stand up and fist my keys. "See ya in an hour or so."

CHAPTER NINETY-THREE
Make It Four

ris climbs into the passenger seat of my car and I feel bad that Jared's in the back. I think she wanted to keep him away from me. I turn to her.

"Why don't you sit in the back with Jared?"

"I don't mind," Jared says. "You're my chauffeur."

"Okay," Iris says, and she leaves me in the front to sit with him.

I want Jared to like her. She's so interested.

I sneak glances at them while I drive in between watching the landscape. The road winds and twists through the canyon, the tall mountains rising on either side. The trees are still dormant, branches extending like clawed fingers, forming a cluttered mat of brown. Snow hugs the sides of the hills, and the roads are lined with it. I'm longing for spring, for green leaves and yellow flowers, but the peek of sunshine over the crests of the mountains is enough for today.

They carry the conversation without me, as I knew they would if they sat together. I don't mind. My brain is cluttered. I'm worried about Iris and Layne, but I'm hopeful. This will get resolved.

⟊⟊ ⁕ ⟊⟊

I have another Portuguese quiz Monday morning. I fumble through it, but I memorized the questions ahead of time, so I don't feel like a complete idiot. I draw upon the phrases I've embedded in my mind. I might not understand anything, but I can fake it.

Professor Dennis tells us something as he collects the quizzes, but as usual I have no idea what. I hear the word "video" and remember we have another quiz tomorrow. This one is on comprehension. Fear stabs my chest. A copy of the video is online, and I've watched it a dozen times, trying to jot down phrases as I listen. I'll have to study it tonight, try to get it down.

I consider contacting Tiago again. But I have a deep apprehension about rekindling any conversation between us. I'm going to see him in a few months. I'm so uncertain about it. We are only friends. That's all I want to be. That's all I can be.

I hope I feel the same when I see him.

After class I meet with the TA in the language lab.

"Hi!" she says in a beautiful English accent. I'm immediately reminded of Tiago and Franklin and every Brazilian I've known who speaks English. "I'm Elisabete." The "t" has a "ch" sound. Elisa-beche. I sit down at the table with her. "I'm Cassandra. Your name is so beautiful." And it's so nice to hear English.

She smiles at me. "What would you like to work on?"

I consider the question. Conjugating the regular verbs isn't too hard. But the irregular ones throw me. And my vocabulary is pessimal.

"Can we do irregular verb conjugation?" An idea strikes me. "And then maybe go over the video we're having a quiz on tomorrow?"

"Yes, of course."

We spend the next twenty minutes on verbs. Because she can explain it to me in English, I get more clarity and understanding in that time period than in a week in class.

"You know a lot," she says to me. "But you don't speak Spanish?"

I admitted to her my mistake. I shake my head. "I study like crazy. I feel like I should be dreaming in Portuguese by now."

She laughs. "That will come. You are doing so well. I meet with a lot of students and your understanding is ahead of theirs."

"Really?" I feel a touch of pride. "I feel so behind."

"Let's watch the video."

She helps me after the first time to see what words I was missing, where I wasn't hearing the ending of a sentence and the beginning of the next. We watch it again and she asks me more questions, and then she switches to Portuguese and helps me understand that she's asking the same thing, but in Portuguese. My heart pulses in my head and my hands sweat, but it starts to make sense. We watch the video one last time, and I'm much more confident when I answer her questions about what's happening.

"You're going to do great on this," she says. "Don't doubt your abilities."

"Thanks," I say.

She writes my name down to prove I attended the session, and for the first time, I'm excited about this class. Maybe I can do this.

⟲∽⋇∾⟳

Iris texts me while I'm at work.

I: call me when you get off. Need to talk.

All my warning bells go off. There's so much drama at home. What can it be this time?

Me: okay

That's all I think about for the rest of my shift. I study the common Portuguese phrase sheet in front of me, aware I'm neglecting every other class I have. But just like failing Portuguese would sink me, if I ace this eight-credit class, it will save me. There's no happy medium here.

I call Iris as soon as I'm in the car after work. "What's up?"

She exhales. "I think I made a mistake. Can we go somewhere to talk?"

"Yes. I'll be home in five."

I swing into the dorm parking lot a moment later and text Iris to let her know I'm there. She runs down to the car and climbs in beside me.

"Want to go somewhere?" I ask.

"Just the park."

I drive us around the block and pull into the park behind the elementary school. Then I look over at her. "What's going on?"

She pulls off her knit cap, long black hair falling around her shoulders. Her fingers tug on each other, snapping, the skin dry and white from the Colorado winter.

But she doesn't speak. "What mistake did you make?" I prod.

She licks her lips. "Yesterday at church, I talked to the pastor about Layne."

My shoulders tense. "But we said we weren't going to tell."

"I didn't say a name," Iris says, her voice soft. "I wanted advice. I tried to keep it anonymous. But—he said he thinks he knows who I'm talking about." A tremble enters her words. "He said this is very serious. She could get kicked out of PYU."

I drop my head to the steering wheel. "Layne," I whisper. "What do we do?"

"I'm sorry." Iris sucks back a sob. "I just wanted advice. I didn't mean to tattle. She's going to hate me now."

"I thought you didn't care," I say, quietly.

"I was confused. I thought the right thing to do would be to turn her in. Especially because she's still doing it. But ever since he told me that, I realize you're right. Layne is more important here. Not what her actions are."

I couldn't say it better myself. "What's he going to do?"

"I don't know. If we don't accuse her, I don't think he can either. He might try to talk to her. Get a confession from her."

"And if he does?"

"I don't know."

This is bad news. And very concerning. It's out of my hands.

The only power I have is prayer.

I'm not sure it will be enough.

⚬∼⚬

We get our Portuguese quiz results back on Tuesday.

I utter a gasp out loud when I see my score. Ninety-seven percent! I want to squeal. I did it! I'm catching on! I quickly calculate my grade and am excited to see it's up to a high B.

The video quiz doesn't go as well. I'm sweating bullets trying to decipher each individual word and phrase. Still, I studied it with precision and I know I get more than half right. As long as it's a B. I've earned this grade and I want to keep it.

Four more weeks until my midterm in this class.

Four more weeks until I leave to see Owen.

I can think about it now. I'm not going to die before then.

But I feel another immeasurable sadness when I think of it. I'll be there for four days. Four weeks until I see him. Five weeks until I'm away from him again.

Maybe forever.

Damn.

"What did your roommates say about me rooming with you guys?" Abby asks as we leave English class that evening.

"They said it's fine," I say. "We're still looking for an apartment that fits six. Most of the ones we've looked at are crappy."

"I'll keep an eye out also. I'm so glad. It will be so much fun."

"Although," I say, lowering my voice even though I know no one's listening, "we might only need for four people."

"Why? Who changed their mind?"

"Layne." I heave a sigh. "She and Iris are not getting along. And I'm afraid it's going to get worse."

Abby frowns, her lips jutting out as the furrow mars her face. "Why?"

I lift a shoulder, not wanting to get into Layne's private business. "She broke the Honor Code and Iris is struggling with it. And now I'm not sure Layne wants to be with us. It's been tense at home."

"Yikes." I see Abby internalizing that. Thinking.

"Maybe you don't want to room with us now," I say, laughing.

She smiles. "A little drama is good for the soul."

"A little. We're having a lot right now."

"It will settle."

She doesn't act concerned. I wish I had her optimism. Or her blase.

CHAPTER NINETY-FOUR

Decided

For once I'm working on something besides Portuguese when Camila bursts into our room. It's almost ten and her face is flushed. She's wearing long-sleeved running clothes and I know she's been outside.

"It's too cold for that," I say, looking up from my English essay.

She smiles really big. "You're going on a date with me this Friday."

I turn back to my computer. "I love you, but I don't think we should date."

She laughs. "Jordan asked me out."

I smirk. "That's nice. You and my cousin don't need me to chaperone, though."

"He's setting you up with a kid from his dorm. So you have to come."

"Oh, do I?" I keep my eyes on my computer, but I can't help feeling a thread of excitement. I haven't gotten out in awhile. Going with someone I don't know and my cousin and roommate sounds like a safe way to have fun.

"Yes. We bought tickets to the basketball game and then we'll go out to dinner. Are you working? Say no, please say no."

"I'm not."

"So you'll come?"

I consider it for two more seconds. A chance to exchange the stifling, tense environment here for a sweaty, stinky basketball game and food? "Yes."

Camila squeals and prances back out of the room.

"Hey!" I call after her.

She bops back in.

"Were you with my cousin?" I ask, eyeing her with curiosity. She seems too perky for a run.

"He ran with me," she says. "That's when we set up the date."

"And the tickets?"

"He bought them online while we ran."

"I didn't know Jordan can run."

"Eh." Camila lifts a shoulder. "He doesn't do it very well."

I laugh and she leaves again.

As soon as I finish my last class on Friday, I shut down school mode and focus on this date. I need something fun. It's still sub-thirty degrees outside, so I put on long johns with a pair of plaid leggings, followed by an oversized striped sweater.

"What's my date's name?" I ask Camila as she pulls her hair to the side and braids it.

"AJ."

"His name is initials?" I say. I've never been fond of those.

"He didn't choose it. And I'm sure they stand for something."

I will make it my mission to find out.

"Am I driving?" This is normal. I'm one of the only people with a car.

But Camila looks affronted. "That would be rude! No, AJ is."

I brighten. "Great!"

Twenty minutes later, there's a knock at the back door. Camila answers it, letting in Jordan and AJ. Jordan gives me a hug and then Camila, who he holds extra long. AJ extends a hand to me.

"Hi. You must be Cassandra."

I take it, examining him as I know he is examining me. He's tall with curly blond hair, blue eyes, a strong jaw, and a pleasant face. "Nice to meet you."

"Likewise. I've heard all about you. Jordan says you're awesome."

I turn to Jordan. "I'll mail you a check later this week."

The three of them laugh, and I say bye to Iris as we leave.

I haven't seen Layne. She's kept herself scarce.

"Where for dinner?" asks AJ. He opens my door for me, the king of politeness. I've come to expect this in college.

"Italian sounds good," Camila says, getting in beside Jordan.

"No way," Jordan says. "Mexican."

"We had Mexican yesterday," AJ says.

"It never gets old."

"You had gas all night!"

Jordan reaches over and punches AJ's shoulder, and Camila and I laugh.

We end up at the Olive Garden. The boys keep up their antics so I barely have to make conversation. I can't stop giggling. It's so nice to not have to think, to let someone else take the lead.

"So, Cassandra," AJ says, turning to me while we wait on our food. "Jordan told me you used to be vegetarian."

I nod. "Yeah. But I gave it up. And now I love meat."

"Hence why you ordered chicken."

"Yep."

"He also said you like to sing?"

"At least I don't have to introduce myself. Jordan already did." I shoot a mock glare at my cousin.

"I can't help it," he said. "You're so awesome. I had to talk you up."

"He didn't have to work too hard to convince me," AJ says. "Once he said, 'my cousin,' I knew you'd be cool. Though you're much cooler than I expected."

"Because I sing?"

"And you used to be a vegetarian."

"That makes me cool?"

"Food can work for us or against us. I can tell you're someone who makes it work for you."

There's a lot of history behind that. But I don't go into it.

I enjoy every bite of my chicken dinner.

We head to the basketball game after. AJ parks at the Hiland Center, the big athletic building that houses the basketball courts. Dozens of people flock to the entrances. AJ puts his arm on my shoulder, resting it there while we walk. He's tall, like Owen, but lanky like my high school friend Oliver.

"Do you like basketball?" he asks me.

"I've never seen a game," I say. "Do you like it?"

"I love it. I played in high school. Wasn't good enough to play in college, but I still enjoy watching it."

"That's cool. I don't know much about it."

"I'll explain if you get confused."

Jordan shows our tickets at the gate and we climb a set of stairs to the top of the arena. Then we climb down another set of stairs until we find our row. It's like an indoor stadium. It stinks a lot worse than the football stadium, though. Of sweat and old shoes. And it's loud, every sound echoing off the bleachers and the flooring.

The game begins. AJ leans close to me.

"You good so far?" he asks.

"I'm not sure which is our team," I admit.

He laughs. "We're the home team, so we get the colored jerseys. The other team is white because they're away. We have white jerseys for when we play at other schools too."

"Oh. So we're the purple?"

"Yep."

I nod and fall silent. Somehow I can still hear the thumping of the ball on the court, the slamming of shoes. We score a basket, and the crowd around us goes wild.

"Any questions so far?" AJ asks.

I shake my head. "Seems pretty straight-forward."

A guy behind us keeps up a running commentary with his friend. He makes fun of the away team when they drop the ball, but then he makes fun of our team when we lose the ball to a walk. AJ lowers his head toward me several times to make sure I'm getting the plays. His shoulder bumps me, and his knee, and one time he drops his hand to my thigh and rests it there. I keep up with the game, mostly thanks to the funny guy behind me.

The game ends two hours later. We won, and I share the ecstatic high of the other spectators as we walk out to AJ's car. Camila and Jordan are behind us, walking slowly.

"So what sports do you like?" AJ asks. He puts his hands in his pockets, strolling along beside me. The evening air is pleasant for once, in the low forties instead of the low twenties.

"I'm honestly not much of a sports person," I admit. "I'm not athletic. I wish I was."

"Do you like to watch any?"

"I enjoy football. I went to a few games in the fall. And I'm going to the championship playoff in Louisiana next month." Oops. That slipped out. I didn't even mean for it to.

"Wow, you're hardcore!" he says, looking impressed. "Big LSU fan?"

"Yes," I say, biting my lip to hold back my smile. "Big fan."

"Cool! You'll have to tell me how it goes."

"I'm sure you can find out if you want to know."

"Yeah, but I'll want to hear it from someone who was there."

He doesn't know about Owen. I'm slightly annoyed Jordan didn't tell him. But maybe he was afraid it would scare him off. And though I feel no attraction for AJ, this date has been fun. The perfect distraction.

He takes us back to our dorm but instead of going to our apartment, we go to the commons and pull out several board games. We lay flat on our stomachs and play Risk for an hour before Jordan completely wipes the rest of us off the board.

"You cheated," AJ says. "I'm sure you cheated."

"I'm just that good." Jordan pulls out Sorry next. "This one's easy. Maybe you stand a chance."

AJ rolls his eyes and grins at me. "I'll get him on this time," he stage-whispers.

I laugh, and he taps my foot with his.

Hours later, the residential assistant comes down to the commons.

"Time to go," she says to the boys. "It's almost midnight."

I can't believe we played games all night. Camila and I follow the boys back to AJ's car, except it's much colder now. Camila and Jordan stop under the stairs, so I walk with AJ to his car by myself. I don't have my jacket and stand by his car shivering.

"Tonight was a ton of fun," I say.

He reaches over and hugs me. "I loved getting to know you. Can I call you sometime? Maybe we can hang again."

I should tell him no. I probably won't go again. I don't want him to get the wrong impression about me. But I had a great time.

"I'm not interested in dating anyone," I warn.

"Me neither. I'm leaving on a mission trip in a few months."

"In that case, sure."

He gives a fist pump. "Yes!" he crows, Napoleon Dynamite style.

We say goodnight and I head for the building.

Camila and Jordan are still standing under the fire escape, huddled together, whispering. I pretend I don't see them and climb the stairs to our room.

Belatedly I realize I never found out what his initials stand for.

☙ ❧

The sun comes out over the weekend, warming the air to a brisk fifty degrees. It lifts my spirits. We invite Abby to go out with us, and Camila, Iris, Abby, and I head out to explore apartments.

There are far less apartments for six people than for four.

After looking at two dumpy three-bedroom apartments, we hold a mini conference in my car.

"We should look at the two-bedroom apartments again," Iris says. "In case things don't work out with Layne."

I look at Camila and Abby.

"I'm new to this party," Abby says. "I'm just happy to be included."

"I'm still hoping Layne changes her mind," Camila says, her voice slow as she considers her words. "But it's looking less likely. So we should check out the four-bedroom ones again."

"All right." I heave a sigh. I feel like I've betrayed Layne somehow, but I know none of this is on me. Layne and Iris are fighting. I made peace with her.

Iris consults her list, and we look at two more two-bedroom places.

And we fall in love with the last one. It has two spacious bedrooms, a renovated kitchen, and the best part: a washer and dryer in the apartment.

No more running down to the basement once a week to do laundry.

It's not cheap, but between the four of us, we can swing it. Plus it includes utilities.

"It's available June first," the manager says. "I recommend you put a deposit down on it immediately."

"I won't be here in June," Camila says. "I'm going home for the summer."

"Me too," Abby says.

"I'll be here," Iris says. "I'm staying and taking summer classes."

"I'll be gone the first part of the summer," I say. My heart does a little tumble as I realize how close this trip to Brazil is. "For part of May and June. But then I'll come back. I'll be here by July at the latest."

"If you don't take that June spot, it will get rented," the manager says.

"Can we do it now?" Iris asks.

I pinch her arm and give her a look.

"We need to discuss a few things," I tell him. "When can we let you know?"

"I'll get contracts drawn up over the weekend and have them ready on Monday," he says.

Monday. Two days away.

It's enough time for us to decide.

"We have to be sure," Camila says as we walk back to my car. "If we put a deposit down and change our minds, we lose our money."

"Aren't we sure?" Iris asks.

I round on her, not hiding my irritation this time. "We don't know what Layne is planning."

"She's planning not to live with us," Iris says.

I know she's right. But I'm not ready to give up on her. "I'll talk to her this weekend. Depending what she says, we can sign the contract and put the deposit down on Monday."

"Sounds fair," Camila says. Abby nods.

"I like that place," Iris says.

I don't respond.

I like it too.

Looks like we have a place to live next year.

Episode 6: School of Life

A Cassandra Jones Book

OF LIFE, LOVE,
AND OTHER
Noble Pursuits

EPISODE 6:
SCHOOL OF LIFE

TAMARA HART HEINER

CHAPTER NINETY-FIVE

Secrets and Lies

I get to church early on Sunday morning. I want to speak to the pastor. But I'm anxious about causing trouble. I pace in the foyer outside the chapel, doubting myself, wondering if I'm only going to make things worse.

My roommate Layne has broken the Honor Code. She's broken our trust. And I can't carry this secret any more.

Pastor Eric comes down the hall and stops when he sees me. "Cassandra. Good morning."

"Good morning," I say, wringing my fingers together and letting out an exhale.

He stands there looking at me. As if knowing I'm here for a reason.

"Could I speak to you? Privately?"

"Yes."

He gestures for me to follow him, and we go to his office under the stairs.

"How can I help you?" he asks, scooting into his chair behind the desk.

I sit down on the padded one in front of it. "I know Iris talked to you already," I say in a rush. "There's contention in our apartment. I feel like there's a lot of judgment without compassion. I don't know how to fix it."

He steeples his fingers and settles back. "Iris was concerned about one of your roommates."

I nod. "I'm concerned for her too. But I'm more concerned that she's going to feel unloved and rejected by the people closest to her."

"If I tell you the name of this roommate, will you confirm her identity?"

I hesitate. If I confirm, am I condemning her? I shake my head. "I can't. I don't want to be the reason she gets kicked out of school."

"What Iris told me was very concerning. It's not hard to guess who this person is."

"Then you don't need me to testify against her," I say, some fire entering my words.

He smiles softly. "I can't act on assumption."

"That's why there's been no action taken against her," I say with sudden understanding.

"Can you tell me this? Has there been any deviant behavior in your apartment?"

I feel like a deer in the headlights. I stare at him without blinking.

What happens to my soul if I lie?

He reads my answer on my face and looks down at his desk. "Is this behavior frequent?" he asks.

I let out a tiny breath. He's not going to make me tell him. "No," I say, my voice quiet but firm. "It's stopped, and she's promised not to let it happen again."

He lifts his face, and my blood runs cold as I realize he caught me with my second answer. By admitting the behavior stopped, I admitted it already happened.

What did I think I would solve by coming here?

"We'll figure it out," I say, rising from my chair. "Thanks for talking to me."

"Wait," he says, holding up his hand and stopping me before I leave. "I want you to know I'm not here to throw the book at your roommate. I want to help her. If you can convince her to come talk to me, she and I can figure this out together. You and your other roommates don't need to wrestle with this. It's not your responsibility. Let her be responsible for her choices and let me figure out what it means for her."

"Does helping her include kicking her out of school?" I ask.

"Not if I can avoid it. It's the last thing I want."

I study his face and find no guile. He means it. I give a slight nod.

"I'll tell her," I say.

A few more people have arrived at church in the time since I've been in the pastor's office. I step into the chapel and find an empty row toward the back.

"Anyone sitting here?"

I know Jared's voice, so I'm not surprised to look up and see him standing above me. "No," I say, moving my purse to the other side of my feet. "I was saving it for you."

"Nice of you." He smirks and settles in beside me. "Where are your cohorts in crime?"

I laugh. "It's an accurate description of them. They'll be here soon. I came early."

"Why? Wanted extra time to listen to the piano?"

"Wanted to talk to the pastor."

"Ah. The thing with Layne?"

I glance at him. "How do you know about that?"

"Iris mentioned it. It's been bugging her."

"She super upset about it."

"What's going to happen?"

"I don't know. I'm going to talk to Layne tonight. There are some things we need to work through." I arch an eyebrow. "How close are you and Iris these days?"

He pauses, looking reflective. "We have fun together. She's easy to talk to. And I know she likes me."

"Do you like her?"

He blinks at me. "Not sure."

That's better than a no. I snuggle up to him, and he puts an arm around me.

"She's a great person," I say. "She's got some quirks, you know? She's not perfect. But overall, she's awesome."

"Yeah, she's great."

We pull apart as people come in. Layne comes in by herself, and she waves at me before sitting in a separate row. I wonder what she thinks. Church teaches us not to have sex before marriage. But it's clearly possible to believe in God and still do it. If Owen and I slept together, it wouldn't change my beliefs. I'd still get up and go to church every Sunday. If anything, I'd feel a lot more guilty than I did before. The guilt might make it harder to go. But I need this spiritual nourishment.

Iris and Camila arrive five minutes before the sermon starts. Camila climbs over me to sit on my other side, and Iris plops down next to Jared. She whispers to him, and he murmurs back. I want them to get together. I want it because it will keep Jared in my life. And I like having him near.

I corner Layne as the sermon ends, while everyone is making their way to Sunday School.

"Want to go on a drive with me?" I ask.

"Instead of Sunday School?" She looks down the hallway at the people disappearing into classrooms.

"Yes."

She tosses her hair, turning back to me with a smirk. "I'm game."

We hurry back to the dorm, where my car remains parked in the lot. I only use it to get to church if I'm running late, and today I was early. A wind blows around us, cutting through the sunshine and making me shiver.

"Where are we going?" she asks as I start the car.

"I like driving up the canyon," I say. "It's such a lovely day. I can't wait for spring."

"Same," she says. "It's not warm enough yet."

"Spoken like a true Californian," I say, and she laughs.

"Indeed." She gives it a ten-second count, then says, "So why are we skipping church?"

"We have to have a reason?"

"For Miss Perfect? Absolutely."

"I am not perfect," I protest.

"It's not an insult."

I suppose it's not. "Let's go to the lookout."

I drive up the narrow road that overlooks the valley. At the top is a popular make-out spot. I park where we can see the campus below.

"It's supposed to be beautiful up here," I say, peering out the windshield at the dead valley. Brown and brown. Barren trees and roofs of buildings.

"I've always been too busy to look," Layne says breezily.

"I bet." I don't ask her how many times she's been up here. "I talked to Pastor Eric today." I say it quietly. I'm trying to keep her defenses down.

"You told on me?" Her voice rises.

So much for that.

"No," I say, maintaining a level tone. "I didn't talk about you. At all." Kind of a truth. I was talking about Layne the whole time. I just never said her name.

"So what did you talk about?" Her anger has abated, and curiosity replaces it.

"Things in my life that are troubling me."

"Like?"

I shrug. "He did say—if anything should happen—anything inappropriate— that I should go talk to him. And he'd help me figure things out. That kicking someone out of school is that last thing he wants." I'm amazed at the words as they leave my mouth. I wasn't talking about myself with the pastor. But it makes sense that I could have been. And it takes Layne off her guard.

"Why would he tell you that? Did you tell him something about you and Owen?"

"No. Just generic concerns."

"You think I should tell him. About me and Brant."

It's not so much a question as a statement.

"Honestly," I say, "the only reason it's anyone's business is because you were doing it in our dorm. Otherwise, it's no one's business. But if he hears it from someone else, he won't know what the real story is. If you tell him, it might be better."

She considers, tilting her head and looking out the windshield. "I'll think about it."

"Have you thought anymore about rooming with us?"

"Yes." She bobs her chin. "I'm not going to."

"Really?" My shoulders slump. "But we want you to."

"You do. Not Iris. Maybe not Camila."

I can't speak for them. "We're going to put a deposit down on an apartment on Monday."

"Have fun."

That's it, then. It will just be the four of us.

⁂

Layne and I don't say anything else about the living situation on the drive back to the apartment. Instead we talk about our classes and our plans for the summer.

"I think it's so cool you're studying Portuguese," she says. "I'm almost fluent in Spanish, thanks to high school and living in California."

"That's better than me, and my family's from Colombia," I say.

"So why Portuguese?"

My roommates don't know about Tiago. They know about Owen, and I don't intend to muddy the waters by talking about another boy. "I'm going to Brazil for a month this summer. I went a few years ago and loved it. I decided to study Portuguese in school."

"That's amazing. I'm thinking of doing study abroad in Latin America next semester."

I turn to her. "You are?"

"Yes. It would improve my Spanish. I might do it."

"Wow. That's amazing. I want to do something like that."

"So do it."

I think about it. I already plan to do a service mission for church. Can I throw another trip into my education?

Layne grows quiet as we climb the stairs to the back door. I feel the lightness of her mood lifting. I open the door and step into the kitchen.

Camila turns and smiles at us. "There you are!" she says. "I was about to text you! Look who came over!"

My eyes flick over her shoulder and I see AJ, standing tall behind her. Iris is on the couch with Jordan. Layne slips past us and heads into the hallway.

"AJ," I say, not hiding my tone of surprise. "Why are you here? I mean, hi." Crap, that came out wrong. Sounded so rude.

He doesn't miss it, and his smile turns bashful. "Just wanted to drop by. I thought maybe we could go on a walk, enjoy this beautiful day."

I did not expect this. What does he think it means when I say I'm not wanting to date anyone? "I just got back from a drive through the canyons. I want to stay here, if that's okay."

"Sure. Want to play a game in the commons?"

I don't want to do anything. I step around him to the fridge. "I'm going to make a sandwich." I don't mean to act distant, but I'm weirded out that he showed up here. "Want one?"

"No, that's all right."

Instead he stands there watching me make my food.

Camila moves to the couch with Iris, and I spread mayonnaise on two slices of bread. I follow it up with ham and a few cucumber slices, aware the entire time of his eyes on me. Then I sit down at the table with my sandwich and stare at my fish tank. Gurgle gurgle gurgle. The motor of the air tank churns as the bubbles pop to the top of the water.

He pulls up a chair and sits next to me. "It's a nice tank. Whose is it?"

"All of ours," I say.

"It's Cassandra's," Iris says. "She's the one who bought the fish. She feeds them and cleans the tank and keeps them alive."

"And she spends her spare time staring at them," Camila adds.

"It started out as all of ours," I say.

"I have fish at home too," AJ says. "Well, one."

I look at him, mildly intrigued. "What kind?"

"A beta."

"Oh." I lose interest and turn my attention back to my tank. "I see them at the store. They're beautiful but don't do anything."

"You're right. Mine always looks dead."

Why is he so agreeable? "Maybe it is dead."

"Possible. I haven't asked my mom about it in awhile, actually."

"Where's home for you?" Iris asks.

"Kansas."

"Will you go home before your mission?" I ask him.

"Probably. School's out at the end of April. If I don't have my call yet, I'll go home for a few weeks until I get it."

I nod. I'm thinking of Owen, who will have his call soon. When will he leave? Where will he go?

"I'm going on a mission also," I say.

"You are?" AJ tilts his head. "When?"

I shrug. "I don't know. I think I'll finish school first."

"I thought of that too. But then I worried no one would want to hire me if I was applying for jobs two years after I graduated. So I decided to do my mission first."

"That makes sense. Maybe I'll rethink my time line."

"When I get my call, do you want to come to my apartment when I open it?"

I shift to face him. "Why? Doesn't it come in an email? Won't you read it as soon as it arrives?"

"My mom made me promise not to. She said when it arrives, I have to let the whole family know and video chat them so we can read it together."

"That's cool. Sounds like a private family thing, though." Very private. And very familial.

"Yeah, but it would be nice to have someone there in real life."

I'm not sure how to get out of this. I feel Camila's and Iris's gazes boring into my back. It feels very rude to decline. "Um, sure. If I don't have class or work. Don't wait for me."

He smiles, and it lights up his blue eyes. "Hey, that's awesome."

I nod and check the time on my watch, wanting to exit this conversation. "Sorry, I'm supposed to call my mom right now. So I'll talk to you later, okay?" I stand up.

"Yeah." He rises with me and then crushes me in a hug. "I'll talk to you later."

I escape to my room. I hear him and the girls say a few more words, and then he leaves.

Camila flounces in, laughing. "Cassandra! He's smitten with you!"

"This is not my fault," I say. "I told him I didn't want to date."

"He's not dating you."

She's right. But I'm uneasy with his attention.

"How many boys have you spurned this year?" She starts ticking them off her fingers. "Jared. Stirling. Now AJ. Plus you've got two boys in love with you, and you're visiting both in the next six months."

My cheeks burn, and I feel defensive. "It's not like that."

"What did I say that's not true?"

She's got me, and I don't like it. "There's nothing between me and Tiago. He knows it."

"But he's still in love with you and you're still visiting him."

I grab my pillow and chuck it at her. "Leave me alone."

She leaves me, laughing as she goes.

CHAPTER NINETY-SIX

Contextual Clues

We have another quiz in Portuguese Monday morning.
This one doesn't go so well. It's on irregular verb conjugation, and I can't remember the imperative form of *pôr*. The rule is easy: you make the imperative form from whatever the first person conjugation is.

But I can't remember that either.

I guess at the verbs and have to call it good. But I know I missed two. I should be okay if that's all I got wrong.

I listen as Professor Dennis goes over our next essay assignment, and I'm pleased I understand most of what he says. I jot it down and decide to ask Elisabete at our lab just to make sure I got it right.

"Cassandra," he says, startling me out of my note-taking, "*Que gosta de comer?*"

I recognize all these words. We've been practicing using the verb "to like," or "gostar," which is not reflexive the way it is in Spanish. "*Me gosta comer—*"

"*Gosto de comer,*" he corrects.

I cringe. I knew that. I literally just thought how it's not a reflective verb, but habit took over when I spoke. I echo his phrasing. "*Gosto de comer—*" What do I like to eat? Every Portuguese food vocabulary word flees my mind. "*Comida.*"

Oh, goodness, that was awful. I like to eat food? Seriously? He moves off me to ask another student what they like to wear, and a dozen words come to mind. Bread. Candy. Chocolate. Fruit.

Anything besides *comida*.

He must know I'm a fraud by now. Someone who's faking their way through his class, not understanding most of it.

Midterms are next week. I'm almost halfway through Portuguese 101. And I haven't died yet.

After class I go to the language lab and meet with Elisabete.

"How did your last quiz go?" she asks.

"Pretty well, though not the one from today," I say. I pull out my notes. "I've got a low A in the class. I just need to do well on the midterm."

"You will. You know everything."

"That's not true. And I neglect every other class to focus on this one." I show her the notes from class. "Did I get that right? Is that our essay assignment?"

She nods. "Yes. Write it and bring it to me so I can help you correct it. I'm only in the lab on Mondays, but you can call me on my cell phone and I'll meet up with you."

"Thank you, Elisabete. That's so kind of you."

She smiles at me. "You can call me Bete." She pronounces it like Franklin would, turning the "t" into a "ch" sound. Beh-chee.

We spend the next half hour going over what will be on the midterm. Professor Dennis gave us a list of fifty phrases. I'm most nervous for the oral part of the test. He said he'll ask us a question in English and have us translate it, and then he'll ask another in Portuguese. I'm determine to memorize this list.

I take it to work with me, flipping from the English side to the Portuguese side, whispering to myself in between calls. I understand Portuguese grammar, at least, so I'm able to make sense of the sentence syntax.

But there's one sentence that doesn't make sense. The English says, "We give them the chickens." But the Portuguese says, "*Nós damos-lhe as galinhas.*"

Now I'm confused. That's singular. I thought it would be "lhes." I doubt myself, wondering if the indirect pronoun doesn't have a plural form.

I'll have to ask Professor Dennis after class. Because if he asks me that question, I don't want to get it wrong.

I spend some time studying American history when I get home, because I have a nine-week test in there on Wednesday. Most of our grades in history come from small classes with the TA. There are only about five tests total, but they account for a huge chunk of the score. My roommates took the class last semester. I watched them come home with tales of woe and frustration to rival my own feelings about physical science. I can't neglect this.

But I also have a Portuguese essay to write. And an English essay to outline. Just thinking about everything I need to do makes my heart rate increase.

Camila studies on her bed, both of us silent as the night thickens, the only sound that of our fingers on the keyboards.

My phone rings as I stumble along in my Portuguese essay. I glance at it and see Mrs. Blaine's name above the number. My heart skips a beat, but for an entirely different reason.

Saturday is the championship game. Friday I fly into Louisiana and hide out in Owen's house. I want to lie down in that knowledge and soak it up, but I have to get through two essays and two tests first. Then I'll be home-free.

"Mrs. Blaine!" I stand and take the phone into the kitchen. I don't want to disturb Camila. "Hi!"

"Hi, Cassandra," she says, her voice warm. "Are we still set for Friday?"

"Yes!" I curl up on the couch, staring at my fish as they swim back and forth, back and forth. "My flight lands in New Orleans at two."

"Did you email me your itinerary?"

"No. I'm not sure I have your email."

"I'll text it to you."

"And Owen still doesn't know?" I squirm on the couch. I can't wait to see his face.

"Not a thing."

"My coming won't be a distraction, will it?"

"Only in a good way! Email me your itinerary. We can't wait to see you!"

I head back to my room. Camila's gone to bed and turned out the light. I crawl into bed also, my eyes burning. I can finish my Portuguese essay in the morning. I'll just have to wake up early.

I'm almost asleep when I remember we didn't go back to the apartment and sign the contracts. And the next few days will be busy.

Thursday before you fly out, I tell myself. *Do it Thursday.*

⟡

Somehow I wake up early enough to get my essay done before class. I place it on Professor Dennis's desk and sit down to take notes. He spends the class going over the midterm, reminding us about the oral exam and the grammar part.

I understand everything he mentions. Elisabete is right. I know this material.

I approach him after class, standing in line behind the other kids with questions. Some fumble through Portuguese and then Spanish. But at least one falls back to English, which relieves me. I won't be the only one.

He smiles at me behind his wire-framed glasses when I step up. "*Sim? O que é sua pergunta?*"

I understand him because it's so close to Spanish. Which is probably why he phrased it that way. I pull out the study sheet. "This question right here." I point it out. "Shouldn't it be *lhes* instead of *lhe*? Or is there no plural form?"

He looks at it and shakes his head. "It's a mistake. Nothing slips past you. You know *tim-tim por tim-tim.*"

I know this idiom because we studied it in class also. It means "every little detail."

He's saying I know every little detail.

My face warms under the praise. "Thank you."

I work on my English essay and study for all my tests, forming a countdown in my head based on assignments. One essay down, one to go. Two tests to go.

And still work.

Riley calls me while I'm working.

She never calls. We haven't spoken since Christmas. I use my break to call her back.

"I missed your call," I say. "You all right? Is the baby okay?"

"Yes," she says. "We're both okay. I wanted to let you know I'm getting married on Friday."

"This Friday?" I knew it was coming, but I'm still stunned. She's eighteen. I toss that aside. She's about to be a mom. Definitely mature enough to be a wife. "Congrats! Are you excited?"

"I know you won't be able to make it, but I wanted you to know."

"Do you have a dress?"

"It won't be that kind of wedding. I'm pretty big right now, anyway. We plan to do a fancy one later."

"But you'll still wear something nice, right?"

"Yes. And my mom will take pictures. I'll make sure you get some."

I check my watch. "My break's almost over. But I'm happy for you." In truth, I have mixed feelings on the matter. I want Riley to be happy, to be with someone who respects her and treats her well. I want to talk to Owen. Share with him my feelings.

But I have to get back to work.

As if summoned by my thoughts, I get a text from Owen twenty minutes later.

O: what up, killer?

I'm on a call and have to wait to respond. Then I say, *Just taking people's money.*

O: for the better good, I'm sure

Me: regular Robin Hood

I want to talk to him about Riley. But I refrain. I'm going to see him in four days! I'll do it in person.

O: everything good with you?

It's an odd question, and it doesn't fit the banter he initiated.

Me: I'm good. You good?

O: yeah. Think so.

Me: Only think?

O: I'm good.

Something's behind this, but I'm not sure what. I feel like he's probing me also, trying to figure something out.

Me: school going okay?

O: when I remember to do it. My mind is elsewhere

Me: on your big game?

Crap, I shouldn't have said that. I wrack my brain, hoping he mentioned it somewhere. But he barely reacts.

O: definitely more fun than studying

He's so hard to read in text messages. But I need to make another call before my manager takes my phone away.

Me: gotta work. Talk to you later.

O: OK

I turn back to making my calls and studying my Portuguese. But something prompted his texts, and I'm curious what it was.

I don't have to wonder for long. Mrs. Blaine calls me as I'm driving home.

"I talked to Owen," she says, and there's laughter in her voice. "I think I scared him."

"Scared him? In what way?"

"I asked him if he was dating anyone. He wanted to know why I was asking. I said I was curious, because he's kind of private and never talks about girls. And he said, 'you know there's only one girl in my life.' And I said, 'I know, but you're apart and sometimes that makes it hard, so I wondered.' And he said, 'why? Have you heard something?'"

"Heard something?" I interrupt. My heart pounds faster in trepidation.

"That's what I said. I said, 'heard something? Like you are secretly dating someone?' and he said, with a total noise of impatience, 'no. Like she is.' At that point I started laughing. I don't understand how his mind leapt to that. He got annoyed with me and said, 'why are you asking me all this, then?' and I said, 'Because I'm your mom and I want to know.'"

"So he's not." The relief makes me giddy. There's context to his text messages now, also, and I laugh with her. "He texted me. I thought he sounded confused."

"Oh? What did he say?"

I can only recall the gist of it. "He asked if I'm good. But I felt like there was more to it. Like he wanted more information and wasn't sure how to get it."

"Well, now you know." She chuckles. "There won't be any other girl cheering for him at the game on Saturday."

I'm sure there will be. But none of them will be there because Owen wants them there.

⟲⟳⟳

Having an eight a.m. class every day makes me incredibly tired. But it is refreshing to wake up early and have my first class knocked out by nine.

I take deep breaths as I enter the classroom Wednesday morning for my Portuguese midterm. Professor Dennis greets us, hands out the exam, and calls the first student into the hall for the oral portion.

I glance down at my paper. I know the first question. The grammar is easy.

So is the second question.

My nerves calm themselves as I fly through the questions. I remember the vocabulary, I know the sentence structure. It makes sense to me in a way Spanish never did.

The fifth student comes in from the hall, and Professor Dennis pokes his head in.

"Cassandra," he says.

I turn my paper face-down and walk down the aisle like it's a gauntlet. Awaiting my fate.

"*Pronta?*" he asks as I settle into my chair in the hallway.

I nod.

"We'll start with the English. Translate this into Portuguese. 'We eat lunch at my grandparents' house.'"

My mind doesn't fail me. All the phrases I memorized leap forward, and I rattle off the response. He writes something down and asks the next question. And the next.

Then he switches to Portuguese.

"*Quem vai ao cinema contigo?*"

I take a deep breath and decipher his words in my mind. One at a time. "Who is going to the movies with you?"

He makes notes on his pad and I cross my fingers.

"*Meu tio dirige um carro grande e caríssimo.*"

535

"My uncle drives a large and very expensive car."

He asks me two others, and I pull the answers from my mind without difficulty.

"*Muito bem*," he says when I finish. I know that means "very good." He lays the clipboard across his lap and looks at me. "How is the class going for you?"

He asks me in English. I'm relieved and embarrassed he has to stoop to that level for me.

"It's going well," I say. "I study hard. I'm pleased with my grade so far."

"Tell me about your experience with Portuguese."

I don't want to look like a total idiot, so I embellish. "I went to Brazil the summer before my senior year of high school. My friends spoke to me in Portuguese and I picked up a few phrases. I'm going back this summer."

"And you're not fluent in Spanish?"

I shake my head. "No." I don't bother pretending.

He glances down at his clipboard. "On paper, you're flawless. You know the grammar, the spelling, the sentence syntax. You're keeping up with the assignments and outperforming your classmates who know Spanish."

"Thank you," I say, flattered. "I eat, sleep, and drink Portuguese."

He laughs. "If you need any help or have any concerns, stop by my office and talk to me. You're going to succeed. Good luck."

I head back in and finish my exam, but I'm jubilant.

Even my teacher thinks I'm doing a great job.

I go from my Portuguese exam to my English class, where I turn in my paper. Two papers down, none to go. One test down, one to go.

I'm almost out of here.

CHAPTER NINETY-SEVEN

Flight Bump

I t starts snowing on Thursday. I don't feel great about how my American history test went, but everything's over, so I won't complain. I got a ninety-seven percent on my Portuguese test, which blows my mind.

I'm learning this language.

Tomorrow I'll be on a plane to Louisiana, though I won't see Owen until Saturday.

It's so hard to keep this visit a surprise.

Camila calls me as I'm walking home through the snow at a clipped pace, my jacket pulled up to my ears and the hat down over my forehead.

"We need to put the payment down on that apartment before you go."

"Yes, of course." I dread driving in the snow, but I better get used to it. It's a fact of life in Colorado.

"Do we need Iris?" Camila says.

"If she's available. Otherwise you and I can do it. She and Abby can pay us back."

"Okay, cool. I'll be ready when you get here."

"Start my car and warm it up," I tell her.

She does, and after the walk home, I'm grateful to climb into a warm vehicle. We drive over to the complex we liked. I park by the office and climb out of the car, already shivering. A woman looks up from the reception desk when we walk in.

"Hi, yes?" she says.

"Hi," I say. "We were in last weekend and the manager said he'd draw up contracts for us to sign. We just need to put down the deposit."

"Oh?" She glances around the mess of papers on the desk. "Did he put your names on it already?"

"I don't know." I feel dumb as she rummages through different sheets.

"Do you know which apartment it was?"

I look at Camila, and she shrugs. "I'm not sure," I admit.

"Well." She gives up her search and looks at us. "The manager isn't in today, and I don't know what the agreement was. You can come back tomorrow."

Except my car and I will be gone tomorrow. "We can't swing back later tonight?"

Even as I say it, I know it won't work. I have a shift tonight.

"Let me get your phone number. If he comes back today, he can call you."

"Sure."

She writes my number down, and then Camila and I return to the car.

"Why do I have the feeling we're never going to hear from him?" Camila asks, sliding into the passenger seat.

"We will," I say. "He'll remember us. That apartment is ours."

I sound more confident than I feel. But I don't want to search for apartments again.

⟳⟲※⟳⟲

As soon as I get home from work, I start packing for my trip.

"You're going to see Owen on Saturday," Camila sings at me.

Iris comes into the room. "Did you get the apartment?"

I scowl as I fold a shirt and stuff it in my suitcase. "No. The guy forgot to print off the contracts for us. He didn't call while I was at work, either. We'll have to go next week."

"The apartment might be gone by then," Iris says, biting her lower lip.

I throw my hand out in a gesture of frustration. "Feel free to get a ride to the complex. I'll be on a plane. Unless someone wants to drive me to the airport."

No one volunteers for the three-hour journey.

The back door bangs shut, and I hear Layne's voice.

"Hey, you guys."

"We're in my room," I call.

She comes down the hall and steps in. I see her pause, her eyes flitting over Iris and Camila. "I was thinking," she says, still looking at them. "I'd like to room with you guys next year."

"You would?" Iris sputters.

Layne looks at me. "If it's possible." Then she faces Iris again. "I'm sorry for what happened here. I'll respect our shared spaces from now on. And I met with Pastor Eric, and he said I should stay with you. That it will be good for all of us."

"Stay with me?" Iris squeaks out.

"You, Camila, Cassandra. But yes."

Iris's shoulders slump. "I'm sorry I've been so judgmental and harsh. I haven't been a good friend."

Time to exit. I stand up and head to the bathroom to get my toiletries. Camila follows. We don't say a word but take our time, her brushing her teeth and me collecting toothpaste and toothbrush and razor. When I hear the laughing in my room, I head back in.

Both girls are misty-eyed and smiling, standing near each other, and my heart swells with relief.

"So we need a bigger apartment," Iris says.

That. I keep back a sigh. "Good thing we haven't signed a contract yet."

❦

Owen starts texting me on the drive to the airport Friday morning.

O: you in class?

I'm driving, which means I have to wait for red lights to respond. Then I keep it brief.

Me: no

As soon as I say it, I know I should have lied. What else would I be doing at eight in the morning?

If he realizes I should be in my Portuguese class, he doesn't say anything.

O: The championship game is tomorrow.

He's excited and playing it cool. He wouldn't be telling me otherwise.

I have to play it cool also.

Me: yeah? That's right.

O: it's gonna be big

Me: I'll be sure to watch it

I grin at my little joke. He has no idea.

He texts back, but I've hit the interstate and it's snowing. I won't tempt fate, which means he won't hear from me until I get to the airport. That's normal for a Friday, though, and he'll probably assume I went to class.

The Denver airport is much bigger than the regional one near the university. Just parking gives me a minor anxiety attack. I choose the cheapest lot, which ends up being a half a mile away from the entrance. I tighten my scarf around my mouth and hunch my shoulders as I march into the biting wind, dragging my luggage behind me. I remind myself where I'm going and find the motivation to trek onward.

A long line wraps around behind the check-in counter. I have a moment of panic as I check the time. I've arrived when I expected. An hour and a half before my flight. And I'm not checking bags, so I can skip this line.

Security takes thirty minutes, and I'm randomly selected for a pat-down, so by the time I get to my gate I'm fighting nausea.

But I'm here, with an hour to spare. I settle down by a window and look outside at the falling snow. Finally under control, I check my phone.

O: Hopefully coach lets me play

Me: I'm sure he will. I hope he does also. While I know Owen will be happy to see me, he'll be bummed also if he doesn't play.

This time he doesn't answer. Probably in class.

I get comfortable and pull out my computer. I have homework I can do.

Forty minutes later, I realize no one has called my flight over the announcing system. I look up and stare at the gate, worried I'm in the wrong place.

I'm not. My flight's been delayed.

The restless stirrings of panic spike in my chest again. *It's not a big deal,* I tell myself. *Just a delay.* But I glance outside and see the snow is thickening, driving downward at a heavier pace.

This does not bode well.

I try to focus on my school work, but my eyes dart toward the status screen every few minutes. When the flight is delayed by another half an hour, people around me begin murmuring concerns, voicing opinions, and several stand up and walk to the counter.

Camila texts me. *Are you on the plane yet?*

My fingers fly over the keyboard as I share my growing trepidation.

Me: it's snowing pretty bad here. My flight's been delayed an hour

There's no response for a moment, and then an image of the hourly forecast pops up in our messaging screen. Snow. Snow. Snow.

C: It doesn't look like it's going to stop

I swallow hard. I want to cry. The snow can't stop us from seeing each other, not again. Wretched freezing white stuff.

Me: what do I do?

C: how far of a drive is it?

I pull up my map and put in the info.

Me: nineteen and a half hours. My heart sinks into my fingers as I type.

Me: it's not an option. I wouldn't get there until tomorrow and that's if I drove straight through

C: I was mostly kidding. You can't drive in the snow.

Me: truth. So now what?

C: sit tight. Wait and see.

I pull on my fingers, cracking the joints. This is not how today is supposed to go.

Twenty minutes later, a voice comes over the loud-speaker. "Flight five-five-five to New Orleans has been canceled due to weather. Please see the gate attendant for rebooking."

I close my eyes. No. No no no no. This is the stuff my nightmares are made of. I stand and join the line that sprang up in point-two-five seconds, and I'm trying not to cry. I text Owen's mom.

Me: my flight's been canceled. I'll let you know the new info.

Mrs. Blaine: Oh no!!! Keep me posted. Have faith. It will work out.

I don't have faith, not about this. It didn't work out in January. God and the weather don't seem to care if Owen and I see each other.

But I pray anyway, because it's all I've got, and I'm desperate to see him.

I'm rebooked for a flight at three p.m. I'll get to New Orleans at seven p.m., thanks to the time change. I send the info to Owen's mom and then sit in a public space and watch the snow come down and listen as flight after flight gets grounded. Nothing's coming in and nothing's going out.

I'm not optimistic.

The three o'clock flight gets delayed and delayed again, and I know where this is going. Why get our hopes up in the first place? I step into the line when it's canceled, my soul in my toes, all doom and gloom.

There are even more people stranded now, and they can't guarantee me a seat.

"I've put you on standby for the six o'clock flight," the attendants says. Weary lines ring his eyes, and I imagine he's dealt with irate customers all day.

Add me to the list.

"What happens if I don't get on that flight?" I ask.

"Our last flight out is at eight. You'll be bumped to standby on that one automatically."

"And if there's no room?" It's hard to speak past the knot in my throat.

He presses a few buttons. "I have you confirmed on a flight tomorrow afternoon at two. If you can't get on the standby flights between now and then, you have a seat on that one."

I do quick mental calculations. My plane would arrive at six. The game starts at six. I'd be late, but I'd get there. "What are the chances of my flight being canceled?"

"I can't say for sure, but the snow is tapering. We expect to get planes off the ground in the next hour. So chances are good you'll get there."

I nod. I won't rest easy until my plane lands in New Orleans, but I won't give up hope either. I can still make it.

I head to my new gate and check the standby list. There are forty-seven people on it and I'm number thirty-three.

I tell my hopes to sit back down.

CHAPTER NINETY-EIGHT

Number Fifty-Four

sleep in the airport.

It's uncomfortable. A worker comes by and offers blankets to us stranded travelers. I accept one. My contact solution is in my bag, and I switch the contacts out for glasses. I curl up in one of the chairs and secure the blanket around me. I use my jacket as a pillow. This is not how I imagined spending tonight.

But it will be okay, as long as I get there tomorrow.

I am blurry-eyed and groggy as I make my way to the first flight of the day in the morning. I haven't bothered to brush my teeth or wash my face yet. I figure I will have plenty of time if I catch this flight.

And plenty of time if I don't catch this flight.

I don't catch it.

I wash my face and brush my teeth and move to the next gate, then sit in a chair and scroll through the wait list. Even though this is my fourth standby flight, I am still only number twenty-seven. People with airline accounts and priority status keep getting pushed in front of me, and I imagine everyone is as frustrated and annoyed as I am.

I don't talk to Owen. I'm afraid my frustrations will leak through, and I'll end up telling him what's happening. I don't want him worrying about me when he has a game. He needs to be focused.

My roommates text back-and-forth with me, commiserating, feeling sorry for me.

No one feels as sorry for me as I do.

My mom calls and I cry to her, sobbing out my frustrations. She understands. She is the only person I vent to.

The day passes in slow monotony. I struggle to focus on my schoolwork. I'm turned away flight after flight until finally, at 1:12, they call my name.

It's ironic. I only have forty-five minutes until my confirmed flight.

I get on the 1:12 flight.

I text Owen's mom from the plane. *I'm seated. We're taking off.*

She responds right away. *I will be at the airport to get you. I'll sneak away as soon as the game starts so Owen doesn't notice. I'm so glad you're going to make it.*

I exhale. Me too. For a little bit there, I wasn't sure I would.

I let my roommates know next. They've been on pins and needles for me.

And then I allow myself to text Owen. I'll be on a plane for the next three hours and won't have to play superficial to avoid letting him feel my excitement.

Good luck today! I'll be watching you. I'm cheering for you.

He responds almost immediately. *Thanks!*

My stomach is tied in knots throughout the flight. I'm jittery like I drank too much caffeine. I tap my feet and squeeze my fingers.

And then we land in New Orleans, and I let out a giant exhale. I am here.

I speed walk down the gateway and resist the urge to break into a run for the exit.

My eyes sweep the crowd as I get to the bottom of the escalator. Right away I see Mrs. Blaine. She's standing on her tiptoes waving an arm enthusiastically so I can't miss her.

I tug my luggage toward her, and she wraps me up in a huge hug, squeezing me tight. Then she releases me.

"Let's go. The game's already started."

She grabs my hand and pulls me through the crowd, and I don't resist at all.

We throw my luggage in the back of her car, and then I climb in beside her as she exits short-term parking.

"What a night you've had," she says. "I bet you're exhausted."

I take a moment to appreciate the abundant sunshine and lack of snow around me. It's my first time in Louisiana. I pull down the visor mirror and check my reflection. "Does it show?" I put on make up before my flight and tried to make myself look presentable.

"It doesn't matter. I'm going to paint your face purple and put a baseball cap on you," she says with a wide grin. "I can't wait to see Owen's expression when he realizes."

I smile and squirm with excitement, my heart jumping around in my chest. I can't wait either.

"How's school going for you?"

We fall into an easy conversation where we only talk about me. Mrs. Blaine shows as much interest in my life as my own mother, and I know she genuinely cares for me.

We reach the stadium twenty minutes later, only to find no parking. She circles the lot, then the back up lot, scowling and muttering about how they need to put in more parking for the games.

"I can drop you off," she says. "And you can find my family. I'll give you your ticket, it won't be hard."

I am anxious to see Owen. I want to be inside that stadium now, looking for him, watching for the moment when he realizes I'm here.

But I do not want to walk in by myself.

"I'll wait and go in with you," I say.

She nods, and we exit the parking lot to drive half a mile away to someone's driveway, where they're charging five bucks to park. Mrs. Blaine pays it without question.

"I didn't get the chance to paint your face yet," she says. "Hang tight."

She retrieves from the car a tin of purple face paint. She proceeds to smear it all over one side of my face. Then she grabs a container of gold paint and does the same to the other side of my face. She uses a wet wipe to clean her hands, then grabs an LSU baseball cap and shoves my hair up under it.

"Now you're ready," she says.

She smears the same paint on her face and dons another cap. She looks like a college kid again, her curly blond hair poking out the back of the cap.

"Do you have everything you need?" she asks.

I touch my phone in my pocket. "I think so."

"Then let's go."

We take off for the stadium. The noise of the game gets louder as we get closer. I can't make out what the announcer is saying, but I hear the dull roar of voices, the pounding of the marching band on the field.

Mrs. Blaine shows our tickets at the gate. I follow her up the steps and then down another set of stairs to our seats near the field. Best I've ever had in a football game. Owen's dad stands up to hug me when I arrive, and then he directs me to my seat, which is next to Owen's mom. Richard nods at me, and I wave before sinking into the hard plastic and squeezing my hands together.

"Owen's on the field," Mr. Blaine says.

"He's playing?" Mrs. Blaine lifts from her chair.

"Number fifty-four," Mr. Blaine say.

I know Owen's number. I lean forward also, my heart in my throat.

He stands with his back to us on the balls of his feet, his legs tensed to run, his arms bent. I don't see the play because I'm watching Owen, but suddenly he is rocketing forward, running alongside an opposing player as they both anticipate an interception.

It doesn't happen. Play is stopped on the third down, and he returns to his former position. He looks sharp, ready, and I shoot him a text.

Me: nice run! You look great out there!

It's a slow game, but LSU scores a touchdown in the second quarter. The coach pulls Owen out. His teammates high-five him and a number of college kids on the rows behind the bench lean over to pat his head or cheer him on. He takes off his helmet, guzzles water, and dumps the rest of the bottle on his head.

He doesn't look for his phone or pull it out.

LSU scores another touchdown, and the cheerleaders stand up and high kick and throw their pompons. Their belly-baring tops are skimpier than the ones at Preston Y. Their performance is for the spectators, because the football players aren't watching. Owen scoots close to his teammates, leaning his head in with theirs as they point to the field and discuss the next play.

At halftime, the score is forty-eight to twenty-one, LSU winning. The ref blows his whistle, and the coach leads his team into the tunnel beneath the stadium. The band comes out and the dance squad puts on a rousing show. We're winning. I sit on my hands and bounce on my seat, wanting to see Owen play some more.

I get my chance. The coach puts him in after halftime. Both teams are on their A-game, and right away the Texas school scores a touchdown. I boo with the rest of the LSU supporters and cross my fingers they won't make the field goal.

They do.

We're still ahead. LSU picks up speed, and I scream when Owen gets the ball and runs down the field. But he's intercepted and loses it, and suddenly Texas has it again, and they are racing toward our end goal.

"Stop them!" I shout, cupping my hands to my face.

No one does, and they get a touchdown, and just like that the opposing team's score goes from twenty-eight to thirty-four. Then thirty-five.

They are one touchdown away from catching us. The atmosphere becomes tense, riddled with anticipation. A win is no longer guaranteed. I'm breathless as LSU gets the ball and runs it down the field. The running back reaches the end zone and nearly fumbles the ball when a Texas player goes for his feet.

Instead, he tosses the ball behind him to the quarterback.

Who happens to be Owen, ready and waiting.

The other team didn't anticipate him. They swivel and swarm but somehow he evades them. I'm on my feet, screaming as loudly as the people around me, my throat aching, unable to hear anything past the rush of my own voice.

Owen rushes the ball and scores the touchdown.

I shriek and pump my arms and want to run down to the field and hug him. I can't. So I sit down and scream again at the successful field goal.

My roommates are watching the game, and I text them. *Did you see that? That was Owen!*

They answer me back with smiles and thumbs ups.

He plays the rest of the game with plenty of receives and runs, but no more touchdowns. The opposing team steps up to the plate, but they are unable to catch us. We finish the game with a win by fourteen points.

"Come on," Mrs. Blaine says, standing and taking my arm. "He'll have to shower and change. We'll wait outside the locker room."

"Just like high school," I say, flashing back to standing around after games and waiting.

Except I wasn't Owen's girlfriend at the time. Sometimes his make-out buddy, but more often the friend who wished she was more.

The night is dark and cold. I didn't bring my jacket out of the car, but my sweater helps. Bright field lights shine down on the family and friends waiting outside the locker rooms, giving enough light to appear daytime. I fidget beside Mrs. Blaine, my heart pounding harder with each second. I wish I wasn't hidden behind an inch of face paint, but I'm not the only one. Most faces around me are decorated.

Finally the door opens and boys begin to trickle out. They are met with cheers and clapping. They stagger and saunter, and I pause to appreciate their size. Owen's not a small person at over six foot, but some of these guys give Goliath a run for his money. They tower over their moms and girlfriends, dwarfing the miniature humans beside them.

"Owen!" Mrs. Blaine shrieks, and I turn as he comes out.

He's freshly showered, his hair cropped short and glistening with moisture. He wears a gray sweater over jeans, and it astonishes me how he's changed even since November. His jaw is more square, his shoulders filled out. He swaggers like the rest of the players, holding his arms out from his body and coming to wrap his mom in a hug.

If he saw me, he didn't recognize me.

His dad pats him on the back when he releases his mom.

"Great plays, son," he says.

"Thanks, Dad."

There's still an edge between them, a distance, but it doesn't feel as frosty as before. Just cautious. Owen holds his fist out to Richard, who bumps it.

"Yeah, you did all right," he says.

Finally his attention turns to me. I can tell from the casual way he lifts his eyes that he expects me to be Richard's date or something. There's polite disinterest on his face as he extends his hand toward me. And then he pauses, and I know it's hard to see me behind the makeup and beneath the hat, but he's noticing. His family is breathless behind him, watching, waiting.

"Hi, Owen," I say.

CHAPTER NINETY-NINE
Celebrity Status

My voice breaks the spell. His eyes go wide, and he says, "Cassandra?"

"Good game," I say. "I told you I'd watch you."

He laughs once and then grabs me, crushing me to him, smearing my face paint into his gray sweater. "What? You're here?" He grabs my shoulders and pulls me back.

Mr. Blaine is grinning, Richard is smirking, and Mrs. Blaine is crying, her lips spread wide as tears etch down her cheeks.

"I'm here," I say, but I can't stop looking at the streak of paint on his sweater.

He takes my hat off and frees my hair, then he cups my face and kisses me. Doesn't ask if he can, if he should, if I care, and I'm glad, because it means in his mind, I still belong to him. I'm his.

"We're parked a half mile from here," Mrs. Blaine says. "Who's riding with me?"

"Aren't we all?" Mr. Blaine says, but she's looking at me.

Owen breaks away from me and drops his hand from my face to my shoulder. "Where are you staying?" Then he looks at his mom. "Where's she staying?"

"Our house," she says.

"I'll take her." He weaves his fingers through mine. "If that's okay," he adds, glancing at me.

"Absolutely," I say.

"We'll see you back at the house," Mrs. Blaine says.

She ushers the family away, and Owen turns back to me.

"You're really here," he says, awe in his voice.

"Surprised?"

"Yes." He hugs me again, enveloping me in his arms, and I breathe in the scent of his laundry detergent and shampoo and deodorant.

"Happy birthday," I say when he releases me. We're still a week shy, but it's close enough.

"Best birthday ever," he says.

He takes my hand in his and I don't question where he's leading me. It could be the end of the earth and I'd follow. Other players yell good game at him, and students recognize him as we walk, calling out his name.

"I feel like I'm walking with a celebrity," I say.

"The one and only time," he says.

"Why? This the last time we walk together?" I tease.

He laughs. "The last time I'll be a celebrity. This is the last game of the season."

"There are other seasons."

"Maybe."

I hear what he doesn't say: he's considering giving up football.

I'll ask about it later.

We get to the parking lot and I see the car my heart's been yearning for. His tan truck, tucked up and parked neatly in the shadow of the stadium. He unlocks the door and grabs a fistful of candy wrappers, empty drink containers, and dirty socks. He tosses the trash into a plastic bag and throws the socks in the back, then adds his football gear to the backseat.

"It stinks in here," he warns.

I grab his sweater before he can move away, and he lets me pull him back to me. I tug on him until his face is level with mine, and then I kiss him. I breathe him in with each inhale. His hands slide to my hips and he presses me up against the truck, and for a moment we give into the chemistry between us, the heady desire to have it all.

He breaks the kiss off, sliding his body away from mine. He kisses me again, but it's a quick peck this time. Then he moves around the truck to the driver's side, and I climb into the passenger side.

We don't talk about boundaries or concerns or playing it safe. We don't have to. We've had that talk enough, and I have no doubt Owen won't let anything happen between us.

"When did you get here?" he asks, firing up the truck and heading out of the lot.

"An hour after your game started."

"Really?" He shoots me an astonished glance. "How? When are you leaving?"

"I flew in. I was supposed to arrive yesterday, but my flight was canceled and I spent the night in the airport. I didn't expect to cut it so close to your playing time."

"You came just for the game?"

"Yes."

"I can't believe you're here."

I smile, delighted I pulled this off.

He turns into a house with three cars in the driveway. "This is my place. Be forewarned."

"Worse than your truck?"

"Makes my truck look like a spa."

The house is dark, and he flips lights as we enter. None of his roommates are here.

"Consider it a good thing," he says. "They stink."

"Worse than your car?" I joke.

"Way worse."

It's a mess. Dirty food bowls, laundry, homework papers. I ignore it all. "Where's the bathroom?"

"I don't recommend using it."

I just look at him, and he points down the hall.

"On your left," he says.

"You should change your sweater," I say. I see him glance at it as I duck into the bathroom.

It reeks. I wrinkle my nose and search for a hand towel, ignoring the yellow spots on the toilet and the slivers of hair in the sink. There is no hand towel. I find a folded towel under the sink and proceed to wash my face, scrubbing off the paint.

I haven't used the bathroom since I left Colorado. I decide now is not the time to do so.

I leave the dirty towel in the shower and come out of the bathroom. I search the house until I find Owen in a bedroom, shoving clothing into a duffel bag.

"How far is your parent's house?" I ask.

"About an hour."

I'm not sure I can wait an hour to go pee, but I don't want to make him feel bad about the state of the bathroom. "Can we stop and get some food? I came straight from the airport."

"Yeah, sure." He glances at me, then stops for a second look. "I like your face."

"Thanks, I put it on just for you," I say.

He laughs, then he comes to me and hugs me, swallowing me up in his arms. "I'm so happy you're here," he says.

"I'm so happy to be here," I reply.

"For how long? When do you leave?" He steps back and shoulders the duffel.

"I fly out on Monday. I figured you have class, and I do too."

"Monday." He stares at me. "We get one day."

My heart twists. "I'm sorry."

He shakes his head. "It's one day more than I thought. And if you add on tonight and Monday morning, it's two days."

He takes my hand and pulls me back into the hallway just as the front door opens and two guys walk in. They are loud and obnoxious, bouncing each other off the wall, laughing, giddy with victory.

"The goons are here," Owen says, loud enough that they notice him.

And me.

They straighten up, eyeing me, eyeing Owen holding my hand.

"Hi," the tall black one says, nodding at me.

"Who's she?" The white one is so pale he's practically pink, and he's by no means small. Probably taller than Owen but at least fifty pounds heavier, making him appear shorter. "You never bring girls over."

"Be polite," the other guy says, elbowing him.

"This is Cassandra," Owen says, and immediately their expressions change.

"Cass, that's Harrison—" he nods at the tall dude, "and that's Steve."

I mentally match them up to what he's told me about them. Harrison is Catholic and respectful of Owen and his beliefs. Steve is a man-whore who sleeps with anything that moves.

"This is Cassandra?" Steve straightens up. "The Cassandra?"

"The Cassandra," Owen says, and his hand tightens around mine. I feel himself bracing for anything off-color Steve might say.

"Hey, nice to meet you," Harrison says, and he puts his hand on Steve's shoulder and steers him toward the hall. "We've heard a lot about you."

"Thanks," I say.

"Where are you guys going?" Steve calls after us, but Owen already has me out the door, rolling his eyes.

"I was trying to keep you from bumping into them."

"It wasn't so bad." I put my seatbelt on in the car and think about how desperately I need a bathroom.

"Yeah, could have been worse." Owen puts the truck in reverse, then back into park. "Hang on. I just have—" He undoes his seatbelt and then leans over the console, grabbing my sleeve and pulling me toward him. "I just have to kiss you again."

I laugh softly against his mouth before it covers mine. I'm floating, flying as his lips move against mine, opening my mouth to give him entry to my soul. I hold him close, and I don't think I've ever felt so happy in my life.

He pulls back and rests his forehead against mine. "I love you. God, I love you."

"More prayers?" I whisper.

"Always."

He backs the truck out and we leave his house. He finds my hand at the red light and squeezes it. "I should get my mission call soon," he says, quietly.

"Are you excited?"

"Yes. And anxious and nervous and doubting myself."

"You'll be amazing."

"What if I'm not?"

"It's impossible not to be. You're amazing."

He beams at me and squeezes my hand.

We end up at an Arby's. I tell Owen to get me whatever he's getting and then I sprint for the bathroom. When I return, he has three wrapped sandwiches in front of him. He pushes three others in front of me.

"You think I'm going to eat all those?" I say.

"You said to get whatever I was getting."

I snort and move two back to him. "Now you get five."

"I may have seen that coming."

"I bet you did."

We eat in silence for a moment, the only sound the masticating of jaws. Owen takes a long sip of his soda and says, "How long have you been planning this?"

I take a bite and consider the question. "A month, maybe. It was kind of spur of the moment."

He shakes his head. "I can't believe you kept it a secret so long."

"It wasn't easy."

"Tell me about life. Your roommates, classes."

I exhale. "It took a few weeks, but Layne and Iris finally made up. So we're all going to room together."

"That's good, right?"

"Yes, I'm glad. But we were about to sign a contract on an apartment for four people. Now we have to look for a bigger one."

"That's a good problem to have."

"Yes," I say. "It is. Sometimes I have to remind myself of that, though."

"And Portuguese class?"

I brighten. "That's been going amazing! My teacher says I'm doing really well." I proceed to share the highlights of the class as we walk back out to his truck, and I keep talking while he drives us down the interstate toward his parents' home, telling him how I went from being certain it was going to kill me and sink my GPA to feeling like I might not only understand but excel at the language.

He doesn't say much while I talk, and I take a deep breath when I finish.

"Seems like you're excited about it," he says.

"I am. It's the first time I've felt like I'm good at something. And it's a language. I'm fascinated."

"That's awesome, Cass."

"What about you?" Owen's a great listener, but if I want to know what's in his head, I'll have to pry. "How is school?"

He lifts one shoulder. "My grades are fine. But I have a hard time caring right now. I'm leaving at the end of the semester for probably two years and when I get back, everything will be different. I might not like the same things. Maybe I'll like new things. A lot changes in two years. I'll be different."

I hear something else in his words, and I try not to capitalize on it. He doesn't say it, but at the end of the sentence I hear an unspoken, "You'll be different."

I don't point it out or question him because he's one-hundred percent right. We will both be different. Two years is a long time, especially if you're in different places and doing different things.

Instead I circle back to what he'd hinted at earlier. "And football?"

"It's one of those things. I lose my spot on the team while I'm gone. When I get back, I can red-shirt for a year and practice with the team until I've proved my worth and earned a place with them again. But I'm not sure I'll be interested anymore."

I cannot fathom it. Football has always been such a huge part of his life. "Won't you miss it?"

"Time will tell."

He's already different. He's grown up in the past six months. He's reflecting on life, his future, me. I feel it between us. I reach over and rest my hand on his thigh, and he lets go of the wheel long enough to squeeze my fingers before gripping the wheel again.

We make small talk the rest of the way to his parents' house. There's something big and unsaid between us. I don't want to approach it. I just want to enjoy this perfect and beautiful moment of being with him.

Mrs. Blaine greets us in the entryway, smiling broadly, hugging me and then Owen.

"Are you staying the night also?" she asks, glancing at his overnight bag.

"If she's here." He looks over at me, and his gaze is soft, his expression tender. It sends shivers of warm delight through my core.

"I'll put you in the guest room, then. Unless you want to be with Richard? Cassandra, you can have Monica's room."

"Why does Monica get a room and not me?" Owen complains, following us down the hall. "She's here less than I am."

"Ask me again in twenty years when you have daughters," Mrs. Blaine says. She turns on the light in a sparsely decorated bedroom. It has a feminine touch but still feels austere. That will change when Monica comes home for the summer. She'll make it nice. "I'll leave you to get settled, Cassandra. Let me know if you need any water, more blankets, food, anything. Owen, where are you sleeping?"

"I'll take the guest room," he drawls.

Mrs. Blaine leaves, and I pull my luggage onto the bed and sit cross-legged in front of it. The exhaustion from sleeping in the airport and stressing about arriving here hits me between the eyes. Owen sits across from me, and I murmur, "I'm tired."

"How can I help you?"

I shake my head and dig through my bag, searching for my pajamas. It's almost midnight. I need to brush my teeth, take out my contacts, all the things, but I just want to sleep. I yawn and stand up with my pajamas in my hand, knowing if I don't change now, I'll fall asleep in these clothes. Again.

"I've got to do this on my own," I say, waving the pajamas and contact solution at him.

"I believe in you."

My eyes burn so badly. I go to the bathroom and change quickly and pluck the contacts from my eyes. They feel immediate relief, and I put on my glasses before returning to the room.

I'm alone. I place my glasses on the nightstand and curl up on the bed with my phone in my hand, sending off a few text messages to my roommates and to my mom. They want to know all the details, which I promise to give them later. I close my eyes and let the phone drop to the bed beside me.

It jostles a moment later, and I lift my head, blinking.

"It's me." Owen stretches out beside me, and he wraps his arms around me, pulling me into his chest. I relax in his embrace and let my breathing deepen.

I must fall asleep, because I jolt awake when he moves.

"I'm so sorry," I say. "I'm so tired."

"It's okay. Sleep. We have tomorrow."

He pulls the blanket up and over me, and I smile vaguely even as my heavy eyelids flutter closed over my burning eyes. I force them open as Owen kneels at the bed beside me.

"It makes me so happy you're here," he whispers. He leans forward and presses a kiss to my lips, then another to my forehead, letting his lips linger on my skin. "Good night."

I reach out and grasp his fingers, gripping them tight. He squeezes my hand until my grip relaxes, and then he slips away. He turns out the light before he goes, and I'm asleep before he closes the bedroom door.

CHAPTER ONE HUNDRED

Game Night

Mrs. Blaine wakes me in the morning. The scent of sugar and yeast fills the air around me.

"We've got church in an hour," she says from the doorway. "I made cinnamon rolls."

"Oh." I stretch, still groggy but feeling well rested and content. "Thank you."

She smiles at me. "Did you sleep well?"

"Much better than the night before."

She laughs with me. "Come to the kitchen when you're ready."

I shower and brush my teeth and pull on the delicate floral dress I brought. It's too cold to wear the sheer fabric in Colorado, but it feels just right here in Louisiana. The soft fabric brushes against my skin and hugs my slender figure.

I'm in Owen's house. He slept here last night.

I'm giddy with the fact that we are together.

My dark hair falls long and straight down my back. I didn't pack a curling iron and it's still damp, so I leave it alone. I do take the time to put on makeup. I don't always at school, but every time I do, I get compliments.

Today I want to impress.

I'm about to leave my room and go to breakfast when someone knocks on the door.

"Come in," I say, moving toward it.

The door opens, and Owen comes in. He's dressed in beige pants and a green collared shirt, looking both sexy and formal. I smile.

"Hi," I say.

"Hi." He closes the door and crosses the distance between us. His hands fall on my hips as he presses his head to mine, and then he captures my mouth with his. He pushes me backward toward the bed, fisting handfuls of dress fabric in his hands so that it balls up around my thighs. I sit on the bed and scoot back, and he crawls on after me. And then he pulls back, chuckling and glancing down at his

554

pants.

"Crap," he says. "Now I have to change."

My eyes dart to the damp spot on his pants without meaning to, and my face warms. My chest thrills with delight, knowing the effect I have on him. "It's not my fault."

"It pretty much is." He sits beside me and grabs a pillow, hiding the evidence of his attraction. "You're a beautiful temptation. And this dress?" He fingers the material, and it slides open at the slit, revealing my thigh. He lets go of the dress and touches my exposed skin, and every nerve ending in my body ignites. My stomach tightens, my flesh growing hot.

I say nothing. Owen has my absolute trust.

He turns to me and hugs me, knocking me back on the bed but keeping a proper amount of space between us.

"No matter where our lives take us," he breathes against my cheek, "I will always, always love you."

I squeeze him tight around his waist.

There are voices in the hall, and he lets me go, sitting up and looking over his shoulder.

"Go to breakfast," he says. "I'll see you soon."

I nod and stand up, smoothing my dress before exiting the room.

Mrs. Blaine is in the kitchen scolding Richard for something, but she turns the frown into a smile when I sit.

"Milk with your cinnamon roll, Cassandra?"

"Please."

Owen strolls in a minute later, this time in black pants. I smother my smile behind my class of milk, but I can't help smirking at him.

"Shut up," he growls, falling in beside me.

"Owen, don't talk to her that way," his mom scolds.

"I'm just teasing," he says.

"Don't. Respect her always."

"Sorry," he says to me, suitably apologetic and yet somehow still grinning around the corners of his words. "I do respect you."

I know he does.

We leave for church forty minutes later in two cars. Mrs. Blaine sends Richard with me and Owen.

"Worried I'll get lost?" Owen teases her.

"No, I just think Richard will enjoy your company more than mine," she says.

"Right," he drawls, putting an arm around her and hugging her.

She's small like me, only coming up to his armpit. She swats his belly, but her pride and affection for her oldest son shows through.

I share it.

The chapel is smaller than mine at home. We go inside together, not holding hands but bumping with every step. Owen is stopped every few feet.

"Hey, good to see you!" a man says, shaking his hand. "Saw you on the game last night! Great plays!"

"Home for the weekend?" a woman asks two steps later. "I'm sure that makes your mom happy."

"Get that mission call yet?" an old man asks, attempting to fake-punch Owen's shoulder. But his wobbly fist only grazes the side of his sleeve.

"Not yet," Owen says, taking the man's hand and gripping it tight. "Soon, though."

"And who is this beautiful young lady?" Though many eyes have slid toward me with curiosity, it's the old man who finally asks.

I wonder what Owen will say.

"This is Cassandra." He puts an arm around me and hugs me into his side.

"Looks like she's special to you," the old guy says, a twinkle in his eye.

"She is." Owen presses his lips to my temple and releases me.

He doesn't call me his girlfriend. There's a lot more unsaid than said.

How much do labels matter, anyway?

He does take my hand and pull me into the chapel. Then we sit in a row with his family. I sit quietly by as several more people come over to congratulate him, shake his hand, touch him. I lean over and whisper, "Told you you're a celebrity."

He whispers back, "It won't last."

Mrs. Blaine tilts her head and begins telling me about the people around us. "That's Mr. Edwards. He used to work with Owen's dad. That's Jed Hanks. He was Owen's Sunday school teacher when he was ten. That's Alyssa Waldorf. She's been trying to get Owen to ask her out since we moved back."

I hone in on the fair-skinned girl sitting a few benches in front of us. She's already glanced back and clocked me and Owen a few times. "Does she go to school with him?"

"No, she's not in school. Just working. So she only sees him when he's here visiting me and his dad."

"Mom," Owen says, leaning over me, "stop gossiping." He looks at me. "I have zero interest in Alyssa."

"I'm not worried, Owen." And I'm not.

But I know this security is temporary. Someday I will have reason to worry. Someday Owen will be interested in other girls.

Because our time together is ending, and that knowledge pierces my heart so strongly I'm suddenly fighting tears.

I hate that I know this. He's not given any indication. Not said anything. But I know it in my heart.

And if I do, he probably does too.

❦

I want to spend my Sunday doing nothing but talking to Owen, hanging out at his house or in his room, but Mrs. Blaine invites another family over for a game of softball in the backyard and puts us to work cleaning and preparing dinner. She gives me two choices.

"You can play ball, or you can help me peel crayfish."

I choose to play ball.

I change my clothes and head out to the backyard, where Mr. Blaine introduces a family of five boys ranging in age from ten to eighteen. They stare at Owen with adoring eyes. I hide in the outfield, making half-hearted attempts at catching the ball, until Owen calls me out and puts me at bat.

I glare at him as I brandish the bat and ready myself over the home plate. "We're going to lose now."

"We've still got me," he says, unfazed.

The ball comes at me, and I miss.

"Keep your eye on the ball!" he shouts.

I want to smack his head with the ball.

It comes again, and I miss again.

"Don't swing until the ball is in your face!" he shouts.

"If it hits my face I'm hitting your face!" I shout back.

He only laughs.

The ball comes again, and I focus on it, and then I swing, and there's a loud crack.

I hit it.

I can't believe it.

"Run!" Owen yells, and I take off.

I make it to first base before I'm tapped out.

Owen's laughing hard as I walk off the field.

"I thought you would have improved in college," he says.

"I hate you," I say.

He grabs me, spinning me around and tucking me into him. He hugs me against him and brushes my nose with his. "No, you don't."

"I suppose not," I say, going soft against him.

"Hey!" Richard shouts. "Are we playing a game or what?"

"I think it would be the 'or what,'" the oldest of the visiting boys says, amusement in his voice.

I move out of Owen's embrace and sit down on the grassy yard. I'm content in my spot, cheering for the players, until they switch positions and try to get me to play again. I decide it's time to try my hand at crayfish peeling.

Mrs. Blaine is happy for my company and talks nonstop, only pausing to wait for my answers when she asks a question.

Then she says, "Owen says you're going to Brazil this summer."

She shoots me a questioning look. Like she's waiting for an explanation.

My face goes hot. "I'm studying Portuguese in school. I want to go back to Brazil and become fluent in the language, understand the culture more."

"And see a certain boy?"

CHAPTER ONE HUNDRED ONE

Not Tonight

There's no judgment in Mrs. Blaine's voice. Nothing accusative on her face. But I feel it nonetheless.

I stare at the buggy eyes of the crayfish as I remove another shell and drop the tiny fleshy body into the rice. I'm not going to Brazil to see Tiago. "He will be there," I admit. "But he's just a friend. Someone to show me around, help me with the language." I glance at her. "Does that bother Owen? Does he say anything about it?"

"No," she replies. She turns her attention back to the herbs she's cutting. "There's a lot on his mind. He knows everything is about to change."

"He's grown up," I say. "Even since I saw him at Thanksgiving."

"He has. But there's more growing to do. Wait till he gets back from his mission. You won't recognize him."

And then I'll leave on my mission. That sense of impending loss fills my heart again. Once I leave here, when will I see Owen again?

Will we know each other when we do see each other?

After dinner we play card games and eat bread pudding, and it's the best food I've had since Christmas. The other family finally decides to go home, and Richard says to Owen, "Aren't you leaving also?"

Owen checks his phone. "It's only eight, Chard."

"Yeah, but it's an hour drive and you've got school."

"I'm skipping it tomorrow," he says.

"You are?" Mrs. Blaine says.

He looks at her. "Yes," he says, his tone one that says, "Duh."

"Why?" Richard asks, and Owen kicks his leg. "Oh." Richard looks at me. "Because she's here."

"What movie should we watch tonight?" Mr. Blaine says, redirecting our attention.

They argue over which movie and I slip to my room to change my clothes. I smell like garlic and seafood, and it's entirely unappealing. I open the door to leave and find Owen in the hallway.

"My mom," he says, "has done a terrific job of keeping us apart today."

I raise both eyebrows and then give a short bark of a laugh. "I suppose that's true. Think it was intentional?"

"I have no doubt." He takes my chin in his hand and kisses me.

I think he must be right. We'd cause trouble if we sat around and made out all day. "I wanted to talk to you more," I say, breaking away and weaving my hand through his. "I feel like we didn't have any moments to ourselves."

"Again, intentional."

I look over Owen's sweatpants and T-shirt he wore while we played ball. "How many times are you going to change your clothes today?"

He growls and takes my hand, tugging me back toward the living room. "None of your business."

His dad's put on a Western that I don't recognize. Owen and I settle on the love seat in the back of the living room. He sits in the corner and I snuggle into his arms. From here I can barely see the TV.

"Does it bother you that I'm going to Brazil?" I ask quietly.

He squeezes my shoulder. "No."

"Really?" I lift an eyebrow at him.

He shakes his head. "It did. But not now."

"Why not?"

"Some things I have no control over."

I tilt my head, trying to read his expression in the flickering light from the television. "What does that mean?"

He does not answer me. He keeps his eyes on the movie, and when it's clear he's not going to respond, I turn my attention to it also.

It doesn't hold my interest. It would be rude to pull out a book and read, and I don't want to leave Owen and go to my room. What I really want is to unravel the thoughts in Owen's head and lay them on my lap, perusing through each one and examining them to know what's in his heart.

Instead I fall asleep.

I wake when the lights turn on and Mrs. Blaine sends us all to bed.

"Kiss her goodnight in the hallway," she tells Owen. "Don't go in her room."

"Told you," Owen says. "Intentional."

He takes me to the room and settles his hands on my hips, backing me up against the closed door as he kisses me long and slow. All sleepiness leaves my veins, and I cling to his forearms. He ends the kiss and cradles me in his arms. I listen to the steady beating of his heart beneath my ear and press my hand to his chest.

"What's in your heart, Owen?" I whisper.

"You," he whispers back.

I didn't expect that response. It takes away all my questions.

He releases me and opens my door. "Good night, Cassandra."

"Tomorrow," I say.

I crawl into the bed and pull the covers up to my chin, my emotions bleeding in my chest.

I've said too many goodbyes. I don't want to do another.

I've not been asleep very long when something wakes me. I lay in bed, trying to discover what pulled me from my slumber. Moonlight pours through the slats of the blinds on the window, and a footstep whispers on the floorboards behind me. I roll over, my heart rate spiking.

Even in the darkness I recognize Owen's outline.

"Owen," I say, startled.

The door is closed behind him. We are alone in my room.

"I didn't mean to wake you." He comes to the bed and sits on the edge. "I couldn't sleep. Can I be here?"

"Of course you can." My mind flashes back to the nights I've spent with Owen, the times where I've fallen asleep with him and woken in his arms.

There's nothing more romantic, in my opinion.

I scoot over on the bed and pull the blankets back, making room for him. He slides beneath them and enfolds me in his arms, crushing me to him. Only the thin layers of our pajamas are between us, and I feel every outline and curve of his body, but I know he's not here for sex.

He releases me and props himself up on an elbow. The reflection of the moonlight glitters in his eyes, casting shadows on his face. "I want to hold you tonight. Be with you. I won't do anything else, I promise."

I trail a hand down his cheekbone, around his face, under his jaw. "I know you won't."

He drops back down to the mattress and tugs me near him. He turns my body and spoons me from behind. I feel his arousal, and it's probably impossible not to be aroused in this position, but he does nothing to strengthen it. And I don't either. If I rolled over and kissed him, it would ignite a fire and take us places we're not ready to go.

So I don't.

His thoughts are heavy. I feel them. I run my fingers over the hairs of his arm, making little paths, running against the direction of their growth. "Owen," I say quietly.

"Yeah?"

"What is it?"

He squeezes me closer. "What do you mean?"

"I hear your thoughts," I whisper. "They're loud."

He nuzzles his face into the back of my neck. "I'm sorry."

His words make my heart skip a beat. "Why are you sorry?"

"Not tonight, Cassandra," he whispers. Begs.

Feelings and thoughts have been percolating through me since last night, and now they coalesce into a certainty.

He's going to break up with me. He's going to end this.

I stop playing with his arm hairs and tighten my hands on his arms. I suck in a breath and hold it because I'm afraid I'll cry, and if I start crying, he'll know I know.

And like him, I don't want to deal with this tonight. Tonight we are still us.

☙ ⚬ ❧

I wake in the morning when I feel Owen's arms disengage from around me. The sun isn't up yet, but I can tell by the pink color on the horizon that it's close. And I know he wants to get out of my room before his family discovers he slept here.

I tighten my grip on his arms, and he stops moving.

"Are you awake?" he whispers.

In response I roll over. His face is swollen from just waking, his eyes hooded with grogginess. One side of his hair spikes up, and I think he's adorable.

I press upward to meet his mouth and kiss him.

It's as I remember with Tiago. When you want each other, morning breath doesn't matter. Nothing matters.

And we want each other.

His caution from the night before is gone. His arms go around me and we tumble back against the bed, me pressed beneath his body, sandwiched between him and the mattress. We are slow at first, kissing in an exploratory way, his lips brushing my jaw, tickling my ear, grazing my neck. His fingers run along my arm, my hip, my thigh. Taking a thousand years with each touch. My exhale is nearly a groan, and my hands go beneath his shirt, tracing the muscles of his chest.

His breathing quickens. His hands land on my hips, and he yanks me farther down on the bed. It's not slow anymore. Our mouths meet in hunger, desperate desire, and I arch my back, pushing into his touch. He sits back, breaking the connection, and I rise up, my hand falling to his stomach. My eyes flick to the bulge in his pants and I lower my hand, running down his groin and then wrapping my hand around his length.

His hand closes over mine, trapping me there. He leans over me, breathing in quick gasps, not releasing my hand around his body.

"I have to go," he breathes, and saying the words out loud seems to snap something in him. He lowers his head, taking deep breaths, and then he lets go of me and slides down the bed. His eyes rake over my body as he slides past me, and I know his thoughts. I know how desperately he wants sex.

Almost as much as me.

It's impossible to keep it from happening. I lose my desire to stop with each passing moment. If we are together, it's only a matter of time.

If we are together.

He slips from the room without another word, closing the door quietly behind him.

I squeeze my hand into a fist. It feels strangely empty.

CHAPTER ONE HUNDRED TWO

The Call

get up and get ready for the day once Owen's gone. I fly out in a few hours, and my heart's a mess. I alternate between numbness and joy and aching hysteria.

I do not want to leave him. I want to quit school and move to Louisiana and marry him. I want to make love to him and have his babies and raise a family together.

I won't tell him that.

I hear his mom's voice in the kitchen, the low rumble of his dad's response. Richard's sarcastic tones add to the discussion, and then his dad's yelling at him to hurry or he'll be late to school. Richard grumbles back. The front door slams, and Mrs. Blaine yells after him that she loves him.

I do not hear Owen.

I don't feel like peopling. I pull out my homework and sit cross-legged on my bed, immersing myself in Portuguese and American history. The sun is bright and shining outside even though it's only fifty degrees. Birds chirp and shriek. My skin likes it here. I haven't been bathing in lotion like I do in Colorado.

A cry comes from the kitchen, followed by Mrs. Blaine yelling, "Owen!"

I tilt my head and listen. Is he in trouble? Do they have security cameras and she discovered he slept with me? I hold my breath, not about to go out there and find out.

"What? What's wrong?"

His deep voice makes my stomach tighten.

"Get your dad." She's breathless, but she doesn't sound angry. "Get Cassandra. Your mission call came."

"What? It came?"

I can't tell if he's alarmed or excited, but I'm already climbing off the bed and hurrying for the door. I hear Owen down the hall, talking to his dad. I hold back in the doorway, suddenly timid. This is private. A family affair. Should I even be here?

AJ invited me to be present when he gets his call, and I'd known him a few hours.

Mr. Blaine and Owen come striding down the hall. His dad looks more pleased than I've ever seen him, his hands on Owen's shoulders, pride radiating on his face. Owen slows when he sees me.

"Come on," he says, taking my hand and tugging me from the doorway.

Mrs. Blaine has her computer up and open on the counter. She's bouncing on the balls of her feet, anticipation lighting her face. She steps away from the computer to squeeze my hands.

"I'm so glad you get to be here for this!" she says.

Me too. I think. I'm excited for Owen. This is amazing.

But I'm also dreading this. Up until now, him leaving has been all hypothetical. Someday. In theory.

After this it will be real.

We crowd around the computer, where an email box is open. The email sits at the top of the inbox, unopened. *Service mission information for Owen Blaine,* the subject reads.

It's from the church.

None of us move. We stare at it.

"Why did it come to you?" Owen asks. "I thought it was supposed to come to me."

"You must have put my email as the contact," his mom says, swatting his arm.

"Oops."

"Open it," she whispers, leaning into him.

"What if it's not a call?" he says. "What if they tell me they're sorry but I can't go?"

My heart squeezes at his insecurity. This is the part of Owen most people don't see.

Mrs. Blaine rubs his arm. "They wouldn't tell you. They'd tell the pastor. Open it, sweetie."

Owen takes the computer and moves away from us to the couch. He sits down, and we swivel, clustering in closer to him but giving him space.

He clicks the mouse and clears his throat.

"*Dear Owen Blaine,*" he reads. "*Thank you for your willingness to serve as a missionary for the Lord. Your desire to dedicate your time in the service of your fellow man is honorable and acceptable. After studying your interview papers, it's been decided that you will labor in the Chicago, Illinois mission—*"

Mrs. Blaine shrieks. She presses her hands to her face and bursts into tears.

Owen keeps going. "*To the souls with spiritual and physical hunger living in that great city and the suburbs around it.*" He looks up. "Then there's some stuff about what I need to pack."

"When do you start?" Mr. Blaine asks.

Owen checks again. "I report for service on June second."

I catch my breath, my heart skipping beats. I'll still be in Brazil. "For how long?"

"Two years." He doesn't meet my eyes.

I feel the divide growing between us.

He belongs to the Lord now.

"Congratulations," I say, and I put as much happiness and cheer as I can in my voice. "You'll make a great missionary."

He looks up at me, and he smiles, but it's tinged with the same sadness I feel.

I don't want him to be sad. This is a great moment. A happy one he should treasure for the rest of his life.

I step over to him and hug his shoulders. "I'm so happy for you, Owen. It's amazing you get to do this."

His hand comes up and squeezes my wrist.

Mrs. Blaine comes over, laughing, crying, yanking him up from the couch and throwing her arms around his torso. "We have a missionary in the family!" she cries.

Mr. Blaine joins them in a group hug.

I stand on the outskirts and smile so hard my face hurts.

They step back and read Owen's call for themselves, exclaiming over details and touching him, patting him, overflowing with excited energy.

I wait what I feel is an appropriate amount of time and then slip away to my room.

A mission will change Owen. He'll mature. He'll learn to love strangers and sacrifice his own needs for others. It will make him a stronger, better, more confident person and prepare him for life.

But I can't stop the tears that slide down my face while I pack my suitcase. All of those changes will happen without me.

This trip has been wonderful and everything I hoped it would be.

And that makes it more painful than if I hadn't come.

A knock sounds on the door, but I don't answer. I wipe my face on a shirt and wad it up, tossing it in the suitcase. The knock comes again.

"Hang on," I call out. I check out my reflection in the mirror on the wall and scowl.

It's clear I've been crying.

There's no more knocking. I go to the door and open it.

It's Owen. His eyes trace over my face but he doesn't comment on the obvious. "Want to go on a drive?" he asks. "Before you leave?"

This is it. This is where we end things. Suddenly I'm upset. I wish I hadn't come. He would still break up with me, but it would be after weeks of not seeing each other, months of distance growing between us.

Not after two days of love and intimacy.

Saying no isn't an option. If I avoid this, he'll do it on the phone. Via text. Maybe I should jump to the chase and save him the trouble.

He takes my hand and squeezes my fingers.

I cave. "Yeah, sure," I say, as if I don't know what's coming. As if my heart's not breaking.

"Put your things in the truck. I'll take you to the airport after."

I nod and then go through the house, hugging and saying goodbye to his family. Everyone is ecstatic. This is a good day. No one notices my pain.

Neither of us speaks as he drives. I wonder where he'll take us. In Arkansas, I know he'd take us to the white chapel. Does he have a place like that here?

He pulls up to a cemetery. I gawk as I get out of the truck. The coffins are above ground, and massive mausoleums dot the green lawn. Gargoyles and angels stand guard over the dead remains.

Owen gets out and heads for the gate. He waits at the entrance for me to catch up with him.

"Why are the coffins on top of the soil?" I ask.

"The water level is too high here," he says. "Dead bodies used to pop out of the soil during the rainy season. So they stopped burying them and placed them on top or in tombs."

"It's creepy." We walk past a series of angels with horrified expressions on their faces. "But kind of cool. Are they supposed to look serene?"

"Their faces used to be angelic. But after a few centuries of smelling dead bodies, they morphed into expressions of horror."

He's deadpan as he says it, and I have to look at him to know he's joking. Then he grins, and I shake my head.

"Nothing is sacred," I say.

He shoves his hands in his pocket and his eyes dart downward, his countenance growing more somber. "Some things are."

I left myself open to that one.

I don't respond. I sense all the things he's going to say. I'll let him speak.

He doesn't for another moment. I examine the names on headstones and imagine their lives. They are all quite old.

"I have some concerns," he says quietly, and I look at him.

"Concerns?" I ask, and my voice cracks. My heart rate increases.

"About you. And me."

I stop walking so I can face him. A tremble builds up in my core, sending a frosty shiver through my body. "What do you mean?"

His eyes flick to mine but he can't hold my gaze. "You are my biggest distraction."

"Distraction?" My stomach tightens.

He nods. "I think about you every moment. The first thing I do every morning and the last thing every night is check to see if you texted. If you call me, I can't think or focus on anything until I've called you back because suddenly I'm worrying. Worrying the distance became too much. Worrying you're not sure how you feel anymore. Worrying you're with someone else."

I'm astonished and a bit ashamed. "I'm not."

"It doesn't matter if you are or not. It doesn't stop the feeling. And I need it to stop."

He meets my eyes now. I see the set of his jaw, the steely determination in his gaze.

"I'm leaving soon," he continues. "I'll be gone for years. I need to have my head on straight. I need to live in that moment. I can't have those worries tripping me up. I can't spend the days of my mission anxious for them to pass so I can see you again. I need to be there while I'm there. Really be there."

He takes my elbows in his hands. His expression is earnest. He still hasn't spelled it out. I don't know if he will. I don't know if he even understands what he's needing.

"I know, Owen," I say, quietly, speaking past the lump in my throat.

"You know what?" he says, still holding my elbows.

"I know what you're doing."

"What am I doing?"

"You're breaking up with me."

He releases my arms and takes a step back. "No, I'm—I'm—" He's at a loss. "I'm letting you go."

"Right." I try to smile, but the tears blur my vision and make my mouth tremble. "That's what breaking up is." I lift a shoulder and say glibly, "We should be good at this by now."

He doesn't react to my joke. He swallows, hard enough that I see the bob of his throat. "I need you to know that I love you. That my whole soul has fallen for you. I will never love another girl in my life as much as I love you."

"Yay," I say, and I'm laughing but I'm also crying. "Thanks for the consolation prize."

He will love other girls.

But none as much as me.

He steps forward, ready to wrap me in his arms, to comfort me, but I put my hand up and stop him.

"No, Owen," I say. That's not his role now.

He doesn't get to hold me.

He stops, and his expression is wretched. I know he's rethinking things. Wondering if breaking up is the right thing.

But this was on his mind before I got here. If he doesn't follow through now, he'll end up doing it again later.

I'd prefer not to put a bandaid on this wound.

"Cassandra," he says softly. Brokenly.

I blink rapidly, trying to get my tears under control. There will be a time to sob my eyes out.

This isn't it.

"We should go back to your house," I say. "I need to leave for my flight."

"I'll take you to the airport."

"No," I say. One ending was enough. No more goodbyes. "I don't want to ride with you."

He nods once and moves past me toward the parking lot, leaving me to follow.

The silence between us as we drive back to his house is hollow. Wooden. Filled with aching.

He parks in front of the house but doesn't turn the truck off. He faces me.

"The conversation didn't go the way I wanted it to," he says.

"Oh? You imagined a different outcome?"

"Well, I—" he shrugs. "I thought—I thought—I didn't think you'd push me away."

My laugh is tinged with bitterness. "You thought we'd still be close? Maybe besties?"

My words hurt him. I see it on his face. But I see him trying to take it, to not get upset.

"I guess I did," he says quietly. "But that was dumb, huh."

"Yes." I don't hesitate with my words, because I know what needs to be said. "We can't break up and then act like we're together. You can't want me out of your thoughts and then make me your close friend. You can't say you're not my boyfriend and then hold my hand. This needs to be a clean cut. We're done. It's over." The tears fall rapidly from my eyes, so hard and fast I can't stem the flow. "Don't call me. Don't text me. No more ifs or maybes or somedays. Let's live our lives."

He looks away from me out the window. He doesn't answer.

I wait. I mop up my tears with my sleeve and tell myself to get a grip.

"Can I write you on my mission?" he asks, quietly.

My heart clenches.

I should tell him no. This needs to be the end. I can't take the back and forth anymore. Two people who break up as often as we have should realize the universe is telling them it's not gonna work out.

But I can't cut him out completely. "Yes."

He nods. He doesn't look at me.

I need to go. And I don't want to make small talk with his mom or try to explain what went down. I pull out my phone. "I'm calling a taxi to take me to the airport."

He turns from the window. "No, you're not. If you don't let my mom take you, I'm taking you."

"Owen, I—" My fingers shake as I try to pull up the app. My whole body is shaking. "I don't want her to see me like this. I don't want her to ask me what's wrong. I don't want to talk about it."

He gets out of the car and closes the door, leaving me inside his truck. I'm not sure what's expected of me, so I sit there taking deep breaths, trying to stop the hyperventilating sobs that build in the back of my throat. Five minutes pass. Seven.

Then the truck door opens and Mrs. Blaine climbs into the driver's side. She reaches over and hugs me tight.

"Owen told me," she says. "You don't have to say a thing. Let me get you home."

I am so grateful for her words.

That was it. Owen's not coming back. That was our goodbye.

I'm shattered.

We do not speak the entire drive to the airport. I stare out the window and keep my crying under control even though tears leak from my eyes. I will not fall apart in front of her. I wonder what Owen told her. I wonder what she thinks of me now.

I know, in my heart, that Owen did the right thing. Being untethered is better for both of us.

But it hurts like hell.

⚜

Mrs. Blaine wraps me in a hug when we get to the airport. I suck in short breaths. She kisses my cheek and says, "I love you. I know this is hard. But I promise you you're going to be fine."

What a stupid promise. Nobody knows how I'm going to be.

She does not offer me reassurances of Owen's love, or that there's still the future in front of us, or this is only temporary. Somehow she knows that is not what I want to hear right now.

I get through security and go to my gate. I have an hour before I board. I set all my things around me and make a fort with my luggage and backpack. Then I curl into a ball and finally allow myself to bawl.

Owen texts me twenty minutes into my sobfest.

O: Did you make it to the airport? Are you OK?

I will not ease his conscience on this. I will not pretend like we're okay.

I block his number.

CHAPTER ONE HUNDRED THREE

Circling

*C*ircles
The girl standing in the corner
The boys dancing with the statues
The girl painting on the wall
The boy staring at the cross
People all around
Yet disconnected
Solitary and disjointed
Everywhere I look
Everywhere I turn
The girl standing
The boy dancing
The girl painting
The boy staring
Girl standing
Boy dancing
Girl painting
Boy staring
Standing dancing painting staring
Standing dancing painting staring standing dancing painting staring
Stand dance paint stare stand dance paint stare
Stand dance paint stare stand dance paint stare——————

❦

I alienate myself from everyone when I get back to campus.

My roommates know. I couldn't hide this. They tiptoe around me, offering to make me tea or soup, asking if I need anything. I bury myself in my room and pretend like life still has meaning.

There are things to focus on. Classes resume the moment I'm back. I missed two days of Portuguese and spend four hours on Tuesday evening studying and catching up.

It's a good distraction.

I wonder if Owen has texted me. I wonder if he has cried the way I cried. I wonder if he misses me.

I bet the answer to each wondering is a yes. But I will never know because I will not talk to him again.

After a week, Iris brings me a list of apartments with three bedrooms.

It's time to resume life.

"How are you doing?" she asks me as we get in my car to look at places, and she shoots me a timid glance.

"I'm doing fine," I say, quite aggressively. Nobody wants to talk to me right now. I'm the opposite of sunshine.

"Have you talked to Owen at all?"

I shoot her a dirty look just for mentioning his name. "No."

"Do you want to talk about it? You've been so . . . quiet all week."

She means mopey. Depressed. Crying.

"I don't."

She falls silent, and I back out of the parking lot thinking that's the end of it, and then she says, "What happened? You seemed so happy when you were there with him."

I tighten my fingers around the steering wheel and press my lips together. I say nothing. Iris gets the hint, and we continue our journey in taciturn silence.

The apartment is pleasant, small but with three bedrooms and a kitchen. It's cheap, and I'm ready to sign a contract to be done with this, but the current tenant says, "Well, actually, we're not sure all six spots will be available. Some of our roommates might be staying for spring term."

"So how many spots might be available?" I say, leveling my gaze at her.

She shrugs. "Maybe three."

"So this is basically a waste of our time." I turn for the door. "Let's go, Iris."

I don't wait for her. The murmur of voices follows me as I leave the apartment. I have the car running with my hands in front of the heater when Iris finally joins me in the car. I don't ask what was said.

"Next," I say.

Iris gives me the address without another word. I drive in icy silence. I've made my heart into a brick. No one will penetrate again.

༄༄

Shards
Tears of broken glass
Cut across the porcelain skin
Releasing rivulets of crimson liquid
Which stain the pure heart
Stabbing deeper
To the brilliant white bone

Shattered the pieces are stronger
Piercing vital organs
Poisoning rushing rivers of life
Haughty in their crystalline assault
The tiny unseen enemy
Enter the defenseless heart
And slowly bleeds away the feeling
Parasitic draining
And the unsuspecting victim
Is also the perpetrator
With the icy tears of pain

The closer we get to spring, the more sunshine there is. Leaf buds appear on the trees, reluctant to open because they know winter is not over, but they promise warmth is coming.

As the earth begins to defrost, so does my heart begin to thaw.

I miss Owen terribly, but cutting the connection with him completely has helped me accept that we are over. His mom does not contact me, and even though Monica calls and texts, we don't talk about her brother.

My roommates and I still don't have a place for next year, and that anxiety fills every conversation. We are constantly looking, constantly touring, constantly asking. We might not be able to live together.

I spend a lot of time with my Portuguese TA, Elizabete. She says I'm learning Portuguese faster than any of the other students she works with. She invites me to her house for lunch and to listen to music in Portuguese, and the next day I get a 100% on my Portuguese quiz.

And I have finally mastered forward-swimming. Actually, I've gotten so good at it that I'm the fastest kicker in the class. My legs are hard as a rock.

Fliers appear around campus announcing a dance the first week of March. My roommates go from talking about apartments to talking about it who is going to ask them. When Iris asks me Sunday after church who I hope to go with, I say, "I'm not going," and then I go into my room and close the door.

There is no romance in my future.

Something changes inside me at the end of February.

I wake up Thursday and don't feel as if a cannonball resides in my chest. I go to the bathroom to wash my face and brush my teeth, and I examine my reflection. I'm thin and pale, but I'm not dead. I lift the ends of my dark hair and look at my dark brown eyes, and I don't want to see that sad little girl anymore. She suffered and she lost and I'm ready to be someone different.

I change my clothes and go into the kitchen where Iris and Layne are toasting bagels for breakfast.

They both glance at me and give me quick, furtive smiles.

"Good morning," I say, opening the fridge and removing a yogurt. Then I pull the granola from the shelf. "Are there any boys left that don't have a date to the invitational?"

They exchange startled glances. Layne recovers first.

"I'll find out. Are you looking for a date?"

I shrug like I don't care and dig into the yogurt. "If I don't have a date, I won't go."

It's clearly a change in attitude, but neither one comments or points it out. Layne pops her bagel from the toaster and says, "I'll ask around."

I take another bite of yogurt, crunching on the granola I put on top. "I think we should put a down payment on an apartment this weekend. We need to decide, or they will all be taken. Let's pick one."

Iris nods. "I agree."

"Let's do it," Layne says.

"Great." I dump my yogurt in the trash, grab my jacket, and head out the door. I'm ready for change.

I stop by the pharmacy on my way to work and buy a box of red hair dye. I apply it that night.

⊙҂⋐

"How did you get it so red?" Layne fingers my silky locks at breakfast the next day. "When I dye my hair, it barely takes any color at all. And your hair is darker than mine."

"I left it in for nearly two hours," I admit. "Every time I tested a strand to see the color, it wasn't dark enough."

"Two hours!" Iris says. "All your hair could have fallen out!"

"But it didn't." I smile.

I get comments in every class. Abby says we are twins now, and people I don't know tell me they like my hair.

I feel like a celebrity.

I like it.

On Saturday my roommates and I pile into my car with Abby. I'm in a jubilant mood, joking and teasing and making everyone laugh.

"Do you still not have a date to the invitational?" Abby asks me as we pull into an apartment complex.

"Not yet." I look up at the brown sides of the three-story building in front of us. It's a small apartment complex, not sprawling across a block like most of the ones we've gone through. "I'll get one."

The available apartment is on the second story. There's only one door in and a flight of stairs in the walkway outside between the two halves of the building. We step inside the apartment. It has a decent-sized living room and a balcony that looks out over the courtyard between the buildings. The kitchen is small with a nice pantry. But no washer and dryer.

The five of us filter down the hall. A swamp cooler hangs from the ceiling. There are two bathrooms across from one bedroom, and then two more bedrooms in the back. I enter the third bedroom and walk over to the window. It's nearly floor to ceiling and gives a good view of the apartment complex across the street and the mountains in the background.

Camila comes into the room behind me. "It's affordable. If we get six people in here, it'll be about three hundred dollars per person a month. And the landlord covers utilities."

I turn to her. "We should get it."

"Do you want it?"

I nod and then walk out to the living room where Layne and Abby are talking.

"We should get this one," I say.

"Works for me," Abby says.

"Sure, I'm game," Layne says.

The landlord's number is on the whiteboard by the door. I pull my phone out and call him.

"This is Mr. Sanford," he says. "How can I help you?"

"Hi, Mr. Sanford? I'm Cassandra, I'm here in one of your apartments. We want to go ahead and rent it. What do you need from us?"

⟨✴⟩

We wait at the apartment for Mr. Sanford, who comes over with contracts and a receipt book. He gets our names and a deposit from each of us, and warns us that he will list the apartment for the sixth tenant, which means a girl we don't know will be moving in.

Or not. I don't care. I'm just so glad not to have to do this search anymore.

Abby squeals when we walk out and throws her arms around me. "We did it! We have a place to live!"

I smile and pat her arms. "Yes. We can do anything if we really want it."

We walk down the sidewalk back toward my car, and Layne says, "Like get a date to the invitational?"

I lift my shoulders. "I've got a week."

A boy crosses the street and steps onto the sidewalk in front of us.

"Ask him," Abby says.

"Do it!" Layne says.

I look him over. He's tall with ash-blond hair and broad shoulders. I've never seen him before.

Why not? I've got nothing to lose.

"Hey," I say, catching his attention.

He turns, looking up from his phone and blinking light blue eyes at me. His face sports a pleasant arrangement of features, with high eyebrows and defined cheekbones.

"Yeah?" he says.

"What's your name?"

His brows furrow in an expression of bewilderment. I would be confused also if some strange boy started talking to me this way.

"Adam," he says.

"Adam." I flash smile. "Do you live around here?"

"Yeah."

My roommates are silent around me, waiting in breathless expectation. What am I going to do next?

"We're moving in next semester."

"That's cool," Adam says. He's clearly still not sure what to think of me. "I'm moving out before then."

"Do you have a date to the dance on Saturday?"

Those expressive brows lift. "No. Not yet."

"Great. Want to go with me?"

He blinks in astonishment, and his eyes look me over as if just now noticing me. "For real?"

I pull out my phone. "Give me your number. We can meet on campus or I can come here and get you."

"Okay."

He gives me his number, and I program it into my phone, then grin at him. "I'll reach out next week to coordinate details."

"Yeah. Sounds good." He starts to walk into the apartment complex we just left, and then he spins around. "What is your name?"

That makes me laugh. "Cassandra. Cassandra Jones." I continue my walk to the car, my roommates following behind me like a group of ducklings. As soon as we get inside, they erupt into excited chatter, unable to believe I did that. I smile but don't respond, basking in the strange power I never knew I could have.

Maybe Owen was right. Maybe I couldn't really discover myself when I was tethered to him.

CHAPTER ONE HUNDRED FOUR

The Rest of the Story

I am a ridiculous flirt in church on Sunday.

By the time we get to Sunday School, my face is hot and I'm sweating from the exertion of being constantly witty and giggly.

But the power of a woman's wiles cannot be denied. Four boys seat themselves around me.

Including Jared.

I haven't talked to him since I got back from Louisiana thirteen days ago, and I turn to him now, sagging with relief at seeing a familiar, friendly face.

"Hi." I don't flirt with him. We're past that, and I won't do that to our friendship.

"Hey." He gives me a warm smile. "You doing all right?"

This is not a superficial question. I know he is watching my behavior and analyzing my motives. I weave my hand back-and-forth. "Eh. It's been an interesting few weeks."

He nods. Class begins, and I face the front to listen to the spiritual examination of the book of John. But Jared's question broke through my protective mask, and now my heart aches. I was trying so hard to pretend to be okay.

Class finishes, and several of the boys with whom I flirted mercilessly gather around to chat some more. It takes all of my energy to be someone else, and I manage to slip away, claiming to need to talk to someone.

I go out the back door and breathe in the frigid February air, knowing that March is right around the corner. Warmth is coming.

I want to cry, and I hate it.

I walk toward the dorms by myself for about five minutes before I hear footsteps jogging behind me. I don't look back, though the footsteps slow as they come closer, and then Jared is walking alongside me, his hands shoved in the pockets of his long wool jacket.

We say nothing, and I appreciate his steady presence.

I'm curious about his date to the invitational, but I feel like it would be very forward of me to ask. I know this conversation is going to wind back around to Owen and suddenly I want to talk to someone about it. About how desperately I'm aching. So I say, "Owen got his mission call."

"That's great. Really exciting. Where is he going?"

"Chicago."

"For how long?"

"Two years." I say everything very calmly. As if I'm not talking about someone who means the world to me. Someone who I cut out of my life.

But Jared knows there's more to the story. And he knows the questions to ask. "How are you handling it?"

"We broke up."

Saying the word is like taking a hammer to my glass exterior. Something cracks around my heart, around my soul, under my eyes, and tears break free. My chest heaves, and my body shakes. Jared puts an arm around me, his hand on my shoulder, and pulls me into him.

After a moment, he says, "Ever notice how many mailboxes there are outside of apartment complexes?"

I give a strangled laugh and pull away from him, confused by the question.

"Look." He points at an apartment complex on our right. "This is a big one. Look at all those mailboxes."

I nod as I add up the boxes in front of the complex. "At least thirty."

"Yeah, but that's nothing." Jared points at another complex.

My eyes widen as I take in the rows of boxes. "Over a hundred," I say.

"I wonder what kind of mail they've gotten?"

I think of what shows up at my apartment every day. "Junk mail. Coupons. Bills. Insurance statements." Getting the mail is not exciting anymore. Everyone just wants a piece of my money.

"When was the last time you got a piece of mail that made you happy or excited?"

I shake my head. I can't think of it.

"Come on. No special letters? Cards?"

I've gotten birthday cards and Christmas cards from family and friends back home. None of them thrill me. "My best ones have been email."

"Let's pretend that counts."

"It would have been my acceptance letter to Preston Y. No. When I got the follow-up email telling me I got a scholarship."

"Even better than an acceptance letter."

"Yes! Not only was I in, but now I had a way to pay for it!"

Jared holds out his fist to me, and I bump it.

"Great time," he says.

I smile at the memory.

Jared drops me off at the back door of my apartment with another hug. He doesn't say anything about Owen.

I definitely feel better after talking to him.

"I'm flying out to visit you," Mom says on the phone after dinner. "In one week."

"In one week?" I check the wall calendar in my room. It will be March in three days.

Owen's birthday was two days ago.

I didn't call him. I didn't text him. I did nothing.

Except cry, of course.

"Why?" I ask.

"For your birthday," she says.

"Oh." I forgot. My birthday is in ten days. "You don't have to do that."

"Yes, I do." Her voice is firm. "I need to spend time with you."

Translation: she's worried about me.

"I'm handling things all right," I say. "Better than I was."

"That's great, honey. I can't wait to see you."

I decide not to talk her out of it. Besides, it could be fun to have my mom at school with me. "All right. I'll see you then."

My week goes by in a blur of classes.

It's midterms in most of them, except Portuguese, which gives us a day off, during which I write two essays. I aced the multiple choice part of American history, but they grade harshly on the written part, so I give it extra attention. I have an exam in dance, and I'm certain dancing is not my calling.

I also call back the random dude I asked to the dance. I consider telling him it was all a joke, or a lapse in judgment, but as soon as I identify myself on the phone, he says, "Are you calling to cancel our date?"

He says it with just the right amount of humor and uncertainty that I cave.

"No way! It'll be so much fun."

And then we plan it out. He finds it funny that I live in the dorms and says he'll pick me up. He'll park in the empty lot across the street. Then he'll come into the common area where I'll be with my roommates and their dates and we'll walk over to the campus building together.

I'm actually excited about meeting a new guy. This will be fun.

AJ calls me Thursday evening and tells me he got his mission call and invites me over for when he opens it. I'd forgotten about AJ, or I might've asked him to the dance. But again, maybe it's better I didn't. There was no chemistry between us.

"It's so kind of you to want me there," I say. "But I'm working tonight."

"I can wait until you're off."

I don't want to be there, and not because there's nothing between me and AJ. But because I just went through a mission call opening, and it was rather traumatizing.

I can't explain that to him.

"AJ, I'm so sorry, but it doesn't work for me tonight. Open it with your friends and family, okay? And then tell me where you're going."

"Okay," he says, and there's no mistaking the wounded disappointment in his voice. It makes me feel horribly guilty and selfish. I consider going over when I get off work, but then I decide to stake my ground. It's not always about making other people happy.

⊙〜⋅❋⋅〜⊙

As soon as my work shift ends on Saturday, I rush out the door, not pausing to chat with my coworkers.

Except Stirling, who comes out the door after me. "You look like you're in a hurry," he says.

"I am." I unlock my car door. "Have to get ready for the dance tonight."

"Hot date?"

I laughed. "I honestly can't remember what he looks like."

Stirling settles against my car, crossing his arms over his chest and making my rapid get away impossible.

"I am intrigued. Is it a blind date?"

"Practically. No one asked me, so I found the first guy I saw and asked him."

"You did?" Stirling lets his arms drop to his sides. "If I'd known you didn't have a date, I would've asked you."

I don't know that I would've wanted to go with Stirling, but at least someone would've asked me. "Well, next time ask."

"So how about you and I go out to the movies next Saturday?"

I've been putting Stirling off for a while. But now that I sort of told him he should be asking, I feel like I have to be agreeable. "Yeah. That sounds fun."

Stirling moves away from my car and grins. "Great! We can go to my place after and try another cow flavor."

I laugh. It feels like a lifetime ago I was at his apartment trying different juice and ice cream blends. "We haven't done that in a while," I agree. And I'm surprised to realize I look forward to it.

Layne is already working on Iris's hair when I get home. A girl across the hall, Valerie, works on Camila's. I watch them from my vantage point in the hallway, where I can see both rooms at once while I eat a cucumber sandwich. Camila introduced them to me and I find them very refreshing.

"Who is your date, Cassandra?" Valerie asks as she pins another portion of Camila's hair.

"Adam," I say as I stuff the last bite of sandwich in my mouth.

"Who is he? Does he go to church with us?"

"No," I say. "I just met him."

My roommates giggle.

"Oh, that sounds nice." Valerie finishes with Camila, whose hair has been put in tiny braids and tied in a knot at the base of her neck. It's quite becoming.

"Your turn," Valerie says.

I bounce into the room.

"What do you want me to do with your hair?" Valerie asks.

"I like what you did to Camila's. Something like that."

Valerie parts my hair down the side and goes to work making several tiny braids. She works over the straight portions of my hair and ties a dozen knots. Finally, she wraps them in a circle on the side of my head so it looks like a blooming flower right behind my ear.

"It's beautiful," I say, turning my head to admire the braid.

"And now my fingers are cramping," Valerie says. "See you guys later!"

I turn to Layne. I've been home an hour now, and we have half an hour until the boys come get us for the dinner. "Do you want me to do your hair?"

She shrugs. "I'm fine with it the way it is. I've never cared to do it fancy." She touches the bloom attached to my head. "I like this."

"I don't think I can copy it," I warn. "And I think Valerie's fingers are all worn out."

"Yes." She laughs.

We put on our formal dresses and gather in front of the bathroom mirror to put on make up, and I'm reminded of my junior prom at Harper's house, when we went into the bathroom to freshen up, me, Harper, and Betsy. I felt so beautiful that night, so special. It was definitely my better prom.

Although last year could've been great if Owen hadn't broken up with me.

This is the last time I will allow him to break up with me.

I have to swallow hard because I want to cry again and I'm so sick of that.

I'm wearing the same dress from junior prom, but has a much lower neckline than the one I wore senior year.

I can't hide the pearl necklace.

Layne touches it. "Do you ever take it off?"

"I take it off during swimming lessons," I say, and we chuckle.

"But not otherwise?"

I shake my head and focus on my reflection while I put on mascara.

"He gave it to you, didn't he."

She doesn't say his name. And she doesn't even phrase it as a question.

I simply nod.

She doesn't say anymore about it.

We take several pictures as roommates before our dates arrive. They find us in the commons, and I'm pleased Adam is cuter than I remembered. Actually I couldn't remember what he looked like. We take more pictures, and it's nothing but frivolity and light-hearted fun.

We walk to the dinner, which is being served in a building adjacent to where the dance is being held. Adam holds my hand as we sit and wait. Pleasant flutters fill my belly at his touch, but there is still the mingling pain at what I have lost.

I decide it's not a bad thing, to feel the wound of love. It makes the gentle feelings of finding someone else more hesitant, more tender, more aware.

After dinner Adam and I dance until my feet hurt and I call a timeout. We sit in chairs along the wall and he tells me a fish story about how one time he and his dad got lost in Scotland and ended up stranded on top of a snowy mountain with a big lake. Since they had their fishing gear (thinking March was springtime), they decided to fish. But all they got was an old tire that had been chewed up by the Lochness monster.

The story makes no sense, but the way Adam tells it, with his hands spread wide and his expressive features, has me laughing out loud.

"I think I'm ready to go home," I say. "I'm tired."

"I'll walk you back."

I say goodbye to my roommates, and Adam accompanies me to my dorm. I'm sleepy and content and don't say much. He walks me up the stairs to my apartment.

"Thanks for coming tonight," I say, turning to face him in the doorway. "The fact that you said yes to a perfect stranger—it made my night."

"I can't believe you asked me," he says. "I wasn't planning on going, to be honest."

"Obviously, since you didn't already have a date."

He smiles. "It was fun. If you ever need another last-minute date, let me know."

I don't feel any chemistry between us. He didn't make my heart skip a beat.

Then again, maybe it's too soon for that.

"All right," I say.

It doesn't hurt to be friendly.

CHAPTER ONE HUNDRED FIVE
Birthday Visit

pick my mom up at the airport Sunday after church. Her eyes light on me as she comes down the escalator, and something inside me wilts. Just caves in. Mom is here. I don't have to be strong anymore.

She wraps her arms around me. I lean into her, the only one of her children not to surpass her in height. I pat her arm as if I'm the one giving comfort, but I'm so grateful for her presence.

"How are you?" she asks, pulling back to examine me. She touches my hair. "You dyed it red!"

I give my locks a toss, shaking my head back and forth. "You can barely see it now. It looked better when I first did it. I might have to do it again."

"You're so thin. Are you eating?"

The question annoys me, and I pull away from her caress. "Yes, Mother."

"Such a tiny little airport." She looks around our local airport with one baggage claim and only one rental car company.

"Yes. But at least it's here. Thanks for not making me drive out to Denver."

"Of course, hon. How's school?"

I brighten slightly. "This semester is so hard, but I'm killing it in my Portuguese class! I got an A in 101. If I get an A in 102, I'm pretty much guaranteed a great GPA this semester."

"So do you feel ready for Brazil?"

"I don't think about Brazil much," I admit. "I booked the tickets so long ago it doesn't feel real. And I have to finish the second half of the semester first."

"It will be here before you know it."

"I'm looking forward to it. I think."

She waits while I unlock my car, then starts speaking as soon as we're both inside. "You think?"

I lift a shoulder. "It's a little daunting to head to another country by myself when I don't quite speak the language. It was such a spontaneous decision."

"Want me to come with you?"

"You hate leaving the U.S."

She shrugs. "I would do it for you."

It's a kind offer. "Maybe. I'll think about it."

Silence falls between us as I make my way to the interstate. Then she says, "How are you feeling about Owen?"

My shoulders tense. I knew this question was coming, and I dreaded it. "Fine," I say shortly.

"You've seemed so sad. So depressed."

"I'm not. I'm fine."

"Do you talk to him?"

"Mom," I interrupt, shorter than I want to be, "I don't talk to him. Or about him. We are done with each other." The only way I get through those words is by being harsh and cold.

The necklace nestled beneath my collar bone whispers that I'm a liar. I'll never be done with him.

But he's done with me, and that's pretty much the same thing.

Mom doesn't mention him again. I feel guilty for the way I went off, but it accomplished what I wanted.

⟳⟳⟳⟳⟳

Mom comes with me to school all week. I love having her. No one acts weird that I've brought my mom to college. My professors are kind to her, and Professor Dennis especially praises me to her and then talks to her in Spanish, which leaves her flustered and red.

"I don't speak Spanish!" she sputters at me when we leave the classroom.

I laugh. I'm giddy over the fact that I have an A in there. Just like a C would sink my GPA, an A makes it. "I think he's forgotten I don't speak Spanish."

She wants to take me out for my birthday, but Iris and Layne are making me dinner.

"You're so lucky to have such great roommates," Mom tells me.

"I am." I don't rehash the drama we went through with Layne. It's mostly water under the bridge by now. "At church we hear all kinds of stories about people having to change dorms or not liking who they live with. I'm so glad that hasn't been my experience."

"And Camila's a gem."

My heart warms when I think of Camila. "She's my other half." She's been the perfect host to my mom, not once complaining about the cot set up in our room for the week.

I wake up Wednesday morning keenly cognizant that it's my birthday. I'm nineteen. I feel a sharp awareness of time and age creeping onward, and a bittersweet ache in my chest that I prefer not to probe. Camila and Iris sing happy birthday to me before I leave for school, and my phone lights up all day with friends from back home sending me birthday wishes. My mom tells every class I'm in that it's my birthday, and I've been sung to about eight times before we head home in the evening.

"I've never been so embarrassed!" I say to her, but I'm laughing as we climb the stairs to my apartment.

"Happy birthday!" Layne greets me with a hug.

"It smells amazing in here!" I pull past her to see Iris stirring a wok.

"Real Chinese food!" she says.

The door opens behind me and my mom, and Camila comes in. "Look what I got you!" She holds up a six-pack of Martinelli's sparkling soda.

"I love this stuff!" I exclaim. My roommates introduced me to the apple soda, and I can't get enough of it it.

"Every one of these is for you." She pulls out another six-pack. "This one's for us."

Iris sets couch cushions on the kitchen floor. "We're eating old style. On the floor with chopsticks."

"Chopsticks? I guess I'm going hungry," Mom says.

"Me too," Camila admits.

Iris gives them forks, but Layne and I are good with chopsticks.

"Save room for cake," Layne reminds us.

My family calls as we're cleaning up the food, and I get sung to again by my dad and siblings. Then the back door opens, and Abby comes in.

"Happy birthday!" she sings.

"You came too!" I squeeze her tight.

"Jordan's right behind me," she says, and sure enough my cousin comes in on her heels. He and Camila wave at each other, her face rosy, as if they're still not quite sure they can do more than that.

"For you," he says, handing me a gift bag.

My face warms as I blush. "Jordan! You shouldn't have!"

"I had to get something for my favorite cousin," he says, engulfing me in a hug.

"Time for that cake!" Layne says.

She lights the candles, but before we can sing, Cory and Mike come in, followed by the girls from the apartment upstairs. They sing to me, and Layne begins to dish out cake as Stirling and Jamie show up.

"Hi!" I exclaim, hugging my work friends. "You knew about my birthday?"

"Iris called me," Stirling says. "It's been awhile, but I was happy to come."

More kids from church show up, and a few kids from Honors Week that Abby invited. AJ and Adam arrive, and then Jared and Brant and Justin. I'm sitting on the couch next to Stirling, drinking my way through my third Martinelli's, and I scoot over and motion for Jared to sit by me. He does, loping an arm over my shoulders and giving me a side hug.

"This is my mom," I tell him. "Mom, this is Jared."

"Hi, Jared!" she says, like she's known him her whole life even though I've never mentioned him before.

Stirling drops a hand to my knee. "Been a good birthday?"

I look around at my kitchen full of people, the demolished cake, my mom sitting beside my roommates. "I think one of the best," I say.

I refuse to think about that ache in my heart. The one that festers a little more with each beat.

Eventually everyone except Jared, Stirling, Abby, and Jordan clear out. I finish my last Martinelli's and feel slothful as I watch my friends clean up, but they refuse to let me help.

My phone rings, and I glance down to see Monica calling.

My heart pulls at me. I stand up and go to my room to take the call.

"Hi, Monica!" I exclaim. "So great to hear from you!" I'm genuine. I love her, and it's been a few weeks.

"Good to hear your voice!" she says. "Happy birthday!"

I smile. "I can't believe you remembered."

There's a slight pause, and she says, "Yes. Did you do anything fun?"

I launch into a recounting of my day, the delighted embarrassment I felt in every class with my mom, my roommates' dinner for me, and my myriad of friends coming over.

"I'm not surprised," Monica says. "I'm sure everyone loves you."

I laugh at that. "They just wanted Layne's cake."

She laughs with me. "And school's been good? Is it nice having your mom there?"

"Yes," I say, though I'm more hesitant now, leery of where this conversation might go. "Yes, everything's been good." I don't want to talk about how I've been, how I'm dealing. And I can't reciprocate the questions to keep the conversation going, because I'm afraid she'll mention her family, and the floodgates of longing will open, and then I won't be able to close them again. I offer a cautious, "How about for you?"

"Good here too! It's cold. I'm longing for warmer weather."

I relax as we cross into weather talk. "Yeah. I think it's supposed to snow tomorrow."

The safe small talk continues a few more minutes, and then she says, "I miss you. I love you, Cassandra."

My throat closes, and I feel like a lousy friend, but I can't separate her from her family. "I love you too. Maybe we can get together over the summer."

"Of course! What a great idea." Another pause follows, and I feel the ripe expectancy in it.

Here it comes.

"Can I tell you something honest?" she asks.

"Yes," I say, because I won't stop her, I can't stop her, now that she's said that. I have to know.

"I didn't remember your birthday. I was asked to call by someone who prefers to remain anonymous—who cares about you very much. Because that person wanted to make sure you knew you were not forgotten."

Her admission takes my breath away. It's comforting and cutting at the same time. It's what I longed for to make this day complete.

It also successfully opens up those damn floodgates.

I choke back my tears, swallowing back my emotions. "Thank you for telling me," I say. "It means a lot to me."

"I'm here if you ever want to talk."

"Thank you," I say. "I better get back to my guests." I have to hang up now or I will want to talk. I'll want to pepper her with questions that will only lead to misery, and I need to get the floodgates closed. My heart is swelling, my eyes burning.

"All right. Talk to you later."

We hang up, and I collapse on my bed and bury my face in my hands.

Every part of my soul misses him. I ache to talk to him. The only way I function each day is by pretending he doesn't exist.

That pretense just fell apart. He does exist. He's out there in the world right now, living his life without me. Doing all the things people do, and I'm not a part of it.

But he has not forgotten I exist.

I allow myself to sob for a solid five minutes. Then I clean myself up and go back out, my heart bruised and aching. It will take me a few days to put him back in his box.

CHAPTER ONE HUNDRED SIX
The Friend Zone

"Your midterm assignment is to prepare a traditional Seder—or Passover Feast," Professor Walker says in our Bible as Lit class.

I shoot a terrified glance at Abby.

"Isn't that pretty labor intensive?" a boy on the third row asks.

Professor Walker smiles. "Let me clarify. This is a feast we'll make together. I'll give each one of you an assignment. Then we'll meet at my house and go through the celebration together."

It instantly sounds more doable. I relax somewhat.

"Too bad my mom just went home," I whisper to Abby. "She could do this for me."

"That would be cheating," Abby whispers back. "But I'd take it!"

Professor Walker sends around a sign up sheet. A few of the assignments require two people.

"Want to cook chickens together?" I ask Abby.

"Yes!"

I sign us up. "Come over tomorrow. I'll get the ingredients."

I put together a Portuguese presentation after class and then go to the grocery store to shop for our chickens. The recipe has a long list of spices I've never used before. I have to buy whole chickens, and I'm rather alarmed that they contain internal organs. But they're frozen solid, so I leave them in the sink to defrost.

"Nobody touch the chickens," I tell my roommates.

"Ew," Layne says, examining them.

"I think you're supposed to defrost them in the fridge," Camila says.

"Will they be ready by tomorrow?" I ask.

"Should be."

I don't want to kill anyone in my class, so I put the chickens on plates and plop them into the fridge.

"Make sure they can breathe," Camila says, watching me. "Then they'll defrost faster."

"Breathe?" I grumble. "They're dead." But I clear a space around them the best I can.

My phone rings by the fish tank. Camila picks it up.

"It's Jared," she says.

I glance down at my hands, wet with chicken slime. "Put it on speaker."

She does and holds the phone in front of my face.

"Hey," I say. "I'm in the middle of playing with dead chickens."

His pause is not unexpected, in the wake of my statement. "Okay. May I ask why?"

"It's a school assignment," I say, and Camila giggles.

"I'm definitely curious. What will you do with the dead chickens when you're done playing with them?"

"Eat them. Maybe."

"Good luck to you and the dead fowl."

I laugh. "What's up?"

"Are you caught up on the Marvel movies?"

"I think so. Are you going to quiz me?"

"It's a trick question. You can't be caught up."

I close the fridge and pump soap into my hands, then wash them quickly before taking the phone from Camila. "Why?"

"Because the newest one doesn't come out until Friday."

"Ah." I see where he got me. "I guess I'm not, then."

"Want to go with me to see it?"

The invitation catches me off guard. Perhaps it should not. I feel a tingly warning down my spine that Jared might want more from this outing than friendship. But I brush it off. He's become one of my besties over the past few weeks. I look over at Camila.

"Want to see the newest Marvel movie on Friday?" I ask her.

"Sure," she says.

"All right," I say to Jared. "Camila and I will go."

"Great," he says, and the fact that he doesn't react to me bringing Camila along reassures me. We're all just a group of happy friends. "I'll get tickets and text you the info. Mind driving?"

"What are our other options?" I say dryly. "Public transportation?"

"Or walking," he says.

The theater is several miles away. And it's snowing. "Pass. I'll drive."

"That's why I invited you," he says cheerfully, and I laugh.

"Touche."

"I'll let you get back to your nonliving friends. Can't wait to hear what you guys do tomorrow."

I laugh again and we hang up.

"Are you bringing me along as a chaperone?" Camila asks. "Or are you trying to make sure Jared knows he's in the friend zone?"

"Was I that obvious?" I ask.

"Yes. Jared likes you and you keep him two arms' lengths in front of you."

"He doesn't like me," I protest. "Not that way. We got past that."

"But you don't feel comfortable going to the movies alone."

There is truth to her words. "I need to make sure he remembers the dynamics of our relationship."

"That's what I thought."

☙ ⁂ ❧

Abby comes over around three on Tuesday. We have four hours to make four birds. Should be plenty of time.

"All right, little chickens," I say, hauling them from the fridge. "What's first?"

Abby scans the recipe sheet I left on the counter. "Pat them dry and pull the skin away from the meat."

I flinch. "What?"

"That's what it says."

I touch the bumpy pink flesh of one chicken gingerly. "Gross." I grasp the skin and pull, and shards of ice pop off. Abby squeals as they pepper her.

"It's still frozen!" I say.

She comes over to peer at it beside me. "Did you take out the giblets?"

I spare her a glance. "The whats?"

"Giblets. The organs inside."

"No."

"You have to before we can cook it."

I read the recipe. "It doesn't say anything about that."

"Some things it assumes we're smart enough to figure out."

That feels like a deliberate jab, and I shoot her a glare. "All right, how do I do that?"

"Reach inside the neck cavity and pull them out." She gestures at the hole down the middle of the bird. "They should be in a little baggie."

"Have you done this before?" I insert my hand in the cavity, feeling bones and ice scratching at my skin.

"No, but I've watched my mom do it."

"I don't think I've ever seen my mom cook a whole chicken," I breathe. My fingers find a paper bag, and I tug. "It won't come out!"

"Keep trying. We have to get it."

Something is holding it tight. I give a few more yanks before realizing it's frozen to the bird. I throw a panicky glance at the clock. "It's not all the way thawed!"

"Put it in the sink under cool water. It's all right. We'll get this done."

I follow her instructions, grumbling under my breath. If Camila had let me leave the birds on the counter overnight . . .

But deep down I suspect I did the smart thing. Even if it means I'm defrosting a chicken by hand right now.

And there are still three more.

"Hey, the skin comes up now!" I say, demonstrating. The flap of bumpy fat peels away from the pink meat beneath it. "I guess it was frozen also."

"Great." Abby pushes over the garlic she minced up. "Let's get started."

It's messy business, putting this chicken together, and there's a lot of screeching involved as we splatter chicken juices everywhere in our attempts to touch the raw bird as little as possible. Eventually we give up trying to stay clean. By the time we do this three more times and put the chickens in the oven to roast, there are spices on our faces, in our hair, and chicken liquid running down our arms.

"I have to shower," I say. "I can't stay like this."

"Me too," Abby agrees. "Can you finish it from here?"

"I've got it," I promise. I set the timer on the oven. "Want me to pick you up?"

"Yes, please."

I shower quickly while the chickens roasts. When I get out of the bathroom, an intoxicating aroma of garlic, butter, and roasted meat fills our little apartment. Nothing we've ever made has smelled this good.

I check the chickens when the timer goes off, horribly worried they won't be done. But they are. There's no pink, no blood. I won't accidentally kill everyone in my class.

I ever so carefully put the chickens in two large plastic containers. It takes two trips to carry them to my car. I text Abby to tell her I'm on my way, and she's waiting for me in the parking lot when I arrive.

"Oh, wow," she says when she climbs into the car. "It smells amazing in here!" She pulls a container into her lap and admires our chickens. "These turned out great!"

"They did. I'm impressed with us. Maybe we should cook the turkey for Thanksgiving next year."

"That's taking things a bit far."

I laugh with her. I turn left out of the campus drive, heading toward the canyon where Professor Walker lives. It's walkable from campus, but I'm grateful for a car to keep our chickens safe. With my luck, I'd drop them in route.

That could still happen.

We make the five-minute drive to Professor Walker's house, and I remember coming here before school started, when Abby was my only friend and I had no idea what to expect from college. Already I feel like a different person.

We park with the other cars and follow the arrow that points to the backyard. Our other classmates are there, and Professor Walker has a long table out where he is spreading food.

"Welcome, welcome!" He says, ushering us in. "Sign off on the sheet and put your offerings here."

Abby and I both sign off on our chickens and leave them with the rest of the food. Then we sit in chairs on Professor Walker's yard with the other students. He comes around to speak with us when class starts.

"I have a very special treat for you guys today. I brought my friend Daniel Rawson to preside over our Sederfest today. He is a Messianic Jew and well-versed in both religions."

The meal consists of reading scripture passages, eating special foods, and singing in a choreographed fifteen-step celebration.

I am absolutely enthralled by the rituals and symbolism behind every act of the Sederfest. I know very little about the Jewish religion, but I feel a deep connection and appreciation for the history and knowledge they carried over into the modern world.

When we finish hours later, Professor Walker says, "Thank you all for being here. This is one of my favorite activities of the semester. You've all received an A for this project. Don't forget your essays that are due next week."

Abby and I exchange a smile. It's not unexpected. That's the way Professor Walker teaches.

I drop her off at her dorm, *sans* chickens, and head to my dorm. Now I have to work on my Portuguese presentation.

❧

I memorize every word of my Portuguese presentation and deliver it perfectly and then pray no one asks me any questions.

No one does.

I'm given an A on the midterm.

On Friday I load Camila into my car and we pick up Jared to go to the movies. He climbs into the back and sits on the other side of Camila, and I feel confident that we are safe in the friend zone.

Though I have to admit, there's a part of me that wishes he would've sat by me. A part of me that wishes he would touch me. I hate that weak part of me. It hasn't been a month since I was properly held and kissed, but I miss it so much.

Jared sits between Camila and me in the theater, and the left side of my arm prickles with anticipation of his touch through the entire movie. Though his shoulders shake with laughter and he claps his hands a few times, he never once reaches over for me. He doesn't even bump me on accident.

I'm mildly frustrated by that.

Saturday I take Iris grocery shopping after work. We're almost home when Stirling calls me.

"Want to come over? I got some ice cream and a whole bunch of juices."

I glance over at Iris. "Is it all right if I bring my roommate? She's with me in the car."

"Yeah, sure, that's fine."

"Where are we going?" Iris asks me as I hangup.

"Stirling's house for ice cream. That okay?"

She shrugs. "It's fine. At least if I hang out with you and Layne, I get to meet new guys."

"You don't have a problem meeting new guys," I say.

"Yeah, but they're not the kind of guys I want to meet."

"What's going on with you and Jared?" I ask, trying to sound casually curious.

"He's nice to me, and sometimes I think he might be flirting, but I'm not the one that he asks to hang out with." She gives me a pointed look. "You and Camila are the ones who went to the movies with him yesterday. So I'm not sure if he even thinks of me as a friend."

I try not to wince. His actions are very telling. "I'm sure he thinks of you as a

590

friend. Maybe he's afraid of leading you on."

"I'm not interested in him anymore." She sounds frustrated. "I just want to be friends."

I nod like I believe her. I hope it's true.

"Are you sure you don't like him?" she says.

I throw her a quick glance. I could like Jared. Easily. And that's why I won't. I won't give my heart to someone again. "No, he's fun to hang out with. I want to be friends with everyone."

"It's safer that way," Iris agrees.

Safer, for sure. A bit more boring also.

Stirling makes us a variety of flavored ice cream cows and we rewatch sitcoms from the 80s. Again, my evening is filled with laughter, but while it helps ease the ache in my heart, it doesn't fill all the negative spaces where Owen used to be. I have close to zero interest in Stirling, but I so desperately want to fill those spaces that I almost take his hand while we watch television.

And I wonder why I'm more willing to do so with him than Jared.

I don't have to wonder for long. It's because I don't feel anything for Stirling. But I do for Jared. Letting Jared comfort me could turn into something else, and that terrifies me.

I barricade off my heart with my pain and brace myself to be alone.

CHAPTER ONE HUNDRED SEVEN
Gnocchi and Pesto

The next week goes by in a flurry of activity. I have a midterm in Portuguese and nine weeks test in my other classes. I'm disappointed that I only get a 94% on my Portuguese exam. Apparently I didn't study hard enough. But it's still an A, even if just barely. And I vow to study harder for my final in a few weeks.

My roommates invite me to go do karaoke Friday evening, but I decline and instead hole myself up in the library with my history book and my Portuguese phrases. Now that I don't have a math class, these two have become my nemeses.

I carefully translate each Portuguese sentence on my paper, then check the English to see how I did. It's almost perfect.

The hard part is doing it in reverse.

I flip my page over so the English phrase shows and begin the arduous task of translating each one of them into Portuguese. I'm not using my knowledge of grammar so much as I'm simply regurgitating what I've already memorized. I have many phrases memorized. I'm not delusional enough to believe that would qualify me to have a conversation with someone in Portuguese, but I can spout of lines like a freaking actor. I'm anxious to see what it will be like when I get to Brazil. I still don't understand Professor Dennis half of the time in class, and I know he's speaking slowly for our benefit.

Brazil is only six weeks away.

I try not to think about it because I'm filled with both excitement and trepidation.

The table wobbles as someone walks into it, and I look up to see Jared standing there. I smile at the warm flutter of . . . friendship that courses through me.

"Jared."

He shakes his head. "Cassandra Jones. Hanging out at the library on a Friday night. Can there be any greater testimony of your devotion to your grades?"

I laugh. "More like a testimony of my pathetic social life."

He drops his bag on the table and falls into the seat beside me. "I'm sure this wasn't your only option. How many guys did you turn down so you could have a date with the library?"

I laugh again. The heavy weight in my chest lifts when I'm around Jared.

It makes me feel guilty.

"The library and I have a very strong relationship, and it's important to me to nurture it," I say.

"I do not want to come between you and your devotion to the library," Jared says. He unzips his backpack and pulls out a notebook. "Does the library mind if I sit next to you?"

I pretend to consider. "No, I think that's okay. We're not exclusive."

Jared grins, the corners of his eyes creasing, and then he turns back to his notebook.

We study in silence, other than me whispering to myself as I sound out the Portuguese words.

Half an hour later, Jared closes his notebook. "Well, time to eat. Ready?"

I blink at him. "Ready?" I repeat.

"To get something to eat." He stands up, shouldering his backpack. "Come on, let's go."

I don't even think to protest. My stomach growls in acknowledgment of his words. I can't remember if I ate lunch. I put my books away and stand beside Jared, and we walk out together, my hands in my pockets and his holding the straps of his backpack.

"How did your nine weeks tests go?" he asks.

"Fine, I guess. I got a low A in Portuguese, and it was the midterm."

"Yeah, that's a terrible grade. That might be a blot on your college career."

He's all seriousness as he says it, and I shove his shoulder.

"I'm trying to learn this language! Why can't I get it?"

He gives me a sideways glance. "You do realize you've only been studying it for like three months, right?"

I shrug.

"A language! It's not like learning to crochet."

"I can't do that either," I admit.

"That's it, I'm not taking you to dinner." Jared makes as if he's going to walk away from me, but all I can do is laugh.

"Oh, wait." He jogs back to me. "You're my ride."

I grunt and roll my eyes. "I think you're using me for my car."

"Let's make a deal. You drive, I'll buy dinner."

"Absolutely not," I say, shaking my head. "I can pay for myself."

"Don't be so stubborn. Gas is expensive."

"Only if we're driving to Denver."

"I'd rather not, if I'm riding with you."

"Agreed."

But we didn't decide who was paying for my dinner. I tuck that info away so I won't forget it later.

We go up to my apartment and drop off my books, then we climb into my car, and I offer to drive Jared to his house to leave his stuff.

"That's all right. I'm too hungry." He tosses his bag into the back of my car.

I take a good look at his profile while he's turned. He has an afternoon shadow of dark stubble, and his skin is already taking on more color now that we see the sunshine every day. He narrows his eyes in concentration as he fixes his backpack so nothing will fall out, and his jaw tightens as well. Something in my gut twists with a purely physical desire to press my hand to that jaw.

I turn around and face forward.

"What are you in the mood for?" Jared asks, swiveling back around, completely unaware of my scrutiny.

I keep my eyes trained out the front of the windshield and lift a shoulder. "I'm just hungry."

"Like Italian? I know a good place."

Italian food will always remind me of Vicenza's. "I love Italian. I worked at an Italian restaurant in high school."

"Way cool. I worked at a bakery."

"A bakery?" I raise an eyebrow and glance at him, intrigued in spite of myself. "Doing what?"

"Anything they needed me to do. I got good at icing cupcakes."

"Again not something I'm good at."

"Crochet. Icing cupcakes." He ticks it off on his fingers. "We're building a list here."

"Keep going, and you'll figure out how unremarkable I am."

"Pff." He blows out between his lips. "I don't think you know yourself."

I don't respond to that.

I follow Jared's directions to the neighboring city, and we pull into a nice Italian restaurant next to the movie theater. The Macaroni Grill, the sign out front says.

"How do you grill macaroni noodles?" I ask as I park the car and follow Jared down the sidewalk.

"Don't think about it too seriously. It'll hurt your head."

I try to take his advice, but I'm busy picturing someone laying out tubular noodles across a charcoal grill and flipping them with tongs.

Jared grins at me as it knowing what I'm thinking. "Don't obsess over it."

It's dark inside the restaurant, and accordion music pipes through the speaker system. The aromas of garlic and tomato assault my senses, and I inhale deeply while Jared talks to the hostess. She leads us through the restaurant to a table for two.

"This all right?" she asks.

"Yeah, great," Jared says.

I pull out my seat and sit down while he sits across from me. The tablecloth is paper, and I run my hand over it. "I didn't realize how hungry I am. I think the only Italian I've had in the past six months is pizza."

"Which technically isn't Italian at all, the way we eat it," Jared says.

"Yes, I know," I say. "I used to work at an Italian restaurant, remember?"

"Oh, right. So this is all familiar to you."

I scan the menu. "As long as they have gnocchi and pesto."

"Hello, guys." A waiter buzzes over carrying a tray with two glasses of water and several crayons, which he places on the table in front of us. "I'm Wally." He takes one of the crayons and writes his name on the paper tablecloth. "I'll be your waiter tonight. Can I get you guys started with anything?"

"Cheese sticks," Jared says, pointing at the menu. He looks at me. "Are you good with that?"

I nod, though I'm already thinking how any restaurant that serves cheese sticks is not Italian.

"Marinara or ranch?" Wally asks.

"Both," I say.

"Why choose?" Jared agrees.

Wally trots away with the same energy that brought him to our table, and I pick up a crayon.

"I guess we're supposed to color?" I say.

"Are you an artist?"

"Ha. Add that to the list of things I don't do."

Jared laughs. "This is getting to be quite a list."

"Watch my amazing artistic ability." I proceed to draw a tree with the brown crayon. One half circle up, another half circle on the other side. Then I grab the green crayon and make a bumpy leaf top, like a cloud or the bumps of a lamb, but green, connecting the two brown half circles together.

"It's recognizable," Jared says, resting on his elbows to peer at it. "I know it's a tree. My turn." He takes the brown crayon from me and draw a tree trunk. It's thick at the bottom with roots bumping up out of the ground and several smaller smaller trunks growing out of it. The branches sprawl outward, dipping and twisting and climbing like something alive. Then he takes the green crayon and adds leaves, small spheres with points, all over the branches reaching toward the sky.

"If I sneak away now, can I leave with my dignity intact?" I say. "I had no idea I was having dinner with so much talent."

He grins. "Nothing that special. But I do like to draw."

"And you let me touch those crayons. You should be ashamed of yourself."

"I like your tree," he says.

I look from my stick-figure tree to his sprawling fairy-land tree and arch an eyebrow at him.

"For real," he says, but now he's smirking, and I jab my knuckle into his thigh.

Except I shouldn't have touched him, because it does something to me. I yank my hand back, my heart racing, aware that I want to place my palm back on his leg.

Our appetizers arrive, saving me from myself. The rest of the meal passes in non-touching, playful conversation, much of it centering around how much I love Italian food, since I can't seem to stop exclaiming it. Jared orders dessert for us to share, an extravagance I would have skipped, but he insists.

"Two boxes to go, please," I tell the waiter when he comes back to check on us, and he disappears again.

"I'm going to the restroom to wash my hands," Jared says.

I nod, tucking away my curiosity at his need. Maybe he's a clean freak.

Wally returns with the boxes, and I dig out my credit card.

"Can you split the bill, please?" I ask.

Wally blinks. "Oh, I'm sorry! Your date already took care of it."

"He—did?"

I'm not sure what else to say, and then Jared appears behind Wally, sliding back into the bench.

"Thanks for the boxes," he says.

"My pleasure. Have a great evening."

I lean toward Jared as soon as Wally leaves. "I thought you went to wash your hands."

"I did. And I stopped by the host station."

"You paid for me?"

His cheeks flush pink. "I felt bad, I ordered a lot of extras. You shouldn't have to pay for that."

I want to be angry at him but how can I be? "At least let me get the tip."

"I paid that already, also."

"Jared!" Alarm flutters through me.

This is a date now.

As if reading my mind, Jared holds up a hand. "It doesn't mean anything. We're just friends out for dinner and I wanted to cover it."

That's not what it feels like to me, but I play along. "Fine. As long as I cover it next time."

"It's a deal." He pulls out his phone and scrolls through it. "Want to see a movie? There's a new thriller playing next door."

I think of all the homework waiting for me and weigh that against a mind-numbing cinematic adventure. "I should say no," I say. "But I don't want to."

"Then let's go," he says, pushing a few buttons on his screen and then pocketing his phone.

"But I'm buying," I say.

He looks at me, dark lashes blinking over his light eyes. "I already bought the tickets."

"Are you trying to thwart my attempts to help?" I exclaim.

"Yes," he says. "And I'm doing a pretty good job of it."

I narrow my eyes. "Challenge accepted."

He laughs under his breath and follows me to my car.

The movie is a spy thriller about a girl who works for the government and has secret information, and a guy seduces her and steals her secret info, and the rest of the movie is about her trying to keep the guy from spilling the info. It's got the right amount of comedy woven into it, and I like nothing more than to laugh. Jared grins at me every time I do like he finds my amusement amusing.

The movie ends and I don't want to go home. I'm having too much fun. So we drive to the malt shop and get shakes. Never mind that I have chocolate cake sitting in a box in my car.

"I didn't realize how much I needed this," I admit. "Thank you for taking my mind off school."

"I would take you out every weekend if I could afford it," he says.

I wrinkle my nose. "I did not ask you to pay for everything!"

"I let you pay for the milkshakes," he says.

"All eight bucks of them!"

He smiles at me around his straw, and he's utterly adorable, the way the skin around his eyes crinkles upward, his lips pushing up into his cheeks.

The desire to kiss him is so strong that I avert my eyes. I feel like I'm a cheating girlfriend.

But I'm not.

"Tell you what," he says. "Next weekend we can hit the international cinema on campus. It's free."

"I think I can do that," I say, and then I realize what I just committed to. Another date with Jared.

My heart skips a beat. If this keeps up, we'll end up dating without realizing it.

"I might invite Camila," I add.

"Yeah, go for it," he says. "That'll be fun."

I almost think he means it.

He pushes his glass away. "I put in my mission application."

His words have the effect of pouring ice cold water over my head. The shiver spreads over my shoulders and down my arms, through my chest and stomach, and I shudder.

He will be leaving too.

Just like Owen.

It is a reality check. A reminder why I need to keep my heart locked up. Dating isn't fun when it always ends in goodbyes.

"Congratulations," I say, and I scoot back in my seat, already putting as much distance between us as I can. "It will be fun to see where you go."

CHAPTER ONE HUNDRED EIGHT

Just Pretending

I throw myself into my studies the next week. Jared fills my mind. He's become more than a pleasant distraction from the pain. It's like my heart knows if I think about him, I won't be thinking about anyone else.

I have a lot of practice in this, after all. I got over Tiago by falling for Owen.

I got a fortune cookie about that in tenth grade. It said, "Only finding love again will heal your broken heart."

But some people I think you never get over.

I will never get over Owen. No matter how many times I fall in love again in the future.

The acknowledgment that I will fall in love again makes my heart beat with a dull aching note. I can't think about this too much or I will cry.

Camila can't come to the international theater on Friday, but Iris is more than happy to take her place. We get to the theater early and sit on a bench in the hall, Iris between me and Jared. I see how hard she tries around him, joking, laughing, leaning over to include me and then swiveling back to him, trying to prove to him that she's his friend, that there's nothing more in her heart.

And the whole time, his smile grows more and more strained, and I start to think this was a terrible idea. We file into the theater before the movie starts, and Jared doesn't manage to shake Iris. At least he sits in between us.

"Did you take the history test already?" I ask him, trying to come to his rescue. We're not in the same history section, but we're both taking the class.

"I did. Didn't want it hanging over my head. You?" He turns to face me, not quite hiding the relief on his features to break away from Iris's constant chatter.

"Yeah. The computer said I got a ninety-seven percent. That can't be right, though, can it?"

"A ninety-seven percent!" Jared's eyes go wide. "And that's before the curve?"

I shrug. "They won't set the curve until everyone finishes taking the test over the weekend."

Jared closes his fist next to his temples and then spread his fingers out and away from his head as if they're making an explosion. "I am mind-blown. You might be the smartest person I know."

I laugh, but I can't help warming under his praise.

"I only got a seventy-two." He bumps my shoulder with his. "Now ask me how it feels to rub shoulders with greatness."

I roll my eyes but can't keep the pleased smile from my face.

The movie starts and we face forward, and I ignore the warmth generating in the space between his shoulder and mine.

෧෬෯

My history grade is not a fluke.

The arrival of April brings a temperate warmth to the Colorado air. As soon as it hits sixty degrees outside, everyone's wardrobe changes from jeans and sweaters to T-shirts and shorts. I find this amusing because sixty-degree weather is still sweater-weather in Arkansas.

I compromise with shorts and a long sleeve shirt.

There's only a month left of school, and the excitement coupled with the sunshine is palpable in the air. Preston Y skips spring break, so classes end the last week of April.

And two weeks after that, I head to Brazil.

While we email back-and-forth on occasion, I haven't spoken with Tiago since Christmas. I haven't told him a word about Owen.

I also haven't spoken with Owen since we broke up, and it feels like someone stuck a knife in my gut and left it there, just so they can turn it every time it starts to heal and break the wound open anew.

Abby spends more and more time in our dorm.

"My roommate is giving me the cold shoulder now that she knows I want to room with you guys next year," she tells us when she's over on Friday. "I think she's mad I chose you guys over her."

We're having a party. It consists of microwave popcorn and oven-baked egg rolls.

"Well, you did choose us over her. And apparently for good reasons." Layne takes the bowl of popcorn down the hall toward her room. "Let's watch a movie and not think about it."

We take our food and follow Layne to her room, where the five of us spread out on the bed and floor.

I look around at the other girls with warmth and affection. They know me better than any of my friends back home ever did, which is probably something that happens when you live with someone. I'm so glad I'm rooming with them next year because I don't think I could handle a goodbye. These are my sisters.

We're a quarter of the way into the movie when Jared calls me.

I pulled away from Jared this week. He sat by me in Sunday School. I got up to use the bathroom, and when I came back, I sat somewhere else. I know he noticed, but he didn't say anything about it. He hasn't called me all week or come to see me at the library.

So I'm both surprised and not surprised that he's calling me. And I don't know what to expect.

I glance at my roommates, but none of them notice. They're too engrossed in the movie. I brace myself and leave the room to take the call.

"Hey," I say, stepping into the kitchen and closing the door.

"Hey. How's your Friday going?"

I settle into the couch to make myself comfortable. "Great. Hanging out with my roomies."

"Want to break away? We can go do something."

Three weekends in a row.

I want to.

"I can't, Jared. We're having a girls' night. No ditching."

"Hey, that's awesome. I think it's amazing you guys are such a good friends."

He takes it in stride. No tantrums, no whining, no self-pity. Can't there be something negative about him?

"I'm really sorry," I say. "Another time."

"No problem. How about tomorrow?"

I left myself open for that one.

"Tomorrow we're driving over to Abby's house and spending the day with her parents. They're having some kind of pool party."

"I guess people in Colorado don't know it's still cold?" Jared says, and I laugh.

"I think you're right."

"Well, I'd invite myself to crash your girls' night but whatever movie you're watching is probably sappy and cliche."

"You nailed it." I shake my head, thinking of the chick flick playing in Layne's room. "My first choice would be a zombie movie, but Camila is terrified of them."

"Zombies are your thing? I should've seen that coming. Death and decay."

He makes me laugh.

Laughter is the way to my heart.

"I would rather stay here and talk with you," I admit. "But I should go back in."

"Enjoy your weekend. I'll see you in church."

I hang up and hold my phone, feeling like that conversation accomplished the opposite of what I intended. We are pretending to just be friends.

And sometimes I can't remember why.

⬿⬿⬷⬺⬺

We stay up until four in the morning talking in Layne and Iris's room. When we wake up three hours later, the five of us are a tangle of arms and blankets sprawled out in different directions.

"I have an idea," Abby says from where she lies in the middle of the floor, staring up at the ceiling. "Wouldn't today be more fun if we invited boys to my house?"

Her question is met with cheers, and my roommates start throwing out names. I stay quiet. Only one name comes to mind, which is exactly why I can't invite him.

But my roommates can, and they do. Layne doesn't even look at me as she says to Abby, "Don't forget Jared."

600

Abby writes his name on the list without batting an eye. She adds Brant for Layne and Camila requests my cousin Jordan.

The boys come along willingly. But we can't all fit in my car, and Brant can't get his brother's, so we have to invite Justin because he also has a car.

We ride separately, the girls with me and the boys with Justin, driving out to Abby's house an hour away. We have our swimsuits because Abby says the pool is heated, but I have no intention of putting one on. I am extremely self-conscious of my flat chest.

"We have a volleyball pit in the yard," Abby says. "And a theater room with surround sound in the basement."

"We can do a movie double feature!" Iris says.

Abby's as boy crazy as Layne, but Layne paired up with Brant early on in the year, so even though she still flirts with every boy that moves, she hasn't been making out with them. Abby, on the other hand, hasn't settled down.

"Planning on making a move on Justin?" I tease.

She grins right back at me. "Actually I'm planning on Jordan, if you don't mind." She's looking at me, but her eyes slide toward Camila.

"I do mind," Camila says, and we laugh.

"Has he kissed you yet?" I ask. Jordan and Camila have been almost-dating for two months now, and we're all waiting for something to happen.

"And what about Jared?" Camila returns. "Have you kissed him yet?"

"Our relationship isn't like that," I sputter, my face burning.

"Right," Camila says. I look toward Iris for help, but she shrugs.

"You and Jared have been dating as long as Camila and Jordan have been."

"We're not dating," I protest.

But my roommates exchange some kind of exasperated look and give me sympathetic, condescending smiles.

I fume quietly the rest of the drive, irritated that they think they know more about my love life than I do.

The boys are parking in the driveway when I pull up beside them. We pile out of the car and they put their arms around us and crush us to death. The only one who doesn't hug all of us is Brant, who's always a bit standoffish. He looks at us all like we're beneath him and takes Layne's hand. I'm sure he thinks that since they're sleeping together they've reached a place of maturity the rest of us haven't. I roll my eyes inwardly and ignore them.

Abby lives in a single-story rambler with a basement. She escorts us into the kitchen, where her mom has made several casserole dishes of overnight French toast. Her dad cooks bacon on a skillet, and her parents introduce themselves to us while we eat. The feeling is carefree and jovial, so Jared teasing me doesn't feel any more like flirting than the friendly ribbing Justin and Jordan give me.

After we eat we head outside to play volleyball. I prove my terrible athletic ability in the first ten minutes when it takes me four attempts to serve the ball over the net, but everyone makes me continue to play, and we discover I'm not so bad if I play up close to the net where I can spike the ball with both hands. By the time we finish the game a full hour later, I'm feeling much more confident in my volleyball abilities, and I'm hot and sweaty enough that when Abby suggests the pool, I agree.

There's a twenty-minute shuffle while we line up at the bathrooms to change our clothing. The boys take the basement and we take the main floor. When it's my turn, I change quickly into the swimsuit I use for class and scowl at my reflection. I press up on my chest, imagining how I'd look with breast tissue. Even an A-cup would be nice.

"Why won't you grow?" I demand of them.

But I know why. I was cruel to my body when it needed nutrients and calories, and this is payback.

I'm too self-conscious to go out there like this. I grab my T-shirt and pull it back over my head, though it does absolutely nothing to hide my flat chest. I consider staying in the bathroom, but Layne bangs on the door and says, "Come on, Cassandra, you're not the only one here!"

I bite my lip and hold my clothes against my chest as I exit the bathroom.

This gives me the idea to grab a bath towel and hold it in front of me like a shield. I find one in the hall closet and go outside to the small pool, clutching my armor in front of me.

No one is swimming except Abby. Everyone else lounges around the metal table skewered by an umbrella.

"Come on, guys!" Abby calls, splashing at us from the pool. Her freckled skin reflects the overhead sunlight filtering down through the clouds. "The pool's heated!"

No one moves. The boys are getting into a bag of chips, and I relax in a chair beside Iris.

"Looks too cold for me," she says.

I latch onto the excuse. If no one gets in, I don't have to either. "Yeah. It's only April."

But then Layne comes out in a black two-piece, her white belly flashing as she shrieks and cannonballs straight into the water. Abby yells as the water splashes over her face, but Layne bobs to the surface and grabs her, and then they both disappear beneath the surface. They come up spluttering and laughing.

And that ends the stalemate.

All the boys jump in. Camila toes the water, but Jordan grabs her ankle and hauls her in.

"I'm not doing this," Iris says.

"Cassandra!"

It's Justin calling out to me. I look over at him.

"Come in the water!" he yells.

I shake my head. "No thanks."

"Come on, cuz!" Jordan yells. "It's not so bad!"

"I politely decline," I answer.

"Go get her," Justin murmurs, nudging Jordan.

"Don't you dare!" I holler. I clutch my towel closer around me. "I'm still wearing my shirt!"

Jordan hauls himself out of the water. "Better take it off."

"Don't do it, guys," Jared warns. "She'll hate you for it."

"Yes, I will!" I yell.

Jordan doesn't listen. I scream as he launches himself at me. I manage to get to my feet and get two steps toward the house before Jordan's arms go around me.

CHAPTER ONE HUNDRED NINE

Bigger Things

My hundred-and-ten-pound frame is helpless against him. I kick and yell and claw, but he's got me. I manage to shut my mouth before I hit the water.

It floods over my head, blocking out all sound except the rushing of air bubbles past my face. I squeeze my eyes shut and push upward to the surface.

"I hate you!" I yell at Jordan the moment I emerge, splashing water his direction, but I'm laughing. It's not that cold, and I'm reminded of dozens of family reunions when my bigger boy cousins tossed us girls into the water without mercy.

Jordan laughs back and puts a cold, sopping arm around my shoulder. "I know."

Nobody cares that I'm wearing a shirt to hide my boobless status. I don't think they notice.

Iris joins us, and we play chicken and climb on each other and participate in tactile activities with our wet, slippery bodies. It's all fun, all tinged with flirtation, but nobody is exempt, so it feels light and carefree.

Eventually Abby's mom comes out to tell us she made lunch, and we climb out. I wrap myself in my towel as fast as I can, all the way to my shoulders, in case someone should decide now to stare at my chest.

I'm being paranoid. But I can't help it.

I'm the first into the bathroom to change. I don't relax until I'm safely back in my padded bra. I exit the bathroom fully dressed and composed, then head into the kitchen.

Abby's mom made several trays of finger foods, and I help her carry them to the living room. We set them on the coffee table. Abby joins us, and it smells like she snuck in a shower. Her wet auburn hair falls around her face, carrying the scent of lavender and vanilla.

"What movie should we watch?" she asks, sinking beside me on the couch and using the remote to turn on a streaming service.

I shrug. I'll let someone else decide. If I pick, we'll end up with either "Battlestar

Galactica" or "The Walking Dead."

Layne and Brant come in next, and Abby asks them. Together they decide on the latest *Mission Impossible*. I curl up in a corner of the couch. Camila and Iris cuddle up next to me, and Jordan and Justin sit at our feet.

But not for long. As the movie progresses, the boys decide they want on the couch also, and we scoot over to make room. We laugh and giggle as nine people attempt to fit on the cushions. It's not possible, and when Justin and Camila fall off, we don't let them back on. We're a tangle of arms and legs and sweaty heat.

I'm squished between Jared and Jordan, my leg hanging over Jordan's thigh, my side pressed up against Jared.

Jordan climbs onto the floor and leans against Camila.

Now it's just Jared pressing against me.

I pull my legs in and fall sideways into the armrest. Jared rearranges also, his elbow coming to rest on my shoulder. Iris, Brant, and Layne encroach on the other side. There's no place for our extra limbs.

Jared's hand drops into the tangle of my drying hair. For a moment his fingers comb through it before coming to rest in the space between my shoulder blades.

He keeps his eyes on the TV. So do I. It's nothing.

It feels so nice to be touched.

I'm so aware of him.

We watch the movie like that. Just friends.

☙ ❀ ❧

It is the last week of school.

I sit in my religion class unable to believe it's almost over. I have several essays and finals to get through, and then my freshman year of college is in the bag.

It flew by.

It was also the biggest learning curve of my life.

Stirling texts and invites me to come over before work. *For smoothies*, he says. I tell him I will. But first I have a checkout meeting at my dorm.

My roommates and I gather promptly at three p.m. We spent the weekend cleaning, and it turns out an apartment full of nineteen-year-olds hides a lot of grime. Now we hold our breath as the Resident Assistant checks the corners and cupboards.

I am mostly packed. In eight days, we move out. I'll drive my car to Camila's and leave it there while I fly back to Arkansas and get ready to go for Brazil.

I have to get through finals first.

"Things look pretty good," the RA says as she examines the corners of our cupboards. "Remember everyone has to be out by ten a.m next Tuesday. There will be one final cleaning check Monday night."

We nod. We know. All four of us are rooming together next year. The sting of separation isn't real yet.

The RA leaves and I grab my purse.

"I'm going to Stirling's house," I say.

"Stirling, Jared, which is it?" Iris says, but there's no malice in her words. In fact, she's been all smiles since Saturday. I suspect it has something to do with Justin, who brought a chair over to sit by her on Sunday during the lesson.

"Neither," I say, irritated. "We're just friends."

"Maybe you and Stirling are," Layne says.

I don't bother commenting.

"Are you excited to go home?" Stirling asks me as he whips up a grape juice ice cream shake. A purple cow, as he likes to call them.

"This is my home," I reply. "I'm excited to see my family, but I'll only be there a few weeks before I leave for Brazil."

"Are you excited for Brazil, then?" He hands me my glass and sits by me on the couch.

"Yes. And nervous. I still don't speak Portuguese." I give a little laugh. "I've got an A in the class, though."

"Maybe after one month, you'll have picked it up."

"Maybe." My stomach tightens for another reason, a reason I never allow myself to think about.

Tiago.

What will things be like with him? No one here knows about him. I haven't told my roommates or any of these boys.

Is it relevant? He might be so busy with work and school that I never see him.

"Where are you staying in Brazil?" Stirling asks.

"Recife," I reply. "It's a coastal city in the northeast."

"I mean, do you have an apartment? Are you staying with a host family?"

I stare at him and feel a jolt of alarm.

I did not think about this.

Last time I stayed with Tiago's grandfather and I kind of assumed I had a place there. That I'd stay there again.

But Tiago and I haven't talked about this.

Abruptly I realize it's time to break the radio silence. I need to make arrangements, and I need Tiago's help. I'm not old enough or confident enough to do this on my own.

"I'm still working on those details," I say through dry lips. I force a smile to hide my sudden discomfort. "What about you? Summer plans?"

"Staying here with Wyatt. I'll take a term off to go home and relax and then start school again summer term."

"So Wyatt's here the whole time?" Inspiration strikes. I have a favor to ask.

"Yeah, why? What do you need?"

I grin. "Someone to watch my fish."

Stirling laughs. "I should have seen that coming. You and your fish." He turns his head. "Wyatt!"

The bedroom door opens, and his roommate comes out. Wyatt has a mop of curly red hair pouring over his head and into his eyes. "What?"

"Want to be fish parents for the summer?"

"What?" Wyatt's eyes take me in on the couch. "Oh, for Cassandra? Sure. Could be fun."

"Keep them alive," I say. "That's all I'm asking."

"It's a difficult task," Stirling warns. "Cassandra has killed all of them multiple times."

"That was in the beginning!" I protest. "I've changed my ways!"

Wyatt grins. "I can handle a few fish."

He disappears back into his room, and Stirling pokes my leg with his foot. "I think Wyatt has a crush on you. You should hook up with him when you get back."

I stare at Stirling, trying to make sense of his words. He wants to set me up with his roommate? Apparently I was more in the friend zone than I'd suspected. But I recover, hiding my surprise.

"I'm not looking to hook up with anyone," I say. "I like not having attachments."

I don't mean it. I doubt anyone means it when they say it.

What we mean is, I can't be attached to who I want. So I'd rather be alone.

⟳∽ ⚘ ∽⟲

Wednesday I have my final for modern dance, and I spend Tuesday in the basement of our dorm, running through the routine I made up for the final. I'm grateful to both swimming and dance for keeping my body trim and fit this semester, but I know I'm not a swimmer or a dancer. Creating a choreography for this class tested my athletic and creative abilities.

Three more days of school, and it's all over.

Iris comes down to the basement with a bowl of cereal. She sits on the couch and watches me run through my routine. "You're really good," she says, crunching away on her sugary grains. "I think you're a great dancer."

I shove the hair back from my face. "I'm moving three beats behind the music."

"So cut out one of your spins and you'll stay on track."

I suppose I can do that. I did create the dance, after all.

She puts down her bowl and leans forward. "I'll count for you while you do it this time."

"All right." I restart the music and run through the routine again, this time with Iris counting. I manage to stay on beat and get all three spins in.

"See?" She settles back and picks up her bowl again. "You don't need to cut out a spin. Just count."

I nod and exhale, then run through it again, whispering under my breath.

A clap builds from the shadowy hallway, and I straighten up, falling out of my spin and barely catching myself.

It's Jared, and he laughs as he comes into the light. "Camila told me I could find you here."

My face flushes with heat. "Were you watching?"

He lifts a shoulder. "I saw the ending. You look good."

I'm mortified. I turn off the music and slip my shoes back on. "You'll need to forget everything you saw or I won't be able to speak to you ever again."

He runs his closed fingers across his forehead as if zipping his mind. "I saw nothing."

I relax. It's just Jared. "What are you doing here?"

"Well." He shoves his hands in his pockets. "I was looking for you." He swivels

607

slightly to include Iris. "Both of you, actually. My mission call came."

He says something more, but my mind hangs up on his words. I'm falling back in time, into a vortex of memory, at Owen's house when Mrs. Blaine screamed because his call had come.

That was the last day I saw him. The last day I talked to him.

With an effort, I pull myself back to the present moment. I know Jared is saying something about opening his call and I assume he has invited us to be there.

"I think that's awesome!" Iris says, and she stands up and hugs him.

Did I miss something? Did he already open it? Did he announce where he's going?

"What time is everyone meeting?" Iris asks.

"Ten o'clock tonight. We're waiting for my sister to get off work back home so we can video call her," Jared says.

I didn't miss it.

"I'm so excited for you," I say, and I'm genuine. The hurts in my heart have nothing to do with Jared and his call.

"Well." Jared checks his phone. "It's only six. I have four hours to kill and I need to distract myself. Want to go to the movies with me?"

"Yes! Let me put the bowl away." Iris prances from the room.

I consider my homework and the finals I need to study for. "I could use a mind break. I'll change my clothes."

"Okay. I'll wait for you guys in the upstairs commons."

"Are you using me for my car again?" I tease.

He pulls a key ring from his pocket and swings the keys around his index finger. "I borrowed Justin's car. I'm driving."

"Fancy." I grin and scoot up the stairs after Iris.

Iris and I head downstairs together and then follow Jared out to Justin's car. I've never seen so many movies in my life as I have in college.

We have forty minutes until the movie starts, so we stop and get fries and a milkshake.

"Where do you think you're going for your mission?" I ask.

Jared shrugs. "My mind is open. I'll go wherever the Lord wants me to go." He grins as he uses one of the well-rehearsed lines often repeated by future missionaries.

"Yes, but where do you want to go?" Iris says, not letting the topic go.

"Well, if I got to choose . . ." Jared leans toward us as if about to tell a secret. And then he pulls back and shakes head. "I can't say. I might jinx it."

Iris drops a hand on his forearm. "The call is already in your inbox! The location isn't going to change because of what you say now!"

He grins. "Yeah, I guess you're right. Okay. The place I really want to go is Ireland."

"Ireland." I collapse against my seat, playing with the straw of my milkshake. I imagine rolling green hills against a blue sky, castle ruins dotting the landscape. People speaking in a lilting, musical accent. "Oh, my. Ireland would be a dream."

Jared nods. "And we don't get to go where our dreams take us."

If only.

"Why Ireland?" Iris asks.

"I've always wanted to go to Europe. And I won't have to learn a new language. I think that would be hard for me."

"Ireland sounds nice," I say.

We finish our milkshakes and drive to the theater. It's after seven when the movie starts. Jared keeps checking his phone every few minutes toward the end, and his foot rattles as it taps out a rapid beat against the floor. I watch him it out of the corner of my eye, and then I reach a hand out and place it on his thigh, quieting the nervous motion.

He stills. He turns his hand palm up and grabs my fingers and manages to refrain from checking his phone until the movie finishes.

It's a quarter after nine when we get in the car after the movie. Iris's stomach growls loud enough for us to hear, and mine lets out a low rumble. But Jared doesn't offer to stop anywhere or ask if we're hungry. He doesn't attempt to kill more time, just puts the car in gear and heads back toward campus.

I imagine he is too anxious to eat.

Twelve minutes later, we park in front of his apartment. Jared gets out of the car and goes into the house, leaving me and Iris to fend for ourselves. I'm mildly amused. He has lost his head, waiting to open a single email that will deliver his fate for the next two years.

I would be nervous also.

A dozen or so people mill about in the living room when we walk in. Jared stands in the open front door, and he swivels to us. A sheepish expression crosses his face.

"I'm so sorry. I left you in the car."

That makes his friends laugh, and I shrug. "You have other things on your mind."

The right side of his mouth curves upward in a half smile. "Yeah. I kind of do."

"What time do you want to call your parents?" a kid sitting in front of an open computer asks.

"They're going to call me. Make sure the WebCam is facing me. I'll read the email on my phone."

I glance around at the setup and realize this is somewhat of a big to-do. Owen didn't open his call in front of a dozen people. Just his family, and me because I happened to be there.

What if I hadn't been there? Would he have opened it without me? I feel in my gut he would have. Owen already knew he was going to distance himself from me. That would've been the first step. Next, he would've called to tell me after he got his assignment. When? A few days later? A few weeks later? At the same time, he would've delivered the break up blow.

I'm certain of it. I bought myself a few extra moments by flying out to Louisiana.

At the time, I regretted going. But now those bitter-sweet memories fill me with such delicious joy that I'm so glad I got those last days with him.

A few more people show up until there's at least twenty crammed into Jared's living room. I move over to the kitchen, where it's not so crowded. Somebody opens a box of cookies and passes them around, and I take one mindlessly.

Finally it's time. At 9:57, Jared quiets us all down, and I hear ringing on the open computer. Jared sits in front of it and answers the call.

"Hi, Mom! Dad! Hey, guys!"

The rest of us stand there listening as Jared greets his family. Then he moves away from the computer to sit on the couch, and his friend redirects the camera so it's pointing at Jared.

I watch him.

His eyes are glued to the phone in his hand. I read the nervousness in the furrow of his brow and know he's not thinking about anyone else in this room. My heart rate quickens in empathy, and I imagine myself, opening my own mission call.

Someday I will do this also.

I'm not sure when, but it clears my thoughts. Everything happening right now, right here, feels transient. There are bigger things in front of me.

Jared clears his throat and begins reading the same words Owen read months earlier.

CHAPTER ONE HUNDRED TEN
Portuguese Plans

"*Dear Jared Baker,*
Thank you for your willingness to serve as a missionary for the Lord. Your desire to dedicate your time in the service of your fellow man is honorable and acceptable. After studying your interview papers, it's been decided that you will labor in the Madagascar South mission—"

He doesn't get another word out. I gasp, someone on the computer screams, and his roommates yell, crowding around him to thump him on the back and high-five him, wide grins on their faces.

Madagascar. Sometimes I forget how many places there are in the world. How many places to explore.

Jared clears his throat, his face stretched with his smile, and his friends back up as he continues reading.

"*Speaking French and Malagasy to the people of Madagascar. You'll report to the training center on July fifteenth.*"

He keeps reading through the packing list, but I'm thinking how different my sophomore year of college will be. Many of the boys I've known will be gone. Some of the girls.

He finishes with the letter and then sits in front of the computer to talk to his family for a bit. I check the time. Almost ten-twenty, and I still have homework to do. It's a quick seven-minute walk from here.

"Ready to go?" I ask Iris.

She nods, though she looks reluctant. "But we should tell Jared we're leaving."

We join the group of kids gathered around him, waiting to tell him congrats. We're far from the only girls present, and one girl in particular hugs him long and hard, then lingers with her hand on his arm after she pulls away, that air of possessiveness about her.

It's pointless, I want to tell her. *He's about to leave. He's got no room for you in his thoughts.*

Hard truth.

She finally slides away, and Iris wiggles her way in.

"Madagascar!" she squeals, giving him a hug.

Jared's eyes are bright as he hugs her back, and then he turns to me. He can't stop smiling. Excitement and energy radiate off of him.

"It's not Ireland," I say.

"No," he says. "But it's amazing."

"You'll have to learn two languages."

"I'm here for it."

He hugs me, tight, and I shove down the guilt because of how much I enjoy it.

"Thanks for being here," he says, releasing me. "It meant a lot to me."

"It was special," I say. I incline my head toward Iris. "We're going home."

"Oh." Jared glances outside toward the parking lot. "Want me to drive you?"

"No, stay with your friends." I place a hand on his arm, and I can't help feeling like an echo of the earlier clingy girl. But I'm not touching Jared to get his attention or to claim him. I'm touching him because he's my friend and this is part of what we do. "We'll walk home."

He nods. "I'll call you later."

I loop my arm through Iris's and we walk out together. The happy feelings follow us home, but they're coupled with something else now.

Restlessness. I want my turn.

I try to study when I get home but I'm tired, and I fall asleep on my bed with all my clothes on and my history books open in front of me. I wake up in the morning feeling ill-prepared.

My finals have started.

I think I might vomit when I sit down behind my desk for my Portuguese final. I clutch my pencil in my hand and take deep breaths. How can one test determine my retention level? I am a terrible test-taker, and I am terrified of how my grades will turn me out.

But my heartbeat slows as I go through the questions. I know everything on here. I pull the translated sentences from my memory. By the time Professor Dennis calls me out to the hall for the oral section, I only have three questions left.

"You did almost perfect," he says after quizzing me. "The only thing you missed was calling 'cinema' feminine when it should be masculine." He writes my score on his clipboard. "I'm sure you were confusing it with 'película' in Spanish, which is feminine."

I stare at him and feel as if I've fooled him. I've done so well he's forgotten I don't speak Spanish. I nod like that's why I made the mistake and not because my memorization failed me.

"You have an A in the class, of course. And if you intend to do anything else with Portuguese, I highly recommend you take the placement test I'm offering on Friday. You lose nothing if you don't do well, and if you like your score, you get credit for Portuguese 201 as well."

I wrap my mind around that. If I do well enough, this one semester will get me credit for Portuguese 101, 102, and 201.

Sounds like a good arrangement to me.

"What are you going to do next with Portuguese?" he asks.

"Well, I'm going to Brazil in two weeks." My chest tightens as I say the words.

That fact alone is panic-inducing.

Professor Dennis nods. "A lovely country. Unless you want to major in Portuguese literature or Portuguese history, I recommend getting a minor in Portuguese. You get a little bit of everything. Portuguese grammar, Portuguese literature, and Portuguese history."

My eyes widen as my mind lights on the idea. It's exactly what I've been wanting and I didn't know it. "Yes! That sounds so great!"

Professor Dennis grins. "Then maybe I will see you in another class in the future."

I leave his classroom relieved and hopeful. But a sneaking nervousness chokes through my throat, and I know I need to get this phone call over sooner than later so that I can breathe.

⌒∽⚜∾⌒

I call Tiago that night.

"*Alô?*"

A male's voice answers, with the same tenor timbres I've come to associate with Tiago. But it's been too long, and I don't know if I'm speaking to Tiago or his father or one of his brothers. I pull out my limited knowledge of Portuguese. "*Alô, Tiago está?*"

My accent must be evident, even in those three words, because the speaker switches into English, and says, in speech as halting as my Portuguese, "One moment, please."

In the seconds that follow, my heart rate increases tenfold.

I'm suddenly very aware that I will see Tiago in a few short weeks.

What will it be like?

Moments later, I hear someone else pick up the phone.

"Cassandra?" Tiago says, his voice a mixture of pleasure and surprise.

"Hey," I say, calmly and coolly as if this phone call isn't giving me cold sweats. "It's been a while."

"Yeah, it has!"

"How's life?"

"Going well. I'm taking a computer class and an English class. I'm trying to get a job, but it's not going so well. What about you? How is school?"

"I'm almost done with finals. I'm going to survive."

We chat idly for several more minutes, and I relax as I fall into the familiar conversational rhythm. I don't need to be nervous around Tiago.

The conversation jumps into my Portuguese classes, and he asks me to repeat some of my phrases, and he laughs at my accent.

"We'll work on that when you get here," he says.

"You have an accent too," I tease right back. But he's given me an opening, and I launch into the reason I called. "Speaking of when I get there, can you help me find a place to stay?"

It's a loaded question. I can't afford to stay at a hotel for a month. But surely he'll know someone, a friend from church, someone from school, who wants to host an American girl.

It's a lot to ask last-minute, and I scold myself for not doing it sooner.

"You're staying with us," he says immediately. "We're planning on it. We just need your flight information so we can come get you from the airport."

My stomach tightens. I can't do that. But how do I decline without being offensive when I asked for help? "Oh, no, I couldn't impose on your family that way."

"You're not. Your family kept me for nine months. My mom is happy to have you for one."

Sweat breaks out along my forehead, under my arms. I can't stay at his house. I feel it in my gut. But how do I get out of this?

Honesty.

"Tiago, it's so kind of you, so generous of your mom, but I'm not comfortable with it. I need more space."

He's silent a moment, and I know he's reading the implications behind my words.

"I'll talk to my mom. Maybe you can stay at my grandfather's house. Would you be okay with that?"

I let out a quiet exhale of relief. "Yes. That would be amazing. Thank you so much for looking into this for me."

"Of course. Send me your flight information, please. We are so excited to see you."

He and I have not talked in months, and in the back of my mind, I wondered if he had forgotten I was coming. But now I know that is not the case. He's very aware. But he held back, kept quiet, knowing I would reach out when I was ready.

He has been a good friend. We will have a good time together.

I am still anxious about it.

⟨⟩⟩⟩⟩⟩⟩◦※◦⟨⟨⟨

Friday evening finds me at my usual spot in the library cramming for a test. I have one more final tomorrow and an English paper that's due by noon, and then I'm done.

But my final is in history. I will ace it if I can remember the dates and places.

After an hour of studying, I'm restless. And hungry. I consider the cafeteria with its salad options, but I want something sweet.

I want ice cream.

The creamery is ten minutes away, but it will be a good break. I grab my things and shove my backpack on my shoulders, then begin the hike out.

A long line winds itself through the creamery so that I can barely get inside, and I deflate. This could take a while.

I open a book on my phone and manage to lose myself in the story until I get to the display case and can study the ice cream flavors.

"One or two scoops today?"

The question comes from just over my shoulder, and I turn, expecting to see an employee taking orders to help diminish the line.

But to my surprise, it's Jared. He also has a backpack on and looks ready for summer in board shorts and a T-shirt.

I play along. "Two scoops, please, and I'd like extra fudge and whipped cream."

He stays in character. "That's going to be a tall order. Maybe taller than you."

I clutch his arm, laughing, and then I don't let go, because why should I?

We step forward together, and I say, "You cut in front of a dozen people."

His hand closes over mine on his forearm. "But they don't know that. They think I came here to meet you."

He's absolutely right. And I'm happy to fall into this role-playing game also.

He doesn't let me pay for my ice cream ("We don't want anyone to know we're not together"), and when I only want one scoop, he protests, insisting I get two scoops with extra fudge and cream. I sit down at a table with a monster of an ice cream. Jared grabs a spoon from the nearby counter as he sits across from me.

"For when you need help."

"Who says I'm going to need help?" But we both know I will. I can't possibly consume all of this.

He grins at me.

It's not even six minutes before I can't get down another bite. Jared happily takes over.

"What are your plans for the rest of the night?" he asks me as he scoops up hot fudge.

Memorizing dates, drafting an essay, proofreading said essay . . . "Nothing. Studying if I have time."

He nods. "Sounds about like my evening. What do you say we go do something?"

Of course I'm game. I don't let myself consider that almost every Friday for the past month has contained Jared in it.

I don't let myself think how I will miss him.

I'm already missing too many people.

"I need to pick up a few things from the mall. For my packing list for the mission." He stands up and pulls the list from his backpack. I take it from him and scan it. A weight settles in my heart. I imagined doing this with Owen. Shopping with him, helping him get what he needed for his mission trip. Making his leaving a part of me so I could be an active participant.

I didn't get that chance. But I'm happy to do it with Jared.

I hand his list back. "Awesome. Let's get you some rubber galoshes."

CHAPTER ONE HUNDRED ELEVEN

Secret Spot

'␣ve never bought galoshes, and it turns out not to be something in high demand in Colorado. One store at the mall suggests we try online, so we ignore that item and go to the next on the list. Jared wants to touch everything, turn it over in his hand, imagine how he'll use each item in the field.

"I think a lot of this stuff we would find at a camping supply store," I say, looking at how he's supposed to bring his own bedding, umbrella, candles, and an abundance of bug spray and sunscreen. "They might even have galoshes."

He's already bought a waterproof backpack, several notebooks, and a collection of pens that I envy. I nearly bought some for myself but refrained.

Jared nods. "That makes sense."

"There's one not far from here, if you want me to take you."

"Do you mind? I don't want you to feel like I'm using you for your car."

"Oh, I know you are."

He laughs at my response and follows me out.

We find everything we need at the camping supply store. Jared grabs things he's not sure if he'll need, like additional bedding for a cot and a pocket-size umbrella.

"In case I don't feel like putting on this poncho," he says, patting the poncho that's been vacuum- packed into a tiny square.

I look at his collection of rain gear. "It must rain a lot in Madagascar."

"It does." Jared nods sagely. "They have a hot, wet season from November to April which brings in a monsoon season. Annual precipitation is anywhere from eight to forty inches a year, depending what part of the country you're in."

I fight a smile as I listen to him. "Sounds even better than Ireland."

"Ireland?" he scoffs. "There's no comparison. Madagascar is way cooler."

"Ha ha." I'm amazed at his new fondness for Madagascar. I suppose it does something to your brain when you know you're going to live somewhere else for two years. "You won't get to speak English."

"But when I come back, I'll be trilingual!" He beams.

"That is cool," I admit.

We buy all of his equipment, including his special galoshes, and head back to my car. It's been two hours. I hate to call the evening short, but I feel the shadow of responsibility looming over my head.

"I should probably do my homework now," I say, regretfully. "I still have a final to get through tomorrow."

"Yeah, me too. I think I'll go study at the law library."

"The law library?" I shoot him a curious look. "Do you study there a lot?"

"I do. It's not very crowded. And I like the atmosphere. So studious and full of the expectation of success."

"I'll go with you." And then I realize I invited myself along to his quiet study session. "If that's okay, anyway. I don't have to study with you. I can find another spot to sit."

"It's totally fine." He gives me a warm smile.

The parking lot behind the law building is completely open at this time on a Friday evening. I have the pick of the place. But I follow Jared's lead, since he's been here before and knows the lay of the land. The library opens into a wide atrium with steps leading up to terraced levels, full of tables and chairs and surrounded by bookshelf after bookshelf of black binders.

"What is this?" I whisper. There's nobody else here, but the silence rings loudly in my ears.

"I'm not sure." He points to a plaque on a pillar that says, "Case studies." "I've never cracked one open. Do you want to?"

I shake my head. I'm curious, but I'm certain the binders will be full of legalese that will dilute my interest in each case. And if it doesn't, I'll get sucked in and forget to do my homework. "No, I'm good."

Jared opens his backpack and takes out a notebook, a pen, a highlighter, and a textbook. I pull out my laptop.

The quiet descends upon us again as he annotates and I type, the clicking of my fingers on the keyboard the only sound. We don't talk, but every once in a while, I steal a glance at him over the top of my laptop. He's not usually looking at me, but one time he lifts his eyes the same time I look over, and he gives a small smile. I smile back and turn back to my work. Our friendship is companionable. It's easy.

We work for hours. At 9:55, an announcement comes on that the library will be closing in five minutes. Jared stands and begins packing his things, and I close my computer.

"Thanks for taking me around," he says, glancing at me. "I really appreciate it."

I wave him off. "It was fun. Thanks for letting me study with you."

"Now you know my secret spot. You can come here while I'm on my mission."

We walk out to my car in silence. I glance back at the library. It's not my study place. I don't think I would go there by myself.

But I will always think of Jared when I see it.

⟐⟐⟐

I dream I'm back at the camping store with Jared, going down the list of supplies and putting them in the cart. But when I look up to ask Jared something, it's not Jared. It's Owen.

I feel a rush of exquisite joy when I see him, but in less than a heartbeat, even my subconscious mind denies me this pleasure. The sadness blackens my joy, falling over me with a crushing weight.

My eyes snap open, hot and burning with unshed tears.

Owen deprived me of being a part of his experience. I'm still angry. I don't know if I'll ever forgive him.

I get up and shove all boys from my thoughts so I can remember important dates in American history. I take my final and get an 86%.

I don't even care.

Straight after that, I head to the humanities building and turn in my English paper.

I'm done. I finished my freshman year of college.

I almost skip my last night of work, because I know I'm not coming back when I return from Brazil and I don't feel like calling anyone.

Apparently neither does my boss. We don't touch the phones. Instead, Jeff pulls out games and we throw candy at each other. It's basically a closing social but we're getting paid.

I decide I love my boss. But not enough to come back.

⁕

My day is packed on Sunday. We have church in the morning, and then our last roommate dinner together, and then an evening social. A goodbye.

I refuse to speak about it. After nine months with these people, I'm closer to them than I ever was to my friends in high school.

I wear one of my favorite dresses, a sheer, floral-print dress, gauzy with a form-fitting slip beneath it. I join my roommates in the kitchen and we leave together for church.

Outside is green with spring. The sun shines overhead, tiny blossoms opening on every tree. But it's still cold enough I wear a sweater over my dress, and I long for the warmth and humidity of Arkansas.

Or Brazil, for that matter.

My roommates and I are quiet. There is a solemness between us. I wonder what will change over the summer. At least we will all be together again next semester.

I expect church to have the same feel, but it doesn't. it's almost irreverent in the boisterous, giddy attitude in the chapel and Sunday School. I'm relieved. For once, no one speaks about departures.

I take care of my fish when we get home from church. I put them in a container and close the lid, then take them down to my car, followed by the aquarium.

"Now I know we're leaving," Layne says when I come up for the fish food and bucket.

"The fish will be back," I say. "Just as soon as I'm back."

"It will come sooner than we expect," Iris says, stirring her food on the stove. The intoxicating scent of garlic and onion and seasoning fills the kitchen.

I slip my arm through the bucket handle. "I'm delivering the fish. See you at dinner."

"Hurry," Layne admonishes. "I don't want to wait for you."

"I'll take my time just for that," I tease.

She grins at me. There's a lot about Layne that drives me nuts, but we get along well.

I keep one hand on the container of fish in the passenger seat beside me as I drive to Stirling's apartment.

"I'm glad you managed to keep some of them alive until the end of the year," he says as he watches me set the tank up on his counter.

I level my eyes at him. "It was a steep learning curve, but I got it."

"At the expense of the lives of many innocent fish." He places his hand in front of his heart and bows his head.

I laugh. "Collateral damage."

"Tell that to the mothers and the children that you left fatherless."

"There are other fish in the sea," I say, and Stirling comes back with, "But not in your fish tank."

I grin and refill the tank, and I add a few drops of chemicals to dechlorinate it quickly. Usually I just let the water sit for a few hours, but I don't have time for that. When it's been fifteen minutes, I open the container and dump my beautiful fish into the water. They swim around in a fury, exploring the corners and plants as if they've never seen the tank before.

I sigh in contentment. "Aren't they beautiful?"

"I can almost give up my TV for them."

That I cannot picture.

I gather up my things and walk to the door, then turn around. "Thanks so much for everything, Stirling. It was fun getting to know you this year, and I appreciate you and Wyatt watching my fish."

Stirling crosses the entryway and gives me a hug, squishing my empty container between us. Then he laughs and removes it from my arm so he can hug me properly.

"You're a lot of fun. I'm glad we got to work together."

He hugs me a second longer, and my heart does a little double time as a thought forms in my head. What if he tries to kiss me? I don't think Stirling and I have that kind of relationship. What if he does? Immediately, I'm more anxious, my heart rate increasing. Should I let him? Should I turn around and make my getaway now?

He pulls away, and his face is so close. His dark brown eyes focus on me, and then he smiles.

"Call me when you get back. We'll hang out. And I'll give you your fish."

It takes me a good two seconds to realize he's not going to kiss me. Relief is quickly followed by disbelief. Why isn't he? Doesn't he like me? Wasn't there enough chemistry between us? But I smile brightly and say, "I will. You're guaranteed I'll get in touch as long as you're holding my fish hostage."

I turn around and let myself out, berating myself for my confused feelings.

By the time I get home, I have self-analyzed enough to feel calmer. I'm not interested in Stirling. I don't even want his attention. But I felt rejected when he didn't give me any, which made me want it. The whole "hard to get" psychology.

And I can't help but miss the emotional high that comes from tactile connection between two people. My roommates are great, but cuddling with them does not give me the same feeling.

I give a start of surprise when I walk into my dorm and see the empty table. No fish tank.

"Yeah, it's weird without it," Camila says, following my eyes.

"Definitely means we're leaving," Layne says.

Iris put the couch cushions down on the floor and beckons us to sit. "I'll miss this place," she says.

Layne snorts. "I won't. And we'll have a lot more privacy at our next place."

Her statement causes an uproar and exclamations about her extracurricular activities.

"Don't worry, geez, you prudes!" Layne says, shoving her hand through her hair. "I'm rooming with Cassandra. She's the only one who won't give me a hard time!"

I am startled. I don't love the idea of Layne bringing home boys.

But she promised she wouldn't. So I shrug. "We can room together. It'll be fun." And if there are any issues, I can beg Abby to swap rooms with me. Abby won't mind Layne's shenanigans. She might even be up to them herself.

"Oh," Camila says. She looks at Iris. "I guess that means we'll room together?"

Instantly I feel bad for ditching her, but at least she saw the way this played out. I didn't plan it.

Iris puts an arm around her and leans her head on her shoulder. "I can't wait!"

Camila smiles. No hurt feelings here. We like each other too much.

We clean up after eating Iris's orange chicken, rice, and peanut noodles. Cleaning is strange now because instead of putting things away, we pack them. Into boxes, into bins, and then shoved into corners of our rooms until they can be permanently moved.

I find Camila in our room after we've finished cleaning the kitchen.

"I hope you're not upset," I say, coming to sit on her bed with her. "I planned on rooming with you."

"I know. I was surprised—more caught off-guard. But I'll be fine. I know you didn't plan it."

"And Layne might be right," I say, softly so no one but Camila will hear. "I might be the only person who can handle her."

"You're good at letting things slide off you," Camila says. "You're probably the least judgmental of all of us."

I lean backward on the bed, considering those words. "That's quite a compliment," I say. "Tiago used to tell me I was very judgmental. I've been trying hard not to be."

She studies me with astute eyes. She's the only person here who knows the gravity behind my plans to go to Brazil. "What do you think is going to happen when you see him?"

"Nothing," I say. "We haven't seen each other in two years. We are completely different people."

Her lips purse together in a smile. "People change a lot in two years."

"They grow up. Grow apart."

"Like you and Owen will?"

Her words hit me like a sucker punch to the gut, and I sit in shock. Suddenly I want to cry. I feel my eyes burning, my shoulders curling up and inward, trying to protect myself from the stabbing pain in my chest.

"Yes," I whisper.

She sees the hurt she caused and reaches over to grab my hands. "Oh, Cassandra, I'm so sorry. I didn't mean to—"

"No, you're right," I say, yanking away before she can touch me. She wounded me badly, and my flesh feels like its been flayed from my bones. "I'm sure that's what he was thinking when he broke up with me."

In my head, though, I've been thinking there's still a chance for us. He's still the one I'm waiting for. I don't care how long it takes.

But this whole time, he might be thinking like Camila. It was nice but it's over. We won't be the same when—if—we see each other again.

I'm shaken. I stand up and leave the room. I go to the bathroom and close the door, where I hunker down and breathe deeply, working to stave off tears.

Only love will heal your heart again.

The words of the stupid fortune cookie I was given in tenth grade come back to me, and I hate them. I don't want to love again.

CHAPTER ONE HUNDRED TWELVE
Would Have Been Fun

Once again, I have to work to compose myself before we leave for the church closing social. Today is a day of many emotions, and my face wants to show them all at one time. It wants everyone to know the mess I am inside.

I don't want that.

We meet at the pastor's house on the lawn. He's set up white chairs and a platform, so it almost looks like a wedding. But then I see the microphone stand and know we're doing an open mic. We do these at least monthly at church, the chance for individual members of the congregation to get up and share their thoughts, testimonies, and love for each other and God.

I don't usually get up. I'm quiet that way. But hearing the feelings of others always moves me.

So it's no surprise that a lump forms in my throat as Pastor Eric stands and tells us how we've been his favorite group of kids so far (we know he says that every year) and he hopes to see many of us next year. Then he goes through his list, reading off the names of each person with a mission call and where they are going.

Jared. Madagascar.

Brant's name is mentioned, and I'm surprised. I glance over at Layne, but she doesn't react. She never told us, but I'm sure she knew.

He's going to New York.

And then he announces Layne's name.

"Layne Montgomery," Pastor Eric says. "Guatemala City, Guatemala."

I gasp. I'm sure a few others do too, but it's lost to me in my shock. I spin to her, mouth open, gaping.

She lifts a shoulder and gives a small smile.

I have a dozen questions, but I can't ask now. I have to sit through the rest of the meeting. It's beautiful and emotional, but my mind is tripping over Layne leaving. How did she keep this a secret? What does it mean for next year?

I could go on a mission now if I wanted.

Do I want to? Am I ready?

I always planned on going later. When I finish with college. Nineteen feels so young.

But Layne is doing it.

As soon as the meeting ends, I grab her before she can stand, before she can walk away. I sense our other roommates crowding around, but I focus on Layne's face, ignoring everyone else.

"When?" I demand.

Her eyes crinkle with laughter. "When what?"

"When do you go?" Iris asks.

"And when did you do this?" I say.

She exhales, her expression becoming more serious. "I put in an application a month ago, but I almost changed my mind. I didn't tell anyone because I wasn't sure it was what I wanted. Or if I'd be able to go."

"But you're going," I say, flabbergasted. Now I echo Iris's question. "When do you go?"

"A month before school starts."

I'm dumbfounded. "So you won't be rooming with us next year?"

She shakes her head. "I'm only going for six months. I asked to be placed in an orphanage, and they agreed. So I'll be back for winter semester." She looks at me and says, "Can we still room together?"

The reality hits me. "You knew this when we were talking about rooms earlier today!"

She laughs and nods and doesn't flinch when I whack her shoulder.

A line has formed behind us, wanting to talk to her, to congratulate her, and I stand up and move back. I scan the congregants, my family for the past nine months of my life, and the lump in my throat is back. My eyes land on Jared, messing around with Justin and Brittney and Mary. I push my way toward them and I suddenly long to feel Jared's arms around me, holding me close. Close the way we never got to be. Feelings we never developed because I kept him two feet away from me at all time.

I'm fighting tears when I stumble into him, and I'm not sure why I'm hurting again or why I keep trying so hard to control my emotions. He turns when I knock into his arm, and then he does precisely what I want: wraps me up in a hug.

"I'm so glad I got to know you this year," I say, and the tears have broken free, gliding down my face, my heart swollen and overflowing. "You're one of my best friends."

He pulls out of the embrace and wipes his palms over my face. "Me too, Cassandra." He kisses my cheek. His hand pauses along my jaw, and then he kisses my mouth.

It's so unexpected there's no time for me to protest or withdraw or deny him. In fact, I'm stunned into silence as his lips press into mine.

And I remember he's never kissed anyone before.

There's no thought involved as I impulsively kiss him back, opening his mouth with mine, gripping his forearms and pulling him closer to me.

It only lasts two seconds before I step away, breathless, wide-eyed and unbelieving.

I glance around, expecting to see an audience, but no one is looking at us. If they saw, they didn't make a scene.

"I hope you don't mind," Jared says, and I look back to see his eyes glistening. "I've been trying not to do that all semester. But I wanted you to be my first kiss. And I couldn't resist."

My heart warms at his words, and I clutch his fingers. "I don't mind."

He gave me his first kiss.

I'm honored.

He hugs me again, just rocks me, resting his head on top of mine. "I'll keep in touch," he says.

He steps away, and more tears fall when I blink.

"I'll miss you," I say.

I won't see Jared again. I know it. And it's all right. There's a whole world between us we didn't explore, an alternate time line that will never be.

But that kiss was enough to let me know it would have been fun.

⟡

Iris's parents come to get her on Monday. Layne is staying and doing spring term before she leaves for Guatemala. She has a spot in the apartment we rented, but she'll be with other people until the rest of us get back.

I still can't believe she's going.

I pack up my clothes, my toiletries, everything I need for the next few months goes into the front seat. Boxes of dishes and towels and winter clothes will stay locked in my trunk.

I strip my bed and fold the sheets and blankets to put in a box. I trace my fingers over the edges of Owen's quilt. He didn't ask for it back, and I have no intentions of giving it. It's mine. I lift it to my face and inhale. It still smells like him. I fold it carefully and place it at the bottom of the box.

That's where it will stay. I won't unpack it next year.

I load up my car. I'm ready to go, but Camila's parents aren't expecting us for a few more hours. I'm leaving my car there until I get back from Brazil.

"Let's pick up Jordan and go on one last drive through the canyons," Camila says.

"Let's do it," I say.

We pick up Jordan and drive around for an hour singing songs, laughing, making plans.

Jordan just decided to go on a mission. He's still working on his application. He doesn't think he'll be here next semester.

Camila doesn't say much about it with him in the car. I wait in my car while she walks him back to his dorm and they hug.

For twenty minutes.

Finally she gets back in the car and I plug her address into the GPS.

"Did he kiss you?" I ask.

"No," she says. "It didn't seem like a good time, with him leaving soon."

"Didn't stop Jared," I say, and I can't help but give a wistful smile at the memory.

I didn't tell my roommates. They were so busy with Layne they didn't see. And I didn't want Iris to know.

Camila rounds on me. "Jared kissed you?"

"Just a goodbye kiss. But it was special." I'll never forget it.

"Why did he wait so long?" she groans.

I wave her off. "It had to be. I wasn't ready to date him. If he'd kissed me sooner, I would have had to avoid him."

We sit in silence a moment while she digests that. I wait to see if she'll have more questions. When she doesn't, I say, "What about you and Jordan? Did you make plans for after?"

She shakes her head. "Everything feels so temporary right now. We're young, we just met, big changes are in front of us. We'll just wait and see."

Wait and see.

Feels suspicious.

At least she didn't mention Owen again.

I feel a spurt of sadness when I think of him. I've kissed another guy. I don't feel like I cheated, but I do feel like I came to a cross roads and went to the other side. I've accepted that I might not be with Owen in the end.

Might not. It could still happen.

I change the subject. "What do you think of Layne going on a mission?"

She brightens. "Oh my goodness, I was so shocked! I can't believe it! But it will be so good for her!"

"Yeah." I laugh. "Yeah, it will. I wonder how different she'll be when she gets back?"

"It's only six months. Probably not too much."

"I wonder if I should go sooner than later."

She glances over at me. "It's a big commitment. Are you ready?"

That is the big question. In a week I'll be in a Brazil. Two months after that I'll be back at school. I've already chosen my classes. I'm ready to study, to learn, to see what the next year of my life brings.

"Not yet," I admit. "Maybe in a year. I want to get more schooling in first."

"There's your answer, then."

I nod, satisfied. Maybe when I'm twenty I'll go.

We spend the night at her family's house, and the shadow of the memory the last time I stayed here lingers over us.

Days before our first year of college. How excited, naive, unknowing, and fresh we were.

Maybe that's why they call it freshman year.

Camila takes me to the airport in the morning. We hug goodbye, but it's not teary or emotional because we know we're rooming together. We'll see each other in a few weeks.

I fly to Dallas and then to Arkansas. There's a minor hitch with a forty-minute delay in Dallas, but it doesn't affect anything except my arrival time.

Only my mom meets me at the airport this time. The rest of my siblings are still in school and my dad is at work. Besides, it's not exciting for me to come home anymore.

I text Harper in the car while my mom drives.

Me: I'm home and I have one week before I leave for Brazil. Hang?

Then I text Riley.

Me: I'm home. Not for long. But I'd love to see you.

"How did school finish up?" Mom asks.

"Great!" I say. Mom and I talk at least once a week, so she's up to date on everything she needs to know about. "I got an A- in one of my English classes, but I got As in everything else, including Portuguese! And I tested out of the next level. So when I get back from Brazil, I'll start Portuguese 202."

I pause, and Mom says, "Good for you!" in the moment where I'm not speaking.

I open my mouth to say more, but she says, "Are you sure about going to Brazil? By yourself?"

"Mom, I've been living on my own for a year. I can do this."

"All right," she says, smiling slightly.

My phone chimes, and I glance down to see Riley texted. I swipe open the message.

R: hey!!! I'd love to see you. I'm working today but I'm off tomorrow. Come see me.

Me: I will!

I add a bunch of heart emojis. I didn't expect to hear from her so quickly.

Then it's Harper texting.

H: I'm at work! Done at eight. Appleby's?

Abbleby's. Such nostalgia. Oliver and I used to go there when we worked together at the Italian restaurant. I wonder how he is. I make a mental note to ask Harper.

My phone dings again. It's Jared. My stomach does a funny tumble when I see his name.

J: did you make it home safely?

Me: I did. You?

J: yeah. Have a safe trip.

It warms my heart that he's checking up on me. That he cares that much.

Me: you too. Good luck in Madagascar. I know you'll be amazing.

J: I'll never forget you, Cassandra.

I smile at that. Of course he won't. I was his first kiss.

You never forget your first.

CHAPTER ONE HUNDRED THIRTEEN

Babies

Harper and I sit at Appleby's for three hours talking about everything. We both agree I'm terrible at keeping in touch. I haven't told her anything about school, my break up with Owen, the subsequent quasi-relationship with Jared. She's equally annoyed with me and incredibly amused.

The restaurant closes and kicks us out, so we drive to her house to chat some more.

"And you and Miles?" I ask. We're back in her bedroom, and it makes me feel like I'm in high school again, like nothing changed, even though so much has.

She shrugs. "We broke up."

She says it so casually I almost miss it. I press my hands to my face and want to be annoyed she didn't tell me, but I didn't tell her about anything either.

"Ohmygosh. When did that happen?"

"Maybe a month ago."

I laugh. I'm so relieved. "I was afraid you were going to marry him!" Then I realize how that sounds and add, "Not that it would have been horrible."

"Oh, it would have been horrible," she says. "I thought I wanted to marry him. But finally I asked him point blank if he was going to marry me, and he said no. So we broke up."

My heart squeezes. "That must have been so hard."

"It should have been. But it wasn't. That's when I realized how much he doesn't make me feel. And now I'm dating someone else, and Cassandra—he makes me feel everything."

My eyelids flutter. "You're dating someone else?"

She nods. "He's still in high school." She sighs. "So it can't go anywhere."

I narrow my eyes at her. "How far has it gone?"

"Hmm." She lifts a shoulder, a smile flitting across her face. "Pretty far. Pretty much everything except sex. Oh!" She groans and buries her face in a pillow, her long blond hair spilling around her shoulders. "It's so hard not to have sex!"

"Oh, I know." I laugh and squeeze her shoulder.

She tosses her hair back and eyes me. "Did you and Owen? You promised you would tell me."

"No." I think of all the close calls we had. "I wanted to so badly. It was going to happen. And I was okay with that. But instead we broke up."

"Do you think he was trying to keep it from happening?"

I consider his words that morning at his house. The certainty I had that sex was only a matter of time. He probably knew it also. But I shake my head.

"He already knew he was going to break up with me."

"Does he know you're home?"

"No. We don't talk."

"You didn't want to tell him you're home?"

"I blocked him on my phone."

"Why?" Her voice is quiet as she studies me, trying to understand why I would cut this boy I love out my life.

"Because it was harder to be lukewarm. If I let him keep talking to me, he wouldn't be able to forget me on his mission. We might even end up back together only to break up again. We did that at least twice while I was at school. This way, he can stand by his decision and we don't have to go through that again."

"Sucks," she says.

"Yeah," I agree. I search for a way out of this topic and light on Oliver. Oliver and I were super close our junior year of high school. He and his girlfriend didn't get along, and I was his confidant. But she hated me, and once we quit working together, we barely got to talk. "How's Oliver these days?"

"Fine. I haven't talked to him much since the wedding."

"Wedding?"

"Yes, his and . . ." She trails off when she sees my face. "You don't know."

I shake my head.

She stands and goes through her dresser, then returns with a wedding invitation. "He and Claire got married."

I stare at the invitation of Oliver and Claire standing beside a tree together, tall and graceful, smiling at the camera. I can't believe it. But I can. I hand the invitation back with a deep sense of sadness. "I didn't get one."

"I don't think Claire likes you," Harper says.

I nod. It's an accurate assessment. "Did they seem happy?"

"I don't know. They never look like they're happy. But he asked her, and she said yes. So they must be."

"I hope they are." I do. Because I hate the thought of Oliver being miserable for the rest of his life.

I end up spending the night at Harper's. She has to leave at nine in the morning for work, but her mom lets me sleep as long as I want. I head home and feel like a lump on a log in my parents' house. There's nothing for me to do here. I don't even have assigned chores. I bunk with Emily, but it's not my room anymore. I find myself thinking of my dorm, my roommates, my life at school.

I message Riley.

Me: can I still come over?

R: I'm ready for you!

Me: is Lucas there?

R: he left with some friends. He'll be back later.

Good. I don't want to bump into her husband.

I nearly choke on the word, even in my head.

"I'm going to visit Riley," I tell my mom. "Can I use the van again?"

"Yes, that's fine," she says, and I head out.

I've been to her duplex, the one she shares with her mother-in-law, once before, but I don't remember how to get there. I follow the directions on my phone to the other side of Springdale. Things finally begin to look familiar. I park out front and give a knock on the door before sliding it open.

"Hello?" I call.

"Hi." Riley waves from the living room. She's watching TV, sitting on the edge of the couch to do so.

I forgot she's pregnant.

Very pregnant. Riley's hair is longer than I've ever seen it, the strawberry blond spilling nearly to her shoulder blades. Her face is thin, her cheeks pink.

But it's her belly that draws my attention. It's huge, extending beyond her knees where she sits.

"Oh, wow," I say, closing the door and coming into the room. "You look ready to pop."

"Feeling it also." She rises, a clumsy, cumbersome movement that requires her to grab the underside of her belly with one hand and push off the couch with the other. "Still one more week. I'm ready."

I cross to her and we hug, but it's weird, with this baby between us. I expect her stomach to feel soft and squishy like mine, but it's hard as a rock. I put my hand on it.

"So firm," I say.

"Yeah."

I don't know what else to say. I'm astounded to see my best friend so large with child. "How are you feeling?"

"Pretty cruddy right now, actually. I'm so hot." She walks away from me and paces the living room, waving a hand near her face. I glance up to make sure the ceiling fan is on, and it is. It must be the pregnancy making her hot because I don't feel it.

"Want to go somewhere and get something to eat?" I ask.

"I'm not hungry. I've been a little queasy all day, actually," she says. "It's the baby. She kicks a lot and it makes me lose my appetite."

I nod like I get it. But I don't. "What's it like?" I ask. "Having someone else growing inside of you?"

Riley grins. "Amazing. Come here, she's kicking. You can feel."

I can see it. A tiny bulge pushing against the flesh of Riley's belly, visible through the sky-blue shirt pressed tight over her skin. I hold my hand above her, several inches above her skin, hovering.

"Go on." Riley grabs my hand and pulls it down, smashing it down on her stomach.

Again, I'm surprised how firm her belly is. And then I feel it. The little push against my palm. I raise my eyes to Riley's, enthralled.

"That's your baby," I say, disbelief in my voice.

"Yep."

I pull my hand away, but I can't forget what it felt like, that tiny being inside her kicking against me. "Okay, no food. How about a drink? Nothing alcoholic, of course," I add quickly, in case she has any doubts.

Riley laughs. "I can do that."

We head back to my mom's car and I drive us to the nearest coffee shop. Riley is clearly uncomfortable, fidgeting frequently in her seat during the six-minute drive. She rearranges her seatbelt over her shoulder, over her belly, under her belly, off her shoulder completely. She adjusts the air vents so they blow on her face.

"You okay?" I ask as we get out at the coffee shop. I want to help her walk as she waddles forward, but I know Riley well enough to know she will resent that.

"I'm fine," she says. "It's getting more uncomfortable every day." She exhales, huffing her breath hard enough to send her bangs flying. "I can't wait for her to be born. But the doctor told me when it's your first baby, sometimes you go a week or so late."

"Two more weeks," I say, doing the math.

She groans. "I don't know if I can make it that long."

We both order an icy drink and sit down at a booth. Again I watch her fidget, rearrange her legs, stand up and tug on her belly like she can make it smaller.

"I'm so uncomfortable," she says.

Riley's small like me, maybe five-three. Her baby easily takes up a third of her size. She's making me nervous about ever being pregnant.

"You'll have to send me pictures," I say. "I'll be in Brazil."

"Visiting Tiago," she says, her expression brightening as she finally sits still long enough to drink her iced coffee. "How do you feel for him these days?"

"Oh, I'm not visiting Tiago," I sputter. "I'm visiting Brazil."

"And Tiago will be there."

"Yes." I don't mention that he offered for me to stay at his house. That I'll be staying with his grandfather.

"How does Owen feel about this?" She eyes me over her straw.

I wince. She's another person I never told about Owen.

Probably because I didn't tell anyone. I didn't make a public announcement anywhere. "Owen and I broke up," I say breezily, as if saying it like I don't care will make it so I don't care.

Riley doesn't bat an eye. Breakups and hookups are par the course for her. "I'm sorry."

"Yeah." I keep pretending. "So what I do doesn't matter to him. But he knows I'm going."

"And he knows you're going to get back together with Tiago?"

"I'm not getting back together with him!" I'm indignant. "I don't feel that way for him."

"But you did."

"I did." Tiago was my first love. Does that mean I have to fall for him again? The thought angers me. "We are just friends."

Her lip twists in a sly smile. "Tell me that when you get back."

She's infuriating. And now I'm hot also.

She can't be right.

There's a little shiver of fear in me that says she could be.

Riley knows me better than anyone. We've been best friends and frenemies off and on ever since fifth grade.

Sometimes she knows me better than I know myself.

"Ow." She winces and rubs her stomach. "This baby hurts so much. I think she's trying to step out of my body. Shoot." She exhales and passes her hand down lower, cradling her groin.

And then she freezes, her face going still, the color leaching from her skin, leaving her freckles exposed in high definition on her pale skin.

"Cassandra," she says, and I hear the tension in her voice. And something else. Like panic.

"What?" I ask, leaning toward her over the table.

"I think my water just broke."

I know nothing about babies. Nothing about labors, pregnancies, giving birth.

But I know what it means if your water breaks.

Adrenaline spikes through my veins, a heady hot elixir that spurs me to action. I try to keep calm and feel out the situation. "How do you know?"

"Because my crotch is wet!" she snaps, and then she bites her lip, her eyes wide enough to see the whites around her irises. "And I didn't pee myself!"

I believe her. I stand up and place a hand under her elbow. "Okay. I'll drive you to the hospital."

She tries to stand with me but stops with a sharp intake of breath. Her shoulders hunch and her head bows forward, her hair falling over her face.

"Riley?" I say, worrying. Close to panic myself. I see the water now on the vinyl covering of the booth, see the wetness down the legs of her pants.

She straightens up and grabs my arm with her other hand, her fingers as sharp as claws as they dig into my skin. "It hurts," she gets out through clenched teeth.

I swallow and nod. "Okay. Can you walk to the car?" I'm suddenly terrified she's going to crouch down and have this baby in the coffee shop. I glance around and see a few patrons have started to notice us.

"Do you need help?" an elderly gentleman says.

I nearly wilt with relief. "My friend. I think she's going to have her baby."

The patrons spring into action.

"I can drive you," a woman says. "I'll get my truck and bring it right to the door. You sit in the back with your friend."

"Let me get some towels," a worker says, disappearing into the back of the restaurant.

The man comes to Riley's other side. "Let's get her out to the car," he says.

"I can't walk," Riley gasps out.

Another woman comes to my side, practically shoving me out of the way as she gets in Riley's face. She takes Riley by the shoulders and stares at her. "You can do this. Shuffle. One step at a time. We need to get you to the hospital so you can have this baby safely."

Riley nods. Her eyes are glazed over. I know she's not thinking.

For that matter, neither am I.

The woman turns to me. "Does she have family she needs to call to meet us at the hospital?"

My thoughts snap together. "Yes." I haul my phone out. I know Lucas should be the first person to contact, as the baby's father and Riley's husband, but I don't have his number. "I'll call her mom."

The truck lady pulls up out front, and it takes three of us, but we manage to get Riley out of the coffee shop and into the backseat. It takes effort to get her up into the cab. She's hissing between her teeth, clutching her abdomen, sweat beading along her forehead. I'm helpless beside her, good only to dial her mom's number as I let this woman drive us to the hospital.

"Mrs. Isabel? Hi, it's Cassandra," I say when her mom answers.

"Cassie, hi!" she says, and I plow right through her pleasantries.

"Riley's having the baby," I say. "We're on our way to the Springdale hospital. Can you meet us there?"

"Of course!" she says. "I'm on my way!"

My brain does remind me of a few things, and I add, "Can you let her husband and his mom know?"

"Yes, I'll call them right now! Thank you, Cassandra!"

I hang up and take Riley's hand. She doesn't seem to see me, huffing and puffing and staring at the back of the driver's seat. But she squeezes my fingers like she's trying to pop the bones right out.

And I'm scared. I know this is normal. But I've never seen anything like this. Never been friends with someone going through it.

And from the bottom of my soul, I want to call Owen and sob out my feelings. I want to hear his reassuring words, feel the warmth of his love.

I grind my teeth together and keep my pain to myself. But my whole soul aches.

CHAPTER ONE HUNDRED FOURTEEN

Here for It

Three hours later, the baby is born. The doctor says it was a fast labor, for a first-time mom, and I'm about convinced that I'm never giving birth. I didn't stay in the room. Once Lucas and the moms arrived, it became crowded, and I was glad for a reason to leave. I sat in an adjacent waiting room and tried to read a book on my phone.

But as soon as she's born, Mrs. Isabel comes and gets me from the sitting room. She's beaming and takes my hand, pulling me up.

"Come see the baby."

I follow her. It's a little after five in the afternoon, but I feel like I've been in this hospital for four days and four nights.

Riley is sitting up on the hospital bed, her face shining with sweat, exertion, and joy. She radiates love as she smiles down at the pug-faced, fat baby in her arms. Lucas hovers at her shoulder, a handsome boy with dark wavy hair and the same enamored expression on his face as he stares at their daughter. Riley looks up, and the smile directs at me now.

"I did it. I had a baby."

"I can't believe it." I approach but not too closely. This feels private, and I'm invading. "You're a mom."

"Want to hold her?"

She offers the blanket-wrapped pug-face toward me and ignores my stammered protests. I take the small bundle of warmth and my heart melts. The baby has a crop of dark hair and her head wiggles back and forth as her tiny features scrunch up as if she smells something dirty.

But she smells fresh and clean and heavenly. I sniff her tiny head.

I want one.

She stretches her arms and opens her mouth and croons. I hand her back to Riley. "Oh, Riley, she's precious."

"Yeah, she is."

It doesn't matter how horrible the past few hours were. Riley beams.

I've never seen her so happy.

I stay another half an hour and then slip out. I'm moved beyond words, enraptured by the miracle of life and motherhood.

And I swear my uterus is screaming for a child.

Not now, of course. But I know like I've never known before that I want to be a mom one day.

⚬⟋⟋⟍⟍⚬

I visit Riley one more time when she comes home from the hospital. Harper comes with me, and we bring baby blankets, diapers, and diaper wipes.

"She's a good baby," Riley says, and we hover nearby, watching her change baby Ella into pajamas. "Sleeps a lot. But my boobs."

Riley makes a face and pushes on the offending appendages. They are huge. Watermelons sitting on her chest.

"I wasn't going to say anything," I say, laughing. "But I noticed."

"My milk came in. And there's so much of it. It hurts, gosh dang it! And nursing brings relief—but it also brings its own kind of pain."

She keeps talking, but my mind is elsewhere. I'm distracted, and it's Harper who calls me on it.

"Cassandra," she says. "Are you listening?"

"Yes," I say, and then I admit, "No."

Harper and Riley exchange looks.

"What are you thinking about?" Harper asks.

"Brazil." I pleat my fingers together. "I fly out tomorrow." My heart rate increases even as I say it.

"I know," Harper says quietly.

Neither of them say anything. I'm not sure what they're thinking. What I'm thinking.

"I'm super nervous," I say.

Harper takes my hand. "Whatever happens will be fine," she says. "Just relax and enjoy the experience."

I let out a breath and nod.

"You're always trying to make it what you think it should be," Riley says. "Stop worrying about it. Stop worrying about Tiago. There's no right or wrong. It's just life."

She's right. I'm so worried. I'm so worried about screwing up, or making a mistake, or feeling like a fool.

"But don't get pregnant," she adds, and Harper and I laugh.

That would definitely change the course of my life.

⚬⟋⟋⟍⟍⚬

I spend the next morning unpacking and repacking my suitcases. I'm a ball of nerves, anxious energy coursing through my fingertips. Do I have what I'll need for a month?

I don't know what I need.

My mom drives me to the airport, and I can tell from her pasted smile that she's as nervous as I am. If I told her to come, she'd probably buy a ticket and hop on the plane with me.

I don't say a word.

"Are you anxious?" she asks me.

"No, I'm fine," I say. Total lie.

She helps me get checked in for my flight and then hugs me extra long in front of the escalator to go to security.

"If you need to come home early, if you need money, if you change your mind—just call me and let me know."

I nod. "I'll talk to you a lot. Email, texting, whatever."

"Remember they don't have great internet down there," she warns me.

I remember.

I get through the small security line and sit at my gate checking the time. Still two hours before we board.

And then I have another twenty hours of airplanes and airports in front of me. No time to get bored yet.

I pull out my phone and open the app I haven't used in months. The one to talk to Tiago. I hesitate only a moment before typing, *At the airport. See you soon.*

I add a thumbs up and exit the app. I don't want to have a conversation yet. There will be plenty of that, and soon.

Instead, I pull up Owen's contact.

He's still blocked. I wonder, if I unblock him, will a flood of messages arrive, messages he tried to send me?

Or maybe he hasn't tried to contact me at all this entire time. Maybe he is relieved that confusing chapter in his life has ended.

I want to text him so badly. I miss him. I wish I was getting on a plane to New Orleans to spend a month with him.

My finger trembles with the effort not to message him. Do I know his number? I close my eyes and try to conjure the digits in my head, but I can't. Owen is a button on my phone, not a seven-digit number.

And if this contact stays here on my phone, I'm going to do something stupid. Like call him bawling and beg him to reconsider.

This time I have to force my thumb to move. I press it down on the phone. Onto the big red button that says "Delete."

And then he's gone. The contact removed from my phone. With it, any possible way of us reaching each other.

I put my phone away, swallowing hard, ignoring the lump in my throat, aware of the heavy ramifications of what I've done.

Face forward. Chin up. I'm headed to Brazil, and I won't let my wounded heart keep me from experiencing every new adventure.

I am ready to embrace the world.

⚬⟋⟍☀⟋⟍⚬

If you enjoyed this book please consider leaving a review! One word, one sentence, all of these have amazing results in getting Amazon to show my books to new readers and helping me increase my audience!

Thank you!

I am hard at work writing the next year of Cassandra's life!

Available for pre-order now! Of Campus Schemes, Hopes, and Dreams!

Don't want to wait? You can find it in multiple places where I release the stories as I write them, in their raw, unedited, unabridged form!

On Ream

On Laterpress

On Kindle Vella

Can't wait to hear your thoughts!

Advisements: The characters in this book are new adults learning about independence, trust, sexuality, and adulting. Parental discretion advised.

Preview:

Eighteen hours after leaving Arkansas, my plane sets down in Recife, Brazil.

I'm bone-weary. I finished my freshman year of college just days ago. Yesterday I permanently deleted my ex-boyfriend from my contact list. My heart is heavy, and I need sleep.

Today I'm expected to smile and be polite while I greet Tiago and his family, who are putting me up for the next month.

I have no idea how this month will go. Years ago, Tiago and I dated when my family hosted him as an exchange student. We were close, but the time and distance between us forced us apart. Other than a few emails and phone calls, we haven't talked much these past few months. Coming here seemed like such a good idea when I bought the ticket right before high school graduation. I'm studying Portuguese at Preston Yarborough University, and spending a month in Brazil with one of my dearest friends sounded like an exciting adventure.

Maybe I'm just tired, but I don't feel that way now.

I trudge through the line of other weary travelers, blinking against the grit in my eyes. I went through customs in São Paulo, so now all I have to do is exit through the doors and collect my baggage. I remember where to go. I came through here two years ago, the last time I saw Tiago. The air is thick with moisture, a salty, mildewy scent clinging to the walls. I inhale, and the scent takes me back in time.

It smells like Brazil.

People come to life around me when they spot their loved ones waiting from them on the other side of the doors. They brighten, their eyes widening, and they shriek, scream, gasp, or stand in place and cry. My heart pounds a little harder as the reality breaks through my exhaustion: as soon as I get through these doors, I'll see Tiago.

What I feel is a frightening combination of dread and anticipation.

Will he recognize me? My hair is longer than the last time he saw me, but I have it up in a ponytail. I'm nineteen now and ten pounds heavier but still have a baby-face.

Will I recognize him?

I push through the doors and keep moving, taking deep breaths to keep calm as I scan the faces.

I see him the same time he sees me. Even though Tiago has also put on weight and grown his hair longer, it's the same face, the same dark eyes, the same high cheek bones and thick lips. Our gazes meet across the room, and then a smile splits his face. He crosses over to me, parting the crowd to get to my side, and I smile back, but my heart hasn't stopped racing. In an instant he wraps me up in a hug, but he's only a few inches taller than me and his hug doesn't swallow me whole.

Not like Owen's hugs.

Why am I thinking of Owen? We broke up months ago. I might not be over him, but I've moved on. Why is he haunting me now?

Because of Tiago. Because of the drama that occurred between those two boys. Because they are the only two I've ever loved.

Find me on social media! Join my Cassandra Jones fan club on Facebook. Here we can theorize together on what's going to happen, talk about past events, dive into character feelings, and even give me ideas for upcoming books! Find it on Facebook at "All About Cassandra Jones."

Follow me on TikTok for video updates on all my writing activities! @Tamara_writes

Did you find a typo?

Even though I have a critique group, an editor, a beta team, an ARC team, and a proofreader, errors still slip through, and I want to know! If you find one, email me at Tamara@tamarahartheiner.com and let me know which book and what it is, and I'll send you your choice of one of my ebooks for free!

Thank you for helping me make my books better!

Enjoy this book? You can make a huge difference!
If you enjoyed this book, I'd be honored if you'd leave an honest review on whatever book haunt you frequent.
Reviews are indie authors' bread and butter, and we couldn't do it without readers like you!

About the Author

I live in beautiful northwest Arkansas in a big blue castle with two princesses and a two princes, and several loyal cats (and one dog). I fill my days with slaying dragons at traffic lights, earning stars at Starbucks, and sparring with the dishes. I also enter the amazing magical kingdom of my mind to pull out stories of wizards, goddesses, high school, angels, and first kisses. Sigh.

I'm the author of several young adult stories, kids books, romance novels, and even one nonfiction.

You can find me outside enjoying a cup of iced tea or in my closet snuggling with my cat. But if you can't make the trip to Arkansas, I'm also hanging out on Facebook and Instagram but usually TikTok as @Tamara_writes. You can also visit me on my website, tamarahartheiner.com. I look forward to connecting with you!

Made in the USA
Coppell, TX
12 January 2025

44059313R00371